ADVANCE PRAISE
for

March 1917
The Red Wheel, Node III, Book 1

"*The Red Wheel*, Aleksandr Solzhenitsyn's epic of World War I and the Russian Revolution, belongs to the Russian tradition of vast, densely plotted novels of love and war set during a time of social upheaval. An extended act of author-to-nation communication, this multivolume saga poses the question, "Where did we go wrong?" and answers it in human and political terms, but with a mystical twist that is unlike anything else in Solzhenitsyn. Like *The Gulag Archipelago*, *The Red Wheel* subjects the nation's past to forensic investigation and moral review. The epic is an intricately formatted synthesis of fiction, documents, and analysis. Scenes of life and death in the trenches, palace intrigue, political conspiracies, street riots, and families in harmony or conflict are interspersed with cinematic Screens, newspaper clippings, archival documents, and learned essays on a variety of historical topics. *March 1917*, the epic's third "Node" or novel, shows the outbreak of revolution in Petrograd (Saint Petersburg) as the beginning of a great national unraveling from which all subsequent catastrophes necessarily followed: Russia's Year Zero. There are dozens of plots with dozens of historical and fictional, public and private personalities from every social class and cultural stratum under the setting sun of the Russian Empire. The Tsar and his family, courtiers, ministers, parliamentarians, conspirators, military men of every rank, businessmen and beggars, intellectuals and ignoramuses, workers and peasants, criminals and terrorists, Realists and Modernists, priests and atheists, ascetics and libertines, lovers and haters, they are all here, to shape or to witness history. Among the historical figures are Tsar Nicholas II, the Bolshevik leader Vladimir Lenin, and the future head of the Provisional Government, Aleksandr Kerensky. This translation beautifully conveys the distinctive flavor of Solzhenitsyn's prose, with its preternatural concreteness of description, moments of surreal estrangement, and meticulous detailing of the nuances of human relationships in the shadow of encroaching chaos. The novel's reliable, unreliable, and even mendacious character voices, its streams-of-consciousness, and its experimental flourishes possess the same vividness and freshness as they do in Russian. Think *Anna Karenina* and *Doctor Zhivago*, with Dostoyevsky's *Demons* thrown in for good measure."

—Richard Tempest, University of Illinois at Urbana-Champaign

"There is no doubt that *The Red Wheel* is one of the masterpieces of world literature, made all the more precious by its relevance to the tragic era through which contemporary history has passed. Moreover, the impulse of revolutionary and apocalyptic violence associated with the age of ideology has still not ebbed. We remain confronted by the fragility of historical existence, in which it is possible for whole societies to choose death rather than life."

—David Walsh, Catholic University of America

"Scholars may debate whether Russian culture is an integral part of Christian civilization or whether it should be allocated its own separate place. The five thousand pages of Aleksandr Solzhenitsyn's *Red Wheel* comprise one of those pyramids of the spirit (the other being *The Gulag Archipelago*) that makes living Russian civilization stand out from other large-scale cultural constructs that shape the literary landscape. In his insistence on conveying to his 'brothers in reason' his vision of the inexorable Russian catastrophe of the twentieth century, the author frequently abandons the narrative form to address the reader directly, grabbing him by the scruff of the neck mid-text. His grandiose picture of this catastrophe and the cultural continent that perished in it is not confined to the pages of the book; making sense of it requires additional time — including historical time. Unfortunately, this time is incomparable to the length of one man's life."

—Alexander Voronel, Tel-Aviv University

"As the great Solzhenitsyn scholar Georges Nivat has written, Solzhenitsyn is the author of two great 'literary cathedrals,' *The Gulag Archipelago* and *The Red Wheel*. The first is the definitive exposé of ideological despotism and all of its murderous works. *The Red Wheel* is the definitive account of how the forces of revolutionary nihilism came to triumph in the first place. It is a sprawling and fascinating mix of philosophical and moral discernment, literary inventiveness, and historical insight that sometimes strains the novelistic form, but is also one of the great works of moral and political instruction of the twentieth century."

—Daniel J. Mahoney, co-editor of *The Solzhenitsyn Reader:*
New and Essential Writings

"In his ambitious multivolume work *The Red Wheel* (*Krasnoye Koleso*), Solzhenitsyn strove to give a partly historical and partly literary picture of the revolutionary year 1917. Several of these volumes have been translated into English, but the present volume appears in English for the first time. The translation is very well done and ought to give the reader a better understanding of the highly complex events that shook Russia exactly a century ago."

—Richard Pipes, emeritus, Harvard University

THE RED WHEEL

A Narrative in Discrete Periods of Time

The Center for Ethics and Culture Solzhenitsyn Series

The Center for Ethics and Culture Solzhenitsyn Series showcases the contributions and continuing inspiration of Aleksandr Solzhenitsyn (1918–2008), the Nobel Prize–winning novelist and historian. The series makes available works of Solzhenitsyn, including previously untranslated works, and aims to provide the leading platform for exploring the many facets of his enduring legacy. In his novels, essays, memoirs, and speeches, Solzhenitsyn revealed the devastating core of totalitarianism and warned against political, economic, and cultural dangers to the human spirit. In addition to publishing his work, this new series features thoughtful writers and commentators who draw inspiration from Solzhenitsyn's abiding care for Christianity and the West, and for the best of the Russian tradition. Through contributions in politics, literature, philosophy, and the arts, these writers follow Solzhenitsyn's trail in a world filled with new pitfalls and new possibilities for human freedom and human dignity.

Aleksandr Solzhenitsyn

MARCH 1917

THE RED WHEEL / NODE III
(8 March – 31 March)

BOOK 1

Translated by Marian Schwartz

UNIVERSITY OF NOTRE DAME PRESS

NOTRE DAME, INDIANA

Published by the University of Notre Dame Press
Notre Dame, Indiana 46556
www.undpress.nd.edu

Translated from book 1 of books 1–4:

"Март 1917" (I)
© A. I. Solzhenitsyn, 1986, 2008

"Март 1917" (II)
© A. I. Solzhenitsyn, 1986, 2008

"Март 1917" (III)
© A. I. Solzhenitsyn, 1986, 2008

"Март 1917" (IV)
© A. I. Solzhenitsyn, 1986, 2008

Published in the United States of America

Library of Congress Cataloging-in-Publication Data

Names: Solzhenitsyn, Aleksandr Isaevich, 1918–2008, author. |
Schwartz, Marian, 1951– translator.
Title: March 1917 : The Red Wheel, node III (8 March/31 March), book 1 /
Aleksandr Solzhenitsyn ; translated by Marian Schwartz.
Other titles: Krasnoe koleso. Mart semnadtsatogo. Kniga 1. English |
Red Wheel, node III (8 March/31 March), book 1
Description: Notre Dame, Indiana : University of Notre Dame Press, 2017. |
Includes index.
Identifiers: LCCN 2017006656| ISBN 9780268102654 (hardcover : alk. paper) |
ISBN 0268102651 (hardcover : alk. paper)
Subjects: LCSH: Russia—History—February Revolution, 1917—Fiction.
Classification: LCC PG3488.O4 K67613 2017 | DDC 891.73/44—dc23
LC record available at https://lccn.loc.gov/2017006656

∞ *This paper meets the requirements of ANSI/NISO Z39.48-1992*
(Permanence of Paper).

Publisher's Note

March 1917 (consisting of books 1–4) is the centerpiece of *The Red Wheel*, Aleksandr Solzhenitsyn's multivolume historical novel on the roots and outbreak of the Russian Revolution, which he divided into four "nodes." *March 1917* is the third node.

The first node, *August 1914*, leads up to the disastrous defeat of the Russians by the Germans at the Battle of Tannenberg in World War I. The second node, *November 1916*, offers a panorama of Russia on the eve of revolution. *August 1914* and *November 1916* focus on Russia's crises, revolutionary terrorism and its suppression, the missed opportunity of Pyotr Stolypin's reforms, and the souring of patriotism as Russia bled in the world war.

March 1917 tells the story of the beginning of the revolution in Petrograd, as riots go unchecked, units of the army mutiny, and both the state and the numerous opposition leaders are incapable of controlling events. The present volume, book 1 of *March 1917*, is set during March 8–12. It will be followed by English translations of the next three books of *March 1917*, describing events through March 31, and the two books of *April 1917*.

The nodes of *The Red Wheel* can be read consecutively or independently. All blend fictional characters with numerous historical personages, usually introduced under their own names and with accurate biographical data. The depiction of historical characters and events is based on the author's extensive research in archives, administrative records, newspapers, memoirs, émigré collections, unpublished correspondence, family records, and other contemporary sources. In many sections the historical novel turns into dramatic history. Plots and subplots abound.

The English translations by H. T. Willetts of *August 1914* and *November 1916*, published by Farrar, Straus and Giroux in 1989 and 1999, respectively, appeared as Knot I and Knot II. The present translation, in accordance with the wishes of the Solzhenitsyn estate, has chosen the term "Node" as more faithful to the author's intent. Both terms refer, as in mathematics, to discrete points on a continuous line.

In a 1983 interview with Bernard Pivot, Aleksandr Solzhenitsyn described his narrative concept as follows: "The *Red Wheel* is the narrative of revolution in Russia, its movement through the whirlwind of revolution. This is an immense scope of material, and . . . it would be impossible to describe this many events and this many characters over such a lengthy stretch of time. That is why I have chosen the method of nodal points, or Nodes. I select short segments of time, of two or three weeks' duration, where the most vivid events unfold, or else where the decisive causes of future events are formed. And I describe in detail only these short segments. These are the Nodes. Through these nodal points I convey the general vector, the overall shape of this complex curve."

Dates in the original Russian text were given in the Old Style, according to the Julian calendar used in Russia until 1918. In the English translations these dates have been changed, in accordance with the author's wishes, to the New Style (Gregorian) calendar, putting them thirteen days ahead of the old dates. The March 1917 revolution thus corresponds to the February Revolution in Russian history (Old Style), just as the revolution that placed the Bolsheviks in power in November of that year is commonly referred to as the October Revolution.

In the "screen" sequences in this book, the different margins represent different instructions for the shooting of a film: sound effects or camera direction, action, and dialogue (in italics). The symbol "=" indicates "cut to." Newspaper headlines of the day, common in other volumes of *The Red Wheel*, are not included in the present book because the Petrograd newspapers had stopped publication during this period.

*   *   *

The English translation was made possible through a generous anonymous donation to the Solzhenitsyn Initiative at the Wilson Center's Kennan Institute, which is gratefully acknowledged.

The two maps of Petrograd and the Index of Names have been adapted and revised from the versions in the French translation, *La Roue rouge*, Troisième nœud, *Mars dix-sept*, tome 1, with the kind permission of Fayard and approval of the Solzhenitsyn estate.

Contents

THURSDAY, 8 MARCH

FRIDAY, 9 MARCH

MONDAY, 12 MARCH

CONTENTS / xix

8 MARCH
THURSDAY

[1]

Nikolai spent sixty-six days at Alix's side in the contained stillness of Tsarskoye Selo, by his presence easing her immeasurable grief over her loss. (Fortunately, the winter lull at the front had permitted this absence from GHQ.)

Troubled, restless, and grief-stricken, Alix had communicated to Nikolai her sense of an impending stretch of disasters and misfortunes that would not be overcome quickly.

There was another disaster as well: the poor man's death had drawn a line of misunderstanding between Nikolai and Alix. They had always had different views of Grigori, his essence and significance and the extent of his wisdom, but Nikolai had never insisted on this, sparing Alix's feelings and belief. Now, though, Alix could not forgive her husband for not handing the murderers over to justice.

When on 30 December, at GHQ, during a military council with the supreme commander about the plan for the 1917 campaign, the Emperor was handed a telegram about Rasputin's disappearance and possible death, he was, in a sinful way, privately, actually rather relieved. After all the anger that had built up, he was tired of listening to the endless warnings, revelations, and gossip—and now, all of a sudden, this object of public hatred had himself vanished, in some fatalistic way, without the Emperor having to make any effort whatsoever, without an agonizing conversation with Alix. It had all passed—of its own accord.

He took an artless view of things! He couldn't imagine that almost immediately he would be forced to abandon both this military council, which had taken so long to organize, and GHQ—and rush to be with Alix for a full two months—and earn a hail of reproaches: his indifference to the elder and deliverer's fate had led to the very possibility of this murder, and not only that, he had no wish to punish the murderers!

Half a day later, he himself was embarrassed that he could have felt relief at someone's death.

Indeed, murder was murder, and the long harassment and evil tongues had progressed to poison and gunshots—and there were no mitigating circumstances whatsoever for not putting them on trial. But the fact that the prick's sting had issued from such proximity, from among the grand dukes and even soft-spoken, gentle Dmitri, whom he had raised practically as a son, beloved and spoiled Dmitri (whom he kept at GHQ and would not send to a regiment), rendered the Emperor powerless. The more inexpressible and blood-related the offense, the more powerless he was to respond.

What monarch had ever landed in such a fix? His only buttress was the distant, mute, and invisible Orthodox people. Whereas all the spheres close to him—educated and godless—were hostile, and even among men of state and government servants one saw very few who were zealous in their work and honest.

Even the hostility inside the dynasty itself was striking. Everyone detested Alix. Nikolasha and the Montenegrin sisters had for a long time, but even his Mama had always been against her. Even Elizaveta, Alix's own sister. And naturally, his Lutheran Aunt Miechen had never forgiven Alix her fervent Orthodoxy and on the occasion of the heir's illness had laid the groundwork for her own sons, either Kirill or Boris, to seize the throne. Then there was the string of unmaskers that had appeared this fall and winter among the grand dukes and duchesses, who had lectured the imperial couple, with rare effrontery, as to how they were to be—as had Sandro, once upon a time Nikolai's close friend, when they were young. Sandro had gone so far as to say that the government itself was bringing on a revolution and a government was needed that was to the Duma's liking, that apparently all classes were hostile to the throne's policy and the people believed the slander, but the royal couple had no right to drag their own relatives into the abyss. Even his brother Georgi had echoed the same: unless a government responsible to the Duma was created, we were all going to perish. Grand dukes could think of themselves. When things were going bad for them, they could go to Biarritz and Cannes. A sovereign did not have that luxury.

Now he was ashamed before Russia that the hands of the emperor's relatives had been stained with that man's blood. But so stifling was the dynastic condemnation all around that he could not find the firmness in his breast to respond with a legal blow. Even his Mama had asked him not to open an investigation. Nikolai could not find in himself the ruthless will to prosecute them harshly under the law. Given the gossip that had arisen, any ordinary legal action might be interpreted as personal revenge. All that Nikolai could bring himself to do was to exile Yusupov to his estate and Dmitri to Persia, but Purishkevich—nothing even happened to him; he boarded a hospital train for the front. Even these mild measures were met with mutiny by the dynasty, a hostile collective letter from the entire large family of grand dukes and duchesses, and Sandro came and shouted right at the Emperor to stop this murder case.

How utterly they forgot themselves. They no longer considered themselves subject to the state's judgment or God's!

But then Alix breathed fury, saying that Nikolai had been criminally lenient toward the murderers and his weakness would ruin both his realm and his family.

An unprecedented, prolonged tension, an unremitting resentment, had lingered between him and Alix these two months at Tsarskoye. Nikolai tried to yield and oblige in any way he could. He authorized all the special arrangements for the murdered man's body: a guard and burial right there in Tsarskoye, on Anya's land. Hiding away from everyone, as if they were hunted pariahs in this country and not its Tsars, they buried Rasputin at night, to torches, and Nikolai himself and Protopopov and Voeikov were his pallbearers. Nonetheless, Alix was not entirely mollified, and a heaviness remained in her heart. (She now took lonely walks to grieve and pray at his grave. Malicious people spotted her and sullied the grave in the very first days. A permanent guard had to be posted until a chapel could be raised over that spot.)

So passionate and insistent were Alix's reproaches of his weakness and incompetence as Tsar that Nikolai's faith in himself was shaken. (Not that it had ever been solid since he was young; he considered himself a failure at everything. He was convinced that even his trips to see the troops, trips he loved so, would bring those troops military failure.) Even little Aleksei, who was not yet engaged in adult matters at all, exclaimed in grief, "Papa, are you really not going to punish them? They hanged Stolypin's murderer, after all!" Indeed, why was he so weak? Why couldn't he summon the will and decisiveness of his father? Or great-grandfather?

Especially after Grigori's murder, the Emperor could not agree to any concessions for his opponents and society. They would think that it was because he'd been freed from that influence. Or see, he was afraid of being killed, too.

During these hard winter months, under his wife's reproaches and coming to his own senses, Nikolai decided on drastic steps. Yes, now he would be firm and insist his will be carried out! He removed Justice Minister Makarov, whom Alix had not liked for a long time (and who had been indifferent and sluggish at Rasputin's murder), and Prime Minister Trepov, whom she had objected to greatly from the very beginning, saying he was cruel and alien. As Prime Minister he appointed dear old Prince Golitsyn, who had helped Alix so much in prisoner-of-war matters. And he had stood up for Protopopov. Later, just before the New Year, he shook up the State Council, replaced some appointed members with more reliable ones, and appointed Shcheglovitov State Council President. (Even in this refuge for worldly-wise, honorable dignitaries, the Emperor had lost the majority and had no influence. The appointed members as well as those elected were playing the liberal game here, too, more and more ruinously.) Moreover, he intended to move at last to decisive governance and defy public opinion, no matter the cost. He would even intentionally select as ministers individuals whom so-called public opinion detested—and thereby demonstrate that Russia would accept these appointments perfectly well.

It was high time for a bold step. In December, congress after congress raged—the zemstvo, the towns, even the nobility—competing to be the loudest in defaming government and Tsarist power. Even Minister Nikolai Maklakov, once a favorite of the Emperor, whose reports had always been a joy for the Emperor, and with whom working had been inspiring, but who had been dismissed under pressure from Nikolasha, had now written most loyally that these congresses and all the hooting in the press had to be understood correctly, that this was the beginning of a direct assault on the state's authority. Maklakov presented a memorandum from some loyal men regarding how to save the state, and Shcheglovitov sent another just like it. These loyal men had plenty of nerve, so why had the Emperor lost his?

And now from many other sides, even from Uncle Pavel, news had come in that throughout the capital, even among the Guards, people were talking openly about preparations for a coup d'état. In January and February, the Emperor had been nurturing the thought of a preventive strike: bringing back his best, firmest ministers, dissolving the Duma now, and not reconvening it before late 1917, after the Fifth had been elected. He had already instructed Maklakov to compose a formidable manifesto dissolving the Duma. Which Maklakov had already composed and submitted.

However, as always, debilitating doubts flooded the Emperor. Need there be an escalation? Need the risk be run of an outburst? Wouldn't it be better to let matters proceed peacefully, run their course, and ignore the bullies?

What about the coup? That was all just talk. No Russian would agree to a coup in time of war, not even the State Duma. Deep down everyone loved Russia. And the Army was boundlessly loyal to the Emperor himself. There was no true danger, so why provoke a new schism and resentment? Among the names of the conspirators, the Police Department had submitted such prominent ones as Guchkov, Lvov, and Chelnokov. The Emperor wrote that public figures were not to be touched, especially in time of war.

Never before had such an aching loneliness been felt around the Tsar's family as after this ill-starred murder. Betrayed by relatives and slandered by society, they retained only a few close ministers, though they, too, were hated by society all the more. Even loyal, close friends like aide-de-camp Sablin were few and far between. With them they spent Yuletide, winter evenings, and Sundays at sparsely attended dinners and teas, sometimes inviting a small orchestra to the palace, sometimes a movie. In addition, they had their inimitably diverse outings in the Tsarskoye vicinity, and even a novelty: snow motorcars. In the evenings, Nikolai read aloud a great deal to his family and solved puzzles with his children. Although since February the children had been falling ill.

Alix spent those two months nearly prostrate, as if she herself were the deceased. She learned and knew almost nothing other than Grigori's death, and her loyalty to her sorrow was more and more of a reproach to Nikolai every day.

The family was Nikolai's favorite milieu, and he could have spent a couple of years this way, in untroubled seclusion. He did not miss a single mass, he fasted, and he took communion. However, due to his proximity to the capital now, he could not entirely avoid affairs of state administration for those nine weeks. During one of those weeks, a conference of allies opened in Petrograd. Nikolai had no desire to appear in that hubbub, so General Gurko acted as the senior figure from Russia. On the other hand, the Emperor was thoroughly fed up with the length and harshness of Gurko's reports. (But he did have to receive the conference delegates at Tsarskoye—and Nikolai tensed and agonized terribly that they might also start advising him on domestic policy.) Every weekday, the Emperor also received the few ministers and prominent figures he especially liked, and with considerably greater pleasure.

However, whether because the funereal note did not abate in their home all those weeks and the headaches and sobbing over the murdered man dragged on, every man has his limit, and at last Nikolai was drawn to the straightforward and unconstrained life at GHQ, which also meant no ministerial reports. A few days before, Mikhail had arrived at Tsarskoye from Gatchina (his wife, a lawyer's daughter, already twice divorced, was neither allowed in nor recognized), and he had said that dissatisfaction was mounting in the army. Why had the Emperor been absent from GHQ for so long? Somewhere the rumor had even popped up that Nikolasha was once again going to take on the Supreme Command.

Could that really be? It was drivel, but dangerous drivel. Truly, it was time to go. (Here, too, was the unfortunate fact that his previous stay at GHQ had also been brief. He had spent his name day with his family at Tsarskoye and had not returned to GHQ until 20 December, and on the 31st was called back by Rasputin's death, and there he had been until now.)

But it was far from easy to beg leave of Alix. She failed to understand how he could abandon her in this grief when new assassinations might follow. They agreed that he would go for just a week, or even less, so that on 14 March, that unhappy anniversary for the Romanovs, the day of his grandfather's assassination, he would return to Tsarskoye and they would once again be together. This time she did not let the heir accompany his father because he was coughing for some reason.

Nikolai consoled himself with the fact that he was leaving the Tsaritsa under the protection of Protopopov, who assured him that everything had been arranged, there was no threat in the capital, and the Emperor could travel calmly.

Once the departure was decided, the weight of reproach that had divided them for two months suddenly fell away. Alix warmed and brightened, delved animatedly into his issues, reminded him not to forget whom in the army he should reward and whom replace—and viewed Alekseev's return to GHQ after his long illness with particular mistrust and distaste. What was the point? He shouldn't. He was Guchkov's man and unreliable. Decorate him and let him take an honorable rest.

But Nikolai loved his hard-working, unconceited old man and didn't have the heart to dismiss him. He couldn't possibly say that; it would be too awkward. Was he linked to Guchkov? Well, Gurko, in the very same position, now in Petrograd, according to a dispatch from Protopopov, had met with Guchkov. And he was linked to the Duma. (And ten days before, during a report at Tsarskoye, he had burst out in a voice like a trumpet at Jericho: "Emperor, you are destroying your family and yourself! What are you preparing for yourself? The rabble will not stand on ceremony. Dismiss Protopopov!" Never before had there been one so frenzied near Nikolai, and he already repented having agreed to take him on.)

Yesterday, after noon, Nikolai was riding to the train station—as always to the bells of the Cathedral of Our Lady of St. Theodore. Both he and Alix were inspired by the ringing of the bells. On the way, they stopped in at the Church of Our Lady of the Sign to make their reverences.

Just then the sky cleared, and the vivid, frosty, and joyous sun promised a good outcome for everything.

A pleasant surprise awaited Nikolai in his compartment (actually, this was their custom): an envelope from Alix placed on a small table next to his travel kit. He began reading avidly, in English:

"My very Own precious one! With anguish and deep pain I let you go— alone, without sweet Baby's tender companionship! Verily God has sent you a terrible hard cross to bear. I can do nothing but pray and pray. Our dear Friend does so in yonder world for you—there he is yet nearer to us.

"It seems as though things are taking a better turn—only, my Love, be firm, show the master hand, it's that what the Russian needs. Love and kindness you have *never* failed to show—now let them feel your fist at times. They ask for it themselves—how many have told me: 'we want to feel the whip.' It's strange, but such is the Slav nature: *great* firmness, hardness even—and warm love. They must learn to fear you—love is not enough. One must play with the reins, let them loose and draw them in . . ."

The whip? That was terrible. That was unimaginable, unspeakable—not even to be threatened. If *this* was the cost of being emperor, then he could do without being emperor at all.

To be firm, though—yes. To show an imperious hand—yes, in the end that was essential.

"I hope that you can come back very soon. I too well see how 'the screaming mass' behave when you are near. Duty calls, just now, *more* here than there. So do be home in ten days. Your wall, your wify remains guarding here in the rear.

"Ah, the loneliness of the nights to come — no Sunny near you — and no Sunshine, either."

Oh, my dear! My treasure! . . .

How his heart was eased that once again no clouds lay between them. How this fortified him emotionally.

As always when traveling by rail, Nikolai took pleasure in reading, which he found relaxing and refreshing, this time in French, about Julius Caesar's Gallic War; he was in the mood for something far afield from contemporary life.

It was cold outside, and somehow he didn't feel like moving, and he didn't leave his car at all for the entire journey.

Nikolai had noticed more than once that our tranquility or its lack depends not on remote, albeit major events but on what is happening right where we are. If there is no tension in the environment, in the immediate hours and days, then one's soul brightens. After his Petersburg cares of state and without distressing official papers, it was quite glorious to lie in the train's dear rocking and read, with no need to see or talk to anyone.

Late that night he reread his favorite, the marvelous English story about Little Boy Blue. And, as always, tears came to his eyes.

Documents – 1

TO HER MAJESTY. Telegram.

GHQ, 8 March

Arrived well. Fine, cold, windy. Am coughing rarely. Feel strong again, but very lonely. Thoughts always together. Miss you awfully.

Nicky

TO HIS MAJESTY

Tsarskoye Selo, 8 March

(in English)

Well, now Olga & Aleksei have the measles. Baby coughs very much and eyes ache. They lie in the dark. Our meals we take in the "red room." Can imagine your awful loneliness without sweet Baby. So sad he and Olga can't write to you, as must not use their eyes. . . . Oh my love, how sad it is without you – how lonely, how I yearn for your love and kisses, precious treasure, I think of you without end. Do wear the cross sometimes when making difficult decisions, it will help you.

. . . Cover you with kisses. Ever

your very *Own*

[2]

SCREEN

In the plundered Petersburg sky,
scraps and tracks of it between the overhangs of the joyless fac-
    tory roofs —
the sun has broken through. It's going to be a sunny day!
The drone of voices.
    = A warm day even. Scarves pulled back from women's heads,
        mittenless hands, no one huddling or hunching over, they
        bustle about freely
in line, forty or so people,
at a small shop with one small door and one small window.
Extricating himself from the small door is someone who has al-
    ready bought something. Each person, first one, then an-
    other, is carrying two or three loaves of rye bread,
big, round, well-kneaded, and baked, with a dusting of flour on
    the bottom —
oh, so many being carried away!
So many being carried away, and so few left! Before you can
    squeeze in, your eyes peer over shoulders or from the side
    through the window:
        *"Lots of white, women, not that that's any good to any-
        one. But the rye's running out! No, there'll be none left
        for us."*
        *"Folks say as rye flour's been banned altogether and
        they won't bake it no more. There'll be a pound of
        bread per snout."*
        "Where'd the flour go?"
        *"The Tsaritsa's floggin' it to the Germans, they've got
        nothin' for their bellies."*
The women, angry voices, drone on worse.
    A sensible old man with an empty sack under his arm:
        *"And there's nothing left to feed the horses. They're not
        letting oats into Petersburg. And a horse, if you keep it
        on bread, it's twenty pounds a day, no way less."*
And out of the small door, a woman. She spreads her arms wide
    on the threshold: They say they're out.
The next three start going in at once, not that you can squeeze in.
A woman's shrill voice starts screaming:
        "What about us? We waited for nothing?"
A scarf slips, but hands are free. Eyes search: do what? throw what?

= Ice shard, chopped off, a chunk at the pavement's edge
Frozen on? No, no, it'll come up.
She grabs on to it and throws overhanded like a woman, with
both hands—
whomp!
= And the little window just – crash!
A ringing.
to little pieces!
= The salesclerk bellows like a bull, from inside, through the shards,
and out of nowhere comes a second chunk! Hit, miss—
everything starts spinning! the commotion! People try to dodge
through the door, but that many won't fit.
A general roaring and banging.
They throw whatever they find through the broken window,
right on the street. We don't need anything: white rolls!
candles!
red cheese wheels!
smoked fish!
bluing! brushes! laundry soap! . . .
And all of it on the ground, on the beaten snow, underfoot.

* * *

An excited hum.
= A sweeping crowd of workers throngs down the brown workers'
avenue.
Added to the throng is another throng from a side-street. Lots of
women; they're the angriest.
A crowd of several hundred pours in, itself not knowing, nothing
is decided,
past a single-story factory workshop.
People peek out, through windows, through window vents. To
them then:
"*Hey, ammo man! Quit working! Join us.* **Bread!**"
They linger alongside and try to persuade them:
"*Quit, ammo man! As long as there're lines—what
work? Bread!*"
For some reason ammo man doesn't want to, even moves back
from the windows.
"*Oh you, dimwit bitches! Hey, have you got your own
shop or something?*"
"*Every man for himself, is it?*"
A thickset old workman comes out on the stairs, hatless.
"*Regular hooligans you are, eh? Everyone's got his own
head. It's our own bins you think we're assembling
shells for?*"

A piece of ice at him:
>"*Your own head?*"

The workman grabs his head.

A guffaw.

= Throng of adolescent workers.
>They're off! Like on the attack!
>And in the wide-open factory gates—what can you do with a horde like that?—they run around the guard, spin him 'round,

run around the policeman—

Eee! through the factory yard!

Eee! through all the doors and all the workshops!

>Voices from a children's chorus:
>>"*Quit working! Come outside! . . . Everybody outside! . . . Bread! Bread! Bread!*"

= The guard grapples to close the gates,
>to pull the gates' tall, strong halves together,
>while half a hundred hale workers are running in from outside—
>with all their strength!—

it creaks,

>and one half tears off its hinge, its corner scrapes as it leans atilt,
>now everyone who wants, go on in.
>The policeman puts his hands on one
>but he gets it with a stick. A stick!
>The drone of voices.

*　　*　　*

= Bolshoi Prospect on the Petersburg side. The five-story buildings look fused, unyielding, lined up in order of size. Straight as an arrow.
>All the buildings are fancy—balconies, ledges, and decorated surfaces. And not a single tree anywhere. A stone canyon.
>Downstairs is Filippov's bakery, magnificent. Three double plate glass windows and, behind that, pastries, cakes, pretzels, and fluffy loaves.
>A young petit bourgeois man brandishes a crowbar,
>people run away from him, protect their eyes,
>how about like **that**?
>Crash! the plate glass.
>And on to the second.
>Crash! the second.
>And the crowd pours into the store.

= And inside everything is lacquered and properly fitted out, not
   like in ordinary shops.
Some nice black bread? It's crowded in here. But the fluffy loaves!
And the pretzels! So white! And sweet! . . .
Is this what you don't want? A stick strikes the glass counter!
Is this what you don't want? A stick at your cakes!
The genteel public staggers back, aghast.
The salesclerks are nowhere to be found, they've fallen back.
Smash the white! Smash the sweets! If we're not eating, you're
   not either!
Don't rile us, you devils! . . .

         ✻   ✻   ✻

Ringing,
= from the Finland Station down a side-street, a streetcar makes its
   way through the hubbub of excited people in the street.
A small group of workers is standing around, looking like bullies. They curse:
        "Where're you shovin'? Can't ya see?"
The streetcar conductor is standing on the front landing behind
   the window, like an idol, turning the long lever in his box.
A bright idea! One worker jumps up to him, onto the front
   landing—
Don't you understand Russian? Kicks him aside,
tears that long lever off his box—
and showing the people from the step, shakes the long streetcar
   lever
over his head!—
And gaily hops off.
They saw! They understood! They liked it!
The streetcar comes to a halt. It can't move without that lever.
It looks out through the three front windows,
and the conductor in the middle, his forehead on the glass.
= The whole crowd is laughing!

         ✻   ✻   ✻

= And on Nevsky, what a nice, frosty, sunny day for a stroll! A few
   dashing sleighs glide by. With sleigh bells!
So many people on the sidewalks, including the most genteel:
   ladies with their purchases and maids, officers with their
   batmen. All kinds of ladies and gentlemen. Lively conversations, laughter.

It's somehow even too dense on the sidewalks. In the street, all decorous, no one hindering the cabbies and streetcars, but on the sidewalks they squeeze together—not strolling but pushing forward to the demonstration.

Ah, here we have the petty bourgeois, and the workmen, and the common women, every stripe, pushing into the fancy crowd, and this in the middle of a workday, on Nevsky!

But the genteel public doesn't disdain them, and so together they sail along, like a single fused body. They've come up with something entertaining; the faces of young men and women students beam. The crowd isn't breaking anything, it's sailing together down the sidewalk, faces both pleased and mischievous, and mournful voices, as if they're burying someone, like an underground moan:

"Bread . . . Bread . . ."

They've appropriated it from the women workers, transformed it into a moan, and now all together, more and more broadly, even those who never put rye in their mouths, and yet they moan sepulchrally:

"Bread . . . Bread . . ."

But they titter with their eyes. And laugh openly, and taunt. Petersburg's inhabitants are always somber—which makes the gaiety that's come over them even stranger.

Little boys run to the edge of the street, where they march and drum and horse around:

"Give us bread! Give us bread!"

= Here and there police details along Nevsky. Worried policemen. Where there are mounted police, too.

There's nothing you can do, you can't find fault. It isn't an infraction. A foolish position for the police.

*   *   *

= And down Nevsky, down the Nevsky arrow shining in the sun, in the line of receding streetcar poles—

these streetcars, for some reason these streetcars are too close together, there's some obstacle, no getting through:

A string of them, lined up. The public is looking out the windows like fools and doesn't know what's next.

One front landing empty.

Another empty landing and a front window smashed.

While down the street go five young bucks, workmen or petty bourgeois, carrying five control levers—long ones!—

brandishing them like weapons,

to general laughter. From the sidewalks the genteel public laughs!

= Seeing this, an assistant police officer,
   without fuss, quickly cuts through the crowd—
   walks confidently, as the authority, and doesn't much look to ei-
      ther side,
   he's not expecting anything bad, and if he is, then he's brave,
   he reaches to take a lever away from one man—
   when another lever strikes the back of his head—
   and twice!
   The officer spins around and drops, unconscious, there, under-
      foot. Gone.
= The genteel Nevsky public laughs and laughs! So do the female
   students.

                    *   *   *

= The ribbed cupola of the Cathedral of Our Lady of Kazan.
   Its famous square between the arches of the classical arcade
   is jammed with people, still with the same cheerful appeal and
      plaintive wail:
         "Bread . . . Bread . . ."
   They like this game. Grand fur hats, bowlers, stylish ladies' hats,
      simple kerchiefs, and black peaked caps:
         "Bread . . . Bread . . ."
= And along the cathedral's sides stand the dragoon details on
      their noble, imposing steeds.
   And their officer, dismounted, speaks to a high-ranking policeman,
   leaps into the saddle, gives an order
not too loudly—the crowd can't hear—
      and the dragoons move off in groups of six, at a round pace, and
         so stand in groups of six in one place, and another,
      they're riding onto the sidewalks! Straight at the public!
      The horses' heads and chests rise up like cliffs!
      and they themselves are even taller!—
      but they aren't angry or shouting, and they're giving no orders—
      they're just sitting there, in the sky, and coming at us!
= There's nowhere to go, people of all estates scatter, dash off in a
      wave—
   away from the square, into nearby passageways,
   through front doors and gateways. Some collapse into a snowy
      pile. A whistle from the crowd.
   And the horses step proudly through the empty places.
   But as soon as they ride away—the crowd returns to these places
      and sidewalks.
   The rules of the game! No one is angry at anyone. They're
      laughing.

= But alongside the Ekaterininsky Canal, on the far side of the
    Kazan Bridge—
half a hundred Cossacks, young bucks from the Don—with
    lances.
Tall! Well built! Frightening! The dashing, menacing Cossacks
    scowl from their steeds.
A high-ranking official drives up to an officer:
> *"I am Major General Balk, the city governor of Peters-
> burg. I order you to disperse this crowd immediately,
> at full gallop—but without the use of weapons! Clear
> a path for wheeled and sleigh traffic."*

= The officer is quite young and inexperienced. He looks awk-
    wardly at the city governor.
Awkwardly at his detachment. And listlessly,
so listlessly, it's amazing they move up at all, let alone at a full
    gallop, but they do move
at a walk, their lances pointing straight up,
at a walk, their steeds' hooves slipping on the slippery pavement,
across the wide bridge and down Nevsky.
The city governor gets out of his motorcar and sets off alongside
    them. He walks alongside them—and unable to restrain
    himself, himself orders:
> *"Full gallop!"*

Do Cossacks really take orders from an outsider, and one on foot
    at that?
Well, the little officer sets his horse at a trot.
So the Cossacks, they do, too.
But the closer they get to the crowd, the slower they go . . .
Slower . . . This is not scaring them . . . Their lances all straight
    up, not pointing forward.
And before reaching them, they halt altogether. The joyous roar
    of thousands!
the crowd roars with delight:
> *"Hurrah for the Cossacks! Hurrah for the Cossacks!"*

This is something new for the Cossacks, hearing this from city
    dwellers: "hurrah!"
And this in the Cossacks' honor. They beam.
And pass on by the two Konyushennaya streets.

= But the crowd hasn't come up with anything:
the rally hasn't started, there's not a single leader—and all of a
    sudden an ominous clatter,
frightened faces turn to the side:

= from Kazan Street, skirting the cathedral and the standing street-
    cars in a large arc,

louder clatter!
>> a mounted patrol, a dozen or so men—but at a gallop! A gallop!
Fanning out, though without baring their swords—at a
gallop!
= Convulsed fear! And without waiting for them!
The crowd runs, scatters in all directions—
as if blown away! Nevsky is clear—all the way to the Duma.
= They never do bare their swords.

[3 ']

(THE BREAD NOOSE)

Through the great, earthshaking Duma speeches of November 1916, through the palisade of hasty inquiries, protests, clashes, and new elections, the State Duma never did take up the food question, which in any case was too particular for politics in general. In mid-December, a certain Rittikh was appointed the new interim minister of agriculture. He asked for the floor and respectfully apologized to the Duma for not yet having had time to consider the matter and for being unable to report on measures. They scolded him as they would any government representative, but rather lazily, for they themselves expected nothing to come of their own Duma discussion if it was too specific. Yes, the food question was important, but in the *general*, not the specific, sense, and thus the main flame of politics escaped the Tauride Palace, which was fettered by Duma procedure. Rather, the main flame of politics roared up first here and then there as it ran through society, and even more so in Moscow. There, three congresses had been scheduled for late December, all three on the topic of food: the Food Supply Congress itself, and congresses of the Union of Zemstvos and Union of Towns (to say nothing of all the other concurrent public meetings, as the joke then went: if the German outdoes us at technology, we'll beat him at meetings).

The food supply was discussed with a quaver in the voice. The government didn't dare forbid the Food Supply Congress, although both the government and those assembling understood that this wasn't about food, that Russia had always been supplied with food even without us and it would somehow continue to do so. No, it was about those assembled discussing first and foremost the *current moment* and somehow expressing themselves more sharply about the government, and in that way *shaking things up*. (The previous revolution had shown that this could be achieved only through continuous shaking.) Knowing all this, too, the government this time summoned up the courage to forbid the other two congresses before they even began. City heads, zemstvo figures, and eminent merchants who had gathered from all over Russia crowded the sidewalk on Bolshaya Dmitrovka, but the police wouldn't let them into the building. While Prince Lvov was drawing up the nonadmission document, zemstvo representatives whispered quietly and slipped away to other premises on Maroseika, where they "got down to business," that is, once again, not the boring food part but general considerations of the *political moment*. In a prepared but undelivered speech, Prince **Lvov** wrote:

At the very edge of the abyss, when there might be just a few moments left for salvation, all we can do is call on *the people themselves*. Leave behind any attempts to work together with the present regime! . . . Turn your back on the phantoms! *There is no authority and the government is not running the country!*

This did seem to be the case. (As Shcheglovitov put it, "The regime's paralytics have been struggling rather pathetically with the revolution's epileptics.") Prince Lvov, who was on his way to becoming the top man in Russia and who was greeted stormily, caught up with the zemstvo session on Maroseika, and the resolution passed there was even harsher than his speech. To avoid being dispersed, the congresses of the Unions assembled in private apartments—and initially the police were reluctant to violate the sanctity of the home. By the time they arrived, the resolutions would have already been approved or the vote would be taken then and there, in front of the police:

> . . . The regime, which is ruining and disgracing Russia . . . Irresponsible criminals, driven by superstitious fear, are readying its defeat, disgrace, and enslavement! . . . The people cannot trust this shameless and criminal regime, which has disorganized the country and rendered the army powerless, with prosecuting the war or concluding a peace.

In truth, what choice did the regime have? Either leave immediately (and they had permitted and allowed so much that they might as well go) or else ban these congresses after all?

Also in December a congress of industrial figures gathered, also to discuss the food provision issue. At the tail end of these fiery policy resolutions there were a few words found for Rittikh's initiatives:

> The new government measures only crown the disorder.

For **this** government will never find a solution in anything.

Modest, obscure Rittikh girded himself to delving into the details and finding a solution. In the very first days after assuming his position he ascertained that one-twelfth of the bread needed had been procured: one hundred million pounds instead of one billion two hundred; all the parties and all the press had finished saying and then promptly forgotten what they wanted about fixed prices, but fixed prices loomed over the grain market and locked it up, and the trading apparatus was powerless to extract grain from the granaries; the late autumn congress of agriculturalists, where there had been many chairmen of zemstvos and cooperatives as well as peasants, had insisted on raising grain prices to cover the cost of production, labor, and also transport from granary to station, although, according to the prices given by Progressive Bloc figures, transport was not considered to involve labor or even to exist, and was paid, so be it, for a delivery of twenty versts, even if it was transported ninety, and over impassable roads.

But they had missed their chance to raise prices this winter. The countryside would only be expecting even higher ones. Rittikh took the liberty of paying for cartage from granary to station immediately, as of December (carriage paid, that is, the price being calculated at the granary and the delivery on top of that)—for which he was angrily rebuked in the State Duma. "You're wrecking fixed prices!" This measure of Rittikh's notably increased the influx of grain, but not enough to feed the Russian army and Russian rear until autumn 1917 with a solid reserve. Fixed prices remained lower than market prices, and once the winter road was established, the countryside started sending grain to town, where it was immediately sent back to the countryside and there disappeared. Private trade sought it out there, but at high prices. And the specter of a *grain obligation* or grain levy flickered before the newly minted Minister of Agriculture. He found the resolve to take this step, a step he was not alone in having picked up in the Russian air.

Rittikh had no intention of taking the grain by force. That would be sacrilegious to Russian traditions and a disgrace for the Russian government. How could they, instead of buying the grain, take it from whoever had grown it? A grain obligation was a terrible coercive measure that Russian minds would not accept. No, Rittikh's idea boiled down to

> shifting grain deliveries from the realm of a simple commercial transaction to the realm of fulfillment of a civic duty required of every holder of grain. To explaining to the populace that fulfillment of this levy was for him a duty akin to the sacrifices they were making without a murmur for the war.

The levy included the requirements of the army, pound for pound, and of defense factory workers and their families (as they were already being supplied at many factories). Major centers and nonproducing provinces had not been included as consumers because it was difficult to inform 18 million peasant farms that it was their civic duty to supply the capitals and the North. The figures received

> were also reduced so that the levy would not be difficult to fulfill for any reason.

The provincial zemstvos were supposed to levy their assigned amount among their counties, the counties among the townships, and the townships and village assemblies among the farmsteads. And what of it? The apportionment went very well.

> Initially, I'll be frank, a patriotic impulse was felt. Many provincial and county zemstvos increased this levy by 10 percent and more. (I asked them for this increase in order to be able to feed the centers and North with the surplus.) But immediately following, doubts were brought to the matter, as was a critical attitude toward the levy, and all attention turned to the fact that the levy would be difficult to implement, that too much was being required of each province. Of course, it was hard, and it required a great deal, but gentlemen, after all, war is also hard.

A representative of the hated and despised government had to express himself to the enraged public gently and circumspectly:

> Nonetheless, gentlemen, I think that those methods used to prove the levy excessive are hardly correct. Following the zemstvos' first rush to carry out this levy, all attention was hypnotized by whether after the levy the populace would be sufficiently provided for. This cooled the enthusiasm there had been for the levy and reduced it from a great goal to calculations of measures and weights, how much to leave each one in reserve and how much could be allocated to our army.

All the zemstvo representatives possessed an extraordinary sensitivity to local interests; they were patriots of their neighborhood. But what if the harvest failed and there was a new call-up and a shortage of hands and grain? Be careful, don't send more than you must. . . .

> It's easy to convince today's peasant—now nearly always a woman—not to give up her grain, so her children won't starve.
>
> All the provinces drew up consumption standards 5–7 poods higher than is considered usual in peacetime. But given 150 million people, that's 900 million

poods, that is, the entire domestic grain trade was held back. Provinces like Tauride that always brought in tens of millions of poods were seemingly incapable of contributing anything, and on top of that, it turned out 14 million poods needed to be brought into a rich one like Ekaterinoslav.

Doubt had been sown, and the levy was delayed by so much that it reached the townships not in two December weeks, as Rittikh was so anxious it would, but only in February 1917. . . . Some townships met it, others even exceeded it, and some refused. Rittikh, though, *did not permit requisitions to be applied:*

Too many coercive and decisive measures have been taken against our producer, but—

assemble a gathering once more, perhaps its mood will change, and indicate that the Homeland, its defense, needs this. . . .

At the repeat gatherings the levy often passed. Or else they promised to impose it after the winter crops came in. The levy's first result was that the peasants started threshing the grain they had left in ricks more zealously. The grain supply increased greatly in December and January:

in December, 200 percent of the average monthly autumn delivery; in January, 260 percent. And every week it rose.

The zemstvos, too, got over their hypnosis. If it's required, we'll give it. We'll tighten our belts and get through this. The grain problem definitely moved along and began to be resolved. Rittikh hoped that by August 1917

the levy's great goal would be reached.

(There was no threat of famine in the next few months; the idea was to provide for the summer.)

Meanwhile, 27 February was approaching and with it the long-awaited opening of the State Duma's suspended sessions. Russian society was waiting impatiently for an outburst, especially from the first day. Even more so were Milyukov, the leader of the Progressive Bloc, and the leftist leader Kerensky preparing to bring about this outburst. Their speeches, historic before they were ever delivered, were meant to create this historic State Duma day—historic before it ever happened. The public gathered avidly in the Tauride Palace galleries. What a deafening rout awaited the government in the next few hours! President Rodzyanko himself was already relishing this as much as anyone else, but according to the Duma's wooden charter he could not refuse the minister who unexpectedly asked for the floor. (Practically since Stolypin's day they had grown unaccustomed to a request for the floor from ministers themselves, who were happy to maintain their silence in their box when they were not being thrashed too badly.)

It was Agriculture Minister Aleksandr Aleksandrovich Rittikh, who for some reason had not been removed in the last three months and who had only just returned from a trip through twenty-six grain-producing provinces (having already informed the Emperor of his intentions). He stepped onto the tribune with a conciliatory tone—utterly out of keeping, of course, with the Duma's burning political objectives, and for more than an hour put a damper on its heat, ruining the historic day and the broad political debates on fundamentals with his tedious focus on food—everything quoted above.

For several years the government had been squirming out of its Duma box, and its ministers had avoided attempts to clarify the situation with the Duma—and that had been bad and rightly reviled. But now a minister had come out with detailed explanations, had been patiently present at the day-long debates, and had readily stood up to provide more and more new explanations—and was even less able to please!

Having departed from the tradition of recent Russian governments, which were absent, faceless, and paralytic, Aleksandr Rittikh himself came from the very same educated stratum that for decades had indulged in liberal politics and criticism. Wholly focused on the matter at hand and always prepared to account for himself and offer arguments, Rittikh had been sent by fate on purpose to the final week of the Russian State Duma to show what it was worth and what it wanted. Its criticism had constantly harped on the fact that the government had no knowledgeable and effective ministers—and here was a knowledgeable, effective minister, and on the most important matter—so he had to be repudiated all the more!

No matter how he tried to soften it with his cautionary, even respectful attitude toward the Duma:

> I emphasize that I have decided on these measures not myself but with approval and consent of the most authoritative nature: the bases for the levy were laid out by the State Duma (noise on the left), and they were repeated by the Special Conference—

it was even more offensive that he had taken *our* idea but was carrying it out with the *wrong* hands! He was "skillfully positioning himself under the banner of the nation's cause." Rittikh made himself tedious as well by telling everyone from here, from the Duma tribune, what they already knew: after the warm, mild winter of 1915–16 and the unusually harsh winter of 1916–17, in February there had been nearly three weeks of unrelenting blizzards and drifting, which had brought all rail traffic and grain shipments to a halt. He was especially venomous in having the nerve not to accept the blame for the doomed, feeble government, which had done nothing but prevent Russian happiness:

> But there is no certainty that the deliberate movement of grain supplies will hold. It isn't the spring's impassable roads that are so frightening. That doesn't happen everywhere at once. What is dangerous is the unflinchingly negative attitude toward the actions of the agricultural ministry on the part of a *well-known trend in public thought,* a trend so major that it has the means to insert its view into the very thick of the populace. This criticism has presented **all** measures as having been taken by a government that does not enjoy confidence and consequently are incorrect and doomed to failure. What is the good in holding the flag of no-confidence up to the government no matter what, without penetrating to the essence or taking the trouble to verify the consequences? (Noise on the left. Voices on the right: "Let's listen! What's this?") They want people in the very thick of our countryside to know: Don't do it, don't bring grain, because it's the government calling on you to do this. (Shingarev: "Not true!" On the right: "Bravo!" Voronkov: "The audacity!") I've been reproached for audacity. But I fear this politics more than all the impassable roads. I'm afraid it will wreck the cause. (Applause on the right.) Calculation won't get you the peasant's grain. The peasant now has no need of money. Now, if society were to suggest to the peasantry that the war and homeland required it, then the grain would flow two and four times faster. Where for whatever reason opposing forces have not materialized, we are seeing astounding results.

In some provinces, grain piled up so high, they didn't even carry out the levy by township, for example, in Samara Province, where before December barely 4000 poods were purchased and 19 million were brought in over the month of December.

> But this venom—that this was being done by the government and therefore should not be obeyed—had not penetrated there. If we could all unite on the grounds of this simple sincerity, not worrying about who belongs to what but just whether he wishes his homeland good. . . .

> But what are the critics suggesting? They're not suggesting realistic, direct measures but merely more discussions and congresses. Last autumn there was this huge congress, and it only undercut and predetermined the whole fate of the food campaign, and now desperate efforts have to be made to correct this. I view with fear this policy of divorcing consumers from producers. All the zemstvos have deemed the government's measures correct, the only ones possible even, but the stamp of distrust has been placed on it all: this was conceived of by the government and can only lead to ruin. If, God forbid, this ruin does occur, then, gentlemen, *we will have to sort out where the reason for it lies.* Are we really going to continue to wage a political struggle around this tremendous cause which has such terrible significance for Russia? I anxiously await the State Duma's response. (Applause on the right and in the right section of the center.)

(What made this unnecessary speech dangerous was that it split off the Bloc's right section, which was not necessarily *opposed* merely on principle. He had undermined the Bloc's tactic of uniform psychological pressure on the authorities.)

He waited, sitting in the ministerial box, at the foot of the speakers and facing the deputies.

But the Progressive Bloc, naturally, was not about to discuss Rittikh's trivial statement, and the Duma tabled it by a vote of 2:1. They did decide to hear and discuss the Progressive Bloc's general statement. Although it evidently referred again to food, transport, and fuel, it did so in the *general* perspective, in the sense that none of these issues could be decided as such, but first

> it was essential that the men running the country be recognized as the nation's leaders and meet with the support of the legislative institutions. . . . A regime that every citizen could gladly obey.

As long as this was not the case, without a radical restructuring of the executive authority, they could not discuss food, transport, or fuel. Let this insignificant so-called state answer this question:

> What is going to be done to eliminate the intolerable state of affairs set forth above?

And so, the solemn course of Duma sessions could flow once again, and Russia's leading intellect and leader of its liberals and center now had an opportunity to deliver his own general political, exclamatory speech of the highest and broadest significance—and, naturally, not about bread. **Milyukov:**

> Relations between the government and State Duma are the sole issue of the current moment.

But he did not leave out Rittikh, whose arguments

> have showed us these men's blatant inability to grasp the issue's full breadth
> and depth. Self-confidence, smugness, a free handling of the facts, and disre-
> spect for his audience. There is no sense in a single comment of his speech
> that he understands that the food issue is not only . . .

not only . . . not only . . . about the chewing movements of teeth. The food issue was this:
Why did they persecute the attempts of the Unions of Zemstvos and Towns to resolve agricultural problems themselves, without the government? What was the reason behind shutting down the Free Economic Society of Marxists? . . .

But Milyukov was capable of acting by the strictest scholarly methods, too. Here, if you
please, was a diagram, he was holding a diagram, and showing it to the entire Duma. He
did not give detailed explanations (without higher knowledge, the deputies couldn't penetrate this), but everyone could see the rise:

> Here is a curve rising high up after fixed prices were set. And here it is when it
> starts falling—the moment Rittikh appears.

And from this everyone could see that

> fixed prices brought grain to the market!

That is, when it was profitable to sell, they didn't, but when it became unprofitable everyone immediately began bringing it in. Waterfalls falling up. There was no "patriotic impulse," but once Rittikh offered this benefit and paid for cartage to the train station, then it
became profitable to sell the grain itself below cost. Finally, Milyukov exposed Rittikh's
numbers, too, about the grain procurement rising in December–January by as much as
260 percent over the autumn. No one calculated that way; the comparison had to be made
with the same months of the previous year.

> Mr. Rittikh should not be believed. He distorted an idea by taking it out of con-
> text. And that idea cannot be resolved without a decisive change in domestic
> policy.

But **Kerensky**, in his equally historic speech, barely engaged with Rittikh.

> This gentleman, who many in the Duma here call brilliant, this first disciple of
> Stolypin, cut his teeth on the destruction of the agricultural commune

(dearly loved from afar by Trudoviks and Kadets alike); his entire "patriotic impulse" came
down to a landowners' class conspiracy. In Kerensky's usual muddle, free trade was just as
bad as the levy, nonfixed prices were as bad as fixed, and economic anarchism as bad as
state coercion.

Here, too, with the hall not full, deputies were constantly drifting off to the buffet,
which was the only place the food question arose, whereas the discussion was on politics in
general and the most fundamental policy at that.

Rittikh obediently sat through the day like a patient pupil, hearing nothing more about
food supplies from anyone in the Duma majority, and just this from the minority, the rightist Professor **Levashov:**

> Huge reserves of the most important foodstuffs have been artificially removed
> from consumption and intentionally hidden in the storehouses of city pawn
> shops, banks, and joint-stock associations and companies—in anticipation of
> higher prices.

He cited many cities and examples—hidden reserves of matches, soap, and rice in Caucasian cities, manufactured goods in Stary Oskol, flour and sugar in Turgai Province, 2 million in hides in Nizhni Novgorod, an artificial petroleum shortage from Caspian oil producers—and this was only what had been discovered, while a thousand times more had not been. Some were fighting, but the rest?

No matter what the state was reviled for, though, the liberal Duma members had never accused it of pandering to industrial companies and banks.

And now they had to vote on their inquiry:

What should be done to eliminate the intolerable situation?

The illegality of the changes in the makeup of the State Council had to be discussed as well!

Inquiries had to be made about the illegal actions against the trade unions and workers' organizations. . . .

But on 1 March, the Duma was not in session, although it was a weekday.

And on 2 March, debates had to be held on the inquiries. Here this diligent Rittikh, appearing punctually in the beginning, irritating the Duma majority by his mere presence, now seemed to be taking his place to respond to the inquiry (inasmuch as the food supply was mentioned)—and they had to give him the floor, so here he was again on the tribune and again making his point. He responded to the crumbs thrown at his question in the last two days.

> I simply could not understand what kind of curve it was State Duma member Milyukov was talking about.

(Respectfully, although Milyukov had called him simply "Rittikh," without the "Mr.")

> I studied it with our statistical department and realized, or rather, guessed. Gentlemen, it turns out that the grain has been *commissioned*, but we don't have it. Indeed, when free trade was completely driven from the market, several grain supply deals were made. These deals were as good as the paper they were written on, what came in was deplorable, and the commissions were for spring navigation. I don't believe we can speak of grain receipts when there has only been paper about grain, nor can we take up the State Duma's attention with these kinds of diagrams. (On the right: "Absolutely correct!" The center and left do not support him.) Naturally I was reporting with respect to the grain that is not a matter of speculation but has in reality been received at our granaries, at receiving points near railroads, in warehouses near mills, and in drying rooms.

Here, then, is what we have, as a result of this persuasion and despite fixed prices: 260 percent. But if one calculates as Mr. Milyukov wishes, and compares the months not with the autumn but with the same months last year, then there is still an increase: 196 percent in December, and 148 percent in January.

He was not saying that Milyukov was foolish or dishonest.

> I would not allow myself to explain this using the same motives as State Duma member Milyukov does to explain *my* words and numbers. I explain this by a simple mistake: one of the secretaries . . . . As for the statement of State Duma member Milyukov that fixed prices *brought* grain to the market . . .

at zemstvo meetings they would merely laugh. Rittikh referred to Zhilkin, a member of the revolutionary First Duma, who in the same months as the minister traveled through a number of provinces and published the following in the newspaper: Yes, grain disappeared because of fixed prices, but in December it appeared, as if the spell had been broken.

The Progressive Bloc was silent: If truth is not on our side, then away with the truth.

Generally speaking, to say that fixed prices brought grain to the market, I understand this as a witty paradox.

In Samara Province, after the appeal regarding the army's needs, all of a sudden grain was brought in abundance without any levy whatsoever—and so? *Progressive society* rushed to warn the peasants: "Don't believe it or you're going to starve."

I consider this *work*—even if it is progressive society's, I don't know what to call it—devastating to Russia's interests and very close to sabotage.

What will the peasants' reserves lead to when the land is defiled by our enemy's foot? This may be the decisive moment, and everything down to the last pood should be released in order to ensure success. (Applause only on the right. Milyukov: "Progressive society must be regarded differently.") Does the fate of the war truly depend only on shells and not on grain? Can a decision be put off for even a minute? There needs to be a unanimous appeal to Russia and the peasantry to give up everything for the war and victory!

But what is progressive society and its Unions proposing? Not paying cartage, stopping the levy, taking stock, taking stock again, and of course, more meetings, and of course committees that don't include peasants.

With committees like that, you won't get a single pood of grain. . . . They've also introduced the term *agrarian*, which covers three fourths of Russia's population. I well remember the accusations that speculation had penetrated to the peasant classes,

so the city's consumers had to be protected from this profiteer. It was the excessive defense of the consumer,

through direct instructions to curtail the producer—18 million farms—that brought about this terrible schism, to the point that the main producer, the peasant, returned from the bazaars with his carts and stopped threshing grain, and this "agrarian" started not bringing anything to market, and if we survived from August to November then it was exclusively thanks to the grain of the landowners, who continued to bring it in.

It is a very unpleasant combination for the Bloc that peasants, too, fall into the "agrarian" category—and you can't separate them out.

Right then there were personal attacks against me as Stolypin's prize pupil. I beg you not to raise me up so high. I say the solution lies in all progressive society subscribing to the general suggestion to the peasants to bring every last bit! I anxiously await your reply, although I have been accused of optimism. But I will bear it without a murmur and will be happy if everything turns against me and not against the cause. I understand that a valve needs opening, and a guilty party must be found other than the critics themselves; the system must be destroyed in order to find the guilty party. Let them attack me, but don't keep rural Russia from bringing in grain! (Applause only from the right and center-right.)

It was a simple human inflexion such as was rarely heard from the Duma tribune except for maybe from unsophisticated, maladroit peasants. Duma members did not accept blame; they always defended themselves, and interrupted others, devastated others, with passion and sarcasm.

True, if only now they could forget party dogma, leaders' smugness, and reckonings and scores with enemies, and wake up. After all, Russia could perish! Everyone should unite and with a single breast call upon rural Russia: Save us sinners, brothers! We've come to blows and made a hash of things. . . . The air of distrust could be replaced with an air of trust, both in distant townships and at hand in the capital, so that people would not start storming bakeries. And this would blow over.

However, even Tsarskoye Selo with its proudly tossed feminine head could not allow even the hint of a smile. And the Duma leaders, dragged down by the inertia of their never-ending quarrels, cries from their seats, and votes, by commotions, discussions, revelations, and inquiries, in this dark, closed hall, a former winter garden that had not a single window onto God's world but only a cloudy glass ceiling through which the day's gleams flickered in, and in the intervals between sessions—eight doors down, doors that opened not directly on the light but to corridors—the Duma leaders could no longer stop, look around, come to their senses, and be reborn.

The hand of the regime had figured things out at its end of the rope, where Rittikh's warm hand had weakened it. But the Duma's distant, indifferent hand continued to pull confidently at its end. And the bread noose was tightening around the throat that fed Russia.

Of course, the hand of the regime had pulled quite a lot as well. The following speakers reminded them how Interior Minister Protopopov had pulled on it by postponing deliveries in the autumn, during the decisive weeks, with his project to confiscate food from the Agriculture Ministry and restore free prices. The leftist **Dzyubinsky:**

> The ineptitude of the levy lies in the fact that it was brought about specifically without consultation with public organizations. Only with the strictly democratic public, while the entire population participates in commissions in strictly proportionate representation . . .

(Though this takes years.)

> I think that the disappearance of grain from the market is merely coincidental with the publication of fixed prices. *Post hoc,* not *propter hoc.*

(Once you get going on those hocs, there's no hocking out of it. . . . The grain for some reason just vanished all by itself.)

> Rittikh violated fixed prices. The producer was *given* a few dozen kopecks per pood.

(Damn it! If you'd dragged a loaded wagon ninety versts through the Russian mud, I'd have given you that myself!)

They unleashed against Rittikh a most learned economist from the liberal camp, **Posnikov,** who in an expansive and erudite lecture explained to the State Duma and the mistaken minister this:

> A food levy is an extremely delicate matter!

(The food requisitioning detachments would soon demonstrate this for us.) And he loftily explained why the peasant delivery to the train station must not be paid for: doing so did not fit rent theory and the theory of market prices.

Yet another longwinded, hair-splitting lawyer from the Progressive Bloc, **Godnev** (in a few days, a minister in the Provisional Government), delving more and more deeply into the essence of things, revealed to us another root of evil: although the Duma had produced a law saying livestock could be slaughtered only four times a week, nonetheless Rittikh had complacently allowed the daily slaughter of cattle in the week before Christmas.

That was all the liberal speakers had to say against Rittikh. This minister had stunned the left wing. They had not been spoken to so convincingly and emphatically since Stolypin's time. In essence, it didn't matter whether Rittikh was right or wrong; he was a Tsarist minister and therefore necessarily foolish, dense, mute, and fearful—and Rittikh had violated their entire code. The speakers did not shy from talking about him as if they hadn't bothered to listen to him, and the same Dzyubinsky shamelessly distorted what the minister, who had just left the hall, had said: Rittikh has accused the peasantry of a lack of patriotism. (On the contrary, he had marveled at their patriotism.) But in this hall, the left could carry on against the right any way it liked, and most of the loudmouths were in favor of this speaker. A rightist shouted from his seat, "A misrepresentation! What lies are these?" But no one had the strength left to protest or discuss. So the lie was made fast in the transcript forever.

A leftist speaker ascended to the tribune not even to get entangled in food details but to tell us this:

> Never has the public atmosphere been so saturated with the thirst for a renewal of domestic political life, never have *nerves been so tightly wound*, and at the same time the country is cloaked in this fog. The harshness of the speeches and the passion with which they're listened to . . .

freed him from the obligation to speak to the point. But look, why aren't they sending police to the front? Did the peasants really need police? . . . And how dare the agricultural minister appeal to the peasants' patriotism if the government itself would not *resign*, as society has been demanding of it for two years? Where, then, was the patriotism of the government itself?

> The true guilty party is the autocratic order. A government that does not wish to resign will be toppled by the people's will and desire!

Savich. A zemstvo activist and Octobrist. As part of the Bloc, he was supposed to agree with the leftists about the government's immediate removal and much else. But he found the courage to object to his fellow Bloc members:

> Public opinion has lost its way on the food supply issue. Very few individuals have grasped the matter fully, dispassionately, and knowledgeably. The issue has been clouded by class strife. For the good of the state, a middle course must be found.
>
> Everything that happened this autumn had deep roots of long standing in the psychology of our country and society. From time immemorial the government, the towns, and our intelligentsia have been used to viewing the countryside as Rome viewed its provinces, as the metropolis does its colonies. The countryside was a reservoir of soldiers and assessments. The countryside was supposed to provide as many goods as possible as cheaply as possible and to

consume the city's goods at the highest possible price. Both the government and the towns chronically cheated the countryside of its fair share. We grew used to thinking that since we exported so much abroad, since we in the towns had cheap agricultural products and firewood, then we had an abundance of all this. But this was an error, and now it has become a colossal mistake. We have never had tremendous reserves. In order to pay the assessments being wrung from them, to buy the vodka they had grown used to, and to acquire second-rate goods at high prices, the countryside was forced to dispose of it not because it had too much but to keep from starving. (Applause on the left: "That's right!") The opinion took shape that there was no need to stand on ceremony with our countryside, that it would endure and provide everything. The war has had immeasurably harder repercussions on the countryside than the town. All grown male hands have been pumped out of the countryside.

(The leftists began to applaud, not envisioning where Savich was going. Now they quieted down.)

The percentage of conscripts there was much higher than in town; they poured capital into industries, and industries were released from their obligation—but the countryside wasn't. The first grain difficulties triggered repressions against agriculture the likes of which industry never experienced.

And so, first they stopped trading. But the horror went further: they stopped **sowing**. Never had it occurred to the towns or the government that the countryside might be in no condition to **provide**.

But in the autumn of 1916, agriculture was finished psychologically. And so began

a major persecution of "agrarians" and a settling of political scores.

The Stock Exchange Gazette proposed *exacting a contribution from agrarians* by lowering grain prices by half a ruble. Their only mistake was that major production could not stop unloading grain on the market because then production would stop, whereas the peasantry could get along without the market.

The polemic on prices set the countryside against the town. A great deal spoiled. The countryside closed itself off. Since it couldn't acquire anything for money, it simply rejected money. Had prices been a little higher, the levy would have been immeasurably easier. But now we can't get along without the levy because we're in no condition to give the countryside the goods it needs in exchange for foodstuffs. The lion's share of what the country has is going to the towns. You're all getting three pounds of sugar a month with your ration card, but the countryside doesn't get even one. And so it is with everything. Now the state has to carry out the levy by force.

(The stomp of boots and rifle butts . . . The inevitable was advancing on Russia. . . . No matter what happened from here on out, Russia could no longer avoid the issue. The entire history of the grain duty was instructive because when necessity arose, figures from the most contrary camps were prepared to carry it out. Only not everyone was given the authority and cruelty to do so.) Actually,

this did not have to mean military requisitioning, which would be plundering, but certain coercive measures would have to be . . . And to insure the countryside from low fixed prices in the future. Give enough that agriculture might not perish. (Applause in the center and left section of the rightists. The Kadets and leftists don't like it.) Otherwise, soon it will be impossible to plow, sow, and reap.

Shulgin: Workers, shop clerks, doctors, lawyers, and journalists—they can all defend their economic interests without fear and remain patriotic, but "agrarians"—never.

We are all to blame for the fixed prices because among us were men who understood full well where we were headed. But the *agrarians* didn't dare object. They had to step aside and let this experiment be carried out. They even gave up their own grain at these low prices. However, the peasantry has proven to be less conciliatory. I think the time has come to reject the idolatry of fixed prices (voices: "Right!") and approve the Minister of Agriculture's actions.

A Poltava representative spoke and proposed that for producing provinces (his own!) a consumption standard be set and the quality of the wheat and rye flour be reduced, for a coarser grind.

The agrarian was proposing a sacrifice . . . But there sat Milyukov, Kerensky, and Chkheidze, and they probably didn't understand that this was a sacrifice. Did they even know what a *grind* was?

The rightist **Novitsky** spoke. Feeding Petrograd and Moscow should not be the greatest concern. That is trivial compared with the state's larger task.

The government should not have agreed so readily to these prices. Creating steady prices for grain cultivated by children on shaky legs! . . . The hundred-million peasant population has sent its men to the army's front ranks. The soldier's wife, bathed in sweat, cooks and feeds her children while at the same time cultivating her desyatin. It takes her three or four days to do what a good mower does in one day and a reaping machine in three hours. While at the same time Groman and Voronkov, who only know the dirt on their shoes, have submitted a protest, the pitiful creation of little city people who don't know the land and don't know great Russia, a protest that grain prices have been set too high.

Dzyubinsky does not know the *business*. I wouldn't let him feed a chicken. The Duma's grain delegates don't know the grain business and should resign.

What a vile insult! And toward the public's leading representatives! The best expressers of the people's interests!

But now, irritated to their core, *agrarians* climbed up on the tribune:

Gorodilov (Vyatka Prov.): As a peasant, I live in the countryside. Fixed low prices for grain have wrecked the country and killed off agriculture. The countryside isn't going to sow grain anymore except to feed itself. Who's to blame for this, gentlemen? The law on lowering fixed prices was promulgated by the State Duma itself at the Progressive Bloc's insistence. We peasants weren't admitted to the Conference, and the Kadets don't know anything about the life of the countryside.

You, gentlemen, are blaming the ministers, but take a look. Who has raised insurrection in the country? The Progressive Bloc. (Voices on the right: "Bravo!")

You, gentlemen, have enslaved us peasants once again and forced the wives of peasants and soldiers to sow the fields and let their grain go at the lowest prices, at a loss. People of other classes want to live at our expense. Everyone who can takes however much he can from the peasant. This is why the country-side has stopped selling anything to the town. Can there really be fixed prices on grain alone? What about iron, nails, and cotton fabric? They get however much they want for them. For merchants and factory owners there are no fixed prices, which are only for the unlucky peasant. You, gentlemen Kadets and Progressive Bloc, lowered grain prices for a purpose, but you're blaming the government for everything. You're sending your authorized food delegates around the whole country. Don't we have local people we can select to administer this work?

(**A Penza landowner**): Before you go blaming the government for everything, take a good look at yourself. You sat on the Special Conference on Food Supplies with no understanding of anything and offered only hindrance. When you join the Conference, you can't represent your party anymore. You don't have any wisdom but you do have plenty of grievances. The people who live in the countryside can't accept that. It's a disgrace! Fixed prices are the single most important cause of our food havoc.

At the local commissions working out prices, there were five city dwellers for every zemstvo representative, and they refused to listen to the fact that the price can't be lower than the cost. The cost of producing grain rose—and I should be in a hurry to sell it at low prices? If the grain did go on the market, then it was out of bitter need, to pay off debts from the summer season.

What kind of patriotism is this, to wreck the country and disrupt the food supply? These gentlemen have no patriotism whatsoever. The men from the People's Freedom Party lack any feeling for popular freedom. What should be done, we all know, but can you tell us **how**? No matter how much I study these gentlemen on the left, I see a great deal of criticism and a great deal of noise but never anything creative.

He objected to Rittikh that even now it wasn't too late to raise fixed prices—and pay for the levy that way. In any event, those prices would be lower than the speculators'. And let them sell any grain over and above the levy at the free, open prices that emerged.

(This plan was being set forth in February 1917 by an agrarian, farmhand, and land-owner. And for this reason it was a reactionary idea unacceptable to the freedom-loving public. But if we reread this through the eyes of the 1920s, we would recognize NEP, which was greeted as blessed freedom.)

(**A Kursk landowner**): The grain was delivered in Kursk Province, but it's lying at the train stations, and it's all raw-ground, mixed with snow and ice. In our foul spring weather, in the rain, it will all rot. First they collected rusks for the army and then they gave them to the rats. Then they demanded livestock be brought to the stations—where they starved to death. There's no fuel, but in Petrograd there's been no letup to the lights, evening commerce, theaters, and movie houses. There are so many extra, idle people in Petrograd. Why are they here? The capital should be unburdened.

(This idea seemed insolent. It was up to us, the capital dwellers, to judge for ourselves, not for some Kursk landowner to tell us. Petrograd was overcrowded, yes, but the crowds of refugees were all the army of freedom.)

(Deputy from Voronezh Province): We have reached the point where there is nothing more to say about politics. In Voronezh Province, too, the train stations are packed with grain, but there are no train cars (and there are freight cars where there is no grain). Official Russia knew very little about thrift and they were confident we could get along without economies, but rural Russia is alive thanks to this thrift. When the trains are snowed under, women, adolescents, and old men come without a murmur to free them with their shovels. In Saratov Province, three hundred bulls starved to death because they weren't given hay, which was being safeguarded "for the army," as if the bulls weren't for the army. Spare the countryside!

"The countryside?" **Kerensky** said, amazed.

Help the *countryside*, while forgetting the city? But *we* live for city culture, after all, without the city the countryside couldn't accomplish anything! The city is the artery of national creativity!

> **Makogon** (an Ekaterinoslav peasant): Who do you see in the countryside? Only old women and children in the summer, and lots of houses have started to collapse. Who do you see in the field? A sixty-year-old gray-hair whose time has come for rest, and his grandchildren, and women. And you want this old man to feed not only the army but all Russia?

While in the cities? All the buildings were full, there were young and middle-aged men, a crowd of idle men, managers and commanders, to spare. And how many of these got a military deferment?

> Peasant children have laid down their bones in battle—but these? Lately, the peasants have come to realize that all of ours have been taken, but others have been given deferments. And what price are they going to pay that old man for a piece of bread—a fixed price or a higher one? They've been paid their life, stayed where they were and saved themselves.

> One minister spoke firmly, and now we're going to be a hindrance to him? Our voice is small, we can't speak, and we're little believed. But you have to understand the truth, and if all this isn't attended to in the future, it could end up a poor reflection.

Naturally, in the Duma transcripts the proportion of what was set forth was different. Every dull type got two pages, but the Kadet professors got ten or fifteen. Naturally, the Duma scholars listened disdainfully to all those dull men, and all the simple men's arguments were like dull water. What a difference their own Milyukov, their own Posnikov, their rent theory. This was the so-called State Duma, the young Russian parliament, but in fact, 80 percent of the Duma's time was taken up by just twenty men, and these twenty random politicians, obviously, were supposed to be understood as the true voice of Russia.

It was good fortune that those twenty included Andrei Ivanovich **Shingarev**, a far from random man, but a giving heart, a sacrificial lamb to our history. However, if you were one of the twenty, then you had to make quick turns and reply frequently. And if you were in the Kadet Party, then you couldn't cease to be a Kadet and had to hew only to the line your party needed you to and defend your leader and your perpetual correctness. You couldn't forget the overarching mission of your party and Bloc: ultimately, grain per se was unimportant; what was important was bringing down the Tsarist government. And if Milyukov could not justify himself in his accursed diagram, then you had to step up to the tribune to help him: Yes, although grain deliveries increased under Rittikh, you could consider them to have decreased in comparison with demand, how much we now needed.

Individual calculations may have been inaccurate.

(Fourteen years ago, before he was a Kadet, this genuine sympathizer of the Russian peasant wrote "The Dying Village," in which he calculated the peasant budget down to a hundredth of a kopeck!) Where party duty guided Shingarev, he stooped and perhaps even distorted. He went out of his way to defend every kind of public committee, especially the Zemgor. He didn't notice how he was contradicting himself:

> What is this puzzlement, as if one could get along without politics somewhere? Gentlemen, your assembly is, after all, political, and you are not the Food Supplies Committee. Politics is the essence of state life. If you eliminate politics, what do you have left? It is the gravest error that there is any state issue to which politics cannot and should not be tied.

At that, he brought his reproach sharply around to the government:

> Do not bring your insane politics into the food question! We have a dictatorship of insanity that is destroying the state at its moment of gravest danger.

But even during his party moments, there was no arrogance or malice in his speeches, as there was with other opposition leaders. He mouthed all the mandatory party phrases, but you heard his rich voice tighten with anxiety over the Russian calamity. He felt these boundless expanses, the vital masses of granary grain held up, and the dark (and rational) peasant distrust for city swindlers. All of a sudden, as if waking up and pulling his free head out of the party bridle, he declared to a stunned Duma:

> The minister is right in saying that you should help, too! Yes, gentlemen, the grain must be shipped. If we have given up our children, our last sons, then we also need to give up our grain. This is a sacred duty to the homeland.

And the anxious and extraordinarily energetic Minister of Agriculture, so invincible in debate, was back on the tribune! But the Duma had no desire to listen to him anymore, and the entire leftist section made a terrible ruckus, demanding a recess.

Rodzyanko: I most humbly ask you to take your seats. (Noise. Voices on the left: "Recess! Recess! This is disrespect for the State Duma!")

Rodzyanko was barely able to quiet them down. Rittikh repeated the first few words of his speech several times:

> Gentlemen, it is with the greatest . . . (Noise on the left: "Recess!") Gentlemen, I will be very brief. With the greatest (Noise on the left) with the greatest satisfaction (Noise on the left: "Duma resolution!"), with the greatest satisfaction, with joy, frankly, have I listened to the part of Duma member Shingarev's speech in which he spoke so sincerely about calling on the people and about civic duty. However, gentlemen, I listened to all the rest of the prolonged speeches by Duma members Milyukov and Shingarev with the greatest bewilderment. After all, the latter speaker is from that party, and what did we end up hearing? Duma

member Milyukov accuses the Minister of Agriculture of criminal optimism one minute and pessimism—I don't remember if it was criminal or not—the next. What are they arguing with me about by constantly trying to prove that I am to blame? There is no argument here. I feel immeasurably guiltier than they can prove with figures. Yes, gentlemen, I am tormented day and night by the thought that I have not done a thousandth of what I should have done in this terrible historical moment. (Applause on the right.) Unfortunately, I am a mere mortal, and at this time Russia ought to have brought forth men of titanic strength. I am to blame for not having that strength.

Without bias: Why couldn't the leaders of the opposition speak the same way? Then it would be simple to come to an agreement. But the titans of the opposition shouted:

>**Adzhemov:** Resign!

>**Milyukov:** There are other fish in the sea!

>**Rittikh:** Can we really be wasting our time on purely personal politics? This is simply terrible. Gentlemen, I dream of someone coming up here who is not an orator but simply a man who loves Russia selflessly. . . . It seems to me—and perhaps everyone feels this—that we are living through a solemn historical moment. *Perhaps for the last time has the hand of fate raised the scales on which Russia's future is weighed.*

But here were Saturday and Sunday, and there were no sessions. Then a Duma member died and there was the obituary, the mourning, the memorial service, and there were no working sessions for three days. Only on 8 March, at noon, when **all that** started on the Petersburg side—no one in the world understood this yet—did a regular Duma session open once again with a discussion of the tedious grain question.

Petrograd bakeries were already being looted, the crowd was stopping streetcars and crowding police stations. Vague rumors of unspecified origin reached Duma members during recesses.

But in the windowless, electric hall, with an early night under the glass tent roof, specialists and experts from the liberal camp kept giving speeches, and on 9 March, after noon, once again Posnikov, Rodichev, Godnev, and, of course, every day, Chkheidze, and every day, Kerensky, and taking a sweeping blow at this boring food issue, throwing up their hands and shouting, "Don't believe this Rittikh!"

>**Rodichev:** Let us be done with him as of today!

>**Chkheidze:** Gentlemen! How can we put the food question in the sense of black bread back on track? . . . The sole solution is a struggle that leads to this government's dissolution! The sole thing that remains within our powers is to give the street a healthy channel!

So ended a two-hundred-year national process whereby a city constructed with the Petrine stick by Italian architects on the northern swamps began to speak for all of Russia. IN THAT SWAMP, NO GRAIN IS GROUND, YET NO BREAD WHITER CAN BE FOUND, while this city itself expressed itself now not in thinkers from the shelves of the murky Public Library, or sharp-tongued State Duma deputies, but in street bullies breaking store windows for not bringing a flood of bread to this swamp.

[4]

Sasha was summoned to 32 Karpovka Embankment and told to ask not for Himmer himself but for his wife, Mrs. Flakserman. This turned out to be on the corner of Miloserdie, an absurd name for a street—Mercy— probably because there was some kind of philanthropic institution on it— and directly across from a hideous black and gray church: a slab of banded stone, the Black Hundreds nest of Ioann of Kronstadt. In the meager lighting on the wretched Karpovka Embankment, it looked like a black mountain.

The smell of just the incense that might come from the church had always nauseated Sasha. This was a psychosis, this faith was like a psychosis. As long as there was God, there could be no freedom.

Sasha walked toward Himmer's apartment intense, collected, and with avid interest. After the war years of scurrying in and out of all kinds of holes, he'd grown quite unaccustomed to a genuine socialist atmosphere! He'd used the three months since he had happily moved to Petersburg for thinking, searching, and recommendations, with the goal of finally meeting some noted theoretician of socialism. Not that he'd been searching this entire time. The first month he had just enjoyed being home, back in Petersburg, and he'd joined the tough competition for Yelenka, whom he'd nearly lost. But after his initial rest, the intellectual vacuum had begun to mount, the lack of serious discussion and serious revolutionary work. It was forgivable to vegetate like a philistine from one out-of-the-way army unit to another, as fate had sent him up until now, but in Petersburg?

However, Petersburg, too, had emptied out during the war years, and men of revolutionary mind were all scattered, used up or hidden away, they'd changed identities; this was not the free, seething society it had been. If the city's socialist circles still had any rudder, they were so much less united or had withered away to such an extent that there wasn't even anywhere to go or anyone to talk with. Many trends could be divined, but there were no notable personalities. Of those there were, Sasha picked out Himmer as exceptional and sought a way to get through to him. Himmer, who signed himself "Sukhanov," was the most important author in Gorky's *Annals*—possibly the only Petersburg journal worth reading. No matter how the censor subdued it, Himmer's grasp was politically keen and his orientation based unabashedly on Zimmerwald.

His apartment was on the ground floor. It was neither Himmer himself nor his wife who opened the door for Sasha but a pleasant, lively young man wearing an infantryman's uniform but obviously a university student, and this immediately gave the air a familiar feel. (Later it turned out he was the wife's brother, who, like Sasha, had also wound up in the army and hadn't been allowed to finish university and was now toiling away in Nizhni.)

Right then Himmer came out.

In that first moment, Sasha was disappointed by his appearance. Not only did Himmer not look like a leader, he didn't even look like an eagle of theory. He was significantly shorter than Sasha and not just skinny but actually puny. His clean-shaven face was a yellowish gray with bloodless lips and repulsively browless. Nonetheless, his face was expressive and energetic, not with the energy such as a strong body confers but with an inner burning and fevered gaze—the kind of burning that only revolutionary thought and none other gives us!—as Sasha determined, recognizing someone of like mind even as he was introducing himself.

"Lenartovich."

His hand, too, was small and frail, like cotton wool.

"I was expecting you to be in uniform," Himmer said.

"I thought—perhaps for conspiracy's sake—not to stand out too much. Is that better? And in general, for freedom. I take advantage of every chance not to put on my uniform."

"Where are you serving?"

"Right now in the Cavalry Remount Administration."

"A cavalryman?" Himmer raised the spots where there should have been eyebrows. (Was he surprised because the cavalry was the least easily propagandized?)

"Oh no." Sasha laughed. "I don't even know how to come at a horse."

"And they keep you on?" Himmer grinned.

"The others there are no more experts than I. You just have to know how to write and shuffle documents. I haven't been there long, just since November."

The apartment consisted of a few very small, directly connected rooms. They passed through the small dining room, which had an uncurtained window on the service yard, where an outside iron staircase slanted across the window, and entered a small study with two shuttered windows and, on the wall, small portraits of Marx and Lasalle and no other foolishness hung the way people like to in city apartments. This directness and severity pleased Sasha greatly. Here they lived for the spirit.

"What's the mood among the officers in your administration?" Himmer asked even before he'd offered him a seat, with great vitality.

Sasha replied easily.

"They aren't laying down their lives to serve the homeland. It's a very large staff. The senior men gather around twelve o'clock to lunch together and chat and by two o'clock they're already starting to leave. Everyone understands that in this war the cavalry is less necessary than having to feed it."

"No, I mean the mood itself?"

"Very free discussions. Out of the blue someone will bring in a caricature from a foreign newspaper showing Wilhelm, his arms open wide, taking the measure of an artillery shell, while our idiot Tsar, getting down on his knees and spreading his arms the same way, is taking Rasputin's measure. All the

officers looked—and laughed. So I can be fairly open. Naturally, the boldest among them only go so far as a bourgeois constitution. And then, that's
just talk."

They sat down.

"Yes, you're right, a certain caution is not out of place," Himmer said.
"Even in my own apartment I'm living sort of half-legally."

"Why did you stop at 'half'?" Sasha smiled.

"Well, because in May of 1914 I was exiled from Petersburg. But I didn't
want to be and didn't go. At the time I should have changed apartments, but
I couldn't be bothered, I was used to this one. I just try not to tease the porter
too much. I usually go through the service entrance and make sure not to
come home too late. Actually, he does know, and he turns a blind eye."

"No particular troubles?"

"No. Even at work I serve under my own name."

The conversation flowed easily, and Sasha summoned his nerve to ask,
"Where do you serve?"

"In the most boring place possible." Himmer did not boast even to a
novice. "In the Agriculture Ministry there is something called the Department of Land Improvements. And in that is the Administration for Irriga-
tion of the Hungry Steppe. So that's where. It's convenient that it's quite
close, right here, at the end of Kamennoostrovsky, on Aptekarsky Island. It's
also convenient that I can do a lot of literary work during working hours.
You know, they have all these irrigators, sprinklers, and spillways, and I understand just about as much about them as you do about horses, but good
people have set it up the way they always do. And they keep me."

"Yes, me, too. It wasn't easy getting in."

No, the first unpleasant impression had passed, and Sasha started to like
Himmer.

He observed with quick, dark, avid eyes.

"Lenartovich. Is that your real name?"

"Yes."

"But do you have a pseudonym, a nom de guerre?"

"Not a pseudonym. I'm not actually doing any literary work yet. . . . But I
did have a nickname. 'Yasny.'"

(That was long ago and little used. What underground work had he ever
had? None.)

"Yasny. Good," Himmer said appreciatively. "It might come in handy."

They sat down across a small square table. In all the time they'd been
talking, no one had come in or tried to offer them anything, made a suggestion of food or drink—and Sasha liked this unaffected way. He could have
tea and a cookie at home. That wasn't what he was after in coming here.
Whether there was a wife somewhere, this room showed no sign of a tending
hand choosing the arrangement or fixing anything. Good. Business-like—
straight to discussion.

Sasha had composed himself well, realizing how important it was not to appear foolish or uninformed. But there was no danger of that; he knew himself.

Himmer did not start asking him about his underground work or his party connections. He might not have had the former, due to his youth, and he evidently didn't have the latter, since he'd surfaced out of nowhere. But he began asking *what he had read,* first running through quickly and then in more detail—which authors, which books, in which languages, and which journals he followed. He asked almost nothing about the nineteenth century but hewed rather closer to the present day. He was glad that Sasha knew German and questioned him on contemporary German Social Democratic authors. Here he was very detailed and had a categorical judgment about each journal.

A lively, outstanding intellect. He raced along in his speech, swift and logical. This was strength!

What interested Himmer most was whether Sasha was a Zimmerwaldist— and Sasha didn't have to pretend. He was a Zimmerwaldist and had been since the war began, even before that name appeared, although in wartime he hadn't been able to get a hold of the *literature* itself. Now he was reading *Annals.*

"Yes," Himmer agreed with pride. "We are simply working wonders. Under police state conditions and during a war we are legally publishing an anti-defense journal, the sole internationalist publication. Of course, Gorky's name helps a great deal."

Sasha sincerely loved Gorky, who hadn't drifted off into literary refinement and was still stirring the foul mess of life. His heart was with the working class.

"And notice, since 1914 he hasn't been a patriot for a single minute!"

Sasha passed the exam more easily than he'd expected, and he managed to shine in the theoretical section with just one of his prepared deep thoughts. But after that it dealt with the actual status of revolutionary circles in Russia—which was what was most important and had led him here, to become part of these tight, closed circles! Somewhere the main underground channel was flowing, somewhere a crucible was blazing—and Sasha could no longer live in dreary detachment. Of course, during the war all this was powerfully repressed and distorted, right?

Himmer grinned drily, caustically:

"Our Social Democratic organizations are in a dreadful state. Not from being routed but from internal weakness. I'd say there is more fuel in the masses than among our Social Democrats."

Truly, he had the broadest acquaintance in all the revolutionary circles of the capital. Thanks to his special position as an interparty literary man not belonging to any one group, he dealt with everyone realistically. His works were popular and appreciated. He was connected not organizationally but personally to all the socialist circles in Petersburg. And as the editor of *Annals* he had the most intensive ties to all trends of the emigration. So that there was not a single (failed) attempt at interparty blocking that didn't involve him.

He knew his own worth!

Remarkable. Remarkable! Sasha had landed right where he needed to be. Under Himmer's wing he would get the lay of the land and understand, and he would choose the most appropriate direction for himself.

"But you must understand," said Himmer, who had an exceptionally confident manner. "The top socialist brass, if I can put it that way, are all in emigration and partly in exile. Here we have at best the socialist officer corps. I mean"—he joked—"not socialist officers, like you, who are the exceptions, but the mid-level command among socialists. So you see it is very middling. They are second-rate, slaves to routine. They have no overview from any political height. The theoretical level is almost nonexistent, and any attempt at a deeper comprehension of events absent altogether. Even the best are drowning—some in the Duma game, some in the hairsplitting over food distribution. I'm not even talking about collaborating with the plutocracy, like Gvozdev and his group. So it's as if everyone were blind and absolutely groping their way around.

"'Down with autocracy!' Everyone understands that, of course, but that's a far cry from a political program. Some are even prepared to support a franchised Duma, which the proletarian struggle most surely cannot allow. Generally speaking, not one of our parties is preparing for a socialist coup or any actions whatsoever. Everyone is daydreaming, pondering, having premonitions. . . . But something must be readied. It's too bad you're not in a regiment. It would be easy to brew something up."

Regimental drudgery—thank you, he'd already done that. But the socialist general was right. Indeed, what could be done for the revolution in the Cavalry Remount Administration? However, he replied confidently.

"I think I can be useful. I'm not in a regiment. But for the revolution"—his voice trembled in the certainty of his emotion—"I'm prepared to join any regiment and come under any fire."

This was, in fact, the case. Sasha Lenartovich had indeed been dragged down by his dreary, imposed slumber these two and a half wartime years. But he believed **it** would happen! How could it not?

"Can the country really forgive all its sufferings, pains, insults, and humiliations at the hand of the autocracy? Even considering such an assumption is terrible."

"Yes," the grayish yellow, browless leader intoned with sang-froid. "It is inevitable, and the stricken tissue is going to have to be excised. But now, given the current upheavals, you have to be careful. Autocracy will bring its wrath down on everyone suspicious, in order to inspire terror. These upheavals could end badly. And if you have any compromising notes or papers, don't keep them with you. Either hide them with others or burn them."

. . . What a man prepares himself for and what he later grows up to be. Nikolai Himmer had been quite frail from birth, he had lagged behind his coevals, he was contemplative and had an unhappy childhood in a broken family, his father being a degenerate alcoholic. His mother, an impoverished noblewoman, a midwife, also earned her living by copying Tolstoy's manuscripts. By age seventeen, Himmer was in the grip of Tolstoyan ideas, he was a vegetarian, and he refused to go to university on principle. He took his criticism of the political regime and economic order from Tolstoy. As he developed further and became more and more leftist, he ended up in Taganka for illegal literature, was released by the crowd in 1905, and felt he was a revolutionary, and then a thoroughgoing Marxist.

[5]

This past winter had been filled with an arch-dramatic struggle and might have ended in a proletarian revolution in Switzerland, which might have spread to all of Europe, had it not been for its base betrayal by its gang of leaders who had stained, blackened, and led the entire Swiss party astray, and above and worst of all due to that scoundrel, intrigant, and political prostitute Grimm. And that old ruin Greulich. And all the other filthy scoundrels.

Characteristically, the superficial, bourgeois view—the kind of view most people and even revolutionaries have—doesn't notice tiny cracks in huge mountainous masses and doesn't understand that, with skill, the entire mass could be brought down through just such a crack. The average frightened man observing the Europe-wide war between million-man armies and millions of exploding shells can't believe that the smallest handful of individuals could stop this iron hurricane (changing its course) if they were maximally determined. True, this does require a tremendous event— a European-wide revolution. But a European revolution might require nothing more than a revolution in a small, neutral, but trilingual country in the heart of Europe: Switzerland. Doing this meant taking over the Swiss Social Democratic Party. And if it couldn't be taken over, then it had to be split up and the battle-worthy portion separated out. All it took to split a party like the Swiss one—opportunists and bookish theoreticians won't believe it!—was just five or so determined party members, plus three foreigners capable of giving the local comrades a program, preparing texts and theses for speeches, and writing pamphlets for them.

So it takes fewer than ten capable, unwavering socialists to overthrow Europe! The Skittle Club.

What the Skittle Club had contemplated in the autumn, the Skittle Club would now launch. After the failure at the November congress of the Swiss party, Lenin — at first seemingly only for the *young people's* psychological revenge — composed realistic, practical theses about their goals in their struggle. The many months' immersion, even the reading of insignificant Swiss newspapers — all of it came in handy here. Later, explanatory sessions began being convened with young leftists around the theses, which they let spread throughout Switzerland. The intention was for at least one local party organization, even the tiniest, to *approve* them, and then it could be legitimately demanded that the socialist newspapers publish them, and in this way the theses would become part of the wider discussion. They searched for a way to print the theses as broadsides and to distribute a few thousand of them (they were all talk and no action, either depressed or dissembling — no one knew how to distribute anything properly).

Should they start publishing broadsides independently at all? But Münzenberg, the main support and youth leader, grumbled that there was plenty of *literature* as it was. (As if they had ever had *that* kind of literature!) Swiss leftists were weak, devilishly weak.

The revolutionary's impatient eye espied another desired crack that promised to yield more, and more quickly: another congress of the Swiss party was coming up, scheduled for early February and devoted (they had forced the bosses to promise this) to their *attitude toward the war*. This was a marvelous opportunity to disrupt and split the entire opportunistic leadership and to fire vital, urgent questions at it in front of the Swiss masses. Was it permissible to bring Switzerland to the brink of war? Was it permissible for the descendants of William Tell to die for international banks? Was it permissible . . . and so on and so forth. A lot could be made of this. The congress was especially dangerous for the opportunists as well because in September of the next year, 1917, there would be parliamentary elections, and no matter how they decided — *for* or *against* the fatherland — the party would inevitably split in the elections or even cease to exist — which was just what we needed!

The opportunists grasped this and began maneuvering. Couldn't the recklessly promised congress be postponed altogether? Couldn't the war question not be decided *at all* as long as Switzerland wasn't fighting, or decided when all the wars had ended?

They still didn't know *how* the blow would be wielded against them, *how* it would be stated, not simply "for the fatherland" or "against militarism" but with merciless determination: war cannot be fought *otherwise* than through socialist revolution! Vote not on the war, essentially, but for or against the immediate expropriation of the banks and industry! The Skittle Club vigorously drew up a resolution for the congress. Platten wrote it, poorly, and Lenin recast it in Platten's name. (Not an easy job, but a gratifying one. All international forces had to come to the aid of the Swiss leftists.)

They had to sharpen every line: Demobilize the Swiss army immediately! The defense of Switzerland is a hypocritical phrase! It is the *Swiss* peace policy that is criminal! Their success could be tremendous. A resolution like this from the Swiss congress could inspire the most enthusiastic support among the working class of all civilized countries!

But the opportunists stirred. It was learned confidentially that the bosses were preparing to *postpone* the congress. Such scoundrels! In instances like this—a preemptive strike! Seize the initiative! They instructed Bronsky to offer a resolution at a meeting of the Zurich organization: "Against a secret behind-the-scenes campaign to postpone the congress! Condemn signs of lapsing into socialist chauvinism!" They had an opportunity to fix the vote—and they made sure the resolution passed! A fine blow against the centrists, who were, after all, afraid of being taken for chauvinists.

Their gang was so brazen, though, even that didn't scare them. A day later they assembled the party presidium and threw down their mask. (Platten, Nobs, and Münzenberg attended the presidium, so everything was reliably reported.) Old Greulich set about defaming the entire Zurich party organization: that there were many deserters in it, he said; that we had vouched for them to the authorities, and specifically on the issue of homeland defense they could have been expected to . . . But someone else shouted that if the party sullied itself in this way, they of St. Gallen would quit! These comrades were of no high opinion of Swiss workers (they even suggested that *foreigners* were behind the trouble). . . . Someone else worked himself to a pitch of chauvinist hysterics: "Get out and take your international congress formulas with you! Discussing the war issue in wartime is madness! At moments like this, any nation unites (with their capitalists) in their common destiny. How can you demobilize the army when it's defending our borders? Yes, if danger arises for Switzerland, the working class will go out to defend it!" (Listen to this. Listen!) But Grimm behaved most shamelessly of all. The chairman of Zimmerwald and Kienthal—and such a scoundrel in politics. "You mean if there's a war we're to start an uprising? . . ." He made vile insinuations against *foreigners* and young people. And uniting with the chauvinists, 7 to 5, with the slight edge for his, Grimm's, centrist vote, they postponed the congress *indefinitely* (read: to the war's end). . . . An unprecedented and disgraceful decision! Grimm's total betrayal.

Oh, you swindler, brute, traitor. It was infuriating! All the more, then, it was time to wage war on the party more than ever! Only one thing remained: to lay Grimm low! Everything rested on Grimm, so now it was important to publicly dishonor him, expose him, rip off his mask.

Just as, in a fight, when the hand searches for some handy object to grab and wield, so a political fighter's mind plucks out the lightning-like twists and turns of possible moves. His first thought was, Naine! It was unusual that Naine, who was not very leftist, had voted for us. That meant it was most advantageous to overthrow Grimm via Naine! But how? Write an open letter to Naine's newspaper and call Grimm a scoundrel *publicly* and say that it was impossible to remain in the same Zimmerwald organization with him any longer! . . . No, not that. Have everyone write open letters to Naine's newspaper, everyone we could find, and bury Grimm for good under that avalanche of open letters and protest resolutions! Every minute was precious. Gather leftists from all over—and aim them against Grimm!

It was a dramatic moment. The loyal Abramovich joined us in La Chaux-de-Fonds. In Geneva, Brilliant and Guilbaux hesitated.

But in Zurich, night after night, leftists and young people gathered and worked out methods of attack. It became clear that open letters weren't enough. There had to be *political murder* so that Grimm never got back up again.

Here's what shape it took. Not losing an hour, they, along with Krupskaya, Zinoviev, Radek, and Levi, scooped up all the forces they had at that moment and walked the many blocks to Münzenberg's apartment, and there, when all the resolute had gathered, Willi called Platten on the telephone and asked him to come over without telling him what it was about, but urgently! He had to be ambushed, caught by surprise. Lately Platten had obviously feared both Grimm and a schism, had resisted learning from international experience, and had showed himself to be too much a Swiss, a limited Swiss, as had Nobs, actually. (Come to think of it, where had they come from? At Zimmerwald they'd simply *registered* as "leftists.") So you see, they had to catch Platten unawares, by the throat.

He walked in, and when he saw Münzenberg not alone as he had expected, but the six of them packed tightly in the little room, three squeezed on the bed, and all of them somber, his large-browed, open face, which was not suited for playacting, expressed dismay and alarm. If only he had found one to be an ally or reassuring! But there wasn't even one. They shoved him and sat him in a corner as far as possible from the door and behind the commode, where he couldn't get out, and the six of them moved closer, some on chairs, and leaned over if they were on the bed. Münzenberg (this was his role) announced in a ringing, impudent voice, "We—all of us here, our group—have decided to break immediately and decisively with Grimm and to disgrace him before the whole world!" Platten had a choice: Grimm or us. Platten started to fidget, but he was trapped, and he started to fret; he looked over all the faces, searching for the kindest, but even Nadya was looking at him like a frozen witch. Platten wiped his brow, squeezed his weak chin, and asked for time to think, he said, but the six didn't budge. They maintained a gloomy silence and looked at him as if he were an enemy (the entertaining Radek had dreamed all this up)—and that was what was most terrifying. Platten was taken aback and succumbed: "No need to do this right away! Send Grimm a warning, a caution." "No! It's all been decided!" Platten was left with a choice: either us, in the honest international alliance, or his Swiss traitor—and we would disgrace them both! Answer! Right now!

Platten clutched his head with both hands. Sat there.

Surrendered.

They instructed Radek to write a discrediting pamphlet, which he could do that very night, in one night, smoking his pipe like a chimney, without the least effort, the sluggard. But he wouldn't. Lenin had to walk around Zurich with him for a few hours to persuade and rouse him to write and write stingingly, as he alone knew how. He was, after all, an incomparable journalist! The next step was to attack Grimm at a session of the International Socialist Commission. Lenin himself did not go in order not to make a show of himself, but Zinoviev, Radek, Münzenberg, and Levi attacked, saying that Grimm's activities in Switzerland were a crime, infamy, depravity! And so he should be expelled from the Zimmerwald leadership! (Dethroned.) Then a few from Münzenberg's Youth International attacked Grimm. Then the idea arose to try to have an intra-party referendum and organize a congress now, in March! The referendum's motivation was the best part of the entire campaign (he had to write it himself): postponing the congress was a *defeat for socialism!*

The reaction! What a ruckus! What a dustup! M-marvelous! The party leaders roared with indignation and threw themselves into refutation! Who in socialism could withstand a bold and harsh accusation in principle **from the left**? A single accusatory voice could bring down a thousand opportunists!

M-marvelous! It worked! This was just what was needed!

At the canton party congress they were also able to collect one sixth of the votes for the leftists' resolution. A major victory!

But it was also the high point of the campaign, which began to fall off.

Grimm attacked the referendum feverishly—and frightened our young people.

The foxily cautious Nobs publicly dissociated himself from the referendum.

And Platten—Platten didn't say a word, the ninny. Now go build a struggle on him. No, he was hopeless. He didn't want to learn how to organize a revolutionary party.

They even refused to print Radek's pamphlet: "If we print it, they'll drive us out of the party!" Oh, you *leftists!* Oh, you warriors!

Grimm, sensing our weakness, assembled an arch-private conference and invited the leftists. Naturally, Münzenberg and Bronsky didn't go. But Nobs and Platten wended their way . . . to their master.

No, three fourths of them had already fallen in with social patriotism. No, the leftists in Switzerland were arch-skunks, weak-willed men.

Sowing confusion, painting over disagreements instead of highlighting them—how vile!

And then there was the outrageous business with Bronsky. They were electing a board at a citywide meeting and some of those elected declined, so they went further down the list—and fortunately they came to Bronsky. Bronsky suddenly had made it! So the brazen rightists stated they could not work amicably with Bronsky, and they refused. Nobs was the chairman and agreed to annul the elections!

And Platten took this slap in the face.

Lenin was sitting in the meeting, silently, but beside himself! He didn't sleep a wink that night.

His nerves were shredded in general, he was having headaches, and he couldn't sleep because of these daily assemblies.

The Swiss party were all opportunists through and through, a philanthropic institution for philistines. Or officials, or future officials, or a handful frightened by officials.

The leftists fled from our help, both in Zurich and in Bern. Only Abramovich's affairs were good, but he was far away. And Guilbaux and Brilliant were wavering.

The young people's leaders, even the pointed, harsh, unbending Münzenberg, were leaning toward a compromise. Münzenberg! Even he rejected Radek's brochure! (Radek had left for Davos for medical treatment, as exhausted as everyone else.)

It would have been funny if it weren't so awful. Evidently, Lenin was seeing the end of his troubles with the Zurich leftists.

But there was no need for regrets, even if it was a loss. He'd always known how rotten the European socialist parties were. Now he'd experienced it himself in practice.

No need for regrets. What had happened would leave some trace. After us, our heirs would create a leftist party in Switzerland!

A meeting of leftists was scheduled for 8 March—and didn't even happen. People just didn't come. No one needed it. Lenin had prepared to make a report—and all for naught. He returned in a rage. A rage that lasted the whole night.

He envied Inessa and Zinoviev and how they could go somewhere and give reports: before you there you see not middle-class socialists but fresh people, workers, a crowd, and you have a direct influence on the masses.

There were numerous other frustrations, too. Alternating friendship and arguments with Radek (he was unbearable when he got into academism), and Inessa and Zinoviev took a hard view of their discord. Then the dispute with Usievich. (He and Bukharin never stopped their arguing, though at least they didn't bring it out in public.) Shklovsky squandered the party coffers. Inessa got the idea of "reexamining" the issue of the fatherland's defense, which meant how many wasted arguments.

In letters. She never did come to Zurich once.

Soon it would be a year. . . .

[6]

People are right: prison and poverty do make you smarter, whatever it takes. In the past, Kozma would get caught for little things, and they'd let him go right away. Now they'd charged him under Article 102 of the Criminal Code: a criminal organization aimed at overthrowing . . .

Kozma Gvozdev was arrested along with the entire Workers' Group on 9 February—but that happened when he'd had pneumonia, so they gave him three weeks to recover at home, so he'd only been carted off to prison five days ago. The others had already been there a month.

Lying in bed at home was a great deal easier. The news filters in, you read the newspapers, and you can send and receive letters. Kozma knew how upset all of workers' Petersburg was over the Group's arrest, and Guchkov sternly interceded for them. A lot of noise was made in their defense, and there was no grief that now they would have to stay in jail for a long time, no heavy punishment should be imposed: no one else was getting punished; everything in the country was drifting along as if drunk. They hadn't even arrested Rasputin's murderers, although it was always easier to imprison our brother, while the higher-ups—well, no. . . . But since the Group's arrest, Kozma felt like his back had been broken and he'd been beaten all over with clubs. Had he done something wrong? Or gone about it wrong? This meant he hadn't been able to pull all the pieces together; he hadn't reinforced things properly. What should he have done from the start? The Bolsheviks shouted, "Strikebreakers! Traitors!" And the major newspapers wrote, "They are genuine patriots"—and so stained them in front of the Bolsheviks. But for us to declare, "No, we are not patriots! We are revolutionaries!"—you weren't going to justify yourself to the Bolsheviks anyway, you'd be a traitor to the state, and they'd drive you away then and there.

So there you had it. We were the patriots.

It hurt, that kind of position. There was no justifying yourself whatever you did, even if you did nothing at all.

Over these months, Tsereteli himself had honored Kozma with two letters from exile. You had to admit, all those years in Siberia, and he understood the matter better than many in Petersburg. Yes, Irakli Georgievich, Kozma replied, I, too, am searching, trying to find something. You see, besides the needs of the working class there are also the needs of industry itself. We want to make sure our struggle doesn't bring it to a halt. And there are the needs of a warring country and army. All this you have to be able to pour down a single channel at once. Somehow they know how to in Europe, so why don't we? Russia's military defeat is going to affect who above all? Us, the workers. You fight and fight for your class, but not so you drag down the war effort.

So, how are you going to make those cannons crack? And isn't it a pity to let them cut down our men in the trenches?

But the French labor minister arrived in December, and although a darkness filled his chest, and his head, Kozma repeated the words of his quick and nimble advisors: "Through you, we have to tell the proletariat and the democracy of France and the entire civilized world how with its own hands the Russian government is destroying its defense and trying to ruin its own country. Given a convenient opportunity, the government would not think twice of committing yet another perjury, of betraying its allies." When German peace offers were announced in December, the secretaries slipped him a speech: "You must gain the proletariat's control over diplomatic actions!" Other members of the group, twenty or so, yielding to a foreign mind, giving speeches here and there—came out with all sorts of things. You had to wonder at the government putting up with it for so long. By January, the group had tried to keep a low profile, fearing that either the Bolsheviks would burst in and smash things, or that the police would, and send them all to Siberia. On 16 January, a letter arrived for Guchkov from the Military District: "The Workers' Group is an antigovernment association discussing the overthrow of the government and the conclusion of peace. Therefore, a specially appointed official must be present at every session of the Group." That was all! During a war like this the government had that right, and the only obstacle would be for leaflets. But Boris Osipych Bogdanov, now the Group's main secretary, urged, "Don't allow this mockery of freedom!" Over the next few days an official kept showing up, so they would cancel the session and assemble on the quiet. The Duma's February session was coming up now, and Bogdanov applied pressure: democracy had to intervene in the protracted single combat between franchised society and autocracy! The time to strike was now! He explained the duality of the situation: if we go on patiently holding back, that will mean letting a fateful moment slip, the unprecedented drop in Tsarist power's prestige; and if we call working Petrograd out on the street, but at an unpropitious moment, that summons could seal the Workers' Group's fate.

All this was now going on not in the Group's sessions but among its members, in secret, and agitators were sent secretly around to the factories to prepare the protest for the Duma's convocation. Right then, they arrested several members of the Moscow group (even Pumpyansky was caught) and raided the intransigent Samara group—and this flustered Bogdanov. The moment of struggle had come and he could not let it slip! So he offered up this—"A letter to the workers of all Petrograd factories and plants"—saying, assemble your assemblies and read and discuss this. The government is taking advantage of martial law to enslave the working class. The people themselves, not the autocracy, must abolish war. The moment's most urgent task is the establishment of a provisional government! Democracy cannot wait or be silent any longer! We have grown up now, and we will not go *there* or *that way*, as we did twelve years ago to the Winter Palace. We will go with imperious demands, and may there not be among us a single traitor who would hide at home from the common cause!

Kozma was desperate for this not to happen—but he couldn't stop it either. How could the Workers' Group keep silent if even rebelling gentlemen were abusing autocracy as vociferously as possible. And no one touched them!

Against his heart, with his last strength, he issued his proclamation.

Even two weeks after this they had not arrested the Workers' Group. The rebelling gentlemen were not touched, but the worker animals were seized after all.

Who gets away with what.

But Acetylene fled, he wasn't caught.

And just who didn't harass the Workers' Group for betrayal. All of them went free, but the Workers' Group was sent to prison.

Prison and penury make you smarter.

Too bad Sashka Shlyapnikov was most likely celebrating. Here, says he, you lackeys—you served, you did, and your service landed you prison. While I always resisted—and I'm at liberty.

Only Aleksandr Ivanych Guchkov defended them: in the arrests' wake he immediately assembled prominent Duma members and printed a statement saying this was a serious blow to the national defense that extinguished the masses' belief in the fruitfulness of our common work and only intensified ferment among the workers. Konovalov spoke in the Duma itself, saying that the Workers' Group was patriotic, serving the defense and to pacify political passions; that the Workers' Group was a bulwark against other dangerous trends in the working mass, and the government had destroyed it pointlessly; and that workers simply could not refrain from interfering in politics when everyone else was, while the government was leading the country straight to its ruin.

Kozma and his fellows in the Kresty prison were sure that Protopopov himself had panicked, since he'd arrested them, and that the government wouldn't last so they wouldn't have long to serve.

What weighed on Kozma was not that they wouldn't be released from prison but how badly he had coped with the matter.

There was no simplicity or straight path in life. Everything was twisted, and everyone had twisted heads. Try balancing between them all.

The Guchkov industrial committee was also opaque. They seemed to stand for the fatherland, but they also were careful to get their hands on the money, and to accrue lots of it. For the fatherland, yes; but they themselves wanted to seize power in that fatherland. That was the truth.

While already under house arrest, in communication, Kozma passed his message on to the factories, trying to persuade them not to call a general strike before the Duma opened. Everyone to their lathes. The longer we strike, the more we sap our forces. Our interests are calling us to our lathes.

Kozma did what he could. He attempted much, let a few things get by, did a few things wrong, made mistakes, and everyone was unhappy with him. But when they imprisoned him, his cares fell away. Rest up now on your prison bunk.

There was no rest, though, something was gnawing at him. Release didn't beckon either: back to the office on Liteiny and all that busywork again.

While they were admitting him to the prison, Kozma had a brush with criminals, too, and that upset everything. There might as well not have been a Tsar, a Duma, or Social Democrats because right here and now they could filch your favorite boots with the patent leather tops, so don't put them on the floor and make sure they don't take them off you. Kozma spent the fourth decade of his life in the gutter, as low as it got. But look, you found out there were people lower than you, dark and unruly, so safeguard your very modest property from them and take care they don't pick you off in the most revolutionary fashion. At liberty, these men lived apart—one or two per village, a horse thief or a known robber, a swindler, a fumbler, sometimes coalesced into gangs, but no one saw them together in gangs, while in prison they are all assembled. You looked and if **those men** ever shrugged as one— what happened then?

Gvozdev was taken to the hospital ward, where he found two from his group: Komarov from the Obukhov, and Kuzmin from the Tube Factory. Too bad Bogdanov wasn't with them. Until they were slotted into singles, they took three cots side by side, where they talked to their heart's content.

In a stone sack—but your thoughts were free.

They talked over all the Workers' Group affairs—and damn if they could figure out what the right thing to do had been.

From the past they brought up so-called Makhaevism. Where had that come from? No one knew, but among Social Democrats, Makhaevism was the only thing they called it and they forbade anyone from knowing. Was it "Makhaevism" because *"makhnut rukoi"* meant to give up on someone? According to "Makhaevism," the intelligentsia was a parasite class living off the workers while aspiring to dominate all of society. To that end, intellectuals were flattering the workers for now, saying that they were the most progressive segment of humanity, but meanwhile they were suggesting ideas that workers hadn't the slightest chance of verifying, let alone appreciating. That's the deceit socialism was: it was all set up for shirkers to seize power. According to Makhaevism, the working class shouldn't take power until it had an education. It could be easily misled. It should only be waging economic struggle.

But after all, Ushakov—our Ushakov, the worker—was still alive, though God knew where. He'd been slandered. He, too, had said, Why should we overthrow the Tsar? A laborer can't hold power because he's uneducated. The gentlemen intellectuals will seize power. We're better off having the Tsar summon the people's delegates and consult with them.

Sounds about right, eh?

But there was also Zubatov, he and the other fellows recalled. Zubatov, too, was berated by the Social Democrats so that he would be remembered not otherwise than as a devil. But he, from his high-ranking police posts, told the workers the same thing: Why do you need a constitution? Or political freedoms? Only your enemy, the bourgeoisie, needs all that in order to strengthen itself, both against the regime and against you. You need an eight-hour workday and higher pay—something autocracy can better obtain from the factory owners. You are its loyal sons, and the government will support you, but the bourgeoisie—it's rebelling against the state.

Might that be right?

At one time, when the three were young and foolish, people say, the Zubatovites took the upper hand in Moscow and beat out the Social Democrats.

But for some reason it hadn't worked out.

Truly, the worker's only hope was his worker brother.

If there was a coup, then there was no getting along without the educated, after all. How could you rule the country without them? After all, not everyone could ply every trade. Running a country was a particular skill.

But trust the educated and they'd quickly make a mess of things.

The Workers' Group had been spun around and confused—and so had the entire worker cause—and even Mother Russia—and there was no solution in sight.

It was late, but there was no thought of sleep; they were good and rested here. Kozma was sprawled out on his cot, hands and feet at all four corners, his loose hair tangled, a little mustache barely bristling from his upper lip— he hadn't shaved during this month of house arrest—and he kept looking at the ceiling vault: whitish-gray and smooth, and where there was a crack, or a spot—he looked at it as if it were something important and sailed under it on his cot, as if under the sky.

He hummed under his breath:

Oh, is it in that flatboat, all fitted out . . .

And the others beside him joined in:

Daring oarsmen, forty-four, aseat.

What is it with songs? They were about something else entirely, but about you, too:

And one of them, a fine young man,
Was pensive and downcast.

And from the other wall they picked it up because it was something we shared, and everyone knew it:

Oh, you, my brothers, comrades!
Stand me in good and loyal stead . . .

And in the whole world, all that was left to ask for, to breathe out:

Toss me, throw me into Mother Volga,
Drown in it my grief and pain. . . .

They kept on singing like that for a while, these slow, drawn-out, sad songs, and his heart was soothed and quieted.

And so, his hair still tangled he wished: my pillow, my friend, carry me away, far into the night!

[7 ']

(EARLY EVENING, 8 MARCH)

To Petrograd's police officials, the events of that day—their origin, course, and conclusion—remained an inexplicably random set of events. Not a single signal from an informant had warned of them, and it seemed none of the party leaders yesterday evening had been cooking up anything in advance.

Except maybe this: revolutionaries were always fussy about the *day*. The 22nd of January didn't work out, and the day the Duma opened didn't work out, and today there was some "international women's day."

A few strikes had begun that morning on the Vyborg and Petersburg sides when the shops there ran out of black bread. Why did they suddenly run out? The bakeries had been issued exactly the same amount of rye flour as on previous days, calculated at a pound and a half per resident, and two for workers. True, no one checked the bakers; the idea of that kind of inspection had never come up. (Meanwhile, many of them started not baking bread but selling the flour to the rural counties, at double the price.) They could have run out for only one reason: an irrepressible rumor that flour was no longer going to be delivered to Petrograd, that soon there would be restrictions on bread in the city, either there'd be less of it or it would be given out by ration cards—a rumor that might have arisen as an echo of the Duma debate and the City Duma's plan to introduce ration cards. This rumor could have been dispelled by a firm governmental explanation, or by introducing ration cards and stable distribution, but nothing of the kind was done and the rumor caught fire: Stock up! Make rusks! And since they were selling as much as anyone wanted, people bought twice and three times the usual, so there wasn't enough bread for some.

Those workers who had been striking since early morning—following well-known and studied tactics, to make it easier for themselves—were on their way to neighboring factories to drive others out. Yesterday, management had itself shut down the large Putilov Works and its wharf—because work procedures had been persistently violated at this military plant for several weeks already and because of the wild demands that seemed to have been instigated by someone to immediately increase wages by half. But over the course of the day, shutting down the Putilov had not spread from the Narva side or affected the capital, so the Narva district had remained calm. At the Franco-Russian Works on Pryazhka, a rally of three thousand gathered. They had their say for and against striking, and there were voices against the war, but some also spoke for it, and everyone railed against the shortage of black bread, but they dispersed calmly, without striking. Neither Okhta, the Gunpowder district, nor the Moscow and Neva sides were touched by the disturbances. Strikes spread where they had begun, in the northern part of the capital, and until the bridge crossings were shut, they had carried over to the Liteinaya and Rozhdestvenskaya areas.

Spreading faster through the capital than strikes that day was a new trick: removing streetcar levers. Everyone liked this, and it spread cheerfully, like wildfire, through the city, so that fifteen or so cars blocked all the lines, and a hundred streetcars headed off for the depots. In the evening, in Lesnoi, the workers toppled one trailer car, but as mischief—and they stood right there, not preventing the police from righting it.

They didn't like the police, and every last one picked up the nickname for them: pharaohs.

Another craze began of smashing shop windows and ravaging, even looting shops. They started with the bread stores and sundries shops, but when a crowd thronged down Suvorovsky or Bolshoi on the Petrograd side and the adolescents up in front started smashing all the store windows in a row—how could the crowd restrain itself? They started looting vegetable stores and greengrocers and scooped up the take from cash registers. In the evening, on Smolny Prospect, they looted a jewelry store, too.

Everywhere, the crowd ran off before the police arrived. Nowhere did the crowd want a beating, and the police dispersed them everywhere without difficulty, but once a crowd scattered in one place, it always and immediately reassembled in another. True, over the course of the day there were also attacks on policemen and on factory foremen, and a few people were sent to the hospital, some unconscious, or with a dislocated jaw, or a broken arm. But apart from the supporters of law and order, no one suffered any injury. For all the dispersals—and on Bolshaya Dvoryanskaya they dispersed a crowd of four thousand, and on Liteiny and Nevsky a thousand at a time more than once—not a single demonstrator was harmed. Nowhere were weapons used, and not a single shot rang out in the city all day. Not a single red flag was displayed all day, not a slogan; the crowd hadn't been prepared by anyone in any way, and it was not seen to have leaders, even outside the Cathedral of Our Lady of Kazan, the capital's most sensitive place, the place most beloved by revolutionaries, the place where everything in Petersburg had always begun.

Early that evening they started restoring order on both the Petersburg and Vyborg sides, the streetcars ran unimpeded once again throughout the city, and Nevsky's usual evening life revived, although the workers were unusually present, *carousing* among the refined and wealthy public, whom they frightened. Patrols of city policemen under officers' supervision "filtered" the public, driving away newcomers coming from the lower-class outskirts, and for young people this once again became like a game, a fairly good-natured game.

So that day both sides began, seemingly inadvertently, a performance they had taken upon themselves.

In the course of the day, City Governor Balk asked for army assistance for the police—and was provided with details from the 9th Cavalry's regiments from Krasnoye Selo and from the 1st Don, which had just arrived in Petrograd and been replenished by new re-cruits. The Don men acted sluggishly, though here and there they did lend a hand.

Since in the afternoon troops had in part been drawn into actions, it was the District Commander General Khabalov who chaired the late-night meeting at the city governor's offices. Shortly before, General Chebykin, the commander of the Petrograd Guards (in fact, but a Petrograd-based remnant, the Guards in name only), had gone on leave, and Colonel Pavlenko—recently arrived from the front and still not fully healed after a serious contusion, ill, and utterly unfamiliar even with the layout of the Petrograd streets—became commander of the Guard units and thus in charge of the capital's defense.

Neither the Police Department nor General Globachev, the chief of the Petrograd Okhrana, had any information explaining what had happened today, nor could they point to motives for the action. They were not ruling out a convergence of circumstances, in-cluding the good weather that had set in. For many months the Okhrana had warned of a mounting revolutionary situation in general. But for these last few days specifically—it had foreseen nothing. Why had it happened at all?

Famine? There was no famine in the capital. Absolutely anything could be bought without ration cards, except for sugar, which could be with ration cards. All was well with butter, salted and fresh fish, and poultry. They should probably announce to the populace that there was sufficient flour.

All other signs were favorable, though, and the Okhrana chief was inclined to assume that there would be no disturbances of any kind tomorrow.

At the meeting at the city governor's offices, no one proposed or undertook any decisive measures. Despite the injuries to a few policemen and factory foremen, no one had sug-gested arresting or searching anyone. The troops were merely ordered to be prepared to-morrow to occupy certain districts of the city.

The city governor wrote it all up for Minister Protopopov, who, actually, could have seen all the day's goings-on with his own eyes.

Did Commander Khabalov have to report to the Supreme Command? Nothing seemed to have happened that would require reporting by a line general.

There was confidence that order would be reinstated tomorrow. The meeting partici-pants dispersed calmly after midnight, going their separate ways from Gorokhovaya through the sleeping, peaceful, dimly lit city.

There was no session of the Council of Ministers that day at all. They usually met on Fridays, that is, tomorrow.

[8]

If you stuck your nose out from under your quilt and opened your eyes, you would see the crudely whitewashed wall of a small wooden house lit by a night lamp, which had recently been startled but not blown out, and gradually swaying, was glowing steady, and with it all the shadows were dis-tinctly outlined on the walls. Full and deep under the frosty stars was the silence of Mustamyaki, a most distant and remote place in Petersburg's dacha region.

This old ottoman, some of its springs collapsed, others poking out, never had dried out properly, never had warmed up from the autumn damp or from the freezing all winter long, although they'd been heating the place for more than a day, not stinting on firewood. This time they spent only one night in Petrograd and late yesterday made their way here. But not on the first Petrograd evening, not en route, not sitting by the fire, not over today's slow, expansive day had Georgi revealed the main thing that had decisively changed the entire situation.

They also took a walk in a light snow and were invited to dinner at another dacha, with a professor's family she knew, and Olda somewhat absentmindedly exposed their relationship, by using the familiar "you," or putting her hand on his arm to warn him off one glass too many—so that her beloved old people could not have guessed that Olda Orestovna was better acquainted with those two than with her companion. "Sic itur ad astra!"[1] said the old man, repeating to Vorotyntsev his first opinion on Andozerskaya's first book.

A woman of outstanding qualities like Olda Andozerskaya had her own particular difficulties in constructing an intimate life. She'd given her best years to her scholarly works and successes, and in this time various possible companions worthy of her had gone off to marry other women. Her very professorship was a hindrance as well. Someone beneath her was no companion for a woman. As they say, marriage is a cap on a woman's head, a cap for a boyar's wife. Olda loved and quoted Marina Mniszech out loud:

> To plunge into life, boldly, arm in arm,
> Neither with a child's blind eye nor as slave
> To my husband's ready desires.

Placing the wrong crown on her head was for life, so better to go uncrowned than let her life perish.

Olda Orestovna had thus been able to establish herself in everyone's eyes such that she met with no pitying glances. Rather, everyone accepted that this uncommon lady did not need the ordinary lot. She wore this polished and flattering armor today, as well, but secretly knew that her inner uncertainty and incompleteness now shone through. Even inhaling the disturbing smell of old book bindings (you open the book—and a blast of the smell! Then it abates but is still discernible), in the happiest hours of work, it had become clear to her, as never before, that she was, in the end, alone. Alone. So undoubtedly superb—but sought by no one?

---

1. That is the way to the stars.

At the very end of October she got the idea of luring this random colonel, which took no effort at all, so gladly and obediently did he oblige—it even threatened to be boring. But he had surprised and engaged her with his combination of courage and inexperience—frisky, unvarnished. Like a clever country boy who hadn't attended the village school because of the plowing, with no notion of what literacy was, for whom a "Г" was just a scythe and a "C" a sickle, not letters, and if you'd taught him, he'd have finished high school. But those six autumn days he'd engaged her as assuredly as if she'd been waiting for only him all her life. He asked questions about all sorts of things: Germany, France, theories, today's university. Only he skipped over her woman's life, as if not contemplating that aspect in general—again out of that same ignorance?

Olda, too, was drawn then, but although she questioned Georgi about his wife, it was more out of a habit of viewing any face or event she encountered from all sides—and she couldn't imagine herself openly linked with this officer. Then he left and wrote rarely but ardently, and those winter months everything grew gloomier and angrier and began to totter, and her own chill hit her harder and harder—and suddenly, so simply, it became clear to Olda that he was the man who could be a husband to her! Anyone from her professorial, intellectual milieu would be measured up: but how would he compare with Professor Andozerskaya?—and if he came out the lesser, that meant she had married out of desperation. But a war colonel? It would never occur to anyone to apply that measure, and everyone would accept it as her eccentricity: marrying an officer! If there wasn't a fine crown on her small, thought-filled head, let it be just a cap, but one from which courage flowed onto her easily chilled shoulders.

She summoned him: come to Petersburg right away. After waiting for the last few weeks and then greeting him the day before yesterday at her apartment on Pesochnaya, she had decided definitively that she would be united with Georgi, that the time for distractions and exhaustive searches had passed, and at her thirty-seven years she could not complain of a misalliance. Of course, they had to wait for the war's end. But given his unhewn, unmilled quality, it would take more explanations, advice, and support until he followed the not at all simple journey of uncoupling from his present wife, and this, too, could mean battles for which he was not at all prepared, of course.

But something she had in no way expected, an absurdity no one could have assumed, he had announced to her only this evening. Once again they had sat for a long time on billets in front of the stove's open door, as if it were a fireplace; they kept adding logs and didn't take their eyes off the fire, in its blissful radiance. By Georgi's side, Olda was cheerfully obliterated in her smallness, the smallness of her hands, the smallness of her feet, and he variously found room for her, folded her, bent her, picked her up, played

with her hair, first taking it down, then gathering it at her nape and plunging into it face first, as if into foam. And all of a sudden, he told her.

Astonishing, unparalleled stupidity! He had taken so long to tell her not
because he wanted to hide it (although he seemed to be afraid), but sincerely believing that this was secondary and had almost nothing to do with
their bliss in this remote building by the dancing fire. He told her that back
then, in November, returning to his wife, he had immediately disclosed it
to her . . .

What? That is—how? Himself? Unprovoked? Why? To what end? Had
he wanted (his heart melted by this new kitten in his arms) back then, had
he in a week been ready to begin the separation with his wife? He had announced to her his *decision*? No . . . So then—why on earth?

The roof had collapsed, a window had been knocked out, frosty air flowed
over them through the gap, and the laws of fire were no longer in effect—yet
he understood nothing, for him nothing had changed. He still pulled her
onto his lap the same way.

But Olda was a kitten no longer, she had become as heavy as a wedge
iron and sank and pulled away and demanded explanations. So much required understanding here. *What* had he had in mind when he told his
wife? (This had been the hardest to get out of him.) How had his wife reacted? And how had he afterward? And she again? It turned out to be a long
story. Olda was smoldering, but Georgi couldn't recount it all precisely because he got mixed up as to what followed what and exactly who said what.
He hadn't thought this would ever be needed. And why didn't he once say
in a single letter . . . ? Well, same reason. It would take a long time to describe and telling it now was quicker. But from this disclosure then in November and up until his surrender . . .

"What surrender?"

. . . how had his relations with his wife and with Olda changed? Did he
understand?

No, honestly, he didn't, and nothing had changed.

Nothing had changed if he had never taken Olda seriously.

And in this letter from his wife, then to GHQ . . . ? Yes, I already told you.
No, you have to remember exactly! Being by the stove's fire had become inappropriate. Let's light the lamp again. And go back to the table. Oh, how
tedious. So then we'll have dinner a second time? Yes, I guess we will. More
questions, and more answers. What exactly did you write her from Mogilev?
Well, that I'll never remember, I swear. I wrote and sent it off straight away.
I don't reread my letters. This is so boring! We were planning to go to bed at
eight and look, it's nearly two in the morning. Well, what about it, what
about the past? Again and again?

Sleep, sleep. He drew her to him and warmed her, himself sincerely not
changing and not noticing, not wanting to believe, that Olda could change

right here, by the stove. He dropped off quickly, deeply, peacefully, so that Olda's tossing sleeplessly didn't disturb him in the least. He dropped off like a happy log, leaving to her all the problems and all the solutions.

Through those nighttime hours, which were already coming up on morning, Olda laid out the full picture analytically, element by element, reconstructing some missing pieces. Pressing close to this hot, silly log that she was finding increasingly essential, she was filled with warmth from him, and as he slept she decided his future even more irrevocably than twenty-four hours before. Since this had happened, there was no putting off what she had previously been willing to let play out gradually.

[9]

"You've been incredibly simple-minded. If I didn't know you, I'd find it unbelievable. You're not a little boy, after all. Naturally you left for the front—and that's fine. Why did you initiate this conversation with her?"

He didn't answer and barely stirred.

"To understand yourself? But you should have done that on your own. You didn't let your own feelings take shape and strengthen. That takes a lot of time, but you had it. You were the one who pushed it away."

Yes, Georgi now understood perfectly well. He was full of regret.

"Burdens like that can't be shifted onto anyone else's heart. But you handed it all over to her, what *she* decided. You handed our common fate over to her."

Well, not exactly. He just . . .

"What do you mean no? See for yourself. How could you think she would decide in your favor, let alone ours? It's the rare woman who won't hold onto her husband no matter what. A woman can't take the high ground and reason dispassionately."

He had nothing, nothing with which to wall himself off from the conversation. And there was no point crawling out from under the blanket into the cooling room. Outside it was overcast.

"These few months you and I should have been checking on ourselves, conferring. And when it became clear to us—then we could have told her."

Well, maybe that wasn't entirely honest, either. . .

"My dear, we needed a period like that. You and I became close much too quickly. I don't think that . . . Not so fast, though! We've robbed ourselves, there's something we don't have now that will take time to get back."

Silently he ran the fur of his chin over her skinny shoulder.

"And naturally, she immediately gave you an ultimatum."

An ultimatum? Hardly.

"But there's that letter! The truest ultimatum: choose immediately! One of us you won't see again!"

"What kind of ultimatum is that, Olda? It's just the cry of a wounded animal."

"That's no wounded animal's cry, you little fool. It's as real an ultimatum as it gets. A challenge and a struggle. Violence against your immature emotion—that was the moment to crush it, when you opened up out of naiveté. She's in a winning position: you and I have nothing but a rosy beginning. . . ."

Not, rosy, scarlet! Words can't . . .

". . . and no past, but you there have ten years, hundreds of cozy habits, shared memories, and friends, and breaking away seems impossible. Destroy everything? Break it off? Explain to everyone?"

"But you know, if that's how she happened to put it, it wasn't out of calculation. . . . Trying to make me come back wasn't about calculation but resolving her grief, even if it meant some sacrifice. . . . She's prepared to concede. . . ."

"**Where** do you see any sacrifice? She's sacrificing what she no longer has. Just confirm that I'm your number one, incomparable! She's taking a risk without risking anything. She knows you well enough, just as you don't know her."

"But you especially don't . . ."

"No, I know! Even from these methods of hers. She 'let you go'—and by doing so instantly triumphed! And threatened suicide. An unconscionable ploy. And you gave in!"

He grew very gloomy.

"Although this affected my fate, too. You see, you gave in—for the both of us."

"Fate! The spring offensive is about to begin. I could be killed, and then there'll be no fate at all, and maybe no me. There'll be no Vorotyntsev left on this earth at all."

She fell quiet.

"Would you be sorry if there weren't?"

"Not before, but now I have been."

"Don't. For death—maybe. But for life . . . I never did want it. A child turns his mother into nothing but a protectress, and this puts chains on everything creative and halts the individual's development."

But there was no avoiding the subject:

"You didn't destroy her happiness, you destroyed her carefree peace. I didn't take her place, after all. She lost you over the years before either of you knew it. Now, she's rushed instead to conquer you all over again."

She gazed with regret at this warrior, this bungler against the feminine fabric. She searched for something less offensive:

"You were a clay digger and so you found nothing but clay. I'm sorry, but you're just a child." She kissed him, stroked him. "That's no way to live, though. You'll perish."

She caressed him rashly—but he was no child. Her entire lecture fell apart, arguments spilled out as if from a broken basket. She tried to hold on to her chain of argument, persuasion now being more important than all pleasures—but no, he no longer heard her.

Again they lay there, in no hurry. If they got up, they'd have to prepare the firewood right away because it had run out. But not getting up—right here, by a shoulder, on an ear, like an angel or an imp, in a quiet, methodical incantation, she could steadily put so much more to him.

He listened and listened and:

"Anyway, this is horrible. It depresses me. Is it really like permanent war between men and women? So cruel, calculated, and hard? I'd thought this was the one place they could relax."

She hadn't convinced him.

Battles awaited him, and he was totally unprepared.

"The way they cleanse a cut—not in hot water or warm but in cold— that's how you and Alina have to clarify your situation. Your mistake is that you let everything dissolve in warmth and turned to mush as a result. But in *these* matters you can't be so nice: it's a sea of warm water, in which everything softens up hopelessly."

"Yes, but . . . You somehow have the wrong idea, that I don't love her. You have to understand, I do love Alina!"

This was what she couldn't accept. It was probably not even so. If he did love Alina (this she didn't tell him), he wouldn't have walked into her arms so readily, after a few glances, straightaway. But a goal had to be set. Which way to proceed. He didn't know how to do that . . . but this would be the least painful:

"Listen, there's no need to be so brutally blunt, don't take it that way. But . . . it would be easier if she did find a consoler. Don't you think so? Is it possible?"

That slipped by him completely—he didn't pick up on it, or ask questions, or notice even.

He wasn't the clay digger but the clay itself, and a clay that sculpted poorly. He should stay here longer. She needed a night and a day, a night and a day, a night and a day to soak into him so that her juices displaced everything else and he couldn't live without Olda in every way. It penetrates. It especially penetrates someone like this. And Olda knew how to penetrate.

Half a day had gone by. They were starving! Go prepare the firewood. They jumped up. Dressed. Brewed tea and warmed cutlets on the fire's remains, the chips. They cheerfully ran off with the sled to fetch a log.

The air was snowy from what had fallen overnight. The indestructible Karelian pine needles were still supporting the snowfall on the branches. On the slippery stretches, Olga took a running start and slid, like a little girl, holding on to his elbow, pushing the snow off the darkening ice with her boots, and Georgi ran alongside her.

Everything in the world seemed merry and remediable.

They tied the log down, dragged it back, and sawed it on the block with a ringing, two-handed saw. Georgi wondered at everything about her: "You're so lively when you run . . . and the way you pull. Let go, I'll do it. You don't saw badly, that's such a rarity."

"I grew up in a very remote county, the country practically!"

Steam was pouring off them. "Come, how is your heart? Let me listen. It's right under your skin, right here, leaping."

And changing his voice and hand: "Enough sawing. Let's go! I'll finish up myself. But let's go!"

[1 0]

*   *   *

Early in the morning, a notice went up on the Petrograd streets:

> Over the last few days, the same quantity of flour has been issued to bakeries for bread baking in Petrograd as previously. There should be no shortage of bread for sale. If some shops are short of bread, that is because many people, concerned about a shortage of bread, bought it to set aside for rusks. There is a sufficient quantity of rye flour in Petrograd. The delivery of this flour is proceeding without interruption.
>
> Troop Commander of the Petrograd Military District
> Lieutenant General Khabalov

This urging was hard to believe. People always believe rumors more than they do the authorities.

Where did this Khabalov come from anyway, with that sassy name, so buffoonish—just plain smutty. And why was the district troop commander giving orders about ordinary bread?

*   *   *

Today the city governor (police chief), Major General Balk, recently appointed, from Warsaw, and knowing little of Petrograd as yet, had been making the rounds of the main points of concentration for police details since early morning. He emerged from his motorcar and addressed the formation with confident words about how police officers would work above and beyond their strength to maintain calm at the front. Responses rang out and the policemen gave appearances that they understood.

But a shadow had been cast over their gallantry. They all knew that they were forbidden to use their weapons, but a weapon could be used against them. They knew of their own wounded and beaten yesterday in various places in the capital. They were supposed to stand at their isolated posts, targets for bolt nuts and rocks, as troops grinned on the sidelines and the crowd saw the state was absent.

A large detachment of city police and gendarmes had been brought together in the closed courtyard of the City Duma, in the very center of the city, but the populace couldn't see it. Balk announced to them that by order of the Minister of the Interior, the two police officers who had been seriously wounded yesterday would each receive a 500-ruble subsidy. (A month's pay for them was 42 rubles, and many workers earned more than they did.)

* * *

Early that morning—workers had barely assembled at the Shchetinin Works at Commandant Airfield—a rally had been called. The speaker made an appeal:

"Comrades! I think we should all proceed as one to our violent mutual cause. Only in this way will we get our daily bread. Comrades, remember, too: Down with the government, down with the monarchy, and down with the war! Arm yourselves as you can, with bolts, nuts, and rocks, leave the factory, and smash shops however you can!"

All the workers went out, burst into the yard of the neighboring Slyusarenko Works, and drove everyone out. The leader continued:

"And now, comrades, let's climb up on the railroad and take a break."

They climbed onto the rail bed and stopped a passenger train. They rested. And then:

"Let's all go to the State Duma together. No one take a streetcar, but start to act against the shops along the streetcar line!"

* * *

On the entire Vyborg side, workers at the Ericsson Works were the best off and the most mutinous. Some went around the bread shops, but the Ericsson men went to Nevsky! Strike! Don't stay home. Let the bourgeois tremble.

Except that Sampsonievsky Prospect narrows after the factory, so with their column of two and a half thousand, the Ericsson men blocked it completely. Up ahead, well short of the Liteiny Bridge, there were Cossacks on horseback, lined up since the last streetlamps, at the first splash of morning.

It was dreadful. If they fell on us with their swords now, they'd chop us down, there was nowhere to go, and no protecting yourself or running away.

However, they'd already gathered and crowded into the narrowness.

A Cossack on the flank, quietly: "Push harder and we'll let you through."

But their officer commanded the Cossacks to ride on the crowd in extended order. The officer cut through, clearing a path with his horse.

But the Cossacks winked at the workers. So they drew together in single file, in the corridor behind the officer. And proceeded quietly, one by one, not pressing and not drawing their swords.

And the workers, in an excess of joy: "Hurrah for the Cossacks!"

For all the factories, the road to the Liteiny Bridge was clear.

* * *

The dispatches simply didn't arrive at the city governor's offices in time. On the Petersburg side yesterday, they had first started smashing the shops, the bread and sundries shops—and once they got away with it, they liked it. Today it was here they picked up where they'd left off. Early in the morning they looted Utkin's butcher shop on Siezzhinskaya—although the argument wasn't over meat but began with rocks at windows, and then one woman went ahead and everyone followed her and they grabbed the chickens, geese, pork rinds, sheep's feet, pieces of beef, fish, and slabs of butter without any money whatsoever and carried it off. (That same day the police started searching the neighboring buildings. Some did have something, but some lived farther away. Oh well, you can't search everyone.)

They looted the tea store at the same time. Tea is light but expensive, and not having to buy tea for half a year is economical. (Policemen arrested two women and one adolescent and carted them off.)

But a crowd was already streaming in from somewhere that morning, out of the side-streets, a few thousand—just people who lived there and various pupils, some wearing their uniforms and some not, and university students— poured out of Bolshoi Prospect onto Kamennoostrovsky, packing the entire street—and sped up as they neared the Trinity Bridge. They tried to sing a song, but it didn't come together, and maybe not everyone knew it.

A Cossack patrol rode at the crowd—which scattered.

Scattered easily and seemingly without offense: you drive us away, and we flee. As usual.

* * *

The nice soldiers were standing at the Liteiny Bridge.

Standing looking not all that gallant, some belted up like sacks, barely stuffed into their greatcoats, but all in the same uniform, rifles all held at the leg—which made them look stern. Standing and silent—and because of that, stern.

But **what** would they do if . . . ?

This was best for the gals to ascertain. Civilians weren't supposed to approach a military formation. It was improper. You there, they might say, why aren't you in our formation? It was dangerous, too. Miss some password there and—a good wallop for you on the spot!

But it was fine for the gals. In twos and threes, arm in arm, they gathered—and rolled right up to the formation, making eyes, giggling and chewing sunflower seeds:

"How's it you men come to be here? The German's not here. There's some mistake."

If this is scary or funny then it's on you, not us. Troops don't have no business on the streets, and we women, the Vyborg here's our home and we're just chewing sunflower seeds.

A soldier in formation isn't supposed to respond. Discipline. He'll just sneak a smile. Gals—who doesn't like them? Young still, not worn out by a factory stint, fresh lips, rosy cheeks.

You couldn't walk right up to the formation anyway; the ensign was pacing up front. Very grim. Though he himself was so very young and slim.

"Your honor, how is it you're so awfully grim? Or did your bride cheat on you? If so, we'll find you another."

He laughed.

"Which one of you is going to take her place?"

"Me, if you like"—and she licked her lips. The conversation was very close, and the girls could hear but not the soldiers, not the police. Another glance to either side: "Listen, did you really come to shoot at the people, eh?"

How he flushed:

"Of course, not! What a disgrace. You've got nothing to fear. We won't touch you!"

The mounted Cossacks were standing cross-wise in a line, at attention. The workers started talking to them, and they responded. Then people started ducking right under the Cossack horses and moving on along like that. The Cossacks didn't stop them. They laughed. Then the mounted police rode up and drove the duckers back.

*   *   *

Meanwhile, the nice sun broke through and started twinkling in a very un-Petersburg way. The frost was easing up and about to melt. Drops slipped off the roofs.

If someone's time had come, it was the adolescents'. Mischief—sanctioned mischief!—that was great! What's what—that was for the grownups to know, not us! They ran down Ligovka with sticks and smashed the sundries shop windows. Smash! Smash!

They smashed six—and ran on. You'd never catch them.

*   *   *

But we, the black masses, gathered, in countless numbers. We set up all along the Pirogovskaya Embankment and covered the Polyustrovskaya and

Sampsonievskaya ones as well. The Vyborg side's factories all began empty-ing out and wended their way from all its side-streets to the embankments — forty thousand or so of us, truly. But what next?

Standing hour after hour and at the end of a bread line was all right. At least there you'd come out with a warm loaf. But what about here? Still, standing at the end was backbreaking, the way they bent you, so give some-one a kick in the head. But it's freer here, you're your own boss. Look, we came and we're here!

The Neva was burning with sun and snow sparks. It both blocked the way and beckoned.

We weren't Petersburg at all, we were just a settlement attached to it, to work for them, the gentlemen. It might not seem so, but it was all for them. Take a look at their clean city — towers, big and small, palaces and parks, all built specially, but our folk they kicked out past the Great Nevka. We'll never have justice. They'll be nice and clean as always, and we'll be all twisted up.

They didn't just block the bridge, there were also police details at the steps off the embankment to the river.

Why are we standing here, you ask? To look at their city from afar again? It was all supposed to be one city. The same streetcars ran there, and for that it was connected by bridges, but look — ask the truth! The way to us was barred! Yesternight on this same bridge, on Liteiny, every streetcar into the city was stopped in the middle of the bridge, which meant local and city policemen boarded and walked the length of the car eyeing the riders. Only they had an eye aimed like a blackjack. At your nose, at your clothes, and show your hands, no need for documents. Get out! What for? Get out, that's all. What for, what am I guilty of? Step lively and less talk. Or else — by the shoulders and elbows. But the rest, their people, the ones closer to the educated folk — they could go on riding, and the streetcar rang its bell.

Nasty things they were, those streetcars, better never to see one in your life. Look what they came up with: not to walk with your feet at all but go from building to building on wheels.

There was nothing to lure us there, to the city. They didn't sell our rye bread, and you couldn't fill your belly on their delicacies, that funny stuff and sweeties — nothing to stick to your ribs. And their clothes were so foolish — expensive but full of holes and not warming. And now they'd blocked us off! Blocked us off as if we weren't human beings, and your heart filled with in-sult: To Nevsky! Get along to Nevsky!

What if we went straight across the Neva? The ice was still strong, not spring ice. Snow knee deep but no one's walked there.

But it was like when a woman sets you on fire, as if there'd never been an-other: you melt, and that's it! We want to go to Nevsky!

*   *   *

At midday, all five telephones started ringing at once in the city governor's offices. Straight across the Neva! Over the ice! Single file! An unbroken file of people! Below the Liteiny Bridge! And above the Liteiny Bridge! To the Voskresenskaya Embankment, in several places! Moving toward the Main Waterworks!

In several places at once! They were blazing trails through the deep snow! They were off!

What were the police supposed to do? They'd been told not to use their weapons. On the granite embankments of the left bank, police details stood by the steps, but if the disturbances were supposed to be stopped without pushing, without injury, and without bruising, how were they going to stop this mass?

Did they have to let them pass?

Here they'd reached the left bank and were trailing up the steps. In some places the pharaohs, arms linked, made it look as though they were trying to detain them; in some, they looked like they'd nodded off and didn't see.

What of it? The lads were walking, not making mischief, and there was no law that said they couldn't walk across the river.

*   *   *

The public had filled all the main streets in the center, and there was barely any room on the sidewalks, an expanded promenade. Once again, a sunny, lightly frosty, cheerful day. Polite society felt a mounting urge to throw something, to spite the authorities. People were waiting for the workers to start something.

*   *   *

A new crowd of seven thousand thronged down Kamennoostrovsky headed toward the center. They had assembled quickly since almost none of them were at work and institutions had shut down, too. The wounded waved from their infirmary windows. Boys and girls shouted, danced, and squabbled in front of the crowd.

A police officer ordered the march to cease. They ignored him.

Then, stepping back with his detail, he ordered the mounted police guard nearby to come out on the street and disperse the crowd.

The horses clattered and the mounted city police rode out in a curved wing. The motley public—workmen and petty bourgeois, and some rather cleaner, and high school students, and university students—quickly cleared the street and started down the sidewalks. Because of this they were tightly packed—and out of this great congestion—already near the end of the street, opposite Malaya Posadskaya—someone fired a gun at the police detail! The **first** shot in all these days!

But he didn't hit the policeman or anyone else, and he pushed quickly into the crowd and wasn't discovered, and the crowd wouldn't give him up.

The crowd had packed the sidewalks, as if expecting someone very important to pass by. Only they crossed the road freely, in a throng.

And now, on the other side, at Malaya Posadskaya now, the same gun, or so it was understood among them, fired a **shot**! A second!

A woman, a random woman, screamed. And fell. Her head injured. But he'd missed the policeman again!

They sent for an ambulance carriage.

But failed to catch the fellow—again. The public was packed tight and wasn't giving him up, wasn't pointing him out.

A modern school pupil at the edge of the sidewalk started shouting that it was the police officer who'd shot the woman.

Right then a police chief walked up and in front of everyone checked the bullets in the policeman's gun. There was still time to verify the truth. All there. And no gunpowder residue in the barrel.

The modern school pupil was arrested.

The woman died in the hospital.

✻ ✻ ✻

How many of us hearty souls started across the ice, but our numbers didn't go down at the Liteiny Bridge. People kept adding and adding to the ranks.

It actually just happened that way, without premeditation. Those in the rear pressed up and those of us being packed in tighter and tighter kept moving forward, right under the horses' heads. And so we went, inch after inch, and the crowd climbed on the horses. The horses snorted, shaking their heads, and stepping back—because horses are aware.

But the mounted police stepped back a little—and naturally the foot police moved aside.

And so inch after inch, inch after inch, imperceptibly, the inches becoming yards, and here they were at the bridge.

The police called out—though no one was moving forward. They simply kept pressing up from behind. We didn't even swear in reply, though here and there someone might have snarled. The women added their bit about bread. If you looked at policemen up close like that more often you'd see they were people, too. You'd think they were doing their job, and they had families and children.

"Are your women standing in the bread lines?"

"Where else are they going to get it?"

"Why don't we see them then?"

"Are they supposed to put on our uniform?"

And now we were almost stepping onto the bridge. Here blocking us also were dragoons, two rows of horses.

What if we broke through now? Would they mow us down? No? Was there a way to read the dragoons' faces? They wouldn't speak up in front of the police.

Because look how far we've made it, so what were we supposed to do now? Retrace our steps all the way?

Somehow, it just happened, without leaders or a plan. People just glanced at each other and let up a shout:

"Hurrah!"

But they didn't budge. Stronger, and from behind, too:

"Hurrah!"

And all of a sudden they drove like a piston across the bridge. This was mightiness, this crowd, it could knock you off your feet. And everyone:

"Hurrah!"

They broke through the police there without even noticing, and on to the dragoons: How about it?

They weren't hitting us! They weren't hitting us! They weren't even putting hand to sword and the horses were stepping back.

"Hurrah!"

They rushed past the cavalry! And headed across the bridge! Across the bridge at a run!

A quarter of the bridge! Half the bridge!

And there, almost nothing, a dozen policemen—and swords nowhere in sight!

But the police colonel's face was brutish. And the others' no milder. They were going to cut us down! Cut us down as best they could, and they were ready to lay down their lives they were!

And the thousand halted before the dozen—not to be the first to lose his head . . .

But someone farther back, who must have guessed what was happening, picked up a jagged piece of ice and threw it at a policeman! The policeman grabbed himself, covered in blood, covered impressively, and dropped his sword.

As his blood flowed, they ran past them. Someone along the way pulled something out of a snowdrift—a shovel! That was even worse if you took a good swing!

They weren't cutting us down! We ran through.

"Hurrah!"

Now to Nevsky! (Though why—we didn't know ourselves.) But those in back were pushed back, and they howled:

"Bloodsuckers! Bread!"

"Oprichniks!"
"Pharaoh mugs!"
But the road was clear for now, and our feet light:
"To Nevsky!"

* * *

It would be wrong to think that city life came to a halt. Everything went on as usual. In the editorial office of *Speech* they were preparing for their annual banquet. Milyukov himself would be there, as would all the KD leaders.

Cavalry Captain Voronovich arrived from Luga (we would soon be hearing about him) and attended the Guards Economic Society—and didn't notice any disturbances, and no one said a word to him.

In fact, many in the city noticed nothing. General Vertsinsky rode through the city in a cab and saw nothing, only hearing noise coming from Nevsky. In the evening he went to the theater, as did many.

The Prime Minister himself, Prince Golitsyn, was surprised when he couldn't take his usual direct route from his home on Mokhovaya to the Mariinsky Palace, for a government session. He had to make a detour.

At the Council of Ministers that day there were various routine matters, and the city upheavals were not discussed. Protopopov did not appear at the session, and the police had handed today's disturbances over to the military authorities, who would be responsible.

[11]

Veronika rang the bell loudly and burst in with Fanechka Sheinis.

"Oh, dear aunts, just for a minute! We shouldn't have taken the literature. This is no time for that. We're putting it back. We could get caught with it, like Kostya!"

Veronika had a swiftness of movement and decisiveness about her, new since last autumn.

"What Kostya?"

"Motya's friend, Levantovsky, from the Neurological. He was giving a speech to the workers, the police grabbed him, and there was a slogan on calico folded in his pocket: 'Long live the socialist repub—'"

"You mean you're planning to give a speech to the workers, too?" said Aunt Agnessa with approval.

"I don't know. We'll see!" Veronika laughed. And plump, good-natured Fanechka said, "We'll see. But why ever not?"

"Veronya, Fanechka, wait, eat a little!" Aunt Adalia fussed.

"No time!"

"Well, here's some pâté. And aspic." She'd put plates on the table. The young women sat down as they were, in their coats and hats, at the edge of their chairs.

While Aunt Agnessa, badly upset, breaking a third match in front of them, in frustration, said, "Look, you've slowed me down! How can we sit at home at times like this! We'll miss everything! What did you see, girls? Where? Tell me?"

The pâté was a hit, though. And with stuffed mouths:

"First near Siemens & Halske, on the Sixth Line. We shouted to them and whistled. At first they wouldn't go, but then they gushed out—oh, about five thousand."

"Oh, more! Seven thousand! They came rolling out the gates. . . ."

"And on to Sredni Prospect! And the mounted police—well, what could they do? They were too few! But very close by there were about ten Cossacks, and the police called for help. . . ."

"But the Cossacks! In front of the whole crowd, not a word in reply! They stood there in silence! They let the crowd pass! And rode behind the crowd, again in silence!"

"Behind! The crowd! As if there were nothing to it!" The girls beamed.

"Right after that they turned into a side-street. They were ashamed!"

"That's astonishing! Cossacks—ashamed!"

"One Cossack dropped his lance—and the crowd handed it back to him, in a friendly way!"

"Really?" Aunt Agnessa took drag after drag on her trembling cigarette and paced around the dining room.

But Aunt Adalia dropped onto a chair and sat with an enchanted smile.

"And then the crowd split up. We went with the part going to the Harbor, and then they started breaking down the factory gates from the outside, to get them out, the horseshoe factory."

"No, even before that, here, on Eighteenth Line, they stormed a shop— and threw the bread on the street, right on the pavement!"

"We've lived to see it, Dalya, we have!" Agnessa was walking around and cracking every knuckle. The *Cossacks* have changed! Well, *their* time's up then!

"The streetcar drivers wouldn't leave the depot this morning. They said to first make sure there's bread!"

"As if they could even go! A crowd had already started to rock one car and topple it. While the soldiers were dragging them back by the shoulders, to save the car. What fun!"

"The high school students were singing the 'Marseillaise' and teaching it to the people!"

"All in all, everyone was in a jolly mood, aunties! Hurry along, you. There's more for you to see! And we're off. If Motya calls, tell him we aren't studying! Nor should he, of course! . . . Sasha didn't call?"

"You have to make them shoot! Get them to shoot!" Aunt Agnessa said as she saw them out. "Otherwise it will all be for nothing. There'll be a little unrest and that will be the end of it."

Fanechka was already pulling Veronya away. The door slammed shut behind them.

"What about Sasha? Can't they force him to put them down?" Aunt Adalia said, terribly worried. "They shouldn't call on an institution, should they?"

"Don't you know Sasha? He would never!"

"What if they force all the soldiers?"

Agnessa lit another but immediately put it out.

"No, let's go! Or else I'll go myself. Just think. This may be the very day they've been waiting for, the very day they've dreamed of seeing on the calendar—all the people who've given . . ."

They listened at the window vent. As if from afar—the workers' "Marseillaise," youthful voices.

"Oof!" Agnessa gave up and went to dress. "They're singing the 'Marseillaise' wrong. They've forgotten it since '05."

[1 2]

On the 9th, a Friday, they called up one platoon of the Volynian Reserve Battalion's training detachment to mount guard on Znamenskaya Square. To command they sent Staff Captain Tsurikov, a dashing, cheerful officer, who was recuperating from his wounds in the reserves and who knew none of the soldiers or even all the sergeants there. To assist they assigned him Sergeant-Major Timofei Kirpichnikov from the 2nd Company of the same training detachment, a wiry man with a rather sullen, primitive face, a short neck, and flat pressed-back ears. A longtime Volynian, since back in peacetime, a sergeant of the kind that knows all about service—and maybe nothing else, but that he knows.

They started from their barracks down the full length of Ligovka and at the last building on it before the square descended to the caretaker's large room, in the cellar, where there was a Chinese laundry and benches where they could sit after stacking their rifles in pyramids. And smoke, but not right away. Outside were two sentries.

The staff captain didn't stay. He went to the Great Northern Hotel to sit at a nice table.

A soldier's life, they were always making them do something: if not training, then sit here, in your belted greatcoats, shoulder to shoulder, crushed together. If you want, be quiet; if you want, say the same old things over and over. Everyone already knew everything about you, as you did them. More than once Timofei had told his sergeant friends, if not the soldiers, about his orphan's life, his ruined family, his saddlemaker father, his stepmother—

and how only in the army had he found his home, and how lucky he was to have ended up in the Guards, in Warsaw.

So that was why they'd put the soldiers there, so they couldn't be seen from outside, as if there were no one there. They were ashamed before the people. And the sentries at the gate—that didn't mean anything.

But they didn't sit for long, less than an hour. Tsurikov ran over and was already shouting from the stairs:

"Kirpichnikov!"

"Here, your honor!"

"Give the order to arms!"

"But what's happening?" Timofei knew his worth, and he didn't snap to immediately to any command for just any officer. He himself had set his sights on ensign school but never got there.

"They're coming!"

"Who's coming?"

"Who the hell knows! Bring them out!"

Well, the command to arms was given, and they grabbed rifles and tramped up the stairs.

While outside there was sunshine and a light frost.

They deployed a front on Nevsky, cross-wise, on the packed, trampled snow.

They saw a crowd moving down Nevsky, down the street. And two flags overhead, red ones.

But the atmosphere was not the least bellicose. The public crowded right up to the soldiers' ranks, from behind and the side, and coaxed them, not desperately but merrily, provocatively: "Good soldiers, don't shoot! Mind you don't shoot!"

Kirpichnikov, looking around to see if an officer was nearby, softly: "Don't you worry, we won't."

What kind of assignment was this in fact? Stand in the middle of the city, in the middle of the people—and fire at the people? Was that a soldier's business?

But just try disobeying an order.

The crowd and flags were thronging, closer. Some dressed more grittily, some more proper, common folk and educated. And they were shouting:

"Don't fire on the people, soldiers!"

But they themselves didn't believe it; they were just playing.

The staff captain was standing not very erect and not looking sternly. He gave no command.

Kirpichnikov walked up to him, softly:

"Your honor, after all, they're coming—asking for bread. They'll pass by and disperse. It's all right."

The staff captain looked and shrugged. He was flying free and wasn't going to be here long. What service was this of his?

Timofei was tired of this, too, but they kept him on in the battalion as someone who trained well.

Those at the front of the crowd faltered. They looked at the officer but didn't go any farther, onto the square.

The staff captain smiled and dashingly, with a wave of his hand: "Pass, I said, pass!"

The crowd split in two and went around either flank of the soldiers' formation. Timidly at first, then more boldly.

Then they started shouting: "Fine fellows, you soldiers! Thank you!"

And then, louder: "Hurrah!"

And then, there, on the square—wouldn't you know, they started toward the statue of the Tsar on horseback. They weren't dispersing at all.

A bad business. We wouldn't be getting any strokes for this.

And over there, some loudmouths had started speaking from the marble pedestal. What about—that was hard to hear from here.

Though they would have liked to listen.

Lance Corporal Orlov, a Petersburg worker, had led him surreptitiously to a certain apartment on the Neva side. A simple, worker's apartment, in the Archangel Michael settlement. Another five or so soldiers from the other reserve battalions went there, too. Two university students explained everything to them, what the tsars were like, all shedding the people's blood and feasting at the people's expense. That's what all the noblemen were like, and all the Petersburg rulers, too. And now, together with some of the generals, they were trading in the Russian soldier's very blood. And committing treason—passing information on to the Germans. Rasputin had been a part of this, and the Tsaritsa had been lolling around with him. That was where we were headed. This whole war was something our people didn't need at all.

Some of this was the truth, and some just talk. And the heart felt a chill.

The staff captain thought a bit and waved his hand: Take them away!

That's right. It was worse now for us to be standing here.

They went back to the caretaker's room for the time being.

[13]

SCREEN

Between the four bronze steeds of the Anichkov Bridge
two live ones race by!—beauties!—
a devil of a cabbie—
light sleighs race, and their riders are
a respectable gentleman, confident and smiling,
and a lady beside him, wearing a fur collar and a broad hat with
    feathers.

But just coming off the bridge the horses shudder, stop short,
    and dance in place,
the cabbie leans back—either astonished or terrified,
= a young workman in an undercoat, his cap askew, is standing in
    the way, unafraid, his hand raised—
and so he stops the horses. One by the bridle—and he walks
    around
and indicates with a sweep of his arm: Get down, I say, get down!
The cabbie's chest swells to bursting, but the gentleman—
the gentleman drops his monocle, smiles, it was just a misunder-
    standing:
        Comrade! Why do this? I'm for freedom as well!
        I'm a correspondent for The Stock Ex . . .
= But the fellow hasn't faced down a gallop for that:
        The Stock Exchange? You've ridden enough! Get down!
= They jerk the gentleman from the sleigh by his elbow.
The gentleman raises a fuss and the lady starts clucking, but
    they climb down, and the cabbie makes his own fuss,
= well! in return, friends jump up from either side:
        Drive!
The cabbie bristles:
        And who's going to pay me?
= The fellow stands tall in the sleigh, swinging both arms freely
    —a slap to the cabbie's shoulders!
        Let's go!
They're off!
And the fellows are off, don't ask the cost, down the length of
    Nevsky!
Down the length of Nevsky

if you look into the distance
= there seem to be a lot of people in the street and the streetcars
    are too close together.
They've been stopped.
= Passengers in the streetcar—
all different reactions.
Basically, though, what? Get out and walk.

             *   *   *

On the Kazan Bridge,
as the Savior on the Spilled Blood comes into view down the
    canal,
a mixed crowd of workers and women from the outskirts, you can
    tell by their clothes, and adolescents.
        Give us bread!

Not all of them, but individual voices try to pull together:
> *Arise, awaken, working people!*
> *Join the fight against capital!*
And a red flag tears upward! Raised there in the middle.
And a young cry, anguished, ringing, lonely:
> *Down! With the police! Down! With the government!*
But they have nowhere to go: the cavalry is right there, the song
    ended,
the dragoons press their horses' chests up to the workers—and
push them aside—that way, along the canal.
Not rudely, without swords—that way, toward the Savior on the
    Spilled Blood.
The flag is gone—fallen, taken away.
A confused din. A dying murmur. And only little boys' merry, harmoniz-
    ing voices:
> *Give us bread! Give us bread!*
= On the sidewalks, the public is more genteel
better dressed.
They watch like sympathetic idlers,
but their joy—that seems to have subsided.

✳   ✳   ✳

Church of the Sign.
Monument to Aleksandr III, on red granite. The fairytale hero,
    the emperor, embedded with his steed for eternity in this
    parallelepiped pedestal.
Heft and permanency.
And fifteen mounted policemen,
well-formed fellows, live cast monuments,
swords bared, no little grins like the Cossacks—
they clatter
    going forward. They aren't in the mood for jokes.
    Oh, they aren't?
From deep among us—a whistle! A howl!
    And right then, across the square from Ligovka, carting sleighs
    drag along, carrying firewood.
A whistle! A howl!
    Someone's hand reaches out—
    snatches a log!
    and fires it at a mounted policeman.
    With all his pride and firmness—a log in the side! Not what he
    wanted?

Our boys throw accurately—nearly knock him off.
His horse starts turning.
And even worse, a whistle straight through the crowd! And shouting!
and ten or so fall on those logs to grab and hurl,
from behind the cart, using it as a barricade.
Two of the mounted men try to get here—but you can't touch us.
A log! A log! A log! they fly like missiles!
Smaller objects go flying, too—maybe rocks, maybe ice.
And a whistle!
The horses spook. They start turning—and carry them off. Their
strength is in their horse—and so is their weakness.
Some gallop off, so the other mounted men aren't going to stay
either—
they turn around—and they're off, to Goncharnaya.
= One horse alone doesn't stir:
Aleksandr's. A horse straight out of a fairytale.
As is He.
= The square is free, and the crowd jams into it from Nevsky.
So what now? A rally!
But where? Why, on Aleksandr's pedestal; there is no other ele-
vation.
They clamber up every which way.
You held us tight, and now we've broken away!
They're shouting—whatever someone comes up with, the people
are all random, not a single loudmouth:
Down with the pharaohs!
Hurrah!
Down with the oprichniks!
The crowd all spills onto the square and into Nevsky's mouth,
blocking it,
half a hundred Cossacks.
Slightly sideways on their horses, condescendingly. Dandies.
As it happens, it's as if they were at our rally, too.
With us!
Brother Cossacks, thank you! Hurrah!
Hurrah!
The Cossacks grin, pleased.
And the hurrah thunders. Hurrah!
What about them? Should they do something?
Ah, they decide to bow.
Bow to all sides.
Like artists.
Some remove their cap and bow their forelocked head.
With us! The Cossacks are with us!

[14]

One sorrow always crowds out another. Measles, like a dark fire, spread to one child after another—but raised the mother and her utterly broken heart, and made her firm on her feet, and everything heartbreaking and oppressive, everything that had kept her from getting up for more than two months, was pushed back.

It began with the eldest, Olga. Her whole face was covered with a red rash, and badly. At twenty-two, this was no childhood illness. It was very dangerous. Then Aleksei, with a rash not on his face but in his mouth, and it affected his eyes. Measles overtook them all at once, from oldest to youngest, and it became clear that the rest were unlikely to avoid this fate. Even they were coughing suspiciously. She separated the children, but it was too late. Today Tatyana had over 100° and a bad headache—and she was the main nurse, so capable, her mother's indefatigable helper in all practical matters. Thank God, the two littlest were still holding out. Aleksandra Fyodorovna had landed in an all-around battle, with enemies on all sides (though she had grown used to that over this last year), but there was little help and it was not decisive. Having darkened the patients' rooms with shutters and put on her usual nurse's dress, she went from one to the next with a newly restored firmness of step.

The first day that same measles spread to an adult, Anya Vyrubova, who would have a very hard time of it. Since that terrible 30 December, they had removed her from her lonely little house and kept her at the Aleksandr Palace, concerned that she might be killed the way Grigori Efimovich had been. She had long been receiving threats, and she was utterly defenseless, on crutches. Now she had taken ill with her two constant nurses, in another wing of the palace, which it was not easy for the Empress to reach through the length of apartments, so they wheeled her in a chair, and she would sit there an hour in the morning and an hour in the evening. Anya came down with a terrible cough and a burning internal rash, but most of all, she couldn't breathe and was afraid of suffocating, so she sat up in bed—and on top of everything else she was mistrustful and easily given to panic. She implored the Empress to ask the Emperor for his most pure prayers on Anya's behalf in her very first letter. She very much believed in the purity of his prayer, and she hoped he would go pray to the Mogilev Mother of God. (Anya had great faith in that monastery icon and had taken her diamond broach to it.)

In and of themselves, the nursing duties not only presented no difficulty for the Empress, she had considered herself a born nurse even before her hospital practice in this war. Sometimes she visited other patients unannounced, and she herself had cared for her own: Anastasia from diphtheria and Aleksei through all his illnesses. But now she herself was so sapped and broken, on the threshold of forty-five she referred to herself as a ruin.

Thank God, Aleksei was not acutely ill; for him any illness was all the more frightening. But what was going to happen to him in general, since their Friend's death? They had killed Him, the Only One who could save the heir. Now all she could do was wait in agony for inevitable misfortune. Grigori had once predicted that six weeks after his death the heir's life would be put in grave danger and the entire country would be on the brink of ruin. True, nine weeks had passed now, but her fear had not dissipated.

Just this black autumn, their Friend had predicted something better, that we would emerge from all that was bad and overpower our enemies. Yet, when at their last meeting at Anya's little house the Emperor had asked upon their parting: "Grigori, bless us all," their Friend had suddenly replied: "Today, you must bless me."

Had he had a foreboding?

In December the Empress, with a presentiment of something, saw him nearly every other day. She was seeking support in the deadly hounding that besieged her. The capital's hatred and malignant gossip had thickened around her—and the Tsar's family met with those closest to them under cover of night and secrecy.

On the very day of the murder, the Empress sent Anya to take Grigori an icon brought from Novgorod. Upon her return, Anya told her that late that night their Friend was going to meet Irina at the Yusupovs'. The Empress was surprised. This was some mistake. Irina was in the Crimea. But she thought nothing of it and failed to warn him. How a fog can overtake us! On the morning of the 30th, Grigori's daughter, who lived with her father, telephoned. He'd left late the previous night with Yusupov and had not returned. She had thought nothing of this either. Two hours later a call came in from the Ministry of the Interior: a policeman on duty had reported that a drunken Purishkevich had run out of the Yusupov home declaring that Rasputin had been killed. Later, a military vehicle without lights drove away from the home. Here, too, though, already realizing that something bad had happened, the Empress could not believe in the death of this man of God! Afterward, the murderers themselves telephoned (though she still didn't know they were murderers!): Dmitri, asking that they be allowed to come for tea at five o'clock. She declined. Then Yusupov, asking for permission to come by and explain, called Anya to the telephone. She wouldn't allow that; he could send his explanation in writing. That evening they brought Yusupov's shameless, cowardly letter, in which the lying grand duke swore that Grigori had not been to see him that evening. There had been a party and they drank too much, and Dmitri Pavlovich had killed a dog. Only two days later, near an ice hole close to Krestovsky Island, did they find Grigori's galosh, and later divers found his body as well. He had been bound hand and foot with a rope, the fingers of his right hand were formed as if to make the sign of the cross, and he had bullet wounds and a laceration from a spur—they'd beaten him with a spur—but the bound man had been alive when they threw him in the water. His lungs had still been functioning because the autopsy found them full of water.

The rotten capital grinned, and everyone congratulated one another: "The evil spirit is no more!" "The beast has been crushed!"

Wasn't this murder? Wasn't this the same instance of terror for which revolutionaries were properly executed? Grand dukes were murdered and revolutionaries executed, but the Grand Dukes murdered a common man, along with the shrill, perverted Purishkevich, and everyone was full of praise and no one anticipated punishment! Even worse, the distraught, weakened Emperor could not bring himself to lay a hand on the murderers! How could he forgive a villainous, cold-blooded, premeditated murder— and not punish anyone? Not even arrest, let alone try them—but forgive them? But then there was no more justice in the state and no defense for anyone else! After all, the ruthless plans could creep further; there was hatred enough. That was why Nikolai Mikhailovich had given a warning at GHQ in November: *The assassination attempts will begin!* So was this the Grand Dukes' shared plan?

In all these years the Tsar's family had never feared such attempts. Not even after Stolypin was killed had there been any. That seemed a thing of the past.

How could we allow ourselves to be trampled underfoot?

There was no end to the Emperor's forgiveness and weakness! Perpetually concerned only for peace and harmony, the Emperor would not let rage build inside him.

Not only did the dynasty not feel accused, it felt itself the accuser! The whole family of grand dukes demanded at the top of its voice that the Emperor not dare punish the murderers—as if there was no crime in the murder. Calling each other, gasping over the telephone, and writing through the mails were the noxious Maria Pavlovna the elder, her erstwhile sister Elizaveta, and Princess Yusupova, the murderer's mother (the Empress was delivered her intercepted letter to the Emperor's sister Ksenia saying it was too bad they had not followed through and gotten rid of *everyone they should have*; now there was still *her* to lock up!).

From beginning to end, the right tone had never been found with the dynasty, the monarch's large family, or high society. There had been no closeness even with the Dowager Empress, especially since the mama listened to all the capital gossip. Many other offenses edged in as well. Maria Pavlovna had once asked for the Tsar's daughter's hand for her playboy son, her roué Boris. The Empress had declined this marriage in horror, saving her little girl—and earned herself a new mortal enemy. The two Montenegrins, Militsa and Stana, with whom she had once been so friendly (she and Stana had fretted in the next room while the 30 October Manifesto was being signed), and even especially on the sacred ground of mysticism, and around Monsieur Philippe and later Grigori Efimovich. The Montenegrin sisters had long been fierce enemies, plotting how to place their Nikolasha on the throne. She had no heartfelt ties, or even friendly feelings with any of the great many grand duchesses or dukes—except perhaps Uncle Pavel, although he was offended by the punishments. Here they had loved Dmitri like a son—and this was how he had repaid them! Everyone had their own scores to settle, their own reasons for offense, and even the nun Elizaveta, Aleksandra's own sister, had long become an irreconcilable foe and had no wish even to listen to any explanations about Grigori. Slander by the grand dukes raced to join up with high society slander. Grand Duke Pavel's adopted daughter, Marianna Derfelden, spread a rumor that the Empress was plying the Emperor with spirits, others said with Tibetan herbs. How defenseless the royal couple was against this malignant gossip! Where, how, in what form, and to whom could it be refuted that the Emperor drank only a man's usual glass at dinner?

That sad winter at the Aleksandr Palace, they had allowed themselves a light distraction. They had invited a small Romanian orchestra for three concerts, in Anya's wing—and the entire capital was already spreading malignant gossip about orgies in the palace.

They were in such a hurry to cast aspersions! After Nikolai Mikhailovich's visit to GHQ, the ever huffy and offended Viktoria, now Kirill's wife and previously the wife of the Empress's brother Ernst, went to Tsarskoye and by right of kinship boldly lectured Aleksandra Fyodorovna about what she should and shouldn't do. The extravagant Sandro, Ksenia's husband, tried to obtain an audience with the Empress when she was laid out flat in bed that winter, exhausted by all she'd been through—and the Emperor could not refuse him. His only defense was that he had been silently present during Sandro's accusatory, abusive, repulsive, and mendacious monologue.

"Lord, what have I done? What have I done to them?" Aleksandra would sob or despair after these meetings, letting her face fall into her hands. She was powerless against a dynasty that had closed ranks.

That entire winter was a time of letters and denunciations. Indeed, one of the Vasilchikov princesses, not even using paper befitting the highest correspondence, tore a sheet off raggedly from a random notebook and in a careless, hasty hand, dashed this out: "You don't understand Russia. You're a foreigner! Leave us!"

"There is a hunt under way against your wife. How can you not understand?" the Empress exclaimed to her husband.

Having forgiven all who had done her wrong, all who had impudently lectured her, not even stripping court officials of their uniforms, even forgiving Rodzyanko for spreading the transcript of his conversation with the Emperor, he did only this in her defense: he banished that Vasilchikova and the painfully talkative Nikolai Mikhailovich, who had exceeded all bounds for gossip among the grand dukes, to their estates.

But he had nothing to offer in defense of his spouse against all the other attackers.

The Tsar's displeasure could be expressed to the entire family of grand dukes only by not sending them presents that Christmas.

The Emperor was no defense for his spouse.

She had no defense. Only God and prayer.

She especially loved and was consoled by Psalm 36: "Fret not thyself because of evil-doers, and be not envious of them that work unrighteousness; for they shall soon be cut down like the grass. Commit thy way unto the Lord, and rely upon him. Cease from anger, and forsake wrath. For evil-doers shall be cut off; but those that wait on the Lord, they shall possess the land."

It goes without saying, all these months the entire Duma clique and all the Unions never let up in their attacks, and their illegal congresses raged on in Moscow, defaming the regime. The Empress could have banished Lvov, Guchkov, Milyukov, and the malicious Polivanov to Siberia with a clear conscience before all of Russia, and this would have been only to Russia's salvation! How could domestic betrayal be tolerated when there was a war going on? But the Emperor not only undertook nothing against them, he sought some way to concede to them. Without consulting with his wife, he removed old Stürmer, and several times he endeavored to sacrifice even the devoted Protopopov. He took on as premier the perfidious Trepov, who was flirting with Rodzyanko, and allowed himself to be guided by him (whereas he should have been hanged!). How many more sincere attempts at persuasion did it take to convince the Emperor to drive out the last hostile ministers and take on the honest Prince Golitsyn and the gentleman Belyaev finally as War Minister!

When he was there, in Tsarskoye, the Emperor conducted all affairs and audiences himself. When he went to GHQ for a few days (letting him go meant more anguish and terror for the mistakes he might make), he left a note and a list of appointments, albeit secondary ones. The Empress might not have carried on for her husband, especially given the children's illness, but she considered it her duty to drag through his schedule.

And so today, after changing her light nurse's dress for a heavy woolen one (whichever one, the Empress did not care very much, and during the war she did not have a single new thing sewn), she went out into the hall and despite her infirmity and preoccupation tried to be sufficiently attentive while receiving a string of importunate foreigners—a Belgian, a Dane, a Spaniard, a Persian, a Siamese, and two Japanese—which took an hour and a half—followed by other urgent ones—and then the assistant palace commandant, General Groten.

The problem was that although no one told the Empress anything, yesterday at evening tea she had learned from her close friends and guests, aide-de-camp Sablin and Lili, the wife of aide-de-camp Dehn, that there had been disturbances in Petrograd and bread stores had been looted. But the Empress would have liked to learn these things through her own officials! She summoned Groten and instructed him to clarify with Protopopov what had happened there. Protopopov telephoned his assurance that it was nothing serious. Early this morning, people said, the disturbances that went on were even worse, and they had called up the Cossacks. Groten went to see Protopopov and brought reassurance that the disturbances were already letting up. All this had been put in the hands of the military, with General Khabalov, and tomorrow all would be calm.

More than once that day the Empress was called away to the telephone. The day pulled her in such different directions and she felt a need for peace, to glance in at her favorite Church of the Sign, in Tsarskoye.

She wanted to take along her two youngest daughters, Maria and Anastasia, but the doctor found suspicious symptoms in their throats. Oh well, so be it! She went without them.

It was only four below zero, the sun was pale, and the air felt utterly marvelous, stunning, as only clean frosty-snowy air on the very eve of spring can be.

In the church's afternoon dimness and quiet, she dropped to her knees. She lit candles for her entire family and prayed for everyone. She hoped the candles' flame would carry her prayers to heaven! Especially for the weak-spirited Emperor. So that in his present difficult solitude at GHQ, without the warmth of his wife and son, and facing a string of unavoidable affairs of state, he himself could be unwavering and steadfast and have the firmness for which the country thirsted.

For evil-doers shall be destroyed. The seed of the wicked shall be destroyed. But the salvation of the righteous is of the Lord.

[1 5]

For Sasha Lenartovich, Likonya was a kind of enchantment, a temptation. Her bafflingly enigmatic, alluring eyes had played before him all these years, although he had only made two brief visits during the whole war. When he did have the chance to see her, any meeting struck him in the heart as if for the first time! Each time she was new! That small face concealed an immeasurability of enchantment, every hour turning into something new.

Sasha realized that Likonya—everyone called her that, though to him and her she was Yelenka—in no way suited the direction his life had taken or the scope of the anticipated struggle. He well imagined the true ideal of the Russian woman:

> For passions neither low nor base
> Do you hide your riches in your heart.
> Our suffering brothers seek your face
> To take in love's great cause their part.

A woman should be a helpmeet, a comrade-in-arms, and herself an energetic agent for the common good.

According to all Sasha's views, a woman didn't dare play the kind of revolutionary role in life that Yelenka had taken on—or at least, if she did, she ought to be a revolutionary herself. But Yelenka had given herself up to the most perverted bourgeois fashion, the distasteful modernist style, so that even amenable Veronya could not sustain their friendship and they had made a complete break. Sasha couldn't get her out of his thoughts for a single day, though, and despised his weakness—nonetheless he couldn't. Every free minute he burned with thoughts of her. He even understood that she was openly imitating the enigmatic Komissarzhevskaya, that all this might be just a pose—but he was besotted.

Had it not been for the war and the army and had he been in Petersburg all these years, maybe he'd have been able to bend her to his spirit and will and point her in the right direction, and even cultivate her for himself and conquer her utterly. But there was nothing he could do from the army, while she was in Petersburg in the middle of all this poison. She wasn't the least interested in him and hadn't done the slightest thing to attract him. She answered his letters rarely, briefly, and casually—and he, just as senselessly, kept these letters and even (to his shame) kissed them, feeling a tenderness for the very pages.

Submit to his will? Not on your life! She didn't even take her own mother into consideration and lived by her own lights, not her mother's (her father had died long ago). During the war years, as one might guess, she became intimate with someone and separated just as easily, but Sasha, like a haunted fool, admired her photograph from afar. Never had he behaved so unindependently, so contemptibly, in anything.

Oh well, everyone has his flaws. In other respects, Sasha was an extremely successful individual, so defects had to catch up with him somewhere. All the better that it was this and in this form, which in part he even found pleasant: a handsome vice. A bizarre flower on a revolutionary.

But burdensome as well. It took up so much extra time and effort. The transfer from Oryol to Petersburg itself this autumn had entailed such fuss and not always admirable methods designed to appeal to and ingratiate himself with influential people, albeit perfectly progressive ones, but he'd have preferred not to have gone to them. In Oryol, too, he was already an officer in the bureaucracy, and had it not been for Yelenka, he wouldn't have been drawn here, and he could have finished out his service there until war's end. He had a decent setup, and there was a lively Zemgor circle there with the very best public aspirations. However, then he would have had to give up on Yelenka altogether.

But although he had come, he hadn't achieved a thing. To vie for her here, he would have had to give up on reasonable leisure, on reading useful, important books, and instead play a role not his own, spend time in strange company and even personally degrading circumstances.

But that's exactly what Likonya was like. Evanescent? Changeable? You couldn't let her out of your sight. You had to be by her side all the time and focus steadily on her.

Today had been a particularly desperate instance. In broad daylight, on a weekday, when all working people were at work, the entire theatrical and—as if that were not enough—the entire quasi-theatrical world had gathered there, at the Aleksandrinsky Theater, a daytime gathering of nocturnal specters, to attend a dress rehearsal of some supposedly incredibly special performance, four years in the making, by the director Meyerhold based on Lermontov's *Masquerade*—such that you might think Meyerhold had done something greater and more important than Lermontov. There was no point trying to talk Yelenka out of going. She couldn't miss a festival of art like that! But he also couldn't join her because tickets for this kind of celebration, naturally, weren't sold, they were passed out preferentially among the known members of this spectral world, and anyone who couldn't prove a top-notch understanding of the stage's nuances or hold a dialogue in ecstatic oohs and ahs naturally couldn't get his hands on a ticket.

Not only that, like all practical daytime people, Lenartovich did have to be at work, after all. Although he could, of course, ask for time off.

It was in moments like this that he felt so acutely that he couldn't hold on to Yelenka. That she, like a specter, was slipping away—even if he encircled her with his arms—and was moving with her rocking, wobbly step through the world of these specters, to which he would never have access. And of course the world was not spectral but all too real, where no eyes or hands could miss a beautiful woman. There would be a multitude of tenacious and importunate smart alecks there.

This whole atmosphere of refined spiritual beauties, languorous verse, anguished music, soft tones, soft furniture, and half-gloom—it led to abstract dreams and forgetting about harsh reality. Sasha truly and clearly understood that his entire attraction to Yelenka was ruinous, that she was not the right girlfriend for him, that if he was to maintain his convictions and revolutionary path he naturally would have to be the first to give her up.

But not only could he not give her up, he couldn't sit there at work today, imagining her there in a strange, slippery situation. He was jealous. He felt sick. He was senselessly but steadily drawn to at least go there for her departure, meet her in the vestibule, see who she was going with. And attempt to spirit her away from her escorts, if only then. (How shamefully superfluous and awkward you immediately were. . . .) But perhaps she would come out alone.

Performance end might be at around four in the afternoon, when it was still light. But what if it were half an hour earlier? He couldn't miss it. Sasha came up with an excuse for leaving, but three in the afternoon seemed too late, so he tried to slip out of the office even earlier.

Meanwhile, on the streets, the previous day's disturbances continued. It was a sunny, cheerful, not very cold day that in no way impeded any demonstrations, and all the sidewalks were crowded with student youth (few studying, the fine fellows), some workers, and ordinary inhabitants.

On these agitated streets, Sasha's feelings were ambivalent. He beamed at the studentry pouring out—he was an intimate part of them—but his greatcoat might make them take him merely for an oppressor who tomorrow would be given an order and would disperse them, fire at them.

The only way to clear up this kind of misunderstanding was by entering into conversation in each separate place and expressing his sympathy for the crowd. There was still time before the theater, and he felt such joy at merging with this crowd and imagining himself a student once again.

The sidewalk was completely filled with youth. Students, male and female, chanted gaily and loudly:

"Give us bread!"

Then they started singing it to the plaintive Stenka Razin melody:

"Why do we have no bread?" And they laughed.

Sasha so wanted to have fun with them, but his uniform didn't allow that. Instead, he stood in their crush and smiled meaningfully at them. The girl students' merry eyes understood him and shone affably.

A company of young men from the Don strode down the street, also cheerful for some reason, smiling and even engaging with the sidewalk.

The young people began shouting:

"Well done, Don Cossacks! Hurray for the Don Cossacks! Our defenders!"

And the Cossacks nodded, pleased.

Sasha didn't understand and asked his neighbors. They explained to him that today in various parts of the city the Cossacks had demonstrated that they did not support the police but sympathized with the crowd.

Was that so? Now that was news! An unprecedented turn!

Oh, how much more youthful strength, how many more possibilities. If in the third year of the war demonstrations were held with mischief in mind, as if in jest, playing at disruption but not disrupted.

But this was no joke. Turning to cross the square, an injured mounted policeman on a raven steed galloped by wearing a black greatcoat and a black-plumed black dragoon hat and with a bloodied face. He could barely keep his horse.

The Don men shouted after him, mocking him:

"What happened, pharaoh? Get it in your ugly face? Hold onto the mane now or you'll be pushing up daisies!"

Yes, it was a stunning turn! Sasha walked on under this grand impression, even forgetting his purpose.

There you had it. Someday, in his lifetime, in his youth even—what if? . . .

Revolution! The magic word! Sung to us so often in our childhood! The marvelous flickering of red banners on tilted poles through the smoke of rifle volleys! Barricades! And Gavroches on the barricades! The taking of the Bastille! The fiery Convention! The king's flight and execution! Supreme self-sacrifice and supreme nobility! Heroes cast in sculpture! Words cast in the ages!

What earthly feeling could compare with that of a revolutionary? This shining rapture swelling your breast and lifting you above the earth? For what greater cause could we be born? What happier hour could intersect the life of a generation? Sad and dim were those lives that had not intersected with revolution. Revolution was greater than happiness, brighter than the daily sun; it was the explosion of a red dawn, the explosion of a star!

Sasha might well have been a Gavroche in '05, when he was already fifteen, but there were only barricades in Moscow, and Gavroches did not travel from one capital to the other. All the rest of the revolution passed invisibly somehow, without these banners bursting through the rifle smoke, more in the intelligentsia's stories and impressions and in the brief exchanges of gunfire during bank robberies or the shots fired by daring terrorists. The '05 revolution had been defeated because it had been poor in sound and color.

At that time, what hope had Sasha had of living to the next revolution? Great, authentic revolutions do not grace the earth very often. Did he face the prospect of dragging his life out colorlessly in the hopeless Russian abomination whose first and most agonizing aspect was army service? Not four years in the army—four years of stultifying nightmare for Sasha to live through, a protracted illness. He wore his uniform like shackles on an iron collar. Those military commands and military training were imposed on him like a violent contagion, and he tried to forget it, not to know it, to push it away inwardly, especially formation and the delivery of fire. Fortunately, he was able to transfer to innocuous assignments in the rear and so preserve himself for the future (but what kind of future would it be if there was no revolution?).

But! The immortal dialectic! No matter how much Sasha despised his military uniform, he grew used to it. And to military gestures. Even to saluting. He'd even noticed that it looked quite good on him. (Even Likonya liked it.) If the uniform was sewn to measure (and he had had it sewn well in Oryol), it made him look manly, there was no arguing that.

Why in fact would the intelligentsia, which always despised athletic and military exercises and lacked physical labor—why would the intelligentsia give this manliness and action all to their enemies—the officers, the police, and the state? An intellectual couldn't even defend himself from physical insults. Joining battle with everyone meant having muscles and military organization. Instead of soft laxity and a house coat, the how-so's and my-my's, to be smoothly shaven, fit, belted, and with a firm, decisive step. What was wrong with that? It only helped conquer the world. (Likonya liked it, yes, but not enough for it to pull her away.)

[16]

In Petersburg the range was especially marked: from late autumn, when there was almost no day, to the dawn of summer, when there was almost no night. Here especially marked toward spring was the swift increase in light—which Fyodor Dmitrievich followed vigilantly every year, joyfully remarking on its arrival and registering its tokens. Spring meant going soon to the Don. To all appearances, Fyodor's principal life sailed along in Petersburg—but no, the whole time his soul was on the Don, longed to go to the Don!

So, too, today, still quite a wintry day but sunny, and by midday there was an amiable and ringing, even resonant dripping from the roof, and this first sure knocking of spring, its many stealthy steps, struck at his heart. But his observant eye had espied the light's vividness and depth days before.

He was glad it was spring, that he would soon be limbering up behind a plow in the field, with a shovel in the garden—and even sooner, before spring, move his novel along! In the village there was nothing but work, and you couldn't write. And this spring, they'd agreed that Zinaida would come to the village. Get to know his sisters. And the Don life. See the farm. What would happen? What? It was sweet and scary both. All the more reason to write and polish his precious, heartfelt pages.

How much of the Cossacks has been seen and lived, and the Cossack himself—but here one had come forward and was constantly in his mind's eye—a dark forelock, tall, not terribly benevolent—as he rode up to the watering place and met his neighbor's wife. This Cossack woman was a combination of several village women whom Fedya himself had bedded in huts, next to wattle fences, and under carts, or simply caressed with his eyes. (One of them he still held dear, only she was illiterate and would never read this novel.)

Fyodor Dmitrievich Kovynev continued to lodge with his landsman at the Mining Institute and to work as the institute's librarian—so he had a roof and a steady, decent salary such as literary work could not provide. His happiest and most important hours, though, were when he was able to write. But all the happiest telephone numbers were literary: the editorial office on Baskov Lane, and with its associates in various places in the city. From his distant corner on Vasilievsky Island, which he could not always leave for his beloved editorial office, that trip took a long time—so he sometimes liked to telephone and learn the news.

Anyway, walking through Petrograd now only upset him. Everyone was so bilious and nervous—assistants in shops, officials in institutions, the cabbie smoking right under the fare's nose, and even the carters beating their overtaxed horses and then sitting right on top of their load. Soldiers fitted out as sentries hung around the Gostiny Dvor and the Passage, absurd to look at. Had they deserted their post or the guardhouse? Also, the city authorities had graciously granted soldiers free transit on the streetcars, out of respect for the fatherland's defenders. So now, if a soldier had to go one block, he waited for a streetcar. Idle crowds of them would take over an entire streetcar and were actually put out that the civilian public, too, wanted to ride. They ignored the conductors, packed the cars, and hung in clusters from the landings.

Yesterday, Fyodor Dmitrievich hadn't left the institute, although he'd heard people were looting bread stores somewhere and ravaging sundries shops. Today over the phone he'd learned that the police weren't letting people down Nevsky and, as always in these instances, his heart immediately fell still in joyous hope: could this be the *beginning* of something? All society, all his surroundings, all Fyodor Dmitrievich's Petersburg friends lived in this constant hope, that one day it would *begin*.

A weekday. Getting away from work was inconvenient, but he couldn't just sit there. At least a brief walk through Vasilievsky!

He set out, and the weather itself drew him on. He set out, with his no longer soft face catching the first sunny warmth and his cap and shoulders willingly collecting drips from roofs.

He had a good walk but only saw a paltry youth demonstration on Bolshoi Prospect that no one dispersed and no one detained. And one stopped streetcar.

He returned to work. But rumors kept coming in all day, agitating him. As soon as he closed the library at day's end, Fyodor Dmitrievich headed for the center to see with his own eyes. Whether anything came of *this* or not, his own eye would pick up and retain all of it. In his notebook.

But no matter how far he walked toward Kazan Square, he saw nothing in particular. Kazan Square was entirely jammed with people, but even there nothing was actually happening. They weren't shooting or beating anyone or swinging whips or riding their horses over people. Occasionally mounted Cossacks would drive the waves of people just a little across the flowerbeds toward the colonnade—but riding carefully—and then everything would go back to the way it had been.

Seeing mounted Cossacks on Petersburg streets had always engendered torment and ambivalence in Fedya. A torment that they'd been sent here to play executioner, a disgrace as if it were he himself, he himself who bore this brand. (They can't get the kind of police they need and so dump everything on the Cossack name!) Nonetheless, he felt joy and pride at the mere Cossack appearance and the snorting of their superb horses raised and acquired on the Don.

Today, though, the Cossacks were behaving quite kindly, no one from the crowd was berating them, and this soothed Fedya's heart.

Here and there stood closed gray ranks of soldiers with crimson epaulets. The crowd pressed right up to them, sometimes shouting "hurrah" at something—but no one took any action. It was all good-natured, involving either curiosity or mild squabbling.

Nothing serious was going to happen.

Fedya himself was suffused with this peaceable, good-natured mood and no longer expected anything and so recorded in his invariable little notebook only characters, clothing, and expressions.

The sunny day shifted without a wrinkle into a red sunset, although gathering a chill. Red betokening joy? Or perhaps blood? Above the city's edifices a scarlet light lay on Nevsky's five-story buildings and the glass Singer cupola. And sad, like any sunset as its melting warmth cools.

At first the people's peaceable good nature, and then this sadness, advanced, and advanced some more, toward Fedya's heart. And at the crowd's peaceable dispersal he, too, set out for home, already contemplating only his private thoughts.

Was he really on the irrevocable verge of marriage? Why was he always going on about his "fifth decade"? It wasn't as though he was fifty! It was the right time for a man, his prime. Imagining himself, a free man, with a ring on his finger, was impossible. And sweet! To be joined and merged indissolubly and forever. It was flattering to take a young wife, and so much passion lay ahead.

But so did desperate terror: to destroy by marriage not so much his life as his writing. Generously are we awarded life, but also stingily. Every age comes once, never to be chased down again, and every choice at life's crossroads is almost irrevocable. You could miss out on—but never win— an entire world. Up until now, Fedya had always taken salutarily cautious decisions—no and no. But Zinaida had come boring, rising, splitting through—and notched herself into his life.

As he had hers. What had he done? He had destroyed her son by his reluctance to join her in the country and summoning her to Tambov. And in Tambov he hadn't supported her. He seemed to be doing quite the wrong thing. After that he'd nearly finished her off with his foolish lie about "someone else." And so—they'd been sent smack into each other. Destiny, evidently.

That winter Zinusha came to Petersburg and was as affectionate and receptive as he'd always dreamed a sweetheart might be, without striking outbursts. Here, unlike in Tambov in the fall, she seared him through and through. He and she united so solidly and comfortably, he was prepared to devote himself to a woman like that.

And Zinaida would willingly take Petya on as a pupil.

But like anyone in a new situation, she simply hadn't foreseen how much alienation and hostility she would meet with in the village—as a Russian. It was anything but easy to make his sisters and everyone else like her and for her to accept her Cossack destiny as his wife. It might be a great success, but it also might not.

She had wanted to marry before the Don, so they'd arrive as man and wife, but Fedya knew that could not be. That was impossible.

Fedya plodded on with this new irritation, failing to notice the now ordinary Nevsky, and came out at the Palace Bridge. A cooling sunset rose up the Peter and Paul Fortress spire higher and higher, narrower and narrower—trickling off its point and into the sky.

No matter how you lived, no matter what choice you made, there was the aching feeling that in love you could never make the right choice. Ever.

Only one thing was true and right: his little notebook with the first chapters of his Don novel. He had to hurry up and sit back down to it—and luxuriate over every line.

[17]

At the beginning of Syezzhinskaya Street, near Kronverksky, lay a solitary overturned motorized streetcar. There must have been a lot of people there when it was being toppled, but now even the little boys had had their fill of sitting and jumping on it and had run off. Passersby scarcely stopped, and few even slowed down, as if the sight of a streetcar toppled in the middle of the street were an ordinary thing. Maybe before this they'd seen something even more unusual—or were expecting to wherever they were hurrying.

One tall passerby wearing an engineer's cap and dark cloth coat and carrying a leather map case over his shoulder, the way officers do, did stop, though, hands in pockets and his fur-less cloth collar turned up at the neck. And stood there, as if next to someone prostrate.

The streetcar was an earthy, dirty green color, like the hide on some large animals can be, and it lay like a large working buffalo, gasping its last, or having gasped its last, in the dirty snow. Its glass brow was cracked: before they beat and felled the animal, they'd battered its brow. The side it had been dropped on was crushed and crumpled, cut by shards of glass. Far behind its back and unnaturally dislocated lay its trunk with a rope attached. Four dead round iron paws stuck up along the ground—and you could see how the rails had been damaged when the paws were wrenched out. Also, the unlucky animal's belly, which no one ever sees, its hidden danglings splashed with street mud, was now on display for derision.

Its masters had not tended to the injured animal. Everyone had abandoned it.

So what now? How easiest to raise it?

Obodovsky leaned toward the body and through its top windows viewed what had happened to the lower side, and walked around it, and glanced at the conductor's platform and felt the bow collector. It was almost twilight when he plodded onward.

He didn't have far to go. They lived right there on Syezzhinskaya, just before it curved onto Bolshoi Prospect.

Nusya greeted him with her usual warm, soft hug and a kiss on the lips. And with the instant rapport that had developed between them she sensed her husband's gloom, instinctively prompting her to tone down the excited stories she'd prepared.

Today Nusya hadn't gone far, but she'd seen a lot right there, nearby. She listened to his dejected description of the fallen beast—and she did know, in fact, how that streetcar had been stopped. It had been proceeding under guard, a police officer on the front platform demanding that the conductor not stop but drive on. But two pieces of ice from the crowd had wounded the officer in the ear, and the conductor had jumped off the other side and then all the passengers were forced off.

Pyotr Akimych was eating his dinner as usual but without noticing his food, moving all the skin on his head and his ears as he chewed, nervously.

The crowd! A strange, special being, both human and inhuman, all legs and heads, but where each individual was released from his usual responsibility and was multiplied in strength by the number in the crowd, who stripped him of his will, however.

What there'd been most of over the course of the day here, in the district, was window smashing: the bread bakery on Lakhtinskaya, Yerofeev's bread store on Hässler Prospect, Utkin's butcher shop, Kolchin's sundries store, and the fruit stores—out of malice. Every crowd had someone, adolescents or adults, who absconded with the receipts. Small groups, apart from any crowd, had also looted the butcher shop and tea store on Bolshaya Spasskaya.

Pyotr Akimovich had also been told of similar instances in the Okhta area—people smashing windows and absconding with receipts.

These receipts spirited away in many places, then, all over Petrograd, made the events irredeemable, as did the gunfire. Tomorrow they would have to go on smashing and stealing to keep them from searching for the perpetrators.

And what had happened in the center! That he had seen for himself. He never thought he would live to see this: to stand by the Kazan Cathedral, at the sacred center of all revolutionary students for thirty years now, and see them singing openly, no one bothering them: "Arise, awaken!" They unfurled the red flag and his heart leapt involuntarily, to the old beat.

A human shuttle-boat consisting of two pairs of eyes, a man and a woman, they were always as one, they agreed about everything, and with the cord of their gaze and the cord of their feelings they invisibly put each other right as to how to hold on under the lashing coming from different sides. Their bipolar magnetic arrow pointed through these stormy forces.

And the key to the story, the key to their attitude toward everything they'd seen that day, turned.

In many places, the Cossacks had done nothing to hinder them! They had let an entire crowd of adolescents and women cross the Nikolaevsky

Bridge. The Cossacks' neutrality was the most astonishing thing of all. Nothing like that had ever happened before!

An ecstatic presentiment gripped him.

The looting of stores was vile, of course, but that kind of thing always happened during a mass movement.

"Was there really any of that in Irkutsk in '05, Petya?"

"Not in '05, but in '06 there was everywhere."

They felt torn.

That fallen, senselessly spoiled streetcar, the marvelous work of human hands.

After the Workers' Group's arrest, Obodovsky had been so indignant he himself would have given a drubbing to the Ministry of the Interior, the insensate building itself! Dimwitted asses, they were incapable of developing or understanding what Gvozdev was and could be for them! Not understanding nuances was the sign of asses!

But here, had it really been **ours** who had risen up—in the nick of time?

And once again all those *Social Democrats*—such an ugly word—were seething now—both those acting high-handedly and those winding abstrusely among a dozen amendments and stipulations?

"So, should we go to the barricades, Petya?"

No, it was not the Irkutsk mood.

At the same time, there was the fear that everything put in place since '15 was about to collapse—all the military equipment, all the artillery training. What would happen to our spring offensive?

These disruptions at certain defense factories, at the Putilov, were even suspicious. Did one sense a hidden hand?

No, the government's second day of inaction was suspicious. Not a single shot, not a single arrest. As if it were a planned street performance. Was this really a grandiose provocation? Would there be unimaginable reprisals? Had the government really been idle intentionally, in order to provoke even greater disruptions—and then drown them in blood?

For a hundred years to come? For another hundred years! Our unlucky country!

Might the opposite be true? Were they wavering? Would they make concessions? Remove the idiot Protopopov? Agree to a responsible administration?

Might all this horror abate at last? Or even collapse?

Immovable and inviolable—and suddenly collapse?

And a bright society of equal rights come where stupid bureaucrats on fat salaries displaying stars on their chests didn't block all paths? And no one indifferent to the public good?

His heart leapt: Oh, triumph, revolution!

And fell back: During a war like *this*! How inopportune! Insanity. . . .

"Nusya, I was standing near the Kazan, in that singing under the flags, and believe me, not only was I not glad but like a reconciling priest, I was prepared, with arms outspread, to try to say to the crowd: Brothers! Stop! Bear up a little longer! This is not the time! This is only a gift to the Germans! Wait until our spring offensive! This will all be over soon, and then . . ."

[18]

That he simply could not leave Alina was perfectly clear to Vorotyntsev. Not that he'd been planning to! He himself was amazed by the happy catch in his breath when Alina wrote that she was setting him free. . . . No! he was responsible for her and would care for her, and it was his duty to restore her equilibrium, which he had so unwisely destroyed. (How could he have told her? He didn't understand it himself.) A weak thing, she'd been so crushed it had taken her months to recover. She kept sending him letters of reproach, first feeble, then furious. But he wouldn't let himself get irritated and replied persuasively, as to a child, wrote often (one more kind of writing added to his staff writing), and only when she got the idea of coming to see him at army HQ did he firmly refuse. That would have been unbearable.

He deserved all her reproaches, yes, in full, but please, they had become so castigating that he no longer recognized himself in this scoundrel. And although he had been the one to tell her everything and had not left her, after all, she demanded more, over and over, and as an essential condition that he return to her the confidence that he thought her the best and incomparable. But his conscience made it hard for him to lie in this case. She wrote to him as if he had gone off to summer camp rather than the Field Army, where he might have perished long ago and where his good fortune had already been strained. How angry she was, how horrified that others, too, would know—it occurred to him that apparently it would be easier for her to lose him dead than having left her for another.

The spring offensive was drawing closer, and all the officers rushed to take leave in the winter, while they were alive, and Vorotyntsev was offered leave, too. At 9th Army HQ for just three months—he hadn't given a thought to leaving. In the very first moment he pulled back. See Alina? In the thick of this squabbling? Not on your life. But if . . . but if what? Now, after all, not from the regiment. While he was alive, indeed. . . . Did that mean he would never hold Olda close again? Impossible! But she was constantly calling to him; either she'd send something she'd drawn—little animals, a mysterious little girl with green eyes, rebuses—come and we'll solve them together—and he had managed to get himself a dozen days, three days there, three back, and bypassing Moscow raced straight to Petrograd—and didn't even tell Vera, not to embarrass her, better she not know.

All the way there he had had no doubts about his trip and could only think: six days, the length of a single sigh. It wasn't enough. But the moment he reached Olda's building, it all rose up as if new, with even more strength and heat, as if they were both younger and naughtier.

It was as if these meetings, this eddying funnel, were what he'd always lived for. He felt all newly fresh from the inside: his chest was different, his breathing different, his eyes different, and he was utterly happy.

But now, well, it wasn't as easy and cheerful as looking at rebuses. This time there was a nagging feeling. There was also a special ritual here, a talking-listening ritual. Especially the entire train trip to Mustamyaki, when they were doomed to just speaking. Yes, Olda knew lots of things, but in a pedantic way that made anything interesting immediately boring. As if the contour of her experience already encompassed the main of life.

In his letters to Olda, Georgi had omitted his explanations last autumn with Alina—what he'd disclosed and what had come of it. That was something you couldn't communicate in a letter, and even in a story, whether or not you could, so much of it was difficult and unnamable. At the time, it had worked out well. Alina didn't go to Petrograd and he didn't have to think about it. Like any miscalculation, it was unpleasant, but to hide this now, at their meeting, also seemed dishonest. It was torture. Even here, he didn't tell her right away.

And now—he could never have predicted how upset Olda would be, how she would start questioning him in detail, cross-questioning him, and have so much more to say about it that there was no going to sleep. And since early morning, eyes barely slit open—over and over again. These around-the-clock conversations had begun to weigh on him. It was so pedantic, so tedious—and now there were reproaches as well! Because of his mistake, Olda had concluded that she would now direct him according to her own lights and dictate a plan for how he should act. Occasionally there would be that tone that if she didn't tell Georgi the harsh truth right now, no one would. She thought for him as if he were already her husband, spoke as confidently as if she considered him her husband, as if they'd already been to the altar. Almost the way it had been assumed when they'd visited her professor neighbor, and Georgi thought, "No. If he were free now—would she be that direct? No. Was there too much of the insistent, the imperious even, about her?"

Meanwhile her entire plan came down to the fact that he should fight *for her*. And Georgi felt awkward objecting. But she took his silence to mean he was absorbing what she was saying and went on to develop it further.

Actually, if she was murmuring this—in a melodious, persuasive voice—on his shoulder, then fine. He didn't really have to heed her remonstrances; he could skip some of it, not respond. These irksome requests slipped past him, but she was the girl with the green eyes. Not as green as colored in with pastels, but with a hint of green. At this everything doubled. He sensed

Olda beside him like a treasure, and he probably would always await her summons and languish without her. There remained a perpetually nagging feeling that he owed a debt to Alina, but none to Olda.

She was the one who'd said time was a priceless helper, and she was the one who'd been rushing him, saying there was no more putting it off now. Putting off what?

Then Olda began lecturing him horribly about how destructive kindness was in private life, how cuts have to be cured with cold, and how Alina needed a consoler. . . .

Still afraid of offending, Georgi didn't let it show, but his heart ached.

He hadn't noticed exactly when or exactly why, exactly what the stimulus had been. Maybe he'd woken up with an inexplicably aching heart.

Why that first layer of emotional constraint appears—we don't always notice that. Yesterday, when they were strolling through deserted Mustamyaki, its houses closed up for the winter, when they went to see the professor, something was already weighing on him, dragging him off.

During the day they'd run to fetch a log and merrily sawed it—but something had squeezed and squeezed, relentlessly.

If you don't watch that kind of constraint, it's easy to make a mistake. This squeezing similarly can come from both a presentiment of disaster in the future and remorse over what has already been done. The two shadows are very similar.

Was it Olda's attempts at persuasion? Apparently not. Although they were a part of it. But there was something more encompassing.

When he had gone to split wood and was already standing, steaming in just his tunic, in a pile of fallen blocks with a yellowish, splintery body, he was suddenly taken—seized!—by a terrible melancholy that stole his heart away and blackened the snow, and suddenly he couldn't bear to remain in this piney, snowy, dacha silence.

He argued with himself that this was crazy. He'd traveled two thousand versts for this intense solitude, and all the rest was always his. But he wasn't persuaded. Inside him the darkness grew and he crumbled, and nothing could console him.

Had it been weaker, he would have taken fright and shied from telling Olda and made the effort and stayed.

A few hours ago there had been joy—and suddenly it had crumbled for no reason.

He brought back an armload of split firewood, dropped it by the stove, and said, "Olda, I don't know why, but my heart is heavy now, and I don't feel right. I have a presentiment of something, something bad."

He walked away without waiting for her reply. He brought a second armload, dumped it on the first, and then: "Let's leave early, all right?"

"No! No!" She came to life. "It's so quiet! So nice! It's so rare we're together!"

But she saw his face. She walked up, snuggled close, and looked up: "Let me reassure you."

Georgi—in a weary, almost broken voice: "You see I don't know . . . I don't . . . All of a sudden it's hazy."

But even her face now was unhappy, and darkness gave chase across her small forehead and her eyes.

But it can happen. Things can calm down as suddenly as they begin.

They'd been planning to leave here Sunday afternoon. Now it was Friday, and actually after noon.

Olda's mood became very dark, offended even. She pressed her lips sternly.

It can be shameful for a man to pursue something based on a presentiment or doubt. (He did not give Olda even a hint of his doubt.) "All right, we'll stay, and then we'll see."

The early northern twilight wasn't far off. They fired the stove red hot and sat on chocks in front of the open firebox, intent on the fire. Georgi was ashamed that suddenly he found staying there a burden. What woman had ever given him one tenth the joy Olda had?

Once again she tried to talk a lot, now about other things, but he hushed her so she would be quiet and held her long and tenderly in his lap, pressed sideways to his chest, to his very heart. For some reason if he pressed and held her like that his unease dissolved. It was dark in the little house, and there was just the one light—from the burning logs, like in a cave twenty thousand years ago: We're sheltered from dangers, we have food, we have fire, and if I, a strong man, am so comforted by your embrace, then how much you must be! All it takes to fend off enemies, frost, hunger, and death is warmth and harmony between us. Not words. We might not know how to speak yet.

Oh, what sweet evenings they'd had—but none more gratifying than this.

And the tender, tender and quiet night, the whole time embracing.

[19]

He knew it. Mikhail Vladimirovich knew that popular indignation was bound to explode! Even the French delegation had recently said, "You deserve a better government than you have!" Now, governmental politics had begun to yield its fateful fruits! It had aroused mistrust for the state apparatus among all thinking Russian circles! With each passing day, the regime lagged further behind society's consciousness! The government's fateful separation from the people was this government's fault! By its manner of issuing commands it had sown the first seeds of the future revolution! Since 1914, the State Duma president, as well as others, had prophesied that the government would not be able to cope and would make many mistakes!

Indeed, all the supreme power's instructions seemed to be aimed at the specific goal of muddling the country's situation even more. One could say without a moment's hesitation that the government was run by the circle around Rasputin, who himself was serving the interests of Germany!

What else could one expect from those contemptible people whom chance had put in power and who did not know how to manifest a single lofty impulse? They did not have enough love for the people to abdicate voluntarily. That selfless love for the people that every heart of the people's representatives bled—and Mikhail Vladimirovich's huge, anguished heart tenfold! The government had brought about its own ruin because it had resisted any public initiative, the efforts of the whole of society to assist in the common disaster—without any ulterior motive, with the sole goal of supporting the government in its time of trial! An invisible hand had brought the people irritation and mistrust!

The sinister personification of this criminal policy was the abominable Protopopov, a turncoat and double-dealer! The entire State Duma and the entire Progressive Bloc were offended that this prominent, so very successful member of theirs had turned out to be such a base traitor, had greedily rushed to the government's camp, but Mikhail Vladimirovich Rodzyanko's offense was double, and personal as well. This despicable man had for years been Rodzyanko's right hand in the Duma presidency. Not only that, Rodzyanko had proposed him as minister of industry and trade. But imagine his astonishment when Protopopov, returning as head of the Duma delegation from a foreign journey, did not bring his report to Mikhail Vladimirovich but was summoned to the Emperor, *bypassing* him! Thus began their mysterious and disgraceful negotiations with Stürmer about the Ministry of the Interior. Mikhail Vladimirovich's indignation knew no bounds.

And now—popular resentment had burst forth! Yesterday there were disturbances in Petrograd that Mikhail Vladimirovich could not have failed to notice: workers were quitting their factories and proceeding in large numbers to the city center—although, with an unknown purpose, not to the State Duma, for some reason. Today, justly (and with a sense of vengeance) anticipating a continuation of the disturbances and wishing to divine this popular movement, Rodzyanko left the Duma debates to blaze without him for part of the day and personally went to where the movements had begun: Vasilievsky Island and the Vyborg side. He himself observed the tremendous agitation of women workers, evidently due to some irregularity in the sale of bread. Once again the crowds were proceeding toward the center with some unknown purpose in mind.

If there was one thing Mikhail Vladimirovich had always had in abundance, it was initiative and energy. Others might, but he could not be an indifferent spectator to the collapse of statehood! Before his automobile could return from across the river, his perceptive eye had already pictured the entire scene: the criminal and helpless government had tasted the fruits of its wicked policy! What had burst out was exactly what the best public figures had always predicted!

If you looked deeply, the problem wasn't bread, of course, but popular offense at the way the government had insulted the people's elected representatives. The problem wasn't bread disruptions but the populace's political mistrust for the authorities. Why should there suddenly not be enough bread? Because the population wasn't bringing their grain to the market. And why weren't they bringing their grain to the market? Because they didn't trust *this* government and feared the authorities' inept instructions.

So the problem wasn't bread, of course, and the situation demanded a radical cure. But even on the narrow bread issue one could render the people decisive assistance while at the same time pressuring the government in principle, and at the same time inflicting the most powerful defeat on Protopopov. After all, Protopopov had fought consistently to take food supply away from the Agriculture Ministry and give it to Interior—so now take the bread issue away from all state officials and hand it over to the Petrograd City Duma! This would mean simultaneously putting it in the reliable hands of the public, who would take up the cause carefully and ardently—and once again show the entire capital—the entire country!—that the government was inept, incompetent, and doomed.

When something began to sizzle in the capacious chest of Rodzyanko (who took a dim view of anyone applying declensions to his name), it was the rare person who could resist that roaring flame. So it was now. The energetic Duma leader first rushed to Rittikh's apartment. The latter had caught a chill and was staying home with a bad cold. Pressuring him with his prominent position and the significance of this home visit, the Number Two Man of State easily obtained the Minister of Agriculture's consent. Preoccupied with the vast shipping of grain from distant corners of the country, Rittikh easily conceded its distribution within the capital and saw no public landmines lurking there.

Now he had to move deep inside the government in such a way as to sidestep the traitor and scoundrel Protopopov before he found out and guessed. Rodzyanko had convinced Rittikh; his fervor simply melted any resistance to the idea that only swift action could save Russia. He must go to the War Minister immediately and through him influence the Prime Minister, Prince Golitsyn.

Although this path was inexplicable from the legal standpoint, Rodzyanko's volcanic breath kept forcing it through—and a couple of hours later, in his luxurious Duma office, Mikhail Vladimirovich received a telephone call that this evening, in the Mariinsky Palace, there would be a meeting on his proposed plan. A meeting not for the record but for a practical deal.

That evening, the emergency meeting was held in the blue velvet hall. The indefatigable, steely Rittikh reported the same thing he had in the Duma. That the reserves of rye flour in Petrograd totaled more than half a million poods (not counting the military storehouses, where there was significantly more). Even given a Petrograd population inflated to two and a half million, this, for consumers of rye, meant a pound of bread a day per person, if there was none brought in at all. That the worries manifested by the population were groundless and stemmed merely from alarmed rumors. That the snow-storms' drastic disruption of the railroads was behind them and tomorrow a hundred train cars would arrive from the suburban station of Lyuban, and the obstructions at junction stations would be resolved, in March there should be no fewer than 35–40 train cars arriving every day, and each car would mean thousands of poods of flour. That the problem was more about horses, of which there were as many as 60,000 in Petrograd, and a large portion of the grain was fed to them. On the other hand, meat—there was 180,000 poods of meat, and the same amount with army plenipotentiaries, and a thousand train cars of frozen meat were on the move from Siberia, more than the refrigerators of Moscow and Petrograd could even hold.

Rodzyanko listened to this and insisted that the food supply matter should be handed over to city self-government immediately.

To which the government agreed.

Shcheglovitov, the State Council's coldly balanced, firm, and resourceful president, also supported his usual opponents instantly.

It turned out that no one was opposed!

True, a few articles of the law would have to be changed to expand the rights of city self-administration. But the government set about that very night composing a draft and tomorrow would report it in the Duma. With the breath from his noble breast, Rodzyanko assured them that the Duma would approve the draft with all due haste. Shcheglovitov promised he would not hold back the State Council.

In warm unanimity, they approved it unanimously (something that had not happened anywhere in a long time). True, it would take several days, a couple of weeks, for the procedure—Rodzyanko knew his Duma balkers and loudmouths who went on about irrelevancies—nonetheless, the victory he had gained today was tremendous! Finally, the grain matter would pass into the honest and efficient hands of the public!

He had managed to be everywhere today, had continued to run the Duma—and had saved the capital from famine!

[20]

Yesterday, at the Mogilev train station, the Emperor had been met by the usual complement of staff officers led now by Alekseev, who had returned before his leave had ended, while Gurko had left for his Guards Army. They had not seen each other for nearly four months, and the Emperor was glad to see the unpretentious face, so unlike an official with its feline whiskers, of his unfailing chief of staff once again. They embraced warmly. But the traces of ill health were still evident on him, and he was holding on by sheer will. The Emperor took him to task for hurrying so from the Crimea—he might have stayed another few weeks to recover. But Alekseev expressed his wish to participate personally in all the preparations for the spring offensive.

He had only just returned and had not yet had a chance to scrutinize matters. At the administration offices they spoke for half an hour, not on official topics but in general. Nikolai was left to himself for the long evening, in a solitude he'd grown unaccustomed to.

All the same, the break from Alix was never complete. Every few hours something passed between them. So it had been yesterday evening, when two telegrams had rushed in: one from Aleksei saying he felt well and was sorry he wasn't with his father and hadn't gone to GHQ; the other from Alix saying Aleksei and Olga had come down with the measles. Nikolai sent a telegram immediately in reply.

So it had happened, it hadn't spared them. That suspicious cough, that little cadet who had played with Aleksei ten days ago. And now that it had begun, everyone would probably catch it now, and it would be better for everyone at once, only without complications. He was glad he hadn't brought Aleksei here. What would it have been like for him to be ill here? But also how unsettling it would be for Alix now! She should curtail her official audiences, using the measles as an excuse.

He began sorting through his things and putting his room and the adjoining sleeping room—it was so lonely by Baby's camp cot—where his small things, photographs, and knickknacks were laid out—in order. How his heart was warmed by his son, and what hope—and constant alarm—was mounting in him!

At dinner he saw all the allied military representatives, whom he had missed over the past two months. He told them of his children's measles, and everyone was very sorry. Old and bearded General Ivanov was at dinner— such a dear, and such a marvelous storyteller.

With the evening hours the loneliness took an increasing grip on Nikolai's soul. There was something elevating and very reassuring to it. The silence here was such that no human sound could reach him, and he could hear the windowsill's iron cover when it moved in the wind. But he missed Alix's presence and the peaceful half-hour of patience every evening with her all the more keenly. This silence—it was oppressive. He would have to find occupation. And he would have to revive the domino playing in the evenings.

He hadn't seen his Sunny in more than twenty-four hours—and he was longing to write her a letter. Yesterday before bed he had begun to write, and today he added for Aleksei a new delight: a decoration from the king and queen of Belgium presented by their envoy; he would be delighted by the new little cross.

Meanwhile Alix's last admonitions, repeated in the letter of hers he had found in his train car, took on more definition and meaning for Nikolai: Be firm! Be lord and master! The time had come to be firm.

Yes, she was right—so with great emotional effort Nikolai prepared to be unfailingly and exclusively firm. Yes, he already felt firm. Yes, he did. This time he had arrived at GHQ absolutely firm.

But he should not overdo it. Being lord and master did not mean snarling at people right and left every minute. Very often a calm and pointed remark was perfectly sufficient to show one person or another his place. Even more often, it took only clear, firm goodness and fairness, and people would grasp, understand, and think in the best way possible.

With this awareness and these thoughts—on how to learn to be newly, royally firm—he had concluded his letter yesterday and last night—and with this awareness he had awoken and started the new day.

But the day had brought no sign of spring: overcast and windy, and then thick snow had fallen. Enough to chill the soul.

Yet another telegram arrived from Alix, about the children's health. Apparently Tatyana and Anya Vyrubova now had the measles.

A GHQ day—strictly ordered, taciturn, and quiet. Despite the bad weather, Nikolai's soul began to even out. Life here was a type of relaxation: no audiences for ministers and none of those tangled, tense problems, claims, and conflicts with the Duma. He went to see Alekseev to hear his report about the fixedness of the fronts, about minor incidents, reformations, and generals' appointments, and all the decisions had been prepared in advance. Then, a pleasant hour-long luncheon with his suite. They wanted to take their usual ride in motorcars out of town, but the snow was falling very thickly so they didn't go.

Due to this snowstorm, the day Petrograd train was late, and with it Alix's anticipated letter—and he very much wanted that letter.

He sent a telegram: Don't tire yourself out running from one patient to another; my cough has lessened; tenderest of kisses for everyone.

Somehow he filled the time until evening tea, when they brought a letter from his Sunny. He read it eagerly: all the details of the illness, which rooms they had been put in, where they had their breakfast, where their dinner. Aleksei and Olga were sad that their eyes hurt and they couldn't write their father, but Tatyana (the only one like her mother—in her will, discipline, and dark hair), not having succumbed to the illness yesterday, attached a brief letter from herself.

Alix was suffering over how terribly lonely Nicky was without his sweet Baby—and how lonely she herself was without her husband.

She reminded him in particular that if he faced difficult decisions he should wear the little cross she had given him, which had already helped in September of '15.

At eight in the evening, dinner with the allied military representatives and select men of his suite as always.

After dinner he sent Alix one more telegram: thank you for your letter, ardent greetings to all the patients, sleep well.

After sending the telegram he still felt its inadequacy and sat down to write a letter in reply.

He thanked her again for her dear letter. He had just been talking with Dr. Fyodorov, who had asked how the illness was progressing. He found that for children, especially Aleksei, a change of climate was absolutely essential after they recovered, after Easter. It turned out he had a son, too, who had also had the measles and then coughed for a year—because they hadn't been able to take him away immediately. To the question of where best to send the children he named the Crimea! Well, Nikolai himself had thought the very same! Magnificent advice! And what a rest this would be for you, too, my darling! Indeed, after the illnesses the rooms at Tsarskoye would have to be disinfected, and you are hardly going to want to move to Peterhof. So much better the Crimea! They hadn't been in so long—not once since the war began.

Nikolai imagined this happy new arrangement for the family come spring, and he relaxed warmly over his letter. So many joyous Livadian details arose, you couldn't write them all. But we will think all this through calmly when I return.

I hope to return soon—as soon as I assign all matters here and my duty is fulfilled.

My heart is suffering from our separation. I hate any separation from you, especially at such a time.

Well, my dear, it's late already. Sleep peacefully. May God bless your sleep!

[21']

(EARLY EVENING, 9 MARCH)

The plan for the capital's defense had been drawn up back in 1905. At the time, though, an entire full guard not taken for the Japanese war had been stationed in Petersburg, tens of thousands of select men too good for that purpose. Now the entire guard had gone to the front, and following Polivanov's idea of pulling reserves to the major cities, they had brought to Petersburg a garrison of 160,000, the majority under the guise of a "guard"—but these were worthless, freshly recruited troops, and the reckoning was entirely on the police, the mounted patrol, and the gendarmes—something over a thousand in all. Khabalov had refused to accept more reliable combat troops last month because there were no barracks and reserves were packed in everywhere. Back in November, though, Interior Minister

Protopopov had boastfully shown the Emperor a colored map of Petrograd divided into six-teen districts, each with its own military unit and police attached to it. But who would re-port to whom? Protopopov had many concerns, and he decided that in the event of some-thing serious, it would be to the military. (The police, who were specially equipped to guard the city, would report to ignorant, transient soldiers.)

When today at half past twelve City Governor Balk reported to General Khabalov over the telephone that the police had not been able to halt the gatherings and movements on the main streets, Khabalov groaned and reluctantly decided, Fine, the troops will take up the third position. Tell your subordinate officers that they are now to report to the mili-tary district chiefs.

He promised that for ease of joint administration, he himself, with others from HQ, would move to the city governor's offices today. Balk telephoned Protopopov, who added nothing. However, War Minister Belyaev advised Khabalov that if people crossed the Neva over the ice, the troops should shoot so that the bullets struck in front of them. No, the Em-peror had objected without reservation. They had to make do without firearms.

And so, the commander's HQ were set up in the city governor's offices, at 2 Gorokho-vaya Street, and Balk's office was filled with military men. Police officials curtailed the re-ception of visitors, but wealthy citizens kept telephoning for reassurance. There was no space or buildings for troops near the city governor's offices. A gendarme division was brought into the small stone courtyard, and arriving troops were positioned on narrow Gorokhovaya and on Admiralty Boulevard.

What should they do about the crowds? Well aware of their own impunity, in one place those scattered by mounted detachments without the use of firearms immediately concen-trated in another place, and these movements continued for several hours straight, down the entire length of Nevsky from the Nikolaevsky Train Station to the Moika.

Police dispatches streamed into Gorokhovaya. There were crowds of a thousand, of three thousand, and today for the first day red flags appeared here and there. City policemen had been wounded on Liteiny Prospect, on Znamenskaya Square, and on the Petersburg side, some gravely, and over these two days twenty-eight policemen had suffered wounds and in-juries, but neither the police nor the troops had fired a single shot; they had not wounded anyone with firearms or harmed anyone during their dispersals. By the Kalinkin Bridge, as elsewhere, the crowd attempted to upset streetcars, but the city policemen intervened, and for that they had iron bolts thrown at them, and of the adolescents doing the throwing, seventeen-year-old Rozenberg had been arrested. The police wanted to put a guard on the streetcars for the evening, but the streetcar workers wouldn't work like that and took the empty cars to the depot. Streetcar traffic came to a halt.

The second day, continuous disturbances rolled through the capital. Of 300,000 work-ers today, as many as 200,000 went on strike, but by evening everything began to quiet down, and when all the police chiefs and all the military district chiefs gathered at the city governor's offices, the situation once again did not seem serious, as it hadn't yesterday. After all, hadn't the crowds dispersed and calmed down, as if nothing were going on in the city? Maybe today the crowd was somewhat angrier than yesterday, but in general it was good-humored, spontaneous, made up of random inhabitants, with no agitators, leaders, or or-ganization whatsoever in sight.

Perhaps it would all work itself out. The peacefully inclined Khabalov, who was not prepared for battle, and Colonel Pavlenko, who was recovering from a serious wound, and the heads of the Okhrana and the Gendarme Administration who had come for the second meeting today would have liked to believe that. This morning at Khabalov's apartment they had all been assured by food plenipotentiary Weiss and the city's chief that the daily norm of flour was being released, it had not dropped, and bread was being baked. There were no obvious reasons for mutiny. There had been disturbances dozens of times before, and they had always ended.

But what if it all happened again tomorrow? There was no directive to use firearms, which meant continuing the same bloodless tactic of dispersal tomorrow. Only had the Don Cossacks shown a reluctance in disbanding the crowds? Then call in the Guards cavalry regiment from Novgorod Province. (That winter there had been a debate about the Cossack regiments in Petrograd. GHQ had demanded they go to the front, and the Court wanted them in the capital.) "Why don't the Cossacks disband them with whips?" Khabalov wondered. The Cossack officers there replied that they didn't have whips, that this was a combat regiment from the front. "Then give them each a half-ruble and let each make his own."

Someone asked what the mood was among the troops. The question itself was inappropriate. Troops were troops. What kind of "mood" could they have? Okhrana General Globachev interjected that he would like to know the mood among the troops, but back before the war General Dzhunkovsky had sent out a directive with the highest approval about how the Okhrana was forbidden to maintain agents inside the troops. No efforts since had been able to change that, and the Okhrana could not know the harmful elements that were undeniably there.

In general, according to agent reports, the left's *top leadership* had been flabbergasted by how auspicious the situation was for them. Today they decided that if crowds gathered again tomorrow, they would agitate vigorously and, if they found sympathy, they would expand the disturbances to a display of arms.

That might happen. And it might not.

But what if they tried to arrest the instigators tonight, by going to their homes?

Were there such instigators, though? That remained unclear. Swoop down like the wind on nighttime apartments and indiscriminately arrest every fortieth man? A legitimate state could not permit itself such a thing. In any case, the Okhrana would conduct a few searches. Among the workers, naturally. Higher than that they wouldn't dare go.

Balk asked, since many policemen yesterday and today had suffered in isolation, not to post them singly anymore but in twos. Khabalov gave his permission.

What else?

Here they all were sitting together, the capital's military and police leaders appointed by the Supreme Power, and in addition to them their superiors, Ministers Protopopov and Belyaev, who had remained more than calm these last few days. The men sitting here — what could they chance or propose that was more decisive or effective? What could be undertaken in general against the jostling popular crowd? The only thing more decisive would be to cut them down with swords or to shoot. But the memory alone of 22 January 1905 hung heavily over them all. Columns in the liberal newspapers alone made the governors pale and attempt to justify their measures. All the more so now, at the war's height. How could they shed their own people's blood? They couldn't bring themselves to raise a hand, and Belyaev warned that corpses on Nevsky would make a terrible impression on our allies!

Explain things to the mob? The commander's order had been posted everywhere. And when Balk called on the workers' delegation from the Liteiny Bridge to go with him and look at the grain receipt books—they wouldn't. Although the evil rumor let loose was having its effect. What if they stopped baking bread? Who was hiding flour behind high walls?

The Petrine scars, that drawing of lines which our Dutch emperor was so proud of, had become permanently embedded and eaten their way between the Russian estates.

Instead of a disposition of troops for tomorrow, should they take a chance and throw troops into work this very night? Send details to the military bakers to bake double, triple the bread from military reserves and have troops deliver the additional bread to the bread shops so the people could see: Look, we're not coming to disperse you but to feed you and heap you with bread!

Who would dare chance that? This was the purview of Actual State Councilor Weiss.

What these authorities were implicitly obligated to do was report in full and in writing to their superiors about the previous day's events.

However, the Petersburg's city governor's daily reports could not deviate from the model established by Nikolai I: first, the movement of the sick from hospital to hospital; then, accidents involving military officers; and only at the end briefly about events in the capital—which there shouldn't be. These reports were written by a special, capable official who knew the form well and had very handsome penmanship. Major events had no place in this report. And had there even been any major events?

The Minister of the Interior was himself in Petrograd and was himself informed about the disturbances even without this report. But he would have considered it a loss for his position to report seriously to the Sovereign about such insignificant events as this running through the streets. After all, he had always assured the Emperor that dealing with rebels cost him nothing. What was there to fuss over writing about now?

Along military lines today, as yesterday, General Khabalov definitely found nothing to report to Supreme GHQ. His troops had not fired a single shot, they had not suffered a single injury, and they had not carried out a single serious maneuver.

Thus, on 9 March as well no report about capital events was submitted to the Emperor.

It would be very close to the truth to say that on this deceptively quiet evening of 9 March, capital authorities had already lost the February revolution.

[2 2]

For half of February the Bolsheviks had been calling the workers out on Nevsky—but they hadn't come. And all of a sudden they'd thronged themselves, unbidden. No, the popular element was like the sea, unpredictable and uncontrollable.

They had been called to Nevsky and Kazan Cathedral intentionally, to distract them from the Menshevik call to go to the Duma on opening day, as the Workers' Group had called for before its arrest. And again something unforeseen happened. The workers did not react to the Gvozdev group's arrest or rise up, but they were adamant about going to the Duma on 27 February. This Menshevik scheme had to be frustrated no matter what. Better they go nowhere than to the Duma! The Bolsheviks promoted their standard resolution to the masses: Don't support the Duma. Instead, stop the war and bring down the Tsarist government. "A government of trust" was a bourgeois slogan and would only weaken the proletariat's revolutionary movement. The State Duma was abetting the war and powerless to bring the people relief, and the Mensheviks were treacherous in summoning you to the Tauride Palace. No one should go to the Duma. Everyone to Nevsky!

But the Interdistrict group split off; they didn't want any kind of demonstration now. The working class wasn't ready for revolution and the army wouldn't support them. Generally speaking, they were factionists and didn't want to act in common. Not only that, they evidently had a lot of money, were paying their strike committees, had nearly taken over the Putilov Works, and were going to stand independently. They'd also gathered the best young writers and were putting out leaflets more often than anyone else: "Bread!" "Equal rights for Jews!" and "Down with the war! Down with the war!" But "down with the war" was hard for the working masses to understand, and the Bolsheviks were more circumspect about that slogan.

But there were also the Menshevik internationalists, who had their own position, the hair was split in four, and social democracy was in total disarray.

But for half of February the Bureau of the Central Committee and Petersburg Committee had been fighting all of them—and they succeeded: on the 27th the workers did not go to the Duma!

Shlyapnikov himself jealously verified this. He put on a bourgeois coat and hat, took a girl student by the arm as if she were a young lady, and for a long time strolled with her down Shpalernaya, waiting to see whether there would be a mass movement. No, there wasn't, except for about five hundred people, and then only the servants from the grand houses, the caretakers, and passersby stood around in curious clusters.

Why didn't the workers go to Nevsky? The top Bolsheviks themselves were to blame. They had outwitted themselves. In order to separate themselves from the Mensheviks more decisively, they decided to change the day to the 23rd instead of the 27th, to the anniversary of the trial against the deputies. But no one remembered or understood that these were the last days of Shrovetide, and by law not even all the military factories were operating. All the workers were at home eating pancakes. Who were you going to draw out for a demonstration? When they suddenly remembered this, they moved the strike to the 26th, but not everyone knew this and they were unable to notify everyone.

Fine, "to Nevsky" didn't happen, but neither did "to the Duma"—a Bolshevik victory anyway.

Then yesterday, all of a sudden, it just happened! Wonderful! Caught flat-footed, the BCC and PC gathered wherever they could and held meetings: Shlyapnikov and his blunderers Molotov and Zalutsky, and the core of Sormovo men as well—all were aghast: no one had summoned the workers, so why had they come? Street demonstrations were always good, though. No matter how they ended, they always led to an exacerbation of the struggle. Something always happened during a street demonstration. These last few days the soldiers had kept very passive, mildly pushed the public back, mildly blocked their way, started up conversations, and a few had even scolded the police. Good! Being stationed at demonstrations always demoralizes troops; they listen to the demonstrators and pick up things. Although the crowd still lacked malice. How could they be turned forthrightly away from their bellies and toward political demands?

Both those days the authorities had behaved quite sluggishly—with an astonishing lack of decision. Not a single shot, and not even a single arrest. A rumor had cropped up among the comrades that this was a government provocation, that they were deliberately launching the movement and letting it grow so they could drown it in blood later.

But Shlyapnikov didn't believe this from the outset. The authorities' actions, and especially today's importunate announcement by Khabalov, intimated the authorities' true weakness, very much like that sudden weakness on 13 November, when he had overcome them without any forces! They were simply unsure of themselves; they didn't know what to do. Meanwhile, by not countering the movement in any way, they were losing.

But what were we to do? How could we take over the movement and outflank the other Social Democrats? What pivotal slogans should we offer? We had one pathetic leaflet about the brutal bourgeois gang in preparation, and that was handwritten and might have political errors. But the moment might be the most decisive and even more important than it was in November. How could we keep from making a mistake? This time would pass and all would be clear in hindsight. But what about now?

Oh, Sanka Shlyapnikov didn't have a head like Lenin's! And alas, oh so wise Sashenka wasn't even here!

What was clear was that we couldn't let things cool! We couldn't let the strike end after just a few days! We had to take the struggle to the limit, to clashes with the police (where that didn't happen, instigate!), to street battles, even to a bloodbath! Even if it ebbed, that bath would not be forgotten or forgiven. Even a defeat was a victory!

But a movement that arose everywhere so unexpectedly and at once could not be steered! They had no way to influence it, no people, not even liaisons for each district. As everywhere, people here loved to chatter, and cocks like Vaska Kayurov fluttered up, but the public had nothing to offer, no genuine revolutionaries. And now, instead of leading the masses on the street, they'd placed all their hopes on mere spontaneity, while they themselves gathered in apartments on the Vyborg side and talked themselves sick about which tactic to pick, a tactic no one might ever use. Shouldn't all Russia be supporting us? Shouldn't a general, Russia-wide strike be called? And who should be sent when we couldn't deal with Petersburg itself? Connect with the army? We haven't been able to do that for the last six months; you're not going to in a day.

Pfah! We swaggered when we faced defencists, but we ourselves are powerless.

All Shlyapnikov could do was roam the capital and see for himself what was going on. The street was more important than indoor contemplation. In the afternoon they weren't letting people across the bridges, but by evening things were subsiding and everything opened up. Both yesterday and today, Shlyapnikov had gone to Nevsky in the evening to mill about and observe.

Yesterday there had been an ease, the situation felt normal, everything was open, everyone was strolling, and even the police were escorting the young workers from Nevsky as if it were a game.

But today there were no strolling soldiers or even officers. Obviously, they had gone on barrack status. Sometimes Cossack platoons rode out. And later, the streetcars, cabs, and motorcars quickly thinned out noticeably before their usual times. But the pedestrians on Nevsky didn't, and Shlyapnikov saw there many workers at a completely wrong time, but there were no police to drive them from the genteel capital street. In these surroundings, the dandyish, sauntering public, although no one seemed to be directly inhibiting them, did not feel free to amuse themselves and also vanished. Confectionaries, cafés, and restaurants closed early, and the luxurious shop windows that had always traded until late in the night went dark.

Khabalov's morning notices had been partially ripped off here and there.

Nevsky's bourgeois spirit had been broken—and without a fight, in the dark. The ignorant mob had taken over. People clustered.

Suddenly, at the corner of Nevsky and Liteiny, where streetcars had stopped crossing, several clusters moved in from different directions—and there was a crowd! And something was found for the first speaker to stand on. Shlyapnikov didn't recognize him, but he was clearly experienced. He shouted confidently and powerfully and got to the point right away, not with the Mensheviks' silly slogans, and was probably an Interdistrict man:

". . . The godforsaken night of government reaction! . . . The delusion of the fatherland's defense! . . . They got off cheap with their victory in '05! But we've gained experience in the last twelve years! Down with the handful of bandits who plotted war! The dissolute government . . ."

He carried on glibly. And people listened without objections. Shlyapnikov discovered that slogans could now be advanced more and more boldly. The Interdistrict group had outstripped them again.

" . . . We will take vengeance on the tyrant on the throne, the tsar-epigone! Ruin to the Tsarist hangers-on, the nation's murderers!"

Right then everyone heard it, although the hooves were stepping softly over the snow: the Cossacks were riding down Nevsky from Znamenskaya straight toward them.

The speaker fell silent. And slipped away. Everyone stirred and turned around. In the silence, the horseshoes were even more audible.

But the Cossacks were riding oddly, in extended order, singly, not only not taking out weapons but not even holding their sword hilts or drawing their whips—with a quiet step, as if wondering where they should go now.

The way a horseman in a fairytale might ride.

The crowd started moving toward the sidewalks but didn't run away, and many even remained in the middle of the street. They weren't afraid. In these last few days, hope had arisen for the Cossacks.

Silently, with the same slow step, still singly, the Cossacks carefully rode between people, though a few got pushed by a croup—and so they rode through the thinned crowd, and once in the open, closed ranks and proceeded on their way, without slowing or looking back.

And from the crowd, from the sidewalks came applause and shouts: "Bravo, Cossacks! Bravo, Cossacks!"

The crowd closed ranks again, and the same speaker climbed up and continued, saying the army had to be drawn into the revolutionary struggle.

Then they went their separate ways, without coercion, and shouted, "Tomorrow, back to Nevsky! . . . Come to Nevsky tomorrow!"

Shlyapnikov did not intervene in any way. Now he was taking long strides down the darkening, emptying street. He had more than five versts to go to the Pavlovs'.

He hoped the workers' ardor would not die: stir them up another day—and another day—and another day, and no going back to work.

It felt like racing along on the wings of joy. Now he would tell his comrades, who were gathering at the Pavlovs' for the duration of the night.

But for some reason Aleksandr Gavrilovich noticed that he didn't feel a full, genuine joy. Seemingly this was just what he had been waiting for, living for! and now . . .

Or had he begun to tire of it? How many months had he spent under surveillance, changing his attire, using a false passport? He had traveled again to Moscow and the Volga, where he saw nothing but weakness. Nothing was being readied anywhere, and no Russia-wide strike could be instigated now, he knew. But in Petersburg, there were secret meetings in lawyers' apartments—with Chkheidze and Kerensky, who went into hysterics about how the Bolsheviks were sectarians and Shlyapnikov on 27 February had ruined the triumph of democracy that had been readied and had aided the Tsarist government.

Perhaps it was true that he hadn't always done the right thing. There was no one to ask. Or was he simply weary of the underground life?

Now, these last few days days, he had been seized for some reason not by joy but, as Sashenka put it, melancholy.

[23]

Georgi awoke with his chest aching once again, tugged by a melancholy worse than the day before.

All the joy rescued just yesterday sitting by the fire had evaporated. He wished he could leave. But yesterday she'd been hurt. How could he do that to her again? Olda wasn't used to being toyed with. But staying until tomorrow noon seemed just as empty and inconceivable.

And, he had woken up early, as if for spite.

Soon after, so did she.

Their eyes met, and already all was not well. Something held back had settled in their eyes, separating them.

If the silence lasted just a little longer there would be a tiff. But if he spoke—would she go on about Alina again?

A little push:

"Shall we go to the city?"

And she, unexpectedly:

"All right, let's go."

They didn't light the stove. They went outside, where it was even warmer than in the little dacha.

And down the path.

So, Rasputin was killed. So what? While he was alive, rare was the person who didn't dream of him being done away with! At first there was rejoicing, especially in educated society. Everyone congratulated one another, and there were even receptions and banquets.

"Our staff officers went looking for champagne to drink, too."

Yes, a murder had been committed that seemingly had been unanimously desired by all of society. Actually, was this really the first murder that society had applauded? But it had not been to the good at all. Weeks had passed and things got worse than with Rasputin. Now there was no one else to blame. And there was the stain that grand dukes had killed him. And no one had been punished—another stain.

"That's for sure. I went around the companies in one new division and chatted. An old soldier stood up: 'I wish your honor would tell us why it is the Emperor's relations who killed Rasputin are going scot-free and there's no trial against them?'"

107

Yes, indeed, the laws weren't even fitted to anything so savage as arresting grand dukes for murder. You can imagine how the defense would abuse and defame the throne.

It was amazing Rasputin had lasted so long—maintaining his tone and role. He had even given advice. And the advice had been taken.

"And at what level? How could he have risen as high as advising on state matters?"

"That means he had a natural sobriety of mind. And the ability to respond without blundering. And religious ecstasy, obviously. The despicable, peasant outsider, he knew how to convince the bishops to elevate him. You can't blame it all on the women. Only the bankers toyed with him."

"But no matter what his common sense, it demeans each of us subjects that matters of state could be decided at that level. And every man has to wonder what kind of monarchy we have."

"Of course, it's all a terrible misfortune, enough to more than try the heart's patience."

They arrived at the train station early. There were just a few people on the platform and humps of trampled snow. There was still little of the northern light. And gloomy firs dense by the station.

"But still, you've changed since autumn. You don't support all this the same way."

"No, you're mistaken. Supporting the throne—in that I haven't changed. Now it's still more necessary than then for firm, loyal men to close ranks. After all, there are so many intelligent and firm men, but they're all scattered, they don't know each other—and they're powerless."

Her purse out of the way above her wrist, she entwined her gloved fingers—and there was impotent supplication in that gesture, but strength as well.

"Oh, they don't need our help. No one's asking for it. And there's no one to offer any—no means or access for a hundred versts. You couldn't figure out a way **how**."

Olda's eyebrows and forehead trembled together:

"So you mean there's no point trying to save the country?"

"The country should be saved. But strengthening the throne that lacks the will for it is utterly impossible. How can someone without a will be helped? As soon as you ally yourself with the throne you're shackled to all its accumulated, adhered junk."

"No, you're not a monarchist," she said ruefully. "You said the same thing in the autumn. And the time to take this up was then, to support it."

The train blew its whistle as it approached. Its cars rocked and drew to a halt. They boarded. The dacha car was meagerly heated by a stove in the middle, and there were people sitting close to it.

"Are you going to be cold?"

"No, I'm fine."

He hesitated. And:

"Then . . . I didn't tell you everything."

"How's that?"

Even now you couldn't express everything. It would take too long.

"I have had all kinds of thoughts. But they're vague. It's all turned out to be so very very complicated. And there's no finding allies in Duma circles."

"You're not going to hang on the Duma's every word. Rasputin was just a godsend for the Duma. Not those mighty 'dark forces' they used to blow out of proportion. Rumor always exaggerates excess, that's the law of rumor. And dirt sticks at every level. It started to be very advantageous in society to speak out against Rasputin. Anyone who says he was Rasputin's victim immediately becomes society's darling and is assured ardent support wherever he goes."

He liked this even, restrained passion of hers, the way she always spoke about anything to do with public affairs. With her head slightly tilted back.

Rumors had swarmed in Petrograd—and what rumors. That Rasputin's murder had opened a new epoch of terror. People even said Protopopov had been shot! They'd tried to poison General Alekseev! There was a plot to kill the Empress and Vyrubova! Not just anywhere but among the elite they argued whether only the Empress would be killed or the Emperor as well. They were already naming the regiments where the plot was being readied. Then saying that it was a plot of the grand dukes and there would be a coup d'état and then, by Easter, revolution. About plots among the Guard—from a dozen places.

"And you think there's an iota of truth in it?"

"I think it's all chatter. But it's going around. It's as if at the allied conference in January they'd resolved to take the Russian government under their wing and give Englishmen and Frenchmen a seat at the Russian General Staff."

Vorotyntsev winced.

Frail Karelian trees out the window. A stream's snowy valley.

The rumors pressed and tormented, and not a day passed without their empty bitterness. First: a separate peace would be signed by February. Then: a rail and general strike was anticipated. Then: look, in half an hour they'll stop producing current and the streetcars will stop. But who was saying this? A chamberlain wearing a courtier's uniform suddenly called— true, in small company—the Winter Palace a snake pit! There were a great many traitors among the courtiers in general, and they spread the most rumors, humoring society. All kinds of vile things about the Tsar's family supposedly holding orgies. . . .

"And all this freely and out loud?"

"Entirely! Now they say anything they please."

Still the same scanty conifer trunks in the snow—and suddenly a granite boulder would bare its teeth.

It seemed easier while moving. Herein, probably, lay the whole problem: it required movement.

But no. Yesterday's sucking emptiness was still inside him.

The awkwardness between them seemed to have abated. Once again he admired her pliant little head and her expression of strict judiciousness, which suited her very well. But their conversation sounded odd, like friends meeting in a train car. What had happened to their mutual, united joy?

What had there been right before the murder? These congresses of the rear's hothead heroes who had no intention whatsoever of discussing anything practical but only to vote for some previously prepared venomous resolution—and unleash it throughout Russia in swarms of proclamations. Even if they didn't vote on it, it would still be unleashed. For instance, that the government was *intentionally* leading Russia to defeat in order with Germany's help to do away with the 30 October Manifesto! The universal thirst to pass for liberals gripped the nobility as well, and anger was expressed at congresses of the nobility, where "shameful regime" was considered a sane definition of the Russian state. And there was no strong, weighty voice to thunder out: You must stop! Don't lie like this!

The stationmaster's blue cap. The dairymaids came in with their buckets.

Up until now they hadn't noticed or heard anyone. But now their ears opened up. And in the train car, which was already quite full, they picked out conversations about certain Petersburg disturbances: smashed stores and stopped streetcars.

Vorotyntsev went on his guard, but Olda shrugged it off.

"This happens, too. It did in February, too, on the Petersburg side."

But then they distinctly heard that today the streetcars weren't running anywhere at all.

There then, did that mean the horse-drawn streetcar from Lanskaya to the Stroganov Bridge was probably not running either? Then they couldn't get off at Lanskaya, as they'd thought. They'd have to go to the Finland Station.

Some petty bourgeois behind them was telling a story about how last night, near the train station, he'd turned into a side-street and there, in total darkness—no fires, not a sound—a dismounted Cossack detachment was hiding, lances drawn, only their horses snorting quietly. They were hiding—and waiting.

Was that so? That meant the matter was serious. This was when Georgi berated himself. Why had they rushed? How nice it was there together! What a rarity it was in life and what kind of accursed nature throws all this away and rushes off somewhere?

He guiltily stroked Olda's wrist behind her glove.

She smiled ruefully.

[2 4]

*   *   *

There had been very few streetcars on the Petrograd lines since early morning—and soon after that they were all gone or stopped without their levers.

Not all the morning newspapers came out. On the Petersburg side about eight hundred people went over to the state printing press to disrupt the workers, but they were dispersed by policemen mounted and on foot.

*   *   *

The day dawned at eight degrees below zero, no wind, a light snow.

All the streets were well cleared; the street cleaners had worked zealously, as always.

Haymarket Square overflowed with all kinds of produce and cheap sausage.

On the street walls a new notice appeared from General Khabalov: work in factories must resume as of Tuesday, 13 March (Sunday and Monday were skipped for things to settle down). About the demonstrations and street unrest and the beatings of police there was no mention.

*   *   *

Close to nine o'clock in the morning, the workers of the Obukhov Works on the Neva side stopped work, fifteen thousand or so of them. They went out on the street and started moving toward the city to the singing of revolutionary songs and one red flag, along the way stopping work at the playing-card factory and a porcelain works. On Archangel Mikhail Prospect the crowd was met by mounted police details and dispersed with arguments but then with whips and flat sword blows.

*   *   *

The police, now subordinated to military units, telephoned in reports of their location, which factories were striking, and where there was what kind of disorder. Many military officers didn't even know the factories' names.

*   *   *

A policeman and two assistant street cleaners were walking down Kosaya Line on Vasilievsky Island. A crowd of workers had decided he was leading prisoners and rushed him, took away his sword, christened him with his own blood, and knocked out his teeth.

*   *   *

On the Vyborg side, there were rallies here and there among the striking multitude. A speaker got up, a worker judging from his clothing, but from his language one accustomed to speaking:

"Enough of them exploiting us! Down with them all! The gendarmes! The police! The factory owners! The government! For us the war is death, but for the bourgeoisie it's profit! Enough of them shedding our blood!"

After him a nervous young woman from a pharmacy with a squeaky voice climbed up on the stand. At first they made fun of her, but then they listened more and more: she turned sharply in the same direction—"Down with them! Down! Down!"

*   *   *

Some of the crowd came to *shut down* the Artillery Department's Tube Factory on Vasilievsky Island. Many of its workshops had no wish to strike. Stationed at the gates were reservists from the Finland Battalion Life Guards. People in the crowd made fun of its commander, Second Lieutenant Joss, and one fitter shook his fist at his nose. The second lieutenant drew his gun and killed him on the spot. And the crowd scattered immediately. But Emili Behm, a modern school pupil in the sixth grade, was arrested for possession of a loaded government-issue gun.

*   *   *

Military sentries had been stationed near many government buildings, the post office, and the telegraph office. Also on the Fontanka in front of the house where Protopopov lived.

There were policemen in the center, usually in pairs, at all the usual street posts.

Military units guarded the bridges and river crossings from the outskirts to the center. They also tried to block points elsewhere, but how? Lines of soldiers a pace apart were no obstacle to anyone. The public went around them, filtered through on either side, cursed, and shouted—and ultimately were all let through. The soldiers themselves thought the officer had given a very foolish order. Now the crowd was only assured that they could get through everywhere!

*   *   *

A sleigh cab carrying two officers sped across Trinity Square, and at the intersection with Kronverksky, on the sharp turn, dropped its runner into a streetcar rail gutter. There was a jerk, a screech of iron—and it was stuck.

The cabbie hopped down, and the colonel and captain got out.

And from a far-off crowd of common laborers, half a dozen men moved toward them—ran even, overtaking the others.

What was this?

Going back and forth across the square were various others, also laborers—and they, too, began drawing close.

The police were nowhere to be seen.

There were already stories about gentlemen and cabbies being made to get down—even on the familiar square of their own Russian city, amid their fellow countrymen, the officers faltered—cut off as they were. The captain put his hand on his hilt—though would he really pull it out?

But the laborers came running, as if to play, gaily:

"What is it, gentlemen officers? Or is the square too narrow?"

"What's with you, fool, and your gaping gob?"

They grabbed on amiably enough and pushed them out.

And refused a tip.

*　　*　　*

Meanwhile, on Nevsky, crowds had gathered and were roaming—some were workers from the outskirts but there were many of their own, from the central districts, students, an especially large number from the Psychoneurological, female students, adolescents, and lots from the city's idle public. And, of course, during these three days all the city's scoundrels had gravitated there. Over yesterday and the day before, a sense of total safety had formed among the crowd, which was used to the patrols and the fact that they weren't touching anyone.

*　　*　　*

Many thousands of workers from the Vyborg side had coalesced on the approaches to the Liteiny Bridge today. Going out to meet the crowd down Nizhegorodskaya Street was the old police chief, Colonel Shalfeev, with half a hundred Cossacks and a dozen mounted police guards. Having placed them as a barrier along Simbirskaya Street, Shalfeev rode out alone toward the crowd and tried to persuade them to disperse. In reply the crowd surged toward him, dragged him off his horse, beat him lying there, some with boots, some with a stick, some with an iron hook used for switching rail points. They smashed the bridge of his nose, lashed his gray head, and broke his arm.

And the Cossacks didn't lift a finger. (The crowd had been counting on this.)

Mounted police rushed to his rescue, and there was a scuffle. A strapping fellow swung a large crowbar at a sergeant, who struck the attacker with his revolver butt. The crowd threw ice and stones at the mounted police and then started firing. At that point the police returned fire.

After the first shots, the Cossacks (4th Squadron of the 1st Don Regiment) turned and rode away at a half-trot, leaving the police and Shalfeev lying in the street on the brink of death.

Then other police, mounted and on foot, came up from the bridge and pushed the crowd back.

*　　*　　*

The Petrograd intelligentsia thirsted for events but still didn't believe in anything major. At Gippius's apartment, Kartashev said, "It's all ballet, nothing more."

*　　*　　*

After eleven o'clock in the morning, no more dispatches came in from Petrograd's outskirts. The rout of police stations everywhere had begun. Ranking police officers were in hiding or had been tracked down and murdered.

[25]

They stepped out on the platform. There was a pleasant light frost and a light snow falling. At the train station, all was as usual. But when they went out onto the overcast square, the streetcars really weren't running, and the usual slow line of loaded drays wasn't crawling across the square, and hired cabs dashed by only rarely. Some free procession with a red flag came out of Simbirskaya Street—but there wasn't a single policeman to be seen.

Vorotyntsev was stunned.

You couldn't find waiting cabs right away, so they walked around the building. They were asking incredible fares, five times the usual. They got in a sleigh. Olda was shivering, though it wasn't cold. Georgi straightened the rug on her lap and held both her hands in his one.

They started across the Sampsonievsky Bridge. There were no police at the intersections. There were barely any soldiers. And the pedestrians weren't so much walking confidently as roaming nowhere in particular. Or standing in groups, workers. The streets were full of people but seemed deserted due to the absence of the usual wheeled and sleigh traffic. An overcast holiday. On Posadskaya Street all the shops were closed and the windows boarded up.

The city wasn't radiant, as it had been last autumn, but desolate, gloomy even.

On Kamennoostrovsky, businesses were open and the luxury stores had no lines, but the simpler ones did. No one was storming anything, and you did see policemen here and there, paired at posts. No, the windows of one bread shop were smashed and they weren't selling. Now one did come across cabs and an occasional motor vehicle. But something morbid hung in the air.

Along the way the cabbie also told them that some factories were striking and others barely operating. Or else people were up to mischief: they would see gentlefolk riding in a cab, stop it, and make them get out.

As if to say, careful they don't make you get down. It was a foolish situation, truly—with a lady and against a crowd. What could you do?

A detail of mounted police rode by. People shouted defiantly at them from the sidewalks, unafraid. The policemen did not turn around.

And here was the Pesochnaya Embankment near the snowy Nevka: clean, springy snow under the runners and no destruction whatsoever. Here you could forget yourself and go on.

But the nasty gnawing that had driven Georgi from the dacha wouldn't pass.

They climbed the spiral staircase in their rotunda.

"I'm starting to dislike all this." Olda shook her head.

They threw off their outerwear and immediately embraced, as if they hadn't in a long time. They stood there, swaying silently.

"I'll just make a call and find out what's going on," Olda said.

And from the hall she telephoned one place, another, and a third.

While Vorotyntsev crossed back and forth, smoking, sitting down. This apartment held such a hospitable and embracing coziness for him, but right now, for some reason, his heart wasn't in it.

They'd been foolish to return from the dacha.

He may have been even more foolish to come to Petrograd at all. Hadn't he made the whole trip in vain?

An enlarged portrait of Georgi, done from a photograph he'd sent her from the front, had appeared on the bedroom wall.

With this Olda had recognized him, accepted him, taken him into her home.

But as what?

He was proud of this. And embarrassed.

Olda came in. She'd learned that the workers were not being allowed across the bridges to the center so they were making their way here and there over the ice across the Neva. They had killed policemen in various places. Near the Cathedral of Our Lady of Kazan early that morning there had been small groups of university students, who were driven away. And now a large, excited crowd had passed down Nevsky from the Moscow Train Station toward Gostiny Dvor. A dragoon detachment had prevented the police from disbanding the crowd, and the crowd had shouted "hurrah" at the dragoons.

Good grief.

It was the same sensation as always of there being nothing solid at the top. A kind of gray emptiness. It would be impossible now to lie down, even simply do nothing, chat idly.

"You know what? I'll call Verochka. Why should we hide now?"

"Of course."

He went into the hallway, turned the lever, and asked the young lady to give him the number of the Public Library, second floor, pick-up. He didn't remember it.

They were connected and Verochka was called over fairly quickly. Vera could only gasp into the receiver—but less than he'd expected.

"Oh, how fine that you responded!"

How odd.

"I'm in Petersburg."

"I know! I've known since the day before yesterday."

"How?"

"From Alina. Telegrams. Even telephone."

The earth gave way beneath him.

"Alina? Why? How?"

"For some reason she wired you at army HQ, and they told her you were in Petrograd."

It gave way and he kept falling deeper and deeper. Deeper than imaginably possible. Here was his presentiment, which had not deceived him.

"But what did you . . . ?"

"I told her I didn't know anything. That was the truth. Although, to be honest, I believed her right away. But I was so afraid you wouldn't give a sign that you were here."

He tried to imagine the swift action he should take—and couldn't. Crash! He lowered his voice so it wouldn't reach Olda.

"But what about her?"

What about her now? My God, what about her?

"She doesn't believe me. She's accusing me. She's cursing you. She says . . . Oh, come over, Yegorik."

"No, what is she saying?"

Silence.

"What is she saying? Tell me quickly! Is she coming here?"

"I don't know. No, maybe. . . . Basically, I don't know." Even over the telephone he could hear the agony in Verochka's voice. "Please come as quickly as you can."

"What is it? Something bad?"

"Yes . . . basically . . ."

"But what exactly?"

"Well, there . . . Come over."

Crashing and more crashing, tumbling to the ground.

Everything he'd built that winter—it had all collapsed. And now the whole nightmare all over again? Doubled even?

He held the receiver and fell silent, dismayed. He was so dazed he couldn't think of anything to say. But Verochka said, "What's going on in the streets . . ."

How unlucky he'd been. How had he never thought she might telegraph and not warned anyone at HQ?

"Around Gostiny, there's a big scuffle, we can see out the windows. They've overrun the police, they're beating them. People are walking down Nevsky with red flags."

Yes, there was that, too. But all this he only half-heard. Most important, he couldn't figure out what he should do.

"But you'll come see us today? Nanny is so upset!"

All of a sudden everything in his head started spinning, his entire world. Now he couldn't return directly to Romania or avoid going to Moscow. He could make up a lie about some urgent assignment. But then he should go as quickly as he could. But she wouldn't believe him! If only he hadn't confessed in November. Idiot.

"What's there around the Moscow Station?"

"That's where it's been stormiest of all these last few days. Do you need a ticket? I can go get one, otherwise you'll get pulled in."

Here he was getting more and more mired, and then there were these street disruptions, and you really could get pulled in. It was stupid.

"Yegorik! Well, can you come see us? Then I'll go home. Only avoid Nevsky, don't try to cross it. Come around from the left, from the Fontanka. Are you"—a pause—"on Pesochnaya?"

At last everything had come full circle and resolved. And his breaking presentiment was gloomily replaced by clear action.

"Yes. I'm on my way. I'll be there in an hour."

But as he was giving the lever a quick turn to disconnect, he realized he couldn't go back to Olda with this. Anyway, he could never convey how horrible this was or why. If he did disclose this, she would start lecturing him again about how to be firmer with Alina, and that was unbearable because she didn't understand. And if he did disclose this it would be impossible to leave right now, and he would have to stay and talk and talk. . . . Impossible.

Lying to a lover was shameful, but Petrograd events were giving him his one chance to wriggle out. (What was that he had heard from Vera? He could barely recall now.)

Olda met his face with fright.

"Yes," he muttered, "it's very serious. . . ."

"What is?"

"Around Gostiny. They're beating up police. And there's something even worse around the Moscow Station."

Of course he would have told her everything! If she hadn't frightened him off with yesterday's insistent reproofs. There was a kind of prohibition against discussing all this with her.

"Things have gotten out of hand!" Olda didn't take her eyes off him, and he was afraid she would guess. "What are you thinking?"

He said nothing.

"Well, it's not '05," she tried to persuade them both. "We've already seen this. And in October, the day we met, remember?"

Yes, it was true, it had been similar then. So recently. Back then he hadn't had these small shoulders. In the last few hours he had completely cooled toward her. But now that it was time to part, she was once again dear and desired. *My unexpected happiness! Thank you for everything. But I've turned black inside, it pains me, and you can't console me.* Out loud, though:

"I have to go see someone at HQ, to figure out what's happening. What do they expect? How could they let this happen? There you have it. . . . Autocracy without a will. It's, you know . . ."

Something has to be done. We've said the same ourselves.

Yes, you're right. It's true.

"But you'll be back before evening?" She had pushed him forward but now she was holding him back.

The situation was such, they couldn't part openly.

"If things don't get out of hand. If I'm not needed there."

"But then there's tomorrow at least! Tomorrow is still ours!"

He sighed.

"Well, at least you'll telephone me about what and how?"

"Yes, of course!"

Shall we eat?

No, he couldn't sit still. Everything was swaying and writhing.

"But we aren't saying goodbye yet, are we?" Olda's alarm intensified.

"Who knows?" he said perplexedly with a blank face. "I'll take my bag just in case."

"You're not going to see her, are you?" She suddenly guessed and clutched his tunic.

"What makes you say that?" he said in almost sincere amazement. *Look what it had come to: he was hiding his wife as if she were his lover.*

"That can't happen!" Olda insisted with eyes wide. "I'll be jealous! You're mine now!"

"What's the matter with you? Where is this coming from?"

Here it was: the moment of farewell. She raised her hands and put them on his shoulders, and with shining eyes said, "For me, your appearance is like my second birth. I waited so long! I'd already lost hope I would ever see . . . I felt as if I'd been crossing a desert. . . . All winter I thought of your last glance then, by the bridge. And I believed we'd be together. I believe it now! I love you! I do!"

He removed her hands from his epaulets and kissed them.

He had treated her badly these last few hours, and he would have done worse now if she'd demanded he stay. But here she had set him free easily—and he had a flash of insight. What a gem she was! And how selflessly he loved her! He regretted even that she'd said so little to him. He kissed her again and again, hungrily!

Her upper lip curled touchingly, awkwardly.

"For some reason men attach great significance to a woman's age. But for a woman. . . . Am I really too old for you?"

"I've never touched a woman—as young as you."

[2 6 ']

(THE DUMA ENDS)

The many thick volumes of transcripts of the four State Dumas, for anyone who gets through them, make an incomparable impression out of the river of Russia's public moods during its last eleven years. Even if we didn't have a single other memoir, testimony, or photograph, these transcripts alone indisputably re-create all the shifting concerns and urgings, the collision of passions and opinions, and even the personalities, even the voices of the most frequent speakers, who numbered a couple of dozen.

Having begun these volumes with still total ignorance and total trust, having no opinion or preconceptions whatsoever—from one session to the next you suddenly experience a dreary emptiness from the leftists' harsh and insulting talk, which never relates to the *matter at hand* and never offers anything practicable. One imagines that in Western parliaments even the most radical opposition nonetheless is sensible of the weight of its state and national duty to participate in something constructive and find new paths for the state structure even under a distasteful government. But the Russian Social Democrats, Trudoviks, and many Kadets were utterly devoid of any awareness that the state was an organism with a complex, day-to-day existence, and no matter how you changed the political system, the people who lived in the state from day to day naturally still had to go on existing. All of them—and the more leftist the more caustically—had devoted themselves to nothing but reviling this state and this government. All of them, when they came onto the Duma tribune, were addressing not so much this Duma, and were counting not so much on influencing it in some practical decision, as they were grabbing at the applause of the *progressive*, liberal, radical, and socialist public—whose approval was their heart's desire.

The food supply issue was discussed. This was no time for good or bad harvests, deliveries, mills, or grain prices! As if for the last two hundred years Russia hadn't had a crust to eat. The crisis cannot be resolved if the nobility is in power. Give that power to the Kadets and Social Democrats, and Russia will have its fill. (A few days later the Kadet Nekrasov would groan that they couldn't unload the food—purchased under the Tsar—that had been coming into Petrograd in huge quantities since the winter storms had ended.)

On each discrete tangible issue, there was this wheel-spinning, which had no connection to genuine life, just a strain of accusations.

> **Chkhenkeli:** Our government was and is the people's enemy, that's clear to all. There must be an end to the political system that led the country to the brink of ruin. The hour has come!

(And how unfree this Russia was! Look how not a word was let spoken.)

> **Skobelev:** The entire country detests this state and despises this government.

> **Chkheidze:** It's a government of hangmen, a government of field courts-martial, a government of White terror, arch-reactionary through and through. . . . Any collaboration with this government is a betrayal of the people's interests. The Russia of the people and the Russia of this government are two *incompatible things.* They share no joys, no sorrows, no defeats, no victories. We should follow the path the forefathers of our dear, good friends the French took. The eighteenth-century bourgeoisie did not trade in words. (Skobelev: "They swept away thrones!")

What was there to be shy about if the entire Duma had already stood up for immunity for parliamentary speeches—and had tabled even the state budget and all the Empire's finances until the Duma's Social Democrats were allowed to speak their fill. This verbiage in this red-hot void, which had reached the point of screeching and squealing, arrogantly concerned as well its fellows in the Duma, especially the Kadets, who were always insufficiently revolutionary.

> **Chkheidze:** Gentlemen, you cannot fail to reckon with the *directives from the street.*

The fewer in numbers the handful of Social Democrats in the Duma, the more arrogantly they sneered at the rest of the Duma, first reproving the Progressive Bloc, then arrogantly encouraging it, but most consistently of all playing up their own foresight and erudition and scattering the tinsel of their social revelations. The fewer their numbers, the more lengthily and abundantly they frittered away what was the Duma's time and not their own and, in digressing at length in pointless wheel-spinning, knew for certain that because they were leftists no one would dare cut them off.

> **Sukhanov:** This government is conducting a policy of traitors and fools.
> **Rodzyanko:** I beg you to be more circumspect.
> **Sukhanov:** These are the words of Deputy Milyukov.
> **Rodzyanko:** I most humbly beg you not to repeat such unfortunate words.
> **Rodichev** (*from his seat*): Why unfortunate? (Noise, laughter.)

Or

> **Chkheidze:** I would insist that I not be admonished from the seat occupied by the vice president. This is an abuse of his position. (Applause on the left. "Right!")

> **Volkov** (Kadet): These gentlemen (pointing to the government seats) should be put in prison, for they are the true criminals preventing us from turning all our powers to the struggle against the external enemy. (Applause. The president does not cut it off.)

(A socialist adds): The old regime was too late offering possible concessions. Now, only by stepping over the old regime's dead body is the path toward
bread possible.

Rodzyanko readily smooths this over:

> Your metaphor is somewhat incautious, but I have no doubt that you did
> not mean that in the direct sense.

The socialist did not even bother to vindicate himself, and a little while later he repeated
the same "metaphor," quite unimpeded.

Somehow the hilariously boring Chkheidze, with his rattling pronunciation and his
uncleaned-up language, felt obliged to saddle the Duma for an hour nearly every other day:

> "given the situation that is found in the country;

> "The Bloc has taken the position of a priest who has left his prepared ser-
> mon in his old trousers."

When they removed Stürmer and the new Prime Minister, Trepov, who had not yet
shown himself in any way, came onto the tribune, the Social Democrats wouldn't even
let him make a statement, but shouted and raised an uproar, and then each took five
minutes to be impertinent and rowdy from the tribune, and they were all removed for
eight sessions.

It is very striking that once the Socialists were removed, calm, practical discussion began
in the Duma.

Constantly vying with the Social Democrats not to lag behind in tone, shouting, or
harshness, in reviling the government or disdaining the Duma majority, not to speak a single time less often than Chkheidze, or five minutes less, one man would gesture quickly,
his racing speech chasing down his hobbling thought, with the commonplaces of high
school baggage, cursing and predicting—this one man was a lawyer who had come into
fashion right before the war, the persistent intercessor for the exiled Duma Bolsheviks:
Kerensky. Having assumed leadership of the gray Trudoviks, with an especially good feel
for the peasantry:

> The peasantry have awakened and realized that the sixteenth of June system
> has led to the state's ruin;

he consistently felt he was the voice of all Russia and all laborers, the favorite of Russian society beyond the Duma's walls, and its most brilliant speaker:

> our opinion, that of an insignificant handful here, is being taken into considera-
> tion by European public opinion. You, gentlemen, have so far understood the
> word "revolution" to mean certain actions that destroy the state, when all of
> world history has said that revolution is a means for the state's *salvation*!

Sometimes in the pirouettes of his eloquence Kerensky lingered where the truth lay
and struck accurately at the Kadets:

> If you lack the will to act, then you should not utter overly weighty words with
> such grave consequences. You believe you have done your duty when you utter
> these words here. But when support is prepared to pour out into grandiose
> movements of the masses, you are the first to quash their enthusiasm with your
> "sensible" words! Isn't this a way to keep your warm chairs? The idea of an

imperialist seizure unites you with the regime! Look at those lightning bolts that are beginning to stripe the horizon of the Russian Empire. . . . Be careful with the people's soul!—

exhausted now, all his nerves shot, barely hanging from the tribune.

We have quoted Kerensky disproportionately little, skirting cubic kilometers of idle talk and selecting only that which is relevant to the narrative and thereby presenting him as more focused than he was, as a visionary, even. All of a sudden, pressed by presentiment (actually, it was already 28 February):

> In this last moment before great events . . . we ask ourselves for the last time whether we can save the past's national legacy that has fallen into our hands. The country is already in chaos. We are living through a period of turmoil historic for our homeland, a revolt that makes 1613 seem like children's tales. . . .

Nonetheless, you couldn't deny that the radical leftists were more coherent than the Kadets, who themselves did not keep up with their own figures of speech and had a poor understanding of where they were actually pulling people.

The Kadets were astonished by the unexpected victory of their attack on 14 November 1916, when suddenly they achieved their main goal: overthrowing Stürmer in a few days' time. There had been no precedents for this in our parliamentary life. The Progressive Bloc demonstrated that they were a force that imperial power took very seriously.

However, this victory obliged them all the more to attack more and bring down (first of all, an appetite had been kindled against the despised Protopopov), bring down, knock down, anyone—like Trepov—until they, the people's elected representatives, were invited to join the government.

Meanwhile, unrest had burst out beyond the Duma's walls. Congress after congress was held, and they issued the most terrible resolutions.

> Historical power is standing at the edge of an abyss. The government is leading Russia the way of ruin. . . . Time will not wait, all the postponements history has given us have run out. . . .

Reading Russia turned to the newspapers, and there, on the advice of Markov the 2nd, there were no more blank columns but there was also no story about what had happened. However, people already had the habit and technique of self-information—handwritten, typewritten, and mimeographed. All autumn and winter there flowed through Russia genuine and invented Duma speeches and transcripts of meetings between Duma members and Protopopov that reached even the remote provinces, and now there were the resolutions of all the December congresses, which **Milyukov** called

> the high point of the success we had achieved. Before our eyes, the public struggle has gone beyond strict legality, and the *unauthorized forms* of 1905 have been resurrected.

This high point of success, however, lay outside the Duma. Didn't something have to be done in the Duma, which was meeting half of November, all of December, and the beginning of March? The Progressive Bloc should not have tired of saying:

> The country is in the clutches of madmen, traitors, and renegades.

> **Adzhemov:** The first matter for the future government will be putting the present, treacherously behaving government on the defendant's bench. The

line has been crossed, and the country simply must save itself. At the decisive moment the Duma will be with the people, but *the people will show no mercy!*

The Kadets experienced a hitch and even an inner dismay. What was the right thing to do? How should they use the Duma and their leadership in it? Opposing the government on every issue came naturally. The greatest victory in this regard had been won when through concerted effort they had sunk the Ministry of Health—a ministry already created with a minister already appointed who had already begun his activities, but without the Duma's consent—and for this they abolished it and all its epidemiological and sanitary efforts—to spite the government! They also undermined the plan to introduce mandatory labor, if only in the zone just behind the front.

Forced labor? Police measures? The disgrace! Down with it!

Or forcing idle refugees to work:

Are we introducing serfdom for refugees?

All the more stormily did they protest and undermine the plan to militarize defense plants, that is, deprive workers of the right to strike and resign (on the other hand, they would be fed at the plant). This was serfdom and conscription for the proletariat even more so! This measure was meant to smother the revolutionary movement!

Delicate situations arose as well where the Progressive Bloc could not show its denunciatory anger—each time a question arose about industrial capital and banks. The lone voice of the priest **Okolovich** was heard in the Duma:

> There is a vampire who has overpowered Russia. His repulsive lips are sucking the lifeblood from the people's economic organism and holding its head tight and preventing its mind from working. This vampire is the banks: the Azov-Don Bank, Petrograd International, Petrograd Discount Loan, Siberian Commercial. . . . The banks are financing not the war but inflation. They have taken ownership of many factories. They are holding up the sugar shipments to Petrograd. They are buying up produce and not sending it where there is demand and hunger. There is stock exchange gambling on oats going on. The banks have placed commercial interests above the homeland. The country's entire economy is under surveillance, except for the banks.

But the Duma turned a deaf ear to this voice. The banks were too powerful to challenge. Shingarev had proposed surveillance over banks in the spring of 1916, and the Progressive Bloc had refused. To the public, the government was still to blame for everything, and they could come up with nothing better.

In its turn, a draft law on the township zemstvo, a question of very long standing for Russian development that had been drawn out and slowed, like everything important in Old Russia, crawled out from under the many years of Duma deposits. After fifty-five years of vain attempts to define and create the township zemstvo and eleven years gone to efforts to take it through the legislative chambers—now, in the third, grainless war winter, three months before the revolution, in December 1916, the township zemstvo was squeezing into Duma debates.

The plan to create townships based on all classes of society had been born even before 1861, when peasant reform was only being discussed. The peasantry, which had only just emerged from serfdom and was used to obeying any authority without a murmur, was incapable of defending itself against the state bureaucracy, and the landowners' isolation would deepen their strife with the peasantry; it would be good to unite them in a zemstvo that included all classes so that together they could realize and defend the interests of the land. And the state would cease to be a burden for the peasant.

But the peasants never had a chance to reify their peasant destiny. Many landowners opposed being drowned in the peasantry. Nor did the radical intelligentsia of the 1870s and 1880s sympathize with the plan. Narrow township interests would distract from broader horizons, and local self-administration would only bind democracy's general development (the sweet, boundless sea of politics). Concluding now was

> **Stempkovsky** (a Voronezh landowner): We are not citizens united by a single idea but master and worker, superior and subordinate. There was nowhere for us to come together and talk over future needs, nowhere to merge our interests into one. We always encountered a situation that was not conducive to restoring unity and a good peace. We haven't even taken on the expenses of the township, despite saying how many times that not doing this would be unfair.

Over and above zemstvo dues, they were planning to collect communal dues from the peasants, instead of asking landowners to pay.

The county zemstvo had languished for a very long time: they were so close to the populace, yet so far away. How could they get closer? The eternal argument was whether to begin immediately developing the civic consciousness of the impoverished and illiterate. Or first literacy, then improvement in economic life, so they would have leisure, and then reforms would follow?

The 1891 famine broke out, and this abyss yawned more distinctly: there was no township zemstvo, which would know who to feed and who to give loans. Even ill-informed benefactors couldn't reach out to the starving population without going through the land captain.

Meanwhile, a few peasant members of the county zemstvo acquitted themselves well. They had a vivid understanding of their own position, rights, and interests and expressed distinct thoughts about needs and objectives.

Back in the Second Duma, Stolypin had introduced a plan for a township zemstvo equal for all classes. Ten years later, even Kerensky was forced to admit:

> **Kerensky:** I give his memory its due. He boldly, honestly, and frankly rejected the curia system in the zemstvo and said that it was a flame of enmity being introduced into local zemstvo life.

But the plan got bogged down in the Dumas for a long time.

In Christian, peasant Russia, not a single peasant law or Christian issue ever seemed urgent or important to the four State Dumas of the educated class. If any of them did pass any of them, then they did so only if it meant an obvious triumph over the government. Thus for eight years the issue of peasant equality had been brewing in commissions—and not been granted. But now, was this the time to venture a township zemstvo, when there was a war going on?

Shingarev, fervently: Yes! Yes! It's just what's needed for the war! During a war, all dangers are even more dangerous. Here we are coming up with all kinds of local food committees, but what if we had a township zemstvo? It could see to the inventory of supplies, and the purchase of grain, and the distribution of goods, and the use of refugees and prisoners of war . . . The township zemstvo would preserve us from anarchy.

These debates bored the Duma, but maybe it even bored itself now. The township zemstvo was being discussed—and people were walking freely about the hall, talking loudly, more than half had gone to the foyer and buffet, at times there were only 150 of the 440 men in the hall, often the speakers signed up were not present and even Shingarev was absent.

Sixty years had proved too little for the plan. It was hasty, raw, not thought through, and criticized from both flanks and simply anyone who took the trouble to think about how such a fundamental, comprehensive reform could be carried out without even asking the peasant opinion at meetings.

Even **Kerensky** said as much, that you don't talk about worldly matters at a dying man's bedside. There's nothing to eat in the towns, and we don't know whether we'll be alive— and they're offering us a plan for a township zemstvo. . . .

All of a sudden, the argument ratcheted up to the point of fury, as often happens, and until you get used to it at first you don't understand why.

> **Gorodilov** (a peasant): How can you hold elections for a township zemstvo when the whole population's in the war? It's just an insult. The gentlemen progressives need their township zemstvo so they can plant their own people after the war's over, people who'll fill the countryside with nearly the worst element. But now, in today's township administrations, which are purely peasant, outside elements have no access.

> **Shingarev:** How could anyone sign a circular saying "outside individuals are not allowed into township meetings"? Who are outsiders in the Russian Empire? *Who* can't be allowed in?

And it cuts through like a flame—implied, clear to the debaters, bubbling and burning: Yes, refugees! And Jews! Why would you make them equal zemstvo members to us? To run our countryside? Are they going to work the land?

And with the same unquenchable fire the same ardent tongues licked at the tribune:

> Otherwise, the universal human and popular sense of justice would be violated! By oppressing the Jew, you're giving Germany a trump. What's this about Russia fighting for the rights of ethnicities?

In this Duma (as in all parliaments, actually), the more rightist the speaker, the more of a disgrace to society and the more constrained in his arguments he was. No matter what the rightists said, they were given no faith, no support, not even simple respect. They were easily suppressed by voting, or by the president's remarks, or simply by shouts from the seats, for there were many more leftist gullets, which barely let them talk, interrupted, made it hard for them to extend their speaking time, and more often cut off the debates to keep them from speaking at all and passed resolutions against them in machine-gun order.

> We, the Russian nationalists . . . (On the left: "Prussian!" Laughter.) . . . Speakers not from the Bloc cannot speak from this rostrum, you're constantly interrupting them. . . .

The Duma majority consistently ignored its rightist minority. The young Russian parliament could grasp the idea of voting but found the idea of concordance on which the ancient Russian communal agreement was built alien and strange.

All this was not the main reason why it was hard for rightists in the Duma. They had it tough because they were loyal to a dynasty that had lost its loyalty to itself, at a time when the autocrat seemed bewitched by an inner impotence. It was tough for them because they had to prop up a pillar that itself had begun wobbling. But what path could be indicated when the columns of principles were reeling and the dynasty's vault was tottering? Autocracy without its autocrat! . . . The rightists were in disarray, distraught, prostrate. What if the Emperor didn't need loyal men? . . . What if the Supreme power itself had forgotten and abandoned the rightists? . . . What would they do? Surrender? Concede power to the Kadets without a murmur? They wouldn't be able to hold it. They'd keep moving it further and further to the left. Dissuade them?

Also, one in six Duma deputies was a peasant. (The government had been afraid to give the countryside universal equal rights and thus had deprived itself of a rightist majority in the Duma. Those gray "agrarians" would never have allowed the bread noose of autumn 1916.) The peasants sat there quietly, afraid of casual ridicule, and spoke rarely and briefly, constrained, and with trusting touchingness:

> We have been giving everything to this bloody war—our brothers and sons—
> for over two years. Lord help you vanquish those impudent and bloody ene-
> mies. . . . And nails have gone up to 20–30 rubles a pood. . . .

or with a roughness of speech:

> They're abusing for our whole armed force. . . . What persuasion may be afoot
> for the people . . .

evoking only smiles with their unpolished, unconstructed speeches. Over the years they never got used to the impudent ways of those educated gentlemen in the Duma, to the barking and howling, which would have been so improper at village meetings. Or to the fact that they clapped not in agreement with a speech but if their own man was speaking. And even if something was right but not from their *own* man—most often they kept quiet. Peasant deputies had to scrub through a few years here just to get used to this being the State Duma.

How could this Duma be run in a fine and successful way? The task of Rodzyanko, the uneasiest of presidents. You could see he wasn't sitting idle! Russia's situation was very complicated and could only be taken in from the president's seat. Sometimes go to a secret session of the Bloc's bureau, sometimes don't decline and join the rightists for dinner at Stürmer's. Conceal unpleasant documents from the Duma, or intercede personally and directly with France in discussions about aeroplanes, circumventing all the ministries and the Supreme Command. But tensest and touchiest of all was trying to obtain an audience with the Emperor, each time fearing either a refusal or a chilly reception, or experiencing the humiliation of being crossed off by the Tsaritsa from the guest list for a high-ranking lunch or being given the most uncomfortable compartment on the government train. And all of a sudden, in autumn of 1916, a rumor went around that was a surprise even to him, that came out of no one knew where, but a sweetly and powerfully embracing rumor: the Prime Minister and foreign minister would be RODZYANKO! No one had officially proposed this, and this gracious word had not come down from on high, but he needed to think over the conditions worthy of a great man: seeing the empress off to Livadia; his position confirmed for at least three years; ministers of his own choosing; Polivanov to replace General Alekseev; and the removal of grand dukes from military posts. Unfortunately, Russia would never hear this ultimatum because the rumor remained just that.

And once again to carry himself up the oak steps to the Duma's highest rostrum and in his Zaporozhie bass lazily parry:

> The president himself knows. Don't start your wrangling. . . .

In these dangerous days, trying to avoid a scandal, surround yourself with Duma duty officers (many of them with shaved heads and large faces, like their president), and on that tragic day when the churl Markov the 2nd, waving his arms and shaking his fist, went up to the president, evidently to pick a fight—to find yourself without real protection other than Count Bobrinsky, who picked up a pitcher, all other help being too late.

This regrettable episode occurred after the Duma majority had—for half of November, it's true—been abusing the entire government put together and each minister individually, and **Rodzyanko** had objected perhaps too cautiously (but it wasn't for him to argue with the majority!):

> I most humbly ask the gentlemen Duma members to interrupt the speaker less often. . . .

Chkhenkeli: There's only one solution: revolution!

Rodzyanko: I'm calling you to order for this kind of expression,

but he let him finish, and Markov the 2nd, for his reply "Don't shout!" was removed from the rostrum. And this unbridled deputy walked up to Rodzyanko and declared loudly to him:

> Dimwit! Scoundrel!

Rodzyanko: State Duma member Markov the 2nd has permitted himself to insult your President such as has never happened in the annals of the State Duma. (Noise. Voices: "What insult?") But I cannot . . . (Noise.) However, in view of this circumstance, I will ask my Vice President to propose a measure of retribution. . . .

V. Bobrinsky: For this incredibly serious insult to the president of the State Duma (Voices: "What insult?") . . . I will not repeat this expression. . . .

Markov was excluded for fifteen sessions, the maximum allowed by charter. However, according to the same charter, the guilty party was allowed to explain his action, and Markov the 2nd managed to declare:

> From this rostrum people have had the audacity to insult the highest personages with impunity. And so, in the person of your president, who is biased and disreputable, I have insulted you!

Nonetheless, this episode ended to Rodzyanko's greater glory: applause from the Progressive Bloc and sympathetic telegrams from zemstvos and assemblies of the nobility, city dumas, and the Legion of Honor from the president of France!

Leading the Duma was more complicated than directing a symphony because you had to foresee so much and adjust its tones, methods, and forms of voting.

Even more important, there could be no error in opening a tensely awaited session after an enforced break, as on 27 February. This was even more vexing because Rittikh's speech postponed the central speech by Milyukov, which he would deliver the next day to a less than full hall, without even a quorum of deputies, unfortunately, and without a triumphant confluence of the public.

Milyukov: We, the legislative institutions, have broken with the government. There (pointing to the government box) are but those pale shadows. (Applause. Adzhemov: "And all sorts of trash!") The country has far outstripped its
government. . . . A spectacle profoundly insulting for a great nation. . . . Will
this disgraceful and vexing obstacle be cleared from the nation's path? . . . Gentlemen, not in silence or reconciliation but in the patriotic alarm that fills your
own hearts do I see our salvation. You who know more than I can say from this
rostrum, you know that this alarm is well founded. If in fact the idea takes hold
in the country that Russia cannot win with *this* government, then it will win *despite* its government, but it will win!

(This was said by a major connoisseur of foreign policy on 28 February. The United
States was obviously going to enter the war, and the Allies' victory seemed virtually auto-
matic. Why could it seem so to Milyukov and to nearly everyone? Wishful thinking. Of
course, once you've floated down history's river, found its shores, and measured its depth,
it's easy to criticize. Now that we've paid for everything, we know that the state of affairs was
exactly opposite to what Milyukov said: with *this* government, Russia would inevitably
have won the war and *without it*—it lost.)

Hopes are rushing toward us from deepest Russia. It is we who must not be
content with speeches and must act in an unusual and special way. . . . "All the
speeches have been made. Act boldly!" we are told on all sides. These hopes
touch us deeply but also daunt us somewhat.

This took courage, when on the left the Social Democrats biliously gushed:

What can we call your tactics, gentlemen? You continue to assert that you
are prepared to use only *legal means* to fight the regime that is leading the
country to its ruin! This is worse than any defeatism! . . . Haven't you been saying that this regime is betraying the country?

Oh, this leftist wind, how painfully it cuts the face! And after all, it was true, there was
nothing to say. The Kadets had been blocking it, blunting and sidestepping it:

It is quite deplorable when disagreements arise between us and our comrades on the left, to the delight of sinister forces.

The Kadets' inner weakness lay in the fact that, while merciless in their criticism,
they had no attractive program to offer. More often they didn't have one, and some
points they made scant mention of so that the government wouldn't usurp them. Except
maybe this:

Milyukov: Rid this nation of superfluous watchmen and police. The
people's desire is to send the police off to the front! Why have these well-fed
men remained inviolable?

But then, there was just one thing, just one thing they repeated, and herein lay their
main program:

Rodichev: When men worthy of the people's faith are sitting there (he
points to the government box), men whose very names say to the country, *Wait
and believe*, men who will do their deed or perish. . . .

If only the state would go away, we would step in—and everything would be fine.

What else could you propose, really, other than a *government of trust?*

> **Efremov:** A government like that could work wonders. It would be inspired by the popular soul, and the entire nation would create and work with it.

(Soon we would be verifying this, in the Provisional Government.)

Forestalling the Bloc's leaders, Kerensky scrambled to gain new popularity:

> **Kerensky:** *Who are they* who bring these shadows here (pointing to the government seats).

And more about *those people* above the government. Even in the autumn he had already taken this up, and now look! He had correctly understood that reviling the government was no longer an oratorical achievement. The time had come to revile the throne. He had correctly understood that now *everything* was permitted in the Duma. He had correctly understood that Rodzyanko would not dare give him up. (Prime Minister Prince Golitsyn would request the transcript, and Rodzyanko would reply there was nothing blameworthy there.) All the dangerous sections would be excised. But this moderately gentle section:

> With violators of the law . . .

(that is, the government)

> . . . there is but one path: their physical removal! (Applause on the left, "True!") —

even in the transcript that wasn't cut. Reveling in the level of audacity achieved and the country's anticipated delight, the member of parliament announced what had been heretofore assumed, but now let it be spread in mimeographed leaflets:

> Gentlemen, I can speak freely because you know that by my personal political convictions I share the opinion of the party, which . . .

(now he could admit that he was not a Trudovik but a secret Social Revolutionary!)

> . . . on its banner has openly placed the possibility of terror . . . toward the party that has recognized the necessity of tyrannicide.

After this incendiary speech, who was going to listen to the right's doleful arguments?

> **Levashov:** A handful of heartless, ambitious men is trying to exploit our homeland's difficult position in order to seize power over it illegally and prevent the government from concentrating on the destruction of our mighty foe. . . . The songs of the Jewish press, the hysterical cries of Duma speakers saying the current government cannot lead Russia to victory . . .

Whereas the Social Democrat **Skobelev:**

> Not only to the government or the *central figure* pulling these puppets' strings. (The president does not intervene.) So much has accumulated that the working class could present to the current authorities. Either these authorities and their henchmen are swept aside or Russia perishes. (Applause on the left. The president does not object.)

When parties, parliamentary factions, newspapers, and speakers get used to society and studentry applauding them and avidly following them, they are drawn into competitive play without even noticing it. Each subsequent speaker and journalist, each subsequent statement and resolution, was calculated to elicit amazement, delight, and support — stronger, or at least not weaker, than the previous ones. Such was the inertia of this game. But in order to achieve this, speaking talent, writing talent, and quick wit were not enough.

This continuous surge and warming of public support could be achieved only by using an encouraging series of facts and ignoring the depressing ones. A voice and success could not grow if these series were compared in an honest and balanced way. So this public-parliamentary-newspaper game (which we were observing on the eve of the Russian Revolution but with our weary vision often see in today's West) became a self-absorbed, deceptive procession, the carnival, before toppling over. The eye and foot ceased to distinguish where there was still firm ground and where its spectral, mirror reflection.

In the last week of Russia's State Duma, this rivalry reached the point of desperate anguish. Not a single discussion—about the township zemstvo, transportation, fuel, or food supplies—was carried through to completion but was instead interrupted by some hysterical, urgent inquiry, which would collide and jostle with more and more new inquiries and questions, also not carried through to any decision, one inquiry more pointed than the next; the agenda fell apart, and the speakers, upsetting the unitary flow, each spoke about whatever was burning them.

Konovalov, a prominent textile manufacturer who did not have set prices for his own cloth and a revolutionary figure from the Progressive Bloc, with his gold pince-nez on a long cord, voiced an inquiry about illegal administrative actions, a very long speech.

After that it was **Chkheidze's** turn to jump up, which was his inviolable right, so listen, even if your eyes pop out of your head. It was time to recall the Social Democratic deputies of the Second Duma exiled in 1907. Why wasn't the Duma doing anything about them?

> Has the moment not arrived, gentlemen, when the foreign war, thanks to this regime, gentlemen, is about to become in fact a *civil* war? Gentlemen, I suggest you bear these prospects in mind!

(Why had Lenin reviled this dear Chkheidze so mercilessly?)

The longer the government remained silent, the bolder the deputies became. They reviled the government in words that made it seem as if that government was no more in Russia. In his successful new role as society favorite, **Purishkevich,** too, never tired of making a spectacle of himself, in the last few months having taken a sensational leap from the extreme right practically into the Kadets' arms and gone unpunished for a murder. The tribune was never left empty, and the speakers overflowed with a mounting excess of emotions and words. Skobelev had already exulted from the tribune that there were disorders on Petrograd's streets and people were absconding with streetcar levers.

> **Kerensky:** We demand that you, the authorities, submit to the country's demands and resign your positions!

On 9 March, the Duma was awash in a new and urgent inquiry: What measures was the government taking to resolve the food situation in Petrograd? How could they let slip such a marvelous occasion for heartrending speeches? Then came the food question in Russia in general, an almost academic question, so it could be abandoned. Here was where it was vital. Here, in Petrograd!

An ominous inquiry was submitted. The Kadets' leaders knew that in two hours, at a meeting between Rodzyanko and the government, everything was going to be resolved amicably, in the most favorable sense. Oh no, now there was reason to shed light on the political aspects and ignite passions!

Rodichev: We are in that final moment after which there is no salvation! A government in which you can't tell a minister from a swindler—and all of them were appointed by an influence that we cannot fail to call treasonous. (Applause on the left, "Right!") This is their supreme punishment, befitting the deeds they've committed. In the name of our hungry nation, we demand a government worthy of a great nation's destinies! And call upon men whom all Russia can trust!

How could we get along without Chkheidze now? No matter how many speeches you made, you felt like settling scores and having a peck, too.

Chkheidze: It is characteristic of the government and many of you to ignore the street.

And then—ten times the detail, smearing, and abundant mention that he himself and his faction had always been right, had always known and foreseen this.

What is the resolution of the food question? Disband this government and this system!

Meanwhile at the ready, bursting, not having spoken since yesterday

Kerensky: Yesterday we spoke from this tribune and no one in Russia ever learned that. I have formulated and spoken many times about the ultimate reason for the misfortunes we are now suffering. However, gentlemen . . .

to be fair, he was capable of coming to his senses faster than an SD or even a KD,

. . . now that we have entered this period of collapse, disaster, and anarchy, now that the country's reason has died, in the grip of hunger and hatred, then I cannot repeat from this rostrum what Deputy Rodichev said: The final hour has come, that it's now or never. *Be careful what you say* if you yourself do not wish your words to become deed. We are facing a picture of the state's demise that is all too vivid. Be careful, keep your hands off this mass, whose mood you don't understand. How right we were when we said . . . —

and a great deal about how right they had been when they had said it.

Salvation lies in the people alone, and it is to the people that we ourselves must go with penance

(as we have known, actually, since the nineteenth century).

All of a sudden a priest appeared on the rostrum. He was under the fresh impression of what he had just seen on the streets. A tremendous mass had filled all of Znamenskaya Square, all of Nevsky, and all the adjacent streets, and completely unexpectedly, the passing regiments and Cossacks were greeted by shouts of "hurrah!" One of the mounted policemen was about to strike a woman with his whip when Cossacks stepped in and drove the police away. (On the left, extended applause, "Bravo!" Karaulov: "Hurrah!")

Sit around in this stuffy, closed hall and you'll see nothing!

The leftists applauded. Someone spoke for the rightists saying that it pained any Russian when the legislative institutions did nothing but hurl foul-smelling liquids at the Russian imperial government instead of creating legislation.

On 10 March, at the morning session, the same dutiful, obliging, swift **Rittikh** responded to the latest inquiry. Despite the decline of shipments due to the winter storms, they had had sufficient stores for more than three weeks. There was enough rye grain, and some bakeries had even declared a surplus; people weren't taking it all. There was no shortage of flour, and the bakeries were all being issued the norm. The visible shortage had begun only three days ago, and especially on the Vyborg side. On Rittikh's instruction, a plenipotentiary rode around to all the bread stores and bakeries there and clarified that they all had a reserve of from a few days' to a few weeks' worth.

But something unusual had happened. Suddenly tremendous lines had appeared, and a demand for black bread specifically. Everyone pointed out that the person who bought bread at one shop immediately moved on and stood in line at another. Panic was mounting. Everyone was trying to lay in a supply of bread to make into rusks. Something similar had happened two weeks ago but had passed fairly quickly, and afterward the people were selling big boxes of those rusks.

Now the usual batch started not sufficing, and some of the bread stores and some of the people wanting to buy even more started running out of bread. Even though the total Petrograd supply remaining would last more than two weeks. Special route trains had been scheduled for Petrograd to make up for the shortage. Nineteen trains had already set out, and this was a two-week quantity.

Now, without waiting for a new law, as soon as the Petrograd Municipal Board gets itself organized enough to approve this business, it will be immediately handed over, that same day! If it can be passed today, then it will be done today!

This was verified as follows. When you watched the loaders carrying the sacks, you'd think you could do that easily! But when you started trying to lift a corner of a sack like that with your shoulder—oh, how it pained and flattened you! This here was the first corner of the weight of state that they were giving the Progressive Bloc to lift. And Kadet **Nekrasov** was already making excuses:

We know that public self-governments will not have in its hands many of the opportunities that government organs had.

Shingarev: However, the city might take up this matter if it's secured a grain shipment. How else can it take responsibility before the Petrograd populace?

(The sack was already starting to weigh heavy.)

. . . Perhaps *they* now have one last hope, that having brought the matter to this dire end, they could fob it off on the city?

Expeditious Duma members were also promoting a legislative proposal (studded with phrases saying it was all the government's fault) to be discussed and passed in three days' time. So had they gotten down to business and was the wordmill over, if only for today? Not a chance! But—

Chkheidze: Let's see what comes of what's now being proposed. The food question is more acute in the Caucasus than anywhere else.

Here's what: three days was too long, we had to finish in two, by Monday.

And there was Kerensky! Just a few words, if only to join in: Faster! Get to work!

A few requests: stop the general session so that the food commission can begin its work immediately!

But what about an explanation of the vote? Stopping the session's work required an explanation of the vote. Once again,

Kerensky: The Minister of Agriculture has told us nothing new. But the formula for the transition (so that they could start the food work quickly):

Having listened to the Minister of Agriculture's explanations and finding them wholly unsatisfactory, the State Duma deems the further stay in power of the present Council of Ministers altogether intolerable. . . . Form a government subject to the oversight of the entire people! As well as immediate freedom of speech, assembly, organizations, and the individual . . .

He'd beaten friend Chkheidze to it! What a deft maneuver! But all was not lost. He could make up for it! The explanation of the vote (on ending this session)—

Chkheidze: I have absolutely no wish to object to the formula my comrade Kerensky has announced. However, we cannot deny ourselves a certain right, so to speak, to express ourselves on what the gentleman minister has explained to us. Therefore, I propose not to delay the session, to continue the discussion of this question, and to hear from the tribune one more time. . . .

(Kerensky and Chkheidze one more time and one more time)

. . . and one more time registering in the populace's memory what needs to be said. *Afterward there will be time,* I think, to work out the draft bill on transferring food supplies to public committees.

Ten minutes ago he himself had said that he couldn't stand to wait even until Tuesday and that they should do everything by Monday! And now, let's have debates for as much as a week!

What was terrible wasn't that any demagogue could burst onto the Duma's tribune at any moment and mumble any nonsense. What was terrible was that there was no outcry of indignation, no murmur from anywhere in the Duma hall. That was how battered everyone was and shy before the left flank. What was also terrible was that eleven years of four State Dumas were ending in pathetic mumbling.

At 12:50, Rodzyanko closed the session.

All this was copied out by me from the Duma transcripts of the Russian monarchy's final weeks. All this lies on the surface to such a degree that I am amazed at just one thing: Why has no one presented it before?

This Duma would never assemble again.

Today, having read its transcripts from November 1916 straight through, and previously many many others, what I feel is this: I'm not sorry.

[27]

Today the training detachment of the Volynian regiment sent not a platoon to Znamenskaya Square but the entire 2nd Company, which meant Kirpichnikov had to go all the more. That's what it came down to, no matter how much he didn't want to go.

They said that today we would be there until twelve at night, and a hot meal would be sent over. Don't let people converge on the square.

Once again the company sat in the caretaker's cellar and details took turns going on patrol.

The Cossacks rode out and past in platoons fully equipped for battle. Their look and clattering hooves on the streets were menacing—not just to the crowd but also to the easygoing soldier patrols, whose hearts sank at the sight of these Cossack forays. Even though they had not taken out their whips and were riding through peacefully and to no purpose.

But the police were nowhere to be seen in the thick of the crowd along Nevsky and only stood in a short rank near the train station. They were very few.

Kirpichnikov returned to the cellar rather exhausted. From all his long service, maybe. In war you hold on for dear life, in peacetime they wear you out with parades, and now here they'd thought of something else: running down the people.

The staff captain's orderly again came running to the cellar to tell the company to form up. Right then the ensigns, Vorontsov-Velyaminov and Tkachura, one for each half-company, came running in. In the two years Kirpichnikov had been absent from the Volynian Regiment (after mobilization he had ended up in an infantry regiment, then been wounded, and then been receiving treatment), many former officers had been worn down, and he rarely came across anyone he knew. These men were new.

They climbed out. And the look of the Guards—greatcoats that didn't fit, some lacking proper footwear, let alone an upright bearing.

They formed up, but now diagonally to the side, so that the way from Nevsky to the Aleksandr monument remained open to the crowd, which had thronged there with a red flag and had come to a halt by the monument.

First, they doffed their caps and all sang "Memory Eternal."

Then the shouters started coming out, though from here they were hard to hear.

One elderly soldier, zealous, couldn't stand it and shouted to his officer from the back row:

"Your honor! That orationer—he's screaming some speech!"

Kirpichnikov called him to order:

"Pipe down, grayhair."

If you only understood, if you only knew. . . .

Ensign Velyaminov went to ask the captain for permission to disperse the crowd.

Staff Captain Mashkin the 2nd made no reply. Gave no order.

Kirpichnikov thought that, after all, one could come to a perfectly decent agreement with people. And to Velyaminov:

"Permit me, your honor, I'll go out to them alone."

"They'll kill you."

"Never in a million years."

The ensign wouldn't let him go. He himself went back to the staff captain to ask permission to disperse them.

Oh, another bad ending. Again: What were the soldiers to do?

Velyaminov returned and told the first platoon:

"Shoulder arms! Follow me. Forward march!"

And he headed off, himself swinging his arms and stamping his feet, and they followed behind, listlessly. Then he rang out:

"Firm step!"

The soldiers grumbled:

"This isn't a smithy to be holding a step firm."

Kirpichnikov stayed back with the other platoon, and though he couldn't hear, he could see just fine. There, by the monument, they had raised a red rag and unfurled it overhead: "Down with the war!"

Had they gone mad or something? How could that be—down with the war? What about the German?

After twenty paces or so, Velyaminov commanded the platoon: "Short guard!" He turned them face front, and they set off in a line, rifles tilted forward—straight at the red flag.

The monument's pedestal was red granite and kept clear of snow, and there were common laborers on it.

Velyaminov rushed forward, breaking away from formation—slipped—and fell on his face.

Immediately, they fell on him with a stick and struck him in the back.

Meanwhile they furled and hid their "Down with the war."

The crowd was losing its nerve, too.

The ensign briskly jumped up, walked over, and tore the red flag off its pole—and returned to his formation.

He asked his soldiers who had struck him and was told they hadn't seen.

He turned the platoon, again "shoulder arms"—and went back, to his company.

Barely had they formed up when a group stepped out of the crowd and asked the staff captain to return the flag.

The staff captain politely asked them to disperse.

Velyaminov and Tkachura shouted at them:

"Disperse or we'll shoot!"

One came up in a student's uniform, missing an arm. With his intact hand he poked the badge on Velyaminov's greatcoat:

"We sat on the same school bench, and now you want to shoot me? Go ahead and shoot!"

He offered his chest.

Velyaminov said to him:

"Army service is service. Without it there is no country."

That's right.

Cossacks on shaggy Siberian horses galloped up. They twirled and clattered hooves. They chuckled. They rode at the crowd, but gently.

The crowd surged from spot to spot: a "windmill."

The officers left to sit in the hotel, but Kirpichnikov and the soldiers stayed.

When the crowd pressed too hard and surrounded them, the soldiers begged them to look at it from their difficult soldier's position and to fall back.

Service also meant not always doing what you were trained to do. People wanted bread, and they wanted to talk, so why should they be barred?

An orderly ran up: Go to the caretaker's room for now.

[28]

Over this gloomy winter, yet another sweet, devoted young woman had drawn near: Lili Dehn, the wife of an aide-de-camp, a sailor appointed to command the cruiser *Varyag*, which had been bought back from the Japanese. Just yesterday she had seen her husband off. He had left for England, perhaps for six months, to change machinery, and she had arrived in the evening to sit for a while. Grieved and alarmed (so many German mines en route alone!), she behaved magnificently. And with their similar feelings and absent husbands, a heartfelt understanding arose between them.

Around midnight, Anya sent to ask for her, and the Empress took a wheelchair the full empty length of the palace to see her. She spent an hour and a half reassuring her as she lay in a fever, short of breath, frightened, in a very bad way.

So far the children had had a relatively easy time of the measles; in the mornings their temperature would drop and by evening rise. They all lay in darkened rooms, and their mother went alternately from one to the next, relieving the attendants. There had been no complications so far. The younger girls were holding on, albeit on the brink. Anastasia had a very suspicious throat.

Outside the morning window a light, pleasant snow was falling, with a light frostiness. It fell, soft and carefree, on the untouched snowy masses of the Tsarskoye Selo park. Life could be just that light and carefree!

For someone else . . .

In the morning they handed the Empress a letter from Protopopov, who explained the city's disturbances of the last few days (which apparently had not ended even today?): This is a provocative, simply hooliganish movement of boys and girls who are running and shouting they have no bread merely in order to create a disturbance. Some workers are striking, too, and out of malicious habit are not allowing others to work, either. The Socialists want to use propaganda to impede the city's proper supply. If the weather were cold, everyone would be sitting at home. But the disturbance will subside and pass, Protopopov explained, if only the Duma behaves well.

However, there would never be peace if the Duma assembled. When all together in Petrograd, they were always a venomous element. Scattered across the country, no one respected them.

Just yesterday evening a close, trusted friend, Aide-de-camp Sablin, having seen Protopopov at dinner, had conveyed his reassurances by telephone that all would be well.

See what a minister God had sent! Not an indifferent stranger, like the majority of them always were, but wholeheartedly devoted, not dozing as he watched over the Tsar's interests. And, at the same time, intelligent, daring, energetic, perceptive, and possessed of a great understanding of men and the situation. And, at the same time, a dear, charming, sincerely sympathetic man to whom one could openly complain. In a quarter-century there had not yet been a minister with whom one could converse simply. So unpretentious, simple, and instantly accepted in the close circle of the Tsar's family. So much had he not sought after state ceremony that one could for speed get in touch through Anya and send along important papers. In a quarter century there had never been a minister so pleasantly accepted in the family circle as one of their own, not feeling shy in front of him in their most candid statements. (Perhaps even a subtly understanding, mystical soul kindred to mysterious fulfillments.) It was impossible to believe that this man had spent nearly ten years in the State Duma without its poisoned atmosphere of malice suffocating him. He was direct, candid, straightforward, and pure such as can only happen in Russia, as happens among the Lord's holy fools, not one bit defiled by the Petersburg callousness—and from the first meeting he had loved the Emperor so unreservedly. They had searched long and hard and sorted through so many. The Minister of the Interior was more important than any other, even the Prime Minister! And at last they had found him. He was picked out and suggested—naturally by our sharp-eyed, unforgettable Friend. Protopopov had always understood His heart. Now he remained their defender, somewhat replacing Him, a compensatory shadow.

It was curious observing the Duma's biased, instantaneous turn with respect to Protopopov. First they held onto him as their leader, then cursed and derided him for his loyalty to the Emperor. But society was already so blinded, it didn't see this Duma absurdity.

Protopopov took charge efficiently. To run police affairs he took on Kurlov, who had been callously pushed out after the Stolypin affair. Recently he had arrested a nest of revolutionaries, the "Workers' Group," under the malefactor Guchkov. When the Friend was killed and all of abominable society had roared with delight and Minister of Justice Makarov had not rushed to an investigation, Protopopov had done wonders searching, and his police had quickly found the body, in a distant arm of the Nevka, under the ice, and he had managed to bring the deceased to Tsarskoye Selo with tact and discretion. He had also prevented Yusupov's flight from Petrograd—and would have punished him if the Emperor had had the wisdom and firmness to punish. Using his own staff to inspect correspondence, he brought the Empress perfidious, malicious letters from the grand duchesses in which Aleksandra Fyodorovna bitterly tasted the enormity of human treachery. (And this was why, over and over again, the Minister of the Interior had to be an absolute confidant, on our side.)

Everything would work out if the Duma behaved decently. The root of the uprising and incitement lay in the Duma, not in the street processions. Oh, there was no convincing the peace-loving Emperor that one mustn't forgive the rebellious and even anti-dynastic Duma speeches. Horrible things were being said there that Rodzyanko wasn't even including in the transcript, something impossible to get hold of, but most likely they were releasing it all over the country on mimeos. It was wartime! Such a thing would not be countenanced in England, but here all was forgiven.

Even after spending two months by his side, the Tsaritsa had not transfused her husband with her hot-blooded will. He kept declining to do a man's work of state. He hadn't punished a single Duma speaker or a single loudmouth at the Unions' mutinous congresses. He lacked the decisiveness to get rid of the insincere, undevoted Alekseev. All he had to do was extend Alekseev's leave, but the Emperor found that awkward. So Alekseev returned. Other strangers had been placed at GHQ, too, Lukomsky and Klembovsky, whereas dear Pustovoitenko had been removed—and the Emperor had made his peace with that. He had not even made up his mind to disband Batyushin's biased commission, which had needlessly agitated the Jews and all of society, mercilessly seizing upon first Rubinstein, then the sugar manufacturers, and then poor Manasevich. (In today's letter as well, Aleksandra had asked Nicky to let Batyushin go at last.)

She was writing Nicky a letter, but she had to tear herself away because today once again the Emperor had audiences scheduled, and she had to take her spouse's place firmly and vigorously. Once again she had to climb into her official clothing and receive foreigners once again: one Chinese, one Greek, an Argentine and his wife, and a Portuguese and his two daughters. How infinitely alien they were, as were their grievances during these difficult days.

However, she also had a lively and interesting audience—with newly appointed Crimean Governor Boisman. He, too, had sober thoughts about Petrograd. First, that they should have a genuine combat cavalry regiment here, not lax, undisciplined reserves who in addition were more than half made up of local Petersburg and Finnish folk. (Indeed! No matter how often it was mentioned, no matter how many times they decided to call a combat Guards regiment or Uhlans to Petrograd, for some inexplicable reason none of it ever came to pass or was found a place.)

Second, they should make the striking workers open their eyes, tell them outright not to organize strikes or else they would be sent to the front or strictly punished. This was wartime, after all!

The Empress liked all his thoughts for their clarity and simplicity. It seemed there was no problem and nothing to consider—and she could not understand why official persons were not taking the simplest steps.

The Empress always became very inspired at an audience that went beyond empty courtesies, a report that went beyond specifically female activities and rose from an isolated problem to one of state significance. Her insistent will moved swiftly toward important decisions to strengthen and elevate Russia—and afterward either suggested them to the Emperor in letters or else herself sought the shortest route to their implementation here.

Perspicacious and decisive, the Empress was capable of leading and directing all those who were loyal and just. Long ago, just after arriving in Russia, she had discovered that the people surrounding the Emperor were insincere, did not love him or the country, and were taking advantage of his inexperience. No one was performing his duties conscientiously, and each was thinking of his own advantage. The people around and close to him were so base. She lived with this bitter knowledge for many years, bearing one child after another, trembling over the heir, not interfering in anything. Only with the course of the present horrible war, she could no longer stand off to one side.

But the Empress had been in Russia for twenty-two years and knew the country. She knew that the people loved the most august family. Quite recently in Novgorod the people had shown this so unanimously, with such enthusiasm. . . . The Duma and society should have seen it!

Her trip to Novgorod in December remained not a memory but a vital, inspirational feeling. It was just one day—but she had seen the people's depth, purity, and guilelessness! Enormous popular crowds drawn by love surged toward her motorcar at stops, kissed her hands, wept, and crossed themselves. What open exultation on those thousands of simple faces! And all this to the continuous ringing of Novgorod's ancient bells. Everything around you spoke of the past and you lived those ancient times. Lines of troops, ecstatic high school students in the Kremlin, public prayers in the Cathedral of St. Sophia, the self-revealed Mother of God in the chapel, the Yuriev Monastery and Desyatinny Convent, her visit to the aged nun, her visit to the wounded—she rode and walked from place to place surrounded by unbroken popular ecstasy, so much love and warmth everywhere, a purity and unity of emotions, and a sense of God, the people, and antiquity. The Empress's expanded heart filled with exultation at this mutual loyalty: Hers to the Orthodox people, and the Orthodox people's to her.

Was that really in Novgorod alone? What about before the war, when she and the Emperor sailed down the Volga? The populace had walked into the water up to its knees and shouted greetings and love to them. And look, even during war, university students in Kharkov had met her with a portrait and torches, unharnessed the horses, and pulled her carriage themselves.

What pitiful attempts by befogged Petrograd brains could outweigh this? Only society and the public of Petersburg and Moscow were opposed to the royal couple.

[2 9]

*   *   *

What made this day different was that there was none of the good cheer or play of the two preceding. There was no more chanting, "Bread! Bread!" and the looting of shops had flagged. The people were wholly confident of the troops' and especially the Cossacks' friendliness. (Women would walk right up to their horses and straighten their bridles.) For the third day straight there had been no losses among the demonstrators—and the people no longer feared the police, either. On the contrary, the people were confronting them, and with mounting malice.

Confidence had abandoned the police. No one was for them, not even their superiors, and their few numbers, lost in crowds of thousands, were supposed to hold something back.

The power of the street had begun to be felt.

*   *   *

Large crowds had broken through all the outer cordons around the city's center, where the main action was playing out. Here, locals were massing, especially along Nevsky. On the sidewalks, clerks and ordinary residents stared at the street processions, neither sympathizing nor disapproving. People shouted to them from the street:

"Why are you standing there? Come down off the sidewalk! Hey, you, bourgeois, come down off the sidewalk."

*   *   *

The number of young people in the crowd—intellectual and quasi—had increased. Separately, singly, but in many places, red flags began to appear. And when the speakers stood up, they shouted not about bread but: Thrash the police! Bring down the criminal government that has gone over to the Germans' side!

*   *   *

On Znamenskaya Square what was now a continuous rally went on and on. The crowd changed and the speakers changed, but the rally went on. And all of it around the monument to Aleksandr III.

It would be impossible to imagine anything more incongruous than this solid, immovable, and indifferent figure of the emperor on a hero's frozen steed with its head set low, surrounded by tall metal lampposts and, nearby and behind, a small five-domed church.

The speakers could not be heard for the din and hurrahs. The entire square was full. Near the train station and on both sides of Ligovka were Cossacks and mounted policemen. A police officer bared his sword and shouted, "Disperse! I'm breaking this up!" The crowd neither believed him nor moved. The police officer waved his sword at the Cossacks: "Break this up!" Sullen-faced, they rode forward but not seriously. The crowd flowed around them and then back again—to their old spot. Or sometimes the mounted police, sabers bared, galloped at the crowd—which rushed about and squeezed together—but struck no one.

No one knew what to do about the crowd.

*   *   *

Nevsky was packed with people, a sea of heads and red flags.

Army trucks that happened onto Nevsky couldn't get through. They crawled slowly behind the red flags, as if joining the procession.

*   *   *

Across Sadovaya and around Gostiny Dvor were solid formations of armed soldiers. But the crowd, was being pressed up to the soldiers, still from behind, their chests facing the presented, tilted bayonets.

Behind them, people were singing revolutionary songs. The female students in front told the soldiers:

"Comrades! Put away your bayonets and join us!"

The crowd was pressing. The soldiers exchanged glances—and began pointing their bayonets up so that they would no longer poke.

"Hurrah!" The crowd pressed up even more, and all was confusion.

*   *   *

A large crowd was gathered by the Cathedral of Our Lady of Kazan and the Ekaterininsky Canal. Among the proper public there were also some very agitated ladies, and they too were arguing in clusters and impromptu rallies. There were virtually no common women in the crowd, but there were lots of female students.

A Cossack snatched a red flag as he flew past, galloped about fifty yards with it, and ripped it off its pole. The standard-bearer ran after the Cossack, begging him to give it back. Unbeknownst to his superiors, the Cossack threw it down and the flag was scooped up and pocketed.

The crowd started throwing empty bottles at the police. Then they fired half a dozen shots at the policemen; one was wounded in the belly, another in the head, and others were injured by bottles as well.

A police officer responded with two shots. The wounded policemen were taken away.

*   *   *

At the corner of Nevsky and Mikhailovskaya, inside The Baker, a coffee-house, a police supervisor was on duty. People took a good look and started throwing bottles and rocks at the coffeehouse and broke three windows. They made their way inside to the policeman, took away his sword, and broke it. The café lowered its iron shutters.

*   *   *

Some of the crowd went down Kazan Street toward a courtyard where policemen were holding about twenty-five arrested men.

Right then a platoon of Cossacks from the 4th Don Regiment rode up with an officer. The crowd faltered.

But the Cossacks cursed the policemen:

"Hey, you! You're serving for the money!"

They struck two of them with their scabbards and someone else on the back with a sword. The arrested men were released to the crowd's roar.

*   *   *

A military unit bypassed the Moscow Train Station, taking Ligovka on its way to embarkation. The soldiers marched with full gear, sullen, paying no heed whatsoever to all the agitation and shouting.

*   *   *

At the Anichkov Bridge, a young man wearing a student cap pulled something out from under his coat, knocked it against his boot—and threw it under the mounted police, in their midst. A deafening crack—and the horses were blown to bits and the riders thrown on their backs.

*   *   *

On Znamenskaya Square, under Aleksandr III's heavy-footed steed, the rally flowed on and speakers poured off the red granite pedestal. Next to it was a large red flag.

A police officer, Captain Krylov, rode in from Goncharnaya with five policemen and a detachment of Don Cossacks. He sat on his steed like a good
cavalryman. He bared his sword and lifted it high—and rode into the crowd.

The others followed: policemen with and Cossacks without swords
drawn, lazily.

The crowd yielded and swayed—the flight had started flowing around
the monument: "They're cutting us down!"

They weren't, though. Krylov rode ahead alone, as if trying to fetch what
was most precious to him on the tip of his sword.

No one prevented him from riding all the way to the flag.

He tore down the flag—and started driving the standard-bearer before
him, back toward the train station.

Past the policemen. Past the Cossacks.

Suddenly, a sword blow to his head from behind knocked him off his
steed to the ground, where he dropped the flag.

Mounted policemen rushed to his defense, but Cossacks pushed them
away.

The crowd let up a roar, exulting, waving caps and handkerchiefs:
"Hurrah for the Cossacks! A Cossack killed a policeman!"

People finished off the police officer with whatever came to hand—a
caretaker's shovel, their boot heels.

And his sword was passed to one of the speakers. Who raised it high:
"Here is the executioner's weapon!"

A Cossack hundred sat on their steeds, accepting the grateful cries. Later,
near the station gates, they raised a Cossack up. The one who did the
killing?

A different one?

*　　*　　*

As a young man, Krylov had served in a Guards regiment. He had fallen
in love with a girl from an impoverished family, but his mother, who was
rich and had high connections, would not give him permission to marry.
He presented his fiancée to his regimental commander and obtained his
permission. He presented her to his fellow officers. She was charming and
well bred, and the officers accepted her. So Krylov married. Then his
mother appeared before the regimental commander saying, If you don't
force him to resign, I will file a complaint against you with the War Minister and higher. The commander called in Krylov, who himself decided that
he had no choice but to leave the regiment. He began searching for work in
other departments—but his mother had been everywhere and closed all
paths to him.

He had but one choice left: join the police. . . .

*   *   *

He lay there, killed. Eyes shut. Blood from his temple and nose, down his neck.

Everyone walked up and looked.

*   *   *

Liberals and Black Hundreds, ministers and the State Duma, gentry and zemstvo—everyone has merged into a single enraged gang, raking up the gold and feasting on the people's bones. Explain to everyone that the only salvation is a victory for the Social Democrats.

Bureau of the Russian Social Democrat Workers'
Party Central Committee

*   *   *

[30]

It was so good, she was terrified.

Thunderstruck.

She didn't want time to go on: it would inevitably bring worse. This soaring state would subside—and go away.

Just sit and enjoy it, with not a thought in the world.

Not a one.

So many thoughts, and all of them good.

Much was impossible, but Likonya didn't want the impossible.

She'd seen him on Ekaterininsky Square and gone weak in the knees. She'd realized that if she didn't say something now, she never would. And she would always regret her hesitation.

Somehow her legs bore her all the way. And somehow her throat was able to speak:

"I wanted to tell you. . . . I'm happy to have met you. And now I hear you're going away. . . . So you see I . . ."

He was very friendly. But the usual superficial words.

They started walking side by side. Her arm was shaking, so he squeezed it sympathetically.

But the alley was short. This was the end, and the parting.

He said that what she'd said was marvelous, that there was no need for regret, and he thanked her.

Thanked her *for what?* She was stunned.

And that he had liked her very much right away, too.

But if that were so, why hadn't he once looked at her specially or said something special?

Although between acts, he'd more than likely laughed, aloof. And canny. There weren't any like that here. Tall! High boots. A light beard. (And a light heart?) Such a straight back! And with a Volga freshness. In theater-speak—a shining eagle. That had flown here from a windy expanse.

"You're not leaving for good, are you?" she asked.

No. Right now he was only leaving for five days or so. Then he'd be right back. He generally found himself in Petersburg from time to time.

He kissed her hand.

It all lasted perhaps two minutes. And now there were too few hours for her to make sense of it all.

There was so much of everything, this could not be compared with anything, this was too much!

Likonya had always preferred not telling others everything (and keeping things to herself). But now she wished she could tell him everything!

And she could. She wanted to: everything.

And even suffer from what was left unsaid.

Who should she thank? . . .

[31]

The present Interior Minister's situation had its easy, charming aspects and its intolerable difficulties.

The easiest aspect was the royal couple's sincere affection for Protopopov. How the kindness of our superiors warms us! And how cheerful you feel when you are confident of a friendly disposition toward you from the utmost heights! And what a surge of emotion that had been when last summer, at his first audience, the Emperor had enchanted him so—after everything hostile and malicious that had been said about the monarch in Duma circles—and at the same time to see that he was enchanted by you! More than likely, it was better tactically to conceal his admiration, but the honesty and candor of his nature did not allow that, and Protopopov said everywhere that he was enchanted with the Emperor, thus earning himself irreconcilable foes. But how could he not admire him with all his heart after he had come to know closely this slandered, most august family, not only without cunning, intrigues, malice, or decadence, as their enemies ascribed to them, but living in such heartfelt simplicity—in love and prayer! What a delightful ritual was established: after his report to the Emperor to have the happiness each time to visit the Empress and simply speak with her, not necessarily about his service, about anything at all, about the physiocrats. That high regard was established between their souls which crosses over to the unearthly and mystical. All society gossiped about the Empress with laxity and hatred—and they didn't know how intelligent, cultivated, and firm she was as a woman, in a foreign way, her English disposition.

The minister's chief difficulty was the harassment that came from society and his former Duma friends. Now all Duma comments and mentions of him were mocking, contemptuous, and hateful and treated him as beneath not only the level of a statesman but even that of a human being. Probably never had so much filth been poured on a single minister in a single country as was on him. Accommodating and digesting all this abuse and finding responses to it was impossible. All he could do was inure himself to it and stop letting himself feel. (But he could not stop feeling!) He was hated not for his activities or inactivities but simply for being in this post and being loyal to the Emperor, for what was called betrayal and desertion, inasmuch as the Duma considered itself at war with the regime, and he had been the Duma's deputy president! He had agreed to accept the ministerial post straight from the Tsar's hands. There was no slander they scorned! Although Protopopov had reported to his Duma colleagues in detail about his meetings with the Germans in Stockholm at the time, and they had accused him of nothing, the moment he was appointed minister they spread the slander that he had played up to the Court with his connection to the Germans. All that was forgotten! That Rodzyanko himself had interceded for Protopopov about the ministerial seat, that the English king and English press had given Protopopov an ecstatic review when he traveled there with a parliamentary delegation, that he had been praised by Sazonov, that Krivoshein had also recommended him for the government—all forgotten, leaving only hatred! Now no trifle could be forgotten; he was blamed for everything.

But if they persecuted him that pitilessly, he had something to answer with! They knew him—but he knew their weaknesses as well! They hounded him, spit on him, and sicced others on him, but he would teach them a lesson! Just wait! They would come to regret their deed. As once he and they together had been thoughtlessly indignant at the throne's actions, so now he was smothered in indignation over what the Zemgor was up to. They were unconscionable and brazen in pushing normal state power out of all state life. They operated on public funds alone, strewing money about heedlessly—and here they were lying and giving everyone the impression that this was money collected by society. When Protopopov decided to publish whose money was involved, the shameless liberal newspapers would not one of them publish it because it wasn't to their advantage, the blackguards! Since the Japanese war, the Union of Zemstvos had failed to account for eight hundred thousand rubles—which meant they had spent it on private needs, and only that. The government was cowardly and kept approving all their insanely luxurious budgets, which exceeded the ministries' estimates on all points—and on top of that they had the gall each time to request a few million in "reserve" capital, above and beyond the budget!

So it was with the food supply. Protopopov knew why the matter had to be taken away and given to the governors. Under the guise of food provisioning there had been deception and a collapse of state power: the Agriculture Ministry would be put in the zemstvos' full power, but the zemstvos were not the former, simple, separate zemstvos; they had been joined into a Union of Zemstvos and engaged in nothing but politics. Protopopov had stewed in their pot for ten years, so how could he not know what went on there? Anything to spite the regime! Anything to snatch some for themselves! During a war, whoever distributes food sets the country's mood. The governors were disheartened. They had been deprived of rights in their own provinces, and food and fuel plenipotentiaries were seeing to arrangements instead. Oppositional elements made up the local food supply committees. All they had to do was announce a strike of weighers and warehouse employees and all the grain was halted, for the whole country! If all grain storage were returned to the governors, then the zemstvos would have to serve honestly instead of their oppositionist speeches.

Having spent time on both warring sides, Protopopov understood all this particularly well. But the hounding had doomed him to impotence—and he couldn't bring himself to do battle over the food supply.

On the other hand, he frightened Duma members with rumors that he was going to disband them, that the deputies would go to the front not, as they boasted, with hospital trains, but carrying a soldier's roll. Or that he himself would confiscate landowners' lands, without them—and this frightened the Duma most of all. Without them? (In 1905, when the workers seized his textile factory, but he was chosen director—even then he had organized meetings and handed out pamphlets saying that landowners' lands should be forcibly alienated.)

Indeed, the government's power was boundless in comparison with the opposition—this Protopopov had realized when he came into power. But for some reason everyone's daring had simply gone missing.

Happy plans swarmed in his head—to gain glory and triumph by dividing up the landowners' land. But another time he had the idea of granting full Jewish equality and circumventing the Duma on this, too! (He had already released an initial circular in Moscow.) He would carry out his powerful policy on the waves of public gratitude! He would have great need to get close to the Jews. This would allow him to rely on capital and industrial circles. (He had hastened to free Rubinstein as well, so as not to throw the banking world into the opposition.) He himself was a factory owner, and he understood the power of financial and industrial circles.

He wanted terribly to do something great and good for everyone! He knew it was no accident that he had been appointed to this post. By the Emperor's gracious will he had suddenly soared not as Minister of Trade and Industry, as he had dreamed, but as Minister of the Interior! Not for nothing had he been called upon to save Russia! However, he could not proceed decisively from any point. Everything inside him trembled and swirled out of pride, happiness, and fear. He had a gendarme uniform sewn—but only dared wear it at home. He also had great need of the rank of major general, and through an intermediary requested it from Alekseev—who would not award it, disgusting man.

Even industrial and banking circles had let him down. Counting on them, Protopopov had done things in a big way, putting out his own newspaper to defend and clarify the government's actions, such as was so essential. (After all, it was better not to open the other newspapers; each flung mud on Protopopov.) The most fashionable writer, Leonid Andreev, had agreed to head up this newspaper, *Russian Will* ("will" in the sense not of undisciplined freedom but of an imperative to action), other major writers had promised to collaborate, and banking circles had given money without stint. And the result? From the very first issue, this very same *Russian Will* had cast off its obedience and bitingly attacked Protopopov! A brilliant intention thwarted!

He could not put a stop to the newspaper abuse through his power as Minister of the Interior since his ministry had long not had any power over the press, not even censorship. In both capitals, there was only military censorship, which saw no threat in the ministers' defamation.

The leftists reviled Protopopov—but so did the rightists, with whom he was not close due to his past activities and whom he condemned for not acting decisively enough against sedition. Purishkevich, too, who actually seemed to have hopped over to the left, furiously reviled him in the Duma. Protopopov tried to respond menacingly, but Trepov forbade him to reply. The ministers feared a clash!

When had they conceived such hatred for him? It was a mere five months ago, in September, that he had been appointed, but they had hounded him so hatefully that the frightened ministers had convinced him to go to GHQ and ask to be relieved. Aleksandr Dmitrich made the trip— but only strengthened his position with the Emperor. Just since Christmas he had become a full minister.

They themselves, all of them, had hounded, chafed, and not spared his delicate soul! They themselves had hardened him! "You are wrecking Russia!" they shouted at him. He replied selflessly, "Then I shall perish beneath its ruins!" He had become a lion in the throne's defense!

He wanted to inflict a fatal blow on them all! He realized that the main revolution was seated in the military industrial committees and the Zemgor, but he couldn't make up his mind to touch high-ranking men like Guchkov or perceptive ones like Kerensky. (Although there had been Okhrana agents' reports that Kerensky had spoken about a coup to his Trudoviks directly in a private apartment.) In late January, Protopopov decided to arrest the Workers' Group. If only to throw a bridle over the revolution's face.

Battling revolution and being master of the Ministry of the Interior were all well and good, but to do that he had to master police work, and Protopopov did not have that kind of knowledge (he kept mixing up those Bolsheviks, Mensheviks, and internationalists and never could remember). He needed a strong adviser and helper. To the point, there was such a man: Pavel Grigorievich Kurlov, a supreme connoisseur of the police who had suffered unhappily in the Stolypin affair, losing his high pension, and was now in bitter suspension. Through the Tibetan doctor Badmaev, who treated them both, they had come to an agreement that autumn. Kurlov had promised help, support, and training. It was Kurlov who had had the idea of disbanding the Duma with an iron hand, while simultaneously carrying out popular measures for the Jews and peasants. The Emperor had agreed to Kurlov. Fine, I was angry at him over Stolypin for two years, and then I wasn't. He and Kurlov agreed that Protopopov would take him on as a colleague and restore his former post as commander of the Corps of Gendarmes and later to the Police Department.

But it was not to be. A rumor broke out instantly: "Kurlov again!" And although the Kadets had never had any regrets about Stolypin, now they were horrified and hissed. Fearing even more bitter Duma attacks against himself without adding this splash to the red-hot skillet, Protopopov decided against publicizing the appointment. Kurlov was merely "at the minister's disposal" for a couple of months and signed some documents for him — and was forced to retreat into the shadows, although with a newly secured pension of 10,000. Protopopov lost a loyal friend and remarkable specialist.

On the other hand, the position of Minsiter of the Interior was greatly eased by the fact that in Petrograd, as in all places that were part of the theater of military actions, his ministerial power was nil, none whatsoever. The military authority — previously Commander-in-Chief Ruzsky and now District Commander Khabalov — made all arrangements and was responsible for everything. Thus, all the present street disturbances did not affect Protopopov and he did not have to rack his brains. A fortunate thought flashed: advise Khabalov to issue a notice saying there was enough bread in the city.

How should he run the Ministry of the Interior? He could run it so that his head spun, his eyes saw white, total despair overtook him, and he felt like collapsing, especially if he read all the documents and dispatches; it would take years to grasp, understand, and endure this. But sometimes, after a kind audience with the Emperor and encouragement from the Empress, or after a visit to the Tsarskoye Selo infirmary to see the attractive nurse Voskoboinikova, a surge of happiness and faith in himself, or a pleasant dinner in friendly company, Aleksandr Dmitrievich would be bathed in a soaring, sailing lightness — so that he instantly hovered above all the insults, misunderstandings, and difficulties and drank his fill of the happy awareness of his own omnipotence, success, and triumph. In moments like this, running a ministry only seemed difficult, and in fact no matter how you stepped, how you directed, either things would be fine or would somehow work out on their own.

In this winged state, he had sailed through the previous night with the pleasantest of dreams in his ministerial residence on the Fontanka (the building had been under guard since yesterday) and could count on maintaining this high note all day today.

During the morning hours, he spoke with one official and then another, looked at this file or that—and his cheerful lightness never quit him, and he joked, pardoned (by his nature he had always been indulgent toward human shortcomings), forgave mistakes, was charming, and knew it. (But there had been a lot of mistakes. Even the minister's correspondence had not been handled well during his troubled ministerial months.)

Right then the Empress delighted him with a telephone call from Tsarskoye. This special telephone to Tsarskoye was here in his office always and was never idle; they would talk for hours even. The Empress wanted to know more about these unpleasant street disturbances.

Actually, Protopopov himself did not have a lot of detail, and the reports from the city governor were disjointed, and from yesterday, and had not been updated today, but since he wished with all his heart only what was pleasant for the Empress, and she wished to be reassured, he sent her excellent reassurances over the wires in a cheerful, carefree voice. (In English, as was customary between them.)

Shouldn't you telegraph something to GHQ as well, Aleksandr Dmitrich? After all, the rumor will reach them and they'll exaggerate it and start to worry there, too.

He agreed he should.

Soon after, the city governor telephoned that a police officer had been killed by a Cossack on Znamenskaya Square. Oh, how dreadful! And why by a Cossack?

The poor police. Here was yet another one of the problems Protopopov had not managed to solve. Looking at imperial Russia from the side, even from the Duma benches for ten years in a row, he never would have thought or believed that the police were so utterly impoverished, that policemen were paid only a little more than manual laborers. This was why nearly everywhere was understaffed, the police could cope with nothing without the army, and the police function was being handed over to an inept army. The rural watchmen were generally scattered singly over the face of the Empire, having lost any military aspect, and the police authorities did not even have the right to combine them into county detachments.

Some order had to be issued to inspire the mounted gendarme guard.

Today he worked in his office, and he had many individuals and petitioners to receive, as always. The time had come for his friendly appointment with Gendarme General Spiridovich. Now Yalta's city governor, he had been summoned by Protopopov himself a week before by telegram, at the Emperor's behest. It was quite clear that the Emperor's intention was to appoint Spiridovich Petrograd's city governor, replacing Balk. Kurlov, too, had been asking very much for him since autumn. Spiridovich arrived, but meanwhile the Emperor had left for GHQ—and postponed his audience without announcing his decision directly. And so Spiridovich was left waiting in Petrograd for the Emperor's return, and Protopopov was not authorized to tell him anything officially, but he could make up for that with the heightened affability that came to him so naturally.

"Aleksandr Ivanych! My dear friend!" Going beyond the usual protocol, with two outstretched hands, he greeted the tall, dashing, tight-lipped, reddish-haired general with the gentle but determined step. "Look, I'm like a good-natured sphinx in your path. I received you on the first day of my arrival at the ministry—and you went to Yalta. And here I am receiving you again in order for you to rise still higher—though I myself don't know where. Believe me, I don't. Ha ha ha!"

He did not let the cat out of the bag, nor had he yesterday at dinner. And he asked his dear guest to sit.

"But I am sincerely pleased that this unfortunate Kiev event has not reflected on your brilliant career. . . . This event that so poisoned the life of my hapless friend Pavel Grigorich, who is, after all, your friend as well. It did not affect you, and you came out of it beautifully. And here he was already returning to his former influence—but alas, alas, he was forced to leave us. . . ."

[3 2]

Apparently, this Stolypin episode of five years before, like the sticky skin of a slain dragon, could never be ripped cleanly off General Spiridovich.

Nothing stung him more unpleasantly than mention of the "unfortunate Kiev story," even if in the most well-intentioned way. How many times had he been wounded by even a sympathetic inquiry to which, if he replied, he would have had to pull out over and over the explanation that this had not been within his competence, that he had been so busy every hour and minute guarding the Emperor's person that he could not be catching terrorists, and so on. But even when people didn't mention it, he thought he caught the tacit reproachful memory of the event in their eyes. What especially infuriated Spiridovich was that even those who should only have rejoiced at Stolypin's death—even they expressed false regret or exaggerated devotion to the law.

Spiridovich himself began experiencing irritation bordering on hatred for Stolypin, because of whom he had become a constant object of blame.

Yes, only poor Kulyabko had suffered and been knocked out of a career. It had not reflected on Verigin, who during the war had become the civilian superintendent of Arkhangelsk, the window on Europe. Spiridovich's own service—the lofty task of guarding the Emperor's person—had not suffered at all, of course. But Kurlov had, unfortunately, endured much. Having received Supreme forgiveness after the Kiev story, he once again surfaced among prominent officials in Riga—and once again fell tragically under investigation for abuses. Since the autumn he had once again surfaced among the deputy ministers of the interior and the head of the Corps of Gendarmes—and once again fallen, this time due to Protopopov's weakness.

But right now, in front of his minister, who was so fantastically close to the royal couple, this beaming, confident official, on whom his career wholly depended, Spiridovich could not feign a cold or perplexed expression but chimed in with regret over Kurlov.

Having circulated for so many years in the highest circles, Spiridovich possessed an unerring ability to forge solidarity with his interlocutor, be it a grand duke, an important official, or an influential lady. His art was in making everyone like him.

Right now, too, Spiridovich was watching with all his attention, taking it all in, and trying to understand this almost legendary minister. With his professional eye Spiridovich saw very well that Protopopov was in no way suited to his post. It was almost a joke. As a long-time officer in the police service, an original gendarme, and even a theoretician of security matters who had studied the habits and principles of revolutionary parties (and written two books about it), Spiridovich knew that the Ministry of the Interior was a specialization—and what a specialization! He realized that Protopopov was in no way prepared for this service and even in these few months had not been able to master affairs. Clearly, Protopopov could hold on only with Kurlov, whom he had now betrayed. Protopopov's flightiness and weak will skidded across the surface. Spiridovich also had information through acquaintances in the ministry that the new minister was so negligent that his direct subordinates could not get in to see him for weeks and documents got stranded for months. He had also read how the press had given Protopopov a good tongue-lashing, and he knew all the gossip, that he was accused of psychic abnormality and that he supposedly summoned Rasputin's spirit through spiritualist séances—to ask him for state advice. These last few days in Petrograd he had heard jokes from people he met about how Protopopov was a braggart, loudmouth, windbag, bluffer, and worthy fruit of the State Dumas. But such was the caprice of the Supreme appointments, and who would dare argue! Behind Protopopov stood the undoubted trust of the royal couple, and success always wins people over. How could Spiridovich not join forces with the victor? This would now be his superior, and he had to oblige him as best he could (and divine his weaknesses). These few days in Petrograd, Spiridovich had heard his fill of gloomy conversations, presentiments, predictions of plots and coups (they even named the regiments, officers, and grand dukes), and new anticipated murders of highly placed persons. Even people in court uniforms jabbered freely about all this, and for three days in a row, street disturbances had been boiling up in the capital—and here the Minister of the Interior himself was simply beaming and rejoicing at their fortunate condition! This vivacious blond of average height, with a well-groomed, curled mustache, his face shaved clean, and amazingly beautiful eyes—languishing brown and vibrant, but with a hint of sadness—possessed so much charm and spoke so beautifully, was so lacking in even a shadow of concern, had such untrammeled vitality and quickness (No, he wasn't stupid! And no, you could never prove abnormality), such concentration on his interlocutor, and such frightening candor, unusual in official circles—no, this man was holding on tightly! He knew something for certain, he was reliably sure of something!—and all the gossip lost its relevance and he had to bow before the man's blinding official success. Luck could not be judged!

For General Spiridovich, all this held not psychological but rather the most vital interest. During these days his career was being decided, and he didn't want to make a mistake now. For ten years he had been the head of palace security and in everyone's eyes was ready for administrative promotion. But no matter how exalted his honorable service in Yalta and no matter how visible he was to the royal couple, their gratitude and appreciation for him had barred any promotion. For two years he had been trying to find a way out and up. Spiridovich had dreamed of a city governorship, but Petersburg's—it was for this precise seat that dozens of candidates were vying. Palace Commandant Voeikov had always backed and encouraged Spiridovich. However, it was the Emperor's special disposition that had undermined him. Last autumn the Yalta city governorship—which included the Crimea's entire southern shore, all the places where the Tsar stayed, the grand dukes' estates, and the royal hunting ground beyond the Yaila—suddenly opened up. The Emperor entrusted Spiridovich with his favorite place to live and said he wouldn't appoint anyone else! Thus made happy, Spiridovich simply could not refuse. Seeing him off and giving him a signed photograph (a few of which, actually, hung in this office, and the Empress's, too), the Emperor expressed his envy that he couldn't abandon GHQ and go there himself. But precisely because the royal couple was not living there now, Yalta was turning out to be a professional dead-end. (Actually, he had managed to introduce himself there to a dozen grand dukes.) Over the past few months Spiridovich had written a few letters and had received a few encouraging him with regard to the Petrograd city governorship. So that the summons now was not unexpected. He understood they would be appointing him to Petrograd to replace Balk. And here, treated so kindly by Voeikov, he would have received actual confirmation if only the Emperor hadn't left for GHQ. Now, although Protopopov was pretending he didn't know about the appointment, this was all a sweet, transparent game. Indeed, Protopopov had won him over with his regard. (He'd had a Duma nickname: Sugarman.)

However, as he walked around Petrograd these days and listened to the crowds' shouts on the streets, Spiridovich sensed that these events would affect no one as intimately as himself should he be appointed. Perhaps it was just as well the Emperor hadn't had time to appoint him. Let all this pass

without him. He didn't feel like taking on the capital in this agitated state
(even though he could gain fame by subduing it).

However, the street disturbances were getting out of hand, the Duma
speeches glowed red-hot, and in Petersburg salons there was the same
gloomy, nightmarish air—and suddenly the entire scale of values as it had
presented itself to Spiridovich all these years and last few months in Yalta
had begun to wobble. A sensibly calculated ascent might lead not to success
and honor but to a shaky position difficult to defend. Of course, Spiridovich
was the star of security, not the muddle-headed Balk, and if he were sitting
at 2 Gorokhovaya today, he wouldn't be so helpless and these disturbances
might already have ended. But if not? . . . He was prepared to fight using
tested methods, but what if given the present public revulsion those methods had already failed? Wouldn't it be more judicious to contemplate this in
advance, before the Emperor returned to announce his decision, to contemplate this here and now, taking advantage of his audience with the Minister of the Interior—and then choose another line for himself? Make some
kind of lateral move? Or return to Yalta? If the game was suddenly lost here,
then why engage in Don Quixotism and push to the front with lance in
hand? And if it wasn't at all lost? How could he tell that now for sure?

Spiridovich unleashed all his equally enchanting graciousness—and focused on unriddling the Minister of the Interior.

But lively, smiling, friable, and chameleon-like Protopopov was even
more enchanting, delivering monologues, tossing his head back, and rolling his eyes.

No, he definitely knew something!

Taking advantage of the exceptional welcome at his audience, Spiridovich, in violation of hierarchical etiquette, spoke cautiously about society's
troubled mood and, here, on the subject of the street disturbances.

But like an old personal friend, Protopopov put his hand on his shoulder
and with sincere simplicity, his eyes glittering:

"My dear man! My dear general! When was our public and when was
our Petersburg society ever not troubled? When were they ever satisfied?
Can they ever really be satisfied? You may rest assured that the people do
not—of course do not!—share the intelligentsia's moods. But who are the
people? The peasantry is utterly inert and closed in on itself. The workers are
in the grip of others' propaganda. The *rightists*—as men and as influences—
do not exist. This is a myth, an empty name. No one has organized them.
The clergy is living on a pittance, humiliated and stifled. Tell me, where are
the strata in Russia on which the government relies or can rely? Not the
banks!"

But up close his eyelids were puffy and sore. There was a subtle haze of
perfume.

"There is just one buttress: the spell of the Tsar's name! The people are
generally indifferent to the various parties and programs but not to the fact

that they have a Tsar. And that is our hope. One can hope that all this will pass. It has so many times before!"

And suddenly—agitated, half-ecstatic, with blinding eyes:

"Of course, if need be, we will flood Petrograd with blood! To save the Emperor, we would sacrifice our life."

But he calmed down just as swiftly.

He examined the plan for a major overhaul of Yalta itself and generously allowed Spiridovich not to skimp on office expenses and receptions. Finally he examined a map of the planned addition of land from the Yalta city governorship to the palace department—to expand the royal hunting grounds in the Crimean foothills.

[3 3]

The night before, Himmer had made several telephone calls, trying to convince notable comrades from each socialist group to assemble at three o'clock on Saturday at Sokolov's apartment on Sergievskaya. Kerensky and Chkheidze promised to be there, but Himmer also wanted to bring in the most unpersuadable ones—Shlyapnikov from the Bolsheviks and Krotovsky from the Interdistrict group—because at that meeting he thought to unfold his audacious theoretical plan, or if not a plan, then at least a statement of the question.

Nikolai Dmitrievich Sokolov, who was short and bald-headed but had a thick, strictly rectangular black Assyrian beard, held the most zealous revolutionary convictions but, like Himmer, also did not fit in any party, collaborating with them all. Since he was a well-known lawyer in the capital, the police had never dared violate the boundaries of his grand, richly furnished apartment—and it was the second refuge after Gorky's where Socialist representatives could meet openly to discuss positions and bicker (they never did manage to join forces). Gorky was practically an open Bolshevik, and not everyone would go to his place—Kerensky and Chkheidze, for example—because they were afraid of encountering insult there.

Before the others had gathered, Himmer led Sokolov into his study to try out his sensational new theory on him.

Actually, there was no urgency whatsoever, but these urban disturbances, for the third day in a row, which were not at all new, having happened a hundred times before, reminded him, nonetheless, that one day the genuine, long-awaited events would catch them all unawares.

Himmer had a favorite pose: speaking ardently, at length, and insistently, leaning forward, as if drilling into his interlocutor. In these instances Sokolov would lean back, chewing his lower lip over his beard, and could listen for a long time. He did not have patience for listening to many, but Himmer he respected for his perspicacity (and the knowledge he gained from him).

Here is what had disturbed Himmer of late: We were turning all our attention to propaganda, slogans, and forcing the movement, but who among us was studying theoretical problems? (He alone. In Petersburg, at least.) We shouted "Down with autocracy!" and "Down with the war!" and thought that all the rest would somehow come about. But how? We simply were not discussing the problem of power, which was the chief problem. If there were suddenly a coup, if only a palace coup, and autocracy were in fact to fall or stumble, who would seize power? Without a doubt, the bourgeoisie and no one else. Power should, of course, become bourgeois, otherwise any revolution would perish. Because democratic Russia had been scattered, the proletariat could create fighting squads but not state power. The seizure of power by socialist hands would mean the revolution's inevitable failure. Above all, what was the point when all franchised Russia had also closed ranks for the struggle against Tsarism?

As long as the war was under way, though, there was here an additional and important difficulty: socialist power would not have any moral right to prosecute the war. It would have to end it immediately, and this would mean, apart from all the difficulties of state power, taking on additional new tasks that were beyond its strength: demobilization, mass unemployment, and putting industry back on a peacetime footing. These were beyond our strength and scope, and socialist power would collapse immediately. Therefore, here, too, it was tactically correct to lay the war and the tasks of foreign policy on the bourgeoisie, and in the meantime fight to end the war.

This was quite an audacious thought, and he felt like testing it on his colleagues. The secret was that franchised circles could in no way accept the slogan "Down with the war!" They were supposedly fighting Tsarism for the war's more successful prosecution. Regarding the war, the Milyukov-Guchkov camp would accept no compromise. If a coup were to occur as a movement against the war, internal dissension would kill it. The question of power was not whether to give the bourgeoisie power but *whether the bourgeoisie would agree* to take power. If they refused, it would be a catastrophe. Its mere neutrality would kill the revolutionary movement by handing it over to the elements and anarchy. (Over there, the disturbances were already more like looting.) Any "Down with the war" would be put forth by franchised circles to rout reaction. And here he was, Himmer-Sukhanov, a consistent Zimmerwaldist, internationalist, and defeatist—today he had come to a conclusion and had summoned the nerve to state it out loud: in order to drive the bourgeoisie on to take power more boldly, in order to force it to seize power, we socialists had to put a damper on the "Down with the war!" slogan and perhaps, temporarily, even withdraw it!

This was a devilishly bold decision, a fantastic pirouette! But Himmer was good at pirouettes, being small of stature but powerful of mind, and now he was planning to bring this up for general socialist discussion. This was very bold, but at the same time this was how it had to be done. There was no other way! Outwardly, did this look like a betrayal of basic principles? Well, in fact, it was a brilliant tactical step!

To Himmer's joy, at some point bald, baffled Sokolov began to nod at him a little, first with his eyes and then with his whole head. This inspired Himmer greatly to continue and develop his monologue. Finally, this anti-defensist, this internationalist-Zimmerwaldist, was nodding at him that—yes? Yes. They had gotten carried away with rejecting the war and laid themselves open not only to the loss of a united front with the bourgeoisie but even to a schism within their own ranks. Because even the populist socialists, Peshekhonov's set, would break away at that slogan. But today, defensist Menshevism held sway. Yes, to rescue unity, the brakes would have to be applied to the antiwar slogan. If . . . if it weren't for the Bolsheviks.

Sokolov was himself the Bolsheviks' best friend, there's what. But Sokolov's approval wasn't worth that much because, unfortunately . . . unfortunately, he wasn't that smart.

Oh, those Bolsheviks! Direct, inflexible to the point of folly, incapable of thinking deeply, they merely scraped popular slogans off the surface. Such was Lenin in Switzerland (the beloved and awful foe-ally!), and such was Shlyapnikov here. There was going to be a struggle with them. And there was no assurance that . . .

But Sokolov reassured him that out of the mouth of such a well-known despiser of patriotism as Himmer, such a theory would not sound maliciously counterrevolutionary. Which was good.

These past few days there had been a spontaneous popular movement, but who among the revolutionary centers could reach an agreement with anyone about anything? Turmoil and confusion. Privately they salivated over the idea of creating a Soviet of Workers' Deputies like in '05, but . . . but . . .

Right then Kerensky's characteristic ringing, strained voice reached them from the living room, and both rushed to join him.

Chkheidze hadn't come. Kerensky had come only as a knight of his word, because he'd promised, but he had absolutely no time. After the Duma session now there was a meeting of delegate representatives, and in an hour he had to . . .

Because Kerensky was always running himself ragged, giving endless speeches, and having nonstop discussions, by contrast for a while he liked and was able to accept a more relaxed position in an armchair: his wrists hung from the armrests, his long, narrow crewcut head hung back and stopped still, he held his tongue and even, there, closed his eyes. In moments like this, Kerensky rested up for new impulses and leaps, but all appearances to the contrary, he heard everything said quite well and missed nothing important.

And what was said—now fresh faces had arrived—was that nonetheless the flood of disturbances was unusually great this time. There were nearly continuous rallies on the central squares, leftist orators on Znamenskaya Square were speaking nonstop and unimpeded. Everyone was citing autocracy as the source of all disasters and of the food havoc. The Cossacks weren't knocking anyone down, and one, people were saying, had even ridden at a police officer and lopped off his head. But what was most remarkable was that the residents of the central neighborhoods sympathized, and this would create a favorable situation in the city's bourgeois section. The general mood being created was that the entire civilian population was as one against the military-police authorities, which was remarkable! The authorities' actions, on the contrary, displayed no decisiveness whatsoever, no planning. Their inaction was heartening. All Petrograd, every bureau and editorial office, was doing nothing but talking about the events. The movement was spilling over—and freely! And . . . and what?

And what? No one knew. How much could all this be steered?

All that was said made no noticeable impression on Kerensky, who had turned to stone, not shuddering once, not exclaiming. And this cooled many here. Who if not he would know best? The most brilliant democrat in the Duma! After all, everyone here wanted not so much to tell him what everyone knew as to hear from him what no one knew. Here he had come from a meeting of delegate representatives, that is, from a meeting of just the leaders of the Duma factions, to which a total of ten men had been admitted. Before that he had spent a few hours in the Duma session, and had probably spoken, but that no one knew either. Most interesting of all were the Duma corridor conversations, who had overheard whom—and that absolutely no one knew, but that was where the winds of history blew, and therein lay the entire interest!

Did Himmer not know Kerensky (and admire him, and at times envy his active role)? How many times had he holed up in his apartment, spent the night in his study, talking long past midnight, when Kerensky remained the precarious gentleman in the colorful Uzbek robe, or coughed away in the chilly apartment wearing just a jersey, like a high school student. How much vicious bickering there had been between them, never agreement, and constantly revived disputes. Himmer was sufficiently accustomed to Kerensky's bombastic outbursts, but he also knew well enough his depressive infirmity, when he stumbled and found it so hard to carry on as the thunderclap exposer of the regime. Himmer predicted an even greater role for him in the future. Given his popularity, leftism, radicalism, and inexhaustible oratorical temperament, he could not fail to become the central figure in the future Russian revolution, if their generation lived to see it; he would predict it, without always believing it himself, but Kerensky only chuckled, denying it (though he himself was definitely affected). Himmer even knew the details of Kerensky's illegal participation in underground SR affairs, how he had dauntlessly abused his deputy position and had already been mixed up in police evidence, and the last few months through a certain provocateur he was implicated in a story so sticky that he was threatened, as he used to boast, at the expiration of his deputy authorities next autumn, with if not the gallows then hard labor—and it was more sensible not to think about re-election but rather about emigrating in time; and even his recent bold speech against the throne, from the Duma tribune ten days ago, which was printed nowhere, might have been a mad attempt to perish gloriously in this trap. Himmer was used to it, he knew—but he could never anticipate at any moment the strength and movement with which this violently fiery political impressionist might suddenly switch from pensiveness to an eruption of thoughts and words.

So it was now, having sat immobile through these stories about the allegedly incredible flood of movement, Kerensky seemed to inhabit once again his narrow, youthful body after some invisible flight, looked at those gathered with tremendous significance, and said:

"The Progressive Bloc, gentlemen, is moving irrevocably to the left! Although the bourgeois deputy mass is panicked and bewildered. It is making no attempt to stand on the crest of events but rather is trying to avoid them. And this opens up unprecedented opportunities for democracy!"

His quick glance caught fire, his long face lit up, and his head turned easily on his thin and even overlong neck that was however gripped by a tall starched collar since he had only just been in the Duma—and he began to speak, without preliminaries, instantly ablaze and possessed—about the dazzling combinations that now could be made out of the shattered Duma kaleidoscope, and it was evident how he loved this Duma life and what a virtuoso at it he was.

In this pure inspiration, this cascading stream of speech, Himmer caught new confirmation of his own plan. There! Perhaps the Duma was in fact not lost for the purposes of the proletariat. Kerensky's insights into the future always gave listeners a thrill. This youthful deputy's almost machine-gun speech carried them away and bowled them over.

Himmer felt shy. He couldn't bring himself to bring up his theoretical discovery now, although Kerensky as a revolutionary defensist could in fact have appreciated his idea. But he could also knock it down completely.

They asked questions about the Duma, talked about the Duma, constructed proposals about various positive opportunities—and suddenly Kerensky leapt out of his armchair in a diagonal direction, as if chasing a flittering moth—no longer staying for further discussions but merely remarking as he went that he was rushing off to the seething Duma, but in an hour they could come see him on Tverskaya for news—and left, practically ran away, for his obligations and opportunities.

An hour later Himmer and the Socialist Revolutionary Zenzinov were on their way to Kerensky's. Such was the irresistible, excited atmosphere that the only thing left to do was to prowl around the whole day until its end and late into the night, to go from island to island and later definitely to Gorky's on Kronverksky, only to find out something new, keep finding out what's new.

Kerensky lived behind the Tauride Garden, so they had to go that way down Sergievskaya to Potemkin Street and then take either a left to Shpalernaya or else a right to Kirochnaya—all blocks near the Duma. It was odd: things may have been seething under the Duma cupola, as Kerensky himself had said and described, but this seething had not been conveyed to a single block here. In all Petrograd now there were no quieter, more peaceful blocks than those close to the Duma, the Tauride blocks.

No, the State Duma was neither the movement's center nor its hope, and for some reason not a single person had felt compelled to go there.

[3 4]

In the morning, a professor arrived at the empty library where Kovynev languished and assured him that he had just seen a genuine Cossack attack on Nevsky. Fedya hid a grin. What could a professor understand about a Cossack attack? "They cut them down?" Whether they did or not, the professor hadn't seen because he quickly turned into a side-street. But their swords had glinted. He'd seen it himself.

Fedya's heart sank. It sank because this meant nothing would happen. It was all hopeless. It sank even more over the Cossacks. He felt himself to be nearly the most responsible person in Petersburg for all the Cossacks; after all, it was he whom decent people would be reproaching for every Cossack misdeed. Yesterday by the Kazan Cathedral he'd thought the Cossacks were waking up and would stop acting as guard dogs. Did this mean they were back at it? . . .

He felt a fog, a pull, and once he was free of the library, rather than sit down to his beloved notebook (tomorrow was Sunday, the whole day his own), he again wandered over to Nevsky, or rather, he didn't wander but stepped lively.

Soldiers and police formed a barrier on the Nikolaevsky Bridge, but somehow they weren't stopping anyone; just so people went separately. The sidewalks on the bridge over the snowy Neva with the frozen-in vessels were full, like a proper street.

It was overcast now, there was very little frost, and a fine snow was barely falling.

Fedya expected trouble soon after the bridge, traces of fighting. But there was nothing of the kind, and nothing suggested disturbances anywhere in the city. He walked down the English Embankment, crossed Senate Square, and walked past the War Ministry's lions toward Gogol Street. People were going about their business with their usual preoccupation, carrying purchases, packages, paper bags, briefcases, sheet music.

Only down Admiralty Prospect, to the shouts of scattering boys, did a broken wall of Cossacks ride by, though without touching anyone. All the way to St. Isaac's Cathedral and back.

Parked by the Wawelberg Bank were a few polished motorcars awaiting their rich riders. Right then, after gawking at the intersection of Gogol Street, Fyodor Dmitrich was nearly run down by a cab that raced up behind him quite unexpectedly and gave a harsh shout too late:

"Watch out!"

Fedya leapt out from under the horse itself, which pulled up short; Fedya hurled a curse at the driver, and he back, and his eyes almost took in two young ladies having a private conversation in their swift sleighs, while at the same moment he heard behind him, ever louder and harsher:

"Watch out!"

Again he dashed aside, but this wasn't a cab, it was a mischievous worker type in a Finnish cap, and he was shouting not at Fedya but at that same cabbie, in response and warning. He also managed to frighten the ladies: two little heads turned simultaneously across the middle, suddenly remembering that there was street life—and the worker fellow stuck his tongue out at them.

Fyodor Dmitrich stepped back into the first wall niche and recorded it all.

Nevsky was quite free today from streetcars, which hadn't come out, having been brought to a standstill yesterday, looming over their surroundings—and was spacious for its full length and seemed broader than usual, and for some reason there were no crowds to be seen, contrary to what he'd been told, nor was it blocked off by army formations, but cabbies and private trotters raced along, motorcars snorted, and the avenue's usual public walked densely on the sidewalks, now without any admixture of worker types' quilted jackets; there were officials, elegant ladies, officers, high school students, errand boys, merchant's wives in short fur coats, and shop clerks—and all the stores were doing a brisk trade, since it was Saturday evening, and not a single window was broken, and there were policemen standing here and there, but the only unusual thing about this was that they were in twos.

Unfortunately, everyday life had flooded the unshakeable capital unabated once again.

Perhaps that was for the better, so the Cossacks wouldn't break his heart.

In the snow's light haze, the idle streetcar poles receded into the distance.

At the wide spot near the Cathedral of Our Lady of Kazan, Fyodor Dmitrich was still hoping to see yesterday's sea of heads. No. There was still a crowd, but not such a vast one. And it wasn't doing anything. As if it were about to disperse. On the trampled snowy square the black figures were separate, each unto himself, Barclay de Tolly and Kutuzov, and the arcs of the ribbed colonnade led back toward the cathedral.

Well, if that was all there was by the Kazan Cathedral, then it wasn't anywhere.

Yesterday, like its amazingly vivid sunset, had not been repeated.

True, mounted detachments passed by twice, in both directions, first a Cossack half-squadron, then a mounted guard. They rode for some reason

down the full width of Nevsky, from one side to the other, right up to the
sidewalks, letting their strength be felt—but not threatening in any way.
The public, unafraid, would move aside, and the cabs and motorcars would
stop briefly—and once again everything would move.

He went no farther. Quite tired and partly frustrated as well, Fyodor
Dmitrich returned home as twilight was falling.

Here, soon after, one of his friends from the editorial office notable
among the populist socialists telephoned him at his apartment all excited.

"Well? Did you hear, Fyodor Dmitrich? On Nevsky . . ."

"What on Nevsky?" Fedya replied with a grim chuckle. "I just walked its
full length, to the Anichkov Bridge. There's nothing there."

"People are saying that on Znamenskaya, near the train station . . . There
were shots. And your Cossacks cut down a police officer!"

Oh, the stories people tell! They're making it up! The Cossacks—a police officer?

"Now, I didn't go as far as Znamenskaya. You mean right there?"

"Witnesses are saying . . ."

"There are too many of those witnesses, they've multiplied. Like old-
timers. Don't believe anyone."

And they were silent on the telephone. It was precisely because he
shouldn't believe that he so longed to!

"There's no comparison with yesterday. It's let up," Fyodor Dmitrich assured him. "That means we don't have the forces. But *they* are strong. Do
you know that story of Chekhov's, 'Too Soon'? Impatient hunters arrived at
sunset and stood and stood—no, they weren't flying, it was **too soon.** . . ."

How many human lives did it take? How much emotional strength in
order to endure and wait? Would this *ever* happen at all, if only in our
grandchildren's time?

They were sadly silent on the telephone.

[3 5]

Betrayal is disturbing, like an underwater mystery, like love. Does love
have a reason? Does betrayal?

Back then, in October, Vera herself saw this betrayal born. Her brother
was stunned and seduced from one glance to the next. One evening it took
fiery possession of him. At the Shingarevs' she looked at the uneven bright-
ness of the two brows, and her pride in her brother that Andozerskaya appreciated him was blocked by her fear that this woman had simply taken him,
openly lured him, and he had accepted her glances questioningly but readily.
Then he had vanished for five days, nearly until his departure. After he returned, he offered no explanation. It was understood but not said, and Vera
could not cross that line first. Later, the insane telegram from Moscow that
Alina might turn up out of the blue. Did that mean she'd found out?

Vera now faced the moral right to behave a certain way or not. If she were going to make reciprocal efforts, she would have already tried to exert her pull on Mikhail Dmitrievich. However, she didn't dare presume this right for herself. Although she knew emotionally and intellectually that this would be the only happiness for them both, she didn't dare interfere and encourage the way it flowed of its own accord, in a way we could neither see nor foresee. Her faith allowed her only to wait for what God would send and to hope. As nanny said, our lot is in God's hands.

Georgi had been alive for forty years and married ten, and it was as if he had never lent more significance to his marriage than to a customary, generally accepted aspect of life. Whereas Vera saw in marriage a greater mystery than simply two people's amorous convergence. Marriage meant a different quality of life, a doubling of the individual, and a fullness unattainable by any other means—a perfect fullness, insofar as fullness could be perfect for someone.

She had not seen this doubling and new fullness in Georgi.

For the last four months, Vera had known nothing about her brother. He had written only once. She ran into Andozerskaya from time to time at the library and greeted her, but her rustling told her nothing. And now, all of a sudden, everything had come gushing out of Alina, in telegrams and reproaches, and instantly Vera was castigated as a confederate and harborer of betrayal. While denying this in words, in her heart she had accepted this role—already accused, well and so be it. (He had always wanted to make friends of her and Alina, and now he'd made them quarrel.)

In her heart she did and didn't accept it. You could not concede to those closest to you where conceding was impossible in general. If you admitted that betrayal could be right under any circumstance, then life of any kind at all came to a halt. One must bear, if not the joyous burden of love, then simply duty; otherwise all was confusion and collapse.

But here were her beloved brother and the very unbeloved Alina. There was so much about Alina that Vera didn't like. More than anything she was repelled by her intense, nervous pride, behind which Vera sensed that Alina did not always love Georgi but rather herself and that she wanted him to express his love for her in public. There was so much Vera didn't like it was easier to name what she did.

A scattered and confused feeling arose in Vera.

She could not bring herself to telephone her brother and convey Alina's threat, which she herself did not believe—a threat of suicide. But when he arrived at Karavannaya, now quite embarrassed and even lost, she could hide it no longer.

Georgi immediately turned gray. He dropped onto a chair, not even trying to hide the torment that was moving and tugging at him. His energy and usual confidence deserted him, his firm lips lost their definition, and the skin on his forehead sagged over his eyes.

"You see, I wouldn't be able to live then, dear Vera!" he said frankly.

He had but one wish: to race to see Alina as quickly as he could, instantaneously. Delay would be only more unbearable. I must go quickly! Quickly, a ticket!

But Vera wouldn't let him go to the train station. He had skirted Nevsky, and he had no idea what was happening on Znamenskaya! A Cossack had cut down a police officer there today! In his lost, defeated state—and nothing had been decided, after all—she wasn't about to let him go rushing off to see Alina. He had to come to his senses, spend some time here, with her and their nanny, and regain his strength.

She immediately took it upon herself to go there and repunch his ticket from Vindava Station to Nikolaevsky Station for him. In the meantime, he should wash up, eat, and spend a few hours at home. Their nanny had already plunged imperiously into her own domain. They hadn't cut off the water yet, but what if there isn't any?

Vera wasn't sure the ticket office on Bolshaya Konyushennaya was open, so she went straight to the Nikolaevsky Station. She walked totally immersed, gripped by this emotional tangle into which she was being pulled. How could she help her brother? He was utterly lost and didn't know what to do, and apparently not only pitied Alina but feared her as well. That was so obvious even over the telephone, even now. What was horrible was not the fact that all this had happened and was happening. What was horrible was that Alina had found out and now there was this nightmare of explaining all over again.

She crossed Liteiny going down Nevsky and noticed nothing special, just dense, animated traffic unimpeded by streetcars in any direction and crossing the intersection on the diagonal. A patrol of mounted police guards loomed over it, two horsemen, not interfering in anything. But she went another thirty paces—and there was a deafening explosion behind her such as she had never in her life heard! Her heart stopped, and before she could be frightened there was a second! Everyone rushed in different directions, and so did Vera, in the direction she was walking, but she leaned into the human wall. Everyone had stopped and was looking around, their fear battling their curiosity. Someone who was taller and keener-eyed announced that two bombs had been thrown under the horses, and the horses and one gendarme had been wounded.

Lord, what was this? Vera pushed her way forward as quickly as she could, toward the train station.

The crowd was very dense at the bottom of Nevsky. All Znamenskaya Square was unprecedentedly flooded with people—agitated, idle, expecting something—since the streetcars weren't disturbing them in any direction from Staro-Nevsky or down Ligovka. They were standing by the monument, holding red flags, waving their arms, inaudible. The police were nowhere to be seen in this sea of people, and neither police nor Cossacks loomed on their steeds.

Inside the train station there were more people milling around than could have been arriving or departing. Maybe they were warming themselves.

Not a lot of people at the ticket window. She stood in line.

Why had he become so weak? Why had he lost his footing? His footing in himself. And in love. Someone who loves is always strong.

The snow had stopped drifting on the Nikolaevsky line so the trains were back on schedule. There were tickets for today's late train, though not very good ones. But Vera decided not to take one.

There were no difficulties with the Vindava line, so she repunched for Moscow for tomorrow at eleven in the morning. Well, that was good.

On the square there was the same ebb and flow. It was a little frightening to go back down Nevsky, but otherwise there would be a lot of twists and turns. Everyone had come thronging. Vera now started down the other side of the street.

In the autumn he had left so headlong happy, everything in him singing. And now he was unrecognizable.

Three policemen were standing opposite Nikolaevskaya Street. No one had touched them.

And on the corner of Vladimirsky there were three more. But the crowd was closing in on them, and before Vera's eyes—they rushed them. One policeman raised his arm and fired his gun, another grabbed his sword, and it flashed high over people's heads, and everyone could see—but then a new shot rang out and the sword came crashing down. There was a crush, a crush, and several shouts—and she could move on. Vera started quickly down the sidewalk without looking around. People said the policemen had been disarmed and that was all.

It was odd. They were disarming policemen as if that was the right thing to do, and life went on as if nothing had happened. The public flowed densely and excitedly down the sidewalks. There were lots of bourgeois wives and worker wives such as you never see on Nevsky. Sometimes they laughed at those richly dressed and shouted curses at them.

Once past the Anichkov Bridge Vera left Nevsky. On Italyanskaya and Karavannaya, all was as usual.

Except for this calamity, what a joy to see Yegor at home! (Could she somehow dissuade him from going to see *her* again this evening?) He was wearing an old house jacket they had kept all these years especially for her brother's visits, and here he was wearing it now instead of his tunic, with his military trousers, but also slippers, so domesticated.

Vera undertook to exaggerate both the delay in the trains due to the drifting snows and there being nothing suitable for this evening, but tomorrow morning he'd have a good seat and for certain. She undertook to exaggerate as well the menace on the square and recounted the incidents on Nevsky. Her brother was stunned. He hadn't seen anything like that when he was riding through the city. Actually, everything today, no matter where you took it from, amounted to the fact that the police were not shooting anywhere, the public were easily disarming the police, and the troops were not intervening.

All this seemed quite serious, but at the same time life was apparently going on as usual.

Their nanny stood in the doorway and gasped. "Right over here, at the Mikhailovsky manège, there are mounted policemen and Cossacks, and the police are saying they're more afraid of the Cossacks than the rioters."

At each piece of news her brother leaned back, frowned, and wondered. If it hadn't been from his sister and nanny, he wouldn't have believed it. (Yes, he did lean back, but he was now frowning around-the-clock, and gray, so you could scarcely recognize him, and his eyes didn't shine.) Most incomprehensible was why the authorities weren't taking any measures whatsoever. As Yegor understood it, the government was in disarray.

He was simply ill—such was his entire appearance. And the house jacket on him was as if he'd put it on due to illness.

Was this the very opening for brother and sister to talk frankly? Not about how it happened, naturally, how he'd come to love her (Had he? That's the point! She hadn't seen this new love on his face), but what he should do now. In and of itself, Petrograd was still not complete proof for Alina. (Yegor now told his sister that in October he himself, out of foolishness, had confessed to Alina. Vera liked the fact that this was so direct. This was her brother!) But the fact that he had definitely not told her about his trip—neither when he left nor from the road. And now . . .

"You see, this is very serious with her," he repeated over Alina's letters, rereading them for the tenth time. "I know her, you see, and when she makes up her mind . . ."

Well—that wasn't so. Or not entirely. Was she injured? Hurt? But not in such despair? his sister coaxed.

"And am I really going to be able to convince her . . . convince her . . . ?"

Her brother's spirits fell. And flattened.

How could she bolster him?

Love itself should have supported him—either there, up ahead, for his wife, or from here, behind her back—a tempestuous love? a resplendent love? But Vera looked and listened closely—and with sadness, fear almost, saw no strengthening signs from either one. Instead, she saw confusion and even emptiness.

You mean this gift had not been given him at all?

Clearly, even to him it seemed sacrilegious to go back to Andozerskaya now. His soul sank in gloom. He said he would spend the night here and go nowhere before the train.

For Vera, this was joy. After her brother telephoned Andozerskaya, Vera telephoned her co-worker and gave her her ticket to the premiere of *Masquerade* today at the Aleksandrinsky Theater. She had bought it so long ago and waited so long for this day—but her brother, he was suddenly home!

She told him nothing of the performance.

Yegor had lost his usual rhythm and vigor. He sat a lot, deep in thought, and paced from room to room very slowly. He smiled embarrassedly:

"So you see how things are turning out, dear Vera . . ."

He was already entirely under Alina's mounting authority. He was now preparing only to see her.

The best thing now would be to sit here this evening and together sort through all the pieces, all the threads.

When he thought Vera wasn't looking, his face was drawn.

He wasn't ready at all.

"And straight from Moscow to the army?"

He perked up:

"Yes, straight to the army."

If only he could somehow skip Moscow.

Their nanny fed them a Lenten dinner: fish aspic, mushroom soup, and cabbage turnovers. She had always eaten with Vera, but now, no matter how they urged her to sit at her place, she jumped up to wait on them. Wait on them not like gentlemen but like little ones who still couldn't hold a spoon or drink from a mug.

Yegor wasn't used to her face anymore, but Vera herself saw the crease of grief—today's, for him.

Their nanny didn't say anything. But she couldn't let herself smile, either.

Yegor said something about fasts, that they didn't observe them at the front, except for Holy Week. Pursing her lips, their nanny, standing, looked down at him:

"And so you haven't been fasting, I suppose?"

"No, nanny dear," Yegor said with regret, even sincerely.

"But you need to more than anyone else!" their nanny blurted out, not dropping her stern gaze.

To his own surprise, Yegor's face softened.

"You may be right, nanny dear. I ought to fast."

"No, not ought to. Must!" their nanny said suddenly. "Now's Saturday. We'll go to St. Simeon's for vespers. And you'll confess. And tomorrow you'll have time for Mass before the train. And you'll take communion."

She opened the window vent, and they could hear bells ringing. For Lent.

But when this prospect suddenly opened up so easily and so immediately, Yegor faltered. Clearly he had very much lost the habit. Or rather, he didn't feel like confessing—right now, on this burning matter.

He kept mumbling, bleating that he might not be able to. Next time, maybe.

They reckoned and indeed, tomorrow he might not have time before his train. Due to the disturbances there would be no transit, and you weren't going to find a cab, or be able to ride.

"Well, we'll pray at home!" their nanny was not going to give in that easily.

In the circle where Vera lived and worked, it wasn't done to attend church or observe the fasts, and even speaking seriously about faith was considered ridiculous. So there she safeguarded it like a treasure she kept to herself.

But Yegor's soul wasn't ready, she could tell. She defended him to their nanny, saying he simply wouldn't have time.

Their nanny walked up to him seated, from behind, so he came up to her chest, and she placed her hand on the top of his head, and in a singsong voice:

"Little Yegor-Yegor. My naughty head you are. But there's nothing to be done. Just wait, just wait." With her other hand she took a corner of her apron and wiped her eyes. "And how is it, sure, no children? It'd be a different life."

Her saying it gave him a jolt. Yegor's eyes opened wide:

"It's true, nanny dear, none. It's the end of the Vorotyntsevs."

"And this one"—she waved her hand at Vera—"I can't get her to marry. Wish there was a little one around, though."

Yegor gave Vera a good look, bright and direct. As if they had always spoken of this easily.

Vera blushed but wouldn't lower her gaze. Their nanny had opened up this simplicity to them.

Had she been too conscientious about collecting references for readers? Had she sat overlong in the corner behind the shelves?

And when you did meet someone—he was married. Or tied.

Oh, how nice for the three of them, all together! If just for one evening! Yegor melted.

"It's nice here with you. I'm not going anywhere."

Nor did their nanny go to vespers. A rarity.

It was already growing dark. Their nanny lit the lamps in her room, called to Yegor, and encouraged him.

"For you extra talk is pure affliction now. Stop and have a little sit over in my room, but without us. And pray. O Giver and Provider of everything good, deliver me from every impulse of the Devil."

[3 6]

Today in Mogilev the weather was windy and gray, and thankfully there was no storm. These snowstorms of the last few days on the Southwest roads had greatly impeded army provisioning. (The reports coming in were that there was enough food for three or four days—but, following army habit, of course, they were making things out to be worse than they were so as not to be left short.)

In the morning a telegram arrived from Alix: The three taken ill have a high fever, but no signs of complications so far. Anya is doing especially poorly, has asked him to pray for her at the monastery. Bread riots in Petrograd, but they are abating and will soon be over.

He went to see Alekseev for his usual report. After so long an interval, it lasted an hour and a half. They surveyed the situation on all fronts and provisioning.

The weather permitted the usual suburban outing in motorcars. He left early, stopped by the Brotherhood Monastery (on a city street nearby, behind a high wall), reverently kissed the miracle working Mogilev Mother of God icon, and prayed separately for the poor cripple Anya Vyrubova, for all his family, and for our whole country.

They drove out onto the highway toward Orsha.

After tea the Petersburg post arrived, not held up today: a precious letter from Alix, yesterday's, and long. And also from Maria. He skimmed them greedily, but he had to go to the cathedral for vespers.

He headed out dressed in his Kuban Cossack uniform.

They sang well, and the priest served well.

Returning, he sent Alix a telegram thanking her for her letter. Now he sat down to reread it several times, considering it with pleasure. So many precious details.

She was running tirelessly between her patients and even kept up the official audience. How much strength she had, despite all her ill health, and how much will to summon all this strength! Sunny!

In her new letter she once again repeated her remonstrances of the last few days: that everyone thirsted and even prayed for the Emperor to show firmness.

All these lonely days it had been churning inside him. Firmness—yes. A monarch could not do without it, and he had to cultivate it in himself. But not anger or vengeance. Firmness must be good, clear, and Christian; only then would it yield good fruits.

In this same letter, Alix reminded him of the mutinous speech of a certain deputy, Kerensky, delivered in the Duma about ten days ago. They said he had practically called for the overthrow of the monarchy there. A deputy and an open rebel. That was quite a paradox indeed. But the Supreme Power had already gotten around quite a few audacious Duma speeches this autumn, be it Milyukov's, Purishkevich's, or the mutinous speeches at the congresses of the Unions of Zemstvos and Towns. And so? So nothing. It had all ended peacefully. People had to be allowed to speak, even to express anger. Their excess energy went into that, and afterward they worked better.

Alix also asked about a post for General Bezobrazov (but after the major losses in the Guards, it would be awkward to post him right now) and then to be sure to write the English king about Ambassador Buchanan's conduct.

She was right to remind him of this. Buchanan had long since crossed the line of all diplomatic proprieties and rules. He had openly drawn closer to all the enemies of the throne and had amiably received Milyukov, who had accused the Empress of treason against the Allied cause; Duma leaders and even grand dukes convened at his embassy and said malicious things while discussing intrigues against Their Majesties, if not plots.

At his last audience, at the New Year, Buchanan had exceeded all bounds when he expressed the idea that the Emperor had to earn his people's trust. The Emperor looked with astonishment into the ambassador's cold, pampered face and fish eyes and replied that wasn't it society that should earn the monarch's trust first? He did not even ask him to sit, and both stood through the entire audience.

Since that day, Buchanan had not changed and was intriguing even worse than before.

Yes, he would inevitably have to write to George. So that he would finally forbid his ambassador to interfere in Russia's domestic life. For this weakened Russian war efforts and, in this way, did not work in favor of England herself. George would understand and correct his ambassador.

To ask more—the ambassador's recall—Nikolai considered too harsh. George would find that irritating and even insulting. But Nikolai kept putting off writing even about the lesser point. Because he loved his cousin Georgie and didn't want to afford him unpleasant moments.

Alix also wrote about disturbances with the bread stores in Petrograd; they had smashed Filippov's to pieces. But now the snowstorms had ceased and everything would soon come to rights.

This very evening, as Nikolai sat over Alix's letter, intending to reply, he was brought a telegram from her which said that things in Petrograd "were not good at all."

There you have it. . . . He wouldn't have known what to think, but Voeikov immediately brought a wire dispatch from Protopopov saying rumors had simply spread through Petrograd that the daily bread ration per person would be limited to a pound, and this had provoked a substantial purchase of bread, workers' strikes, and fairly large street disruptions, marches with red flags, and delays of streetcars; a few police officers had been injured and one police chief had been wounded and one officer killed.

This was fairly serious—and the Emperor frowned. But then he read on that, on the other hand, on the contrary, in some places the storming crowds were welcoming the troops, and now the military leadership was taking energetic measures. Moscow was calm.

Good work, Aleksandr Dmitrich. A smart man. (And there it had begun to seem last autumn that Protopopov's attention jumped around and he lacked concentration, evidently as a result of illness. But he had overcome that, thank God. A marvelous man!)

There was also a telegram from War Minister Belyaev saying that measures had been taken, there was nothing serious, and by tomorrow it would all be ended.

Alix might simply have taken her alarm too much to heart, especially with sick children. Affairs of state had to be perceived coolly, and she always got overexcited.

But Nikolai still could not manage to sit down over a letter to his wife. Such a harvest of telegrams: another from Prince Golitsyn, and a strange one, requesting him either to extend his powers or to appoint someone in his place.

Poor Prince Golitsyn, this position was too much for him. How could his authority be wider than as Prime Minister—and with a signed decree halting the Duma's activities at the ready, needing only a date added?

But where were you to find a worthy Prime Minister for Russia? There was none.

He telegraphed reassurances to Golitsyn and confirmed his authority. . . .

What to make of this? Strikes, disorders, but coming to an end? This had happened before.

[3 7]

She actually felt like dying. Yes, dying, so that nothing else could come take the place of this.

She retreated inward—meaning, retreated into his warmth. He was like a river, like the wind, yet emanating warmth—not even the kind transferred from hand to hand. Everything from him was warm.

She lived on this warmth now, not wasting it.

She could almost always hide a bad mood. But such a marvelous mood was impossible to hide. Anyone who saw her asked, What's the matter with you?

You don't read, you don't do anything. You just sit and enjoy this miracle.

Everyone was getting in the way. Even a revolutionary admirer. Go away and leave me alone.

But none of this might have been. He might not have been there at that moment. Or she might not have had the nerve to approach. (It wasn't like her, to approach.)

Likonya knew she was behaving stupidly in the square. But he had greeted her so kindly.

Might he regret it later?

Why had he said, "No need for regrets"? My God, did he believe she'd never felt anything like *that* before? What had he thought of her? . . .

But here's what she hadn't expected: that he would intervene that day again! An errand boy brought a note from him!

Something bad? She ripped open the envelope with a heated fear.

No, something good. . . .

That he hadn't told her everything in the park and definitely wanted to see her as soon as he returned.

But then it had been too soon! Something good—too soon! (As it was, she was already—drained. . . .) This was too much for one day! She needed time! Time to sort out in her soul what she had been given. Why a note as well, and so quickly?

Now she felt like drinking in the note, too. No, he hadn't thought badly of her, no . . .

She thought she might suffocate! . . .

Temper this . . .

Tonight she would have no sleep at all, that was evident.

Oh, this was how it should be! Not bit by bit, dose by dose, but all at once! That's what I want: all at once! I don't care if I do suffocate!

> My cheeks are blazing in the wind—
> He is chosen! He is King!

The buildup of her feelings and their speed was making everything spin inside her, making her dizzy. Wander all over the room! Fling yourself on the couch! Get all twisted up.

Only the hands of the mantel clock kept showing up in a new place, each time an hour, an hour and a half along.

At night she could read poetry.

> Of happiness, God, I have no need—
> My happiness please give to him!

Yes!

[3 8]

Ration cards for bread! Just after eight o'clock at night, in the City Duma on Nevsky, with its elevated fire tower and irregular flights of stairs thrusting upward, in the Aleksandrovsky Hall, where luxurious receptions were sometimes held for foreign guests, a meeting opened of city councilors and the trusteeships for health and the poor.

But such was the agitation that seethed in men's breasts from all that was happening in the city, and such was the need to talk and listen somewhere, that here, in this safe hall, where mounted men could not swoop in, a significant number of politically *conscious* men gathered from all over Petrograd.

They had hoped very much for Rodzyanko himself, but he just couldn't. Who did come and occupy a seat on the presidium was a steady champion on national food provisioning, State Duma Deputy Shingarev.

The mayor, the conservative Lelyanov, who had called this meeting, did not see the issue as complicated. Everyone—the government, the Duma, and society—had agreed that bread ration cards should be introduced, as had been done in other warring countries. They needed to discuss who the materials would be prepared by and how and who would be in charge of compiling the lists and distributing the cards.

But the first speaker, the well-known liberal Senator Ivanov, impassioned, altered the statement of the question: The present assembly could not and should not be struggling within such a narrow framework—the technical introduction of a ration card system. Since we have assembled, we of course must discuss the overall situation. Why was it the government had taken so long to get around to putting the food supply into the city's hands? Now we had to discuss more broadly!

And so the tone was set! Hearts from every end of the hall responded to him joyously! This was exactly what everyone wanted, to talk and listen *in general*! It was light work to make ration cards; the trusteeships would deal with that.

Supporting this impulse as if from the top, with his monogrammed epaulets, councilor Adjutant General Durnovo urged them not to trust the government's promises, including with respect to bread. Right now they were bringing flour to Petrograd, thirty-five train cars a day. But the government should be bringing in fifty a day, otherwise it was our duty to inform the populace.

Applause. Rejoicing. If an adjutant general was speaking this way, that meant the regime had rotted away. Rotted away!

Councilor Markozov tried in vain to redirect the assembly: Stop the incendiary speeches and let's get down to business instead.

What would that be? This compiling of lists and issuing of ration cards? Was he simply mocking the assembly?

But when he dared say that the government alone was not to blame for the food crisis, so was society, that simply pushed away those who had gathered and they stopped listening to him.

But the assembly was in danger of getting mired in trivial matters. The chairman of the city food supply commission read out a tedious report, listing the train cars, of rye and wheat flours separately, and the train cars by poods, and he also went into the production capacity of the bakeries, and it emerged that the city was fully supplied with flour for two weeks, even if not a single train car more arrived, and they were coming in even during the snowstorm at the rate of three fourths of the norm.

Oh, was that really what they needed to talk about? These boring expositions lost sight of the main point: the state's obtuse inability to cope even

with the bread problem! Had they really gathered in this hall from the mutinous city, some on foot from the Vyborg or Moscow side, just to listen to
these expositions? What was important wasn't the bread itself or the lack
thereof but rather its testimony to the authorities' impotence.

At this, the fiery lawyer Margulies rushed for the tribune, and tongues of
fire began to lick the faces in the hall. He did speak *in general*—about incompetence, stupidity, and police restrictions, and not allowing the working class to be elected to the district food distribution committees . . . which
would mean the workers electing their own Central Committee! Clearly,
he could have cited ten times more, and enumerated government abuses,
but the waving of his arms and the splashes of his voice conveyed to the hall
everything essential—and set it afire joyously and irreversibly!

The next councilor demanded seizing the committees by spontaneous
action, regardless of what was thought in the *spheres*.

Spontaneous action was like an alarm bell in the hall. Spontaneous action was the very essence of the glorious 1905 revolution. Each man and
each public organization did what they considered necessary without asking
the government. This was the approach for Russia! Exactly so had the time
now come to act as well! Patches of light from lit fires ran joyously over the
molded ceiling and walls.

Shingarev stepped up to speak. Always a favorite speaker of society, with
his amazing sincerity and that swelling of emotion where tears, already
close, behind one critical brink, might gush, tears of sympathy for those suffering and tears of matured self-liberation, his uniquely sincere voice
touched every heart. He didn't say "spontaneous action" but defended exactly that: the right of workers and society to decide for themselves, without
the authorities interfering! Yes, the city could take up bread distribution itself, but if the government was going to arrange the supply, they should give
guarantees! But wasn't there a trap here? They had led it to collapse, and
the city was going to take up distributing, but if there wasn't any bread,
would the City Duma be blamed?

Stormy, long applause followed the popular favorite.

Then Shnitnikov, yet another councilor, not a leftist at all, stepped up
and threw the assembly directly into the matter: the present government,
being utterly incompetent, must quit altogether! And a coalition cabinet
should come to take its place!

In the thunderous applause, a break was announced; it was unbearable
just to listen when one felt like walking in the corridors and sharing with
everyone else.

During the break they became even more heated, said this and that and
something else a thousand times over, and after the break the tribune could
no longer countenance boring prudence or dull calculations. Now each
speaker spoke about what he wanted to, and the chairman no longer tried to
stop anyone. The session went along in a wholly revolutionary way.

Kagan, apparently not even a councilor, leapt up and sensationally reported on the shooting. Right here, next to the Duma itself, near the Gostiny Dvor chapel! They had fired into the crowd, killing and wounding people! How could anyone talk about bread now here, so close by, in the Duma? Something must be done, something had to be done, and no later than tonight!

"But what's to be done?" people shouted desperately from the hall.

"I don't know what's to be done!" Kagan panted on the tribune.

Then a new speaker came up and proposed standing to honor the memory of the innocent dead.

The hall rose. And the brief silence mounted ominously.

So the assembly ratcheted up its emotions one more notch.

Once again the speaker spoke for the cooperatives: Was the movement really only about bread? Did workers really need only bread and not a part in governing? We will take it all ourselves!

Right then councilor Bernatsky, a professor, spoke. Here is what he said: Maybe they will avert famine. The government may somehow wiggle out of this and avert famine, but that doesn't matter! We won't let the movement that has begun stop! The revolutionary movement must not stop! It must roll out en masse to the end!

Oh, remarkable! The thought gripped the assembly that this wasn't about famine! But let all this run its course!

In this heated moment—who? oh who? whose light, slender figure suddenly flashed through the hall—over the hall—now recognizable, now tremulously welcomed, and now flooded with a storm of applause? Aleksandr Kerensky himself, speaker par excellence, the beloved public figure and fearless revolutionary, somewhat shielded by legality, visiting us! He'd stepped onto the tribune! And now was speaking out of turn.

He said passionately that yes, there had been an opportunity to resolve the food question, but the dimwitted government, as usual, had not heeded the voice of society—and that opportunity had been lost, lost, lost. Now that the situation was quite hopeless, the government wanted to wiggle out of responsibility and dump everything on the city governments. This seemed like a concession but it was a Trojan horse, and society should not let itself be fooled! The city must set firm conditions so that the government then would not interfere at all in the food supply question. Or in anything else! It should remove itself then entirely! The populace should be given complete freedom to call assemblies about bread. Freedom of assembly!

Right then yet another State Duma member appeared, Skobelev, who had not been noticed at first in Kerensky's glow. This man had boyish good looks and a ringing, pleasant voice, but a foolish face—on the other hand he was a well-known Social Democrat. He explained to the assembly that the food question could not be solved in isolation because it was too closely tied to the political question, and the political question was even harder.

The government's present distress had to be exploited! The government had found its path of struggle with the food crisis: *firing on the mouths to be fed*. But we who were present here had to brand this treacherous method and demand retribution! The government's hands were red with the people's blood and it **must go**!

At this Samodurov, a worker from the Lessner Works, a Bolshevik from the hospital fund, spoke, saying that the modern state apparatus could not be fixed in any way, shape, or form; it could **only be razed to the ground**! Tranquility would come to Russia only when the present government system **had been ripped out at the root**!

Applause.

The atmosphere of '05 is exactly what we *want*! We *want* to breathe that stormy air! Let our ranks become more harmonious! The pressure on the government more violent! So that it topples over!

Once again a slender Kerensky loomed up and sternly called on the assembly once more to stand and honor the memory of the workers who died today.

And the assembly rose once again.

A rumbling ran through it that they were going to bring the bodies here now.

[39]

Today, Saturday evening, at the Mariinsky Theater, Sasha Ziloti and George Enescu were giving a concert. So naturally Maria Ilyinichna went.

And naturally Aleksandr Ivanovich stayed home and relaxed and enjoyed these hours with her gone. Certainly, he had no wish for the street disturbances to detain her on her way home, but that possibility did not trouble him in the least.

Then tomorrow, on the contrary, she would be home and he would go somewhere, just so as not to sit with her on a Sunday evening and feel her sulking. He would pay Kokovtsov a visit and talk about finances perhaps, or go to see another retired man of state. They liked to talk and there was always something to learn from them. He could even go see the young Vyazemskys, the brother or the sister.

Even he was beginning to be scared by the fact that he wasn't simply bored with her but repulsed whenever he looked at her. Then it would pass. There were years, and not so long ago, when they were here in the Petersburg apartment and their paths didn't cross at all. During Duma sessions Guchkov lived here alone, the children were with their governess, and the parents took turns as agreed, amazing their children. They would race to see their Papa, but Papa had left two hours ago and put the key for Mama somewhere. Or they had just seen Mama off but Papa was back. Oh, Papa, how could you be late?

The last few months, since Lyova's death, despite his inability to forgive her—how could she not safeguard the boy? a wooden, unmotherly heart— despite this, on the contrary, with the two remaining younger ones, they began living together.

Together in a manner of speaking.

Maybe because they were older. Because they didn't have the strength to rake over all their misfortunes. Because they had no strength left for drastic individual actions.

But when Maria Ilyinichna was here in the apartment, even if behind three walls, his chest felt like it had an angled stone pressing on it that wouldn't move. Even if she wasn't expected to come into his study and say something, to roil him. So he liked it when she wasn't home.

This is what a bad marriage is: grief—utterly undeniable and ineradicable. No matter how the rest of one's life is going, brilliantly even (though it wasn't . . .), a miserable family life gets embedded like a spoiled lung or liver that can't be replaced, a sickness that doesn't let you forget yourself.

And the constant, years-long, irremediable regret: Why did I marry? Why did I marry at all?

All this coexisted in his masculine soul: to have freedom of movement, not to let his hands and feet be bound—and let them be bound, let them sink in! Unfortunately, these two things never came *simultaneously*. Crowned by the gods was the husband sent both these things *simultaneously*.

But how does it begin? How are these first scratches made on the skin? You don't notice them, like when you've been moving branches aside, and later you look: When did I scratch myself?

Your thirtieth birthday was fast approaching. It was a late, warm Easter. Znamenskoye outside Izberdei, the Tambov estate of the cheerful, numerous, and hospitable Ziloti family. He and nineteen-year-old Masha were riding in a char-a-banc. They drove into a woods and it began to rain. Aleksandr stopped the horse and opened his rather heavy waterproof cloak wide—for Masha. No. No? I mean yes, but for him as well. And with a decisive movement she took it—but only half the cloak. It was that one movement more than any other words, conversations, or glances—she had accepted his shelter, shared it with him, shoulder to shoulder.

And became etched in his soul? Maybe not. Maybe it was her later suggestions that this movement had decided everything. He forgot.

But what a cheerful home! A noble family but strongly oriented toward the arts. Even Znamenskoye itself was special, with its gate tower and its special Church of St. Jacob. Its two exceptional pianists in the parlor without ceremony: Sasha Ziloti and his cousin Seryozha Rachmaninov. Her older brother, Seryozha Ziloti, a naval officer, had fallen in love at the Lipetsk spa and had brought to his parent's house as his fiancée—Vera. This Vera was mad about the theater, which was forgivable for a young girl. No one in Russia yet knew this Vera's last name: Komissarzhevskaya. Her marriage to

Seryozha never happened, but there was so much merriment, infatuation, and noise among these young people!

Another year or two and you, despite your youth, were already a member of the Moscow Municipal Board. And suddenly—a bouquet. For him—from her. From the girl he'd been with in the char-a-banc. . . . A game, and who at that age doesn't play? Reply with a gallant letter. Courtesies easily accessible to someone who has read French novels (and if he also has French blood himself). Masha did not miss a beat: There's something about me you don't like! Tell me what exactly! Oh, perfidious Vera Fyodorovna! I thought she would tell you only what would please you, and she evidently told you everything. Now you've put me on the spot. But it's still a question whether you will be better off if I like everything about you. Another letter and another, and Masha was already trying to elicit from him *just her name!* Just the name of the one you like! Don't answer directly (and what if there was no such specific name?) but something like this: "Here you write that you have changed greatly, then this name might change, too. . . ."

But all this grew hazy and pale and receded. He saw Vera more frequently, and she passed on Masha's letters. They were friendly somewhere where Aleksandr no longer went, but Vera was also friendly with Varya Ziloti, and now Varya had married Kostya Guchkov—and it was to them in their Moscow apartment that the costumeless, moneyless, fameless Vera, having arrived from Vyshni Volochok third class, had her brilliant first theatrical tryout for an ingénue role.

Today several photographs of Vera hung in his office legitimately, as if beyond jealousy: her alone, embracing Masha, and with Masha on a stack of logs by an old provincial fence—Masha with a seeking and Vera an aloof gaze.

Why had his path and Vera Komissarzhevskaya's crossed so early on, through all those Zilotis? But our eyes happen to fall on something, something waylays our will, something tongue-ties us for a few brief hours or days—and something that was let slip later drags on for years? The breast of the warrior and conqueror doesn't sense immediately that it has been given to inhale a scent of superior caliber. The sharp glance of a fragile woman sees something in the distance over the conqueror's shoulders that is more important. The years. This string of women is secondary for you, while she experiences it as the collapse of love and is sick with grief. During those very years when a lead-footed Guchkov was emerging on the political arena, Komissarzhevskaya was taking an airy step onto the theatrical stage, late for a woman. So much coincided: nearly the same age; he had created his own party and she her own theater; he had fearlessly countered the newspaper howl and so had she; he was a practical man—but by what miracle was the artist so precise in practical matters? He was delivering his best speeches; she was playing her best roles. Only he as a man still had many years, maturity, and strength ahead, while she was full of doubt and moving toward a crisis. She had had the daring to cut her theatrical path short when it seemed wrong. (At the time Guchkov did not yet know that he would soon have need of this daring with respect to his Octobrist party.)

Guchkov was not simply an admirer collecting her programs and photographs and sending her huge bouquets like some merchant; the barrier of a loge locked up his rapture—rapture at those tears, too sincere for acting, when the soul snatches up out of a body something weightless but still too weighty for itself, at that bewitching voice that took him beyond his very heart. Often he held her living hands in his own, and he saw her eyes—too blue, too visionary—as closely as two faces can come. But to say, "Follow me!"—that he never could. He didn't dare.

Because *she* couldn't *follow*. Like the rare man, she knew her lot: to follow her own path to the end.

Aleksandr Guchkov, who all his life had been engaged in the movements of tangible masses—party supporters, army columns, hospitals, lathes, capital—was favored with this contact only briefly—with this intense, never cheerful angel who had wended her way toward us and now was moving off.

No, not an angel. She was a woman, and she too was racked by what was most carnal, but what vouchsafed ordinary women undiluted joy led her to depression and to a new impulse—to purify herself and soar. She was a woman, but in her roles she played not women but their souls. With her disturbing voice and frail frame, she brought out—sang out—their unusually complicated souls with great inner anguish, to our eternal puzzlement.

She passed through Aleksandr Guchkov's life as if she were a simple companion, jester, intermediary (a bouquet, a note from Masha, requests to buy something in Berlin for Masha's mama), telegraph kisses to him, and equally to Guchkov the father, but only later, after her death, was it understood that she had passed like an otherworldly shadow in order to leave him with a permanent loneliness, to show him another level of being, not the futile one he dealt with, and another level of possession, not the one a warrior forgets in an hour, but a dried flower that is nonetheless fragrant with immortality and races under his armor—or ribcage? For as many years and battles as he had left until the final one.

She moved through—and melted away. Having decided her next turn—to abandon the theater—at this intolerable fracture she left life, wrapped in a pseudonymous cloak of contracted smallpox. She died very far from Petersburg, as far away as she could get—in Tashkent. She died right during those weeks when his struggle demanded that he summon all his forces, when he became president of his Third Duma.

There was some meaning, some fate (or joke) in the fact that it was Vera who was constantly passing something on from Masha, reminding him of

Masha, inclining him toward Masha: In Masha you'll find the person you need more than anyone. Who could live with someone as crazy as you? She'll always do everything for your happiness. Masha is an exceptional person! There, char-a-banc or no, the shared cover of a cloak, but this forgotten seed would not have been allowed to grow at all had it not been for Vera's constant encouragement: Masha is a choice individual. Take a closer look!

Vera seemed to be making up for what she herself could never give on this earth: she had the husband who betrayed her marry the woman with whom he had betrayed her. And she gave her other friend to Guchkov instead of herself. And having married them, she smiled for another seven years, and joked, and bore their jokes, and invited them to Italy, and visited them at Znamenka. . . .

Guchkov was lost in thought when the telephone rang, finding him in front of Vera's photographs on the wall.

So lost in thought—What were those days in Petrograd and what was this vile government we had, and what was to be done about it?—but the warrior was not allowed even brief minutes of mournful forgetfulness.

The telephone rang. And they informed him that the police had arrived at the Workers' Group premises on Liteiny. They had arrested representatives of the workers' cooperative gathered there and also two members of the Workers' Group who had been spared since the February arrests!

All his melancholy and distraction evaporated, and Guchkov reared up as if his foot had been stepped on! Oh, the endless obtuseness! Oh, how sick he was of them. Curse them! How he hated them. When would we be rid of them? In February they'd broken up and arrested the Workers' Group—and you might as well have smacked into a stone wall. Then in Moscow they'd banned even the congress of War Industry Committees. They were trying to choke all vital activity! They lived in constant fear for themselves. Incapable of anything, they wouldn't let anyone else do their work. He had moved the congress to Petrograd, where it was banned as well. According to police department reports, the congress would begin with an expression of no confidence in the government. (That was the intention; their intelligence was correct.) He complained to Rodzyanko. Rodzyanko got permission for the congress to open. But the local precinct didn't know and came to shut it down. Back to Rodzyanko, who furiously telephoned the city governor: "I'll come myself and throw the officer out by the scruff of his neck!" They opened at last. So now they'd reached out again for the Workers' Group.

But what was this? What had they found fault with? What were they doing?

Yes, the cooperatives had discussed whether to elect a Soviet of Workers' Deputies.

No, you couldn't let them!

He twitched—and called the city governor. He himself wouldn't come to the telephone, and they mumbled that outsider workers from different factories had been present at the assembly. . . . But what if they had?

Again he called Rodzyanko, who also started roaring like a bear into the telephone.

Clearly they had to go right now, that night, straight to the city governor's offices and kick up a fuss.

No, straight to the Prime Minister's residence!

This they could not concede. Specifically because the street disturbances in the city had not been a success and had already cooled down, they had to hold the line at the War Industry Committees and Workers' Group no matter what! This was the useful lever Guchkov had found that could shake the state. For him it was a substitute for the Fourth Duma, to which he had not been elected, and a firm staging ground for the Fifth, next autumn. The Fifth Duma would be his last sure attempt, at age fifty-five, to take his place in Russia and also turn it around and save it.

Otherwise, he had been toiling in vain all these twenty years. There is no torture worse than impotence, to live in a country and not be able to influence its life—in any way.

So you see, he sat home alone that night and dreamed. . . .

[40]

Okhta had been cut off from the city all day. Troop detachments had been stationed on the Peter the Great Bridge, on the Neva embankment, and between Okhta and the Vyborg side and weren't letting Okhta residents go anywhere. Not many started across the river on the ice either because the Neva ice opposite Okhta looked unreliable, and it was spring ice, and opposite Smolny here and there water was already nearly knee high. So all day they didn't know what on earth was going on in the other districts or across the Neva. Someone had gotten through and told stories about large crowds walking through the streets there, troops everywhere, and not a single factory operating.

But Okhta was like a separate town, anything but a capital. Okhta residents crowded through their one-horse streets, gathered in circles large and small, argued, and sometimes speechifiers spoke, whoever had a glib tongue.

Police patrols passed through occasionally, but they weren't up to dispersing crowds as large as that. Occasionally a Cossack patrol would ride through and cut the air with their whips—but just to give them a scare. They didn't touch anyone.

Where Okhta residents recognized disguised police informants in the crowd, they gave them a thrashing.

There was a rumor, though, that this was not going to end well. That if a general uprising were to start, the authorities would detonate the Gunpowder Factory and all Okhta and half of Petersburg would shoot straight up in the air.

Not everyone had dispersed even as night fell. People were noisy and wandered through the streets long after. Here and there they started bonfires with boards broken off government fences.

On the embankment by the St. Elizabeth Community Hospital, a dozen or so Cossacks were watching one such bonfire in mounted formation.

And the people at the bonfire watched them back, making loud fun of them and whistling at them. Because it chafed their gut. Why were they standing there? What kind of overseers were they? Loudly about them:

"Heroes for sale!"

"Curly-haired knighties!"

Children and adolescents, too, would run up close and throw snowballs at them. They felt like whipping the children, but there were adults nearby.

All right, pretend they weren't there. An elderly factory hand who was also tipsy and had a voice like a wail climbed onto a pile of solid snow and talked about '05.

"Minister Witte himself crawled on his knees he did before our Nosar, that he did! But they took it all away from us. And all because of those long-curled dogs!" And he pointed that way, at the Cossacks. "T'weren't for those whips of theirs, it'd still . . . Bastards they are, that's what!"

He aimed a hard stare in their direction. Everyone did.

And all of a sudden the Cossacks—they heard everything!—quietly began to move. Forward. Toward them!

The crowd froze. Running away was disgraceful—but how could they stand their ground? It was terrifying.

Instead of leaving it at that, one fellow saw what was what, snatched a firebrand with his mitt from the fire—and threw it straight at 'em! And accurately: one Cossack barely dodged it, shook it off.

They shouted something threatening.

"You're in for it, you Tsarist toady!" someone shouted desperately as if they were slaughtering him. "Get 'em, boys!"

And they chimed in:

"Get 'em!"

"Get 'em!"

The crowd stirred—one went for a firebrand, another for a piece of ice, a third threw a sharply broken off board. They howled! Whistled!

The Cossacks backed up on their steeds. To the cross-street. Backed up at a march—but pursued by boards and pieces of ice.

And then the Cossacks fled at a full gallop.

"Hee hee hee!" The crowd made merry and hooted. "Got the hell out, you swine?"

In the sky, the northern lights played intensely. Blue and red.

[41]

*   *   *

Before darkness fell, the demonstrators near Gostiny Dvor started singing revolutionary songs and unfurling banners saying "Down with the war." An officer from the 9th Cavalry Regiment's training detachment who had come to the narrow street by Gostiny to rest warned them to stop. In response, several gunshots rang out from the crowd, aimed at the officer, but they wounded one dragoon in the head. The platoon dismounted, opened answering fire on the crowd, and killed three and wounded ten. The crowd scattered.

It was these dead bodies that were later carried to the City Duma.

*   *   *

Only this evening, on the third day of the city disturbances, were the first communiqués about them sent to GHQ, from the Minister of the Interior, War Minister, and General Khabalov. All three dispatches made it clear that although there had been a few disturbances, they were being put down successfully and practically without bloodshed.

Meanwhile, the authorities had lost the day in all respects. The crowd could plainly see that the police had been isolated from the troops and the troops would not put them down.

*   *   *

Quite a few police stations on the outskirts had already been stormed and lost contact with the center.

Police Colonel Shelkin, who had served forty years in one of the Vyborg precincts—the workers knew him well—changed into civilian clothing and a leather jacket, wound a kerchief around his head as if he'd been wounded, and was taken somewhere to hide while the police were being stormed.

A police officer from the remote Gunpowder precinct hid from the crowd in an entryway, bought some rags from the doorman (who demanded 300 rubles), and in this guise, that night, once everything had calmed down, went to his family's home on Nevsky.

*   *   *

By ten o'clock that night, every last demonstrator had left Nevsky and the central streets were peacefully deserted except for military-police posts here and there. There were also patrols of mounted guards, dragoons, and Cossacks.

All the demonstrators had dispersed to their homes and were sleeping peacefully, unconcerned about raids, searches, or arrests.

So went the revolution.

And in the daytime it wasn't too cold, so go on, go demonstrate.

*   *   *

The Emperor's brother, Grand Duke Mikhail Aleksandrovich, and his spouse Natalia Brasova drove from Gatchina to the Mikhailovsky Theater for a French performance. But noticing the accumulation of people on Nevsky and having learned of the police officer's murder that day, under that grave impression, he decided not to go to the theater and spent the evening at the apartment of his secretary, Johnson, writing letters. After the performance he picked up his wife at the theater—and they returned to Gatchina.

*   *   *

Places of entertainment—theaters, movie houses, and the better restaurants—were full that evening, as usual. At the imperial Aleksandrinsky Theater they premiered Lermontov's *Masquerade* in a production unusually sumptuous even for imperial theaters. Preparations had been under way for several years, and it was expensive. At the end of the performance, following the director Meyerhold's conception, instead of the usual curtain they dropped a transparent black tulle curtain with a white wreath—and behind it a skeleton wearing a tricorne walked by silently. The success was grandiose, and Yuriev, in whose honor it had been done, was in rare form. He got a lot of applause, and then they honored him with an open curtain—and he was presented with a gold cigar case with a diamond eagle from the Emperor and a diamond eagle from the Dowager Empress.

However, the public dispersed instantaneously: a quarter of an hour after it was over there wasn't a single cab or automobile to be found and the square in front of the theater was empty.

The city was deserted.

*   *   *

Late that night at the city governor's offices reports were heard and the day was discussed. Commander Troilin of the 1st Don Regiment decisively rejected the idea that a Cossack could kill a police officer. Police officials kept insisting that that was what had happened. General Khabalov, displeased with the Cossacks' behavior over the past few days, decided to keep them in the barracks for tomorrow just in case. He was waiting for cavalry units from Krasnoye Selo and Novgorod to replace them. And the cavalry, in dispersing the crowds, had worn out their horses, which had not been watered all day and had nothing to give.

But what could they do? After listening to the reports from the chiefs of the military districts, everyone spoke out in favor of the energetic use of weapons.

Should they use weapons? Independently, without an order from above? Khabalov reluctantly gave his consent. If the crowd was large and aggressive and had flags—after three warning shots, open fire. And a vigorous new appeal to the population was ordered composed.

The Okhrana reported at the meeting that the rebelliousness was evidently going to continue tomorrow as well, but the leaders still had not agreed on a plan.

Nor had the Police Department. Arrests? Arrest whom? In what numbers? Wouldn't that be worse? No one had reached the point in their thinking of intimidatingly large-scale arrests. Five well-known members of the Petersburg Committee of Bolsheviks had all been arrested because they had gathered at a single apartment. Some had been picked up at the Workers' Group premises on Liteiny. This wasn't exactly inaction.

Protopopov, too, came to the city governor's offices. Everyone was shocked by his hysterically elevated mood and glittering eyes. He delivered a pompous speech of gratitude to the loyal defenders, ordered that his gratitude be announced in a decree on the city governor's office, the dead be remembered in prayers, and subsidies issued to the wounded.

"Pray and hope for victory!"

*   *   *

That evening, soldiers strung a telephone line down Nevsky. They lit fires to keep warm.

*   *   *

The streets were deserted that evening, so hardly anyone saw the rare and intense display of the northern lights. Across the sky, beyond the clouds, flickered tongues of light, bright blue, violet, and red.

[4 2]

At long last, everything in the city was deeply calm. But even during the day no noise had reached the apartment on Mokhovaya, the Prime Minister's official apartment, which was in a fine old building. Now the heavy shutters had been closed, completely enclosing the room's expanse, and inside, each sound was distinct and separate—the ministers' murmured discussions and all the twelve brightly ringing strokes of midnight by the grandfather clock.

Where hadn't this Council of Ministers convened (by no means or even especially this one because its makeup was constantly changing)—in the Winter Palace, at the Mariinsky, at Yelagin Palace, at GHQ, at Peterhof under the chairmanship of the Emperor himself, whether they wore their uniforms and all their medals, black frock coats, or blindingly white tunics? But even the very longstanding ministers here—Bark at three years, Shakhovskoy at two (though the longest serving, Grigorovich, was ill and not present)—they had never convened in this apartment, not under Goremykin, not under Stürmer, and not under Trepov. This government had no visceral memory of the years when ministers were blown up by bombs, and there had been no occasion for them to meet so late and in such secret. Perhaps because Prince Golitsyn had no wish to ride through the city twice, he scheduled the session not for the Mariinsky but here, at his home, once everything calmed down. The ministers' automobiles were driven off the street and into the courtyard so as not to attract attention outside.

No one could have thought they were hiding or reproached them for it. They might not find another time during this alarming day due to the city disturbances. And now, having traveled through the night, it felt as if they had come to another, calm city.

But they themselves understood that they were hiding.

This apartment had rooms intended for formal receptions and dinner parties, but none for a business meeting. They gathered in the large salon and sat wherever they could—at the figured varnished oval table, at the small round one on the side, simply in armchairs, on side chairs, and on the gilt sofa with the dark green velvet upholstery. A chandelier burned, but not too brightly, not so that they could write very much, but then no minutes were expected for this night session. There was no secretary, and the ministers themselves expressed no inclination to take notes.

They did not assemble all at once or steadily. For a while they conversed privately, in low voices, in twos and threes, mostly not about the matter at hand. They had never been a genuinely united government. Each minister could conduct his department's policy fairly independently, reporting to and receiving instructions from the Emperor himself, but the ministers were not briefed on foreign and war policy, and even the Prime Minister knew little about them. And now as well the ministers had been shaken up and refreshed many times; five had been there for two months, including the Prime Minister himself, three only since November. They had not had time to become as familiar with each other as they should, and they anticipated new reappointments and dismissals on a daily basis. None of this inspired confidence.

Among those gathered, it was not the Prime Minister who stood out but the Procurator of the Holy Synod, Raev, a large man in the prime of his years and powers, despite his clerical arena bursting with health, good cheer, and appetite. His unctuous gaze and curled, cavalierly turned-up mustache expressed this joyous zeal for life. He comported himself here nearly more freely than anyone else—it was no mean trick staying in his post for six months, a veteran.

But these frequent replacements made the real veterans, Bark and Shakhovskoy, feel they had overstayed and were outsiders. They were the last of the eight ministers who had dared sign the collective ultimatum to the Emperor in '15 (at the time, that had been a daring impulse). Five had been dismissed long ago, one had died—and they alone had not been allowed to go. They had begged the Emperor to let them resign two and three times each, not waiting to be driven out, but he would not let them. Actually, up until the recent alarming months, Bark himself had held on capably. His path to becoming Finance Minister had been too long. He had once promised Stolypin the Russification of credit, and when he had become minister, he had unwittingly begun to make it increasingly cosmopolitan. He himself had run a major bank and was close to the bankers Manus and Rubinstein, and he would not allow state oversight over the banks. Goremykin liked him, he wasn't impudent toward Rasputin, he avoided pointed disputes in the Council of Ministers, he tried to please the English, and the Emperor considered him irreplaceable. But what was the use of this now, when he keenly sensed the whole edifice wobbling?

Also these last few days, Bark—well-fed and robust, with a fat, widely spread and also curled mustache—had been covered in nervous boils and sat there ill and indifferent.

Pokrovsky sat on the sofa mournful and drowsy, his gaze aloof. He was a favorite of society and an expert on economics, but in November he had been reappointed from State Control to the Ministry of Foreign Affairs—appointed, like everyone now, inappropriately. In these three months he had already asked the Emperor's permission to resign four times—to no avail.

Bald old man Kulchitsky, since January the Minister of Education, who seemed taken straight out of a Griboyedov character from the bygone days of Ochakov, was sitting in the corner with an expression of bafflement, as if he hadn't quite heard or seen, not taking ideas in at all.

No one in the room was smoking.

In all, the government consisted of a fateful thirteen. The Duma simply would not let them create a fourteenth, a Ministry of Health. Only if a given minister—today, the Minister of the Navy, Grigorovich—failed to show up could they maintain a decent twelve. Actually, Protopopov still hadn't arrived and was awaited.

Actually, also summoned to today's session were the military district commander, Khabalov, and the city governor, Balk. They had arrived earlier and were already sitting there, on either side of the grandfather clock.

They sat on either side of the clock turret like guardians of the overwound hands of the ebbing night.

Protopopov was the one who was late, holding everyone up! But during such ominous days, might the Minister of the Interior well be busy with incomparably more important matters?

Protopopov was not on his way. It would actually be better if he never arrived at all and cracked his head open somewhere. Without him, even this colorful cabinet might continue to exist and reach consensus. But not with him!

At last he showed up, wearing a magnificently tailored suit, gray, to match his graying dark brown hair, his magnificent mustache exquisitely curled, to the ladies' taste, and a smooth-shaven face, and as he walked he worked his elbows slightly, as if he were lightly shaking himself off. If not for his stoop, he would have been very well put together.

So, could they begin? Prince Golitsyn was sitting by the wall in a high-backed armchair to support his weak spine. Now they started out with a distasteful explanation. What were those arrests last night and again in that ill-fated Workers' Group? At such an important and critical moment, how could such recklessness be permitted?

Protopopov looked like an actor who has just taken off his makeup and had yet to extinguish the sharp gaze from his complex psychological role or lingering movements, which were too showy for the dull assemblage here. He was still entirely hovering at that great height, and here they were asking . . . ?

No, he definitely knew nothing of this incident.

But how could that be? It seemed to have been especially for propaganda purposes—striking at the same sore spot. . . . Here Kerensky had already grabbed hold of this, as had Guchkov. In the present overheated situation, could we really allow this?

No, no, my friends, the Minister of the Interior knew nothing. (Protopopov had this habit of saying "my friend" even at first acquaintance, and after a dozen sentences, for sure. An excess of good will gushed from him, and so sweetly flattering was his manner of conversing even that he was called "Sugar Honeyson.")

Well, will our city governor explain this?

No, General Balk did not know either.

General Khabalov?

Even more so.

Ah, there, they had neglected to call in the head of the Police Department.

Here you go. Working his elbows a little, Protopopov went over to the telephone and summoned him.

Basically, Golitsyn complained, there had been a dreadful revolutionary rally at the City Duma this evening. They gathered about organizing bread ration cards and moved on to demanding the government's removal!

A few had already heard about this, but Protopopov—no, he hadn't heard.

As a novice in government, Prince Golitsyn was still not quite accustomed to this, but, actually, like any educated Russian city dweller, he ought to have been. Any gathering in a major Russian city assembles in order to demand the resignation of the vile, hated government, but in the meantime to move on to action without any government at all.

If you were not lacking intelligence and abilities, but had joined this accursed handful, what would it be like for you in this government?

At sixty-six, Prince Golitsyn was not yet old, but his gout wearied him greatly and because of it at times he simply had to drag his feet; he limped. His teeth weren't in perfect condition either, so he had a slight lisp. Not only that, he was utterly lacking in any instinct for power, and here he had been in a state of hopeless anxiety from the moment of his sudden appointment at the New Year—an appointment he had neither sought nor expected, and he simply pled with the Emperor for this fate to pass him over. He blackened himself before the Emperor as much as he could and explained he had aged from his long-ago governorships, he wasn't capable, for fourteen years his work had been for the judiciary, the Senate, not the state, so the appointment would be unsuccessful—all in vain. The Empress had recommended him! Right after the New Year, the prince was once again received royally, and he ventured to draw for the Emperor a gloomy picture of men's minds, especially in Moscow and Petrograd, saying even the life of the royal couple was in danger. In the Guards regiments they were speaking openly of proclaiming another tsar! To Golitsyn's astonishment, however, the Emperor replied, unperturbed: "We are in God's hands. His will be done." Then the prince begged with redoubled vigor to resign—and again was refused.

Now, having barely begun, he had arrived at these alarming days, and resolutions about the hated, vile government were raining down on his silver head.

What was this about shooting near the Gostiny Dvor chapel? Right next to the City Duma and just before the start of its session! You couldn't engineer that! How would General Khabalov explain it? We refrained from shooting for three full days, that was our tactic—and at exactly this moment and place we shoot?

Khabalov, low on a soft chair near the clock cabinet, like a guard sitting when he shouldn't, now hoisted his bulky body. This was a general of the soldier type, dull-witted to look at.

We did refrain. But if the troops are armed, then you can't answer for every barrel. The crowd fired first.

But, the prince insisted, this is the one thing we've been standing firm on, that we weren't going to fire.

With a light wrinkle of his forehead and fingering his bared cleft chin, making a hasty remark like a half-missed rejoinder, Protopopov objected that just the opposite was the case: the disorders should be put down by force alone.

So perhaps the minister would shed light on events in more detail?

Alas, Protopopov's animated tone immediately subsided. He was not directly involved in these events. Here was the district commander. Here was the city governor.

Golitsyn tried to hold his ailing body erect and spoke with strict politeness, but he, too, was in agony over this Protopopov, who was like an ulcer. Why had the Emperor bestowed this torment upon them all? At a royal audience nine days ago, Golitsyn had requested in the name of all the ministers, and not for the first time, to rid them of this colleague—in vain.

Then shall we ask his excellency the district commander?

Once again, the ponderous Khabalov rose. Especially after Protopopov's facile, rather scattered manner, Khabalov came across as a heavy thinker. How slowly his words crawled out. How much time they took! Why, it was more like bellowing, and without any clear connection. Here he was speaking—but it didn't all stack up. What exactly was going on and how successfully for the government? What further measures was he proposing? By whose whim had he emerged from the sea of ignorance, the remote Urals territory, and gone all the way to the capital's military district, Petrograd's top post? No one here knew him well, and no one could recall a single battle ascribed to him.

Basically, Khabalov assumed he himself would put an end to the disruptions. Infantry numbers were sufficient, and he would also reinforce the cavalry and call up an additional regiment. Right now he still couldn't report all the details, since as of midnight he still hadn't received dispatches from the heads of all the troop units.

Indeed, how many times had other disturbances ended, so why shouldn't these, too?

Would it be appropriate here to ask the supreme military opinion—War Minister Belyaev? But General Belyaev had arrived shaky of step and was sitting in the corner of the sofa mute, beetle-browed, narrow, sunken-chested, and balding, his little eyes set deep in their sockets, a real "dead head," as he was called in the army. He wasn't looking out of those eye sockets but was deeply self-absorbed; his very authenticity was even cause for doubt: was he a man or a little puppet?

Not only did he not ask for the floor, his entire alienated appearance demonstrated that they should not dare ask him any questions or touch him. If the Minister of the Navy wasn't there, then why he, the Minister of War, was sitting here was unknown. A superfluous man somehow drawn into their foolish politics. His business was to supply a warring army. (He had been appointed minister as of the New Year because he spoke English and French and had the experience of foreign travel on military provisioning.) If the Minister of the Interior had nothing to say, then why should the War Minister?

Then they asked for a report from City Governor Balk. Balk was a specialist in police matters but, unfortunately, he had only recently been appointed from Warsaw, and he, too, was a stranger in Petrograd. Nonetheless, he described the main events of the last three days with the abrupt professional precision of police dispatches, reading from a document the precise places and precise, to-the-minute times.

Suddenly, these events piled up in such numbers and were so terrible that they surpassed anything the ministers had imagined. Although they had been driving through the streets these past few days, they had not come across the main tumult.

So what was this that was happening, gentlemen, might we ask? Some were giving it quite serious thought only now for the first time.

Kulchitsky anxiously trained one ear—and seemed to hear everything.

Justice Minister Senator Dobrovolsky didn't try to hide his sour or possibly desperate grimace. A socialite and bon vivant, he was, however, in agony over his wife's three-year illness (half that time she had been in a coma) and entangled in monetary debts and promissory notes. He had worked so hard for this ministerial post and counted so on setting his affairs to rights—he had only been appointed in January—and now he'd ended up here. So why had he worked so hard?

Oh, what illegitimate incursions, these events distracting him from his main affairs. Energetic little Shakhovskoy's mind was filled with iron supplies, oil billing rates, and purchases in America of new mining machines— and here? . . .

Now bald Krieger-Voinovsky, a passionate engineer his entire life—an expert on traction, motion, and maintenance of rolling stock—had never known a free evening or Sunday. Here he'd had to take over the Ministry of Roads and Railways administration since January. The pipes on locomotives would rupture from severe frosts—and here there were these urban upheavals. What was this? What was the point?

The entire government had certainly not assembled to deal with these irritating Petrograd upheavals. The government had its perpetual problem: its war with the State Duma, not some random urban disturbances.

A complaint was made against the army by the city governor: It was the police alone who were resisting and incurring losses, while many army units were entirely idle.

Khabalov said nothing, as if this had nothing to do with him.

What measures did General Khabalov propose for reinstating order?

The general replied without confidence. Even resorting to the use of weapons. Right now notices were being printed and by dawn would have been pasted all over the city in large numbers saying that gatherings would be dispersed with weapons.

But would that be right? A twinge passed through the ministers.

Pokrovsky, just over fifty, usually rather slack, with sagging eyelids and droopy mustache, and always soft of speech and regard—right then he spoke more firmly than usual, saying that under no circumstances should they allow this to be put down with weapons. Suppression would not help. What they needed was to agree to major concessions.

But this had now become an internal discussion. Prince Golitsyn let Khabalov and Balk go.

Now not guarded by anyone, the clock hands ran far past one o'clock.

The ministers were indignant that the military command didn't know and was incapable of doing anything.

This wasn't a debate and their opinions weren't tallied; this was just sliding around and about. Pokrovsky had the support of society, so his views had to be considered. But the ministers had too little power, the remote Emperor had not empowered his cabinet to make "major concessions." Naturally, certain reforms were needed, but were you really going to change the Emperor's mind?

Kulchitsky trained his ear on each speaker but himself said nothing. Raev had the most satisfied look and Dobrovolsky the sourest, but they didn't get involved. Bark had boils, and Belyaev might as well have been simply drawn on blotter paper: eyes behind a large pince-nez, and a glued-on mustache. Protopopov was resting, his head tilted back handsomely. Rittikh, Shakhovskoy, and Krieger exchanged uneasy comments—all of them pragmatic. But each only knew his own department and had no idea what to do against the restless crowd.

If such a notice were posted all over, what would that mean? A state of siege?

A state of siege would have the advantage that then under law all assemblies would end, but would that mean the activities of the unbearable State Duma as well? Or not?

Would this apply to the Duma? That question was debatable.

Then there was the hope nourished by Prince Golitsyn: Tomorrow was Sunday, and a strike on Sunday made no sense, there was no strike, and they wouldn't throng the streets, each would begrudge his time—and so everything would quiet down, right? So it would end, God willing?

In this government, which had changed so many times over the course of the war, changed and changed again, to the point of a loss of confidence, a loss of significance for each, and in which one half, including the Prime Minister, thought of nothing but how to get out of his position, what could they ever hope for? Moderation, consensus, the passage of time? Was there so much as a tiny cube of genuine struggle left in these twelve breasts?

There was. In Rittikh, the Minister of Agriculture, the second youngest. One of Stolypin's younger associates, he had contended fearlessly with the Duma, such as had been forgotten since Stolypin's day, and now, without losing his worthy look and excellent manners, wearing a pince-nez on his tossed-back head, he spoke firmly, agitated.

He said that the brutal street disturbances and mass crippling of the police could be countered only by force and nothing else, as in any other country, even France, in similar circumstances. If troops were being fired on from the crowd, what choice did the troops have? The disorders had dragged on because the authorities wanted to avoid bloodshed. But horror at bloodshed is deceptive. If the moment was let slip, the streams shed would be incomparably greater, even seas of blood. Only the resolve not to be daunted by a few victims could stop this instability.

He said this quite unbendingly and nakedly. Everyone fell still.

Then Pokrovsky, curling his lips, in a slack voice but with a shade of mockery, responded:

"Nonsense. There you have the path to ruin, 22 January. Only major concessions. And without delay."

Did they have to decide on anything? Oh, how they wished they didn't! Did they dare without the Emperor? But he was at GHQ.

Oh, if only the Emperor would return soon! (He had left only three days ago.)

Right then they were informed of the arrival of the head of the Police Department, whom they had summoned. They invited him to explain.

What legendary police chiefs there had once been! Their entire being strictly aligned with their police service, inspired on a level with revolutionaries and putting their own life on the line for the political order. Actual State Councilor Vasiliev, who had just come in, was—no, definitely not one of them. He seemed uncertain, even pathetic—and Protopopov alone lit up with a fond smile for him. The name "Vasiliev" had never resounded, and now they could not recall how he had advanced or why. (Life-loving Kurlov liked him because he never forgot himself over his service and liked to drink and play cards. Under Kurlov he had risen nicely and then stopped, and now, upon Kurlov's brief return to the ministry, under his wing, had become the department's director.)

It was a ticklish spot, but Vasiliev tried not to besmirch himself in reactionariness; and he rid the Petrograd Okhrana's overly gloomy predictions of the past few months of their pessimism, so as not to distress his superiors. So, too, now, Vasiliev entered this quiet nighttime room not fanned or overwhelmed by the events of the last few days but with an enumeration of his dispatches.

They looked at this Vasiliev. They could tell he wasn't genuine. He left no loose ends, and his arguments held together. They excused him.

Vasiliev, bowing, reminded Protopopov with a respectful look that he was expecting the minister today for Sunday dinner. After all, it was already Sunday—the hands had gone past two o'clock.

And no one could stop their progress.

Oh, what a restful silence in the quieted nighttime capital! If only it could linger for the coming Sunday! And after Sunday as well?

Besides, the main question wasn't the street itself, of course, but the State Duma. That was the center of provocation for the upheavals. It supported the disturbances in spirit, but it could also be the key to calming things down if they could figure out how to turn it, right? Tomorrow, Sunday, there would be no Duma, and that was good. But on Monday strident speeches were anticipated—and how could they be stopped?

Barely stirring on his sofa, Pokrovsky responded in his melancholy way that they had to get along with the Duma, they had to know how to work with the Duma, and there was no living without the Duma.

As wanly as this was stated, it was quite convincing. All these frightened, exhausted ministers wanted to find was a way to get along with the Duma. The Duma speakers' exclamations were stings from a swarm of wasps, and the ministers didn't know how to swat them away.

How could we get on with it, though, Rittikh confidently objected, if after all the speeches on the bread question it was perfectly clear that the Duma had nothing substantive to object to the Minister of Agriculture's efforts, but it couldn't approve them by a vote because no one in the Duma had the moral right to agree with the government.

Meanwhile here, at home, in his desk drawer, Prince Golitsyn already had the Emperor's signed decree suspending Duma activities, which he was authorized to date and publish. But what was right? Suspend the Duma? Wouldn't it be better to reach an agreement? A bad peace was always better than a good quarrel. And then ask the Duma members to use their prestige to bring the crowd to its senses? That would be the best solution to the upheavals.

Pokrovsky, leaning forward on the sofa, weary, said as about something already known: "But for this to happen, the cabinet would have to accept all the Duma's demands. And perhaps even resign."

The hardhead Krieger-Voinovsky: "If this government doesn't suit the Duma, then the most sensible thing would be for it to resign."

And again Pokrovsky, without energy, but this was so clear:

"Yes, gentlemen, that is the only solution! We should all set out immediately to see the Emperor and implore His Majesty to replace us all with other men. We have not won the country's trust, and we will achieve nothing by remaining in our posts."

Intoxicated by himself, Protopopov increasingly was forced to descend to this session from the height where he hovered. He had never indulged the cabinet sessions with long statements, correctly understanding that all matters were decided not here but in other, private and higher, audiences. However, since they had truly begun to believe their own misconception, perhaps it was time to explain.

So he launched into a descriptive explanation, trying at the same time to be charming. The ministers exchanged looks. Was Protopopov's whole exaggeratedly mobile face, sharp, darting eyes, but distraught smile, that of an obvious madman? Lunacy being extremely dangerous for an interior minister.

Protopopov couldn't understand how they failed to understand something so clear. How could they lay down and give up portfolios when the rabble was rebelling in the capital? The Duma was ratcheting up the country's mood, and we weren't going to last to the war's end with it. We had to stop running to and ingratiating ourselves with the Duma! It had become the focus of the revolution—and it had to be disbanded altogether. Not suspended for a brief time but disbanded, shut down, until autumn—when its authorities would end and a Fifth would be elected.

Disband the Duma altogether? The ministers staggered back in horror.

"It's not so terrible!" Protopopov declaimed triumphantly. "Japan has disbanded its parliament eleven times, so why can't we?"

To their relief, though, the question was not that urgent today specifically. The Duma didn't convene on Sunday so it could only be suspended or not as of Monday.

Couldn't they reach some good agreement with the Duma? So that there wouldn't be these incendiary speeches that stung and enflamed the public? Shouldn't they try, tomorrow, taking advantage of the Sunday, to enter into relations with faction leaders and through a private exchange of opinions work out a possible compromise? Probe the moods of sensible Duma members?

Here Pokrovsky had the greatest entrée into Duma circles. And to balance him out—Rittikh, at the opposite end. To somehow reach an agreement that would resolve this situation. Quietly and peacefully.

Tomorrow Golitsyn would try to speak with Rodzyanko himself.

That quiet night—and it was nearly three o'clock—they were so tired and they so wished for everything to be quiet and peaceful.

Unbeknownst to them, that very evening the City Duma had resolved as follows: "this government, its hands red with the people's blood . . ."

11 March
Sunday

[4 3]

*   *   *

As morning broke, the police officer from the Gunpowder precinct who had yesterday bought himself rags from a doorman showed up at the city governor's offices and reported that the Gunpowder police station no longer existed. There was no one to tally the police killed and wounded.

*   *   *

On the morning of 11 March, another new notice appeared on Petrograd's walls:

> Over the last few days, there have been disturbances in Petrograd accompanied by violence and attempts on the life of military and police officials.
> I hereby prohibit any public assembly.
> I hereby warn the population of Petrograd of my approval of the use of weapons by troops in this matter, stopping at nothing to establish order in the capital.
>
> Commander of the Petrograd Military District
> Lieutenant General Khabalov

But since this notice was the third in a row and the first two had not been enforced, it had no effect. If they hadn't fired so far, then evidently they weren't going to.

Not only that, the notice was read too late. It was Sunday and people were in no hurry to get up, in no hurry to go out on the street.

They walked right by the decrees, scarcely reading them.

*   *   *

Today, not a single major newspaper came out in Petrograd.

Yesterday was the first day without streetcars, today was the first day without cabs. Frightened by threats, they weren't going out anywhere.

The factory districts fell still: the factories were producing no noise or smoke, and the streetcars weren't rattling. Only the suburban trains still rumbled. On the fourth day of the strike, all the haze had been sucked out of the air. The sky was remarkably clean.

*   *   *

Today the police had not shown up in the worker districts since early morning, not even the mounted police.

There was a rumor among the workers that the same thing was happening in Moscow and Nizhni Novgorod as in Petrograd, that our side was winning!

*   *   *

The Vasilievsky Island Bolsheviks assembled a meeting on the 14th Line. Prepared appeals to the soldiers were passed out to everyone. Approved was the following: keep up the demonstration speeches and take them to their extreme limits; collect weapons for the combat units; disarm police in surprise attacks.

*   *   *

There was this rumor going around among the city's educated public that the government was allowing all these upheavals on purpose so that it could say this was a revolution and have the right to make a separate peace. Apparently many of the demonstrators were disguised yardmen, not workers.

*   *   *

Only in the very center were there still paired posts of policemen. People were always used to seeing them confident and stern, so it was quite odd seeing them distraught.

On the other hand, more troops had been brought out than in the last few days. All the Neva bridges and trampled crossings over the Neva were guarded by lines of patrols.

But they were letting small groups of workers through, as if they were families.

And where they thronged in large groups, banned groups, they trampled new paths across the Neva.

The soldiers looked the other way.

Workers, men and women both, crowded up to the patrols and tried to persuade them.

All these lines and patrols seemed tormented as well, as if they were ex-pecting violence directed at themselves. As if they even wanted to be broken and disarmed.

[4 4]

Early that morning Shingarev had telephoned several of his acquain-tances in Petrograd who might have seen new street events. Everyone had replied that nothing was going on, it was a peaceful Sunday morning.

But yesterday the City Duma had been at such a boil, it was hard to be-lieve it would disperse, calm down, and empty out. Andrei Ivanych had slept uneasily, he'd had flashes of crowds and gatherings, a feeling of some-thing irrevocably lost. It had never been sensible to wish for new upheavals, but for some reason, out of some inner zeal, he had! It was very odd that they were seeing a calm morning, nothing anywhere. Could he do any work? He did have urgent work, he had materials from the Military Com-mission, and the session was the day after tomorrow. This afternoon at three o'clock was a meeting of the Bloc's bureau. But right now, this morning, he could do a little work.

There was no bread at home because the girls hadn't stood in line for it yesterday, and what there was had been finished off. The Shingarevs didn't buy the fanciest kinds on principle. Andrei Ivanych drank his coffee and ate some cheese, talked to his daughters a little, rejoicing in how flourishing and carefree they were, and promised that this summer they would go to Grachevka together. He went to his study.

His mind wouldn't switch gears just like that due to the inertia from yes-terday's stormy evening and this whole food flurry; Andrei Ivanych was slow to recover from his own speeches in the Duma. In the last few months, he, too, had been involved in the food issue, but here they were, here lay pro-found matters on which Russia's fate truly hung. How had army provisioning for the spring offensive been pursued in the last few weeks since the allied conference? Having worked with the military budget for more than a year, Shingarev could only wonder at these figures, and a year ago he couldn't have dreamed of anything like it. Over the entire war to the end of 1916, we had produced 34 million rounds, and now 72 million had been manufac-tured. In a month the Russian army would begin its offensive — and would stun the enemy with an avalanche of firepower such as had never been seen on the Eastern Front, but only at Verdun.

Actually, this one thing outweighed and determined everything. Includ-ing the certainty of an imminent Russian victory. That meant this entire fever of Duma battles had been futile. Power would remain where it was, and at most they would knock out one or two ministers. How many times, out of seemingly total despair, had *they* wiggled out!

There was plenty of work here on the proportion of official and private orders and on deadlines and payment shares. But Andrei Ivanovich's mind had a hard time focusing on the details, and as he sped through these days, his thoughts flowed in a general sort of way. A general way—and a general vagueness, a mistrust or alarm. The numbers were quite encouraging for a Russian victory, but the mood was still troubled. The report's import was unequivocal, but a creeping feeling blew an anxious chill and impeded patient work.

Right then the doorbell didn't ring, but for some reason there was a triple knock, as if by a bird's beak. It seemed to be at the door, but it wasn't repeated and was nothing like the way people usually knock. Fronya wasn't answering it, but she was farther away. Maybe it wasn't a knock? Andrei Ivanych still went to check.

At the door stood—not a bird, but dressed in a coat and a soft pie-shaped fur hat was someone tall who had shrunk due to a stoop, not an old man by any means but not young either, with marvelous intense eyes by which he was immediately recognized on the well-lit staircase: Struve!

"Pyotr Berngardovich! I thought I'd misheard. Why didn't you ring?"

It was pointless to ask: he hadn't seen the doorbell. He could also fail to notice a full audience: he could arrive for a lecture, go up to the rostrum, get his book out of his briefcase, and start reading it to himself.

He countered with his own amazement:

"Andrei Ivanych, you're sitting at home? How's that?"

"What do you mean?" Shingarev missed a beat.

"I stopped by to see Vasili Vitalich and he wasn't there," he either complained or praised in his sweet, raspy voice. "It's a good thing I remembered you're in the same building."

"But what's happened? Please, Pyotr Berngardovich, come in, take off your coat."

"Why would I take off my coat?" Struve replied with disquiet, turning his head, and turning it again. "I should go." But he stayed right where he was on the staircase. He was holding just a plain walking stick with a twisted knob and nothing more. He had a button undone, his coat was bunched up, and his sparse, reddish, gray-streaked beard hadn't been trimmed, but what was conveyed was far from funny: it was practically dread.

"Go where?"

"I don't know," Struve replied anxiously, and he twirled the cane knob in his fingers.

"But what's happened?"

Struve's stoop and the tilt of his head made Struve's manner seem as though he were looking askance and thus penetratingly, and on top of that through his pince-nez. He responded in an uneasy, deep-chested voice:

"Andrei Ivanych, do you really not sense it? How can you be sitting in your apartment now? I for one couldn't. . . . I even woke up in the middle of the night. . . . After all, somewhere something is . . . Eh?"

He turned his head all the way around, with mistrust, as if he'd sniffed burning, as if sniffing out whether the building here was on fire.

All at once his guest's anxiety and his own sense of urgency converged in Shingarev. Suddenly he felt there couldn't fail to be events, there just couldn't, it was true! It was just that they didn't know anything yet. Everyone who had reassured him over the telephone was wrong. His heart spoke the truth. On the outskirts, inside your four walls, you could sit through it all, miss it all.

It had dawned on him, and now he knew that if he didn't go with Struve he wouldn't stay home anyway, he would have no peace. Of course it was early, ten o'clock, and the Bloc bureau was at three, but there, in the Duma room, he had other work as well. On days like this, the right thing was to be at the Duma, of course.

"How did you get here, Pyotr Berngardovich?"

"How! There are no cabs. I had to hoof it, with my stick."

That was from Sosnovka, from the Polytechnic! Struve was a year younger than Shingarev, but his stoop, frailty, and disregard for his body made people treat him practically as they would an old man. His body was provisional and uneasy housing for his spirit, and it moved around not according to its own needs but as his spirit demanded. Often quite energetically even.

No, now was definitely no time to sit around! Alarm ran over his skin. He told Fronya. He got dressed. Off they went.

He caught himself with the urge to support Struve going down the stairs and stepping across the threshold. But he was fine. He'd gone up without an elevator.

It was a clear and frosty day, minus eight degrees Réaumur. The streets were perfectly calm and even emptier than usual. After yesterday's din, people even seemed to be speaking under their breath.

It's true, it's easier when your legs are moving. So much had built up over the last few days, it was hard to stay in one place.

From Bolshaya Monetnaya they turned onto Kamennoostrovsky—and nowhere did they see traces of disturbances or riots, nor did they come across broken store windows. Kamennoostrovsky seemed especially empty without streetcars and cabs. Did no streetcar rumble and bells make it calmer for the nerves?

No.

"Things will work out," Shingarev reassured himself. (Or was he, on the contrary, disappointed? He felt ambivalence.) Why did they both have the same feeling? The city was peaceful as never before. It was all over. "That's good because these disturbances could have rolled things along all the way to . . . Only things won't work out with our government. It can't be tolerated."

"On the other hand, look how *they* are tolerating it." Struve's reddish eyebrows over his pince-nez magnified his eyes' searching grasp. "Simply angels of patience. They're not shooting, right? After all, no German or English police would put up with this, would they?" As he walked he kept tripping on humps of trampled snow. "Andrei Ivanych, no scrutiny is fruitful until you study your opponent's point of view. Let's put ourselves in their place. What are they to do?"

Just who had Shingarev not tried to sympathize with in his life! That's all he needed—to rack his brains over what *they* should do!

"Quit!" he cruelly knew. "If we have not tolerated them enough, then how much more can we take? The stones will shatter!"

Struve's legs were not stepping confidently. These were not healthy legs weary from sitting.

"Quit?" he staggered clumsily and pushed up his pince-nez. "But that isn't a normal human response. And tell me. What have we left for them to do the last, well, fifteen . . ."

". . . days," Shingarev understood. Struve didn't always finish his sentences.

"So why in this bread muddle must I also give them—"

". . . years!" Struve suddenly finished.

"What years?"

"Fifteen. Tell me. . . . If there's a political upheaval, won't we . . . ?"

"What?"

"Won't we be poorer?"

"Poorer in what way?"

"Ah," he said slowly. "The spiritual organism that arises from the crowd . . . that is a puzzle for the mystics. But what can we mine there in the bowels of the popular spirit?"

Shingarev gave him a sidelong look of surprise. Here was an astonishing man, as he had long known, unlike anyone else. Like everyone else, he had toiled his entire life in the stormy channel of Russian politics, compelled by a powerful current, but unlike everyone else he had also made continuous lateral movement: a governor's son, he had begun from the far left shore, with an anonymous "open letter to Nikolai II," in response to his "senseless dreams." Then, the author of the first Russian Social Democratic Workers Party manifesto and the creator of the Social Democratic Party here. Following soon after, he began talking about God, the first among the Marxists. He had shifted a little to the right, but to the extreme radicals: editor-in-chief of the unforgettable *Liberation*, a merciless, menacing émigré of Herzen-like sweep, the "knight of Stuttgart." However, starting with the first days of freedom in '05—the secret philosopher behind the as yet not contemplated *Landmarks*, and ever since then his life had been a succession of challenges to public opinion. He joined the Kadets with great misgivings, after Milyukov's attempts at persuasion. And continuing, from left to right, he shifted, forded the entire Kadet stream, serving as a member of the Kadets' Central Committee and a deputy in the furious Second Duma (where Shingarev, naturally, did not rise from his seat to listen to the speech from the throne, and Struve did, stunning everyone). Then he slid more and more to the right, angering Milyukov, and finally, the year before last, left the party altogether. From the Duma tribune he proved unfit, too cameral and inarticulate. Basically he never got the hang of practical politics. But he had an articulate pen, and in guiding *Russian Thought*, he confidently continued his same movement, from the opposition to the right, to being pro-government, a patriot. When during the first wartime summer there was need to write a proclamation to the Poles in Napoleonic language in the name of the Supreme Commander, Struve quite unexpectedly fit the bill. And here today he had come to Monetnaya first to see Shulgin, not Shingarev. He was already firmly nailed to the right bank. But at the same time, it was as if he hadn't gone anywhere and had remained wholly one of them.

"So, Pyotr Berngardych, what can we garner from the popular spirit besides the healthiest, most wellspring-like foundation? On it rests our entire faith, our entire activity, twenty—thirty—forty years. . . ."

There was no point arguing; it was clear to both.

But it wasn't clear to Struve. He stumbled as he walked, stopped, and could not immediately find the words to speak. His head tilted and his gaze was aimed upward:

"But will we retain our sense of measure? The free choice of paths— oh . . . Very few are capable of strict freedom of spirit."

"Well, well! Now you're way up high above the clouds!"

Struve pushed his pince-nez up on his nose and looked, highlighting with his gaze what had not been put into words:

"But if we don't achieve **this** freedom, then even the freest political forms will not free us. The possibility of freedom is not the same as freedom."

"But is that what we're discussing?" Shingarev dismissed this. "We should be seating intelligent ministers. Improving the conduct of the war so it isn't lost. Provisioning the front and towns. Elementary corrections in domestic policy. Look what these dummies have been doing! They've made such a mess of things!"

"That's the easiest thing to do: finding mistakes in your enemy instead of yourself. But what if I was the one . . . mmm . . . while sitting abroad, in '04, who tried to prove to Trubetskoy the moral error of the very concept of sedition? But later, returning to Russia, at the height of everything, how could I not have seen that this was . . . mmm . . . a practical concept?"

Struve was worked up in a way he couldn't have been in front of Shingarev. In his throat, sentences seemed to be solidifying and arguing over which would jump out first. That's why he kept stopping, in order to speak more easily. His free hand, the one not holding the cane, made odd gestures, as if looking for something to prop up that hand, too.

"Yes, our rulers have fallen asleep on their watch. But we have hypnotized ourselves on one single shining point. We have opposed the government so passionately . . . and for so many years, as if Russia's main interests lay in this struggle. Or as if one could live in general without a government. If we're smarter, then we should be the first to come to our senses about the caution needed in solving the problem of liberation. . . . Normal evolution rather than a political earthquake. But we have only been waging war against the government, that one war! We have always insisted that the state cannot stand without freedom—but freedom cannot stand without the state! This is the flaw in our consciousness: living in our own country in a permanent state of rebellion."

"Well, Pyotr Berngardovich, I would understand your remorse if we'd wrung their neck. But as it is, they're wringing ours, and it's cracking. And the Tsar? Even without an outstanding mind, he could have ruled us differently from the very start. After all, he didn't have to step over his dead father to get to the throne and at the same time hear the People's Will's ultimatum. His father died suddenly, and the country was truly in mourning. No one disputed autocracy, society was calm, and all they asked was that the zemstvos be recognized . . . and that the ministries' opinions not be the only ones to reach the throne. No one would have reproached the young tsar for his weakness had he met society halfway then. Had he revived the line of the 1860s, then Aleksandr III's slight freeze would even have been justified. Autocracy would have proven that it was strong and could handle everything itself. But the young Nikolai . . . declared his father's hesitation the course for all time."

Struve kept making as if to go. He searched with his eyes, maybe seeing the sidewalk underfoot, maybe not, and checking with his stick, and in despair sought and sought with his hand his dangling pince-nez, which had skipped off on its leash, and put it back on again. His thoughts scorched him before he could pronounce them, and in the very process of speaking he chased them down, and solidified his sentences, planting the next on the last incomplete one.

"He might have done otherwise, but what about us? . . . What instructions did we issue, the League of Liberation? I published them myself. Do not let slip a single chance to exacerbate the conflict between society and autocracy. . . . As Zasulich's shot implied: violating the law is forgivable if that violation is aimed at the enemy. For victory in a single short battle we were not afraid to leave any burden to the next generation. How we gloated over the ministers' murders. We vied . . . with the revolutionaries. Even in Paris . . . a meeting with terrorists. We supported all kinds of terror. Just think of it! And ominously cursed anyone who dared condemn terror. From the government we always demanded nothing but unconditional capitulation! Today it's the same thing. Have we ever really striven for a compact, for reforms? Our slogan has always been the same: Go away!"

"What about *him*?" Shingarev hadn't built up any hatred for the Tsar personally, but when he spoke in general. "He inflated the question of autocracy so there was nothing else left under the heavens. It was his advisors who stated that a loyal zemstvo was autocracy's enemy. Could not even the tiniest bit be conceded to the liberals?"

"How's that?" Struve stumbled and stammered and groped for firm ground with his stick. "And who pushed Svyatopolk away? My *Liberation* reviled him. More than anything in the world, what we hated was compromise! We would send instructions to every banquet to pass harsh resolutions without fail. And how did our League play with the zemstvos? It simply exploited their name and signboard."

This was strange to hear from the recent Kadet, but even stranger was Struve's manner of arguing. It was as if he were absent and not saying all this to Shingarev but rather as if his thoughts were merely bursting out. It was as if he were absent but was the first to notice and turned his head even in fright: they were talking as they would in a room, so alone were they. No one was rattling, squeaking over the snow, riding, or walking around them on the sidewalk; no one saw or heard them. And because of this suddenly they were transfixed by the notion that all Kamennoostrovsky, even the whole city, was listening to them.

"The people are tired," Shingarev explained with regret. "They're resting."

Struve nodded. And he continued to bear his stooped shoulders like a burden.

"Did we ever really treat our historical regime seriously? For us, all the institutions of the past were always just a burden and never a part of a possible future. On the other hand, any revolution was for us preferable to what existed. By revolution we always understood something wonderful and healing. But revolution . . . is always unnatural."

With his free hand he grabbed his long, bent ear. He stamped his feet as if dancing. And plodded on:

"We believed that the highest goal was to preserve our reputation in leftist circles. Our constant mistake was not to distance ourselves dramatically from the leftists, from all the *socialists*."

Finally Shingarev was getting seriously worried. This eccentric could be forgiven a great deal, but not that much. He led him on by the sleeve.

"When we started this war, we had trust in the government. But look how surprisingly and disgracefully it has worked out, that the government doesn't wish its own victory! That the people have to win the war despite the government!"

"No! No! No!" Struve warned him animatedly, his breath so choppy that fluency eluded him. Unbearably, he stopped again to delve more comfortably into his interlocutor. He tilted his head so that the beams from his eyes cut across his brows. "You cannot think this way, Andrei Ivanych. It is the party forcing you! Here it is, the difficulty of freedom: you have to rise above party! Do you really seriously believe in treason at the top or even in court circles? This is party slander proven by nothing!"

No, Shingarev didn't think that crudely. It wasn't treason. But there was indifference. An ingrained lack of talent that could even turn victory into defeat.

"Everything here has taken a one hundred and eighty degree turn. We, the defeatists in the Japanese war, are now the only loyal patriots."

They had now reached the "Vigilant" bas relief. Here was their reminder: you were the losers, but we, the last two on the dead torpedo boat, drowned ourselves rather than surrender.

Struve stopped again and leaned on his cane.

"You're telling me this? I caught a good deal more than yours! When the news arrived about Tsushima, I trembled from joy, and in this I considered myself a patriot. My eyes opened only in Paris when a Japanese agent started foisting money on me. . . ."

The avenue stretched far into the distance, and they came out on the square in front of the fortress. It was impossible to miss how especially clean the air was and how unprecedentedly blue the sky. Could it have seemed that way to them both? Or was the sun shining in a special way now?

Given the spaciousness and special quiet on the streets, and it being so especially clean in the sky, and the sun being so special—something like a holiday was hovering over Peter's capital. A long-awaited one.

"Even today we still think it's easy to run a state."

"Well, it's not that hard!" Shingarev objected cheerfully. "Duma work has taught us a thing or two as well."

"You think so?"

"We're prepared."

"Well, I envy your confidence."

On the right, the Peter and Paul Fortress bell tower shimmered in the sun, all the way to the angel on top. Peaceful, replete with its massiveness, the fortress's fat towers and ramparts dozed, a fortress that had once been menacing but had held no prisoners for a long time, nor would it again. The mitigation of mores had spread to us, as well.

It was brilliant and tranquil. Even overly so.

For some reason it weighed even more.

"But what's left for us? What if imperial power betrays its duty as the Empire's leader? Can we wreck it more than he already has?"

Struve's animation subsided, as if he hadn't been arguing. Meekly:

"We all love Russia—but is our love clear-sighted? With our love, aren't we bringing it more harm?"

"Pyotr Berngardovich!" Shingarev placed his broad hand on the weak shoulder, and his voice started to crack. "To say that we love Russia is a banality and embarrassing even to repeat. But there's this: I love nothing but Russia. I could not bear to learn I had been serving her the wrong way. Loving her the wrong way, incorrectly. I personally have no longing for power, all I want is that Russia fare well. But what if our eyes do see better, while *their* eyes refuse, and because of their bad disposition they refuse to consult, look around, or listen closely? How can we cooperate with them? It was they who precluded it."

Was Struve tired of talking? Was he plunged into thought? He made no objection.

Across the entrance to the Trinity Bridge stood a sparse line of soldiers, but they were letting everyone through freely.

People were still walking, after all. Workers, too, dressed for the holiday, some wearing bowlers.

Shingarev and Struve walked across the bridge's smooth-slow rise, down the right-hand sidewalk, by the concrete parapet, now past the limit of the Peter and Paul Fortress bastions and the embankment line. It was too bright to look left, impossible. But to the right. The Neva was white under snow. On it, a little darker, the crisscrossing paths made yesterday by the many on foot remained. Above the Palace Bridge, still incomplete, with wooden booths disrupting the style, was a black vessel iced in for the winter. Moving on, they could see several of those, past the Exchange Bridge, near Hemp Wharf.

Past the first ternate streetlamp stretched a patterned grill of railings adorned with tiny needles of frost.

Even the Trinity Bridge itself, with its two rows of grape cluster street-lamps—free of streetcars and cabs, nearly free of pedestrians—was incredible, enchanted, and festive in this frozen sun.

They couldn't help but stop and look right, their backs turned to the sun.

Down the left bank, without the usual wheeled commotion or the impressive carriages, the deserted but festive granite embankments stretched past the assemblage of palaces, from the gray Marble to the brown, highly sculpted Winter. On the right, across the Neva, girded by the simple stays of the Palace and Exchange bridges, stood the Stock Exchange, powerful and majestic, like a temple of antiquity, on its elevated granite stylobate, with rostral columns rising in front like marvelous candlesticks and with Vasilievsky Island symmetry moving off down the two embankments. Farther down on the right, in eternal yellow stone folds, the Peter and Paul Fortress remained silent, nor was there any movement on it.

"In our freedom," Struve spoke slowly, squinting, "we must also hear Yaroslavna's lament and all Kievan Rus. And the Moscow dumas. And the Novgorod liberties. And Pozharsky's militiamen. And the Azov siege. And the free Arkhangelsk peasants. The people live simultaneously in the present, the past, and the future. And we are obligated to our great past. Otherwise . . . Otherwise this won't be freedom but the Huns' invasion of Russian culture."

Everything, everything visible was soundless, deeply submerged in an unscheduled, unknown holiday, when from on high, the sky had been cleaned and all earthly movement banned and still in the drawn-out morning of this long day of grace. Generously, the holiday had been granted a triumphant sun.

It was as if the entire spellbound city were contemplating its centuries.

Bustling Petersburgers, always rushing busily—how could they not stop and stand a little longer now? How could they look with anxious eyes and not revel?

However, nothing was happening anywhere. Where had they gone so early, and why?

Nothing was happening anywhere, which was too bad. Shingarev felt sorry that the authorities had won again and were again dragging Russia down the same old rut.

Pyotr Struve's restless head had also been invaded by this architectural certainty of the present, which crowded out the seething past and seething future, forcing him to be silent and reverent.

It was sweet to watch, but there was nothing sweet to disturbed eyes. The holiday was so solemn that the heart had to be wrenched by worry. It was all too peaceful, too unrealistic.

They passed the middle of the bridge. The Field of Mars was already opening up before them, merrily flooded with a sidelong sun. The blinded Engineers' Castle was illuminated but without sharp contours.

"No matter what happens"—Shingarev swept his generous hand—"our people will find the correct path. I believe that. And this correct path will be democratic development. It will take decades of cultural work, which we'll do, as we have been already. You have to believe. You can't let doubts take over. My older brother was constantly agonizing over life's questions—and at twenty-five he poisoned himself with cyanide."

They came out onto Trinity Square and Suvorov-as-Mars. But there was still lots of time before the Bloc bureau.

Why had they rushed out? Where had they gone?

"The cold isn't so bad, but it doesn't have you standing around," said Shingarev. "Know what? Let's stop by Vinaver's. He's right here on Zakharievskaya, not that far away. If there's any news, we'll learn it there. He has trusted friends in leftist circles. If something really is brewing, he should know."

[45]

Maksim Moiseevich Vinaver had graduated from high school and university in Warsaw, but he had begun his law practice almost immediately in Petersburg, in the late 1880s. He had chosen jurisprudence partly because this career posed fewer difficulties for a Jew in Russia, and in part because his many qualities led him toward that: his mastery of oratory, including aphorisms, his ability to speak passionately and argue richly, his powerful legal diagnoses, analytical mind, and sense for the mood of the chamber and court. He chose civil rather than criminal law or political affairs because civil was the freest from state interests. He had a good practice and had become quite well known—and he himself sincerely loved Aleksandr II's judicial system. It's easy to gain fame in criminal defense; there's the reaction of the press and public. But a civil lawyer has a hard time achieving notoriety. Only judges and his colleagues can appreciate him. Passover himself praised Vinaver's first work. Being a Jew, Vinaver had long not been sanctioned to practice in court independently and had been kept to "assistant," but he also knew how to recoup his losses in the Senate, to speak there so that the senators were struck dumb. Not only that, many legal opinions and reviews emerged from his pen.

But his pen—his pen drew him on further! He came to realize that his true calling was not as a lawyer but as a man of letters. His mind was saturated with jurisprudence, but his emotions weren't. His emotions drew him into literature. He began publishing sketches of individuals met on his life's path, and then of major events in which he had had occasion to participate. These books afforded him great pleasure.

Nonetheless, his heart was far from satisfied by this activity. Over the decades he had also been able to lend no less emotional strength and energy to the Jewish movement. Back in the early 1890s he had joined a circle of Petersburg's young Jewish intelligentsia, which was gathering resistance to the advancing sinister forces. Vinaver transformed the Society for the Dissemination of Enlightenment Among the Jews of Russia and headed up its historical-ethnographic commission, its spiritual center, which worked to develop a national self-consciousness and encouraged belief in Jewry's inexhaustible strength. Contact with Jewish antiquity was for these young people what contact with mother earth was for Antaeus. Having begun their activities gloomy and flaccid, they emerged from it fortified and confident. At the turn of the century, Vinaver was already at the center of the fight against Jewish inequality and pogrom propaganda. In Petersburg they created a Defense Bureau for Jews: "We must maintain our active disposition. We are only beginning to reveal our political strength. We have finally found an arena for action! We are organizing fighters." Vinaver's line was on no account to adopt points from individual political parties because Russian Jewry had to be cohesive. "Now is the one and only moment when the decision of our fate may be in our hands!" They made the press their main weapon, both in Russia and abroad, in order to actively attract public opinion in the West, which the Russian government always heeded. After the Kishinev pogrom in 1903, this type of activity of theirs intensified, and in 1906 a special press organ was created in Paris on the status of Russian Jews.

However, it was as a lawyer that Vinaver acted. In Vilna he organized the defense of Blondes, who was accused of murdering his servant for ritual purposes—and won the trial. He appeared for the first time in a criminal trial as plaintiff in the name of the Jews in the case of the Gomel pogrom, causing a sensation among Russia's Jews. There he staged a demonstration, declaring the trial biased—and led out of the trial all the attorneys representing Jews. This oration in Gomel in October 1904 made him so popular among the Jewish masses that he virtually became their Russia-wide leader, and in Vilna in March 1905 he chaired a congress of all Jewish parties and groups and headed up the Union for the Full Rights of the Jewish People. Until '05 he did not engage in general political struggle and kept purely to Jewish matters. But at that point he split from the Zionists, although the majority of Jews joined them, and the democrat Vinaver headed up only the anti-Zionists.

The role of Jewish leader passed him by. At that point he joined the Kadet Party, in which he quickly advanced.

In November 1905, as part of a delegation of Jews, he went to see Witte demanding equal rights. Witte replied that in order for him to be able to raise that question, Jews had to adopt a completely different behavior than what they had followed up until then, and specifically, to reject participation in any general political strife: "It is not your business to teach us revolution. Leave all that to Russians by blood and worry about yourselves." Some members of the delegation agreed, but Vinaver replied ardently that now the moment had arrived when Russia would achieve **all** freedoms and full equality for all subjects—so Jews must do everything in their power to support the Russians in their war against the government.

Since then he had never been inclined to separate Jewish and general revolutionary interests. He just always insisted, in the Kadet Party, and then in the Duma, that the issue of Jewish equality be distinguished from the general question of equality for nationalities as the acutest.

The widespread opinion about Vinaver was that he was a cold mind and an excellent intellectual instrument, that he knew how to find a middle formula of reconciliation for debaters, and knew how to obscure the weak aspects of his opinions and advance the strong ones. But in fact he increasingly seethed with public passion. He felt called upon to be a political leader. This vivid new passion—political struggle—dampened his taste for his former activities, jurisprudence and literature. Vinaver became chairman of the Kadets' founding congress in Moscow and immediately joined their Central Committee, remaining on it to the end. He joined the actual ruling foursome and was also linked in heartfelt friendship with Petrunkevich and Kokoshkin, while in Petersburg all the main decisions were taken in tandem, by Vinaver and Milyukov.

Jewish election commissions were created everywhere for elections to the First State Duma, and Vinaver at first stood for the Jews of Vilna. Later, though, he was given a more distinguished nomination from Petersburg, on the Kadet list—and in the Duma itself he ran the Kadet faction as part of a triumvirate with Petrunkevich and Nabokov.

In its unforgettable seventy-two days, Vinaver gave the First State Duma all his energy, his reserve of mental powers, and the poetry of his soul—and of course his pen. During those high-flying days, he and Kokoshkin together composed a daring address in reply to the speech from the throne, and, on that bitter day, the Vyborg appeal, a thunderbolt.

The First Duma completed its brilliant, majestic procession, the inspired flight of the era, and in a short time overcame all the difficulties of its novelty and had already drawn the contours of a new state order and renewed the entire state edifice when a brutal, perfidious dispersal was inflicted on the Duma—and the entire structure collapsed.

On the brutal day of the First Duma's dispersal, Vinaver was in a cab on his way to see Petrunkevich. He was looking around at people's faces, searching for anger, searching even the dead Petersburg stones for a reflection of the calamity that had come to pass—and there was none! Was this the final chord of a great epic? Such was the response and gratitude of his deaf country. . . . The people had not supported their Duma. Therein lay the catastrophe— and the revelation. He felt like screaming out in pain and horror.

After Vyborg he lost the right to run for election and was thrown out of politics and back into the law, only remaining the number two man in the Kadet CC. Naturally, he did not abandon the Jews' defense. He participated in a number of Jewish publications and cultural organizations, and during the Beilis case actively supplied world public opinion with materials. He held firm through the depressive atmosphere for several years. In this war, Vinaver was once again at the head of the fight for Jewish equality, but without losing his connection to the general liberation struggle.

He seemed to engage—and brilliantly—in every type of activity accessible to him; he couldn't stop at age forty-five. But the fire in his heart and the light in his eyes were perpetually under ash, and for the past ten years it had been as if he were burying and mourning his unforgettable First Duma every day, over and over; none of the others could compare with That Duma. As a result, the tone of his life seemed in a way frustrated.

On the other hand, these last few days had been like a red-hot pyramidal needle, piercing the gray vegetativeness and rising into the sky. Maksim Moiseevich and Rozalia Georgievna lived in bright presentiment and could not sit still. Oh, **if only** this continues all the way! We can't go on living in this boredom and pitch dark! Oh, if only this doesn't end in "disturbances"!

Editorial offices shut down and the capital's spiritual life fell still, but information flowed in over the telephone and from witnesses (servants brought their employers news from the street). During those days they gathered at the Gessens'. The reports were mounting ominously! And all of a sudden they had come to an abrupt end this morning, and everything fell quiet, as if ended.

Had it really ended? Really?

From people in the know, Vinaver dug for hints over the telephone or via messengers: not **expected**? But was anything being done?

It couldn't, mustn't die out so simply, he believed!

Maksim Moiseevich was reading in his study when Roza walked in and said in amazement, "You know, they've come—Shingarev and Struve."

Vinaver raised his eyebrows.

"Struve, too? Did they say they'd be coming?"

"No."

"How presumptuous."

With the present decline in the Kadet Duma faction, over time, once the faction had run out of names or intellects, Shingarev had become the number two man in the faction and had nearly become famous, so to speak, throughout Russia. (Whereas since '06 Vinaver had been increasingly forgotten. . . .) In fact, he was not only from another ideological generation than the founders of the Kadet Party but also an undereducated provincial who never had come in contact with genuine Petersburg culture. Vinaver would never have a serious conversation with him as equals, and they were not at all friendly, although they met at CC meetings and conferences. Whereas Struve—Struve was a longtime, original liberationist, a vivid figure and subtle man—which made it even more unforgivable that he was a traitor. Quitting the leftist camp and consciously moving over to the conservatives—that could not be forgiven! That was reprehensible! When it came to Struve, Vinaver had absolutely nothing in common with him, and he disliked seeing him.

Why had they come so unexpectedly anyway? Like any seriously engaged man, Vinaver didn't like that.

But might they have brought news?

He went out to the parlor to see them and was moderately gracious while also letting them feel his coolness, as he knew how to do. Actually, they themselves were embarrassed and sensed his greeting before they had barely sat down. Shingarev immediately clarified:

"Forgive us, Maksim Moiseevich, forgive us. We've come only for a moment. It's an unusual situation, after all, and this was my idea, to inquire as to what you know about the hidden side of events. Is something going to *happen*? Is something being planned *there*?"

Well, there you had it. They'd brought nothing.

In fact, Vinaver stood out in the Kadet Party and the entire political movement for never having had enemies on the left. Small clashes, yes, when out of hotheadedness they'd tried to foist something excessively impracticable. On the contrary, he had always had allies on the left, and he usually knew more than others.

Round-shouldered, ungroomed, lost Struve and the simpleton Shingarev now wanted to use what he knew?

Vinaver not only could but was obliged to know, had been trying to learn the revolutionaries' secret plan.

But there wasn't one.

He had the secret of knowledge, but the knowledge itself consisted of **nothing**, unfortunately.

Even deeper than this knowledge, however, was his sincere belief that there ought to be something! We had suffered too long under this regime, and the ends to patience were coming!

However, he was not going to sully his name as a failed oracle. His visitors could get a factual answer.

"Unfortunately, gentlemen, I have tried to find out. Nothing is going to happen. *In those circles* nothing is expected or contemplated."

Both faces before him fell not exactly into outright disappointment, but in the shadows.

Vinaver, too, sighed. He had had his fair share of these disappointments in life. His face had a yellow cast, maybe due to the room's poor lighting. His forehead was bald all the way back to his crown. His rounded beard had grayed. His intelligent eyes were piercing. And he said, relenting:

"Nothing is going to happen, gentlemen. Let's go about our business. We lost in '06 and evidently for a long time to come."

[4 6]

On his mother's side, Vadim Andrusov was the grandson of Schliemann, the excavator of Troy, and whether or not he had preserved his unquenchable inquisitive disposition, he just couldn't seem to find his place in life. Graduating from high school before the war, he twice matriculated at the Academy of Fine Arts and twice flunked out. He matriculated at the Faculty of History and Literature, which left him dissatisfied, and switched to law. Meanwhile, the war was going full tilt, and he had to avoid mobilization somehow. Vadim's brother, an SR, felt himself to be a Tolstoyan also and professed Tolstoyan convictions—and became a medic. But Vadim didn't hold out: in '16 he was mobilized from his second year and sent to Krasnoye Selo for accelerated ensign courses. But before '16 was over his courses were, and it was inevitable he would be given the next appointment. With such a puny military education, and still a total civilian, and with no gentry background, Andrusov seemingly could have been appointed only to some down-and-out infantry somewhere two thousand versts away, but no, he was appointed to the imperial guard—which previously had been for men from the wealthiest and most high-born families, but was now randomly diluted—to the famous Pavlovsky Regiment, its reserve battalion, stationed in the capital itself! Not because of any successes of the young man but because there were absolutely no officers. Nonetheless, his was a Guards greatcoat, without outside buttons, and in Guards fashion he had to subscribe to contribution lists, and in Guards fashion take the good conduct exam, that is, be excellent at drinking vodka, for which the Pavlovsky Regiment was famous. How swiftly and drastically can a man's fortunes change. And here you were beginning to settle into your new position, strange though it was. They even let him go home for the night.

Andrusov was appointed to a training detachment, that is, a select unit inside the regiment where noncommissioned officers were trained. There were two other ensigns there and two second lieutenants, who were not that much more capable, and over all of them, Staff Captain Chistyakov, a genuine officer with eyes like pistols. On the Field of Mars, directly in front of their barracks, they underwent drilling and bayonet training. They were taken out of the city for gas training once, but they hadn't gone as far as shooting yet.

Sometime in February their training detachment was sent a couple of times to wander around the city with a brass band and cheer up the population with their music and military bearing. And with the start of the city's upheavals, they'd been sent to the guards' quarters in Gostiny Dvor.

That was where Andrusov was Sunday afternoon when the telephone informed him that an enormous crowd was moving down Nevsky from Znamenskaya Square and had to be stopped. Andrusov took his party out and following the new instruction, in the event of a need to fire, spread his soldiers out prone, not standing, across Nevsky, opposite the middle of Gostiny. All its shops were closed because it was Sunday afternoon and there was no commercial traffic. There were very few people at all. Andrusov himself walked back and forth, in front of the bayonets, and behind him to one side was the trumpeter.

False suns were shining in the sky as they do in winter, four around one, silvery white belts stretching toward them from the main one.

The crowd was quite visible as it started onto the Anichkov Bridge. The crowd flowed unimpeded and dense off the bridge and poured onto Nevsky. Andrusov told the trumpeter to give the first signal.

But the crowd kept coming, advancing—and now had come even with Eliseev's store. Right then Andrusov nodded to the trumpeter, who gave the second signal.

But the crowd paid no heed this time either, or did not understand, or were still too far away—an entire block from Sadovaya, then Sadovaya, and half a block of Gostiny—and suddenly shots rang out! Without the third signal the soldiers behind Andrusov had started to shoot?

That's why they'd been put there, to shoot (lying down you don't shoot in the air), and that's what the trumpeter was for, to give the third signal—but there hadn't been a third! They'd started shooting behind the ensign— watch out they don't hit your feet.

Andrusov jumped back across the shooters—and with his sword in its scabbard started beating the prone soldiers on their backsides to make them stop shooting.

But the shooting had done its work. The crowd was scattering. Some surged toward the Aleksandrinsky Theater and hid behind a ledge of the Public Library; others went to Ekaterininskaya Street, past Eliseev's; still others moved back, some cramming into entryways and building gates. The middle of the avenue was cleared and had become a deserted white strip, but on the snowy pavement lay the dead and wounded.

One Pavlovsky soldier lay as he had been lying. He'd been stitched a bullet from some upper story or roof after the second signal. It was probably because of that shot that the agitated soldiers had begun shooting. That's how it had started.

Ambulance vans rolled up from the direction of the Admiralty and collected the wounded. And then the dead.

Fifteen minutes later, Staff Captain Chistyakov rode up from the regiment in a droshky, his arm bandaged from a previous wound. For all his self-possession, he could not hide the fact that he was shocked and distressed.

Traffic was no longer being allowed down Nevsky.

Soldier details went out to the scattered crowd and tried to persuade them to disperse.

But what was picked up from the crowd, in whispers, hushed tones, and even aloud as it began to flow was this: The Pavlovsky Regiment had disgraced itself!

[47]

All these last few days, Vsevolod Krivoshein, under the pretext of going to the university, had been leaving home in the morning and jostling through the streets to his heart's content, running from swords, lying down on the snow, pressing up to gates—and he had experienced and seen his fill of everything; it was all very interesting, and for some reason he was drawn to the danger. Or rather, you realize there's danger, and you should be afraid, certainly—but there's no fear in you. Only yesterday, when he'd had to run with the crowd from Znamenskaya Square to the shouts of "They're cutting us down! Cutting us down!"—it wasn't the swords them-selves—which, aloft, he hadn't ever seen behind him—but the general un-restrained panic of the crowd, conveyed from one to the next by the roar, crush, press, and jostling, that had so completely gripped Vsevolod. But even this wasn't a genuine fear of death, when you suddenly just cease to live, but the faint notion that dying now was so pointless and unnecessary. He didn't know what he was dying for as he fled with this crowd. (But they kept running, as the roar of triumph and exultation reached them from the direction of the square, at their backs—and then everything stopped and started returning to the square—and they passed on from one to the next that a Cossack had killed a mounted police officer and the rest of the po-lice had scattered. The crowd rejoiced for a long time and nothing more happened.)

Today, though, leaving home wasn't that easy. It was Sunday and there was no university. Also, his father had come home from the Western front— where he now served as a Red Cross representative—in order to be present on Monday at the session of the State Council, of which he had become a member after the Minister of Agriculture's resignation, the usual lot of any-one granted a gilded resignation. His father had traveled knowing nothing about what was going on in Petersburg, and so he was all the more saddened upon his arrival. Immediately the entire atmosphere at home thickened with serious concern—and it became indecent for the younger boys to show any animation or to misbehave.

Of the five Krivoshein sons, the two oldest were already officers at the front. The middle, Igor, was also an ensign now and training for the front. And Vsevolod, called Gika at home, although a student at the university, was still one of the younger boys—with the youngest, who was twelve and still had a governess.

The Krivosheins' apartment, although rented and in an apartment build-ing, was itself like a self-contained house, with fifteen rooms as well as aux-iliary rooms, along both sides of the corridor, which was long enough that the boys could ride their bicycles down it. The formal rooms, whose plate-glass windows faced Sergievskaya, even looked like a museum, furnished with rich, antique furniture and hung with marble bas-reliefs and many old paintings, by artists who weren't the most famous but who were valuable enough that his father had bought many of them. The family had lived here for thirty years. Although later his father was minister for eight years in a row and could have lived in an official apartment on Mariinskaya Square, he preferred his own: this way he eliminated the necessity of giving official dinners and receptions.

Gika sat over his morning coffee with the adults and languished. He tried in vain to invent a reason for why he needed to go into the city. But his father was sitting there so distraught and gloomy, and his mother and aunt were as stern as if some misfortune had occurred in the house—so it was awkward to blurt out something.

"They've brought us to this point," his father was saying. And after a long pause: "They've brought us to this point." And also after a long interval: "Who did? And who did they bring in?" And later, also: "They've walled themselves off from the world and have no idea."

This year he had turned sixty, and he was showing signs of age.

He sent Gika out for newspapers—but only to the corner of Voskresensky, to the newsstand, and he'd better come right back.

There, as far as Voskresensky, it was uninteresting, perfectly peaceful, ordinary. But there turned out to be not a single one of the newspapers, the real ones his father would read; they hadn't come out, just the Black Hundreds' ones—*Zemshchina* and *Svet*—there was nothing to get. He bought *The Government Herald*, which had the appointments, transfers, and instructions, which always interested his father, but it was humdrum and held not the slightest trace of current events.

His father was sitting in the corner of the large rectangular sofa in his study, as if thrust into the corner, as if helpless, white-faced, with a drooping, untrimmed mustache—and this was when Gika realized for the first time just how serious what was going on was. He felt sorry for his father. But he didn't have the habit of being affectionate.

His father was shocked that there were no newspapers. He'd been expecting a stack and had ordered half a dozen. He opened the *Herald* right away—and surveyed it sullenly. Again he mumbled, "They're not doing anything. . . . Things haven't quieted down for three days, and the authorities are looking the other way. . . . We're on our way to anarchy."

Afterward, Gika languished in his room, which had a window on the courtyard. He opened his window vent: no ominous sounds, no gunfire. It was quiet. The telephone in the hallway (they had two in the apartment) rang often. His mama, and aunt, and Gika himself, and the mademoiselle, too, were calling their friends, trying to find out what was where—but nothing had happened anywhere.

Convinced of this, after a difficult, depressing lunch, Gika's father let him go out for a walk—but only in the center and not for more than two hours. The youngest wasn't going anywhere.

216 \ THE RED WHEEL

After a vivid morning with slanting suns, the light in the sky was iridescent and diffuse, as if it had spread into small clouds.

No sooner had Gika broken free than he immediately went to Liteiny, of
course, and down it to Nevsky. Like yesterday, there were no streetcars, but
there wasn't a single policeman or soldier anywhere either—only General
Khabalov's new decree hanging on the buildings threatening the use of
firearms. Here and there it hung next to yesterday's, here and there all three
did, or else one half-pasted to another or half torn off.

So it went, over and over, in boldface: Khabalov—Khabalov—Khabalov—
and it was vexing, as if the Russian government had no other voice for the
Russian people these days, no other signature.

Nevsky was filled with the usual Sunday strollers, streams of pedestrians
down both sidewalks—elegant ladies, officers, university students, civil officials, military officials, women with children and perambulators, wounded
soldiers, clerks, and servants—but also workmen from the outskirts, that's
clearly who they were; they'd never been here before. However, everyone
kept to the sidewalks, and the avenue itself was empty.

Suddenly a crowd appeared from Znamenskaya Square, more than two
thousand of every kind you could imagine, lots of men and women students
and intellectuals in bowlers, but most of all, men workers in simple caps
and women workers in scarves, but dressed more cleanly than usual, not the
workaday rabble—and people poured off the sidewalks to join them. In the
front rows they were holding high two red banners: "Down with autocracy!"
and "Down with the war!"

The march proceeded without anyone impeding it or blocking the road.
It proceeded slowly, filling the entire pavement, encountering no pickets
anywhere. It overtook Gika around the Anichkov Bridge, when before it
passed he crossed to the other side of Nevsky, toward Ekaterininsky Square.
He also thought, in line with his father, What have we come to! Here a
crowd like this is marching—in time of war—with banners like these—
down Nevsky—and no one is preventing them. What does this mean?

As if on purpose, this thought flashed and suddenly he heard from somewhere sharp blows, like jolts, or as if someone was ripping a large piece of
cloth. Gika had never heard anything like it up close and wouldn't have
guessed if the crowd hadn't started rushing to either side, running and
shouting that they were shooting. And as he had recently on Znamenskaya,
Gika started running with everyone else and didn't even have time to be the
least frightened. Only as he was running, seeing how frightened the others
were, did he start absorbing their fright or troubled state.

He had to take cover behind the Public Library. Here the shooting was
more muffled—and evidently the bullets couldn't reach there—and the
crowd stood close together.

Everyone wanted to know what had happened—but not enough to go
back, and from here no one could see anything.

Gradually, though, news passed through the crowd that they were firing from Gostiny Dvor and there were dead and wounded left on Nevsky.

This was serious.

The crowd gradually melted away, skirting the Aleksandrinsky Theater.

Two navy blue student caps drew close together here: a tall student was standing nearby, loudly indignant and railing against the military authority, railing against autocracy, and then he said to his neighbor:

"Colleague, these blackguards have given you a fright. They're firing on the crowd. What baseness, the executioners! They have no shame anymore. Perhaps you have far to go to get home? Where do you live?"

Gika told him.

"That's far," the other said. "There's no crossing Nevsky now."

Meanwhile the crowd was quickly melting away, for fear of what would happen next, on the chance that they might turn this way with their shots. Although they had stopped.

"My name's Yakov. What's yours? Let's go to my apartment. I live nearby. We can wait it out there. You can even spend the night."

"Not likely! I have to get home. They're expecting me."

But he was touched by this invitation, this general friendly warmth from the studentry. No matter how bad things got, you weren't alone anywhere. You had thousands of friends.

They started across the Chernyshev Bridge. An expressionless gray side-street, an expressionless gray Petersburg apartment house, a gloomy staircase with cheerless checkered tile on the landings, a dark corridor with doors off it, a large room with gray light coming from the courtyard, amazingly uncomfortable, to the point of slovenliness, although there was nothing dirty, chaotically filled with furniture and things and, in the middle, a table, but not a dining table, a table with papers and books, and hanging over it a lamp with a bordeaux shade that was turned off. Tobacco smoke hung in the air.

Two students, one male and one female, were already there. Yakov announced:

"Vsevolod. Shimon. Frida. Look, I've brought a comrade, or they nearly might have shot him on Nevsky."

They welcomed him graciously. But the arrival of the student stranger was lost in the discussion of what was going on. Everyone was indignant. They could not find words worthy of railing at the Tsar's oprichniks.

"They finally dared!"

"I didn't think they would."

"And Nikolai the Second"—Frida said biliously, sitting by the window with her legs crossed—"naturally hightailed it to GHQ. As always, of course, he's as far away as he can get from responsibility."

"But he's not going to get away!" Shimon flashed. "The troops couldn't fire on their own say-so. An order was given, and this order, through a Tsarist lackey, was his personal order. And he'll be remembered for it."

"But what's our pathetic crowd worth?" Frida had lit up at the window, not lifting knee off knee. "All they had to do was fire a few times for everyone to run away."

"Yes, but tomorrow it could start in again!" Yakov promised.

"No, no!" Frida said, waving her arms, with an even malicious satisfaction against herself. "This is it! The movement's been suppressed! Tomorrow no one's going out on the street."

Right then two more male students arrived along with a female student. And the discussion began in many voices at once: Had it or hadn't it been crushed?

They tended more to saying it had. And it shouldn't have been started. It should have been remembered that the people were incapable of genuine revolution. Now autocracy would only emerge strengthened from the whole situation.

Gika barely spoke and sat there feeling awkward. The entire tone of their statements was unfamiliar to him and grated on his ear and heart. He'd realized that they'd guessed his privileged, aristocratic background, though they didn't express it in any outward way. Truth be told, he did feel his upperclass background and did feel out of place and ill at ease here. The room and atmosphere were so strikingly different from his at home—he didn't even feel like going out on the street, which was bustling, but wanted to go home to be tranquil and "at home." Most awkward of all would have been if they'd asked him his last name now. He couldn't lie because it would be demeaning to lie, but to speak his name here was impossible: even though it was a liberal one, it was a Tsarist minister and a Stolypin colleague as well. (Two hours had already passed. What must his father be thinking? Gika couldn't tell him he'd come under fire.) Gika sat a little bit longer, for decency's sake, and wished he could get away. (Might it also have been why Yakov had brought him here, that he took him for a Jew? Gika and his oldest brother were often taken for such.)

They were chain-smoking, so smoke was hanging in the air.

If only he could get home, catch his breath, return to the familiar.

Two more came in—and from the threshold they announced that Yulka Kopelman had been wounded on Nevsky and was being taken away in a van.

They exploded! Everyone jumped up and started shouting. This was a living instance, so it struck harder than general regrets. Was he still alive? Would he live? The mood became more ominous and nasty, but also mournful.

How events change! Yesterday and today the pathetic, disgraceful regime had seemed damned to hell, thoroughly weakened and helpless. And here they'd fired in several places so it could regain its strength—and its stinking existence would go on for a long time to come!

"How long will he go free?" they said about the Tsar.

Someone started talking about a certain Grisha:

"You know, that mama's boy, the Zionist? He told me, 'The revolution here doesn't affect us Jews. The Russians can deal with this.' There's a scoundrel, or would you say no?"

They started shouting against this Grisha and against the Zionists, who were true traitors to the common cause and were only looking for a way to dodge the revolutionary struggle.

Right then a young ensign walked in—handsome and slender, with a proud bearing and mustacheless, smooth-shaven, not like an officer.

Everyone knew him, evidently, and started yelling noisily:

"Sasha, what's this going on?"

"Lenartovich, you're an officer! A stain has fallen on you! Is it you now instead of the Cossacks?"

Taller than average, and holding himself very erect, he stood in the empty vestibule space alone, visible to all at full height, having removed his cap and revealed his thick, luxurious, back-combed fair hair.

He didn't answer right away, and in that time everyone fell silent. In the silence he said in a formal way that evoked trust:

"Rest assured. We shall not forgive them this day. Just like the 22nd of January."

[4 8]

Life comes easily to shrewd operators. They always scramble out dry. Such, probably, was Lukin, sergeant-major of the training detachment's 1st Company. Yesterday—it was late already, after midnight, as they were returning to barracks from Znamenskaya Square—there had been an order that in the morning the Volynians would go out again, but it would be the 1st Company, and with machine guns.

Machine guns!

Kirpichnikov was relieved that it wasn't him now. Privately, he asked Lukin:

"Are your men really going to shoot? I suggest it's better not to."

Lukin gave him a gloomy look:

"Tomorrow they're going to hang us, you know."

They never did reach an agreement.

But early in the morning, lo and behold, Lukin went to the infirmary, injured, he said. And there he stayed.

Staff Captain Lashkevich, in charge of the training detachment, arrived. Kirpichnikov reported that Lukin was in the infirmary.

Lashkevich—now there was a gentleman, foreign blood, white body. He wore gold spectacles, but through them stung you with his eyes. His reply was like a sting:

"This is no time to be sick!"

As if Kirpichnikov himself had been shirking.

He flashed: today Kirpichnikov was to be sergeant-major of the 1st Company and hand his 2nd over to someone else for the time being.

That is, for the third day there were changes that meant Timofei had to keep going on and on? What a curse! He felt like howling! I'm completely tapped out. Let me go!

But he couldn't say that to Lashkevich.

There was nothing to be done, so they started out soon after—with live cartridges in their pouches and trundling the machine guns along—and Lashkevich himself joined the company, the first time in all these days. The company descended into the same cellar, but rather than go sit in a hotel, Lashkevich went out to take a look and came back. And he kept Kirpichnikov with him. And ordered him to send patrols around the square and chase away the crowd.

But for half the day so far there had been no one to chase. Timofei was starting to hope there might not be anyone and they'd get by.

There was light in the sky: more than just sun; bands and columns of light.

No, by two the public had started to converge and press in. They had no interest in walking down other streets; it was sweet for them here, by the monument.

They started buzzing, singing, and shouting.

The police wouldn't let them near the train station. There were no Cossacks today at all. And the Volynian patrols were doing a bad job of chasing them away. On the square, Lashkevich railed at the lance corporals that they were ragdolls, not soldiers.

But Lance Corporal Ivan Ilyin shifted from foot to foot and answered him: "It isn't a soldier's business—to chase them away."

Lashkevich jerked as if stung and ordered the lance corporal's stripes ripped off immediately.

How's that? It had taken him years to earn those stripes, and now they were ripped off in one instant? By Lashkevich's will?

Oh, they weren't used to hearing the truth from the people.

Who was supposed to tear off the stripes—Kirpichnikov again?

Well, all right, Ilyin wouldn't let them do it. He stripped them himself.

To Timofei it felt as if they were being torn off of him himself.

It wasn't his company, and Kirpichnikov didn't know this Ilyin, but taking him aside into the caretaker's room, on the stairs to the cellar, he shook his hand:

"Well done!"

But what he felt was strain, tedium: now Lashkevich ordered Kirpichnikov to watch over the patrols.

All right, soldier boy, it's all on you!

He went off among the patrols on the square and politely but hopelessly asked the public to disperse.

"What's it to you?" the workers blurted out. "We're not bothering you. We're not asking you to leave."

What could you say?

Lashkevich also ordered him to tell all the patrols that at the sound of the horn they were to run to the Great Northern Hotel. As he jostled across the square, Kirpichnikov told the sergeants and lance corporals he saw. And to some of them, having taken their measure (it wasn't his company), added:

"Only don't be in too much of a rush."

They wouldn't hang him for it, and if anyone informed, they still couldn't prove it.

Timofei feared for that terrible moment when they summoned them with the horn and ordered them to use the machine guns. What should he do then?

Lashkevich said that he himself would go with Kirpichnikov and with one patrol would show them how to chase them away.

Off they went. The staff captain punched and kicked the first person he came across—and the man fled immediately. Others nearby started to melt away.

But a young lady stood there proudly, as if to say, You won't touch me.

"Leave this minute!" Lashkevich commanded. She stood there without budging:

"I'm in no hurry to get anywhere. And you should be more polite."

Now, what could you do with one like that? And they were all like that here.

Kirpichnikov fell behind Lashkevich and went over to another patrol in the crowd.

"Well, boys, a storm's coming, a great disaster. What are we going to do?" They:

"Yes. . . . Surely, a disaster. . . . We're going to end up dead either way."

No one knew anything, and no one could decide on anything. Timofei encouraged them:

"If they order you to shoot, you can't not shoot. But shoot up."

He moved on to a third patrol.

"As if they didn't beat this into us enough. Think more."

Lashkevich, too, realized you couldn't chase them away with patrols. He ordered the company to be led out of the cellar and form up from the Great Northern Hotel to the monument. The signal to the bugler.

They were led out. In front of the formation he explained, gold-spectacled:

"Here before you are scoundrels who are rebelling on German money while a war is going on. Walk toward them with your rifles atilt. If necessary, beat them with your butts; if necessary, stab them. And if the need arises there will be a command to fire!"

He assigned parties to various spots on the square.

He ordered Ensign Vorontsov-Velyaminov to take his section and stand opposite Goncharnaya and disperse the crowd there. And Kirpichnikov to go with them.

Velyaminov lined his dozen up across Goncharnaya, which was packed with people pressing in from Nevsky. He commanded the bugler to play the signals.

One.

Two.

Three.

The people evidently didn't realize what the horn was for or pretended not to—in any case, they did not disperse.

The military machine is indefatigable, though. If there's a horn, that means fire. The ensign commanded:

"Straight into the crowd! In file! My warning: one! two! three! . . ."

They didn't disperse.

"Four! . . . To seven. Five! . . . Six! . . ."

They weren't dispersing.

"Fire!"

And a volley!

Plaster sprinkled down from upper stories. The crowd shied and yielded—but they couldn't see that a single person had been wounded, let alone killed.

That meant everyone had shot up. Well done.

But the crowd began to mock them.

The ensign got very angry:

"Aim better! At their feet! In file: one! two! three! Fire!"

Another volley.

Again the crowd hesitated and scattered.

But there were no dead or wounded.

The ensign:

"You don't know how to shoot! Why are you so nervous? Shoot calmly."

And they fired another volley!

The crowd again all fled into the passageways.

But there were bodies left in the snow. Some were moving.

They had hit them after all. . . .

The joking had come to this. This was war. On a city street.

The crowd didn't gather anymore or press.

Timofei felt uneasy. So uneasy!

An ambulance arrived and collected the wounded. People helped them and shouted at the soldiers from there. But didn't plow ahead.

The soldiers stood across Goncharnaya, rifles to arms. No one pressed in anymore. But they did crowd and hide in the passageways.

Kirpichnikov had been at the back all this time, and now he walked over to an officer:

"Sir, you're freezing. Go to the hotel and warm up. I'll take your place here and see it through."

Velyaminov trembled, he himself was relieved:

"Indeed, please do."

He walked off quickly. Kirpichnikov sent a soldier after him to make sure he went into the hotel. When the soldier returned and confirmed it, Timofei had waved at the public and said:

"Everyone should go where they need to and quickly."

And to the soldiers:

"As if they didn't whip us enough. Think more where you're shooting."

They passed through and went away, and tensions eased. Goncharnaya was clear. The bodies had been removed, too.

Velyaminov returned:

"Well, how were things here? Did you shoot?" Kirpichnikov showed him:

"See, they've all been chased away."

[49]

Sunday morning, as Shlyapnikov was once again crossing the city on foot, it was very calm, as if nothing had ever happened.

Because it was Sunday? Or were they tired?

Now that there were no streetcars or horses at all, he especially was left to his feet. On Sunday he spent the night at his sister's past the Neva Gate, and now this morning he had to cross the entire city to Serdobolskaya.

It was nothing to cross to the Vyborg side in the morning, and they always let you through in that direction.

He strode down the thousand-times-familiar Sampsonievsky Prospect past buildings, apartment houses, and fences, past the barracks of the Moscow Regiment and then of the Wheeled Battalion. It was peaceful everywhere, and the empty factories were silent.

At the Pavlovs he had been dumbfounded to hear that late that evening they had arrested the entire Petersburg Committee, five men, when they gathered on Sampsonievsky.

There's not needing a conspiracy for you! There's the state's inaction. They were making arrests.

It would have been a rout if the committee had amounted to anything decent. But they were needed like a hole in the head.

The Sormovo men gathered here and convened about what to do. They decided simply that for now all the committee's powers would transfer to the Vyborg District Committee. (The Bolsheviks didn't have another district committee. This was it.)

A debate started up about weapons. The Sormovo men, especially the bully Kayurov, bore a grudge. They should arm themselves! Seize weapons

from the police, as many as they could, and in other places, too. Shlyapnikov replied that you weren't going to get many, you didn't know how to
shoot, and your temper would lead you to use them rashly—and you'd spoil
everything. If you used weapons against the soldiers, you'd only annoy them
and they'd respond with weapons. Our sole true path was friendship with
the barracks. We had to win over the army and steep the sour soldier wool in
revolutionariness. Then when the army itself joined us—then. . . . Too bad
we didn't have party organizations in the reserve regiments. We weren't prepared for anything.

It might well be that the whole strike would end right here. Today, Sunday, they'd blow off steam and calm down—and tomorrow they'd be ready
for work. Without the army even budging.

Nothing more was decided. Shlyapnikov headed out for the center to see
where what, if anything, was happening.

He was wearing a fine soft pie-shaped fur hat, and you could see the tie
around his neck, the look of a petty bourgeois, so there shouldn't be so
much as an attempt to stop him on the bridge.

Not that they were stopping anyone: the crowd wasn't pressing, and for
proper singletons passage was unimpeded.

This was such a pity. Had it all ended in nothing?

But no, there were crowds in the center. And lines of soldiers. And rallies
around them trying to corrupt the soldiers' consciousness.

The area right by Kazan Cathedral was awash with them.

And finally, they were shooting along Nevsky near Gostiny! Everyone lay
down, and so did Shlyapnikov, with a joyful heart.

They were shooting! Good. That meant it wouldn't pass. No matter
what, it would be remembered.

They'd been shooting on Vladimirskaya, too. And on Znamenskaya it
was serious, twenty or so wounded probably, and there were dead.

It would be remembered!

Ambulances whisked on by. High school students showed up—and
someone had the bright idea of wearing Red Cross armbands over their coat
sleeves. Female students were insisting on going with the wounded and
looking after them. Exercising their right of social aid oversight, as everywhere now. The police lost their nerve and let the young women go.

No, the streets had eased up again. And the shooting was over. Over. The
soldier and police cordons tightened.

This, too, was tolerated.

Shlyapnikov walked down one of the Rozhdestvenskaya streets where
he'd made an appointment for a female student to travel as courier to
Moscow. "Comrade Sonya" showed up. He gave her money for the trip.
The errand itself was minor. What could they advise their Moscow comrades? To call them to protest now would be a provocation. Evidently they

themselves would have to end it here and now. That's what all the defensists wanted anyway.

What more could be expected of the movement? And how should it be directed? Here the government had fired and we had had nothing with which to respond.

We were badly organized. How many times has the proletariat been unprepared for any kind of battle? In vain have we rushed, milled about these last few days.

[5 0]

"He must be *rescued*! We must hurry and rescue him! From this woman, who must be thoroughly depraved if she's capable of luring away a married man! Oh, why did you hold me back! If I'd gone right away I could have caught them together! He doesn't know what I'm capable of!"

"Alina Vladimirovna, you would have made things worse."

"This autumn you talked me out of it, too, and I wanted to so badly! And what's the result? You can see. . . ."

"An encounter like that, had it had a scandalous ending, could have attracted publicity."

"Oh, that's worse for those two. I'm not in any service! My self-esteem has already been torn to shreds! *He* dared betray me. Just think! He dared prefer another to me! After ten years of admiration and worship! I'm burning up. I can't sit still, idly!"

"And ultimately, no matter how precisely we've calculated—what if it's a mistake? What if it isn't Andozerskaya after all?"

"Well, I'd offer her my apology. That would mean I had no claim against her. Oh, I didn't have the nerve that time in the autumn to find out straight from him. I was so close and I lost my temper. I would have gone already and painted her quite a picture! As it is, what, are they going to decide there without me?"

That time, Susanna Iosifovna had restrained her at first, but then, as with all of Alina's vivid outbursts, it all broke off, and she felt dead. Her surge of emotion lasted only long enough to write him a letter in Mogilev, and this Susanna approved. Then she got scared and discouraged. How would he reply? And a new surge, on and off again! Feeling like a recuperating woman: the fact that she had been first to break it off made her feel better. She sent the letter and rushed to the hairdresser to change her hairstyle! And her plans to burn through her life! That very evening she went to the theater. May as well go down in flames! Her head was already spinning with rearranging her apartment, and plans for other follies were maturing. But then Georgi's plaintive telegram arrived in response. How much better she felt to find out he was broken.

"But Susanna Iosifovna! What was the point of all this if they're together again?"

"What can I do, dear Alina Vladimirovna? Other than weep with you."

Susanna had now given her valerian pills for the second time today and the tenth in the last few days. She was trying to dampen Alina's burning readiness to run straight away from her and rush to Petrograd—and then again the surge would abate, as if punctured, and Alina would drown in the sofa, her arms dangling, and now, on the contrary, Susanna had ordered strong coffee brought.

Drowning feebly in the softness, Alina complained in a listless voice:

"I've been keeping a journal since those terrible autumn experiences. I write down whether I've slept and how many hours. Now I can see how many of those collapses I've gone through when you wake up with gnawing pain, a living corpse, all interest lost for anything in life. Later, in the middle of the day, things slowly brighten."

The unfortunate woman, her suffering was not feigned. She should have been taught a completely different line of female behavior, but she was stubbornly incapable of mastering it and merely rattled on down her well-worn path:

"How pathetic I was! For eight years I adapted to his way of life, to his activities, and that sacrifice was what ruined me. I should have gone to the conservatory to study. I folded my wings too soon! I needed room to grow, not to be someone else's shadow. But I got used to hearing, You're my special one, you're my only one, you're my little star! And to believing it. I bent over backward for him and only during the war did I begin to live and breathe fully—and right away this blow? Oh, why didn't I betray him first? He would understand what he'd lost in me, but it would be too late! Susanna Iosifovna, after all, we're all individuals, and I'm an exceptional person, but I was so stifled! Here now, without him, I only feel emancipated. Why should I hold myself back for a traitor's sake? You know, lately people have been finding something new in my face, my eyes, they say. . . ."

Even she wasn't listening to what she was saying.

Susanna Iosifovna latched on to her expression:

"You're right to say you've been emancipated. You should try to look on it all that way. Above all, you have to be independent of the twists and turns of this story. When you hurt, learn to pretend you don't. To maintain a dignified silence."

Never once in all these months, evidently, had Alina supposed that this might be the rout of her entire life, but instead had raged that they dared compare someone to her. How could she explain this to her? She was being led by blindness, not courage. Without insisting at all, entirely theoretically:

"Alina Vladimirovna, you know, there is this male trait: at some point some of their attention shifts to other women. Any women they meet. In general. You won't admit that even before all these events . . . his feeling for you had weakened?"

Alina tossed her head back:

"Not one bit! He still idolizes me! You still haven't read a great many of the letters. I can show you! He loves me madly, and he'll repent anyway, but I want his repentance to go deeper!"

"You remember, back last autumn I warned you. . . . But you kept insisting that women were outside his circle of attention."

"But that was true!" Alina's face flashed and she insisted expressively with her eyebrows. "I have no idea how things broke down! What could justify him is only ignorance and a misunderstanding of the feminine soul."

She kept boasting like that, but her look was already lost, and her outburst was lost, and the coffee hadn't helped. She hunched over and sighed.

"Yes, of course, now he's been taken away from me, snatched. . . . Drawn in by a new world he finds vivid."

With a chilled movement of her shoulders—her shoulders seemed to convey any emotion before anything else—Susanna said:

"That means it will take an especially long time for that world to lose its luster and fall apart. It will take methodical efforts and your correct behavior. Most of all, he must never see you crying or suffering. He should always get a sensation of *lightness* from you! Don't reproach him or try to prove anything. Just keep your mouth shut as if nothing has happened. Always, no matter what the circumstances, a sensation of lightness! And also: always be new for him, always a puzzle. Do you understand?" Susanna watched with hope.

But Alina's face had taken on a defenseless, if not tearful expression.

"That's wonderful advice! But how can you follow it if you're all thumbs? If you feel scourged?"

Susanna, sitting evenly on a hard chair, sternly shook her head.

"Not only should you not go after him now, you shouldn't even wait for him in Moscow, if he should suddenly come. In this condition you're not fit for an encounter."

"That's true," Alina, lost and gladdened, got a hold of herself. "I'll go away. I'm actually afraid of seeing him now. And now he won't dare skip Moscow."

"There you go. Very good. By the next time you see him a lot will have come clear and be settled."

"But I'll go—and leave him a firm letter! That if he doesn't break with her immediately, I'll never see him again or his things in our—"

"That's just what you mustn't do!" Susanna promptly fussed. "Don't repeat your moves. He might explode, and the effect would be the direct opposite."

"Now I'm sure it wouldn't!" Alina slapped the firm bolster. "If he didn't explode at the letter this autumn, then he won't now. Either I lose him irrevocably or I win him forever! Va banque!" Her eyes truly lit up with a gambler's passion.

"No! No! No!" Susanna said anxiously. "You'll only make matters worse. Not only that, you'll never learn for yourself, never draw any conclusions."

Alina clutched her temples—and lit up, and prayerfully folded her hands.

"My dear Susanna Iosifovna, if he comes and doesn't find me here, and there's no letter, he'll certainly rush to you to ask questions. Won't you—won't you talk to him? Feel him out, understand, find out? Eh? Won't you do me that favor?"

Here we go getting bogged down in superfluous things and other people's stories. There was absolutely no point to this mediation for Susanna, but how could she refuse a close friend in her grief?

"Oh, thank you, thank you, dear Susanna Iosifovna! This way, I'm sure, will be helpful: a bystander, a calm admonition. Oh, do see him! But"—a slanted wrinkle once again crossed Alina's now proud brow—"please, don't ask him to pity me. I don't want to *beg* for his mercy!"

"Yes, that's it! That's it exactly!" Susanna rejoiced. She stole a glance at the clock.

[51]

How many times—what was the count?—had the Bureau of the Progressive Bloc met in Room 11 of the Tauride Palace? The sessions stuck in memory as if the electricity were always on: in the evenings, even if in the afternoons, there was so little light in Petersburg that they turned on the table lamps under their dark green shades, and circles of light fell on the green velvet, open notebooks, pencils, fountain pens, and jacket sleeves.

They were meeting today as well, despite it being Sunday. Today, though, a brightly sunny day, the light did reach here. Although in it one sensed a sad impermanence falling on the worried faces.

Chairing the session, as usual, was plain-faced Shidlovsky, president of the Bloc's bureau. He spoke at length, and incoherently, as always when his speech had not been written in advance, his meaning was not everywhere discernible, and the flow was exhausting. At his side sat the Bloc's true chairman and leader, Milyukov. Since he could not always make the speeches himself, he directed his excess of mental energy to a penciled record of the theses of all the statements, although he himself saw no significant meaning in it.

How many times in this room over the last year and a half, sometimes half a dozen of them, sometimes fifteen or so—either just their own or with some from the State Council, too, or even guests from the Zemgor—had they assembled here, moved around, heated up, even jumped up in the small space or, on the contrary, drooped and dozed and merely sat through the regular sessions. The talk here was always frank. The oak doors and puttied double-frame windows kept secrets well, and the room had no secret cupboards or draperies. The patient Milyukov pencil noted all the Bloc's peripetiae, fractures, flights, and falls.

Milyukov alone, he was certain, understood all the drawing's lofty complexity.

Today they were at a new break, in the most complicated outline, and Milyukov did not even attempt to lay out this complexity to his mediocre interlocutors.

After his stormy speech of 14 November and the furious burst of union congresses on 23 December, January and February had dragged on in a kind of dull vegetative state. The entire constellation was such that the Duma and Zemgor sank into passivity, despite all their activity. November's mighty blow had been wasted, yielding no conclusive victorious result. If we weren't going to act, the popular masses would stop following us.

Now twelve days of the new Duma session had passed—and apparently they had gained a victory easily over the government again, right?—but again that victory had not been fully realized. They'd lashed, scourged, reviled, spat, and used the harshest words possible to their hearts' content with the kind of energy that rages from irresponsibility. All that remained, as Maklakov correctly said, was to beat the government with their fists. But in reply there'd been a distraught silence, with the sole exception of Rittikh; the government, as always, hid—hid—though it still didn't resign! They hadn't even knocked out the Prime Minister, something they'd achieved so easily in November. It had seemed like a victory, but they had lacked the means and ways for seizing it fully. Next autumn would be the new Duma elections, and the very passage of time was bringing the Bloc the risk of losing a supportive Fourth Duma. Who knew who would win—which meant new men would come. And the Tsar would be strengthened by victory in war.

Yes, it was a pathetic government, but how could it be replaced without some kind of shake-up? How could the government be pushed out without toppling the parliamentary order and letting it reach the point of revolution? An advantageous issue was the difficult food situation, but that could be corrected even before the spring mud season. Neither at the front nor in foreign policy were any major events taking place now on which an effective advance could be made. Rasputin? Even he was gone. The hopelessness of a victorious condition: their string of moral victories over the government was threatening to end in naught. Looming was the nightmare of tomorrow's empty Duma session with the inevitable new inquiry or shout—but louder no longer worked.

True, the gunfire on Nevsky last night and yesterday's dead provided an incontrovertible new platform for attack. Yesterday, hot on its heels, the City Duma had resolved the following: "this government, its hands red with the people's blood . . ."—and that could be developed, and tomorrow approved in the Duma from the Progressive Bloc—". . . this government does not dare show its face anymore in the State Duma, and the Duma is breaking with this government henceforth!" Cowardly murderers, they'd dared to use live ammunition! The Duma had to respond menacingly!

However. However, a struggle with the government requires a sense of measure, especially given these kinds of upheavals! They could not be driven as far as anarchy. Generations had stormed this wall of the regime and beaten on it with battering rams. But what if there were no wall anymore? Careful! The Duma was the country's nerve center. We were running the popular movement and were responsible for it, and it was justly aimed against Protopopov and the Tsaritsa.

Take Guchkov, that windbag Guchkov! How we had relied on his promised conspiracy! How picturesquely and mysteriously silent he had been at meetings. Did that mean it was close? But he kept dragging his feet on an overthrow.

A solution began to be seen now in confidential negotiations with the government. Talk the ministers' heads off completely—and confidentially: they were fit for nothing, their cause was lost, and they should resign quietly, all at once—and the Bloc would take their places. If that meant the Duma also breaking off for a week or two, that could be done. (This was even better since there was absolutely nothing to talk about.)

Precisely these very same extremely important negotiations were taking place this very afternoon, at that moment, between two ministers and two Duma members. However, it was Maklakov conducting the negotiations, not Milyukov. Milyukov was sitting outmaneuvered at a pointless, empty session. It was irritating. He envied Maklakov. He, Milyukov, was the master of diplomacy, after all, and he could wear down the ministers better.

On top of this whole pointless session, the caustic Shulgin had touched on a sore spot. With a special ability to unpleasantly insert his sting, across the very long table on a diagonal from Milyukov, with a smile under his turned-up mustache, he spoke almost tenderly:

"Gentlemen, we are quarreling very recklessly. We have no equals in criticism. We are the kings of criticism! The government has almost fallen and is lying in the dust. You can consider victory already won now, that tomorrow the Emperor will be fully convinced and at last call for *men of trust*. For over a year we have been chorusing unanimously for *individuals whom the entire country trusts*. But tell me, do we have a list like that which we could submit to the Emperor tomorrow?"

He cast a sharp glance at Milyukov, for who here was more worthy of pricks and whose skin was better protected by its thickness than Milyukov?

Yes, of course, this list should have been compiled long ago. But there were so many disagreements, couplings and uncouplings of forces, combinations, and plays of influence, a laboratory of moods and occasionally gossip and scandal, that *naming* a cabinet would mean destroying a great deal and pushing someone aside prematurely. It was more perspicacious not to name one for now. Yes, admittedly, no one knew any true specialists to be ministers. Only Milyukov's general intellectual and political superiority ensured him the foreign affairs portfolio without a doubt.

But Shulgin kept driving at his point:

"Does the 'Bloc's great charter' really have practical issues? Are we really going to be dealing from day one with the Ukrainian press and Jewish equality? Gentlemen, we are going to have to do a better job of waging the war and girding the rear for war. Are we capable of that? After all, government means knowing the apparatus and the methods of administration. Are you and I, for example, prepared?"

There was a seeming contradiction between the first tirade and the second. The first assumed that they didn't know who *these individuals* would be; but the second implied it would be they. Yes, knowing all the speakers and all the figures, it would be hard to imagine where a new government might be recruited from the outside rather than primarily from the Duma leadership.

No doubt, that's how it would be. But even the Prime Minister was not yet clear. Lately they'd been naming the zemstvo's Prince Lvov. (But in essence, Milyukov would also be the safest choice.)

Milyukov responded to Shulgin, but not on this point. He responded that the Bloc's program could not be more practical: to attain power invested with the popular trust. As soon as that power gained a foothold, then the best men would lead each department. Worthy ministers were the pledge of good administration. It was that way in the West, too. But, of course, we have been artificially removed from activities of state, which was why we have had little practice.

He looked to Shingarev for support. Shingarev, unfortunately, was too simple-minded. He always supported Milyukov fully, but he could not be led into any secret spring-loaded move. So, too, now, thinking that he was backing his leader, he replied, his soft hands folded on the table:

"But Vasili Vitalievich, we have touched on this question more than once, though we took care to step over it. This is awkward and tactless. What will people say about us?"

Shulgin performed a somersault with his pencil between his fingers.

"Andrei Ivanych, here you have politics Russian style: Everyone is bad, but no sooner do we get down to business than we feel awkward naming names. This way we will never have anything practical."

Right then the deep-set eyes of black-mustached, black-browed, bald-headed Vladimir Lvov, who was hunched over in his chair (his arms dangling between his knees nearly to the floor?), flashed prophetically, and he advised:

"That's right! The hour has come to name names. That is our right! And we cannot delegate it to anyone."

The quite mad black gleam of his eyes and certain turns of speech sometimes made one worry whether this Vladimir Lvov hadn't lost his marbles,

like the ill-starred Protopopov, who sometimes attracted attention as well,
but they had lowered their guard. After all, they had already applied this
Lvov to clerical affairs: after university he had audited courses at the Eccle-
siastical Academy and had trained the Duma and Bloc to think he was a
specialist in theology, and his gaze was like a fanatic's.

The Bloc bureau was silent. Someone sighed and someone shuffled
papers.

Outside, the day was fading. The tree trunks of the Tauride Garden stood
amid sunken, compacted snowdrifts.

The eight in the room were silent, and not a single sound reached them
from outside, not a single movement. So much had already been discussed
in the last eighteen months. So much! And all on the same point. No one
felt like talking anymore.

And Maklakov had not returned.

[5 2]

Not waiting for Maklakov, they called a break. Some went out to the
Ekaterininsky Hall.

Better than anyplace else in the palace, Shulgin liked this unusually
shaped hall, which had been inaugurated by a ball on the taking of Izmail,
and especially as it was now, as the sunset's last rays fell through the seven
very tall Venetian windows in the western semicircle. It was a long lake of
parquet, a hundred paces long, to the matching second eastern semicircle of
windows, and along its entire length on each side there were eighteen pairs
of Corinthian columns, and even inside the column pairs one could walk
freely three abreast. The parquet, polished on Saturday, shone and reflected
the white columns, and you could even vaguely catch the chandeliers—
seven enormous three-tiered chandeliers from the flat ceiling, rims with two-
headed eagles, and white candleholders all around. This hall was dazzling at
balls and lively and picturesque when functioning as the Duma lobby and
five hundred deputies in formal frock coats, cassocks, and peasant clothing
came spilling from the session hall, while the public—especially the ladies,
the ladies—descended the staircase from the gallery. But this hall was most
stunning empty, on non-session days, when one could in solitude, pensively,
slowly crisscross this incredible overarching expanse and ponder or simply
daydream—dreams here being particularly expansive, and Shulgin being so
inclined. In its emptiness, and on top of that at sunset, this hall linked the
soul exultantly and pensively, with a loftier, harmonious beauty.

Right now, though, Shulgin saw Maklakov enter the Ekaterininsky from
the Cupola Hall almost simultaneously. He couldn't make out the expression on his face, whether satisfied or dissatisfied, at a distance—but at a distance his confident, agile figure, always clothed in a beautifully tailored
but not overly new suit, created an impression of finish. Shulgin broke

away from his companions and walked quickly toward him. He had always liked Maklakov for his wit and aphorisms, the resourcefulness of his quick mind, the cheerful gleam in his eyes, and the depth, subtlety, and agility of his speeches' legal argumentation, which made him so eloquent, the siren of the Duma.

Vasili Maklakov was the most colorful figure in the Kadet Party—but not its leader. He was not a leader in general even, in principle. He asserted the heresy that a party program was not needed at all, that unanimity of thought on all points could not be required but could only coincide with the general direction. He never delivered even a single speech at the faction's behest but only when he wanted to and was himself so inclined. (He chose the kinds of speeches where he could display the most brilliance and have the greatest success.) Naturally, uniting twenty different opinions in an orchestra and keeping them all in the Bloc's channel—that was something Maklakov never could or would do. He had never belonged to the Bloc's bureau. Did that mean he wasn't Milyukov's rival? No, he was. Such perceptive opinions, analytical speeches, and fresh ideas never issued from Milyukov. Maklakov always outstripped him in all his ideas, both when it was time to engage in intensive struggle with the state and create in the Duma an artificially cohesive majority (the very idea of the Bloc) and when it was time to show patience and begin cooperating with the government, as he nearly alone had thought for the last few months—because on the whole he considered gradualism and evolution the law of life. Unlike the rest of the Kadet leadership, Maklakov had even feared the beginnings of revolution, the Kadet leadership believing that those guiding all public opinion could exploit the start of a revolution against the state and then stop it. A darling of fate and the public to whom all things in life had come easily, a successful hunter of ducks and women, always certain of his luck, Maklakov—in part due to these successes, in part due to his legal impartiality when he rose above the arguing sides—was always the first to call on people to listen to what was fair in his opponents' arguments, and so, out of the entire Kadet faction, he was the most acceptable for the government if negotiations were to be held. This was why it was he and the Octobrist Savich who were sent today to the Foreign Ministry on the Pevchesky Bridge for talks with Pokrovsky and Rittikh.

Due to the differences in their views, methods, and mode of action, the relationship between Milyukov and Maklakov gave rise to constant personal tension. Neither of them could replace the other but neither could be reconciled with the other, either.

And how had it gone today? What had happened? Shulgin was anxious to find out. A group of them formed upon their meeting and others joined.

Milyukov stood at a distance, by a column. But it seemed there was already a group here, and Maklakov could and already had begun to report the news—so Milyukov was forced to overcome his reluctance, and without hurrying, as if condescending, come join them.

The fact that Milyukov had the look of a firmly convinced cat in spectacles—many knew that. But Shulgin himself was of the opinion that Milyukov looked like a scholarly Prussian general, only in civilian clothes for some reason. Anyone to whom Shulgin expressed this resemblance laughed, so apropos was it. He held his head firmly, and his gaze was firm, his brow broad and low, with all the signs of firmness, further strengthened by all the doctrine he had learned. And there was also his smooth, graying hair, stiff mustache, and gold spectacles.

Whereas Maklakov was a vibrant, artistic iridescence that at any given moment merely took on a suitable shape. All his features seemed to change at will. Already trailing a string of famous advocatory and political speeches, a smart man, a lucky man, he had not led the party, which may have been why he seemed younger than his forty-seven years; in the charm of his quick smile flashed young, white teeth, and in his quiet but distinct and pure voice, with a slightly French "r," he reported the following:

"Well, gentlemen, the ministers are utterly distraught. We have virtually finished them off. More than half of them are quite amenable to resigning. Of course, that doesn't mean the Tsar will permit the government to resign or reconstitute itself."

"But you gave them an additional good scare?" Milyukov asked.

Maklakov's focused, intelligent eyes left no doubt that everything had been weighed and said.

"Yes, they're eager to dissolve the Duma. But I told them. . . . I warned them that the Duma, if dissolved, would become omnipotent. All Russia would start talking: Why was it dissolved? And in a few weeks you yourself would be begging us to return."

"But for a few days was all right, you said?" Milyukov inquired exactingly. No one could have negotiated better than him anyway.

"Yes, naturally," the delegate of free thought, not the Bloc, looked at him lightly but closely. "Dissolve it for a few days, I said, and we'll have a rest, too. Dissolve it, but on condition the entire cabinet resigns. And in those few days a new Prime Minister would assemble a new cabinet and bring it to the Duma when it opens."

Milyukov didn't object. He always took his time pondering. But apparently Maklakov had been so empowered? This was not all, though.

"But I told them, only God forbid you choose a public figure for Prime Minister."

Milyukov frowned and became forbidding and even turned red:

"And why is that?"

Maklakov, without belaboring the point, explained to everyone:

"What do we understand about administration? We don't know the techniques, we've had no time to study them. *Invested with trust*—that's all well and good, but what do we know besides speeches?"

"But who then?" Milyukov choked. It was too soon to name *individuals*, but public figures—that was the only possibility! With his slight little smile, Maklakov had dismissed all their efforts on his own authority?

And with a welcoming bow, slippery and swift, he said:

"Bureaucrats, naturally. Good, intelligent, enlightened bureaucrats. Let Krivoshein, Sazonov, and Samarin return. But for Prime Minister I advised them only a general would do! Not Alekseev, of course—not enough sparkle. But Ruzsky: he's smart and genteel and has public ambition. He would put together a cabinet politically and appear before the Duma as the representative of the military command, and the Duma would deny him nothing. I guarantee stormy applause."

But now another general, in another form and sense, was indignant, and his eyes filled:

"Vasili Alekseevich, this is unforgivable! You have exceeded your authority! You were not . . ."

On the diagonal across the hall, out of the depths, someone was walking this way. Maklakov hurried to finish explaining:

"Pavel Nikolaevich, this is realistic and the best solution now. This is if the cabinet resigns and the supreme power accepts it. The politician's task is to build using the materials he has. The point isn't for us to come to power no matter what but to preserve the state's stability even in time of upheaval. Power is not among the liberal values."

It was Kerensky walking their way, quickly, a narrow, forward-leaning figure. Keeping up behind him was the scruffy Skobelev.

The group by the column became quiet: the socialists were outsiders.

But Kerensky looked at the group flirtatiously, from a quarter-turn sideways, and as he passed exclaimed:

"Ah, the Bloc! What's the matter, Bloc? Why aren't you taking power?"

And he kept walking. With Skobelev behind him, like his adjutant.

Milyukov and Maklakov did not deign to reply, but Shulgin, always disposed toward joking, said:

"We're afraid we won't be able to cope with the Ministry of the Interior."

"Well, well!" Kerensky willingly screeched. And he waved one hand in greeting, turning his wrist: "A few freedoms. . . . A few assemblies, unions, and so forth. . . . Hurry along, gentlemen, hurry along!"

And he himself hurried along, rushing lightly to the Cupola Hall.

They passed by and Milyukov condemned him even more decisively.

"No, this is unforgivable! You should not have . . . proposed that."

Maklakov raised his drawn eyebrows. And dropped this:

"Pavel Nikolaevich! *Quieta non movere!*"[2]

---

2. Move not what lies quiet (Lat.)—Let sleeping dogs lie.

[5 3]

What made Gorky's apartment on Kronverksky so remarkable was that it was a bustling revolutionary headquarters! In permanent operation and with a perpetual influx of people and news—and inviolable to the police, who dared not encroach on this apartment! In addition, they always fed you (not that you were served, but you could take something to eat, anyone who was there often). People came who were unknown to either the host or the usual visitors—but someone brought them and they, too, told stories. Gorky himself loved this stream of people, stories, and news very much, frequently abandoning his own writing to emerge from his study and mingle, sitting and himself calling on people to tell their stories. True, lots of foolish people came to see him, utter ignoramuses and sots, but there were also many revolutionaries, especially Bolsheviks.

As Gorky's right hand on *Annals*—well, simply the actual editor and principal worker—Himmer was there nearly every day and felt altogether at home. So, too, yesterday he had spent the entire remainder of the day and evening here. So, too, today, having risen late, it being Sunday, he decided there was no better place to go than Gorky's. When the news didn't come to Gorky of its own accord, Himmer would fetch it over the telephone. He would sit down and start calling around to various people he knew—not the most important figures, but still from the bourgeois, lawyerly, intellectual, and literary world and even the periphery of the bureaucratic one.

But today, in the first few hours of the afternoon, sitting at Gorky's, he had been unable to learn anything. And so a small company, including Himmer, another *Annals* associate Bazarov (in honor of Turgenev's), and others, set out to gather personal observations. They needed to go to Nevsky, of course. All the events were there. But at the Trinity Bridge the crowd had dammed up the square. Then again, dense groups were buzzing around the people who had already returned from the other side. Everyone was telling the same story—whether from what they had seen or from other people's words—that today there had been shooting in the city, with live ammunition, and there had been casualties. Some said about thirty; others a few thousand, that all Nevsky had been blanketed.

If that was the case, then it was getting dangerous to go there and perhaps it was better to find out some other way. To wait here a little longer.

Soldiers were walking back and forth on the wall of the Peter and Paul Fortress near the cannons. Were they anticipating military actions? Although shots from there would have swept away the crowd, right now the crowd was observing them with curiosity.

The Trinity Bridge had been partitioned off by reserve grenadiers. Though there was also an officer here, a lively discussion was under way between the crowd and soldiers. They were piling it on thick—about the government, Rasputin, the Tsar, and the war. Some soldiers kept silent and others laughed, but no one put up any defense. No, the leadership could hardly act on suppression using these soldiers. It was impossible to imagine this detachment, for instance, taking aim.

They didn't let them all, the crowd, through at once, but you could still cross to the other side one by one. But it would be surer to return to Gorky's and find out everything over the telephone.

Something interesting was cooking!

But Gorky had sat there by the telephone all those hours. He already knew about the shootings and knew that public circles were shaken yet also distraught, for no one had devised a way to respond to this. And clearly their philistine heads weren't rising any higher than "the most decisive notions."

Now Himmer, too, was hanging on the telephone and starting to call his leftist figures. There was a proposal to gather and discuss for the evening, probably at Kerensky's. Everyone agreed that the leftists should exploit the moment, but no one knew where to start.

The person Himmer could not call was Shlyapnikov, who did not have a telephone. They lived over there in their Vyborg lairs, without telephones. His nerves were shot.

But the telephone mercifully filled a lot of time: on the telephone you didn't seem to notice the time.

[5 4]

It was Sunday—but you couldn't tell, going from one patient to the next. She didn't even go to church for Mass because she'd been tired since morning—and she was more needed here, with the sick.

Taking this the hardest was Anya Vyrubova, given her tendency to panic and focus always on just herself. Every minute she was tended by not one but two nurses at once, and in the morning four children's doctors came, and then Botkin and Derevenko in alternation, and yet another doctor had spent the previous night near her, a doctor she particularly liked. Anya quite occupied an entire wing of the palace, and she demanded that the younger healthy children visit her three times a day, and the Empress twice, morning and evening—and the Empress meekly carried out the desires of this mannered, exhausting, and forever trusted friend.

Marie and Anastasia were proud that they weren't ill and would either sit at bedsides, or telephone their friends to report and learn the news. In general, they were a great help to their mother, but she was afraid these two would succumb as well. All the patients had a bad cough and a bad rash. Baby was covered with it, like a leopard, and to her alarm, he had gotten worse and his temperature was nearly forty.

The Guards crew touchingly sent Olga, Tatyana, and Anya each a bunch of lilies of the valley, and their subtle fragrance now lingered in their dark, curtained rooms.

Generally speaking, receiving flowers during those days had become more difficult, and there were not different ones, their own, in every room as usual.

What was going on there in the city? In the afternoon a sweet note arrived from Protopopov, which he had written at four in the morning, after the ministers' nighttime session. Arrests had been made of revolutionaries, the very top leaders. But the mayor was not coping well in the City Duma with the insolent speeches—and he and the speakers would be made to answer. Stern, energetic measures were being taken, and by Monday everything would be perfectly calm.

Well, thank God. It had been learned from various informants that yesterday afternoon a poor police officer had been killed. But generally speaking the disturbances did not in the least resemble 1905. Everyone adored the Emperor and were only worried about the bread shortage.

The idiots, they couldn't get the bread right.

A letter arrived from Nicky, and she pressed it to her lips. (And the Belgian cross came for Aleksei.) My God, how awful his solitude must be for him at GHQ!

Such a nice sun was shining today—such a nice sun, pure and joyful. All would end well!

The sun lured her outside. The best hour to go pray at the Friend's grave.

She took Marie, the healthiest, with her and set out in the motorcar. The grave was at the forest's edge, on Anya's land. The nice sun shone approvingly, although lacklusterly.

Ever since people had committed that outrage at the grave last month, they had had to set a sentry here, someone on permanent duty.

Because of this, of course, the profound and unimpeded communication with the deceased that one can experience in a solitary visit was lost. But they had already begun to raise a log chapel around the grave—and today it had achieved a height such that, when you stepped inside, you were visible to the duty officer and driver only above the shoulders. And Marie was not visible at all.

The square of logs created solitude. Above was God's sky and the sun, but from the side they could not be seen. A temple-like feeling.

Marie stood stern and silent, understanding.

Aleksandra dropped before the grave mound—to her knees, right in the snow, on the turned-up hem of her coat.

Here she was beside him, she sensed the man of God, she conversed with His spirit and with God simultaneously.

They had killed Him, killed her very soul, and a defenseless, naked existence had begun. It had always consoled her so, sometimes on sleepless nights, to know that His prayers watched over the Tsar's family. His teachings rang in her ears: ask not of your mind but of your heart. Let the mind be in a state of grace. Joy by the throne.

Oh God, yet shall we all feel His departure. Since that day there has been steady collapse. Just as he had predicted. Now all catastrophes were possible. For His murder, all Russia would suffer.

But he did live and did die to save us all.

And now he would intercede and pray for us in the next world.

How they, those nonentities, despised Him! They had gotten what they wanted. . . . From this holy place there now spread serenity and peace.

For a contemplative and mystically sensitive soul such as Aleksandra possessed, there was no impermeable barrier between the next world and this. The effects of our actions, our thoughts, and the will of heaven passed back and forth. A man of God had been killed, but he did not die, and here she was now just as undisturbed beside him as before, during their conversations, when his powerful gray eyes shed a saving light on her. She felt Him wholly here, beside her, and, through the blanket of snow, the earthen mound and the coffin.

The Empress was waiting for a saving miracle for the throne and Russia—from the people themselves, from their righteous men of prayer. (In no way was she more a German—she was less German!—than Catherine, whom this country recognized as great.) And her all-seeing, heaven-sent Friend had been the obvious expression of that all-Orthodox connection and all-national aid.

Aleksandra had always sought mysteries, signs, and miracles—through faith. She awaited them! She believed in them!

But by some characteristic of her nature, or in touching on the unsurmountable true essence of things, she inclined more toward bad presentiments and melancholy. Traveling in the summer of '14 on their yacht to the Finnish skerries, something had sadly insisted in her: Could it be that this is the last time we'll travel so happily together? They had left Livadia in the spring of that year, and everything sang mournfully: Could it be that we will never ever return here? On the evening of 1 August she learned that war had begun—and she sobbed and sobbed, foreseeing inevitable calamities.

Now in December, in Novgorod, she had stopped by to visit the aged nun Maria Mikhailovna in her tiny cell, where she lay on an iron bed with her iron chains beside her. She was 107 but sewed linens for soldiers and prisoners without spectacles. She never washed—and there was no smell. Curly gray hair and a sweet face with young, shining eyes. And what had she seen in the entering woman? She held out her desiccated hands: "Here comes the martyr Tsaritsa Aleksandra!" And she had blessed her. "And you, my beauty, fear not your heavy cross!" A few days later she passed away, as if she had only been waiting for that visit.

Why a martyr? Wasn't the life of a powerful Tsaritsa the furthest thing from that?

That meant she had seen something.

Everything was leading to evil and a fall.

[5 5]

Petersburg was not altogether new to General Khabalov. In the previous century he had served here in various posts at HQ for fourteen years running. Subsequently, for fourteen years of this century, in other towns, always in one military training institution or another, for the education of youth. But before he knew it, life was passing him by. At fifty-five he was appointed military governor of Ural Province and commanding ataman of the Ural Cossacks—immediately before the war. There he had had all of nine regiments, all of which left for the war, and Khabalov could serve calmly in his deeply loyal province. Unfortunately, though, last summer he had been made commander of the overstocked, extremely demanding Petrograd Military District. True, not an independent command, but subordinate to the Northern Army Group, so that the main concerns with this garrulous city, its military censorship, and its truant workers rested on General Ruzsky.

But now a week ago, fatefully, or rather at Protopopov's suggestion, His Imperial Majesty had expressed the desire to make the Petrograd District separate—so that all the weight rested on Khabalov's shoulders. (True, the post was equivalent to army commander and the salary was higher.)

Then all at once all this had begun. A major revolutionary march had been scheduled for the day the Duma opened, 27 February, and Khabalov had had to issue a proclamation saying Petrograd was under martial law and any resistance to legal authority would be immediately halted by force of arms. (That is what he wrote, though he himself didn't know what they would tell him from above, and the order came down: in no instance, not a single bullet.)

Fortunately, the march disintegrated and never happened. But the situation in Petrograd was seriously unsettled. After two weeks of drifting snow, the railroads were struck by temperatures forty degrees below zero, and the deserted countryside couldn't keep up with shoveling out the rails—and deliveries of flour to Petrograd fell, and due to a rumor, embittered lines formed for black bread. (It was a serious matter. Even the general's wife laid in generous stores of flour, groats, and oil.)

In the event of disturbances, a plan was worked out as to how to distribute troops among the districts, and General Chebykin knew all this, and he knew the entire officer corps—but at just this moment he went off to Kislovodsk for a rest. (And the main copy of the plan could not be found without him, either.) Colonel Pavlenko, who substituted for him, was recovering from a serious wound and didn't know Petrograd or anyone here. One way or another, all the commanders of the reserve battalions were ill because front-line Guards units did not let healthy officers go. Also, the chief of the Corps of Gendarmes, General Count Tatishchev, had also absented himself, immediately prior, the very day the Emperor left Tsarskoye

Selo for GHQ. And that was when it had all begun! There was no more going to Ruzsky on the neighboring front for instructions. And you couldn't reach the Emperor. Why disturb him for nothing anyway?

Here Khabalov had been sitting for more than two days not in his office at HQ even but in the city governor's offices, where all the lines of communication converged until the police were routed. Here, in a few adjoining rooms with doors flung open, they all sat: Khabalov and his chief of staff Tyazhelnikov and the concussed Colonel Pavlenko, the command of the Guards troops, and the police authorities. Major General Tyazhelnikov had been seriously wounded and permanently disabled. But his resignation had not been accepted, and he had been appointed here, to District HQ, with a still unhealed wound, by the Emperor's own order. Pavlenko had been so concussed that he had trouble getting out his words, and he could not always be understood by those near him in the room; when he spoke over the telephone he could hardly be understood at the other end. A string of completely irrelevant people—city dwellers coming with their fears or ridiculous requests and in their crush only getting in everyone's way—kept pouring in.

Khabalov felt as if he had landed in a cauldron where he had been stewed for days and days, and there was little he himself could do. Everything that happened—voices reached him, faces popped up, decisions were requested—everything happened through the drone of this alien cauldron.

He could never have imagined a situation such as now, had never been caught up this way: it was as if regulations were no longer in effect. He had troops—and seemed not to. Unruly crowds roamed everywhere freely, themselves not knowing what they wanted, because apparently they didn't want bread, either. Occupied the day before yesterday and yesterday with how best to arrange for the baking of bread, today the general had stopped fussing about bread and had lost heart. Khabalov fell into a state that bore him, pushed him, spun him around, and all to this drone, and the only thing that kept him going was the hope that eventually the day would end and things would calm down for the night, thank God—and then he could go home to sleep after covering the telephone with cushions. For the time being, you had to sit here and pretend you were steering events.

Things had gotten so out of hand that arriving officers were meddling with unsolicited advice: a captain from Gatchina, he had a motorized detachment, eight armored cars, he said, with reliable officers and soldiers, even merely passing through the streets they would have a powerful effect on the crowd.

"Be so kind, captain, as not to prevent the authorities from performing their duty. It is not your place to offer advice. Return to your unit!"

Also from time to time Khabalov was called to the telephone by the War Minister, the puppet General Belyaev, who kept asking for reports on what was going on in the city—although he himself could undertake nothing—it was Khabalov all the same. The reports dribbling into the city governor's offices could not all be verified, and some were simply false.

Now Rodzyanko himself called Khabalov, but why? What subordination necessitated answering him? "Your Excellency, why are you shooting? Why this blood?" "Mr. President, I grieve no less than you that we have had to resort to this measure, but the force of things has compelled us." "What force of things is that?" "Since there is an attack on our troops under way, they cannot be a target, and they, too, must use weapons." "And where is this attack on troops?" He enumerated for him. "Forgive me, Your Excellency, the policemen themselves are throwing squibs!" "And what is the point in them throwing squibs?"

A battle in the city! Where had this ever been heard of? How should it be waged? Khabalov, in any case, didn't know.

Yesterday Khabalov for a long time had been unable to believe that a Cossack had killed a police officer. If that was so, then how had that happened? What should be done?

Last night the disturbances reached such a scale that Khabalov had to report in detail by telegraph to General Alekseev at GHQ. Sunday morning had started out so hopefully, and Khabalov had reported that the city was calm. But since midday anyway people had been making their way, collecting from the outskirts, and all of them had gone to Nevsky coming from the north and east. Clashes had begun in the side-streets, so far only with the mounted police. But pieces of ice, stones, and bottles had flown at the troops—and how much were the troops supposed to stand? In a few spots on Nevsky, from Gostiny Dvor to Suvorovsky, they fired, first in the air and here and there with blanks—but the crowd did not disperse as a result and merely mocked them, already used to their impunity. Then they fired straight into the assemblage. But even those who did scatter, leaving the dead and wounded on the pavement, did not run far but hid in nearby courtyards and side-streets and again began to gather. What should he do?

After Znamenskaya Square was cleared, they gathered in the lanes near Staro-Nevsky and from there fired around the corners at the military details. Nonetheless, they got by without major attacks by the crowd on the troops, and there was hope that the crowd's ardor was cooling and now would soon be extinguished. Nevsky was already clearing out, the armed patrols were taking control, and the cavalry was riding out, so one could expect a favorable conclusion to the day. After all, the first gunfire had had an overwhelming effect on the crowd.

Then all of a sudden a report came in over the telephone about an incredible event: the 4th Company of the Pavlovsky Life Guards Reserve Battalion had rushed out of the building of the Office of Palace Stables, where they were quartered, onto the street, without their officers, firing straight up and shouting, had gathered on Konyushennaya Square—and from there had begun to move along the canal toward the Cathedral of the Savior on the Spilled Blood.

Telephone calls followed more telephone calls—with reports and inquiries about what to do. From here the advice was naturally to try to persuade them, remind them of their oath, and to summon the Pavlovsky Battalion's commander.

Instead, a report came in saying that the mutinous company had clashed with a mounted police guard platoon, had dropped to the ground and fired on it.

Khabalov found this new information altogether questionable. Why would soldiers be firing at a mounted police guard? The unrelenting boom and buzz allowed for any silly lie.

It was reported that the company was demanding that the entire Pavlovsky Battalion be returned to barracks and stop firing in the city!

This could not be happening!

It was reported that Colonel Eksten had arrived. But while he was trying to persuade the mutineers, a crowd gathered behind him and from there a student fired a pistol at the colonel, wounding him seriously in the neck.

Now that was something!

Nonetheless, it turned out that the company had been calmed by the persuasions of the regimental priest and had allowed themselves to be returned to barracks.

Thank God.

Now the barracks were locked, and the officers were with their soldiers. Little by little they agreed to surrender their rifles, too. There were far from enough rifles for everyone there, one in ten perhaps; but even of those, twenty-one had disappeared! They had disappeared from the barracks, which meant they had gone to the city's crowd. And perhaps the soldiers themselves with them? They still hadn't taken a headcount.

What was the commander to do in this unusual instance? He reported over the telephone to War Minister Belyaev, who demanded a field court-martial that very minute—and the instigators shot.

How's that? And at which end was he to begin?

The company was too large for an investigation and trial: there were apparently about eight hundred men there. They called the prosecutor at the district court: Is a field court-martial possible without a preliminary inquiry? Apparently it wasn't. But you couldn't question eight hundred men in a week.

Then it became clear that there were fifteen hundred not eight hundred, so inflated were the reserve companies, more than a normal battalion. But then forgetting about the inquiry, there turned out to be no building in the Peter and Paul Fortress that could hold fifteen hundred.

He called the War Minister yet again about the hopeless situation.

It was decided to lock up at least the instigators in the fortress.

[5 6 ']

(THE PAVLOVSKY MUTINY)

Every turn of thought Rodzyanko, Milyukov, and Kerensky had has been preserved for us (albeit written up later, in emigration), and each step they made has been brought down to us. But the thoughts, actions, and very names of the fifteen hundred soldiers in the 4th "marching" Company of the Pavlovsky Reserve Battalion were not recorded, justified, or clarified by anyone and have entered our history only in an ossified flare-up and its brief end result. No one left notes or stories; the usual muteness of ordinary people. And among the educated, none thought to question them afterward, when the memory was fresh, and create a record. (Our Aleksandr Blok wrote his own pen dry recording the inquiries on the Extraordinary Commission of Inquiry, where a sensation was expected.) Only a brief group letter from the Pavlovsky men to the newspaper has been preserved. In the scorch of those days nothing was confirmed in documents, but if it had been, would it have made it through four years of Petrograd's extinction and half a century of disregard for February?

So, the page has come for describing the Pavlovsky Battalion's mutiny—but it cannot be written without some guesswork.

The Pavlovsky was a "marching" company because it comprised those with the most readiness for active duty, those better trained and recuperating after a front-line wound, that is, soldiers who had experienced war and were waiting to be sent back. All the previous days this company had not been taken out for street detail; it had heard stories but seen nothing itself. However, due to the haste in reinforcing the Guards reserve battalions, the company had also acquired freshly mobilized Petrograd workers, who retained their vital connection to the city and some of whom saw people they knew, and leaflets and proclamations were brought to other barracks. We know that discipline was lax in the barracks, and even before this outsiders had gotten in and called on them to support their brother workers. During this spate of urban upheavals, agitators could penetrate the barracks at night as well and tell stories and appeal to them.

There is evidence that on Sunday, after midday, a group of workers steamed toward the men on duty at the gates of the 4th Company, straight from Nevsky, probably. They ran up and told them that the Pavlovsky men had just fired along the avenue. It's clear that they were blaming *these* men for *those*. How could they stand for their regiment firing on the people? (These agitators themselves were not ambitious, or very sophisticated, for none of them published in the next few newspapers, which were eager for any stories or gossip about February, so we do not know the details.) Well, and the obvious hung over them, of course: "And here you are feeding the bedbugs on your triple bunks!"

The 4th Company had some who had fought under Pavlovsky regimental banners—and some, albeit not everyone, were full of regimental pride. How could that be? "Your regiment is firing on the people!" From educated men we have vague scraps: "They're leading you *the wrong way!*"

Was it the soldier's business to fire on the crowd? (And what were your police doing?)

And look: the 4th marching Company dashed out and started running to the street! (There were also men, Petersburg men, driving them out.) At first, of course, only five or ten, but then several hundred—and there, look, all fifteen hundred. Some did stay back in the barracks, and some in the yard, and some past the gates. At first, maybe, without rifles, but they quickly grasped that they should take their rifles, however there were only a hundred for the fifteen hundred, and those were probably rifles of various models. They ran out without understanding exactly what should be done other than stop them! Our Pavlovsky men must not fire at the people! All the Pavlovsky companies must be returned to barracks! They must not fire at all!

But once they flooded out, no one knew where to run. That meant they would bunch up, stop, someone would shout, someone would wave a rifle, someone would light up, someone would wipe his nose.

But their noses—their noses still looked alike, not the former select Pavlovsky men but short and snub-nosed, like Paul I, somewhat more of those.

It wasn't yet five o'clock and the shrouded sun had still not left the sky, although it hung low. An hour and a half of daylight remained.

They flooded out, from the former palace stables, from the semi-circular colonnade, onto Konyushennaya Square, one of Petersburg's inimitable secluded places: that corner near the Moika between the circular market with the bas-reliefs of bulls' heads and the little cube of a church where the dead Pushkin lay and whose burial service was supposed to have been held there, but a crowd converged—so that night they took him to the Svyatogorsk monastery. That closed corner where one bend of the streetcar or a hundred steps past the cellar-level Comedians' Halt of the Silver Age (formerly the Stray Dog) led to the vast expanse of the Field of Mars, while from Konyushennaya there seemed to be no exit in any direction. It was buttoned up tight.

But they already knew and realized this—and they thronged, not in formation, any which way, not soldiers but a crowd—and took the direct road to Nevsky, and if they formed up in rows of four, they took up the full breadth of this narrow bank of the Ekaterininsky Canal, between the embankment's railing and the apartment houses. There was no changing direction or going around.

It was less than half a mile to Nevsky, but they managed to run-walk only two-thirds of the way. They stopped not just anywhere but right by the Cathedral of the Savior on the Spilled Blood, across the canal from the fateful spot where a bomb had blown up Aleksandr II.

Their incoherent, noisy, wild flow, with shouts, curses, arm waving, and no order whatsoever, attracted the attention of a mounted police detail guarding the approaches to Nevsky along the canal.

The universally despised police, whom no one supported, their foot component having already been routed on previous days, still managed to hold the crowds back in many places that day using mounted patrols. For all the days before that, the details have been preserved for us not by historians—revolutionary, liberal, or conservative—but only in police reports, with their full accounts and enviable precision. So the clash with the Pavlovsky men would have been known to us in more detail if the police had lasted one more day.

The mounted police guard, ten on horseback, blocked the path of the Pavlovsky stream, but the Pavlovsky men were out to prove something to someone—here, to the police. Rifles began to fire of their own accord, and almost all into the air. Evidently hands on neither side were prepared to fire at a live target.

But the spot was simply impassable, and just two marksmen could hold back a regiment. So the Pavlovsky men couldn't break through to Nevsky and the mounted police couldn't knock them back to Konyushennaya. Yes, there was probably a crush and panic, since there were several hundred unarmed men. They probably forced their way back through their own and crossed the little bridge to hide behind the cathedral. Many were already thinking how to save themselves here rather than stand up for the truth.

No losses were reported among the Pavlovsky men, so presumably there weren't any. But among the police, one policeman was killed, one wounded, and also two horses. At a distance like this, this was less a skirmish than an angry shouting match made even louder by the crowdedness of the street.

Soon the Pavlovsky men ran out of bullets, there not being many more bullets than rifles. And they started to fall back, fall back, from the Savior on the Spilled Blood, back to Konyushennaya Square.

All this took perhaps as much as an hour. The Pavlovsky men had only that quarter-mile along the canal, and their impotence, and their muddle, and now their regret. Why had they started this? Why had they run out of the barracks? While somewhere, inaudible to them, telephones were ringing, somewhere someone was called for and dispatched, they were already moving to cordon off Konyushennaya Square with a company apiece of Preobrazhensky men and Kexholmers, each with a machine gun, and Colonel Eksten, the commander himself of the Pavlovsky Reserve Battalion, rushed there in a sledge.

Meanwhile, adding to the turmoil—coming from Malaya Konyushennaya, Italyanskaya, and Engineers streets—were the people, the motleyest of people, not cordoned off by anyone, so they could press up to the spectacle.

Meanwhile, the light was failing.

When Colonel Eksten, having no higher ground, began to speak loudly and forcefully to his mutineers, not so much exhorting, probably, as upbraiding—close behind them from the civilian crowd a pistol shot rang out, hitting the colonel right in the neck from behind, and at that his speech ended.

From all these days we note how here and there a university student, or even a high school student, a youth with ideas, would take an instigating shot (those who needed pistols had them), inevitably exacerbating the clash.

They carried away the wounded colonel. They did not respond by firing on the crowd, and they couldn't find the shooter. The twilight thickened. Others wishing to exhort the soldiers were not to be found. But out of a sense of duty, the battalion priest had been summoned and was supposed to speak.

We don't even know his name. Nor his previous or subsequent service. Nor a single word or argument from his speech. But who hasn't given some thought to this ever bitter ambivalence of the regimental priest? Who preaches the Word of God and peace to those who carry a sword and at the same time for this sword to better smite the enemy? And now, although he called on his flock verily not to shoot but to make peace—wasn't this in order that others could shoot unimpeded?

Perhaps the priest was pricked by these contradictions and barely spoke. But more than likely, all the ready-made phrases and necessary texts immediately tripped off his tongue and carried him along smoothly. Whether or not he did much to convince the Pavlovsky men, after his speech, now in the dark, the encircled men began to drift gradually toward the barracks.

After the events these Pavlovsky men had had one freedom: to run off in the heat of the moment before they could be encircled. It was frightening for a soldier to run, especially a soldier from elsewhere. Where could he go from the barracks? Where was a haven for a soldier, where would he be awaited and fed? And if he was caught?

Still, twenty-one men with rifles hid. So they knew where to go? Around the rest a ring closed of the same reserve Guards, and they could stay on the square all they wanted, but the only road was back to the barracks.

Which were more a prison now than a barracks. The rifles were surrendered.

The outburst was over, and the day was over, and the barracks were locked—so the Pavlovsky men were left to themselves, for a slow rethinking.

They say officers entered with them. But there were relatively few officers in their company in general and almost no wounded front-line officers. And those rookie ensigns, who hadn't been anywhere yet, and who had been sent here only recently—no one listened to them.

The Pavlovsky men were left in the surrounded barracks alone, gripped and weighed by anguish. What would happen to them now? They weren't little boys. They realized there had been a military uprising, and during time of war. So did that mean death?

The rumor lingered like a chill near the floor that all of them, fifteen hundred of them, had been ordered shot within twenty-four hours.

No one felt like sleeping.

There were the instigators and there were just the gray cattle, nothing whatever to do with them. That sleepless night, a murmur ricocheted from bunk to bunk: "Because of you . . ."

Men don't recognize themselves in these impulsive events—when they run and shout or when they recover from their hangover.

That night many superiors, outside officers, silver and gold epaulets, arrived, more than they had seen in one place in their entire lives.

The soul sinks, as if felled by a heavy weight.

They were formed up in a few ranks in front of their bunks, and formed up again, and divided up, and dragged in for questioning to the office separately, and threatened, and demanded that they name the instigators!

They had just been naming them, in front of each other, to their face. The most zealous had left with their rifles. Some didn't even understand why they'd been shouting and running. The next time they wouldn't run for anything.

Who could show us a torment graver than this crushing boulder of having to choose? Will you speak up and in an alien voice name a comrade so that he might die instead of you? Could anyone who has heard such hoarse voices ever forget?

Late that night, nineteen named instigators were taken away to the Peter and Paul Fortress.

[5 7]

On the telephone, you don't notice the time. Not only that, he took turns with Gorky, and others had also slipped in to call. It had grown dark long before; night had fallen.

Gorky telephoned Chaliapin, by the way, and learned an odd bit of news. Chaliapin had only just had a call from Leonid Andreev, who was lodging on the Field of Mars, next to the Pavlovsky barracks. So he had personally seen out the window an infantry unit advance on the Pavlovsky barracks from the Field of Mars.

If he wasn't imagining it, then what on earth could that have been? A struggle among the troops? Utterly unbelievable!

Himmer feverishly stepped up his telephone activity. He called again and again and began getting confirmations that yes, something had happened around the Pavlovsky Regiment, and there had also been shooting at the Ekaterininsky Canal.

Finally he was in luck: he caught Kerensky himself at home, he having just run in from the Duma. Kerensky announced into the telephone in a gulping-triumphant, shuddering voice that the entire Pavlovsky Regiment had **all mutinied**, gone out on the street and fired on any of their own who were passive and stayed in the barracks!

This was earthshaking! This exceeded all expectations! If this was true, then the Tsarism card had been trumped! A tremendous event!

Himmer walked away from the telephone and tried to find somewhere to be alone (this was impossible in Gorky's apartment, except in the WC, and that not for long) to think through what this implied. Right now there were no strong minds for revolution in Petrograd (Kerensky was superficial, Chkheidze complacent, Sokolov foolish, Nakhamkes overcautious, Shlyapnikov primitive, and the rest even paler). Himmer alone had to mark out the path for everyone about what to do and what measures were essential. But now he had a case of nerves and couldn't think himself.

One thing was clear: the time had come for the major political decisions he had been thinking of constantly!

He might have been able to think it through if he'd had peace and quiet to ponder, but he was again pulled back to the telephone and discussions—and meanwhile a comrade appeared, a genuine witness from the Ekaterininsky Canal, and he recounted everything differently: one small Pavlovsky detachment, which had been sent somewhere for some reason, had been fired upon by mounted police, evidently in error, but had fired back—and then surrendered and let themselves be driven into the barracks.

All that iridescent excitement subsided. This was not a great instance, not a breach in the firmament of Tsarism.

But there was also no need now to take any important decision.

Himmer began trying to get through to Kerensky again. His telephone was wearisomely busy, and the young operator was tired of turning him down. They were simply talking nonstop. It was already after eight when Himmer was connected.

Kerensky's voice was unrecognizable; it was that subdued. Yes, they had been misled. It had been only one company, which immediately surrendered.

And he said into the telephone prophetically:

"Much blood will be shed. They will suppress it cruelly."

And so? Did this mean the government had won today?

Yes, it did.

Did that mean all these days we've been rushing about for nothing?

Apparently so.

[5 8]

On Sunday, as usual, the Emperor set out for mass at the old seminary Church of the Holy Trinity, on a bluff over the Dnieper. The bishop had ceded it to GHQ, so it was called the headquarters church. It wasn't far, and the Emperor gladly went on foot. He liked to go to church on foot, as being surer, though he didn't always have the freedom for that. He went with two escorts and himself wore a Convoy uniform. At the headquarters church a separate place had been reserved for him in the left choir stalls, which was half closed off from the church by a column and large icons. It was easier to pray unconstrained when hundreds of eyes weren't studying you. It was nice to go unremarked.

The usual service was under way and he stood there praying entirely as usual. He closely followed the words of everything said and sung, which he had studied since childhood, and in places focused and laid his requests on the wings of prayers. His first request to the Lord, the most extensive and constant, was for our brave troops and for granting them a well-earned victory. The entire life of the state and the Emperor himself now came down to this: He could organize nothing in the country, nor could he even live, unless they emerged victorious from this war. Morning and evening, every day, Nikolai raised up this prayer, and when he prayed he was always visited by the certainty that it would be granted thus. For the country itself, for Russia, and for its glorious and eternal future.

Today was the birthday of his father, a wise and mighty Emperor. Nikolai always remembered this day and always turned to his father for support. It had not been his lot to wage such a horrible war, but he would have emerged from it with a thunderous victory. How could Nikolai assume his powers?

Nikolai also prayed for their family large and small, as he and Alix put it: small meant they themselves and their children; large meant not the dynasty, no, this kinship seemed to have withered away, but those few dozen people close to them and loyal who served, aided, and sympathized.

He stood there praying as usual, and everything was as usual, no special alarm or disturbances today—but suddenly, from out of nowhere, a sharp pain entered the center of his chest, an inexplicable squeezing, a squeezing, along with a piercing upthrust. Either an acute pain or an acute fear. Not just a matter of breathing and remaining standing—it seemed his heart was stopping; it felt as if his heart had ceased to beat and everything in his body had stopped. Nikolai braced against the railing behind him to keep from falling. He would have called to someone, but that would have required taking two steps and poking his head out. And also, it was undignified to call for help right away for nothing visible.

It gripped him so and held on terribly. But during these minutes, fortunately, he recalled that this had happened once before and it had eased up after about ten minutes. That was when he had learned about the catastrophe with Samsonov's army; it had been an attack of angina then. It would pass. After the surrender of Lvov, too, his heart had acted up a little.

It would pass. Any moment. But it didn't, and he lost his sense of time and didn't know how long it had gone on. He gripped the railing, but he couldn't hear his heart at all, and the pain was so bad he couldn't move, and copious cold sweat appeared—and suddenly it entered his mind that this was how men died, that this could be dying.

In this feeling he found the strength to break away from the railing and step aside toward the image of the Blessed Virgin—and drop to his knees before it and nearly fall, brow-first, to the rug to pray for help—but if he were to die, then he would die this way.

Then suddenly—suddenly it all passed, just as suddenly as it had come over him! His heart was distinctly working again! There was only a residual weakness throughout his body, so that it was easier to stay on his knees than to rise. Nikolai wiped the sweat from his brow.

It turned out that all during the attack he hadn't heard a word of the service or the singing, but now he did, and from the gap he could tell that the attack had lasted not two minutes but nearly a quarter of an hour. They were already singing the Cherubic Hymn.

No one had noticed the incident.

That was good.

He finished on his knees and rose.

But the weariness lingered in his body for a long time. And Nikolai returned from the cathedral by motorcar. And with the thought of somehow spending Sunday quietly and peacefully.

Generally speaking, Nikolai was a perfectly healthy and even young man. He not only felt well but as the years passed he felt even better, as his doctors found.

It had passed, and he no longer felt like telling Doctor Fyodorov. He was somehow embarrassed to cause alarm. If it happened again—well, then.

Due to the brevity of the Emperor's stay at GHQ, the report of Alekseev, who had also prayed at mass, had been planned for Sunday as well and was supposed to take place after church. The Emperor did not cancel and went to hear it.

By now, after three reports, they would seemingly have discussed everything important that was happening with the army. Everything was going fine, only the supply of provisions on the Southwest front had been disrupted. All army affairs had, in essence, already been directed. The day after tomorrow he might perhaps even return to his Sunny at Tsarskoye Selo. She was very worried and lonely.

Alekseev also handed him Khabalov's telegram. Yes, in Petrograd . . . Well, what about it? This was the first telegram from Khabalov. He reported—still just for 8 and 9 March—that there were about 200,000 striking workers. This was a lot, although the strikers were forcibly removing those still working. They were stopping streetcars and smashing windows in streetcars and shops, and they had broken through to Nevsky—but they had been dispersed, moreover the troops had not used firearms. (This was correct. This was as the Emperor had ordered. The last thing they needed was to repeat the horror of that terrible 22 January.) On 10 March they were also driven off Nevsky. One police chief had been seriously wounded, and one police officer had been killed while the crowd was being dispersed. They listed eleven cavalry squadrons, which was more than sufficient.

Right then the Emperor noticed a note that the telegram had been delivered to GHQ yesterday at six o'clock in the evening. Why was it that over the entire long night, what was now nearly a full day, Alekseev had not reported it? He wanted to ask, but he glanced at Alekseev's conscientious and even exhausted face, which even seemed to have a hard time wearing its spectacles, so unwell he was—and decided not to distress the old man. He probably hadn't yet emerged from his illness, and it was probably hard for him to get up at night. That meant he hadn't considered it important. Indeed, there was nothing special here.

Before lunch he received and read a healing, tender letter from his beloved Alix, yesterday's. My God, how unspeakably she pined! But also how much consolation, joy, and firmness always poured from her letters. She, too, wrote about these disturbances—but also to understand them as nonsense, the excitement of little boys and girls. And here were very true thoughts: Why didn't they punish the strikers for striking during time of war? And why had a ration card system still not been introduced for bread? This Nikolai himself did not understand and had not been able to achieve. There was simply some kind of spell on this food question, which was proving intractable.

For some reason one always encountered too many obstacles between a will expressed and its execution.

She wrote everything truly. Everything did have to be arranged gradually.

Protopopov ought to have given—and naturally was giving—Khabalov clear and categorical instructions. Just so old Golitsyn didn't lose his head! All this was outside his usual realm.

And how much did tending to sick children cost her, poor thing, and with her health?

Nikolai forgot himself and livened up over the precious letters. (There was also a sweet note from Nastenka, the youngest.)

This time he very much missed having Aleksei at GHQ, his pranks and chatter. What a consolation and diversion he was!

But it was time for lunch. Sunday lunch was also full of people, including all the foreigners present. He had to talk a lot, and listen, but always about irrelevant trifles, setting aside any serious thoughts. Actually, the Emperor had mastered this ritual well, trained to it over the last quarter-century.

After lunch, first thing, he sat down—and wrote Alix a letter in reply.

The weather was sunny and frosty. He decided to go for a ride. They brought the motorcars around, started for the Bobruisk highway, and stopped at the chapel built in memory of 1812. He took a walk there. Clear, bracing weather. His body retained no trace of the day's heart contraction. No, he wouldn't tell the doctor yet.

When they returned to GHQ, it was already time for tea.

Then he received a certain senator.

He thought that it would be too long for Alix to wait until tomorrow for today's reply so he decided to send her a telegram right away thanking her for her letter. How he missed her! How he wished he could return to them!

He sent it and then they brought two telegrams from Alix, one after the other. One was entirely familial and restrained (Alix was always very shy that so many military men were reading their telegrams), and the other, later, was openly alarmed: "Very concerned regarding the city."

Precisely because he knew her restraint in telegrams, he could understand how *very* much this meant.

But why were there no official telegrams? Alekseev hadn't brought anything, and it was awkward to go to him with his wife's telegram.

There were grand dukes at GHQ now, but they had all become alien to him, and he didn't feel like talking to them.

It was growing dark. They dined—all in the same measured, abstract routine.

However, alarm was radiating through his chest. Alix would not have done this for nothing.

After dinner he sent her another telegram thanking her for her telegrams and firmly promising to leave for Tsarskoye in two days.

They sat down to play dominos.

Toward the end of the game, Voeikov, the palace commandant, arrived, also holding something, and his face made it clear he wanted to report to the Emperor. Nikolai stood up and went out with him to his study.

The telegram was from War Minister Belyaev: a few military units were refusing to use firearms against the crowd (who had ordered them to use firearms?) and were even going over to the side of the rebelling workers. (This was a disgrace! Could this be?) Nevertheless, Belyaev assured him that the situation would be pacified.

But Voeikov was worried. He reported to the Emperor the mood of the entire suite (neither at dinner, nor in direct report, naturally, had anyone dared express this) that the situation in Petrograd was very alarming.

Nikolai himself no longer knew what to think. But maintaining his self-possession, he promised nothing and returned to finish playing dominos.

However, the fact that the situation in Petrograd was so alarming played in him more and more.

Going to Protopopov was unnecessary. That clever man knew and would figure everything out himself. Golitsyn he had already telegraphed yesterday, but Nikolai lay no great hopes on imbuing him with courage. However, directly along the military line, Commanding General Khabalov (whom he only knew in passing) had to be imparted firmness.

He wrote a telegram and handed it over to be sent:

"I command that tomorrow the disturbances in the capital, inadmissible in a difficult time of war with Germany and Austria, be stopped. Nikolai."

[59]

These last few days, Mikhail Vladimirovich had done everything humanly possible to moderate the popular upheavals and halt the bloodshed. Even during his hours of intense supervision of Duma activities, he did not tire of participating in events by telephone, understanding his responsibility, that during this distant absence of the Tsar, he himself, the number two man in Russia, essentially became number one. He telephoned that dullard Khabalov and warned that he would blame the police. He called the city governor and said he himself would go and put the fear of God into that police officer who had made the arrests. He called the War Minister: Why weren't they dispersing the crowds with water cannons? (Belyaev himself didn't know, but he liked the idea. He called Khabalov, but the reply was that there was a ban on summoning firemen because pumping water would only rile the crowd.)

This afternoon, Rodzyanko had met with the exhausted Prince Golitsyn, supposedly for talks, although what kind of talks could there be between them? The entire country was divided into two unequal parts: one was the people, the army, society, the Duma, and at their head Rodzyanko, so full of strength; the other was the squabbling ministers led these last few weeks by this decrepit prince. Not talks, rather Rodzyanko insisted that the government in full quickly submit its resignation. But Golitsyn replied that he would be happy to, he dreamt only of peace, but he feared the unseemliness of what would look like a disgraceful escape. The Tsar's servant couldn't quit his post in a moment of danger. In the obduracy of monarchical service, if you didn't listen closely to the stormy popular breathing, it did look like that, yes. But if you couldn't instantly save Russia in a single day by an announced ministry of public trust, then at least Golitsyn should rid his cabinet of that scoundrel and knave Protopopov! Then all Russia would breathe freely! Ah, yes, Golitsyn grieved, he himself would be happy to be rid of Protopopov, but he had been placed there and kept on *not by him.*

This was true. However, glancing at the gracious prince, Rodzyanko could not help but remember the three variant decrees Golitsyn held, which he had shown him in a moment of candor: to completely dissolve the Duma and schedule new elections next autumn, to dissolve it until war's end, or to declare its adjournment for an indeterminate length of time. The government had no power. None! However, any day now this debilitated old man could bring about the Duma's dissolution and a historic outrage would have been committed. If Rodzyanko was going to be cautious in his unwieldy turns, he had to take this reciprocal threat into account as well.

Rodzyanko perceived any threat to the State Duma with the keenest alarm, even more keenly than if they had threatened to kill him! He felt his throat being choked by the danger of the Duma's dissolution. After all, the Duma was the sole source of truth in Russia, the sole torch for its restless minds. The Duma deputies were the sole expressers of the people's will. If this Duma was dissolved, who would maintain courage and fortitude in the country, especially given the military failures? In the event of the Duma's dissolution, a profound gloom would ascend in the country, and the whole country would be handed over without oversight to Protopopov, the Tsaritsa, the Rasputin circle, and the German spies! The matter would certainly move along toward a separate peace and disgrace for Russia.

For himself, Mikhail Vladimirovich saw no other outcome then than arrest and exile.

These gloomy previsions had been whirling around for months, ever since the November conflict with the state, when they'd succeeded in driving out Stürmer. They'd also heated up in December after the outspoken public congresses. And in January Rodzyanko had invited a few marshals of the nobility in and asked them outright, in the event of his predictable arrest (exile to Siberia or even hanging), to stand in his place guarding the Homeland's interests. If the Duma could be sacrilegiously dispersed, the nobility could neither be dissolved nor dismissed.

These previsions had been whirling around for months, and Lvov, Chelnokov, and Konovalov had called on the President to come to their Zemgor congress in Moscow to say it all in public. Rodzyanko realized that a step like that could alter the course of history. But he didn't go. It was enough that in the autumn he had written the Emperor a cautionary letter about the danger of the Tsaritsa's meddling in Russia's governance—and the letter was passed from hand to hand. Since February, because of his ways and importance, he had seen a means of saving the fatherland more directly: a formal memorandum to the Emperor, which must happen immediately before the Duma session opened. Rodzyanko's reports to the Tsar could be said to be epochs in Russia's history. Who if not Rodzyanko, in his comprehensive January written report, had opened the Tsar's eyes to the course of the entire war and conscientiously laid out everything he had learned from the brilliant and amiable Brusilov: why Brusilov was not to blame for the halt of the 1916 offensive; how on the Romanian front matters were much worse than with Brusilov; and although he did not name Alekseev directly anywhere, the material itself indicated that Alekseev was to blame for all the mistakes. Never before had Rodzyanko felt himself such a connoisseur of military questions as in this report.

How insulting it was whenever the Tsar responded ungratefully with a dry reception, as he had the last time, two weeks ago.

Rodzyanko had prepared that February report with somber decisiveness. At last, everything should be expressed distinctly and thoroughly, so that the Tsar would be frightened and shrink from dissolving the Duma once and for all—and do everything he could to strengthen society's forces. This had to be the greatest and most pivotal of all the President's reports. If the Emperor wouldn't read or let it be read in full out loud, then he would manage to speak the best phrases and main thoughts from memory.

That victory in the war was impossible without immediate and radical change in the entire system of governance was the conviction of all thinking Russia. Russia was gripped by alarm, and this alarm was natural and even essential. Adding bitterly that our public alarm had already been conveyed to our allies. Much in the country had been spoiled so irrevocably that now even if geniuses were drawn into governance, they could no longer fix very much. Nonetheless, a change of faces and a change of the system of governance was pressing. The populace would trust new faces! The Emperor could not learn the truth from the present ministers, only from the President. And here it was: not only did the Duma have to be preserved, but its powers had to be extended for more than five years in order to cover peace talks after the war as well.

But the Emperor was withdrawn and irritated and refused to accept Rodzyanko's truth. He would start a cigarette and then discard it. Rodzyanko reminded him in vain of his former good advice—and the Emperor replied that he regretted accepting it. Then the President, seized by anger now, said:

"Your Majesty! What you are doing is provoking the populace. All kinds of impostors are giving everyone orders. You have been led down a most dangerous path. There is not a single reliable or honest man left around you. And you, Emperor, will reap what you have sown."

Even today, his chest pounded like mad at the mere memory of that audience.

And today—once again a perfidious blow was being prepared against the Duma.

Gasping for breath under the high ceilings of his apartment, gasping in its nearly hall-size rooms, Mikhail Vladimirovich, without putting on a coat or covering his partly bald head, went out as he was, a bullish figure, onto the expansive balcony over Fuhrstadtskaya Street, directly opposite the Serbian embassy.

This, too, was a symbol. He lived and watched over the oath of allied loyalty.

If the Duma held the people's hopes, then even more so did the President hold them inside himself. That was what he felt: his chest was the collective chest of all Russia; his bulky figure, its mighty corpus; his bell-like bass, its voice. A rare combination when the entire popular will is clearly collected in a single person.

He himself had always obeyed the impulses of his tremendous heart.

Right now its impulse was that, given these events, he had to accomplish something very great. Energetically save Russia.

As a unique figure, he had to act, without consulting anyone, uniquely.

In his position, there was one single action to take: the Number Two man in the state, he had to go to the Number One.

Even though the Emperor didn't want to listen.

Go to him with an ominous warning.

And a rational argument, perhaps the last.

He had to fire a thunderous telegram off to GHQ! Deafen him, even perhaps exaggerating slightly, but so as to draw the Supreme Commander out of his lethargy. (If only he could see himself! Why did he ever take on this ruinous Supreme Command?)

But would he really heed him? Even his mighty voice? How many times had he banged away at the monarch's insensitive consciousness?

Who else could he call on for assistance? Who would join him?

Then the President had a bright idea: Don't send the telegram to the Tsar! Not to the Tsar, he's hopeless! Instead, send it to several Army Group commanders. First of all, to Brusilov, with whom he had a marvelous mutual understanding; Brusilov would support him energetically. Then to Ruzsky, who had always been well disposed toward the Duma. Well and, for the command, he would have to include Alekseev, unpleasant man though he was. That was enough. No need for Evert, the reactionary. Telegraph them and call on *them* to join together and for *them* to implore the Tsar!

Brilliant! Then the telegram wouldn't be a personal step but would be spread through society, to appear for judgment, disgrace, and witness!

What would the Tsar say then in front of everyone? He wouldn't wiggle out of it! He would heed the commanders!

What a plan!

Phrases tumbled out like rumbling chariots! Rodzyanko trod from balcony to study—and with a feather-shaped, four-faceted, foot-long red pen sketched inch-high letters that would not fit into any telegraph blank.

There is panic in Petrograd due to a total distrust of the government, which is incapable of bringing the country out of danger. The hungry crowd is starting down the path of spontaneous and irrepressible anarchy. Transport, food, fuel? What's there to say. . . . Events are unfolding that will be impossible to contain, at the cost of bloodshed. . . . The life of the country in its most difficult moment . . . Russia is threatened by military defeat and humiliation. . . .

(And if the Duma is dissolved as well, the army will simply **refuse to fight**. So Brusilov had said.)

. . . The sole solution is to call on *someone whom the entire country can trust.* . . . Whom all Russia, inspired by trust, will follow. . . . In this terrible hour, unprecedented in its dire consequences, there is no other way out onto a shining path. . . . Delay is akin to death! . . .

(And this Someone, this Someone. . . . Well, they'd have to figure that out themselves.)

The Duma President is asking His Excellency to intercede with His Majesty. . . .

Grandly conceived!

He thought it over—and sent it to Evert as well.

[60]

Throughout his life, Vaska Kayurov had been given only positions of responsibility when it came to revolution. A Sengiley boy, son of a village weaver and threadtwister, crushed by patriarchal religious life, as a little boy he seriously considered becoming a schemamonk. Later he read his fill alternately of Yeruslan Lazarevich and Rocambole, but as a carpenter at a shipworks at age twenty, those terrible "socialists" frightened him like devils. Their kind didn't believe in God and didn't recognize the Tsar. Only after he'd grown up and married, past his twenty-fourth year, did he come to know these socialists at the Sormovo factory—and before you knew it, he'd taken on his first responsibilities, as paymaster for Sormovo's Social Democratic organization. (There he also got to know the writer Gorky, at whose apartment he himself was given 100 rubles by the singer Chaliapin for the treasury, only his name wasn't to be recorded.) At the time, he even took part in printing leaflets, after which he had to leave the factory, and in the town of Sormovo the only work he could get was at the workers' cooperative—where Kayurov became even more important: The cooperative's book and ironmongery departments distributed illegal literature, explosives, and weapons. Vasili himself personally kept 265 pistols and also exchanged the SRs' dynamite for leaflets printed for them at the cooperative printshop. But after the Sormovo free republic in the autumn of '05 and the December battles there, Vasya Kayurov had to make himself scarce and go to his native village of Terenga, where he did not sit idle either but in time created an illegal Social Democratic circle—for which he was put in prison and cruelly not released even to help his family bring in the harvest but rather exiled under open supervision to Samara Province. Later, right before the war, he moved to Petersburg as a patternmaker, for New Lessner, and later for Ericsson—and once again he was not passed over for the important position of director of the insurance movement. Immediately before the war, when they were kicking up a row on the Vyborg side, Kayurov had put up a barricade nearby on Yazykov Lane, and during the war at Ericsson he had fought irreconcilably with Gvozdev's Liquidators, even using a stool. Thus he gradually advanced in the Vyborg Bolshevik District Committee, and in the last few weeks had even been its secretary.

But last night the entire Petersburg Committee had been arrested, and this morning Shlyapnikov had appointed their entire Vyborg district committee in full to be the new PC.

The Sengiley-Sormovo boy had risen to heights he had never dreamed of: running all of Petersburg!

He could burst! What could he throw himself into? But it was Sunday: some were scattered in their homes, some around the city, and he couldn't assemble workers for a talk or even the rest of his district committee. Vaska hurried to race down Nevsky and Ligovka.

The Tsarist satraps were shooting; their hand did not tremble! And right then some idiotic armored car had driven through the streets, its clank and iron rumble literally sowing panic among the workers, even though it didn't fire. In the armored car's rumbling, the vivid colors of their as yet, evidently, unfulfilled dreams evaporated. The worker upheaval had obviously been liquidated.

Kayurov stopped by the barracks to see the Cossacks; on the streets they had behaved sympathetically. But in talks they made no promises.

And so the day passed. In the evening they decided to assemble the district committee. But after the PC's collapse, was any member's apartment safe? Might they be arrested? They decided to go to the vegetable gardens after dark.

There they tromped around in the snow, talked things over, and tended to think they should end the strike.

If they didn't decide that, the workers would probably end it tomorrow themselves.

Then Kayurov made out someone jostling among them wearing a soldier's greatcoat. He roused everyone: "Who's that among us? Why is he here? He heard everything we were saying!" Why, that's a friend, someone said. "How can unverified comrades be allowed into these kinds of sessions when extremely important questions are being discussed?"

The comrade turned out to be from the armored division.

"Then why aren't you helping us? Was that your armored car riding around today?"

Yes.

"We were scared witless! Why did you go out on the street, encourage the police, and sow confusion in the workers' ranks? So now, comrade, leave our session!"

He walked off into the darkness. They kept at it some more after he left, but still couldn't decide on anything. The frost was intensifying, and anyone who wasn't wearing felt boots could feel his feet freezing.

We were wrong to let ourselves be chased to the garden, scared of our own shadow.

"All right," Kayurov declared. "Tomorrow morning a little earlier, beginning right at seven o'clock, gather at my apartment. There we'll decide what's what."

[6 1]

In unofficial conversations—such as he rarely had, and when he did they were always brief and only with individuals from his close circle—General Alekseev would say of himself, "My mother was just a cook. I'm a simple man, from the lower depths, and I know the life of the lower depths, but the heights of generals are foreign to me." To say nothing of dynastic strata and high society.

This would be said sincerely and was largely true, although he wasn't exactly a cook's son, merely a descendant of a serf, but the son of a poor infantry staff captain, a participant in the defense of Sevastopol. And the academy he graduated from was an inferior one, Cadet School. He'd begun his service just before the Turkish campaign as an ensign, and in nine years he hadn't even been promoted to company commander. But without gentility, without connections, and without patronage he rose by virtue of his rare diligence and persistence, achieving everything in life by his own efforts alone. Usually people entered the Academy after three years of army service; Alekseev entered after eleven. After the Academy, however, with his painstaking and precise ways of delving into every matter, he soon became a professor of the history of Russian military art at the Academy itself. Then the Japanese war broke out and Alekseev left for it already as the army's quartermaster general, that is, deputy chief of staff, and there he rose through his success in staff positions, which seemed created just for him, and was already a major general. Then, in the 1911 maneuvers, the Emperor took a great liking to his thoroughgoing analysis of the operation. This impressed the Emperor (he always liked these modest, hardworking, untroublesome men)—and manifested itself during the war. At its outset, Alekseev became chief of staff of the Southwest Army Group under Ivanov. Ever so frenziedly precise, with attention to every question, be it major or minor, but among the generals uncommonly unenvious and even, apparently, not very ambitious. He masterminded the Galician operation of 1914, which Ruzsky and Ivanov only spoiled but took all the glory, Ruzsky winning an adjutant generalship and the modest Alekseev merely a St. George's Cross 4th class, such as junior officers receive. But although he had borne an unintentional offense, he did not let himself be poisoned over it. Nor did he know how to bring up his own merits. But the Emperor's trust and kindness did not fail him, and in early 1915 he took over from the ill (or reluctant?) Ruzsky the High Command of the Northwest Army Group (still not divided then into two groups, the Northern and Western), thirty-seven army corps—three quarters of the entire warring Russian army—and this in a year when they would have to retreat from the Warsaw pocket, retreat for four months along the entire front without ammunition and with a shortage even of rifles, took on his ordinary shoulders a burden such as the Russian army had never known. Many hotheaded officers accused Alekseev of a "mania for retreat," saying he was "preserving the life force but drowning the spirit," and he himself, despondent, considered himself worthy only of dismissal or demotion. The tactic of continuously slipping away from multiple encirclements, which he gave himself credit for, suddenly seemed to him, based on the results, a tactic of capitulation. In August 1915, he asked Nikolai Nikolaevich for permission to resign: "My hand is luckless." On the contrary, though, during those days dismissal hung over Nikolai Nikolaevich himself, and the Emperor, accepting the Supreme Command, appointed his favorite the Supreme Commander's chief of staff—and Alekseev's ill-wishers said, "He surrendered all our fortresses to the Germans and was given a promotion."

Given a Supreme Commander like the Emperor, who had not led a single operation or a single organizational matter, Alekseev became, in essence, not chief of staff but the unchecked Supreme Commander of all of Russia's forces. Even having risen in this way, however, he had not changed in the least—not in his manner of work, not in his even, calm treatment of subordinates, and not in his indifference to the highly placed public, and he did not come to think of himself differently than before, and his head was not turned in the least. As before, at any lower headquarters, he was prepared basically not to rise from his desk, not even for lunch and dinner, and die like that holding colored pencils over a map or a pen over a document. He knew but one interest: detailed penetration of every question and its precise and substantive solution. He was so devoted to his work that he could not allow any part of it to slip past him. No one could help, no one could ease his labor, and besides, then he would no longer feel independent. Nor did he know how to select aides. He avoided all consultations, even with the Army Group commanders. Consultations fogged his thinking and shook his will, and the decisions taken as a result were mediocre. He had to put together and solve everything himself, personally grasp everything down to the trivial—and, even better, write out all decrees, in his own tiny, precise, and even hand.

But the more seriously Alekseev treated every question, even the most trivial, the more he got bogged down in them all. Occasionally Alekseev was gripped by the desperate insight that he simply could not cope alone.

But the Emperor, during his daily hearing of reports, consistently agreed with his chief of staff in all things (sometimes, perhaps, distracted, sometimes not completely understanding), and if he did intervene, then only on certain personal appointments. (The Emperor often forgave guilty generals and was inclined to reappoint them to equivalent positions and even to their former posts without a second thought as to how their subordinates would regard them now.)

The Emperor was attached to his squint-eyed friend's patient, even personality and quiet soul—which was much like his own. He simply had come to like Alekseev. These kinds of sympathies in the Emperor could be deeper than his disposition toward a minister's worldview or political line. He respected this general's military experience and knowledge, and Alekseev's unfeigned religiosity evoked a special, heartfelt trust. He not only prayed zealously and stood on his knees for a long time and bowed to the floor in his inconspicuous place by the column in the headquarters church, but even (the Emperor knew) in his office, and not only did he cross himself before each meal and after, but prayer and faith were for him a constant and insistent requirement.

In the same way was Alekseev bewitched by the Emperor's gentleness, sincerity, and simplicity, which were especially surprising on the throne and especially palpable in their close daily contact. In addition, he could not help but be grateful for his confidence and extraordinary promotion. Nor could he help but sympathize with the Emperor, seeing up close his difficult position both against raging society and with the grand dukes. To Alekseev himself, the appearance and conversations of all these excellencies and titles were nauseating, and not only was he not drawn to be among them and sit at imperial dinners, as he was constantly being invited, but that would have been a great burden for him, an impractical loss of time and a distraction (and revulsion)—and he had asked the Emperor to allow him to dine in the staff officers' mess once and for all.

Alekseev's attachment to the Emperor was sorely tried, however. Last summer the Empress, arriving at GHQ, took the general by the arm and, leading him around the garden, tried to persuade him to give Rasputin access to headquarters. With embarrassment (usual for her when she had to explain herself in Russian, but the general didn't know a single foreign language), she tried to explain to Alekseev that he was being unfair to the "elder," that this was a holy and marvelous man and by visiting GHQ he would bring great happiness to the troops. Alekseev did not yield, however, and replied straightforwardly:

"The moment he appears at GHQ, Your Majesty, I will be compelled to leave the post I occupy immediately."

The Empress jerked her arm away and moved off without saying goodbye.

It had seemed to Alekseev that since that moment the Emperor had cooled somewhat toward him. (Although he himself, back at the beginning of their stay at GHQ, had shyly asked Alekseev the same thing and received a refusal but had not taken offense. Alekseev had even been so bold as to try to convince the Emperor to push Rasputin even further away, but he patiently replied that this was a personal, private matter, and Rasputin held no post.) However, Alekseev could not allow himself to be made a laughingstock by letting Rasputin visit GHQ.

The time had come in Russia when no educated man could limit himself to his own affairs because politics would invariably cut into them. If he did not take an interest in politics, out of disgust, then once he had become the Supreme Commander's chief of staff, politics would become very interested in him. Indeed, who could get away from public notions if, the moment he learned to read and write, to say nothing of in high school, the first thing any Russian subject would learn was that our government was good for nothing. Society and the educated class had always acted by force of argument, by a logic that was difficult to counter. Their free, willful, clever tongue would persuade, and there was no finding a sensible answer as to why, for example, Rasputin or other absurd individuals and puppets could crowd around the throne. If all the famous, proud grand dukes constantly felt the powerfully shifting public wind, then how could a quiet, unexalted general of humble origins remain impervious to this wind?

The person with the social insights, only harsher, was primarily Alekseev's wife, who could not bear the Emperor himself, spoke of him with a quiver of contempt as of a wolf in sheep's clothing, a hangman, a head cracker, an outcast of nature, an emotional cripple, a spiritual dwarf, an idol sent only to complete all the infamies of the Romanov dynasty and that he was Nikolai the Last. (A richly illustrated book was even published in Europe with that title.) As it was thought in all liberal circles, so it was thought in Alekseev's. In unofficial conversations with his own generals Alekseev heard his fill of all kind of political extremes that he in his heart did not share.

But his wife was so unable to control herself with respect to the Tsar that the spouses out of good sense had established that she would never come to GHQ when the Emperor was there, so she would not encounter him even for a minute and cause any frowns. The Emperor wondered why it just so happened that his chief of staff's wife always came when he was gone, and once he even asked jokingly, Could she be avoiding a meeting? Alekseev replied that in the Emperor's absence he simply felt freer. But after this he summoned her once during the Emperor's stay.

Although these convictions, his wife's and his colleagues', did not acquire a hold on Alekseev, they did have their consequences. They pressed on him sideways and dislocated him. Because of them he twice gently refused the title of adjutant general offered him so as not to be ascribed to the "palace clique," and he did not wear the Order of the White Eagle, but the Emperor liked his refusals. He put them down to modesty. He could scarcely imagine that General Alekseev might have his own separate political sympathies. But last Easter the Emperor himself brought adjutant general epaulettes and aiguillettes as a present—and Alekseev had to accept, although he murmured in embarrassment, "I'm not worthy, not worthy. . . ."

This whole malfunction, though, did not hinder Alekseev's irreproachable military service. He placed military considerations above any politics, didn't care for "domestic politics" in general, and didn't understand why they were needed. But the complexity of modern war encroached on all sides, and Alekseev had to sit in long session with ministers arriving at GHQ or figures from the rear and discuss finances, industry, transport, provisioning, food, and horse breeding. And although in these studies he was increasingly inclined toward (and tried to convince the Emperor of) the necessity of a single dictatorship for the rear, which meant restrictions on the Zemgor Union, his relations with the Zemgor, as with all liberal figures and Duma members, remained the very best. (Nonetheless he gently recommended to Prince Lvov that he reduce the number of Jews in the Zemgor to a decent proportion.)

General Alekseev's appointment as the Supreme Commander's chief of staff was in Russia that rare event when the imperial choice and society's sympathies coincided. The Emperor considered him a loyal servant of the monarchy; Duma members, a secret republican. From his origin and the people around him, society guessed in him one of their own, and constantly praised him, and he was glad of this bilateral confidence. Given the peculiarity of his reciprocal position, Alekseev was even beginning to see the possibility of reconciling the Tsar and society. He made up his mind to give the Emperor advice on civil governance—prohibit blank spaces in newspapers, which irritated everyone, and discharge Stürmer, whom society found so unbearable—and modestly influence the Emperor to stop listening to bad advisors.

But this was not what was wanted of him. They wanted more. Whether it was Guchkov, or Konovalov, or Prince Lvov, whoever from that side spoke with Alekseev, it seemed to them that they encountered in this quiet general full agreement that much in Russian life was being made worse by the government or *sinister forces*. And they began treating the general rather unceremoniously, or even uncivilly. They started hinting at certain plans: either to arrest and exile the Tsaritsa, or to force a ministry of public trust out of the Emperor. Someone in the rear, in Petrograd, was apparently supposed to carry out these actions, and Alekseev at the proper moment was to occupy a position that aided the plan. Alekseev was speechless at these forward proposals and always objected that no overthrow was permissible in time of war because it would create a mortal threat to the front.

Guchkov used Alekseev's name simply as an address for his accusatory letter, which he let pass from hand to hand, not intending it for Alekseev at all.

That letter badly taxed and nearly ruined the good relations between the general and the Emperor. Alekseev experienced both humiliation and danger to the point that he felt he was on the verge of resigning his post. But the post was precious to him not in and of itself but for the sake of the work it opened up, for the sake of the decisive blow in March 1917 against Austria, its total collapse, to which so much had led from Alekseev's first days at GHQ. This Guchkov letter business so shook Alekseev that his old kidney disease flared up—so much so that in November he was preparing to die. He had already taken Communion and the chilling shadow of Departure had already set aside all those petty cares and separated him from the war he had waged so intently. Feeling at peace, Alekseev surrendered to the Lord's recall: he had labored for Russia his entire life without seeking anything for himself.

After Communion, though, he began to revive, and the Emperor mercifully released him to go to the Crimea and recuperate for a few months. He would still have time before the great offensive.

However, the undue familiarity of public figures proved to be such that they found ways to see Alekseev even in Sevastopol, where he spent a month between life and death before starting on the mend. The general was visited there by Prince Lvov, who began a conversation about a change in internal procedures and the mood at the front in the event of an overthrow. But Alekseev felt both exhausted by his illness and emotionally harassed by these improper solicitations. The Guchkov letter had taught him how these frivolous conversations could end.

In Sevastopol, Alekseev began receiving materials to work on relating to how the main operation was being readied. By 5 March he had arrived at GHQ himself, still with a temperature, half-ill, so as not to miss the final month of preparation. This offensive had become his entire life's cause. He had never prepared anything comparable in importance. For the success of this offensive he canceled and would not give assistance for the taking of the Bosporus, as the sailors were asking. For the success of this main offensive, where every unit would be needed, especially the Guards units, Alekseev had for many months resisted the Emperor's requests (he often did not have the will to insist but only asked) to send strong Guards units to the Petrograd garrison.

And now, still not fully recovered, he had returned to Mogilev five days ago and managed to see the Emperor, who also had not been at GHQ for two months. Either the Guchkov letter of that autumn or the long separation had taken its toll: if the former firm, trusting relations with the Emperor were being restored, then only gingerly.

Alekseev immediately threw himself into total work—and once again weakness overcame him, his temperature rose, and the doctors demanded he lie down for a few hours a day.

It was at this time that the upheavals in Petrograd began to which, however, there was no reason to ascribe any grave significance. The Petrograd authorities themselves and the government had not even reported on them at all for two days; the first report was from Khabalov last night and pointed to the upheavals' episodic nature. The second, this afternoon, was no more alarming, although in one place a platoon had been forced to open fire.

Late that night, at ten-thirty, an explosive telegram suddenly arrived from Rodzyanko with ominous expressions. But Rodzyanko had always expressed himself excessively, with the insufferable self-assurance that he alone knew everything. There was also this transparently crafty attempt to exploit the Petrograd upheavals in order to promote himself as Prime Minister.

The Emperor did not like being disturbed late at night, and Alekseev did not see any reason to be overly concerned. He felt chilled and was glad to lie down. Tomorrow at ten-thirty there would be his regular report to the Emperor, when he would report on the Rodzyanko telegram.

[6 2]

* * *

In Petrograd, all day, anyone who had a telephone made a great number of calls. Learning and passing on news. Everyone was advising everyone else to stock up on water and fill their bathtubs. Other people's tense, hasty conversations crossed up and were heard obliquely in the telephone. The telephone operators replied unintelligibly, forgot the number taken, and asked again in nervous voices.

* * *

Some said the soldiers were being put in police overcoats to make it look like there were more police. Others said the police were putting on soldiers' greatcoats because they were ashamed of their uniforms.

* * *

Toward vespers St. Isaac's bell rang out, and the setting sun's rays fell through its lofty windows. But there were few people inside: women, elderly men, and devout soldiers.

* * *

Karabchevsky, the well-known lawyer, set out by motorcar with his wife and a guest for the Mariinsky. But although it was the balletomane subscription and an outstanding ballerina was dancing, the theater was fairly empty. Anyone who didn't have his own carriage or motorcar would have to go on foot, and return at night. (It never occurred to Karabchevsky that he himself was riding for the last time, that tomorrow they would take his motorcar and drive it away.)

After the performance, they intended to go dine, as usual, chez Cubat— but they didn't. The streets were bleak.

Pickets. Bonfires.

*   *   *

Late that night, after the theaters, Prince Leon Radziwill's home on the Fontanka was brightly illuminated, and waiting in front of it was a long line of carriages and motorcars. The ball being given by the princess was in full swing.

*   *   *

That evening at Kerensky's apartment behind the Tauride garden, several leading Socialists gathered to discuss.

Kerensky himself had been in a gloomy mood all day, except for the brief hour with the Pavlovsky mutiny. He was sure the upheavals would be brutally suppressed and the Duma wholly dissolved. Then he would lose his deputy immunity—and he would be arrested straightaway for his latest impudent speech.

But even Krotovsky from the most desperate Interdistrict group stated categorically that there was and would be no revolution of any kind, the movement would come to naught, and they needed to prepare for a long period of reaction.

All chances for a revolution had collapsed. Help could not be expected from anywhere.

*   *   *

Shlyapnikov made off for the Vyborg side through the deserted streets, past the line of soldiers on the Liteiny Bridge, to the Pavlovs' apartment.

People were saying the workers on the Vyborg thought they'd had enough of going to the slaughter on Nevsky.

From a neighbor woman: something seemed to have happened today in some regiment, some kind of mutiny. But no one had heard anything more. Shlyapnikov, too, had been in the city and hadn't heard.

*   *   *

That night a bluish searchlight from the Admiralty tower beat down on a deserted Nevsky.

[6 3]

According to the Julian calendar, Likonya's birthday was 29 February, unlucky Saint Cassian's Day, once every four years. But when she grew up she began to find something special in this. Birthdays came into fashion instead of name days—but you couldn't put your finger on her birthday, it was always right there and not there at all. Now her friends had gathered on Sunday, fewer than usual, due to the city's upheavals.

The gramophone sang of love, and they danced.

Likonya danced, too, but less than the others, and she wasn't entirely with them. For her, this celebration wasn't really a celebration, and this wasn't what a celebration was about. She kept what was happiest deep inside her. Two people looked at her demandingly, and Sasha, too, tried to pull her aside and suggest something about the shooting, about the moment. But she moved cautiously, so as not to break or break open what was inside her.

All of a sudden it hit her: what if *nothing had happened*? Secretly slipping back to her room, she looked at the note.

It had! All this was so. He had kissed this hand, filled her soul with heated ecstasy—and now it had barely cooled off, like warm wax. It filled her up inside.

Likonya was glad she could feel this way! (She'd been afraid she couldn't.)

Again she moved among her guests, smiling.

And imagining his smile—so triumphant, generous, and warm.

But did he smile at everyone else that way, too?

He probably didn't even like poetry.

But he did like the theater.

They changed records. She responded, having missed the question.

Then, in the group, he had spoken to someone, vividly and freely, and she hadn't heard it all. And for the first time she had the feeling that she didn't want him to talk to anyone else—only to her.

She needed to see him so badly! Right now, if he were in the city, she would have abandoned them all, her party guests, and run to his hotel through the snow in her good shoes, holding her dress so as not to trip—past those patrols that had been set up, with their bonfires.

And she would have stood at his door: Do let me in!

[6 4]

An extraordinary session had been scheduled for the Council of Ministers late tonight, and once again not at the Mariinsky Palace but at Prince Golitsyn's apartment on Mokhovaya. Once again Aleksandr Dmitrievich Protopopov arrived late, having lingered at a pleasant dinner with Vasiliev, the head of the Police Department. Protopopov walked in wearing his lilac suit, in the dessert excitement—and Golitsyn's apartment seemed to him even darker than yesterday, even more frightened and dull, and there were fewer people: none of those summoned, and not all the ministers.

Protopopov joined them in a mildly triumphant state. The street upheavals were evidently winding down, the gunfire had sobered up the crowd, even before twilight silence had fallen in the capital, and military details were in full control of the deserted streets. Vasiliev also reported that during the day, besides the five most important ones last night, another 141 revolutionary instigators had been arrested. Who exactly they were, Protopopov did not ask. He had a poor sense of the revolutionaries, but the fact was that they had been arrested, perhaps not 141, but the results were evident. Clearly, it was all over.

He was quite surprised to find among the ministers a completely different, distraught state. Immediately before, Pokrovsky and Rittikh had reported about their negotiations with Duma members and Maklakov's reply that there could be no question of dissolving the Duma altogether because there would be a public outcry. It was all right to adjourn it for a few days, but the government had to resign immediately, and as a body, and the new ministers had to be "acceptable to the country" and the new Prime Minister popular—best of all would be General Ruzsky.

How's that? The Duma's dissolution no longer depended on the Supreme imperial authority but, quite the opposite, the Duma was dictating that the government itself dissolve? The ministers were so tired, and so indifferent, and some themselves so wanted to resign, that apparently they were prepared for dissolution? Golitsyn had no determination for anything. Little Belyaev sat perfectly still, silent, as if absent or lifeless. Pokrovsky was inclining toward resignation. (He himself, of course, was counting on ending up in the new government.) Nevertheless, Shakhovskoy did remember that in August '15 dissolving the Duma had also seemed terrible, but it all went calmly.

Protopopov, having jumped up with amazement at one, another, and a third, reached a state of nervousness—and began an agitated speech to them. Did they really not understand that the Duma was stirring up the street, and until it was dispersed, nothing would quiet down? But even if an agreement were reached with the Duma, that did not solve the street. What the street needed was the government to be firm, and now it had been, and the result was evident. For example, only today the Police Department had arrested . . . well more than a hundred revolutionary leaders, and that had had an effect. And then, how could the government dissolve itself? There was no form for them to sign and go their separate ways. Did that mean composing a collective request to the Emperor, as in August '15? That way we were only going to anger His Majesty thoroughly!

Protopopov certainly realized that they were prepared to sacrifice him alone. But he also knew the Tsar's will behind him! There—they believed him, and all his strength came from there. . . .

But Prince Golitsyn, although he had a readied decree signed by the Emperor declaring a Duma recess, still could not bring himself to add tomorrow's date to it. Did this mean that tomorrow morning the abusive speeches would flow forth once again?

While the ministers were contradicting one another, the prince was called out. Returning a quarter of an hour later, he reported that three decisive and even indignant rightists from the State Council had arrived: Nikolai Maklakov, Shirinsky-Shikhmatov, and Aleksandr Trepov, lately the Prime Minister in this very cabinet. They were insisting that the Duma had exceeded all bounds and salvation lay only in its immediate dissolution.

The discussion leaned that way. They voted, some amazed at their own daring: had they lit a Bickford fuse on a quiet night? Golitsyn, limping, went to the other room and brought back the decree—and right there, in front of everyone, inserted tomorrow's date.

Protopopov could not conceal his glee: here was the final blow, all that had been lacking for victory!

Another question arose. Shouldn't martial law be declared in Petrograd? This would impose a ban not only on all street assemblies but also on leaving buildings during certain hours.

But all the previous days this measure had seemed too drastic, and today—perhaps it wasn't needed anymore since there was now calm. It would anger many.

Besides, martial law required a strong and authoritative military leader. Obtuse, clumsy Khabalov could only bring them more new disasters.

Then should they petition the Emperor to replace Khabalov? Here they did have the War Minister (who had not uttered a word). Ask him, for now—to do what? Speak with Khabalov, inspire him.

They also discussed the food situation—and the entire discussion wound down. There didn't even seem to be sufficient light in the parlor to see brightly and clearly. They decided to disperse to their homes. Prince Golitsyn now had to telegraph the Emperor about the Duma recess and telephone Rodzyanko this very day.

Admiring his own free gait, his own ease as a man subordinate to no one—here, in the capital, right now, not subordinate to anyone, whereas the entire capital was in his power—Protopopov walked out the front door and onto the deserted street, where a military patrol was on duty by Golitsyn's home, and crossed to his waiting motorcar.

He was free to go home now, but he thought it would be appropriate close to midnight to visit the city governor's offices under his charge. It was always useful for subordinates when higher authorities made a surprise visit, and right now there were even grounds to praise them, and in fact right now they had all gathered there.

He gave the order to go to Gorokhovaya, not tiring en route of enjoying the comfort of an automobile and the inclined leather-cushioned back, and to hurry. He gave an order to drive past the Mikhailovsky Palace and then to Bolshaya Konyushennaya in order to bypass the always distasteful City Duma.

There were night sentries at some intersections and here and there small bonfires against the fine night frost. Mounted Cossack details were patrolling. A searchlight had been hung on the Admiralty tower, and it cast a spectral light down the length of Nevsky. The avenue, which usually seethed with a crowd at this time, was empty. Other vehicles went by occasionally and private closed carriages, but it was deserted. Near the Admiralty, too.

Aware of his own singularity and centrality, Protopopov, his head tilted back, walked into the city governor's offices and then into the military-police conference. Everyone rose, greeting him, Khabalov heavily, but Protopopov lightly told them to sit and continue and sat down beside City Governor Balk. (Protopopov had appointed him here from Warsaw at the request of the physician Badmaev.) There were thirty or so military and police officials and a very vivid and harsh light on the whole room.

It was a clear-cut military discussion. The district heads' reports had just ended. They had been reassuring in nature: Many similar disorders had been seen in the last few years, and we had always dealt with them, but it couldn't be done without casualties on both sides. Although some military units were exhausted. And so, Captain Mashkin the 1st, here representing the commander of the Volynian Battalion, complained that the Volynian men had been at their posts every day from dawn until late at night, all day without hot food, and were returning to the barracks hungry.

"However," the city governor objected, "everyone today admired the Volynians."

Mashkin smiled but said heatedly:

"Yes, it's true, they acquitted themselves excellently. But they're terribly worn out. And after all, they have to do this every day. Look, tomorrow at six o'clock they have to be roused again, and that's not easy."

He himself and many others here looked weary.

By the way, an order had to be issued to repair the transformer on Znamenskaya Square. The crowd had incapacitated it with rocks, and now the entire square was in total darkness.

Protopopov indicated he would speak and expressed satisfaction both with the troops' actions and with their level of cooperation with the police. He'd thought he had a lot to tell them, but somehow nothing came to mind. He wished them further successes.

The meeting took a recess, and he spoke separately with Khabalov, who was sluggish and gloomily dispirited, especially by a fresh wire from the Emperor—directly to him! The first message directly to him! The Emperor categorically demanded that all the disorders in the capital be stopped tomorrow.

Tomorrow! And what if they started again? What could a general do? If only he had his Ural Cossacks here! Now he was waiting for additional cavalry and Cossacks, which hadn't yet arrived.

Someone near him kept bringing up the idea of calling in armored vehicles to defend the city. Khabalov gloomily refused:

"I don't know who would be sitting inside them. Maybe the same kind of revolutionaries. The mood among the technical crews is unreliable."

Wishing them success, Protopopov left for home. He was relieved that the Emperor had placed the full burden of the dispersal on Khabalov instead of him, which was just: the military authorities had the power.

However, he did think the Emperor would be pleased at his own report on matters. He decided to compose a telegram to GHQ immediately, that very night, to the palace commandant, who would take it to His Majesty. All in all, the day's results had been positive: most of the day had been calm. Up until what time? Well, let's say three. (Protopopov didn't remember exactly.) Then some significant clusters formed. After the firing of blanks aroused only the crowd's ridicule, they had had to resort to live ammunition. And then by, say, a little after four, Nevsky had been cleared. But then the 4th Company of the Pavlovsky Battalion had gone out on its own say-so to punish its training detachment. . . . No, leave that part out. It would hurt the Emperor to learn this. But what about this: today 141 party figures had been arrested, among them five of the leaders themselves. That would be to the minister's credit.

What nights! Continuous meetings, and yesterday he'd written a letter to the Empress and yesterday he'd composed a telegram to the Emperor. Today as well. Honorable but not light was the minister's burden.

All the military men had left the city governor's offices. Khabalov was so tired that he yawned openly, started home toward the Liteiny Bridge to sleep, and ordered them not to wake him under any circumstance.

Those who remained at HQ for the night started arguing over how they were to understand whether the mutineers had a guiding center or whether it was all chaotic.

According to Okhrana reports, the workers, dispersing in the evening, had told the Preobrazhensky men, "Damn you to hell! Here we are doing our best for you and you shoot at us? To hell with you! Tomorrow morning we're going to sleep in and after dinner we'll be at work."

It was time for staff officers to sleep, too. The duty officer stayed by the telephones.

Between two and three in the morning he decided to wake up the city governor: General Globachev, head of the Okhrana, had called for him. Very alarming information had come in: the crew at the 2nd Naval Depot intended to slay all their officers tomorrow morning, as soon as they arrived at the barracks for exercises.

The city governor rushed to telephone Khabalov—in vain. No one came to the telephone. That meant he had arranged to sleep so that calls wouldn't reach him.

He sent his officer off to warn the depot commander.

[65]

The Moscow Life Guards Regiment, renowned for its valor at Borodino, where it held out in a bayonet infantry square against Murat's cavalry, had from then on been called the Moscow Regiment. It had been quartered in Petersburg long since in barracks on the Vyborg side. And now, there, its reserve battalion found itself in the very thick of the worker upheavals, in the most dangerous place.

The reserve battalion had swelled due to the steady stream of untrained reinforcements—as many as six thousand men now—until it was now larger than the combat regiment it was supplying. So its companies were unimaginably large, as many as fifteen hundred men. The regimental barracks could not hold numbers like this. They built three-story bunks and held them in stifling conditions, and recruits were lodged as well in various private buildings throughout the Vyborg side, thereby losing their connection to the battalion. The companies numbered as many as fifteen hundred men, but there were all of 150 rifles per company—and those were taken away by whoever was going on sentry duty or details. There was nothing left to train them with, unless you were to make wooden rifles, and besides, there was nowhere to train them in the city on the pavement to entrench or shoot, just to march. So the outsized companies sat pointlessly and uselessly, in wintertime, in enclosed spaces with nothing to do, but on the standard-issue ration, bored and embittered. Of the four companies, the 3rd was especially difficult. In it were some recuperating soldiers, and counting on their influence, they had transferred to it all the punished and badly behaved young soldiers from the other three companies, and they had also assigned entering factory workers, even from this same Vyborg side, who had lost their deferment over some misdemeanor or crime. The recuperating soldiers were overwhelmed there—and being transferred back to the front in any case. So the company, instead of remaking a nasty element into soldiers, had itself degenerated and broken down—and now it had not been given a single rifle and was not sent on any details but was being kept in their closed cauldron.

For a time, their Sunday strolls with the band had helped calm the worker neighborhoods: a detachment of musicians accompanied by a small formation would walk around the Vyborg side for a few hours without explanation and attract some of the populace with their marches, and people willingly joined them. But for the last few days the mood had no longer been such that a band could be sent out, but only a guard to important places. Especially important was the Liteiny Bridge, where a major post was set up to cut off communication with the city center; and pickets were also posted at convenient nearby medical clinics. At the head of each such detail were not young ensigns but the company commanders themselves, who today had been absent all day and had returned to the battalion late. For the last few days all training in the battalion had been stopped.

Tonight, Colonel Mikhailichenko, the battalion commander, had been called into Guards HQ and had not returned until eleven o'clock—when he assembled the ranking officers. Captain Yakubovich, commander of the 3rd Company, couldn't come because that afternoon, near the Liteiny Bridge, his leg had been injured by a police officer's horse and he was laid up. But among those who did appear, Captain Nelidov, the commander of the 2nd Company, was using a cane: after a wound to his cingular vertebrae, his leg had atrophied from the hip, and he had a hard time walking. And Captain Dubrova the 3rd, in charge of the training detachment, suffered from brain trauma after a bad contusion at Tarnavka. (Tarnavka was yet another famous battle of the Moscow Life Guards, and had also taken place on 8 September, like Borodino, except in 1914.)

The commanders assembled in the officers' meeting room, and Mikhailichenko told them what he had himself learned. First, the events in the Pavlovsky Regiment. This was depressing. Just yesterday, this had seemed impossible. Now that it had happened, it seemed perfectly possible, even given the current state of the battalions—and inevitable. And it was even more likely to happen right there, where the Moscow Regiment was, in the middle of the worker neighborhoods. Second, large crowds were anticipated for tomorrow, and the combat subunits had to be ready as of four o'clock in the morning to be called in to suppress.

An order is an order. But all the officers gathered realized that on the sprawling Vyborg side, which was packed with tens of thousands of mutinous workers, they had no means for carrying it out. Utterly inexperienced ensigns, either worthless ones from the reserve or young ones who had just completed accelerated courses and who themselves still had a lot of learning to do. Too few trained sergeants. A pitiful allotment of rifles. A dangerous and mutinous rabble in the 3rd Company—both the untrained, who didn't know how to hold a gun, and even the unsworn young soldiers in the other companies—all in all, they were worse than nothing. Besides, since autumn, anonymous revolutionary proclamations had been filtering into the companies and even the officers' club by post. Most were destroyed, but some did reach the soldiers.

Rather than sending our soldiers in to suppress, they themselves had to be guarded as a group under threat.

Nor were there enough senior officers. Also, it's true, living in quarters at the officers' club were the two Nekrasov brothers, native to the regiment: Captain Nekrasov the 1st, but with a wooden leg instead of his lost one; and Staff Captain Nekrasov the 2nd, who had come from the active regiment on a brief leave.

It was an early standby so they needed to adjourn and sleep.

But no sooner had they left and gone to bed than Colonel Mikhailichenko again summoned them all after one in the morning. They assembled, now exhausted.

Why they were summoned: Guards HQ had informed him that a telegram had been received from the Emperor. All disturbances had been ordered stopped tomorrow. The Guards HQ hoped that the Moscow Regiment would carry out its duty honestly.

[6 6]

Guchkov was even sick of it by now. Wherever he went, he was either asked outright when the coup would be, or it was obliquely hinted at, or they didn't dare but they shot him searching glances as they would to someone who knew an extraordinary secret. Previously, he himself had done nothing to prevent rumors from seeping through, and had spoken, even in the presence of women, and everyone had avidly soaked it up. The more freely he spoke, the more vaguely was the path to implementation drawn. And now he had said too much. He needed to be more restrained. Everyone so wished for a coup d'état, or perhaps just for this acute sensation— "a coup!"—because everything was stalling.

So, too, today, Guchkov had spent the evening at Kokovtsov's, who, of course, didn't dare ask him anything directly, but did hint, draw him on, and give him meaningful looks.

Generally speaking, Guchkov had noticed the following characteristic in retired men of state: great decisiveness and even mercilessness of opinions such as they had never manifested before when they were in their posts. This had manifested itself now in Kokovtsov, too, usually always so disciplined, his imagination quite straitened. Guchkov had observed this even more in the deceased Witte, bilious and hate-filled unto death, who had been so lost in the heat of '05 and so perceptive in hindsight. But might this characteristic even be inevitable for such figures? Guchkov was learning from his elders' experience; he was honing his own statesmanlike abilities on them. He found it very interesting with Kokovtsov today as well, and he returned home by motorcar through the quieted, deserted streets, here and there with soldiers' patrol bonfires, late.

He had already noticed in himself more than once this strange fatalism for our clearest plans—that they would either crash or yield results opposite of intended. How did this come about and why?

A plot? It kept not coming together, kept being put off, kept being out of his grasp. Nothing advanced, and no dates set. Despite its prescribed simplicity, this had proved an elusive enterprise, with many probabilities and deviations. And yet here in Petrograd there were crowds of thousands, there was gunfire on Nevsky, and a Pavlovsky company had mutinied. The abyss was showing its gullet: how close it was and how it could swallow up everything.

A plot was more necessary than ever, more urgent than ever. But it still hadn't come together.

Much now depended on General Krymov's anticipated arrival in a few days, no later than the end of March. Guchkov couldn't cope without the general's hand.

He returned home so politically inclined that he didn't feel like talking to Masha right now, or even seeing her.

He stopped the driver as he went down Sergievskaya before reaching Voskresensky, to his corner building. He walked the rest of the way. He quietly ascended the small staircase to the second floor and quietly unlocked and locked the door.

Silence. And straight to his study.

He turned the light on—and saw his white bust of Stolypin first in front of him.

He looked at his stone eyelids.

Now **this** was a man who had done everything at the right time and place. He wouldn't grumble later.

That was what Guchkov wanted. He had put the bust there for its unfailing encouragement. He would have liked to be another Stolypin. After his achievements he was prepared even to end up the way he did.

He lay down and turned out the light but couldn't sleep at all.

Through the wall he could sense Masha, even the threat of her entrance—which he so didn't want. As it was she impeded his thoughts, disrupted them even through the wall.

No matter what you do or where you aim, marriage crushes you like a block.

How had this come about? To what end? How had he not seen?

For ten years after that charabanc and spread cloak under the spring rain there had been no contact except through Vera some banter and assurances from this dangerous intermediary that for some reason Masha Ziloti really was the woman who would do everything for his happiness.

But when they met ten years later, Masha stunned him with her frank outburst: she had loved him all these ten years! Had lived for him alone! Waited! Without hope!

Such a direct confession rattles your heart. It was truly astonishing: to love and wait from nineteen to twenty-nine without hope! It was a crime to trample on love like that. If someone has been waiting for you so many years, then you have a kind of duty. And then, Guchkov's father liked her, it turned out. So did all his relatives, and everyone approved. You're almost forty, and dissolute, and you have to settle down someday. It's actually pleasant to think of yourself in this way: settling down. To declare and feel yourself of an age at last.

Truly, it was a wonder: she had loved and waited for ten years! A special nature, indeed. She would do anything for my happiness.

Shouldn't I doubt and worry genuinely not about my own fate but about what would become of her? After all, you're restless, and living with you could not be a bowl of cherries.

Indeed, that was right when it happened: in spring 1903, the happy pre-wedding concerns were overtaken by the summoning alarm of war: in Macedonia, an uprising against the Turks. How could he not go and help? Hadn't it been a long time since the Transvaal, since his limp had healed? And his chest ached: Macedonia!

Here it was, the first encumbrance, the first time he'd had to take someone else into consideration. The time before, he'd told his father nothing in advance, but only once en route: I couldn't have done otherwise, not when a national cause is at stake. When I return, I'll smooth over my guilt before you. But now, he had to persuade and get permission from his fiancée, explain how it could be that, after ten years' waiting, she had to suffer this additional separation. In those most joyous pre-wedding months—Why? What Macedonia, destroying the entire ritual, destroying all the bride's festiveness? Had he thought about *her*?

Oh, you reckless head, you hadn't learned to think about *her* as well. . . . But Slavic blood was being shed! . . . . For the first time, your will was about to snap and you didn't know what to do. . . . After all, it was a silly little delay—May, June, July. Maria Ilyinichna, my darling, don't judge me. You know I'm mad. I'll never forgive myself if I miss this campaign. I can't live if I don't go!

He begged off from the pouting lips until September. From every station, a postcard. From Adrianopolis, a gold coin with a profile of Alexander of Macedonia and a phrase worthy of etching in stone: "If not for you, I would be him. Alexander." (This is still youth, when you like your own name, and also that kind of coincidence. But when life nauseates you properly, you're deadly serious when you rush to the telegraph: just don't name my nephew Aleksandr!)

After all, an oblique banning cross had been placed as a warning sign: his younger brother Konstantin was married to her sister Varvara, and now according to church law it was forbidden for any of the other Guchkov brothers to marry any Ziloti sister.

But all those prohibitions had been ridiculed in educated circles long ago and dropped. (Much later he would think that his grandfather had been right, that only the Old Believers still had strong families. All the intelligentsia had these families grown apart, and the children off God knows where.)

Actually, he hadn't had any luck beginning his married life. His wedding trip to Imatra in October: cold rains, sitting miserably in hotels. And that very winter, before they could make their home: the Japanese war. Mashenka, how can I not go?

Naturally. . . . That's what you're used to. . . . But you have new obligations, too—a husband's. Sometimes you have to look at things from my point of view. What about me? Back to Znamenka, under my parents' roof? It's an insult, as if I weren't married and nothing had changed.

You're going to have a son. Lyova!

These were critical years for Russia—1904, 1905, 1906, and 1907—and Guchkov had the sense that he had been born for and would prove useful to these very years. But he had lost his former freedom of movement and decision, and could only think: How is Masha? Where is Masha? Always dissatisfied again. How could he mollify her? He carried her photocard around in his wallet. In folding tents, train compartments, and hotel rooms, he set it before himself dozens of times and accreted with the habit of being married.

It was a natural thought: it would be easier to draw her in as his accomplice, to try to explain his steps to her as an equal. A Russian wife is often just that. Look: why was society's contempt for the Japanese war so bitter? Look: the unhectic Russian path of the consultative Duma and Assembly of the Land—and how to convince the Emperor of this. Look: detailed impressions from an audience with the royal couple. The unrestrained rancor of the First Duma isn't us. I know you're going to be angry with me for my possible decision to join the Stolypin cabinet, but I will do my best to change your mind.

Sasha, why do you think a ministry is a calamity? I fully approve! I'm prepared to share all the Petersburg burdens that arise from that! I'm prepared to rally the ranks of your circle and like minds!

You've understood and sympathize? Oh, what happiness! And in this way, patiently, their life as a family began to shape up.

But he did not join the ministry. Instead, he came out in support of the Stolypin position against terror. And the entire pro-Kadet society fell upon him, pecked at and persecuted him. His horizons dimmed.

Dolefully and slowly: How is that? But I was dreaming of being a society lady.

Dear Masha, I'm so touched by your sympathy in my affairs. But "society lady" does not fit my notions of a wife and mother. What is loftier and sweeter than the lot of a faithful domestic mate?

Astonishing reasoning—a domestic mate! For you I gave up the entire world of art! I thought I'd find in you another dazzling world, but you've locked me up at Znamenka to bear and raise children. . . . You no longer need to admire me.

Really? . . . When did he ever make that promise—to admire her? He'd said: share my life's journey. Wherever it leads.

From young woman to wife—how quickly one's understanding is transformed and one's rights increased. You struggle to explain to her the subtleties and difficulties of public decisions, why you can't follow a profitable path but must endanger yourself—and you get these oblique replies, oblique in their suddenness and incongruity, like a plate flung across the room, straight from the shoulder.

And when your soul longs to converse—you sit down to write to someone else. Even a female someone. . . .

While she lives a muddled rural life, suffering without conversation or interaction. A society lady?

Oh, he'd been too hasty! From the outside it was impossible to believe. After all, he was no youth, he had long seemed impervious. And approaching forty, having accomplished so much already, why shouldn't he allow himself the luxury of a family?

But at one year and two the wedding white had been charred and you found yourself bound and unhappy.

Where did the ten-year maidenly anticipatory love evaporate?

And had it ever been?

They had forgotten how to understand each other in general. She had outbursts of stormy indignation, and frequently. You were already afraid to ask her anything about herself, sure every question of yours would be met hostilely. And you didn't feel like talking about yourself: you had no doubt that had lost its interest for her.

With Lev and Vera's first little steps (Vera was his favorite, in honor of the other Vera), the parents' union was already stumbling. What joy when a cheerful, carefree letter would burst through from Masha—oh, my darling, if only I could keep you so cheerful your whole life! If you want, I'm prepared to repent of many things.

But again an oblique distortion in reply, another broken plate. Suffering! Suffering such as the world had never known! But what made it so? My dove, start off on the right foot! I'm covered in holes received in battle, my forces are leaking out, and I get no support from you.

Raise your voice and she hears better, sees reason somehow. But God forbid in a weary moment you should call on her for simple mutual compassion—that weak voice was the least to reach her. Persuading her gently was utterly impossible.

She was abrupt in her whims, first too loud and loquacious, then tactless and impatient, an erupting volcano. The guests were already gathering in the parlor, and the dining room table was set for dinner. Masha in a loud whisper was playing out a scene of jealousy. Then Guchkov with insane calm, looking her in the eye, began pulling on the fully set tablecloth. Objects fell, Masha woke up, and the maid ran in to pick up and wipe off.

Marrying at such a mature age—and so short-sightedly? Where are we looking in that crucial moment? So certain when you were deciding and so troubled afterward! How had he been caught? How had he shackled himself to a stranger for his whole life? When you give all your abilities at distinguishing, judging, and deciding to the social struggle, war, and wanderings and you're drawn that way with all your passion, you become blind to what's at a mere arm's length, and hideously helpless against any other sphere. The more unmistakenly you're used to deciding and acting in big things, the more blindly you err in this little thing, and this little thing, this third-degree, subsidiary mistake entirely unrelated to society was enough to weaken you in no time, confuse you, consume your strength and drown you.

How had he looked into her face and not noticed before the heartless, loveless cruelty, the firm, unmissible expression? If you looked at photographs of her young, it was already there: the odd, practically frozen grin, the upper teeth always lifelessly bared. But he hadn't noticed and was used to it now.

Now their separations due to his work were stretching into separations of revulsion. His wife was at Znamenka, and Guchkov was in their ill-kept Petersburg apartment with a bad cook or going to restaurants. Or the children were here with the governess while Masha was in Moscow. Meetings were even worse than letters: the mutual faults and reproaches, and lies rebounding, too. (*His* lies. After all, when a wife takes one step back, her husband takes two, though it actually works the other way around, too.) The nanny, who did not approve of Maria Ilyinichna and considered Aleksandr Ivanych "one in a million," would soon suggest to little Vera that her father had "two hundred illegitimate children." No sooner would they meet under the same roof when all the cheer he had accumulated, all the accelerated action, would weaken and dull. And his immediate thoughts were about how soon he could leave and how many more days were left to go. Had a less similar couple ever been joined in marriage? They separated, and the letters were even worse than the meetings. It would be less tortuous to write to the most distant stranger than to an abortive intimate. Money, possessions, clothing, agreements on how not to let their paths cross, without even a formal "Love" at the end—and all that was left was the children. The questions were only about them. As they got older, separate pages to and from them. In your absence the children are kinder and cling to me more. Tell our daughter that I think about her constantly. (It was for Verochka that her papa's archive was being assembled, so that one day she would get to know her father.) Or an argument about governesses: are foreigners all right? They did need languages, yes, but Guchkov considered a steady Russian influence even more important. And why this traditional *music* for each child? Or the unschooled nanny wrote the report about the children, although Maria Ilyinichna was there, too. Or it would fall on him to take the children down Nevsky to look at the decorations for the Romanov festivities. It was bearable when the children

were busy with their own activities: Lyova would sell half of the little dog Jim
to Vera on an installment plan, until her fourteenth birthday, and they negotiated for a long time. But they looked up and wondered why papa and
mama were always apart and there was never complete happiness.

However, there is this feature to family discord: its nonlinearity, its nondi-
rectness, which is especially hard on men. Women are nonlinear. It's they
who introduce this looping around, this backing up, these returns and glim-
mers of false hope. Seemingly, everything had been torn asunder and was
hanging by just a few fibers when suddenly it was put back together and was
healed. Could that really happen? You started to believe. All of a sudden: I
embrace you tenderly! I love you! And the kisses themselves. And a third
child was on the way. (If perceptive ladies observed from the outside that
you were in turmoil—then nothing of the kind, you see!) But even before
Vanya's birth it was clear that it was all a mistake, all ashes, and they should
separate.

Not divorce. That was impossible because of the children and due to
Guchkov's special position. As Masha assured him, all Russia had its eyes
set on them, and they would not forgive him a divorce. But to separate dis-
creetly, to protectively end this mutual torment that had not left a single living spot in your soul.

How pitilessly you destroyed my entire life! And what did you give in return? I'd hoped to act by your side, and you flung me to the edge of existence! You couldn't, wouldn't fan the coals of your feeling in order to shed
light on my long-suffering soul. . . . In the very first years my sufferings were
bright and encouraging, but now? . . .

But when were they ever encouraging? And why didn't she say they were
encouraging *then*? Instead of flinging away then, too?

Vera Komissarzhevskaya's death marked a string of losses. Had her soaring also supported and somehow given meaning to his marriage to Masha?
Without her it became altogether unbearable. By the end of that year, 1910,
Guchkov was in discussion with Masha about just one thing: how to make
it more painless for everyone and for the children. But she asked him,
please *don't kick* at the past and finish the portrait with Cavos. That is my
last request! (How many there had already been and were yet to come: I
will never ask you for anything more; this is my last. . . .)

But somehow Masha knew how to wiggle out of things and change so
that despite the most definitive, indisputable ending it turned out not to be
the ending again. When it appeared not as an avoidable possibility but a
certain split—Masha was shaken for the first time in a way Guchkov had
not been able to achieve with arguments in the six years of their discord. It
was as if for the first time she started to hear and look at herself.

. . . I admit I have earned your dislike. I'm not laying the debacle of our
life on your lie alone. The first days of our discord were my doing. Although
I find much here that is mitigating for me.

But had she thought she could live in discord and rely on his fidelity? It was as if she'd been asking forgiveness but had taken a turn without him noticing and once again was aiming reproaches at where the guilty party turned out to be—at him. So much had been said before that he could not now remember how to justify his actions. So much had to be said that nothing could be, and the dialogue's mistress was once again Masha. He had lost his will for trading reproaches over and over when separation was inevitable.

Inevitable, but for some reason not done. Inexplicably, their life together was holding on by a few last threads and wouldn't drop off. Somehow they were even able to reach unprecedented agreement and see in 1912 together, at home.

However, in the last few hours of New Year's Eve, he up and left as if freeing his neck from a yoke.

Blaming himself, of course. But he couldn't not leave. Forgive me the pain I've caused you. Caused you. My own excessive sufferings have made me insensitive to the sufferings of others. The children—that's all we have left.

That New Year's seemed like a complete break. For good.

But fingers and hands tie new knots, though exactly how is inexplicable. Family problems are characterized by endlessly new and shifting thoughts. Maybe I didn't do the right thing with her, maybe I lacked patience, maybe I should have had more trust and drawn her more into my work.

He invited her to come along to the unveiling of the Stolypin monument in Kiev. "You loved him, too, after all."

(Or—the same as you did me? . . .)

On whom does one's life's companion not leave a mark? Perhaps, given another wife who would mollify and forewarn him, Guchkov might not have been so devastatingly impatient toward the empress as well. In his battle with Alix he sometimes crossed boundaries one shouldn't against any woman.

The string of losses and failures stretched out, entangled with illnesses as well. The year 1912 brought Guchkov the loss of Russia's trust and his loss in the elections to the Fourth Duma. The year 1913 was the failed split of the Octobrist faction, which did not move Russia along at all. The year 1914 was the unfortunate war, including its first trials: the Lodz pocket and the voluntary decision to stay with the wounded and defend them if they were destined for captivity.

It was liberating for a soul constantly given to large-scale struggle to see again the contrast between these scales: in what insignificance could I have been wallowing? What there could have poisoned me that way?

Having experienced this ascent anew, to pity his unlucky companion for never rising this high, never knowing how petty her offenses or how pathetic her claims. To pity and—forgive her, in the broad masculine form—that is, to *beg* forgiveness. When the world trembles in this way—can an indentation filled with a spouse's tears survive between gigantic craters? And to the rumble of weaponry in the outskirts of surrounded Lodz, with what may have been the last courier to Russia—and what may have been the last letter in his life: My dear . . . forgive me . . . All our life I caused you . . . I cannot stop thinking about our children. . . . Sincerely loving you . . .

But there was no encirclement. Guchkov did return—and to his ordinary Petersburg life even, and, unfortunately, even to family life. Wasn't anything preserved? Could anything be understood from those Lodz notes? (That he was to blame?) According to the laws of nonlinearity, crossing more and more new thresholds of a final split, they once again would look like a proper family. They met acquaintances in Moscow or, at the springs, they inquired about each other and received answers. A general of his acquaintance added a postscript: "Kissing Maria Ilyinichna's dear hand" . . . From journeys: Masha, I forgot my papers, I forgot my boots, please send. . . .War, many events, much movement, and 1915 is passing without him being suffocated. (Only suddenly, out of jealousy, Masha rushed to his Red Cross hospitals, sowed confusion, and put Guchkov in an awkward position.)

Just how long would this go on? But the illnesses that had beset him methodically for many years—his feet would swell, his hands would ache, then his heart, or his liver—suddenly converged, became one, and in early '16 a solemn death hung over Aleksandr Guchkov.

It seemed so similar to the Lodz pocket. In the face of eternal parting, it's natural to reconcile once again and beg forgiveness.

No! There was another law. Why, in addition to all life's trials, was I also sent the trial of a spiteful wife? Heartless, self-serving woman—why were you sent to me as an eternal cross and curse? Why have you eaten away at my life? Leave me at least to die in peace. Don't come near me. I don't want to see you!

Not a chance! Due to his weakness, carelessness, and distraction with something greater, he didn't sunder his wedding rings in time, and now they lay like shackles on his sunken yellow chest. Maria Ilyinichna seemed to rejoice in his mortal illness and threw herself into tending him as if it were plunder. "A feverish nightmare," Burdenko called her. A funnel cloud of fuss! Not only going to see his doctors but also his enemies, and Badmaev, Rasputin practically, for help. An arrogant face: she alone knew how to save her ardently beloved husband.

To lie sentenced to death under a whirlwind of irritating concern and to be helplessly astonished that he could ever have been reduced to this, he, a soldier. They were already bringing the sacrament, and in a few days you'd be gone, but *she* would be trodding the earth for half a century more as your friend, your memory, your interpreter.

This was more like a caricature of his life than his real life: not at all the one he should have led. But for some reason, this was how his life had turned out. Because of his marriage.

How could he have failed to cast it aside despite all his efforts? But he himself had chosen this.

What settled in her deepest of all was her distorted interpretation of the past. The linkage of facts wasn't what had been but what was accessible and convenient to her narrow mind. You could argue, you could rage, you could dig in your heels, but she would never admit how it in fact had been, starting from those first ten years of apparently loving anticipation.

But he didn't die. He rose from his bed. And on doctors' advice headed for the Crimea. And she, too, of course? He cut her off unswervingly: No, my dear, I'm not going to lie powerless like that any more. You'll stay in Petersburg, find a good excuse, and act out the public comedy however you please. . . . But I'm prepared to die for you! . . . No need. Live. . . . What about the other ladies who pounce on everything? What about society, which is already sniffing around our family life? How can you, for all your nobility, humiliate me so publicly? How can you deal me this slap in the face so calmly?

Her status as a lady was a function of her organism. In order to be a lady she was prepared to eat away him.

How many times had he conceded, and how many times had he been weak—only not now!

That's all right, she came up with the boys' illness and Verochka's operation. But wasn't all that possible in the south as well? Everyone will be perplexed and blame me for not going with you. . . . My torment is going to increase because I'm going to have to answer ten times a day why I didn't go.

He left. Quickly—alone, to begin recuperating. Only after a gnawing marriage can one understand what happiness it is to be entirely alone.

But as during that definite indefinite rupture five years before, so it was now: she was overcome. She sensed the separation wouldn't end unless all Russia and all the Earth turned on its head.

From Petersburg to the Crimea for Easter: my life—and my love for you—also began at Easter. Here, love is ending without having given or been given **anything**. How many times have I said farewell to you before, but every corner of my soul is full of you, and ripping out each one makes me scream in pain. And now it has reached the main nerve. I wish I could understand why it is my love was barren. I dream that you could for one moment, right before your death . . . Christ be with you, I hope you find what I was unable to give you. . . .

No, this grabs the heart of anyone who hasn't read the like fifteen times and hasn't learned to see the cold malice on her face. I mustn't be mollified. Being mollified means falling back into pettiness.

I'm sending your Easter letter back. It singes my hands. If you're going to have your revenge on me, don't make our children your weapons of revenge.

. . . In my condition—do you still dare demand something of me? Give me advice about the children? Have you ever overcome yourself for them? You were the one who deprived yourself of them!

That was what he wrote, and what she wrote, not supposing the suddenly horrific meaning of these words: that in a few months these words would come true—and they would lose Lyova to meningitis. She was so self-absorbed that she overlooked their son. She let him go, let the ten-year-old stand up on a full-grown horse and fall.

You can win all of Russia—and lose your marriage.

[67]

It was already after one. There were only Cossacks riding through the empty city and Volynians had arrived at the gates of their training detachment on Vilensky Lane. Kirpichnikov brought them to a halt, faced the formation front, and reported to Captain Lashkevich.

Lashkevich stepped off the sidewalk toward the formation.

"Your actions were poor, showing no initiative whatsoever. In war there must needs be both shooting and initiative. Well, thank you anyway. Disengage to barracks by platoon."

The platoon commanders led them—it wasn't his company anyway—and Kirpichnikov remained with Lashkevich, who reprimanded him, too, for hiding all day, dodging, and acting improperly.

Another officer can be like one of your own. But this one was a stranger, a viper, a lord. He wasn't going to forgive any failure of yours.

Tomorrow was Timofei really going to have to go again? Yes, tomorrow was his 2nd Company's turn.

Both ensigns came up and asked whether they should go collect the bullets from the soldiers. But it was late and Lashkevich said:

"That's all right, the platoon commanders will collect them themselves."

The ensigns said goodbye and went in different directions, home. But Lashkevich accompanied Kirpichnikov to the chancellery. Behind his gold spectacles he was tired, his face sunken. But once he started reading the document he straightened up, as at "attention." And he told Kirpichnikov in confidence:

"The Emperor has ordered an end be put to all the disturbances tomorrow."

And he calculated:

"Tomorrow a party will start out from your company at eight o'clock. Wake them at six. I'll arrive at seven. But right now the 1st Company has to eat quickly and go to bed."

Kirpichnikov:

"The men haven't had dinner or supper today, and they haven't had their tea."

But Lashkevich was too absorbed:

"Doesn't matter. This isn't the time to be drinking tea."

Timofei, hopefully:

"So I'll be with the 1st Company then?"

"No, the 2nd," Lashkevich ordered. And he left.

Well there, he knew it. The fourth day running for Timofei in this dog's service. No one else had had this happen to them.

The company barracks were separate. In the 1st they ate dinner and supper together. And went to bed. Timofei went back to his own 2nd.

There they were already asleep in their two-tiered bunks. There was a lamp by the orderly and also two small ones at the other edge. A small lamp in front of the company icon. The lower bunks were all dark.

Timofei sat down on his separate cot in the corner, leaning on his bedstead. He drooped.

The man on duty brought him his, in a heated pot. He started eating without feeling or thinking.

At least not about food.

He'd hoped not to be going for the fourth day in a row and that the burden would fall from him on its own. But it hadn't.

His buddy, Misha Markov, a platoon commander, cater-corner, on a nearby bunk:

"Timosha, how's it going?"

He called him over. Misha wrapped himself in his overcoat, walked over barefoot, and sat down beside him on the cot.

"Yeah," he said.

They were silent.

"What's going on? The generals are betraying us. And so is the Tsaritsa — with Grishka. Over there, Orlov brought it and you read it. Who needs war? Not us."

"Yeah," he says.

"And our bayonets — in the people's bellies? They aren't leading us in a cause. Today there were dead, and wounded. . . . Misha, I can't look the people on the streets in the eye. How can this be? What are we doing? And our officers? Here you are having a rest, while I have to go again tomorrow. . . . You know, I . . . I can't anymore. Eh?"

Markov hung his head.

"Why torture ourselves like this?" said Timofei. "It'd be better not leaving the barracks from the start. . . . Would you be willing not to go?"

Would he ever! Over broken steps and uphill. Markov — in one breath:

"But what'll happen?"

"Come what may? We're pinned."

Oh, it's hard. Hard for a man to put himself in the way of the ax.

Timofei yawned deeply. And sighed.

"But if it's our lot to die in battle—isn't it the same thing? What's our life worth? We could have lain down at the front a hundred times, like lots of men. But they shifted us here—to shoot at the people. Everyone at everyone? What kind of life is that?"

Misha had a conscience. Like a peasant, he pities both a human being and an animal. In one breath:

"I suppose I agree."

The words had been spoken. The line crossed. Now what? Now they had to do something.

Timofei told him to wake up the other three platoon commanders and bring them here, to his cot. And he told the company duty officer not to let anyone into the room. And when the duty officer came around (he made the rounds at night) to report right away.

The five gathered, their old greatcoats over their drawers. They sat down. And Timofei—he alone sprightly—said to the four he'd awakened:

"How about it, men? Our fathers, mothers, sisters, brothers, and brides are asking for bread, and we're shooting at them? Blood was shed today. Tomorrow there could be more, and on our count. And the Tsar doesn't care. He's ordered us to put it down tomorrow. And the Tsaritsa is passing military secrets to the Germans. I suggest that tomorrow we **not go**. Eh?" He surveyed their faces. "I personally don't want to go."

He didn't say he'd "decided" because he hadn't yet. So, what did they think? Without them it was impossible.

They were silent.

There were more than a few sighs.

And glances. Oh, how frightening to be bold for the first time!

Misha Markov said he wouldn't go. He was supporting his sergeant-major.

Thus the tide turned. Then Kozlov said he wouldn't go.

Then so did Kanonnikov. And Brodnikov:

"All right, we'll stay with you. Do what you think best."

Timofei rose from his cot and kissed them all.

"All right, men! We'll go to the front and they can kill us there, but there's no such thing as dying twice. We won't betray each other and won't let them take us alive. Death is only scary at first."

He called to the orderly in a hushed voice. Now he ordered him to pull the detachment commanders separately from their bunks and tell them not to dress. Only quietly.

Although they'd been asleep, they showed up quickly, some with footcloths around their feet, some barefoot.

In a semicircle, some squatting, some standing. And Timofei told them quietly, but so that it was clear to everyone there:

"Men, you're our helpers. We, your platoon commanders, have decided not to go out tomorrow to shoot."

While he was saying this to the fifteen or so, it wasn't a slow dream anymore. He himself believed something would happen. He spoke as about a done deal.

And right away Orlov the lance corporal, a Petersburger (Timofei had already managed to explain to him separately), said firmly:

"We won't go for anything! This is right."

The others didn't get their say. It was a done deal.

"Fine, then look at me. You do what I do. You'll carry out my sergeant-major commands, and only that. And now I am the sergeant-major of the 1st Company, too. So that . . ."

They decided to get up at five o'clock, not six. To assemble the men by platoon and explain: we've taken an oath to strike the enemy and defend the homeland from Wilhelm—but not to strike our kin. Of course, our men aren't soldiers; they're rabble, slobs, but still. If they agree, get them fitted for guard duty. And we'll get a hold of ammunition.

The platoon and section commanders went off to bed.

Though not to sleep, of course. . . .

Kirpichnikov summoned the quartermaster, a junior sergeant, and ordered him to go early to the battalion instructor tomorrow and get as many bullets as possible, supposedly on order of Staff Captain Lashkevich.

In that company the ammunition hadn't been taken away, which was good.

But! Kirpichnikov suddenly worried about word suddenly getting out now. If just one man went to the duty officer at the chancellery, they were done for. Had he announced it too soon?

He instructed the company orderly not to let a single man out to go anywhere under any pretext.

Now on the cot he and Markov discussed what to do if no one joined their detachment: We'll put one section opposite each window to fire out the window. We'll put one machine gun through the window across from the gunsmith's. And one on the stairs so as not to let anyone in from the yard. No one will take us, not the infantry and not the cavalry. Maybe the artillery.

Right then the orderly ran in.

"Sergeant-major! You're wanted on the telephone!"

Something bad? Had they found out?

Kirpichnikov went and Markov followed. Markov, too, put his ear to the receiver from the other side and listened.

Lashkevich's voice:

"Kirpichnikov! The men—are they all asleep?"

Oh, he's an impatient one. He's picked up on something.

"Yes sir, all of them, your honor."

"All's calm in the detachment?"

"Yes, sir."

"Make a tally of how many bullets were fired. In the morning the quartermaster should go to the instructor to get the live ammunition for the 12th."

That was just what we needed, and here was the order.

"And wake them at seven tomorrow, not six. Formation at ten 'til eight. With weapons. Expect me."

He let him go.

An extra hour. Then we'd wake ours an hour later, at six.

It was already four in the morning. Time to lie down.

Markov detached the bayonet from his rifle and put the loaded gun under his blanket. And kissed it.

"This is my faithful wife."

Timofei, too, had no wife. The company and battalion were his entire home. True, his weapon's metal was cold, but his heart suckled at it.

"Why put it there?"

"Just in case it starts earlier."

"What if the duty officer comes in? Is he going to count rifles? You shouldn't."

"No! That's what I want."

They lay there. They couldn't sleep.

Line up directly with weapons, he'd said.

The lamp went out in front of the icon.

Fine, the air'll be cleaner.

You could almost hear, just barely, whispers and low voices through the barracks.

It wasn't scary when the decision was being made. Or when they assembled the section leaders. Here's when: when it is all done, when everything is cut off, and the last two hours remain. And you, alone with yourself, you can't call out to anyone—while on the other side of morning there might be a noose dangling for you.

It's a terrible moment, as if death were nigh.

He said to Misha nearby, across the aisle:

"If the other units don't join us tomorrow, they'll hang us."

"Yeah . . ."

"Still, it's better to die a soldier than kill innocents, right?"

"Yeah . . ."

"Under all the Tsars, that's how it's been. They've never cared about the people."

Oh, it's so hard to start! Starting—starting is hardest of all. But someone has to.

"Even a dog that never barks one day will."

It was easier that they were young and neither had a family. On the other hand, when you're young you're sorrier for your life.

"All right, Misha. Let people later remember the Volynian Regiment training detachment."

* * *

TWO SORROWS TOGETHER, A THIRD SORROW SHARED

* * *

12 March
Monday

[68]

When everything is decided before sleep, it's more easily gauged than on waking. No matter how they dared to do the desperate, they still had to drop their head to their welcoming pillow, if only for two hours—and get some sleep. It was all still calm and very far away.

But once the man on duty started shouting rise and shine—harshly, bawling his head off, as he was supposed to—and all the electricity went on, then even Timofei himself struggled out from under the stone that had dropped on top of him. Oh, Timosha, Timosha, what have you started and why?

Well, it seemed there was no getting up and shaking himself off. If he'd been alone, not in front of his comrades, he'd probably have renounced it all and shouted, "Dismissed! Go to bed!"

The soldiers didn't know anything. A soldier doesn't know what time he's awakened, only his body feels, Ugh, this seems early, ugh, they're shorting me on sleep.

But a word once spoken can't be taken back. He and Misha Markov lowered their feet to the floor in unison, across the way, and looked at each other—and he could tell for real that it was the same for him, the same, he'd have been fine renouncing this if it hadn't been for Timofei.

But neither could be first to say so.

If only it weren't for the platoon commanders. And the section leaders. They'd already been pouring generously. And what they cooked up overnight had now taken its own course, regardless of them.

What on earth have we done? What's going to happen to us now?

One comfort: head under the tap, and take in the cold water, take it in, and a little more on the withers. It sobers you right up.

You pull your head out from under the tap a different man. If it has to be, it has to be—and that's right.

Drive them all on—come on, wash up! No moping, everyone under the tap!

Meanwhile he realized he'd made a mistake about getting them up. Why did he get them up at six o'clock? He'd thought they'd need time to get ready. But what was there to get ready? Dress, collect their things—ten minutes. There was no getting bullets before half past six, and the kitchen wouldn't feed them any earlier. The best preparation for work is sleep. He'd miscalculated, fool, and he was sorry for himself and everyone else.

After washing and bed making the soldiers waited and wandered around—but there was nothing else to do. It wasn't time to line up, and it was too early to have a word. That meant they could sit down, they could lie down dressed.

They paced around more and more sluggishly. And lay down.

Some now lay however they landed. Some maybe went back to sleep.

And some maybe didn't know a thing—and they just collapsed. But if the section leader whispered something in your ear—you think you'd sleep much? You have one head and one hide, still not hacked, still not pierced—who wouldn't feel sorry?

Now Kirpichnikov grasped what the two dangers were. First, what if for some reason they didn't give them the bullets? If they didn't, that was it, that was the order. If they just wouldn't issue them, then we won't take the men out, which will make it even easier for us, our conscience will be clean and we'll spend the day in the barracks. But what if they didn't give them because they'd guessed? Then what? They'd come and take us bare-handed, and we'd be lost over nothing.

But how could they guess? Herein lay the second danger. Had anyone slipped out, even in the night? He shook the orderly—no, no one. Platoon and section leaders—check your men. All accounted for?

Yes.

They sent reliable men for the bullets with the quartermaster.

Let no one else out.

It's taking so long. Will they give them the bullets? Or not? They wandered around, lay down, and dozed—while Kirpichnikov worried.

He and Markov waited and waited, exchanged looks, watched the wall clock. Oh, weren't they coming?

But at seven o'clock, they came tromping down the hall loaded down with small lead cases.

Oh you, our plumbs—not lead but gilded! With you we're men, with bullets even a soldier is a human being! So we can still stand for a while!

They doled them out to the platoons and sections—and stuffed their ammunition belts full.

And put the extras in their greatcoat pockets.

Now Orlov, the most loyal, would go with four carriers to the kitchen for their breakfast. He'd take a look around.

[69]

Just before dawn, Kozma Gvozdev was sleeping on his prison cot—and dreaming.

He dreamed he saw an old grayhair in bast shoes sitting on a big white rock wearing fresh, well-washed hemp clothes. His foot bindings and every cord was clean and white.

By all accounts, an ordinary village granddad. Only his gray hair was very long, pulled back on his head, and there was a special shine off it, having been thoroughly washed, hair by hair, and blown about.

The granddad was weeping—and so bitterly, so distressed. Had he buried his old woman? Had his hut been burned down? Had his entire nest been smashed? He was weeping, not a glance for Kozma, weeping, and the tears rolled down—you could see each one separately—down his wrinkled cheek or stopped at his gray beard.

Kozma felt sorry for the granddad. He went up to him.

"What's the matter, granddad? Why do you weep so? Come now, don't kill yourself."

The granddad had been holding his head in his hands. But now he raised his eyes—and those eyes set Kozma to trembling and turned his insides to ice: this was no ordinary granddad, this granddad was a saint.

And he was weeping not for himself but for him, for Kozma, whom he pitied.

"But why are you weeping for me?" Kozma endeavored to console him further. "Do not weep for me. Soon they'll let me go."

But the wisdom in the old man's eyes turned around—and Kozma froze again and realized that no, it would not be soon. Oh, not soon not soon not soon. Longer than a man's life.

And so the granddad centenarian did not utter a word. He dropped his head and sobbed. How he sobbed!

Then Kozma felt even icier. Might he be weeping **not for me**? There could not be so many tears for me alone.

So who were they for?

This was too much for one heart to hold.

When he woke up his entire insides were gripped by cold and grief.

[7 0]

After breakfast, Kirpichnikov ordered the 2nd Company to line up fully armed in the long, second-floor hallway. The machine guns stood on the left flank.

He stepped out in front of the formation—still without any medals, although he had been wounded once, with flat, closely set ears, a big nose, fat lips, a low brow, and eyes hard open. Trying to stand grandly, though he was perplexed. And with a voice accustomed to clipped commands, not speeches, in a voice rather faint and strained:

"Well, what's there to say, brothers? . . . These last few days you've seen plenty yourselves, and used your rifle butts, and squeezed triggers, too. . . . We ask, haven't we had enough of shedding people's precious blood? Moreover, there's something obscene going on at the top. . . . Haven't we had enough of bowing to these freeloaders plaguing the life out of us? Wouldn't it be more just for us not to go against the people? . . . I'm certain other units will lend us every support."

This was what he wasn't sure of, but he couldn't call men to a doomed cause.

No one said anything coherent in reply, but there was a buzzing. Which seemed like approval.

"So here's the thing. Do you trust me? And will you carry out my command?"

They responded that they did and would.

"So here's the thing. Respond to all the junior officers who come just as you're supposed to: 'Good day, your honor!' Don't let on. But don't respond to Lashkevich's greeting. Instead, everyone must shout only 'Hurrah.'"

He himself didn't exactly understand what would happen after that, but if they shouted "hurrah," then there was no way back for anyone. This would weld them together, and they would join in step.

They stood in formation. Their hearts were pounding. They awaited the worst of battles.

At ten 'til eight, the ensign arrived. Kirpichnikov gave the command as if nothing were going on, with an excess of mettle even:

"Atten-shun! Eyes front!"

The ensign saluted the sergeant-major and saluted the formation:

"Good day, men!"

They bellowed as they were supposed to, but not overly harmoniously:

"Good day, yr'honor!"

"At ease!"

"At ease, and collect yourselves."

But now everything was off and running. Kirpichnikov approached cautiously, with a sideways step, in part in order to remind everyone.

"Well, yr'honor, didn't our Volynian lads act like real heroes yesterday?"

"Yes," he said.

"And today we'll be doing even better. Wait and see how well they do today." But his own voice was trembling.

The men all stood quietly, stock-still. Everyone understood—except the ensign.

Shortly after eight, the orderly ran up to say Staff Captain Lashkevich was approaching.

All the soldiers turned to Kirpichnikov. But he only squinted harder and raised his arm slightly, so that everyone could see he was thinking for everyone.

Lashkevich didn't come there first, though; he went to the chancellery. He extended everyone's life.

Five minutes later he came straight here. Gold spectacles, eagle-eyed, with a bite. The ensign ordered:

"Atten-shun! Eyes front!"

He reported. Lashkevich accepted his report. Everyone armed—just as he'd ordered. He greeted the formation.

And all of a sudden the entire formation, as one, though with some lagging, roared:

"Hurrah!"

The captain actually arched his back. And went on his guard—at the formation and at Kirpichnikov. Quite unexpectedly, he smiled, gently laying out his words:

"What kind of form is this, Kirpichnikov?"

Whether it was better to phrase his answer this way or that, Kirpichnikov never got the chance, when from the formation Orlov, the Petersburg lance corporal, shouted:

"Enough blood!"

The captain immediately stuck his right hand in his pocket. That meant he had a gun there. He started walking back and forth in front of the formation, pacing, gazing into their faces. He was probably looking for whoever had shouted. But didn't find him. And stealthily asked none other than Markov:

"Can you explain what this 'hurrah' means?"

So Markov was the first who had to explain. One step between them. Markov raised his head, and as into an abyss, by now without "your honor," because they were past that now:

"It means we're not going to shoot anymore! We don't want to go shedding our brothers' blood for no reason!"

Ah! Lashkevich fastened his gaze—he'd found him! Leaning a little closer to Markov:

"What's that?"

After what had been said, what did a soldier have left? There was nothing to say, four-eyes would outtalk him. And—**present** arms! From his leg, as it stood on the stone floor—he took it in both hands, his bayonet atilt.

No, not right at his chest, but, well, take care.

Lashkevich did. He stood up straight again and arched his back. He stood opposite Markov a little longer—and began to pace. His eyes—penetrating and keen—went from face to face, face to face.

Right then two ensigns came up, Velyaminov and Tkachura. They saw the training detachment leader was out of sorts for some reason. The first ensign filled them in at a whisper.

And Lashkevich, no longer up close, taking in the entire formation, in a ringing voice, but desperately rather than threateningly:

"Soldiers of the Guard! His Majesty the Emperor has sent a telegram to the capital's troops. He asks the troops to stop the disturbances, which are disrupting our fighting army!"

He had grasped at the Tsar, that meant.

Silence.

The formation stood as if shackled. A formation is a habit, though.

Markov was lowering his bayonet. He lowered it. He brought it to his leg, like everyone else.

Right then, Velyaminov:

"Captain, sir, permission requested to leave. I don't feel well." Without turning his head, his entire gaze on the formation, Lashkevich told him icily:

"Go."

He left quickly.

Left? Did that mean he was going to tell the other units?

Apparently, if it had occurred to Lashkevich just to turn his head to the door—they would have already spilled out in throngs. But he stood erect, focused on the formation. Still hanging in the air was "His Majesty the Emperor."

The formation stood there.

And Kirpichnikov, in his separateness, but constrained by the same formation, did not dare disturb it. He stood and was at a loss.

All of a sudden someone's rifle butt in the last rank struck the stone slab. And in a bass voice:

"Leave us. We don't want to see you!"

In imitation, another rifle butt, somewhere else: Bam!

They'd found a way! Another rifle butt and another on the stone slabs! An unprecedented, unheard-of, ominous rumble down the hallway! And it reverberated!

Lashkevich hunched his shoulders. Not quite enough yet. And then Kirpichnikov bawled at him:

"Get out!"

Suddenly—quickly—Lashkevich turned. And quickly walked off. Down the stairs. Down the stairs there.

The ensigns had vanished as well.

A victory? That had been the hardest part: how to take that first step. How to treat their own commander. And now he'd gone, been driven away?

They'd left—and now they'd call for an attack on us.

Kirpichnikov rushed to the window, where he could see the courtyard.

He pulled out the sealed frame and opened it wide: Where would he go?

And now they fell out of formation. But not everyone, some stayed in place.

They broke open a second window, too.

They saw Staff Captain Lashkevich come down the front steps and quickly cross the yard to the gates and the street. Did that mean he was gone? Did that mean he was going to battalion HQ?

Orlov, not Kirpichnikov, shouted:

"Get him!"

That wasn't anything they'd planned, but that's what happened.

A good five rifles were raised, Orlov's, too, and banged through the open windows.

And—the staff captain collapsed in front of the gates, on the trampled snow. Without so much as a jerk.

Dead as a doornail.

Oh ho! . . . What was going to happen now?

Some froze. Some ran down the hallway:

"Hurrah!"

What "hurrah"? Only now was it all beginning. Only now had the cord been cut: not when Lashkevich ran out—but when he fell. Now there was no turning back for anyone here.

Now we'd mutinied, irrevocably! What was going to happen?

Kirpichnikov shouted over it all and waved his arms. In your places! Line up!

They assembled and lined up.

But what now? That night they'd thought they would take up their defense at the stairs and windows. But that meant locking yourself in a trap. That's what they'd thought when they were afraid to take that step. But now that it had been taken? . . .

Outside! Call on the other companies! The more we come together, the less they'll fall on us. Now it's all cut off, now the only way out is to call on the others!

Kirpichnikov hollered his command:

"Company right face! Forward, march!"

They tramped, poured down the stairs. Into the yard!

By the time they reached the yard, there was no formation. They'd scattered in various directions and were wandering like drunks, like madmen.

They shot in the air for no reason.

Some shouted "hurrah."

The buglers played the alarm.

Kirpichnikov sent Markov and Orlov to the other training detachment company to call on them to join in.

[7 1]

The train arrived in Moscow very early in the morning, and in a still empty, early streetcar, Georgi made his way home to Ostozhenka.

His heart had been quiet and eased that Saturday evening among his kin. Yesterday morning on the streets of Petrograd everything had calmed down. But that somber squeezing of the heart in Mustamyaki—that had not let go. What had that been?

But in Petrograd everything was overshadowed by the horror that with his own hands he had wrecked Alina's fragile recuperation. And now it was going to start all over again? And on what a new scale!

He hadn't felt his usual sprightly grace for even an hour. There was a confused murk in his soul. A constant impediment.

The closer to home he got, the more oppressed and gloomy he felt. And by the time he was going up the stairs in the gray morning light, his heart had contracted and was pounding. Not having found—or having lost—what exactly he would first express, do, or say, he turned the doorbell twice.

Alina was probably still in bed. He waited for her steps but didn't hear them. She didn't come.

She might be trying to prove something.

He rang again.

She didn't come.

Again. She had to have woken up. But she didn't come.

Again. Or she had to have real restraint. Or . . . maybe she wasn't there?

He thought—and turned cold and his insides collapsed. Oh, God, really? Oh, God, had she really . . .

He rang! He rang! He rang!

Silence.

God, could she really be lying there in bed—dead? All of a sudden he pictured it so clearly and irrevocably that it could not be otherwise! Yes, that was it exactly! How many instances like this there are, when they lock themselves in. She had threatened to do it, after all.

He could already see her dead, prone on the bed, and this suddenness passed through him in a slantwise shudder. What if—our entire fragile life was facing this turning point.

He didn't ring anymore but tried to catch his breath and think clearly. He wiped his forehead. But what if she just wasn't there? A simple idea: go quickly to the church portress and ask.

The old woman was already on her feet. She wasn't surprised. Yes, here, she left you the keys. Yes, she went away. I don't know where.

Phew. Relief. She was alive.

Even triple relief: nothing had happened; she wasn't home right now and there would be no stormy scene; and he didn't have to make an effort to say anything, to explain.

But then, before he reached his floor: what if she'd deceived the portress? And locked herself inside with other keys—and . . .

He hurried up the last flight.

He entered—like a thief into a stranger's empty apartment? Or like a relative into a crypt? Was this feeling inside him or was there a waft of the grave in the air?

Without taking off his coat—forward, quickly, right away!

The dining room. Empty.

The place where her note had been set out the last time. The same frame and photograph: Alina in a broad-brimmed hat with a proudly raised head, handsome and happy. No note.

But lying there were large tailor's shears opened as far as they would go. He looked for a note on the sideboard and elsewhere—and didn't see one. Quickly to the bedroom!

Not there! The bed was neatly made. Not crumpled. Oh, what relief! He'd pictured her prone.

The whole bedroom was tidy. Not like in the autumn, not a flight. His eyes involuntarily across the floor: No crumpled papers, as then? No. He looked and searched some more—on her bureau, her vanity.

Then he saw it: her nail scissors standing in the middle of her vanity mirror, leaning, *propped up* by her powder box. The same way—the two blades opened as far as they would go, until they hurt, it seemed, and even their tips were curled. No, it was these twisted blades that were aimed like stings at the viewer—a jab!

Now also on the bureau, on the lace runner, he saw another pair of scissors—also opened as wide as they would go!

This couldn't be a coincidence, could it? They stood too intentionally on the vanity.

He should go on, to his study. Georgi's desk was cleared, emptied, as always when he was away, his permanent objects in a widely spaced half-oval. Only in the center of the desk, in the middle of the empty space, were his large scissors for cutting maps—splayed, its points spread as wide as they would go.

No, this was no coincidence. But what might it mean?

His first thought suggested itself, rushed in without him ever looking: it was a suicide warning, after all. I'll kill myself!

Why this thought? There was nothing here about suicide other than pointy tips, which were probably for poking out eyes. But the thought had come.

He walked around—everywhere. And everywhere he found more and more: on the kitchen table, in the foyer under the mirror—as many as eight scissors, all the scissors there were in the house! And all of them identical: tips spread desperately apart!

It was some kind of ominous hint, if not of death.

Georgi was no longer relieved that Alina wasn't home but found this turn of events worse. Something was wrong. . . . For some reason she . . . Better she'd been here. He wished she'd splashed him in the face.

Or maybe it was a sign of their separation. Look, the way these blades, which had come together before, had now been spread as wide as they could go—in the same way now we had separated as far apart as we could go, and our wedding rings had been scattered—and it was over?

For a moment this thought brushed him like a warm tail.

He wandered pointlessly, helplessly, from room to room, still not having taken off his coat and sword.

He closed one pair of scissors and another.

And then opened them again. Let it be the way she left it.

No, it was ghastlier. This was more like she'd gone off the deep end. You wouldn't think of standing them on end if you were in your right mind.

Had Alina's mind dimmed?

God, how his heart sank! Such desperation—and there was nothing he could do.

He felt so heartbreakingly sorry for her! And it was he who had led her to this.

He needed to chase her down, make her see reason, calm her. But where should he go? Where was she?

If he only had something from her! A letter, even the worst letter!

Nothing.

Only then did he have an idea: there was still Susanna! Maybe Alina was with her.

Without locking the door, he ran down the stairs to the telephone.

But he thought better of it. It wasn't even eight in the morning, and he couldn't disturb her so early. Half past eight at least.

He went back. Took off his coat.

Walked around like a lost soul.

The apartment was like a wasteland. And such murk.

Had she really gone off the deep end?

How everything ached and hurt inside. Oh, it would be better if she were **here**!

He couldn't do anything to himself, for himself, find her, find a place for himself.

At half past eight he still thought it was too early.

He could at a quarter 'til.

When he did go to telephone at a quarter 'til, they said that Susanna Iosifovna had left and would be home by four.

He'd missed her!

Now an entire day of neither knowing nor understanding, of longing. . . .

[7 2]

Yes, until just recently Vorontsov-Velyaminov had been a university student, but even more recently he'd completed the accelerated courses for the Corps of Pages and received his officer rank. Yes, he had heard society's call perfectly well—but he was also an officer of a Russia at war. These last few days his heart had been breaking, but he could not allow a mutiny in the capital, especially during time of war! Among themselves, the young officers cursed that scarecrow Khabalov: the milksop, he'd allowed chaos in the city. But now the army, too, had been affected. Yesterday, the Pavlovsky, and today, right now, in the hallway, he and Lashkevich had been standing in front of a mutinous formation. Velyaminov guessed—and plausibly begging off—took the steps three at a time—and across the snowy hummocks at a run—he burst into the battalion chancellery—and ignoring all regulations demanded to see Colonel Viskovsky. Mutiny in the battalion! The training detachment was refusing to obey!

Was that so? Could that really be? Well, for now, they reported.

Anything but immediately, the flabby, white-bodied Colonel Viskovsky came out, one of those who, having served a long time, had somehow never had his mettle tested and had merely risen comfortably in the ranks. Previously in marvelous Warsaw and now in Petrograd.

Well, was that so? Those impatient young men didn't know that an officer's primary traits are circumspection and sang-froid. How could it be that soldiers from a Guards regiment were refusing to obey orders? That was an impossible event.

But that was true! And minutes had passed! But Captain Lashkevich had stood there resilient in front of the formation—and even so could not think of anything! Help, we need help there, and quickly!

But the colonel plunged into contemplation at this nuisance.

The ensign was so bold as to blurt out something else without hearing his own words. And the colonel did budge.

The telephone. He asked to be connected to the city governor's offices.

What nonsense is this? At hand an entire battalion, so why the city governor's offices?

"This is Colonel Viskovsky, commander of the Volynian Life Guards Reserve. . . ."

(This all had to be pushed through!)

"May I ask for General Khabalov?"

But the general, it turned out, had not yet arrived from his apartment. But what's happened?

How could he reply? And could he just believe the ensign?

"Well . . . look . . ."—the colonel drew out his words—"I'm supposed to send the training detachment on detail through the streets, but it—"

Right then shots were heard nearby, in a cluster. Ensign Kolokolov ran in and said brokenly, wildly:

"Colonel sir! Captain Lashkevich has been killed! The detachment has mutinied!"

The colonel was dumbstruck. Now something had undeniably happened. But how could he repeat this to his superiors over the telephone? Oh, what a mess.

From there, from District HQ, they could find nothing to say. After all, General Khabalov hadn't arrived yet, and events such as this in military units were not provided for.

Then more officers ran in, young ensigns, then older ones, too. . . . The mutinied company was entering the yard! . . . The yard was all turmoil and disorderly movement! They were shooting and trumpeting! . . . They all had weapons but they weren't going out or forming up. They themselves were obviously perplexed and had no plan. . . . They weren't touching passing officers. . . . Captain Lashkevich's corpse was lying there. . . .

Everyone stood in front of the colonel, legs straight.

But he was lost in contemplation. Actually, the other officers, too, were like strangers in this reserve battalion. Either they had just been appointed, a few days or weeks ago, or they'd just recuperated and were anxious to leave as quickly as they could for an active regiment. This was not their place. They didn't have their familiar loyal sergeants, and they didn't know the soldiers by name — it was as if it weren't their unit.

Colonel Viskovsky was dazed. He didn't send anyone to the mutineers to try to persuade them, nor did he send anyone for support.

He'd turned rigid. He saw Captain Mashkin the 1st and called him into his office to confer.

The officers talked nervously and, in front of the clerks, paced and smoked. Spirited Tsurikov would have rushed to the courtyard himself, but he couldn't without an order. Staff Captain Mashkin the 2nd refused to condemn the soldiers. The soldiers had been led to the same point as Russia had. Tkachura clenched his fists: it had all happened in front of him, and he could just as easily have been shot himself.

But they weren't leaving the office. Then the officers became defiantly indignant. Some ensigns had been in military service for all of six months, but even they understood that . . .

Right then, Ensign Lyuba ran in — but in what a state! Already changed into civilian clothing. Otherwise, he said, it was risky getting through. The dodger! So quickly! So this was what awaited us as well? Outrageous!

Before they could reproach or question him, though, the colonel returned.

Now the voices would not quiet down. They demanded orders! But the colonel, disheartened, himself asked:

"District HQ is issuing no orders. What should we do?"

But it was so clear! Energetic, angry voices shouted:

"Call up a machine-gun crew!"

"Have the other companies cordon off the yard!"

"Call in the artillery from the Mikhailovsky Academy!"

"But, gentlemen," the bewildered colonel objected weakly, taking no offense at the tone of their advice. "Might not the soldiers themselves reconsider and give up the perpetrators?"

"Why should they reconsider?" they shouted at him.

He went back to his office.

His adjutant called Guards troops HQ but could get nothing coherent out of them.

The officers paced and smoked as if shackled now to the chancellery. Their verbal exchanges were brief. So far they hadn't been burst in upon—but what might happen? And how could they not put down a military uprising?

"But can we fire on our own soldiers?"

While *there* lay Lashkevich, his face in the snow.

Closer to half past nine, a sergeant ran in:

"The training detachment is going onto the street with weapons!"

They informed the colonel.

Now he knew even less what to do. And he was no longer counting on District HQ. He went out to the officers.

"Gentlemen, we must admit that events have gotten out of hand. We can do nothing to help. I recommend that you all disperse to your homes."

He himself got in his motorcar immediately.

So there you had it! The disheartened officers remained.

[7 3]

The interior minister's apartment on the Fontanka near the Panteleimonovsky Bridge consisted of two halves: on one side of the mirrored and carpeted staircase, his official apartment consisting of a reception hall with marble columns, a billiards room, his study, and next to that an extra bedroom, where Protopopov had slept today; on the other side of the staircase, his private apartment, which connected with the official one by a separate entrance.

All these months as minister, Aleksandr Dmitrievich somehow had taken to going to bed late, not before three or four in the morning. His audiences dragged on, and then dinner with someone, and more visits, supper, and at night he wrote up his plans—so that the minister's day began, well, at one in the afternoon. And today he'd hoped to sleep in, but for some reason awoke at nine.

Over the course of his life, only irregularly had Aleksandr Dmitrievich enjoyed family life. He and Olga Pavlovna already had two daughters when his dear Uncle Seliverstov was killed and he inherited a textile factory in Simbirsk Province. Protopopov was away from his family for a long time, traveling to Paris on the pretext of studying the state of affairs in the foreign textile industry. But over the course of two years, the manager lost half the factory's value, so Protopopov himself had to settle on his estate next to the factory and both build and undertake reforms. There they had lived like landowners, held feasts in the garden on Olga's name day, and nearly married their older daughter off to an up-and-coming minister—but then he did not become minister and the marriage was called off. And now, unimaginably, it was Aleksandr Dmitrich himself who had become a minister!

So here he was lounging about, squinting at the carved ceiling, and going back over it all. Going back over how he had risen so high and how he should manage what he had yet to do.

Actually, his future had been revealed to him in part by a perceptive seer, the astrologist Perrin.

It had all started like this. The year before last, Perrin had been in Petrograd and stayed at the Grand Hotel. Aleksandr Dmitrich learned about him through the newspapers, and he had always been interested in the world of psychic phenomena. They went to have him tell the fortune of his daughter's fiancé—but Perrin turned to Protopopov himself and immediately predicted a great future for him. He said quite accurately, "You created yourself. Always follow your own impulse. It's true!" Indeed, soon after this Aleksandr Dmitrievich was chosen to be vice president of the State Duma, and a year later minister. Stunningly predicted! Last summer Perrin had once again come to Russia, but for some reason he was suspected of being a German spy and he was deported without the right of return. Protopopov never did get to see him again. But when he was appointed minister, Perrin sent a letter: "Under your administration, a strong, new, and happy Russia will arise. Your path will not always be strewn with roses, but you will overcome all obstacles!" Really? The fact that it was not strewn with roses was something to which he had to reconcile himself. Perrin also wrote: "Every time you're threatened with danger, I experience a nervousness and will be acting at a distance by telepathic passes, which will make you experience a sleepiness." (Here and now, perhaps.) He predicted dangerous dates for Protopopov: the 27th, 28th, and 29th. On those days, it would be best not to leave home and to receive only those close to you. But those dates passed perfectly safely. (After the Workers' Group's arrest, the movement was beheaded for a long time to come.)

Occasionally there were also self-appointed seers, of course. Three weeks ago, Rittikh had told Protopopov at a meeting of ministers: "Your fate is looking you in the eye, which is what the Romans feared. Safeguard yourself against it!" Something unpleasant had even run down his back. But Rittikh was no seer.

Fate! Aleksandr Dmitrievich had always felt fate hanging over him. When he was dangerously ill for so long—myelitis, neurasthenia, softening of the skull—he had treated himself steadily with Tibetan herbs, followed by a two-year course of hypnosis with the psychiatrist Bekhterev. Nonetheless, he had yet to achieve stability of mood, and disastrous, weak-willed, gloomy declines followed by a euphoric soaring condition when you don't take disappointments to heart remained his lot. How fatefully he had played his cards back when he was a cavalry captain. Fatefully he had been made rich from his inheritance. And fatefully and at length had he loved women and subdued his intended.

In the fierce clash between the Duma and the Supreme Authority, who could ever have risen so amazingly and balanced that way on the tight wire, to the rumble of fury below—and achieved such mightiness? No one had ever achieved or combined this. Like an Alcibiades. Yes, Aleksandr Pro-

topopov truly was a fateful individual, with a fateful destiny! Under his administration, an unprecedented Russia might well rise up!

Unfortunately, in his five ministerial months he had unjustifiably done
very little—due to the wild situation, the wild public defamation, constantly being pulled in all different directions. On the other hand, how
clearly and intelligently he saw everything, how many simple opportunities discovered!

Oh, power! Power is not the same as speechmaking in the Duma.

But power can break you, too. Take the New Year's reception at the Winter Palace. Who could have expected? With the very best and most affectionate of feelings, Protopopov had tacked through the crowd of guests toward
Rodzyanko's broad shoulders: "Good evening, Mikhail Vladimirovich!" But
before he could utter his New Year's congratulations, Rodzyanko growled,
shaking like a truck: "Don't come near me! Not for anything, never, under
no condition!" But Protopopov did not take offense. He embraced Rodzyanko around his expansive waist. "My dear man, we can find agreement
on everything." But Rodzyanko kept shaking and growling, attracting those
around them: "Don't touch me! Step away. I find you repulsive!" All Aleksandr Dmitrievich could do was joke in a cheerless voice: "If that's so, then I
challenge you. . . ." But Rodzyanko didn't get the joke: "Please, just so your
seconds aren't gendarmes!"

For the past two months Protopopov had avoided any meeting with him.

But now, things were marvelous. Today the Duma had been dissolved,
and now he could live and govern.

When Tsarskoye Selo trusted you and was well inclined toward you—
that alone healed. Only there would you warm your soul. The only way you
could get anything done was if you were in contact with the Tsar's family.
During these months of defamation, he had been drawn all the more toward the Tsar's narrow circle. It gave him joy to justify this lofty trust.
Which was even firmer in the female half of the palace.

How wonderful life was when you loved and were loved, and how wonderful life would be without political passions and grudges!

There was an unpleasantly fierce knocking at the door. Aleksandr
Dmitrich shuddered and pulled up his blanket.

Who was it there?

His valet. The city governor was summoning him urgently to the telephone and had asked him to be awakened.

Ah? What's this? Yes, they're having . . . disturbances there. But by the
fifth day they should be over.

And so, reluctantly, forcing himself, he got up, put on his terry robe, and
tied his tasseled belt.

He moved to his study, stepping softly in fur-trimmed slippers. While
he'd been lying there, it hadn't seemed early, but now that he'd been summoned, it did.

Immediately in the receiver, Balk's driven daytime voice. That in the best battalion, the Volynian Life Guards, the training squad had mutinied and killed a model officer!

Oh, how cold he turned inside! He still hadn't properly understood— well, an isolated episode—but his tone! His tone?

"But it's a single isolated incident?"

"I still don't know! Tonight we expected a mutiny in the 2nd Naval Depot; there was a dispatch from the Okhrana about a secret meeting of sailors."

"So this is . . . a matter for Khabalov. . . . Or Grigorovich."

"We weren't able to reach Khabalov all night. He wasn't answering! And Grigorovich is ill. We ourselves sent to the depot. . . ."

Oh, so much at once, so aggressive and unpleasant! His instinct was not to accept all this into his unprotected life so early in the morning, still with that bed warmth, not fully slept.

Balk was asking for instructions! Decisions! His call was a question!

But what could the Minister of the Interior do? What did this have to do with him? All this had been handed over to the military authorities.

He didn't know what to say.

The city governor was waiting.

Yes! He remembered—and how inopportune this was:

"We just sent a supreme decree on the dissolution of the State Duma," he complained to his subordinate for some reason. And for some reason, he asked, "What do you say to that?"

"Oh, if only that had been done before!" the city governor exclaimed. "Now it can only do harm!"

His heart sank. Oh, how dreadful. Oh, how truly dreadful!

"Well, we'll see, my dear. . . . Well, God willing . . . Well, perhaps things will calm down by nightfall."

[74]

Kirpichnikov could not figure out what to do next.

Clearly he had to bring other units in: you're already up to your neck, so why not up to your ears? The more we take, the less they'll punish.

If only they hadn't killed Lashkevich. Now . . .

But half an hour passed, and another half an hour—and where was a single training detachment supposed to go? A handful.

Markov returned: the preparatory training detachment didn't want to go out.

Well, sink or swim! Kirpichnikov himself rushed over there.

He ran into their quarters:

"Hurrah!" But there was a gnawing in his heart.

No one was supporting his "hurrah." They didn't see any cause for rejoicing.

"Come out, brothers! For freedom!"

They wouldn't. They weren't taking out their weapons. They were sitting on their bunks sullenly.

Timofei felt his powers desert him, as if his arms and legs wouldn't work. The first step had been easy—but now the second? They'd all be hanged.

Then he called over a handful of sergeants and in a moderate voice (there was no strength left in his voice, either) tried to persuade some of them to help raise the preparatory. Let the sergeants give the order or convince them. How could you not support your own?

The sergeants hemmed and hawed: you go convince them. Break your oath and go out on the street with rifles? It's all over for us, but those in the barracks are of course safer.

"But brothers!" Kirpichnikov's voice strained. "Today they're sending us out to kill people, and tomorrow they'll send you! You should have seen how the crowd rushed back after a round—while the killed and wounded were writhing in the snow. You should have seen it!"

They started off, though reluctantly. One sergeant and then another to their men: I guess we should get dressed and go out. Though reluctantly.

All of a sudden, new noise and shots fired in the yard! Kirpichnikov dashed into the yard—and it was seething! They were firing in the air! Orlov, the ugly mug, went up to him, his eyes popping:

"The whole 4th Company came out!"

"How did you talk them into it?" Kirpichnikov shouted in his ear. "I can't get the preparatory to."

"The worker way!" Orlov shouted. "Punch 'em in the neck! They'll get it!"

And on he went to the preparatory.

In the stone yard, amid the stone streets, the shooting cracked and tore up their ears. But it was merry:

"Hurrah! Hurrah!"

Someone scrambled onto the stone wall, and over the wall were the Lithuanian and Preobrazhensky soldiers, their yard. They shouted at them from the wall, waving their arms and caps. Though they should have understood the shooting themselves.

That's right! There wasn't a minute to lose. Here, in the yard, they'd lock them in and mow them down with machine guns. And they didn't have that many bullets. They had to raise the Preobrazhensky men, their unit here, and maybe the Lithuanians—but first of all their own main Volynian companies, who were in other barracks.

What was also amazing was that more than an hour had passed, and they hadn't rushed over or separated us off. If we left the yard, we'd be saved.

Timofei started shouting:

"Shoulder arms! Shoulder arms!"

A commanding voice, though not deep. But right then they wouldn't hear even a deep voice. They were all hollering, each for himself. He started waving his arms. Stop it! He picked up his rifle and demonstrated:

"Shoulder arms!"

Right then the preparatory came pouring out, too!

An unprecedented formation bunched up—not by squad, not by platoon, not even by company, just in columns of four, sometimes five. Kirpichnikov started shouting:

"For freedom! Forward, march!"

The column swayed—and was off. As if wild or drunk, not in step. Without checking to see who stayed in the yard and who slipped back into the barracks.

Kirpichnikov started running toward their head, to catch up. Leading company columns was nothing new for a sergeant-major, only there had always been quiet and obedience, an officer walking alongside, a route indicated to the sergeant-major, but here—fling it open! Either the whole city is yours or it's the gallows!

He ordered them down Vilensky Lane to Fontannaya—to bring out their own Volynian 1st, 2nd, and 3rd Companies. If we reached them in a column like that, wouldn't they shudder? With every hundred joined to us, it gets easier and easier for us—and what if we raise the entire battalion?

He looked around—only platoon sergeants here and there with the column. Not a single officer anywhere. They'd vanished! Ah, they're afraid of us! Afraid of our soldier host! It's even scarier for them!

But the lane was short, and we'd take it at a march, and to Fontannaya was even shorter. One wall of the lane was all barracks; the other was a few small houses, very few inhabitants, the lane was empty, they didn't see our Volynian march, battered and torn, and not up to proper dress.

Suddenly, two young people ran toward them, a he and a she—running toward both those in front and Kirpichnikov, and they were pointing behind themselves:

"They've got machine guns waiting for you there!"

Where exactly? On Znamenskaya? How many machine guns? Kirpichnikov didn't ask, and they didn't say, and each step took them closer to the machine guns, and there was no time to think, and it would be strange if they weren't waiting for them. Placing his hand to the side of his mouth, Timofei cried out:

"Left turn, march!"

Those in front heard. And obeyed. Those on the left marched in place, those on the right marched, looking and wondering: Where are we turning?

"Back down the lane!"

A crazy command, you'd think it was the wrong time to slacken the formation. But they obeyed and continued that way. Actually, they didn't have enough obedience for a lot of commands. (He regretted that they had their own machine guns somewhere and hadn't brought them out. Why hadn't they sent scouts ahead, down the lane, to check? He hadn't thought of it. He'd gone straight to "left turn"! The lane was narrow, and there was nowhere to go. Two officers with two machine guns could knock us all off.)

Where should they go? Again past their own yard, where machine guns could have been set up.

No, there was no gunfire.

"Onward!" he waved to those in front. "Onward!"

But he had to think fast because here was the intersection. This was the right way! to the Preobrazhensky and Lithuanian men, and farther on were the sappers. All our hope lies in raising them — otherwise we'll perish.

"Left turn!"

Left, down Paradnaya.

For now, a little late, he detailed them to get the ammunition cart ready, rush it to Hospital Street, and try to seize our Volynian arsenal — and bring us bullets!

He himself ran up, and out in front, stepping backward:

"Brothers! If we don't raise the Preobrazhensky men now, it's curtains for us! We have to raise the Preobrazhensky at all cost!"

They turned into their yard. The bristling column continued, rifles in hand, bayonets skyward — you wouldn't stop them at the gates!

And they didn't because they weren't locked.

But in the yard the buglers sounded the alarm. And the cornetists.

The Lithuanians rang the regimental bell.

An attack on us? No, this was them encouraging themselves, as they had all hidden. From us. Our neighbors hid from us, driven from training to their barracks.

The large Preobrazhensky yard was empty.

The Volynians streamed in, a crowd now.

All the doors were locked. The windows on guard. Someone peeked out.

The Volynians were standing in an unfamiliar yard — and it wouldn't be hard to pick them off from above.

But the upper floors were silent.

These Preobrazhensky men now were either our brothers or worse than Germans, and in order to save ourselves we'd have to strike at them.

Here was the Lithuanian arsenal nearby. They had to take it.

But for now, anyone with a good pair of lungs, it was time to practice:

"Hey, Preobrazhensky!"

Markov:

"Join us!"

"Join us — for freedom!"

"Join us — or we'll fire!"

Silence. The doors locked. Strike? Break in?

The whole matter hung on the Preobrazhensky cornices.

Orlov started yelling:

"Darn it! Why'd you arrest your Pavlovsky comrades? Where's your Guards conscience?"

"Join us—for freedom!"

"Hurrah?"

Silence.

Not waiting for a command, the men took it upon themselves to fire a few shots into the air at them and at the roof.

"Hey! Stop! Don't hit the windows!" men shouted from there.

From one upper window, a fat-faced Preobrazhensky sergeant pointed, as if to say, Wait, don't shoot. We'll open the doors right away!

[75]

Vanya Redchenkov was by nature very quiet, but a giant by stature: a couple of inches shy of seven feet. When in February they started taking those born in '98 into the army, the Spas-Klepiki military chief enrolled Vanya in the Guards and didn't send him off right away, like the army boys, but let him go spend another two weeks at home.

Ivan rejoiced at the delay. Two weeks between family walls is anything but superfluous, and twice he still had a chance to drop over to where the young girls gathered in the village. But Ivan's father, a former platoon sergeant in the Guards Cavalry Regiment, put him in his place: "Oh, sonny, don't rejoice. They'll knock these two weeks out of you yet. There's iron discipline in the Guards, and you'll get a slap upside the head from your sergeant."

The boys selected were brought to Ryazan, to the cathedral, and took the oath. From his towering height, Ivan also raised his whole arm and put up two fingers, too, promising with his entire soul, and vowing, but Mitka Pyatilazov, from the same township, quickly struck down Ivan's arm with a knife-hand. "What's with you?" "Nothin'. Don't stick out too much. Hold back something for yourself, just in case."

They took them across Moscow. Their troop train was waiting in Zamoskvorechie on a reserve track, and from there they could see the Kremlin. They waited just past Tver, too—and two identical fast trains with handsome blue train cars passed them by. And every last dunderhead put two and two together: "The Tsar's headed out! To lead the troops!"

Soon after, they were brought to Petersburg itself, and they were led from the station, fifteen hundred young heroes, down the busy main street. Their mouths gaped at the incredible buildings, and the people on the sides gaped at them and were no less amazed: "My God, where did they grow them like that? How many more people we have!"

They were led straightaway to a huge stone barn—a "manege," or manège, where they "maneged" the horses. And started getting divided up into regiments—by some excellency, not just a general, a grand duke, they said. They lined up, and he walked up and down and decided which regiment from each one's face. He had a quick eye. One glance—and he'd chalk a number on the man's chest. And behind the general-duke came another officer, a Guards guard, over seven feet tall, who would see the number over the general's shoulder and immediately shout: "Semyonovsky!" Or: "Volynian!"

Then they explained to Ivan, there's a brief: everyone in a regiment has to be of similar appearance: the dark ones for Jägers, the gingers for the Petersburg Regiment, the snub-noses to the Pavlovsky Regiment, and the straight-noses for the Preobrazhensky. That's how Ivan Redchenkov ended up in the Preobrazhensky.

On the second day they were taken to the bathhouse and outfitted. After the warm cap and warm fur coat they wore at home, the freezing wind of the parade ground was unbearable in a soldier's greatcoat and cap. He rubbed his freezing ear in formation—and a sergeant boxed his ear, and Vanya remembered his father regarding the Guards' iron discipline. He also dawdled at commands or in formation was the fifth in a group of four.

On the third day, though, suddenly there was no iron discipline. They sat in their oral exercise, while the platoon and squad leaders were sullen and kept whispering among themselves. And it reached the new recruits that there had been blood on Nevsky.

Then, that night, all the sergeants were called away somewhere.

On Monday morning, no sooner had they started driving them out in the yard for exercises than shots rang out nearby. And they were driven back, into the barracks. And all the doors were locked. Take off your coats, take off your boots, sit in your bunks, and don't go near the windows—while the duty officers and first sergeants stayed by the windows.

There was a rumor: *"They're already here in our yard!"*

Good gracious, does this make any sense? Germans have broken through to Petersburg? What are we doing sitting on our hands?

But there were shouts in the yard, and they sounded like Russian.

The bugle was playing something Russian.

Right then the sergeant-major swooped down and started yelling in a stentorian voice, as if they'd done something wrong, as if sitting here had been their idea.

"Get dressed! Get out! No one is to remain in barracks! Quickly!"

But no sooner did they get coats and boots on than a few soldiers they didn't know wearing peakless caps—which meant they were Volynians—ran into the barracks and started banging their rifles on the ceiling until their heads hurt.

"Everybody out! Out! Every last man! There'd better not be a single man left in barracks!"

They drove them out, whoever they came across. Even rifle butts to backs. There was nothing to be done for it. Their boots dinned on the stairs.

And in the yard—a horde! Some ours, some not.

They were shooting in the air.

Some were so unnerved, they were shaking. But more stood there, heads down: Oh no, we're in for it now.

[7 6]

Not that any of the combat generals had been trained to deal with popular upheaval, nor could they have done so. But it fell to Khabalov. Yesterday, the Emperor's telegram had upset him so profoundly, he went home for the night and unscrewed the bells on the telephone so they couldn't wake him; his weary, no longer young, almost sixty-year-old body demanded a respite from so many disturbances.

And he did sleep, albeit not enough. Nonetheless, early in the morning he tightened the bells—and the little hammer started striking them immediately: in the night, another sixteen mutineers had returned to the 4th Company of the Pavlovsky Battalion and been put in the guardhouse. Really? He didn't want to leave it at that. In line with his usual scrupulosity, Khabalov decided to go and interrogate the mutineers himself: How could this have happened? Who had instigated it?

He went. He interrogated them. He interrogated the platoon sergeants and the squad sergeants. Not that there was anyone there to sort this out, and if he were to . . . But a telephone summons found Khabalov even there. The commander of the Volynian Battalion reported that the training detachment had refused to go out to perform their service, and its leader had been killed or else had shot himself in full view.

Something new! Khabalov could find no other way to command than the certain:

"Try to keep this from going any further. Return the detachment to the barracks and try to disarm them. They must stay in and not go anywhere."

He took his motorcar to the city governor's offices.

There, the first thing he learned was that Colonel Pavlenko had fallen seriously ill from the tension of these days, an attack of angina, and had not reported for service. And here he'd just started getting the feel of things. Who could take his place? He was suggesting the commander of the Moscow Life Guards, Colonel Mikhailichenko. Well, all right.

About the Volynians, meanwhile, the city governor's offices already knew that not only had they refused to surrender their seized weapons but they'd gone out on the street and been joined by a Preobrazhensky company and a unit of the Lithuanian Battalion, and also factory workers, and all of them were moving off somewhere.

Who was supposed to pacify all this? Troops and police had been positioned through the districts, but they couldn't cope. This same Volynian

Battalion was supposed to restore order over there—but who would do so now? The entire district from Liteiny Prospect to Suvorovsky and the Neva, where there was nothing but barracks, military institutions, hospitals, and warehouses, was in fact considered a military stronghold and had been no cause for worry, and the workers' demonstrations hadn't gone there.

But Khabalov's total reserves were quite limited, and he could not assemble them that quickly. Thanks to HQ chief Tyazhelnikov, who didn't want to leave it at that and early in the morning had called up two machine-gun crews, one of which had already arrived.

They analyzed the Petrograd map, broken down into sections—this unwieldy piece where you didn't know how to proceed: you couldn't use artillery—not that there were any cannons—and machine guns weren't all that attractive. Should he call up a battery each from Pavlovsk and Peterhof?

But he couldn't avoid firing. The Emperor had ordered this put down today.

If people went at the troops saying "Down with the war!" and "Down with the Tsar!"—then how could they not shoot?

Right then an armored company commander burst in with a report. His armored vehicles were being repaired at the Putilov Works (which was idle) and they might quickly assemble one or two of the many and take them out on the streets, but he'd been given orders to disassemble them even more.

Khabalov frowned heavily. Again these armored vehicles. He was sick of this new-fangled contraption. They didn't fit with the old known tactics, and there was something disreputable about them. He got rid of this captain by sending him to see a general in another building, at District HQ— the general in charge of the armored vehicle unit.

Assembling troops against a mutiny was one difficult task. But the second was whom to appoint at its head? Sad to admit, but in the 160,000-strong Petrograd garrison, he couldn't think of a single healthy senior combat officer. They were all at the front.

Right then, fortunately, it was reported that someone had spoken with the Preobrazhensky Regiment, since over there, on Millionnaya Street, right now, they had a combat colonel, Kutepov, a hero of the Guards battles on the Stokhod and aide to the commander of the Preobrazhensky Regiment, who was here on leave from the front.

Khabalov and Tyazhelnikov considered possibly sending the commander's motorcar for him. It was ten minutes. All right then, bring him here!

A marvelous solution. Among all the cripples they'd found a genuine, brave, and popular officer. He couldn't refuse because everyone on leave reported to the District commander.

Their hopes rose. Otherwise, who the hell knew? Otherwise, what were they going to do? Here those mutineers would run all over Petrograd, maybe even coming this way, to the city governor's offices—and who was going to stop them?

They counted out, assigned, and selected a detachment for Kutepov. An Oranienbaum machine-gun company was expected from the station. There was also a company from the Kexholm Regiment. There was one free squadron of dragoons from Krasnoye Selo. Now they considered which regiments could supply more.

All the regiments and battalions were fragile, with unreliable companies and without a sufficient number of rifles, and they didn't know how to shoot.

Oh, they had not prepared for troubles like this!

[77]

The Volynians were busy for nearly an hour with the Preobrazhensky men: some got it in the neck, some were shoved from behind, and the quartermaster colonel—who wouldn't give them bullets—they hoisted him on their bayonets and stabbed him through. The other officers quietly evaporated, as if they'd never been there. They broke into the ammunition depot and took the bullets, as well as the rifles and four machine guns. Corporal Fyodor Kruglov of the 4th Preobrazhensky Company, fat-faced and violent, helped a lot. They liberated the guardhouse. "Everyone out! Strike anyone who's not on our side!"

The more the Volynians succeeded, the more they were buoyed, the more carried away, undaunted. Onward! Onward! More! But many Preobrazhensky men sagged after the very first few minutes. What was going to happen now? No fist was going to drive them out of the barracks. Kruglov's company all came out, under his thumb, but overall they drew out few of the Preobranzhensky men.

The Lithuanians, too, came spilling out (having stabbed one of their own officers to death)—but not all, certainly not! A unit of Volynians, furious, ran back, to the Vilensky, to drive out their own remaining companies, those bearded blunderers.

But the rebels' lead section moved onward! They spilled out onto Paradnaya—and onward! onward! Opposite the Tauride Garden they turned onto broad Kirochnaya.

This was no longer a formation but a fierce soldier mob that had nothing to lose; many voices commanded, but they did not uniformly obey. Not that they could hear the commands. In the Lithuanians' armory they collected lots of blank cartridges—which they now peeled off into the air continuously, as they went. These shots served as powerful encouragement. And their unity: **We!** Answer them all like this! Strike anyone not on our side!

Down Kirochnaya they ran toward Liteiny. Various civilians and many adolescents joined them. Little boys came galloping from every direction.

Still, Kirpichnikov placed one machine gun at the column's tail, opposite the garden, facing back. But no one attacked from that direction.

Along the route were the Guards sappers' barracks.

A few shots from their windows.

Is that so? Let's fire on their building! Get the machine guns. Now!

Into their yard! And they did place the machine guns! And gave a warning burst!

The sappers were already running out toward them anyway.

And we toward them.

A sapper lieutenant raised his hand: "Don't shoot your brothers!" Who? Shoot who? And they shot him on the spot.

And they killed a sapper colonel.

Then the sappers began to join them in earnest.

And they have a marching band! There's just what we need! Come out with your horns!

The band set out in the lead of the mutinous crowd! And the horns sang out!

The music did more for their mood than the shooting! Passersby removed their caps and bowlers—people waved scarves and aprons from windows—and everyone shouted discordantly: "Hurrah!"

They continued on—not knowing where or why themselves. And so they flowed—down Kirochnaya. They passed a nest of their own battalions—but what next? Who next?

They came across a gendarme division building, where there were about fifty gendarmes not on detail. They, too, appeared to join in (but afterward drifted off in different directions). They, too, had bugles hanging on the walls, but there was no one to blow them.

Their building was stormed.

Some did the storming, and others continued on! Then they stopped and these ones caught up. Whoever was at loose ends shouted, shouted as one. Occasionally you could make it out:

"We don't want lentils!"

They had to shout something. Because lentils had replaced buckwheat in their ration.

By the time they rolled their way to Znamenskaya, new music was coming from there! Who was that?

Ours! Volynians! Our very own Volynians, those other companies, and others! They'd been stirred up.

Kruglov bellowed, though only nearby did they hear:

"Well, men, now it's coming together!"

[7 8]

Had it not been for the war, Vladimir Stankevich would have been a lecturer of criminal law and a left-left-liberal journalist. Public foment had always attracted him. After the First Duma was dissolved he organized a rally—and got the same three months in Kresty Prison as all the other Vyborgers. Under the Third Duma he served without compensation as secretary of the Trudovik faction, those dull, distraught deputies. Beginning with the Fourth, he became all the friendlier with Kerensky. Before the war, he and Himmer had put out a rag of a journal. Stankevich's leading idea was, why the quarrels and mistrust among liberals, radicals, and socialists? We have only to unite and Russia's future is ours! He would have liked to make a unifying bridge of himself. As we always think, it's our inclination that's the truest.

But war broke out, and suddenly Stankevich didn't recognize himself. His upbringing, inclination, and milieu notwithstanding, he did not stagger back from this war as something alien, Tsarist, and imperialist but rather saw it as a catastrophe of world proportions that raised the question of Russia's very existence, and peaceful peoples had to stand up to a fully prepared Germany. But Russia's victory would *reinforce reaction*! his friends objected. Let it reinforce whoever works more for the homeland's salvation, he would reply. Defeat, on the other hand, would be Russia's death. It didn't have to be a victory. Let the war end in a draw—even that would dissuade everyone from a repetition for a long time to come. But even for the sake of such an outcome, "sympathizing" with the war wasn't enough. He himself had to go to war.

He abandoned his lecturer position and, ridiculed by Kerensky, set out alongside the young men as a volunteer to the Pavlovsky military school and humbly learned to march in formation, which he just couldn't do, and patiently folded his uniform on a stool for the night to exactly so many inches width, length, and height, as he was supposed to. Upon graduating from the military school he had refused the chancellery-judicial position, as he was immediately appointed, in Petersburg, and petitioned for a transfer to sapper work (still knowing nothing of the sapper business), to go to the front—and in two years he became such an efficient and practical military engineer that he accumulated an abundance of field fortification experience, began lecturing in officer schools, and wrote a pamphlet on machine-gun closures and a report on engineering defense activity that went to GHQ and was disseminated to army groups' HQ. (His idea was that the front's position should never be fixed for a minute but should press relentlessly at the enemy's front.) Old sapper chiefs were indignant at his restless personality, his friends taunted the "Lecturer of field fortifications and geometry"—and he liked it when they did, proud of his new engineering more than his old legal work.

Now he was teaching in the Guards sapper battalion in Petrograd. Just as all sappers are the busiest people in the army, so too he was during these March days so busy with his work that he completely missed the three days of city upheavals, didn't even know about them, and only on Sunday night did his former Party friends tell him over the telephone about the events and the shooting in the streets. At this, Stankevich woke up from his engineering. And felt his old revolutionary wings. Last night he had come up with a plan: to try to incline the sapper battalion officers toward the State Duma—and so bring over the entire battalion.

But on Monday morning, before he could start for the barracks, he had a call from Kerensky's people saying that the Duma had been dissolved, Protopopov declared dictator, and there had been an uprising in the Volynian Battalion, where, after slaughtering their officers, they had set out for the sapper battalion barracks. He had to divert them to go toward the Tauride Palace, in support of the Duma!

Stankevich decked himself in full gear and hurried to the battalion. But when he turned off Liteiny onto Kirochnaya, he saw well down Kirochnaya a disorderly crowd of soldiers seething opposite the sapper barracks—and then start rolling slowly this way, toward Liteiny. Above their heads fluttered two dark flags.

He was too late!

Suddenly, all his confidence quit him. Both his confidence as an officer earned through war and his former left-democratic confidence. Here, seeing with his own eyes this angry mass moving this way, he didn't feel he was on a level such that they would listen to him—either as soldiers would their officer or the people would their leader. Everything he'd spent his life on suddenly didn't seem like enough, like anything, and he was face to face with something elemental. He was no one, just a target.

So he took a few steps toward them and stopped.

Right then a sapper sergeant ran up from the crowd, recognized him, and shouted, panting:

"Your honor! Don't go there, they'll kill you! The battalion commander's been killed! Lieutenant Ustrugov killed! And there are more . . . lying by the gates! Anyone who survived has fled!"

Did you ever! What if he had been on duty there today?

The volcanic breath of the elemental! It swept and burned everything away, the officers, now dead, he had just been planning to persuade in favor of the State Duma, and lead these soldiers there, the soldiers who were now advancing, a crowd obedient to no one, judged by no one, responsible for nothing, knowing none of its own heralds or protectors—and Stankevich, who had always considered himself one with the people—now he could not rely on them.

He had to save himself and quickly, that's what.

Here, at the top of Kirochnaya, there was an engineering school for ensigns—so he stepped in there. In nervous anticipation he started calling Kerensky at the Duma, but no one answered his telephone.

Meanwhile, the crowd, with a howl and infrequent shooting, moved on—and part of it surged into the ensign school. They fired one shot in the hallway and shouted that the cadets should drop everything immediately and come outside!

The cadets didn't want to go. Pale, Stankevich was a stranger here, not in charge of anything, and he could go into a classroom and wait it out behind the door. But the school's head, an imposing general, had to go out to the soldierly throng. He began politely trying to convince them that the school's status was special. If they stopped the officers' training, there would be no one to build fortifications.

The maddened soldiers wouldn't let him finish: Stop the lessons! And come outside!

Helplessly shrugging his full shoulders, the general told his men quietly:

"All right, you may go, gentlemen."

"Where are we supposed to go, Your Excellency?"

"Wherever you like. I don't know."

The soldiers who'd come, who were rifle-less, took down the rifle pyramid there—and poured onto the street and went on.

Stankevich felt so humiliated—that he'd hidden and not intervened—that he now hurried to catch up with the crowd on the street. Merging with them from the side was not the same feeling as standing to meet the stream.

In the crowd he saw many sappers, too, and he raised his voice with an appeal that sounded unbearably false even to him:

"Brothers! Let's go to the State Duma! It's right here. Close! It's on the people's side!"

"Let's go"—as if he'd been with them the whole time and with them had stormed the ensign school?

This was a correct idea, his root idea, to join the people and the liberals—but why did it sound so pathetic and artificial?

Few heard him, and they looked at him suspiciously. Where was this little officer luring them?

Others looked in his direction and confronted him.

"All right, hand over your weapon!"

What could he do? What?

This was not how he'd imagined fraternizing with the people at the dawn of freedom, but this was what happened.

He handed over his sword. And his gun.

Right then a frightening, angry soldier emerged from the crowd, grabbed the unarmed lieutenant by the lapels, and started shaking him and threatening to kill him straightaway. He railed against some other officer who'd insulted him and who should have been killed, but he'd kill this one instead.

And he would. Stankevich didn't struggle. He was gripped by mortal apathy. So this was how his brilliant life was ending at twenty-seven.

But another sapper broke in and started dragging the enraged man away.

"Don't touch him! Don't touch him! This is our officer. He's good. We know him!"

[79]

Kutepov was still asleep when his sister (he was staying with his sisters, on Vasilievsky Island) said through the door that the Preobrazhensky officers' club was asking for him on the telephone. In that first minute he so didn't want to get up that he asked his sister to talk to them. She returned and announced that Lieutenant Maksheev was asking him to come to Millionnaya immediately.

He didn't give a reason. He'd have done better to speak himself. But something altogether serious and, likely, connected with the city's upheavals. Lieutenant Maksheev, the battalion adjutant, was one of those convoluted minds that wanted a responsible administration and more rights for the Duma, and Kutepov had felt a disdain for him ever since his statements at an officer club breakfast the day before yesterday. The officers themselves were reading printed appeals from some Duma factions. What reforms when people were throwing rocks at the police?

But although more than half the officers were new, not genuine Preobrazhensky men, any Preobrazhensky man arriving from the front would of course go first to the officers' club to walk between the kindred walls, to talk, to dine.

So much for leave. He dressed with military swiftness. But how could he get there quickly? There were no cabs or streetcars. His sister went to persuade the cabbie who lived in their neighborhood. He agreed to go for his neighbor lady's sake.

And he drove smartly—not to please his passenger so much as to keep from being stopped either going or coming back.

They sped across the Palace Bridge, where there was an extended barrier of soldiers that barred no one. They skirted the reddish-brown Winter Palace and drove straight to Millionnaya. Although the greater part of the Preobrazhensky Regiment's barracks were now on Kirochnaya, the officers' club, following long tradition, remained on Millionnaya, adjoining the old barracks. That overcast morning the square around the Aleksandr Column was deserted.

In the club, Kutepov saw many disturbed officers—including those who should have been at battalion barracks on Kirochnaya. He learned that mutinous Volynians there had burst into the barracks of a noncombatant Preobrazhensky company and forced them to join them. The colonel in charge of the regimental tailor shop had tried to drive them from the yard but had been stabbed to death.

They had called in Kutepov for support. But where was the commander of the reserve battalion, Prince Argutinsky-Dolgorukov? Summoned to his commanding officer. But the other gentlemen officers, from Kirochnaya, why were they here? They didn't report to Kutepov directly, but due to his position in the regiment they couldn't refuse to carry out his orders: to head immediately for their subdivisions.

That much Kutepov had managed to cover when a motorcar came for him from the city governor's offices with orders from the District commander to come see him immediately.

And again—across the overcast square, past the Aleksandr Column, past the General Staff, they cut through the head of Nevsky, the square's lightly frosted grating, and here were the city governor's offices. A gendarme captain was waiting for Kutepov by the doors on Gorokhovaya and led him up to see General Khabalov.

In the large room were several generals and police staff officers (though Argutinsky was not among them), and taking in the sum total of their faces and the air in the room before he did individual faces, Kutepov could see that they were dismayed, distraught, and helpless. The jaw of the ponderous General Khabalov himself was frankly trembling during their conversation.

As always given a correlation like this, Kutepov felt even more resolved and responsible.

Khabalov announced to him in rather awkward words that he was appointing him head of the punitive detachment. Punitive? Kutepov had never commanded such a thing, had never supposed he would. And why punitive right away when they simply needed to put things to rights?

But Khabalov was already making arrangements over a laid out map of the city:

"I am ordering you to cordon off the entire district from the Liteiny Bridge to the Nikolaevsky train station. And anything that happens in this area—drive it toward the Neva and put it to rights there!"

If you ignored the usual grid of streets—how narrow they were between the ponderous buildings and how full the buildings—yes, this was a single, broad peninsula in the Neva, three by three versts. But if you remembered how crowded the city was, even more packed by the war . . .

"To cordon off this area I'll need at least a brigade."

Khabalov was either annoyed or didn't want to give him his reserves, intending them for something else, and said he'd give him what he had on hand. All there was to take from the building of the city governor's offices was a single Kexholm Battalion company and a single machine gun. Then he would move down Nevsky Prospect and gradually pick up the other subdivisions posted there. If he met the machine-gun company on Nevsky, he was to take half of it, twelve machine guns. One more company of the Jäger Battalion would move directly toward Liteiny Prospect.

Kutepov was surprised but did not attempt to argue. It was what it was. He only asked:

"And this machine-gun company—will it shoot?"

Khabalov had information that this was a good unit and would do everything.

Oh well, there was no time to lose. Kutepov stood up and left. He immediately liked the Kexholmers on Gorokhovaya—a smart company. His experienced eye made no mistake. Fine, let's go.

It was a strange feeling. He'd never gone into a military operation through a peaceful city. Using weapons was the most obvious action in the world—but in Petersburg? Hadn't enough Russian blood been shed at the front? Actually, this had all happened somewhere (distant shots could be heard), but on Nevsky not a single thing, no signs whatsoever. People were going about their business, only fewer than usual, and there was no street traffic.

The sky was changeable: first brighter, then thicker. But there was no break in the gray clouds anywhere.

He wished he could be at his front-line positions. Why had he been in such a hurry to take leave? It's an especially awkward position when you play a part that's not yours in a place that's not yours. It was a shame, and you can make a wrong move.

But he couldn't make a mistake.

From Gostiny Dvor he took a company of his Preobrazhensky men, which was sitting there as if in ambush, and another company of Preobrazhensky men from the Passage. He greeted each in front of the formation and asked their officers what condition the company was in. They praised them.

He himself knew that the present reserve battalion was the disgrace of the Preobrazhensky, such that at the front they had put together another reserve battalion and had retrained all the arriving reinforcements, giving them a martial look and spirit.

Now, on top of this, yesterday they'd been given no dinner, and today had not had a bite to eat.

Argutinsky might have thought of that. On the front lines they provided food even to cut-off units, and under machine-gun fire.

Poor soldiers! He ordered the officers at the first halt to purchase sifted flour bread and sausage for the soldiers. (Another peculiarity of urban actions.)

Kutepov himself walked not on the sidewalk but down the middle of Nevsky, ahead of his troops, not embarrassed by their meager numbers. (He had about five hundred infantry with him, and more were supposed to be added at Liteiny Prospect.)

From his commanding height he had long seen an overloaded unit straggling toward him down the street. This turned out to be that very same machine-gun company, which they met near Eliseev's shop (where they'd gone for sausage and bread). Awkward again! They had no two-wheelers for the machine guns and belts. The men were carrying all this on their bodies and staggering (at the front they moved like this only in connecting moves and when running on the attack). Glad of the halt, they lowered everything to the trampled snow.

Kutepov greeted the machine gunners—and three or four voices responded (out of reluctance? exhaustion?). Separating off half the company for himself, Kutepov asked their staff captain whether they were prepared to open fire at the first order. Embarrassed, the staff captain replied that they didn't have water or glycerin in their cases. (Evidently, they'd poured it out because of the weight.) All he could do was order them at the first halt to find water, buy glycerin at a pharmacy, and prepare for battle.

They crossed the Fontanka and got as far as Liteiny, and still nothing in particular had happened. Only from a far-off section of Liteiny did they hear muffled noise and shooting. At the corner of Liteiny there was even a policeman posted. Kutepov began questioning him as to whether a company of the Jäger Regiment had passed by. He hadn't seen it.

That was bad. Even the small detachment he'd been promised hadn't materialized, the men were hungry, and the machine guns weren't ready.

Suddenly, from an unexpected direction, from Vladimirsky practically, Prince Argutinsky-Dolgorukov rode up in a sleigh cab. Where he had been all this time was a mystery, but he immediately jumped down even before it stopped and ran, staggering in his long greatcoat with a shoulder cape.

Kutepov started toward him across the intersection.

They were on a first-name basis. Agitated, Argutinsky hastened to say that the mutineers were storming the District Court—and were now on their way to the Winter Palace—and therefore General Khabalov had ordered Kutepov to return immediately and defend the Winter Palace and city governor's offices.

However, Colonel Argutinsky's confused agitation and the perhaps total tumult in District HQ was not conveyed to Kutepov at all. The officer, who had spent sufficient time at the front and was sufficiently used to the disarray of superiors and their orders, was naturally skeptical.

"What?" he asked coldly. "In all Petrograd do you really have nothing more than my so-called detachment?"

(He said this with irony, utterly incapable of supposing that this was in fact the case.)

Was he to understand that Khabalov's first order to throw the mutineers in the Neva had now been canceled?

Yes! Yes! And Argutinsky repeated:

"I too beg you to hurry to the Winter Palace!"

But Kutepov stood there intransigent, his left hand on his sword's gold hilt.

"No. Going back down Nevsky is illogical and will have a bad effect on the soldiers. Tell Khabalov that I will go down Liteiny, turn down Panteleimonovskaya, come out on the Field of Mars—and somewhere there will meet the crowd and disperse it."

No matter what kind of crowd it was, disorganized, certainly, it was simply foolish to withdraw and go on the defense rather than attack it.

Argutinsky rushed off in his sleigh. Kutepov, who never did wait for the company of Jägers, put the excellent company of Kexholmers at the head, behind it the less than zealous machine gunners, and then the two Preobrazhensky companies. The dragoon squadron he'd been promised did not materialize either. He couldn't understand where the forces of the entire Military District were.

He moved down the Liteiny canyon, again at the head of the column.

He crossed block after block—and there were no suspicious crowds, or soldiers without a formation, or gunfire or attacks. Actually, any crowd would have seen his column before from a distance and should have made itself scarce.

He resisted the temptation to turn and cross the Simeonovsky Bridge and so move away from the mutiny and shorten his return to the Winter Palace.

[8 0]

On Sundays, as Kovynev knew, strikes lose their meaning and people don't attend demonstrations. Therefore he had firmly decided on that day not to go anywhere either and not to call anyone on the telephone, but to sit and write. However, the breakdown of the last few days and the sidetracking of his thoughts had taken their toll. His work was not turning like a well-oiled wheel but bumping along like an unstripped log rolling over tree stumps. There'd been confirmation of police officers cut down by Cossacks. It was shocking!

But he held out all Sunday, learned nothing, and on Monday had many obligations. He had thought to go to the editorial offices on Baskov first thing in the morning. There was no riding now with the streetcars not running. On foot. Visiting the editorial offices had always been a pleasant chore. That particular atmosphere created by the convergence of people of like mind, the sorting through of the literary news and his own opportunities.

After yesterday's bright sunny day, Monday was born in a wintry fog, cloudy, although clearing, apparently.

Fyodor Dmitrich took the same route—past the Senate, past St. Isaac's. There were patrols out and mounted police riding around. The tension had lasted more than four days—but without any clashes. Actually, it was too early for clashes. No idle crowd of any kind on Nevsky, but everyone going about their business, in a hurry; institutions were open, stores were about to open. Inoperative streetcar poles and the entire arrow of the avenue receded into the frosty fog—so you couldn't see how it ended.

In one or two places Fyodor Dmitrich noticed small clusters examining something, so he joined them—and examined the bullet marks in the streetlamp poles and walls. Yesterday on Nevsky there had been shooting, and now a small boy with a basket on his head was recounting to the grownups who had hidden where yesterday. There had been shooting! But definitely no one took it upon themselves to say why or how it had arisen.

Something *had happened* after all, but amazingly had escaped the eye, diving behind the everyday.

Even now. On the left, from the Liteiny direction—it was as if they were chopping wood. Oh, that was distant shots.

Behind them down Nevsky a thick, even, and precise sound was mounting that proved to be a company of soldiers marching. Marching precisely, smartly even, a trained step and sturdy boots. In the lead, a stately, black-bearded, middle-aged colonel with a dogged look.

Behind the company, on two horses, they were pulling cases with boxes of cartridges. But the soldiers carried the machine guns.

No, something *was happening* after all.

The hour was simply early, but something serious was in the works.

Fyodor Dmitrich continued along down Liteiny. In the distance he could make out a thickening crowd, which had blocked off the entire avenue, something unusual, and thickened around Basseinaya. He reached it.

But found no answer of any kind. Nothing was happening. A line of tall Guards soldiers was standing across Liteiny, allowing pedestrians through, however—while the crowd gawked at the soldiers. All gateways were locked (they said some cavalry officer had ridden past and ordered the yardmen to lock up).

In the last few days, a new form of communication had arisen: an openness and favorable disposition between strangers on the street, and no one was embarrassed to ask or answer questions. Here a beaver cap was announcing:

"Four regiments have mutinied!"

Fedya felt himself crashing and exploding inside, so he could barely keep his feet, when he heard that:

"Where?"

"Yes, yes, they've gone to Baskov, to remove the gunners."

Everyone looked past the soldiers, realizing something. Or was it these soldiers, ranging across Liteiny here, who had mutinied? There was no officer near them. But they were standing too calmly, not like rebels.

But on Baskov, right by the editorial office, artillerymen, yes.

Right then a few rifle shots rang out, muffled along narrow Liteiny, and there was no telling how the bullets flew. The crowd stirred and swayed and someone reassured them:

"They aimed up! Not at people."

Four regiments? Here they were, the shots, now for sure, he himself was witness. So had it **begun**? What was so long-awaited—desired—and only pictured in his dreams—was this **it**?

Bang! Bang! Bang!

Ecstasy lifted him up—not to run to the editorial offices but to fly! Fear was pounding: would they be able to carry it off?

But before he could get away from Liteiny, from behind, from Nevsky, down the muffled stone canyon, dozens of terrifying shots cracked—and it was terrifying, but no one had fallen, no, everyone had fallen and hidden, but out of caution. The crowd had vanished, and the gateway recesses to the gates—all of which were locked—were jammed full. Fedya, too, started running for somewhere to perch. He wasn't a bit scared, he hadn't had time to be scared, only intellectually did he understand that it was foolish and a pity to be killed now by an invisible flying piece of lead death.

An elegant gentleman in a topcoat with a sealskin shawl collar was sprawled out face down in the dirty snow and hiding his head behind an iron post. Fedya had time to think that this was funny and shameful. But he himself didn't manage to slip away and find a spot anywhere: the front doors were locked, too. All the niches, all the uneven places in the walls were filled.

A burst—bang! bang! bang! He didn't have time to hide or run all the way to Basseinaya. Suddenly his ear distinguished among the shots another sound, unbroken, continuous—brass music! Up ahead.

He took a look: far ahead, mighty smoke was rising; something had been set afire. But roughly from the direction of the cathedral the head of a military column emerged onto Liteiny with a band—and turned there to continue down Liteiny. The band never stopped playing its bold, loud march! This march, often heard but not known by name, was conveyed to the nonmilitary man Kovynev with the same soldierly pride the composer had counted on: don't fall, don't run, don't hide—but forward march! Fedya stopped and looked ecstatically into the distance. He didn't think he'd ever heard music more beautiful! What a proud, uplifting summons! The horns' silver sounds and the drum's rumble.

Someone said:

"The Volynian Regiment!"

Fedya started that way, in their direction. More and more new gray files stepped out and turned down the avenue.

But somewhere, a volley was fired at—or over—them.

Fedya couldn't help himself. He espied a wall's outcropping and pressed up to it. And kept looking out. Right then a short, withered general ran up, breathing heavily, and immediately pressed up right beside him.

The shots kept cracking—but the Volynians marched along to the music and not one fell.

The music receded down Liteiny, toward the smoke. And occasionally, gunshots.

His neighbor the general had a noble, delicate, old man's face and a gray mustache. Fedya couldn't help himself and said to him:

"There, Your Excellency . . . you see . . ."

He caught himself on a gloating, triumphant note: You see what they've brought us to. . . . Whether or not the general caught it, Fedya was immediately ashamed of his tone.

But the general pulled out a cigarette from his case with trembling hands—crushed it, tapped it, and didn't light up.

Fedya felt sorry for him. He was one of *them*, but what could he do there, among them? He knew his oath, his duty, he had taken orders, given orders. . . . Had he really been at the helm? He had less freedom than a boy-revolutionary.

Fedya continued on past where he needed to go. The music barely reached him now, that first column was now far ahead, and behind it from the direction of the cathedral emerged not a formation but, with a delay, clusters of soldiers, from the Lithuanian Regiment, apparently.

Fedya himself turned toward the Cathedral of the Transfiguration, with the cannon decorations on its wall, and now saw those soldiers up close. Far from marching heroically, they looked lost and uncertain. A sergeant was nervously driving them on.

Now the source of the shooting was revealed: some Lithuanians, having quit their barracks, were shooting at the upper windows of their own barracks so that those who remained would come out, too. A young man in a fashionable topcoat and student cap, short and pudgy, was standing among the soldiers on Baskov Street brandishing an unsheathed sword. But the soldiers weren't inspired by this, rather they pressed close to the walls and around corners so as not to fall under the gunfire.

One young soldier was lying on the sidewalk by a wall, wounded—but no one was helping him. All the building entryways here were locked, too.

At the end of Baskov, riflemen appeared—harmonious, in step, with their officers—and the disorderly crowd of Lithuanians flooded out of their barracks onto Artillery Street, where they hid.

[81]

In the morning, Colonel Mikhailichenko, commander of the Moscow Reserve Battalion, who had been called to Guards HQ to replace the ailing Colonel Pavlenko, when he left was supposed to have left behind someone in his stead in the battalion. But the next most senior after him, Captain Yakubovich, was laid up with a crushed leg. The other senior ranking officers had gone out with the sentries back before dawn. He handed the battalion over to the head of the supply unit, Captain Yakovlev.

But after he had gone to the city center, Mikhailichenko found himself cut off from the Moscow Battalion and made contact by telephone. They reported from the battalion that on the Vyborg side crowds were gathering and the Cossack details not only were not disbanding them, they were fraternizing with them. All Mikhailichenko could do was confirm the battalion's mission: preserve yourselves and your disposition and ignore the rest.

Only the training detachment remained armed, and then only partially. Just enough to defend the barracks. They were disposed between Great Sampsonievsky and Lesnoi prospects, with gates on both. Yakovlev attached to both gates one trained armed party under Lieutenant Petrovsky and Lieutenant Verigo.

For the next hour Mikhailichenko continued to report over the telephone that Guards units had risen up in the city, the rebels had already mastered the situation—and now everything depended on the Vyborg side, where crowds of mutineers had headed.

He also managed to issue an order sending the last armed letter company to occupy the Military Medical Academy—and at that point the telephone was cut off.

Captain Yakovlev had no choice but to take this last free detachment and himself march with them to the Military Medical Academy.

He left the neurotic Captain Dubrova in command of the battalion in his stead.

Neurotic though he was, he had quite a foul mouth, and the entire training detachment feared him, even the junior officers, when in the morning before formation the door opened onto the parade ground—and the intimidating captain was ominously preceded by his white spitz.

[8 2]

As in a card game, when the players take a drink between deals, now, too, the hands themselves slap down bets, knocking bills around and snatching them up, and their sleeves upset the glasses—so too in this crazy, drunken, reckless state, all that had been planned had gone off the rails and was beyond any stopping or concealing—and if everything did stop, that would probably mean the noose. So let it run on, even if it comes a cropper!

Kirpichnikov no longer recalled and could not tell who had and hadn't joined them. He didn't have a single intact company or crew, not even among those who had been with him from the start; they'd melted away or become spectators on the sidewalks. It was hard to drive the men out of any opened barracks. Timid, from far away, from villages, from other towns, they stiffened, afraid, didn't want to go, didn't understand why they should, resisted. But from each barrack some did burst out: rowdy, boisterous men or local Petersburgers only now just dressed as soldiers, they burst out onto their own streets as to freedom—and the rifles were theirs, so they took the barracks.

Any kind of formation had been lost long since, although somewhere the music kept up, setting the mood, and only the music marched in formation along with those who liked it. Later the music, too, fell silent and dropped out.

What was so unusual was that these were soldiers, not under any command but in a horde, a gang, and each going wherever he pleased, and obeying whoever he pleased, if only himself. People were saying—they'd been loitering somewhere—that some ensign had joined them, but Kirpichnikov hadn't seen him, and no one now was about to listen to him, even if he'd been a general. If Kirpichnikov was obeyed, then it was by the closest handful, and only if that person himself wanted to. And so they ran—in clusters, not crowds, and no one remembered who in a cluster had made what suggestion, but it was taken up. Only Preobrazhensky Sergeant Kruglov with the reddish brown beard on his broad jaw did Kirpichnikov manage to pick out and remember. Liberty had made him utterly brutal, as if he had been in prison, had languished in the army—and had just been waiting for today's liberty. He waved his bayonet, hollered, and issued a stream of commands. He, too, had his own sizable cluster.

And so they ran, not understanding where they should go. No longer Volynian, Lithuanian, Preobrazhensky, or sappers but hundreds of mixed and diverse soldiers, worse than drunk and only correctly grasping that stopping would mean the end and they'd be executed. They had nothing to lose. Ever onward!

And so they ran, and few were silent, but everyone shouted something on the run.

Each intersection divided them, and divided them again, and again, and they couldn't all head off together, and liberty and desire were drawing them every which way—but at each subsequent intersection, and at each subsequent one someone again merged in from among the lost or the new. There were a lot of side-streets here, and the streets came often, one after the other: Fuhrstadtskaya, Sergievskaya, Zakharievskaya, Shpalernaya, and each pulled in some stream, and each later would lead to the main Liteiny Prospect.

Ever onward! Join us! The more of us there are, the less to answer for. Ever onward! There's no going back to the old!

On Kirochnaya they stormed the ensign school. The general there was amiable and wasn't stabbed. And the ensigns were driven outside!

The public was also crowding pretty well on the sidewalks, with more running out of their buildings, and raising their arms and shouting. Who shouted what exactly, no one understood or was even listening. Ears blocked, head buzzing, chest bursting, hands and feet feeling like someone else's—quite an intoxicating feeling.

Gathering more and more new blocks as they went, Kirpichnikov's cluster ran off—ah!—to a prison? Bars on windows. That meant it was a prison, and that was exactly what we needed: All of *them* surely wanted freedom! And all of *them* would be for us!

The House of Preliminary Detention, they said. So, people arrested recently.

The doors, iron clad, were sturdily bolted. How to open them? With rifle butts? We'd just smash our butts to splinters. A crowbar? Where could they find one? Take one from the yardmen? Yes! (They ran off.) But there were almost no courtyards on Shpalernaya; it was all official walls. How could we open it? How?

What was bad in Petersburg was that it was all stone, and there was no setting a corner on fire.

Cursing, howling, shouting, pounding! Ringing the bell nonstop, to deafen them! What of it? They were a handful, and five wardens were on duty there with two revolvers. It was much more frightening for them against us. All they could do was gaze out the windows at our might. We were free to thrash them all day long, or scatter in a minute—but where could they go, in a prison? Few can bear it when people are battering at the door.

Ringing. Knocking! There, someone threw a piece of ice and smashed their window. A shout:

"Ho ho ho ho ho ho! Op'n up, damn you! The people've come. Op'n up! Op'n up or we'll slaughter 'em all!"

But then someone, a sapper, had a good idea:

"Open up or we'll blow you up with dynamite!"

What of it? We have rifles and we have machine guns. Why not dynamite?

In the prison—terror. A guard shouted through the door: Will they let them go in peace?

Open up and we'll let you go!

And they opened the ironclad doors wide!

And our men burst in, banging their rifle butts, yelling even worse! At a run, from floor to floor, down the corridors, freeing everyone! Every last man, whoever was there! Every prisoner was a help for us!

Some poured into the prison, and some continued on, and the clusters split up.

Meanwhile the sky was brightening. More cheer for our cause!

Farther along, past the intersection with Liteiny, was the Munitions Works and an ammunitions depot behind a tall brick wall and the same kind of forged iron gates. We opened up those, so let's try these others.

"Ho ho ho ho ho! Op'n up, or we'll blow you up with dynamite! Op'n up, damn you . . . damn you . . . !"

There was probably a guard there, and police. But there were plenty of our workers, too!

They banged, beat, and hollered—and those doors opened wide! Inside! The police ran away. But facing them was a combat general who had gestured not to let them in.

Three or four bayonets at full tilt—stabbed the general through and through and tossed him up. We have nothing to lose!

Noth'n t'lose! Hanged for a sheep as a lamb!

Some to the ammunitions depot: sack it, arm themselves, and pass it out. Now we needed guns, oh, how we needed them, our one hope!

But spinning in other heads was—where do we go from here?

Flock straight to Nevsky? No, we're too puny, they have their main defense there.

But here was Kruglov's handful, running down Liteiny. Kruglov had his cap set at a tilt, his jaw still jutted out, his face burning and twisted—more! onward!

And here was Orlov's handful.

They joined up: Let's take the Liteiny Bridge! Push through to the Vyborg side! There are plenty of our people there. Only there can we get stronger!

As far as they could see from here, the bridge was free and there were no troops or police in front of it.

But farther on there was the crest, and they couldn't see past the crest.

Here, nearby, the crowd was seething, workers from the Munitions Works, stubborn nonstrikers, but they were being chucked out. At the entrance control post they were now stepping over the general, a lesson and exhibit for all; the rest of their bosses had run off.

Only it would be hard for us to drag the machine guns with us to the Vyborg side.

But here was a truck coming down Sergievskaya. Had it come for ammunition? Someone was the first to realize and shout:

"Hey, that's what we need!"

The truck? Right! That's what will carry the machine guns for us!

The driver won't dare object.

But out of nowhere some small fry ran up—and climbed on to wind red ribbons around the truck and fix a little red flag on the cab.

So now we had a banner. Well well!

One had a red scrap pinned to his collar; another had one impaled on his bayonet. That meant we had a new distinction. How cheerful! (And even more daring.)

Kirpichnikov called to his men—Orlov, Markov, Vakhov—and they set out, set out for the bridge. At a run.

Already on the bridge—but on the avenue behind they were firing in the air, you couldn't stop them.

Someone has to get to those birdbrains and tell them to stop what they're doing.

"What are you doing? Stop shooting! We're all going to die because of you!"

There, past the bridge, if there's a guard, they'll think it's us attacking them. And they'll shoot back at us.

They ran and ran across the bridge, hunkered over, ready to fall to the trodden snow at any moment if anything happened.

Run! Run! We've won. We've won. But stopping here, on the bridge, means it's all over. If we don't keep moving and drum up new assistance, it's all over. The noose!

All of a sudden, someone buried his face in the pavement. He thought, a bullet? Get up! There aren't any!

And at a walk, at a run, here we were past the bridge's midpoint.

Now they saw it: there, beyond the crest, a line of soldiers. With machine guns. And Cossacks to one side, too.

Well, we're done for. They're going to mow us down here defenselessly.

Throwing their hands up, Kirpichnikov and Orlov shouted to them, to the picket:

"Don't shoot! We're on your side. Don't shoot!"

The cluster eased up. No, now—run. Our only salvation is going forward! (And there our truck with the machine guns will pull up.)

The Cossacks had spread out and formed up into a short wall, and they were riding toward us slowly.

They would hack us down easily.

Though they hadn't touched anyone all these days.

"Brother Cossacks! We're on your side! Don't touch us!"

Riding slowly.

But not drawing their swords. Or trotting on the attack.

[8 3]

In the morning darkness, on their way from the barracks, two watches from the Moscow Battalion had been walking with their company commanders for a long time together down Lesnoi Prospect and Nizhegorodskaya, and Captains Markevich and Nelidov had had time to talk.

Because of the early rising, and their lack of sleep, and the darkness, it seemed colder than it was, but Nelidov was ashamed to lag behind the formation, and marching with his damaged leg was hard.

His morning memory first brought up yesterday's revolt in the Pavlovsky Battalion, time and again taking this turn: Why didn't it happen to us? He sensed his lack of confidence and trust in the soldiers, half of whom were entirely unknown to him.

Dismal.

Their unlucky wounds had borne them from direct, open, honest battles to these cramped, murky streets.

What kind of Cossacks were these? The 1st Don Regiment was now, in all Petrograd, the sole combatant unit—with active, trained, and nonwounded personnel. And how had they conducted themselves? On Saturday, Nelidov had had to conduct the inquiry into the beating death of Shalfeev, a police chief, at the Liteiny Bridge. It was immediately discovered that the beating took place without hindrance thanks to the total connivance of the Cossack detail present and observing. When Nelidov went to the Cossack disposition in the Mikhailovsky manège, they sullenly declined to present witnesses or answer questions.

At the corner of Nizhegorodskaya and Simbirskaya they parted ways. Nelidov led his party to the Turner Clinic, arranging with Markevich that he would come out to assist if there was shooting from the bridge.

Small parties also peeled off for the Finland Station and Kresty Prison.

While Captain Markevich led his picket toward the bridge.

His main objective both yesterday and the day before had been not to let the crowd cross the Liteiny Bridge from the Vyborg side to the center. No one yet had come since early morning, and there'd been no need for a cordon. When morning fully dawned and movement started from the Vyborg side, workers began to move up—and he posted a cordon against the Vyborg side. However, after yesterday's event in the Pavlovsky Battalion and the major unrest in the center, it was well to be prepared to defend the bridge against the center, too. He didn't have the forces to defend the bridge on that side or to spread out across the bridge, so he placed his riflemen and machine guns from this side, in order to meet a breach, if there was one.

He let his men go warm up in a nearby cellar in rotating groups.

Then, to Markevich's surprise, a Cossack detail rode up, a quarter of a hundred, which there hadn't been yesterday. In general, the detail was supposed to report to the infantry, but Markevich was not counting particularly on Cossack obedience. Was he going to block off the bridge with them if it was known that Cossacks would let the crowd go between them and under their horses' bellies?

Distinct gunfire started coming from the Liteiny side.

Thicker and thicker.

Drawing closer.

What if it surged this way? Then open fire with both machine guns.

Markevich's main line stood guarding against the Vyborg crowd, but the crowd heard the shooting, too. Its agitation mounted, and they might attempt to break through.

What kind of soldiers did Markevich have? Barely one that was genuine.

On the humped square before the bridge, next to the Neva's broad expanse and under the dismal Petersburg clouds and a puff of fog, Captain Markevich felt he and his picket were helpless and insignificant, much weaker than with his platoon in a few sections of a trench. There was no one else to reinforce them at this key bridge, on this wild expanse.

Across the Neva, the solid din was mounting, as if comprising many voices.

But the bridge remained empty.

Meeting any possible movement from there was rather the point of sending the Cossacks across the bridge. That was their whole purpose, so here was their assignment: at least to admonish them—since he was not about to open fire immediately at a distant crowd before he could see them.

He told the Cossack ensign to move out in full formation, and if people ran this way, to stop them and push them back.

The ensign gave the command listlessly, and the Cossacks dawdled and took too long occupying their position.

While from the other side, men appeared, running this way, from behind the bridge's rolling curve and the frosty vapor—not a sinister worker crowd but gray soldiers.

Retreating from a crowd?

They were shouting something and waving their arms vigorously, clearly signaling not to shoot.

But red scraps could be seen on their bayonets.

"Forward, Cossacks! Push them back!" Markevich shouted to the ensign.

But rather than rush with lightning swiftness, as they knew how, the Cossacks made their way at a walking pace, reluctantly—and didn't even manage to get onto the bridge; all they did was block off all visibility to the machine guns and close the scope of fire.

But people were already running down the bridge!

But the machine guns couldn't fire.

And would they? Hesitant faces.

Should they open fire without warning? There was no bugle to warn of fire.

Markevich commanded the riflemen to be at the ready.

They were—but they had no confidence. No confidence at all.

Behind them, the restrained crowd was making a hostile din.

Meanwhile, the throng on the bridge had reached the Cossacks and pulled even! But not only did the Cossacks not stop them—with their swords, or whips, or horses, or coordinated movement—no, in their new manner they yielded to either side, flowing around, and revealed the onrushing throng forty paces from the machine guns.

So this was it?

Was it too late?

Markevich signaled and commanded the machine guns to fire.

But they didn't.

And the runners were already twenty paces away!

They were running and shouting—a wild soldierly disarray—but without an attempt to fire or take up bayonets.

The machine gunners never did strike.

The riflemen lowered their rifles.

[84]

No general session of the State Duma had been scheduled for Monday morning. Rittikh's report could be discussed further just as well on Tuesday. No one felt like plunging into the unending and impassable township zemstvo, and there was the feeling that this wasn't the time. On Friday, as usual, Chkheidze's call to continue the very general discussion of the government and the moment had been ignored. All that was scheduled were sessions of a few commissions starting at eleven o'clock.

And so the deputies, who did not yet know about the blow inflicted in the night, did not all assemble and, following their Petersburg habit, did not assemble early. Only those who had heard tell of the early-morning military mutiny made haste. Some who lived nearby, like Milyukov and Kerensky, had no trouble reaching the Tauride Palace on foot. Motorcars were sent for others, summoning them. And so Shingarev and Shulgin arrived from the Petersburg side, and Shidlovsky was brought under the flag of the Red Cross; otherwise he could not have made it through.

On that foggy, frosty, modest Petersburg morning, no events somehow were forecast or desired. The humiliating news landed on their doorstep, one learning from the next: the Duma members no longer existed as a body. No matter how rude they had been to the authorities over the last two weeks, and before that all those autumn months, nonetheless they had not expected such decisiveness from the bewildered and frightened government!

When they'd disbanded the First and Second Dumas, they'd hung locks on the doors and posted a precautionary guard, and the deputies had had nowhere to assemble and collude except in private apartments. This time the government had been content with this bold move of daring to send the decree to Rodzyanko and never thought to shut the palace itself. After all, this wasn't a dissolution of the Duma but merely a recess for four to six weeks, until "no later than April."

In some places there were Duma duty officers with badges around their neck; in others, the doormen, who ran with smiles and haste, as usual, to take the deputies' coats. In the Cupola Hall they kept a moderate electric light; in the Ekaterininsky there was none at all, and for a long time the hall remained dark through the slow Petersburg dawning, and the parquet glinted murkily here and there, only slightly reflecting the white columns.

The deputies wandered around distraught. How confidently they had proceeded toward the rout of the unfit government—and suddenly they had stumbled. They needed instruction from their leaders. But their President was somewhere no one could see him, behind the oaken mass of his presidential door, and no one knew what he was deciding there. The Bloc's leaders were discouraged and dodged any leadership; they slipped away to their own room to convene and emerged only to get the news. But the deputies strolled through the halls, met, separated, and again drew together in baffled and indignant clusters.

The next to come reinforced the rumors: yes, some company had mutinied! People were saying they'd killed an officer! No, two officers. An entire battalion had mutinied! Two battalions! And all this not far from the Duma, in the Liteiny area! People were saying an entire crowd of mutinied soldiers had thronged toward Liteiny Prospect. They were murdering policemen!

The greater the sweep of events reported, the more all the Duma members felt the silence and bewilderment of their palace, which had been so ominous and noisy and implacable—up until the last day.

Except for this one sole last day.

What persistent upheavals, though, and there was still no end.

No, it was preternaturally strange that they weren't trying to put them down!

There was something artificial here.

Ah, might this not be playacting?

What do you mean, gentlemen? It's perfectly clear. First, they purposely hid the bread in order to provoke a major famine rebellion, and then used this rebellion as justification for being forced to conclude a separate peace! That's exactly what they're about to foist on us. That's also why they're dissolving us, to untie their own hands, because the Duma is a restraining, patriotic force. Before we can assemble again, a separate peace will have been signed!

In the dark and alarmed halls and passageways of the Duma, the mood was ghastly. Behind the entire Progressive Bloc, behind the liberal Duma, dark forces had been creeping toward a perfidious betrayal of the great cause of the Triple Entente and their own homeland. And the Duma members could do nothing to prevent them. They had turned out to be quite unprepared, quite powerless, and all they could do was stand in clusters and discuss, like ordinary people.

Even the leftists themselves, Chkheidze and Skobelev, felt that all had been lost and only a miracle could save them.

"Member of the State Duma" is a very resonant and honorable title at home in one's province and even in the capital's press. But in its own separate palace, among the mass of five hundred men, a member of the State Duma is a grain of sand. His individual appearance and voice mean little, and he can't unite with others without the Duma leaders. But in these fateful, troubled, and unconscious minutes, there were, in fact, no leaders. It was known which doors they were behind, but no one dared disturb them; Duma members were very unequal in stature.

The Bloc bureau's members were sitting in Room 11 in a daze, in disarray. Just yesterday afternoon they had met in this same complement, in these same chairs, at this same green velvet table, and had seen the tortuously stalled situation—but what a peaceful, unappreciated day that had been, it

turned out, yesterday! Whereas today . . . Was this in fact a coup d'état? The
Emperor's decree displayed only disdain, since it was well known that the
Emperor was at GHQ and could not have signed anything since yesterday.
This was outright mockery!

How should they respond?

Doubly oppressive was the unfortunate coincidence of the Duma's dissolution and the unsuppressed upheavals in Petrograd. It was now, when the
Duma release valve was so needed, that it had been shut off. Oh, that could
make things even worse!

But even before, when reasoning theoretically about the Duma's possible dissolution, the Bloc's leaders had agreed not to undertake any displays
of any kind because, in fact, they had no real power to offer resistance. All
their power was in speaking from a dais as long as there was one.

Now that rebellious soldiers were running through the streets and killing
policemen—now the conciliatory decision had to be strictly observed. The
Duma had thrown out highly explosive words in recent months and
weeks—but precisely so that there wouldn't be an explosion on the streets.
Now that the exploding had begun, the Duma must not let one additional
spark fly.

So the situation was sad, desperate, and uninspiring: they would have to
wait it out.

They sat there downcast and idle, and caustic Shulgin suddenly said:

"In my opinion, gentlemen, our Bloc has ceased to exist."

Right then, black-mustached, coal-eyed, unbalanced Vladimir Lvov,
about whom no one, including he himself, had known two minutes in advance what he would blurt out—in favor of the radical rightists or the radical leftists—proposed in an ominous voice:

"Let's not disband! Let's convene, like the Convention!"

But they hushed him and looked at him as an obvious madman. Especially disdainful was Milyukov.

Today, Milyukov was confronted by events in the morning, still at home.
He lived at the far end of Basseinaya, and as fate would have it, the long-
awaited popular movement was born not just anywhere in the country but
cater-corner from his windows, in the Volynian barracks. With great circumspection, taking side-streets so as not to run into anyone, he had sneaked
into the Duma. And here they'd dissolved it! With his political experience,
Milyukov saw more clearly than anyone how helpless the Bloc's position
was and how untested the situation, which had to be studied logically its full
length and breadth, and new supports found. In any new situation, caution
above all always outweighed everything else for Milyukov. The hardest
thing was to orient oneself in the present.

The faction leaders still lacked the strength of spirit to go out to their
deputies.

In the entire palace, perhaps Kerensky alone had not sunk into emotional distress during these hours—having been gripped by the courage of despair. After his recent insanely daring speeches in the Duma, he had assumed an investigation was being secretly prepared against him. But street upheavals had begun! And these upheavals could rescue him from all of it! Although, according to revolutionary reports, no one had contemplated anything serious for these days—but what if?

He had heard about the Duma's dissolution and the reserves' insurrection from telephone calls when he was still at his apartment that morning—and from his apartment he had telephoned whoever he could in order to influence the troops to rebel even more—and to go to the State Duma!

But now he was rushing about the Tauride Palace, with his wasp waist, on springy legs, in a surge of desperate strength. Might this be the great moment? Out of bread riots a military revolt—this could be the mighty event! But these mutinous soldiers without officers, without a goal or a plan, needed a leader. They needed a pointing hand and a fiery speech! And there were ten, twenty, a hundred such speeches already seething in Kerensky's inexhaustible, albeit narrow, chest. His arm was itself already stretched out in an imperative gesture. He felt shudderingly that he could become these mutinous soldiers' leader!

However, he himself could not take the first step. He could not seek out these mutinous soldiers in the streets, where he would have no pedestal, lose his position, and become yet another riled Philistine. No one would hear him in the din or notice him in the crush.

These injudicious soldiers had to figure it out for themselves and come here, to the Duma steps. But there was no way they could figure that out for themselves (reservists, they probably didn't even know the Duma very well, did they?). That meant someone else had to direct them here and shout amid the crowd: "To the Duma! To the Duma!" After all, one person's cry is often enough for a crowd.

Glued to the telephone, Kerensky called and called. He called his SR and leftist lawyer friends, asking them to go there, to the crowd, or send someone, whoever was handy, even one of their servants, and shout, "To the Duma! To the Duma!"

There, soldiers led by no one were raging; here, the shadows of indecisive deputies loitered about. Despising the ossification of the Progressive Bloc, which had never dared take a step in anything, Kerensky rushed like a burning spark from telephone to window, and the next, and a third, where he could see better, and to the door, and sent someone quick to check the neighboring blocks to see whether they were coming. Weren't they coming? Getting nearer?

If they weren't, the end would be terrible!

[8 5]

Whether or not there was university today, after Gika had wormed his way into the shooting on Nevsky yesterday, there was no leaving home for him. However, his older brother Igor, a newly fledged ensign in the Guards artillery who was home on leave from Pavlovsk for a few days, was getting ready to go to the barber shop—and under the pretext of just going out with him, Gika, too, dashed out.

The street was very quiet and uncrowded, and they needed to go in a quiet direction—toward the Tauride Garden, but as they got closer to Voskresensky Prospect, where his father had again told them to look for newspapers, the brothers heard up ahead on the right—maybe not from Fuhrstadtskaya but farther along, from Kirochnaya—a long, unprecedented sound of great force and closer to a human voice. No individual voice could go on that strong and long, but a hundred voices? A thousand? A long cry or howl, ebbing and flowing, but not stopping for a second. Only a crowd could shout that way, and a very agitated crowd. The sound was coming closer. The voices were male, but they were shouting heart-rendingly high.

And long. And still did not break off.

Occasionally rifle shots struck.

Gika's heart soared joyfully. He so wanted events! He so wanted something drastic and vivid to happen, even if it was to the detriment of many and even himself, but something special no one had ever experienced before that would astound everyone!

So the brothers hesitated at the corner of Voskresensky, again not finding any newspapers at the kiosk and listening perplexedly. At that moment a young infantry sergeant, very good by his face, walked up from Fuhrstadtskaya. He clicked his heels, stood at attention, saluted Igor, and said:

"Your honor, don't go that way. There's a rebellion over there, on Kirochnaya, Volynian and Preobrazhensky men. If they see an officer, they kill him."

Igor straightened up and tensed, as if he were being threatened then and there and had a barrel pointed at him. As if he should draw his sword right now.

But the sergeant kept standing like that, now "at ease."

Ensign Krivoshein thanked him, quietly.

And stood there for a moment, his head tossed back proudly, his brow dark and furrowed, distorted from the humiliation, listening to this terrible, mounting howl punctuated by shots.

But Gika wanted to go farther, onward! Gika was curious to go there! (They weren't going to kill him.) To see something you'd never see again in your whole life, something incredible!

But his brother stopped him with a piercing, changed look he hadn't had before his military service. Through clenched jaw he said:

"We're going back."

Gika tried to contest his liberty, but seniority was highly developed in their family, and his father certainly would not have let him go.

All that his father, and his professors at the university, and his contemporaries had said had led him to a single, certain opinion: we were in a situation that required a **solution**.

They returned home and went to see their father in his study and told him about it.

Their balding father, with his drooping, split mustache, and puffy, enflamed eyes, with a look that was not sleek, as it would be for going out, but homey, and wearing a homey jacket—only shook his head and said nothing to his sons.

For observation there were still the windows at the front—from the larger parlor and dining room, through tulle curtains. Gika and his younger brother began standing watch at the window, and the adults would check in with them. Their apartment was on the fourth floor, and Sergievskaya Street was narrow, but still they could see the pavement.

Before half an hour had passed, they made out through the open window pane the same din of multiple voices approaching. Their elderly maid dragged the younger ones away.

"Vsevolod Aleksanych! Kirill Aleksanych! Move away. Stop! God forbid they see you in the window and shoot—and kill you. Rebels! You never know what to expect from them!"

So the disorderly crowd thronged, in the direction of Liteiny. There were civilians, too, but more soldiers, which was strange in itself, but even stranger because they lacked officers or formation, and because their rifles were held every which way: shouldered, across the shoulder, atilt, under the arm, bayonets poking up, sideways, and down. They'd had their freedom for two hours, and their techniques had already broken down. The soldiers were new recruits, only recently fitted for their greatcoats.

Igor stood there, biting his lips. He was suffering from this view in his own way, as an officer.

People in the crowd were talking loudly, animatedly, chaotically about what they had run through, or what they should do now. They were shouting out to and advising each other—when all of a sudden, up front, someone shouted forcefully:

"Go back! Go back!"

The entire soldier crowd rushed back, nearly stabbing each other with their bayonets.

They were swept toward Voskresensky, and did not appear again.

Their father, too, stood through this scene at the parlor window. And said perceptively:

"A revolution I see. But I don't see a counterrevolution."

Indeed, in the capital, in the orderly, strict city, the soldier crowds had been kicking up a row for two hours—and no one had appeared to stop or subdue them.

Outside, then, nothing had happened yet. But the maid brought a visitor into the hall to see their father—a short man wearing a fur coat with a rich collar and a briefcase so stuffed it was rounded. The sons recognized and greeted him. It was Rittikh, the current Minister of Agriculture, their father's close colleague of many years.

The maid helped him off with his coat. Then he removed his galoshes, wiped his pince-nez, and combed his hair in front of the hall mirror and the small lamp. His dark hair, very neatly trimmed, lay in a thick wing. During this time, the study door opened and out walked their father, extending his hands simultaneously both amiably and reproachfully.

"Aleksan Aleksanych! Where is your government? Is it even watching?"

Rittikh replied in a modest and even youthful voice:

"The government wants to assemble on Mokhovaya. But I'm not sure this will yield any benefit."

"Why on Mokhovaya? And what for?" Krivoshein asked almost indignantly.

"That's just what I'd like to know!" Rittikh replied in the same youthfully guilty way. "The latest call to me just now was from the seventh form at the Corps of Pages. They wanted to rush to Tsarskoye Selo to defend the Tsar and asked which regiment had remained loyal, in order to join them. I explained to them that the Tsar was not at Tsarskoye and they could not get through as a group. And what regiment is loyal? Does the War Minister know that? Aleksandr Vasilich, I have found it not sensible to remain at home and back on Saturday took all the most important papers from the ministry. Would you permit me to spend a few hours here with you and make telephone calls and find things out?"

"I'm very pleased to have you, Aleksan Sanych! More than anyone."

Their father led his guest to his study.

[86]

Captain Nelidov's sergeants informed him that there was continuous shooting on the far side of the Liteiny Bridge.

He stepped out into the clinic courtyard and listened. Yes, there was.

They listened more. The shooting wasn't getting closer, but it also wasn't dying down at all. Something major was happening in the Liteiny area.

However, quite nearby, at Captain Markevich's, it was quiet, so he didn't send out messengers.

Nonetheless, the persistent shooting across the bridge was an ominous sign.

Nelidov decided to take his party out to reinforce Markevich.

His party was sixty sergeants and lance corporals from the 2nd Company, which Nelidov had taken over temporarily, quite recently, from Captain Stepanov, who had left for the Caucasus due to illness. In the reserve battalion, during his long failure to improve, Captain Nelidov's duty had been daily exercises with the undertrained ensigns in the use of machine guns, hand grenades, tactics, even regulations, the history of the Moscow Life Guards Regiment, and the rules of officer conduct. Commanding a company, especially fifteen hundred men, was too much for him in his present condition, and now he was in for it. He hadn't had time to get to know almost anyone, even these sergeants. Right now, it being their turn at the regimental church, the sergeants of the 2nd Company in this week of Lent were fasting and released from details. But there was no one to take for sentries who even knew how to shoot, so he had to take those sergeants from their fasting for sentry duty.

Or rather, even though they made bad riflemen—all of them being from the reserves and not active—they were better than his untrained soldiers. Better shooters, but no kind of fighters. They served diligently but so that they could remain as trainers of new recruits and not end up at the front themselves.

Nelidov lined them up on Nizhegorodskaya Street and led them, pushing the crowd aside, himself in front with a stick.

But before the party could reach the end of Nizhegorodskaya and come out on the square before the bridge, Nelidov saw that there, a little higher up, disorderly soldiers from various regiments had surged this way with shouts of "hurrah," waving their rifles in the air, some even over their heads.

This running was insane—neither an attack nor a retreat—and before Nelidov could register it and understand, he saw just behind them a truck driving up with a red flag. This little red flag didn't explain anything; it just confused him. On Nizhegorodskaya he saw trucks with little red flags every day. They transported cartridges and shells from the firearm stores cantonment, and the little flag was a sign of that. For thirty seconds Nelidov accepted that this was the same kind of highly explosive official vehicle—and did not give the command to fire on it—and indeed, no one was firing anywhere, not even Markevich. All that remained was to figure out what kind of soldiers they were and why they were running.

He lost thirty or sixty seconds in all. When he realized that the red flag meant revolution, and machine guns had been placed there, and there were red scraps there, too, he summoned his party quickly onward to seize the vehicle and not allow it to open fire!

But at that very instant he was surrounded by a crowd of soldiers, separated from his sergeants, nearly knocked off his feet, had his stick taken away, was struck in the chest by a bayonet-less rifle, and had a revolver put to his head!

It was all over! How ingloriously and senselessly, how foolishly. All of a sudden—the end. With his accustomed military grip, Nelidov preserved his will to act: but his ailing spine locked, his leg numb, seized up, and there were two barrels up against him.

Someone else raised his sword over the captain—at close quarters, where he couldn't strike.

But a sapper ran up and grabbed the arm with the sword.

"Wait, comrades! Maybe he's with us!"

Why "with us"? Because Nelidov hadn't had time to give the command to fire?

But the laws of unforeseen deliverances are unpredictable, and there are so many of them. The sword vanished, and both barrels jerked away. Now they weren't killing the captain. They weren't even asking whose side he was on. Everyone hurried on farther.

He was flooded on all sides by a mixed crowd of soldiers and workers and couldn't see ahead to Markevich. A truck drove by.

Nelidov looked around. Without his stick he couldn't get moving and he couldn't reach it to pick up either—and where was his party?

Just the one decisive sergeant was by his side and was already handing him his stick. And the rest?

He burned with shame: to have more than a platoon and not offer resistance. He could have dispersed the entire crowd with a handful of peacetime soldiers.

But this one here, this party, let itself be pushed back, and now seeing that they weren't finishing off their captain, they approached looking guilty.

So guilty that they didn't want to join the rebellion but also didn't want to act against it!

Now, with their numbers, 120 shoulders, they pushed the crowd aside. Though the crowd was busy with its own shouting and exulting, shouting:

"Comrades! Liberate Kresty!"

"Comrades! To the Finland Station!"

And streams split off to go there.

But everything was so jammed, so packed—all he could do was retreat with his party to the clinic. They were not prevented from doing so.

When they all entered the courtyard, they set the gates firmly shut.

The sergeants were greatly relieved at how the matter had ended and were quite cheerful.

But Nelidov was full of anguish: A bunch of women! Where were the real soldiers?

He went to the telephone, reported to the battalion about what had happened, that the bridge had been broken through, his suppositions about Markevich, and that the mutineers had gone to Kresty and the Finland Station. But the main forces more than likely would attack the Moscow barracks because the truck with the machine guns had driven off in that direction.

He formed up his party in the yard and tried to encourage them and bring them to order—but no. He couldn't possibly take them out on the street for actions. Better they had stayed here and fasted.

[87]

The Moscow Regiment barracks were densely surrounded by factories and worker blocks. Had they been filled with armed and capable soldiers, they would have been a lock against any disturbances here. But in their current state they were a besieged basket of chicks.

Not only that, there was the 3rd Company, where so many were from the Vyborg side. Not only that, when the Moscow formation happened to pass down a narrow street in their gear, the women in the shop lines on both sides shouted, "Where are they driving you, boys? When will there be an end to this?" They even grabbed an ensign by his greatcoat sleeve.

This environment and this mood of the workers' side were very much felt by the soldiers.

By ten in the morning the sentries sent out to various places on the Vyborg side had begun reporting over the telephone about large crowds everywhere. Even from the Moscow barracks you could see them flocking down Sampsonievsky.

Captain Nelidov telephoned to say that the Liteiny Bridge had been broken through by rebels.

Captain Dubrova ordered that Lieutenant Verigo's party be sent down Lesnoi Prospect toward the Finland Station and Petrovsky's party stand outside the Sampsonievsky gates. Verigo was a combat officer, but Lieutenant Petrovsky had just come from the reserves, had no battle experience, and was sluggish.

It was toward his party down Sampsonievsky that the truck with the two machine guns and red flag drove, with a dozen soldiers and workers under the leadership of a dissipated beast of a Preobrazhensky sergeant.

The truck ran straight up to the battalion's very gates, and a few men jumped down to open them.

Petrovsky commanded his men to come to the ready, and some did — while others started scattering behind piles of snow and lying down.

Petrovsky commanded them to fire, and those remaining fired two volleys, evidently into the air, wounding no one.

The truck started backing up toward the Church of St. Sampson. Men ran that way from the gates, and the worker crowd reversed itself, flooding after the truck.

But those salvos caused another disaster. After all, it was clear to those who'd heard them that they were firing right here — the Moscow Battalion, their own — which meant into the crowd, right?

The reservists locked into their barracks started getting agitated, especially the shaky 3rd Company.

To calm them down, Captain Dubrova thought to send the regimental priest, Father Zakhari, who happened to be on leave in Petrograd and was in the barracks that day — and truly, what better could a priest be doing?

What did they keep them for? He instructed that the company be calmed at all cost.

Fifteen minutes later, the priest returned red in the face, distraught, powerfully upset, shaking even. He reported with difficulty that he had never encountered convicts like the 3rd Company in his life, that they were so brutalized that no word, neither God's nor man's, could moderate them—and they would undoubtedly soon break out of the barracks and go on a rampage.

The shell-shocked Captain Dubrova began to feel the priest's agitation being conveyed to him like a muteness seizing his arms, legs, and even tongue.

He sent the priest back to the same barracks, but the priest refused, saying nothing could make him go.

But even Dubrova felt he was the wrong person to go calm them down personally, he might have an attack of nerves and lash out, which would only be worse.

All he could do was send the young ensigns hanging around with nothing to do to the 3rd Company, as they had been to others. To say we didn't know who fired, it was outside, only not our men (in no way could he reveal that it was ours, or everything might blow up).

Right then the battalion duty officer, Captain Vsevolod Nekrasov, on one wooden leg, reported to Dubrova, one thing after another.

First, that the Finland Station had been surrendered to the rebels.

Next, that Lieutenant Petchenko had telephoned from Kresty. The mutineers were pressing them to open the prison, the soldiers were refusing to fire on them, and he had been forced to yield and surrender the prison.

It was ghastly. The Vyborg side, which was already brimming with hostile worker crowds, had had all its key locations fall into the hands of the mutineers who had broken through. The Moscow barracks were hopelessly surrounded.

Right then firing could be heard from Lesnoi Prospect—extended and revived. This was Lieutenant Verigo's party returning fire.

Dubrova decided to reinforce him with his last and completely untrained party—Ensign Shabunin's. To it he added after him four free young ensigns.

They exited the gates onto Lesnoi.

The shooting continued, and it was reported that Lieutenant Verigo had been wounded in the belly.

[88]

Farther along, in front of Kutepov's detachment, down the right side of Liteiny Prospect, stretched the barracks, with only its windows on Liteiny, but its doors and yard on the parallel Baskov Street. Artillery Lane took a turn at the end of the barracks, and at that corner Kutepov saw a group of officers from the Lithuanian Battalion.

Overhead, on the barracks' upper stories, windows were being smashed (shards were flying), and frames busted out—meanwhile these officers were not intervening in any way. Coming even with them, Kutepov halted his lead detachment. A colonel from the group walked up to him, and he turned out to be the commander of the entire Lithuanian Reserve Battalion, that is, one of the dozen senior commanders in Petrograd at that moment. He explained that a mixed crowd of soldiers had come down Baskov Street toward their barracks—soldiers from the Lithuanian Battalion, from other barracks, and the Volynians, led by civilians, and they had broken into the yard by force and demanded that all the soldiers join them.

"But those are your soldiers, colonel!" Kutepov exclaimed in an undertone, leaning toward him, so that only the two of them could hear. "What measures are you taking?"

The colonel was ashamed, he didn't try to hide it.

"There's nothing I can do. What can I? The crowd. The soldiers are going over, there's no support. And we're just a smattering."

All this could be imagined but not forgiven. An officer can't do nothing and doesn't dare run away.

Up ahead, a column of blue-black smoke was rising in the vicinity of the District Court and on a weak draft was spreading out over Liteiny. There, up ahead, they had heard machine-gun fire, and individual bullets had flown this way down Liteiny.

Why the Winter Palace? Could they really get away from here? This was where the entire essence of the day had occurred—to lose the soldiers or not? Kutepov quickly sought a decision, which was not long in coming. (He sent one of his second lieutenants to find the nearest telephone and call the city governor's offices to say what the situation was and that the detachment would remain here.)

He separated the Kexholm company by three paces in the platoon column and also moved it up, shielding himself with it down Liteiny from the front, and ordered them to open fire immediately if attacked from that direction. He also sent a scout out ahead—to the area of the Cathedral of the Transfiguration, the Hall of the Army and Navy, and Kirochnaya Street. He turned one Preobrazhensky company with four machine guns to the right, a little behind himself, to close off Basseinaya Street and the back end of Baskov. With one platoon and one machine gun he locked the exit from Artillery Lane. (And suddenly discovered that the machine guns weren't loaded. Today Kutepov had lost the habit of seething and screaming. Everything had gone to hell. But he looked angrily at the commander of the machine-gun half-company. This idiot or blunderer kept repeating that there wasn't any water or glycerin in the cases and they hadn't been able to get any and couldn't fire. That meant all twelve machine guns were merely for show. Well then, thanks for that, at least.)

The left side of Liteiny was lined with solid buildings that did not appear to be hostile in any way. Thus Kutepov walled himself off and created a small suspended zone—but it was his small suspended zone.

All this time, a number of the Lithuanian soldiers had been jumping through the broken first-floor windows and onto Liteiny—more often with rifles and even in sentry gear—and had gathered there on the sidewalk in nonhostile clusters. One could surmise that those jumping out were not ready to join the mutineers; those ready to join were pouring onto Baskov. However, the officers of the Lithuanian Battalion continued to stand around their colonel and were not giving these friendly soldiers any instructions whatsoever. Kutepov sent a Preobrazhensky sergeant to bring over ten or so of those soldiers. They presented themselves precisely and smartly. The most voluble of them stated that there was such turmoil in the barracks, they didn't know what to do. They didn't want to violate discipline and would like to remain where they were, but they weren't being allowed to do that and were being driven out.

It was these soldiers who were the next reserve. He could increase his number fourfold or tenfold, only not with officers like this! Kutepov ordered the yardmen from across Liteiny to unlock two courtyards—and ordered the commander of the Lithuanian to assemble all those soldiers in the yards, bring them to order, and line them up.

Now he faced a harder task: getting the soldiers away from the mutineers. At this moment one Kexholm sergeant reported to Kutepov that even there, on Baskov, the crowd of soldiers driven out was standing perfectly peacefully and calmly, and one sergeant from the Volynian Battalion was asking one of the gentlemen officers to come over. Then the Preobrazhensky sergeant who had been sent came back and said that the soldiers wanted very much to fall in and return to the barracks, to their usual life, but they were afraid that since they had run out they would now be condemned and executed, and the Volynian sergeant asked one of the officers to come calm them down and line them up.

The men were paying for someone else's sins!

Kutepov called over the Lithuanian colonel and said to him:

"Most of them there are your soldiers, after all. I'm amazed. Are you really afraid of your own soldiers? It's your duty to go rescue them."

But the colonel shook his head in a melancholy way. He was frightened, and his fear had not passed.

That Volynian sergeant was afraid to come here for fear of being arrested. The officers were afraid to go there for fear of being torn to pieces. Everything was swaying, as on a scale.

"Fine. I'll go," said Kutepov.

Leaving everyone at their commands, taking one more look at the stretch of Liteiny where not a single civilian had flashed by, taking one more look ahead at the black column of smoke near the District Court—time was a-wasting—he set off at a stroll down Artillery Lane.

Here quite a few soldiers had crowded in, and Kutepov went past them alone, without orderly or adjutant, and around the corner of Baskov there were lots of them and everything was jammed. Right then, just on the corner, a sharp Volynian noncommissioned officer walked up to the tall colonel. Holding his salute tight, he reported that all the soldiers wanted to return to barracks, but they were afraid they'd be shot now anyway.

An enormous thousandth's scale was hanging—and a tiny weight was enough to move it one way or the other.

But Kutepov knew he possessed the presence to speak to entire regiments. Stepping into the crowd of soldiers, standing a head above many, he announced loudly:

"Anyone who now lines up and who I now lead back will not be shot!"

The dozens in front heard, and their despondent faces burst with joy, and they rushed toward this confident colonel! There wasn't the slightest suspicion that they'd rushed hostilely. No, they had looked into his black eyes, fully wide open and bright, and they grabbed him in a way they wouldn't dare grab an officer, be it their own or a stranger, and carefully, with many hands, lifted him up, lifted him on their outstretched arms and interrupting each other:

"Your honor! . . . Your hon . . . ! Repeat your favor! . . . Repeat it to all of them! . . . One more time!"

From the upraised soldier arms, Kutepov now had a good view over their heads of all of short Baskov Street, which ran into Basseinaya—and was completely packed with standing soldiers from the Lithuanian and Volynian battalions, a few soldiers in artillery uniform, and he also made out a few civilians. He immediately interpreted them for himself, of course. And from his height, with all the power of his commanding voice, he stated:

"Soldiers! Those individuals who have pushed you into a crime before your Tsar and homeland are doing this to benefit our enemies, the Germans, with whom we are at war. Do not be scoundrels and traitors, but remain honest Russian soldiers!"

And from various sides, voices:

"We're afraid they'll shoot us now! Because we went out."

"No!" Kutepov responded in a loud voice. "Anyone I lead in now will not be shot!"

But a few voices—from among the civilians?—immediately provoked them:

"Comrades! He's lying! They'll shoot you! There's no going back for you!"

But Kutepov held his own, looking left and right:

"I order you to fall in! I am Colonel Kutepov of the Preobrazhensky Life Guards Regiment, just arrived from the front. If I lead you back, none of you will be shot! I will not allow it! Sergeants! Line up your soldiers!"

And he ordered those below him to lower him to the ground.

All Baskov Street stirred, and the crowd stirred, trying to sort itself out—but it was hard to do that in such close quarters. Now the sergeants came up with all their bearing and saluted sharply:

"Your honor! They're very confused. Some companies don't have sergeants. Allow us to fall in by barracks name."

But right beside him, ten paces away, at the corner of Baskov and Artillery, there was a hat shop—a dozen civilians were skipping out of there now—and Kutepov's keen eye immediately picked out among them clerks from the General Staff. On one of the clerks he noticed a revolver at his waist. The clerk's time to fight had come!

He could have detained them. The soldiers would well have done that for him. But Kutepov didn't want to bring confusion to the main movement.

That same first Volynian sergeant shouted: "Volynian soldiers of such-and-such companies, follow me!" And he led them into the courtyard opposite. Other sergeants in other places commanded the men to fall in by barracks, but there were also cries:

"They'll shoot you! Strike him!"

He should have had those men seized. . . .

Some of the soldiers did not sort themselves out but ran to the unblocked end of Baskov, toward the Cathedral of the Transfiguration. The other, larger portion successfully dispersed by barracks.

Kutepov kept about twenty Lithuanians from among those who had lifted him up close and led them down the freed-up Baskov toward Basseinaya, where his Preobrazhensky company was blocking the way.

He ordered the lieutenant to use one platoon with a machine gun to close off Baskov now, so that more didn't show up from there, and to protect from outside penetration the gates where the sensible sergeant's two sizable companies had already gone. He sent to have conveyed his gratitude to that sergeant and the sergeant's temporary appointment to command both companies.

If Kutepov had not moved the thousandth's scale all the way over, he did seem to have staved things off.

Now he had to return quickly to Liteiny. They had started shooting from the Munitions Works on the Kexholmers who had been moved out in front.

Kutepov ordered the Kexholm company to open return fire, fire on the Munitions Works, and start advancing, come out on Kirochnaya Street, and with a single half-company range down it, and if there was a crowd there to scatter them with gunfire. The other half-company was to go toward the Munitions Works and (Petersburg memory: that was also where the treasury was!) to check on and strengthen the guard in the treasury. (This was not just a heap of stones but the capital's lifeblood.) One Preobrazhensky company was to go ahead, in parallel down Baskov, toward the Cathedral of the Transfiguration, and clear the adjoining side-streets.

The Liteiny Bridge wasn't all that far away, and the smoke from the District Court was spreading thicker and thicker and filling the streets' upper stretches, which made the entire scene greatly resemble the front.

But the officers reminded Kutepov that their companies had not had a hot meal today, and the Preobrazhensky men had not even had dinner yesterday (he had forgotten to ask Argutinsky how he could have failed to feed his companies on detail!).

He had had no luck at all telephoning the city governor's offices. Just then the Preobrazhensky quartermaster staff captain turned up, and Kutepov sent him urgently to see Khabalov and demand the immediate provision of food for the soldiers. And to ask him to send battle-worthy machine guns, not ones like these.

And finally, to get an explanation of what was going on. Who was where, and what was going on in the rest of the city?

[8 9]

When news comes crashing down on us, we can't always take it in at that moment. Protopopov was standing by the telephone in his morning robe and slippers. One officer had been killed in one training company—a military incident that had nothing to do with him. He even wondered whether he should go back to bed. But no, the morning was spoiled. Alarm did not set in immediately. He walked listlessly to the bathroom to gather his forces from hot water. But before the tub had filled, as he stood beside it to the noise of the faucet, he was stung! Not by today's event but by yesterday's. Yesterday, Sunday, when he was dining at Vasiliev's, who had assured him that the revolution had been beheaded and 141 revolutionaries had been arrested, he had said in passing that he was planning not to spend the night at home, worried about being seized by revolutionaries in revenge. This came out so unexpectedly, Protopopov was amazed. Did this mean we weren't the masters in the city? What was there to fear? "But they know all our homes," Vasiliev had said.

Yesterday Protopopov had forgotten this, but now by the tub he suddenly remembered, and the correctness of this thought was revealed to him very clearly: they knew all our homes! And who didn't know the residence of the Minister of the Interior, 16 Fontanka! Here, by the entrance, terrorists with bombs had kept watch in droshkies and tracked down ministers—successfully. And this was with the state in full power. What about during the present instability?

He became so upset that he could no longer step into the tub and calmly relax in it. He became so upset that he was now amazed that he had lain in his bed calmly and slept through all these nights of disturbances. Of course, there was a guard, Preobrazhensky men were posted there, but if a mutinous company were to approach, wouldn't they seize him anyway? If the Volynians had rebelled, then why not the Preobrazhensky men from his guard?

It was shuddering to picture his body seized by an enraged crowd.

It was *him* they hated! Him! He was the one who shouldn't remain at home!

Protopopov felt that today even given favorable circumstances he would not spend the night at home.

And so he began the day—underslept, unwashed, and on an empty stomach. He dressed and went to his study. He couldn't collect his thoughts. What should he do? He couldn't take up his usual everyday affairs. Yesterday the Pavlovsky and today the Volynians? This was something he could in no way have anticipated—military insubordination! No such information had come in—and where could it have come from? The Emperor had revoked the system of political informants in the army. Someone, someone's acquaintance who had gone into the army, might happen to send a letter. That was all the information.

The day had begun—and the Minister of the Interior was fated not to work or govern but to try to find out the news. Not from responsible state officials but from duty secretaries, from officers on commission, from couriers who had just been somewhere and seen or heard something from others. Then he himself had to telephone the Police Department and the Okhrana.

Everyone everywhere was horrified. No one could have anticipated this. One military unit after another had gone over to the rebels. One street after another had been seized, and now even the Arsenal, and they were absconding with the weapons!

Wasn't there any plan to suppress them? Why wasn't the military putting them down?

Very nearby, mutinous soldiers were roaming throughout the Liteiny sector! At any moment the crowd might come storm the interior minister's residence. This was a natural first thought for mutineers!

Not just spend the night, he couldn't even stay here in the daytime more than an hour. He had to leave, flee—but where?

Going to Voskoboinikova's was very tempting and safe but also awkward because there was Tsarskoye Selo and the Empress was expecting something from him. But what? What could he do?

His duty to the royal family and himself was to hide just this: the most important documents. Drafts of letters to the Emperor. And the Empress.

Vyrubova's letters to him. From Voeikov. (He had already been gathering them up and hastily stuffing them every which way into a large file.) Yes, and these photographs here taken then for the royal family of them fishing Rasputin's body out of the river and photographs of the dead man. This was one of the highest moments of Protopopov's career! But this must not be left behind. It was compromising material.

And here was how to preserve it. He called in his agent, Pavel Saveliev, formerly in the Semyonovsky Regiment, then a gendarme, an exceptionally firm and taciturn man. He could always be trusted with secret assignments, to meet with people clandestinely and with many confidential matters.

So Protopopov called on him. He locked his study. It was extremely alarming. He handed him the case and explained that he was to keep it all safely at his home.

He looked into his firm, honest face. He would not give him away.

He let him go.

Protopopov unlocked his fireproof safe. There lay his military code, which he would let lie, and something else, yes, and 50,000 rubles wrapped up simply in newspaper. This money had been thrust upon him quite recently by Count Tatishchev because Protopopov had let him look at secret papers for twenty-four hours—accusations against Khvostov (the nephew). These 50,000 rubles the Empress had later designated to provide for Rasputin's family. Should he give it to Saveliev? He'd left. And there was no need to lead people into temptation. It could stay here.

He locked the safe, put the key in his desk, and now locked the desk as well. This key he would take with him.

That was everything.

Everything? He hadn't had breakfast. But he didn't feel like it. His throat was dry, he was burning up inside, and his hands were trembling. Where could he go immediately? After all, they could burst in at any moment. And with the boiling of the unjust hatred he had somehow aroused in all society— it was he for whom it was most dangerous to fall in the rebellion's hands!

He walked back to his apartment. His wife sat him down to breakfast. He could barely swallow. He explained to her that he couldn't stay here any longer.

But where would he go? And under what pretext would he leave the ministry?

Right then he was called to the telephone. He picked up the receiver.

City Governor Balk. He spoke harshly, flinging his sentences. He informed him that the rebellion was growing unimpeded and swiftly, they had already seized the Vyborg side, and mutineers had seized the Finland Station. Colonel Kutepov's single detachment was holding out against the upheavals, but it was too late now to lay their hopes on it. By tonight total anarchy might descend on the capital.

My God, what horror! Aleksandr Dmitrich's heart plummeted. He didn't understand what he could say to Balk or why they were tormenting him and asking questions since all power had been handed over to the military.

"Ah . . . and what, in your opinion, should be undertaken?" he inquired.

Instead of minding his own business, the city governor ventured that he should warn the Emperor about what was happening and send reliable mounted police to Tsarskoye Selo to guard the family.

This advice was overly familiar. Sending mounted police meant exposing the capital, whereas they simply wanted to avoid a battle. There were lots of troops at Tsarskoye Selo, and the guard there was sufficient. Informing the Emperor of military events was the direct responsibility of the military authorities. He was also certain they had already called up troops for assistance. So certain that he said:

"By nightfall fresh forces will have arrived from the front. Can you hold out until tonight?"

The city governor promised.

"May the Lord God protect you. I'm very glad you're calm!"

And he unburdened himself of the receiver.

Report to the Emperor? There was nothing in this unclear situation to report, and it was unthinkable to charge oneself with the primary weight of this gloomy news, since it might yet be fixed. As recently as last night he had sent a telegram to the Emperor—and now he had better wait at least until evening.

Why did he say fresh troops would arrive by nightfall? He didn't know that. It's just that it couldn't be otherwise! He wanted to believe it.

But where could he go? With every quarter-hour the streets got more and more crowded—and there were fewer and fewer chances of getting away at all.

They hated Protopopov so! He was the first person they would tear to pieces and would not spare!

Another call! Oh, he hadn't walked away from the telephone!

Prince Golitsyn. Now assembling the Council of Ministers. For safety, at his home on Mokhovaya again.

This was marvelous! Here was the solution! This was quite close as well, and he could reach it by back streets, without hindrance. Only he had to put a non-uniform topcoat over his frock coat.

Leave the ministerial building not by the front door—that was too obvious, and there might be surveillance by the revolutionaries—but by the back. And continue on foot.

Without warning the sentry or the clerks. The motorcar—it could drive over to the prince's later.

His last thought was that maybe he should write, send to, or telegraph the Empress.

But he had nothing comforting to tell her. He himself didn't know or understand anything.

[9 0]

Just the day before yesterday, the Empress had told Lili Dehn to come see her in Tsarskoye on Monday. This morning, at around ten, Lili was still in bed when she heard the telephone ring. She did not rise all that quickly to get it, and the Empress asked:

"Lili, do you mean you've only just risen? But I want you to arrive in Tsarskoye on the ten forty-five train. Today is a marvelous morning. We'll go for a ride. I'll meet you at the station. You can spend some time with us and still return to Petrograd on the four o'clock."

"Oh!" was all Lili could manage to respond, and she rushed to dress. She put on a few rings and a bracelet, grabbed her gloves, kissed Titi, whom she left with the nanny—and rushed outside to catch a cab.

No such luck! Lili had completely forgotten that there had been disturbances in the city over the last few days, and now, no matter how much she looked out for one, not a single cabbie passed by, not even on Sadovaya. The streetcars weren't even running. Nothing but disturbances!

Just then, however, a sailor who lived nearby was pulling out, Captain Sablin, also an aide-de-camp, like her husband, and a very close friend of the Tsar's family. She waved and waved to him with her little hand—and he noticed and took her in his carriage.

"Are you going directly to Tsarskoye Selo?" she asked him.

"No, I wasn't planning to today."

"Then please, take me quickly to the train station. The Empress is going to meet the train and I mustn't be late!"

Sablin told the driver to hurry.

The streets were the usual streets, and there was nothing special about the people passing.

"What news, captain?"

"Nothing in particular. Only this odd bread shortage. And yesterday there were gunshots on Nevsky. Today I heard some coming from somewhere as well. But I think everything will sort itself out before too long."

With his charming, endearing smile and his good cheer, conveying his reassurance and a thousand greetings to Her Majesty, Sablin escorted Lili onto the platform—just as the train was about to depart.

But in the compartment Lili saw Madam Taneeva, the wife of the head chamberlain of the sovereign's chancellery and the mother of Anya Vyrubova, whom she was traveling to visit in her illness.

Other than her daughter's illness, nothing worried Madam Taneeva, who knew no Petrograd news.

The first alarmed face they saw—near the peaceful Tsarskoye Selo station adrift in shimmering snow—was the Empress's face. Her first alarmed words were:

"What is happening in Petrograd? I have heard the situation is quite grave. Is that true?"

But they definitely could tell her nothing serious.

The carriage set out. The morning was magnificent, vanquishing; the sky was as blue as Italy; and the snow everywhere lay in a deep layer and shimmered with joy. They wanted to drive through the park, but there were too many snowdrifts there, so they went down the streets.

Lushly snowy Tsarskoye was as peaceful as ever, and the occasional court carriages with their drivers in red liveries added to the festive mood.

They met a captain from the Guards crew who had been stationed at Tsarskoye Selo for the past few weeks. The Empress ordered the driver to stop, called the captain over, and asked him about the danger. The captain smiled and assured her there was no danger whatsoever.

Well, thank God, she had more than enough of her own private ones: Aleksei had taken a turn for the worse this morning, his temperature had not gone down as it was supposed to in the morning, and spots had appeared in new places. Evidently he was not going to get off with a mild case. They arrived at the palace, and the Empress sent Lili to visit her two ill daughters while she herself headed for the heir. Their outing was postponed; they were not in the mood.

There was an elevator between the first and second floors, which the Empress always used to visit the children; the stairs were hard for her. But today the elevator was broken—and whether or not something grave was happening in Petrograd, they had been unable to summon a workman.

By nature, Aleksandra Fyodorovna found it hard to limit herself to family cares when state concerns loomed. Yesterday she had sent a telegram to the Emperor, out of her usual telegraph shyness—how many hands would pass it along—expressing herself with restraint that she was very anxious about the situation in the city. However, the night passed and there was just the one affectionate telegram, and not a reply. Apparently, the Emperor had more reliable information at his disposal. The Empress tended to accept that it was all trifling, but last night a major right-wing journalist, Burdukov, had obtained an audience with her—and presented the situation in Petrograd to her as catastrophic. That's who had frightened her.

But GHQ was silent and had undertaken nothing. Protopopov had not reported anything either—and he would if there were anything! . . .

But the Empress did not sit long with her son—she was summoned. General Resin, commander of the Combined Guards regiment protecting the palace, and General Groten, aide to the palace commandant, their faces gravely pale, reported to her that the Volynian and Lithuanian battalions had mutinied, killed all their officers, and left the barracks.

A mutiny in the Guards? That defies belief!

But the generals were awaiting instructions from her.

What could she instruct them?

How many times had it come to pass that she had had to decide without a man? Oh, she had had a feeling when Nicky was leaving that he shouldn't go, that without him things would go badly!

Had she not been a woman and at age forty-five with more than her share of illnesses, had it only been her spirit alone, she was prepared for a simple action: to jump on a horse herself!

But Protopopov was silent! Only on his assurances that everything would be perfectly fine had Aleksandra Fyodorovna agreed to let her husband go to GHQ. It was assumed that Tsarskoye would remain the concern of the Minister of the Interior, and every day there would be news or even visits (after all, there was also Protopopov's tender attraction to one sister in Anya's infirmary, this unrequited love of elderly hearts so touching). But now—this was the fourth day Petrograd had raged—and where was the hand of the Minister of the Interior? Where was the uplifting ease of his voice, which conveyed even over the telephone? Right now, only the telephone could be quick enough. And where was he?

There had been no call from Protopopov, so she decided to telephone him herself. With events coming so thick and fast, his number might have been busy—but it was free.

Free—but he didn't answer.

Call and call! the Empress demanded of the telephone operators as she herself sat in her bedroom under a portrait of Marie Antoinette.

Some chance clerk picked up the phone. He reported that the minister had either walked or driven out, but no one knew where he had gone and no one knew or had seen anything.

Even stranger.

Or had he jumped into the thick of it and was decisively putting down the rebellion himself?

Each minute hung suspended, though, filling with weight, before falling.

GHQ, too, was silent.

There was only one thing the Empress could do—not sparing Nicky's heart, no matter how painful it would be for him to read it: send him a telegram immediately (written sweepingly):

"The revolution has taken on horrifying proportions. I know that other units have joined it. The news is worse than it has ever been."

This would be a blow to her husband's heart, but she could not put it off any longer.

But also—what could she undertake? Tend to the children and wait for intermittent news from the city.

Oh, those vile Duma creatures! It was they, after all, who had agitated and stirred all this up!

Oh, her heart could not take this! The minutes passed like hours. And the hours?

But GHQ was silent. As if the Emperor knew nothing or else too much.

City events had so violated the normal life of the state that the Empress could not call or receive any state official—as she had in recent months—to question, direct, or instruct. She could not summon anyone—and they were not coming themselves. No one had made himself known, or come, or even telephoned. Even Sablin, one of the most loyal—could he really not have come with Lili? The Empress fed on random information—from Volkov the valet, from the ladies' maids, practically from the palace servants (there were no newspapers, after all!). Suddenly she found herself not the mistress of an enormous country but a mother of sick children cut off from everything.

Suddenly they reported to her that Adam Zamoisky, His Majesty's aide-de-camp, was requesting an audience.

Zamoisky? But he was at GHQ. Where had he come from?

Count Zamoisky . . . the Empress had never liked him. At the beginning of the war, he had volunteered for the army as a private, but naturally Niko-lasha immediately snatched him up for GHQ, promoted him to cornet, and then for no reason at all—a Vladimir cross with swords, and since last year an aide-de-camp. He was taking advantage of his position, she believed, in order to bring up Poland more often.

Well, summon him!

The Zamoisky she knew walked in, but with an unfamiliar, unusual, dramatic look—and that immediately spoke to her heart. His coming was not usual, nor was his stern look, which maintained its pride through his low bow of respect, or his rather dry tone as he pronounced these passionate words:

"Your Imperial Majesty! Finding myself by chance in Petrograd and being a witness to events, I considered it my duty not to return to GHQ but to appear before you and offer you my epée."

And he stood there, with a gallant dignity.

Oh, Polish pride! It is incomparable! His simple officer's sword hung at his side—but truly, yes, at this moment it could only have been called an epée. Tears came to the Empress's eyes.

"I am grateful to you, most grateful!" She held her hand out to be kissed.

She had a mass of troops in her guard, and a single sword and a single revolver added nothing for her—but it added so much to strengthening her spirit! As long as there was loyalty like this, there was hope.

(She had never distinguished this aide-de-camp in any way. She had even impeded his frivolous wife's move to Mogilev in order to preserve GHQ's strict morals and manners.)

But it was from Zamoisky that she now learned for the first time this terribly shattering Petrograd news and the general picture—that all the prisons had been opened wide and all the fugitives from the prisons had stood at the head of the rebellious movement, which the Duma, naturally, had joined.

Above all, the Cossacks! The unshakable buttress of the Russian throne had betrayed it and turned up on the same side as the rebels!

After the loss of the Cossacks, there was nothing to hold onto.

Added to this, then, were reports over the telephone with Benckendorff and the ladies in waiting. According to their stories, half the city, if not its entirety, had been seized.

Now, for the first time, the unbending Empress, who had never surrendered to or subjected her husband to the demands of all this riffraff and educated rabble, melted, as in the face of a volcano. At one in the afternoon she sent the following to the mysteriously silent Emperor:

"Concessions inevitable. Strikes continue. Many troops gone over to the side of revolution."

About the Cossacks—she could not say a word!

[91]

Ensign Georgi Shabunin liked working with soldiers—like the children he might have taught, had he only graduated from the university in peacetime. They were the most genuine people Shabunin had ever dreamed of serving, bringing light and knowledge. But he was fated not to go from the university to the people, deep into their remote villages, but to spend several months in ensign school—and now the People themselves had come to him, to the packed barracks on the Vyborg side. When not on duty, Shabunin often spent the night at his battalion's disposition, in the company chancellery, staying with the soldiers for their evening off-duty hours, writing letters home for them, teaching them a little literacy, and talking—but not in a revolutionary vein by any means. Shabunin felt good and free with the soldiers and somehow could not get used to his officer's existence. The senior officers caught him on oversights and reprimanded him. Even in the past few days he'd been humiliated by the battalion commander in front of all the officers. The commander had summoned them all to the library of the officers' club with their weapons, called Shabunin out, and stated that a few days before, on a streetcar, he had not been bothered to fully salute a sailor, a captain first rank, but had only risen slightly from his seat and saluted half bent over. Shabunin flushed red under this reprimand. But there in the streetcar it would somehow have been unseemly and awkward to leap up and give a full salute, and his sword got in the way.

All these past few days of many dispatches to pickets and sentries, exercises in the battalion had nearly stopped, but Shabunin had attempted to work with those who remained. So, too, today with half-company C of the training detachment he had begun training exercises on rifle handling. They were holding one nearly for the first time and still had no idea how to load it or shoulder the stock.

So, too, today he knew little of what was going on in the city or here, around the Moscow barracks—when suddenly they all heard frequent rifle shots nearby—and their battalion did not keep blank cartridges!

But no alarm was raised through the battalion, the shots died down, and Shabunin continued working.

Half an hour or more passed, and shots rang out from Lesnoi Prospect, and a lot of them. Cross-fire.

Right then Shabunin was summoned by the training detachment chief, Captain Dubrova. His ever ominous face was contorted. He stated that the rebels were ranging throughout the Vyborg side—and Ensign Shabunin and his half-company were to go out immediately as a detail to block off Lesnoi Prospect outside the gates—and not to let any outsiders onto barracks grounds.

Shabunin made so bold as to remind him that his half-company was today having only its second lesson with firearms—but Dubrova ordered him to be quick about carrying out his order.

While he was lining up his oafs, two other young ensigns came up to be under his command, Kutukov and Yanitsky, came up to him.

As they were leaving the gates in the wooden fence for Lesnoi, a sleigh had pulled up with an unconscious and deadly pale Lieutenant Verigo, who was severely wounded, in the belly. And there was an ensign, from the detail, with the sleigh.

The formation parted, letting the sleigh through the gates. The ensign stayed there.

But where was Verigo's detail, or what was left of it? Where had it dispersed?

The enemy was nowhere to be seen, either; Lesnoi was nearly empty. And down the other side of Lesnoi were vacant lots, a long fence, and behind it the Finland railroad.

Shabunin ordered them to form two lines across Lesnoi, closer together to the right of the gates, less so to the left.

He himself stood with the right-hand line.

Right then, suddenly, a polytechnic student wearing a student cap and a thin coat appeared from around the corner, walking toward the line with a quick light step.

He was so dear, so much like him, so familiar, his step and look so easy, that Shabunin saw in him one of his own men; he was still not properly used to the fact that he himself was wearing a greatcoat and was himself a stranger.

But the student, surveying the cross-wise formation, which did not impede individual passage, immediately picked out Shabunin and walked right up to him.

Shabunin did not know this student, but felt as though he did, so familiar, typical, and bright-eyed was he. His manner of speech was familiar, too, the way he asked easily and loudly, so that the soldiers heard, too:

"Gentlemen! Are you really going to fire at the **people**?"

An abrupt and astonishing question! At the martyr People, at the People before whom we are eternally guilty for a dozen educated generations. Of course, Shabunin wasn't going to shoot at the People or let anyone else. But this general, universally known People—where were they today on Lesnoi?

They were in this smooth-faced, inept, timid half-company, which was listening for what the ensign would say in reply.

Shabunin's heart remained open and even yearning toward this student—but in front of the soldier formation and the other ensigns he could not answer him in those terms. Concealing his own membership in that same order, restraining his look and tone, the half-year of military service having changed him somehow, he tried to reply sternly:

"Move along so we don't have to detain you."

The student jumped, as if he hadn't expected that answer, but more theatrically. And walked through. And moved off.

So they stood on a deserted Lesnoi. There were only individual pedestrians, whom they let through.

Later, from around the corner, from Tobolskaya Street, they began hearing shouts. Then a flatbed truck with a red flag on the cab started backing out of there, inching this way, full of civilians and soldiers—and at the edge of the bed were two machine guns, and the gunners were silently aiming them this way, at the half-company. Red trimmings also fluttered on the soldiers' bayonets, and some had attached scraps of red cloth to their chest or sleeve; others had wound it around. So it was all very theatrical and unusual, as if they meant to entertain the half-company and of course not fire on it, defenseless as it was.

But the recruits, you could see, were scared to death, and a shudder ran through the ranks.

Shabunin commanded the lines to come to the ready.

They did.

No, they only started . . .

No, some did and some didn't. . . .

No one did, and the formation disintegrated!

They started running through the little wicket in the gates.

All this in an instant.

The line on the other side of the gates started disintegrating as well—and went through the same wicket.

And the truck kept backing up, aiming its machine guns.

A big-faced Preobrazhensky sergeant with a red flag on his bayonet jumped down off it.

"Surrender, your honors!"

There was no time to think and no way to open fire, not that there was anyone to do so: the formation had disintegrated. They'd run away, squeezing, pushing through the wicket, shouting.

There was also shooting from off to the side, apparently from the railroad embankment.

All the four ensigns could do was retreat toward the same wicket.

And squeeze in behind the last soldiers.

And bolt it shut.

But the half-company was so possessed, they lost their minds. They wouldn't listen to the officers—but they didn't run away either—and now they rushed to defend themselves over the fence: from a nearby stack they grabbed logs and threw them back, over the fence.

The soldiers were out of control. Outside, the crowd was hollering and howling—and so were the soldiers here.

But the machine guns outside had not fired through the wooden gates. (Might they not know how to operate the machine guns either?)

From the other side they started pushing and rocking the gates hard and with a bestial howl.

A narrow passage led from the gates to the barracks parade ground between the manège and the arsenal—Thermopylae. And there the four ensigns remained.

They exchanged glances and got out their revolvers.

And held them out to fire—retreating, retreating from the gates.

But the gates creaked and cracked—and crashed!

A crowd of black coats and gray greatcoats flooded in, all in red scraps.

They'd broken in! But they saw the revolvers raised at them.

Silence.

So young, boys really, straight from their school benches, step by step the four ensigns retreated with their pointed guns. For some reason, it fell to these four recruits to defend the hundred-year ground of the Life Guards regiment—and more ringingly than the roar that again rose in the oncoming crowd, another sound reached their ears:

"Gentlemen! Are you really going to fire at the people?"

But they didn't have to think that far. Out from the slowly advancing crowd a worker with a distorted face and wearing a black cap with ear flaps leapt forward—and fired his revolver at them first.

He missed.

Then Shabunin quite confidently shot him in the forehead, which was hidden by his cap.

And he collapsed into the snow face first.

Another second of silence, cutting short the crowd's cry.

And the four officers stepped farther back, retreating.

The Thermopylae between buildings was over already, and behind the ensigns the broad parade ground opened wide but offered no assistance.

They could have remembered that there was no assistance to speak of.

On the entire rebellious Vyborg side, they could expect no assistance. From the Guards battalions in the center? But here a Preobrazhensky sergeant was at the machine guns. From the Field Army? But not today. All this flashed through Shabunin's mind, like birds. His entire abortive life and his joyous activities.

For some reason, this foursome of skinny men wrapped in fresh belts and even with whistles in the bird's nests on their shoulder straps, were supposed to hold back this crowd for one and all.

When a second worker jumped out with a revolver, Shabunin fired first and he fell on the snow.

The crowd let up another howl—and together rushed them all at once.

Not out of fear, which didn't have time to hit them, but out of simple, sensible consideration, all four of them—whether or not they had fired— turned and ran light-footedly across the parade ground, still holding onto their ungainly swords.

But someone shoved Shabunin in the back, as if with a huge log—and a fiery splash from his head blazed up to the sky.

[9 2]

Colonel Kutepov's appearance greatly encouraged everyone in the city governor's offices: his indisputably prepared and martial look was such that you couldn't really explain which small features it was made up of, but it was immediately clear to each general here that this colonel stood out from all those here for the distinctness of his decisions, the clarity of his commands, and his getting right down to business. Not only was he not amazed, or hesitant, or trying to beg off—he accepted the order as if that was why he had come to Petrograd from the front. Ten minutes later he had left to carry it out.

The mood at HQ was much buoyed, and they now anticipated an end to the upheavals.

However, news arrived that the rebels were already crossing the Field of Mars and going toward the Winter Palace! There was no detail left whatsoever to repulse this new threat apart from bringing back Kutepov, who had been sent away. Argutinsky-Dolgorukov went to chase him down and turn him back.

It didn't matter where he moved—just so he kept going. All Khabalov's HQ reserves and all its possibilities had been exhausted, and he could not strip his headquarters completely of all security. All they could do was follow along on the city map and guess what might develop further.

But the only way they could find out was over the telephones. This was how they learned that the Munitions Works had been seized and a general bayoneted in the process. The House of Preliminary Detention and the District Court had been routed and set on fire. The fire chief, who had gone there with a fire crew, called to say that the crowd wouldn't let him put it out. Khabalov ordered a second-line crew to be located and sent there to drive away the impeding crowd. (But apparently they were neither located nor sent.)

Despite there being fourteen Guards reserve battalions stationed in Petrograd, it seemed no reserves could be pulled in from anywhere. Some battalions replied that they had no free companies at all, or no reliable companies, and there was no one to send. The Finland Life Guards replied from Vasilievsky Island that they had two reliable companies, only they were being used to hold back the remaining battalion, to keep them from mutiny. No one wanted to take a risk and send anyone. Nor would Khabalov risk accepting the order.

Right then the class inspector from the Nikolaevsky Military School reported that his cadets were worried; they wanted to go out on the street with rifles to establish order!

This gave Khabalov a scare. That's all he needed, involving cadets! There was no avoiding his responsibility to them. He ordered the colonel to lock the gates and doors and not let the cadets out under any circumstance! He sent the same instruction to all the academies. He was a specialist on cadets; he had worked in education.

There were no reserves, and there was this: there was no ammunition, not even a dozen cases of cartridges. No one could have anticipated a clash in the city. There were no depots left in the center besides those already seized by the rebels, and the rest were on the outskirts and inaccessible.

There had been more than one telephone call from Kutepov about needing to worry about feeding the soldiers. Easy to say! But feed them from which reserves? And where were you to find field kitchens nearby?

Khabalov realized that he had to act somehow, but he could neither see nor envision any possible line of action. Most of all, there were no reserves whatsoever. He sank into indifference and ossified there. What would be would be. He might survive it.

The only thing he did think was that the Emperor, after all, might not know of even yesterday's events with the Pavlovsky Battalion. To say nothing of today's. So he needed to wire him at least briefly—although he was frightened to take this on.

He composed a telegram and conveniently added that it was essential that he immediately send reliable units from the front.

There were no troops in reserve, and everyone was demanding security be sent. The telephone exchange on Morskaya Street, here, near Gorokhovaya, was demanding it. This was the most important of all, so they sent a platoon of infantry and forty horsemen. The Lithuanian Fortress, the penitentiary, was demanding it. But there were a dozen prisons in Petrograd—and did they really have the strength to defend them? Even Prince Golitsyn had demanded security, not for the Mariinsky Palace, which was understandable, but for his own residence on Mokhovaya Street. Khabalov faltered and said there were no reserves. How about just twenty men or so, to lock down the block from both directions. Twenty men wouldn't mean help, just bloodshed. Mokhovaya was right by Liteiny, in the very thick of it.

The Liteiny area was lost, evidently. But now they began telephoning from the Moscow Life Guards, from the Vyborg side, saying the rebels had broken through the Liteiny Bridge and tremendous crowds were jamming Sampsonievsky Prospect, and of the resisting officers, some had been killed and some wounded, the companies were unreliable, and the best thing was to keep them in the barracks.

Were they losing the Vyborg area, too?

This was especially bad because the rebels had left behind them Okhta and the Gunpowder district, but if one of the powder factories were to catch fire and blow up—there would be nothing left of Petrograd. They had a new problem: how were they to push the rebels north, away from the Gunpowder district? But again they devised nothing. There were no trained troops anywhere.

City Governor Balk had already reported to Protopopov that morning by telephone, but it was useless because he only asked in reply: "And what, in your opinion, needs to be done?" He asked him to hold out until evening, when fresh troops would start arriving.

But the Emperor had demanded that all the disorders be stopped today.

There, among themselves, at the city governor's offices, they were supposed to find and save everything.

At their service for this they had three telephones, which were in constant use.

Over one of them, Prince Golitsyn, the Prime Minister, had summoned General Khabalov urgently to his home on Mokhovaya.

Well, I never! . . . Leave headquarters—and how would I get there anyway? Khabalov went.

But the telephones—the telephones kept working overtime. After all, these were the telephones of the city governor's offices, which everyone knew, and if anyone didn't know the number, the operators connected them. Scarcely had they fended off one conversation when there would be another call. And everyone invariably required the city governor.

Countess Witte telephoned, worried about her residence.

Undistinguished residents telephoned with the same concerns.

Countess Ignatieva telephoned to say she was praying to God to grant the city governor strength.

Trepov, the former Prime Minister, telephoned with encouragement. He knew Balk's equanimity and was certain order would be restored.

Lelyanov, the mayor, telephoned in a very good mood and extremely gracious. He begged the city governor's pardon for tearing him away, but at a session of the City Duma just now it had been decided to hand over to the city all provisioning, and he as chairman of the commission had scheduled its session for tomorrow at four o'clock in the afternoon. So would it be convenient for the gentleman city governor to be present at that time tomorrow?

An officer from the front telephoned. The crowd could be successfully dispersed with ordinary smoke bombs. (But not only did he and Khabalov not have such bombs, this was the first time they had ever heard of such a thing.)

Then two officers burst in demanding a vehicle to remove the wounded and killed. The untidy look produced a bad impression on the public. Other unknown officers gathered in the waiting room as well. The mood was thickening. A captain of the Kexholm Battalion was sobbing hysterically.

A Frenchwoman and her maid broke through, importunate and unhappy because today she could not get white bread anywhere and black made her ill. Balk gave an order and she was brought a French roll on a tray. The guest was thrilled and left radiating gratitude.

But the reports from Kutepov had stopped.

Khabalov returned from the ministers even more downcast. He had heard it all on the streets, seen it with his own eyes.

No, new reserves still had to be pulled in from somewhere, and the best place for this was Palace Square.

They began telephoning around to the battalions—the Semyonovsky, the Izmailovsky, the riflemen, Jägers, and the grenadiers.

[9 3]

Early that morning people had come to see Kayurov and said that the workers were converging on the factories! But among themselves they were still discussing whether they would go back to work or continue the strike. At a moment like this they needed a *leaflet*, but they didn't have a leaflet!

There wasn't anyone among the Vyborg Bolsheviks who could write a leaflet himself. Maybe Gavrilych had one? Anyway, this had become too big for them to decide for the Petersburg Committee. Kayurov wasn't afraid of the responsibility, but he was a little bit apprehensive. He didn't recognize Shlyapnikov's primacy, except for his foreign languages, but then again he did.

So they rushed Pashka Chugurin (because he was quick on his feet) there, to Serdobolskaya: they needed a leaflet immediately!

But they themselves were sitting on Yazykov Lane, in Novaya Derevnya, and discussing whether or not to go out to work. They discussed it for a long time. Shurkanov, old and bald, from the Aivaz factory, spoke well and even with tears in his eyes. (Shlyapnikov had maligned him unfairly as a provocateur, but he was loved in the Vyborg District Committee.) He said to carry on no matter what—and without stopping!

Chugurin brought back from Shlyapnikov that they were writing a leaflet! But who was writing it? Gavrilych himself, actually, since there weren't any specialists handy. And he ordered not going to work under any circumstance but to go organize rallies near the barracks, in order to infect the soldiers, so that they could hear our speeches over the fence. Also, send couriers with notes to them in the barracks. Notes about what? Whatever comes to mind: Support the people! Down with the officers! Down with the war!

Yes, now you regret that we have no party organization in the barracks.

But if we go after the soldiers—and entirely without weapons? If we start something serious, then we need weapons, so how can we barehanded? . . . Here's what, Pashka. Go back to Shlyapnikov, talk to him about weapons for the last time, how we have to stock up, otherwise the cause is lost. And bring the leaflet! Go on!

Pashka ran off.

Well, they dispatched Khakharev to organize a rally near the Moscow barracks on the Lesnoi side, where the fence was low and had gaps.

While they themselves decided to meet in continuous session and await events.

No one should go to work, the men said.

When they went out to answer nature's call, there seemed to be shooting across the Neva. It was far from here, but it seemed as though there was.

Oh, the terror had probably begun, and they were shooting revolutionary forces and reveling.

Right then Pashka ran back in. Gavrilych said there were to be no weapons, no going out as combat militias. So we'd have twenty revolvers. So what? The soldiers will wipe us off the face of the earth. We're no force. But talk the soldiers into coming over with their weapons—there's your solution.

Of course, where was he to get a weapon? So much for your solution.

The leaflet had been written, here was the document, and they were taking it to the printer's now—so it would get read at meetings.

They read it. He'd learned to rattle these off splendidly. You say he really wrote it himself? ". . . Tsarist power has led Russia to the brink of ruin. The people have been robbed. There is nothing to eat and nothing to live on. The Black Hundreds regime is busy looting the people. They're answering the workers' demands with lead . . ."

Say it, and it brings a lump to your throat!

"Continue the general strike!"

That's right!

Khakharev returned from the rally at the Moscow fence. They'd talked and talked but it hadn't helped. The soldiers wouldn't budge, locked in their barracks.

But across the Neva the shooting was fiercer. And closer.

What should they do?

Let's wait for the leaflet.

They waited, and waited some more, and meanwhile they had lunch and went about their business—but the session was considered to be more or less ongoing.

All of a sudden Shvedchikov returned, quite ecstatic.

"Men! There's a soldier uprising in the city! They've already crossed the Liteiny Bridge and freed Kresty! There are prisoners everywhere!"

The joy! They were jumping! Leaping! Shurkanov was kissing them all, and he nearly smothered Kayurov.

And we're sitting here? Come on—let's get going!

Kayurov himself rushed to the Moscow barracks. There was already shooting there! And our reinforcements had already arrived there!

Not only that, the Moscow soldiers, one by one, some without rifles, some with, had been squeezing through the gaps or over the fence here, on Lesnoi. But then, were they themselves feeling afraid or awkward for having abandoned their unit? They shifted from one foot to the other and didn't know what to do with themselves.

But Kayurov, who was born decisive, certainly never lacked in that regard. Although not imposing in height, he had a penetrating voice. He shouted to them:

"Why are you standing there, comrade soldiers? Line up!"

They started pushing and lining up rather indiscriminately. And laughing at Kayurov. What do you mean line up? Facing which way? How many rows?

But Kayurov didn't know any more of these commands, not a one.

[9 4]

On the night of the 11th to 12th, the Emperor was not disturbed by new information from Petrograd and so slept peacefully, as usual.

The first alarm was in the morning, reported by the palace commandant, Voeikov: yesterday's evening telegram from Protopopov. Or rather, it wasn't that alarming. It reported that nearly the entire previous day the order had not been disturbed in Petrograd. Only toward the end of the day they had had to disperse a gathering, first with blanks, but the crowd threw rocks at the troops and pieces of ice, so they'd had to resort to live ammunition and there were casualties. All the crowds were dispersed, although individual participants in the disorders fired on the military patrols from around the corner. The troops acted zealously. Only the 4th Company of the Pavlovsky Regiment had gone out independently. (A mysterious expression: Gone out how? Where? Why? An independent movement without an order from above? A nonmilitary term.) But the Okhrana was enjoying great success. They'd arrested more than 140 party figures. (Rather grandiose even, then it's all put down?) Control had been established over bread and flour. And as of Monday they expected some workers to return to the factories.

And Moscow had been completely quiet all this time.

No, nothing serious.

Protopopov had been a happy find. What an effective, indefatigable, and resourceful man. How many ideas had he advanced during his very few ministerial months! True, the general situation was so tied up, there was little he could implement. And how Alix liked him! There had simply never been such a successful minister. It was a great relief that he was there now, in that post. He would not fail to do everything needed and would provide Alix with moral support.

His telegram was rather reassuring. Only what was this about the Pavlovsky's independent movement? Hadn't they done something unworthy? How would the Pavlovsky Regiment then wash away this stain?

And the crowd's stones at the troops? Unimaginable.

After an early breakfast, the Emperor was planning to go hear Alekseev's report when a staff officer brought him two telegrams.

One was from Prince Golitsyn, submitted today at two o'clock in the morning. That as of this date, as he had been authorized, he had discontinued the activities of the Duma and State Council until the month of April.

That was good. During disorders, it was better that the Duma not function. It was what was bringing the entire situation to the boiling point to begin with. An astonishing assemblage! Not simply enemies of the throne, but enemies of the Russian state. During time of war they were stirring things up, detonating them, and not reckoning with anything.

But the second telegram was very odd, nearly inebriated. It was signed by a Colonel Pavlenko, whom the Emperor, despite his extensive military memory, did not even remember. It turned out he was now for some reason the acting head of the Guards reserve units in Petrograd. (But where was General Chebykin? Oh, yes, on leave, apparently.) The entire telegram was to report that the Pavlovsky reserve battalion commander and his ensign were injured by crowd. And that was it. No information about the rest of the Guards, whether Pavlenko was truly in charge, or about the entire Petrograd situation—or about anything else.

It was odd. But his heart missed a beat: the Pavlovsky men again? Did this bear any connection to the company going out? . . .

At half past ten, as usual, the Emperor proceeded to the HQ building for the next report from General Alekseev about the troops' military actions.

He looked somewhat warily at Alekseev's familiar, rather crude, sergeant-majorish face, anticipating whether he wouldn't have something alarming about Petrograd. But he didn't say so, no, thank God.

He inquired about his health. Although Alekseev responded positively, from his face and shoulders it was evident that it was not that good and he looked chilled.

However, the overall military review went smoothly and contained nothing new.

The Emperor saw all the more clearly that since his illness Alekseev had already made up what he had missed, which meant that the Supreme Commander's further presence at GHQ was not that necessary and he could return for the time being to his poor, lonely Alix.

At the end of the report, Alekseev handed him, first, a telegram from Khabalov in his own name and apologized for not reporting it earlier. It was yesterday's daily but had arrived after yesterday's report. Because it was Sunday, he hadn't wanted to disturb His Majesty, and last night he had felt unwell and had had to lie down.

Oh, of course, the Emperor immediately forgave and did not reproach him. He could understand when a man was neither young nor in good health.

The telegram had been submitted nearly twenty-four hours ago: yesterday at one o'clock in the afternoon. And its entire content referred to the day before yesterday, the second half of Saturday. That all kinds of crowds had been scattered by the police and army ranks many times. Near Gostiny Dvor they had waved red flags saying "Down with the war" and from the crowd people had fired revolvers at the dragoons, who had been forced to open fire on the crowd. Three were dead, ten wounded—and the crowd had scattered instantly. After that, they had blown up a mounted gendarme with a grenade. Saturday evening, however, had passed relatively peacefully. Meanwhile, there were 240,000 workers on strike.

The Emperor rubbed and smoothed his mustache between his thumb and middle finger. He did not reproach Alekseev for the delay; reading it, he didn't have the heart to. Nonetheless, that was too many striking. All these incidents, as they gradually came to light, had somehow built up. Actually, they were compensated for by the calm of the other telegrams, from Protopopov. Actually, all this was a long time ago, the day before yesterday, and since then nothing worse had happened.

Indeed, Khabalov's telegram ended by saying that since the morning of the 11th all had been quiet in the city.

But the ailing Alekseev, gloomier than usual, screwed up the slits of his eyes and continued. Here was what Rodzyanko had come up with: last night, he had sent Alekseev—and, as it turned out, also the commanders-in-chief at the fronts, dragging them, too, into the discussion—an agitated, even panic-stricken telegram saying that the disturbances in Petrograd were assuming ominous proportions. That the government was in total paralysis and incapable of restoring order. That Russia was threatened by disgrace and the war could not be won unless (as always for him and the entire Duma) some individual was charged with governing whom the entire country could trust. (Read: Rodzyanko himself.)

Oh, that alarming, pressing, self-confident fat man! How weary the Emperor was of his incessant, unceremonious lectures. At one time there had been a good joke about him: if he were invited to a royal christening, he himself would climb into the font. Why did he have to listen to his confused, fussy advice rather than heed the telegrams of the duly charged authorities? All these last months, no matter how much the Emperor had heard Rodzyanko, the situation was always "more grave and acute than ever before."

Here, however, was a new and unexpected move, that Rodzyanko's telegram had been intended not for the Emperor directly, and not for Alekseev alone, but had gone directly to all the commanders-in-chief at the front—"the fate of Russia's glory and victory is in your hands, Your Excellency"—and all the Excellencies now had to save Russia by supporting Rodzyanko's profound conviction before His Majesty. A bizarre and daring maneuver. Why not directly? Why via the generals?

Nikolai fingered his mustache in irritation.

The rather perturbed Alekseev's embarrassment was not lost on him. No longer glancing over at the maps of the fronts hung up in the small room, he grimaced awkwardly with his spade-like whiskers. He felt awkward for himself, as the unwitting addressee (always for some reason the addressee for public figures, the cursed Guchkov came to mind), but even more awkward, apparently, for Brusilov. Brusilov, who had received this telegram that same night, at one in the morning, and without even going to bed, without even putting off thinking it over until morning, had immediately forwarded the Rodzyanko telegram to GHQ, not simply to inform the Emperor but also with a decisive addition, that by his duty and oath he saw no other solution than what Rodzyanko proposed! (But what could he see or not see from the Southwestern Army Group? How could a military man behave in this way?)

The Emperor took a puff on his curved meerschaum. How could such different news be coming from the same city at the same time? The government was confidently governing, not even asking for assistance—while the Big Drum assured him it was in paralysis?

If there had been anything truly alarming, Alix would have warned him within an hour or two. But there had been no telegrams from her today.

The Emperor was increasingly amazed at the confused, evasive look on Alekseev, who had not objected to either Rodzyanko or Brusilov. So had he joined them?

The Emperor was used to standing up to public loudmouths. But it was an unusual and dangerous feeling when his own generals, behind his back, had also been enticed by *them*, as if they had struck the Supreme Commander himself in the back.

What did they understand about this issue—Russia's Supreme Power, its eternal legitimacy, its indivisibility and the division over which the Emperor had agonized with such difficulty for a good two decades? How easily everyone took it upon themselves to advise!

No, the embarrassed Alekseev didn't dare advise. He merely submitted all the papers as he was supposed to, the honest old man.

The report was exhausted and the Emperor left.

At twelve-thirty, as usual, the regular high lunch was held for the allies' military representatives and GHQ officers, and naturally, not a word was uttered by anyone about the Petrograd events, inasmuch as the Emperor did not bring them up.

Among the principal virtues of a monarch, Nikolai believed, was never to talk about anything serious at the wrong time, in the wrong circumstances, and with anyone other than the individuals who were appropriately qualified and charged. Self-possession and impartiality were also understood by him as the best part of the etiquette of a monarch who bears his divine burden and full responsibility for all final decisions.

If the suite, which may have known something more about Petrograd, was exchanging whispers, no one dared raise his voice or speak to the Emperor directly. There were perhaps also agitated, if not downright frightened faces.

Just as invariably, the Tsar's drive in the country was supposed to follow afterward, the weather being excellent, sunny, and windless. Two motorcars pulled up and the suite's closest members were already going out to them — when the Emperor, already in his greatcoat, buttoned up, was brought a new telegram from HQ.

This was from Khabalov and perfectly fresh, submitted an hour ago. The last one from him had been addressed to Alekseev, but this was directly to His Imperial Majesty. The Emperor opened it standing, by the stairs, and read it, but they were looking at him. And because they were looking, not only was his face unperturbed but he somehow didn't even read it with full attention; he felt like sticking it in his pocket quickly and going.

Here was when everything was explained. Khabalov reported about that very same Pavlovsky company, which had declared to its company commander that it would not fire on the crowd. The company had been disarmed and arrested. (What a disgrace for the Pavlovsky men!) Evidently, the commander of the Pavlovsky Battalion was wounded in this incident, which was what had come from Pavlenko.

But Khabalov's telegram did not end there. Today a Volynian training detachment had also refused to go out against the mutineers, as a consequence of which its officer shot himself, and the detachment, drawing away a company of reserves, headed for the location of the Lithuanian and Preobrazhensky battalions, where other reserves joined them.

He had read many lines. The short telegram did not seem short because its content went beyond the bounds of anything that could have been anticipated. Unprepared for this and already inclining to move on and go down the stairs, the Emperor finished hastily without wholly grasping its meaning. There was even an assurance that General Khabalov was taking all available measures to suppress the mutiny but thought it essential to have reliable units sent from the front.

Maybe he should have stayed back and reread it? In general—go back and speak with Alekseev? But all this was happening annoyingly in front of those ready for the outing—and a return like that, a cancellation of the drive, would have looked too out of the ordinary.

The Emperor slipped the telegram into his coat's inside pocket and walked down to the motorcars.

They drove down the Orsha highway. Marvelous weather and a merrily blinding sun, but not enough to melt the snow. The abundance of light and the sun's height were already springlike. Nikolai looked around and rejoiced and tried to overcome the bafflement rising in his heart.

When they got there and were taking their walk, he felt like pulling out the telegram and rereading it; he had not grasped everything in it. But once again this would have appeared unusual and would have frightened his suite.

That's all right. God grant all ends well.

The conversations on the stroll were everyday, ordinary.

In full view of everyone, the Emperor was mysteriously calm, as if he knew nothing alarming, or, on the contrary, he had already resolved everything and taken all sufficient measures.

[9 5]

Through these rooms, over and over. Circling slowly. Walking. Sitting.

His study gave him no pleasure; in it, Georgi could find not the slightest thing to do. Nothing to force himself to do.

These rooms, over and over, now more hers than his. Though not hers either. Nor, seemingly, shared. As if the air of a crypt wafted from the threshold as you crossed.

Might she be hiding at Susanna's again? Or has she rushed to Petersburg?

Of course, the freest choice would be to find fault with her running away so you could leave. Abandon everything in a minute—and go back to the front. They hadn't met—well, that was fine, go, and consider yourself at liberty.

That was what he should do.

But he already knew that relief would only last for the first short hours. Depression would come over him afterward. And pity for her, gnawing pity.

There was no getting away from that. That would claw, overshadow the whole world, and you'd rush back halfway there anyway.

Not just leave, in these hours he was incapable even of going outside to distract himself, get some fresh air, sober up.

Or was he waiting for her to walk in? Return?

He remembered how it was seeing each other the last time—right here, in the middle room, that evening after the Smyslovskys—and how she had *looked* him in the face. Why had she done that?

He felt utterly ill.

Alina's dresses hung in a row in her wardrobe. Two or three dozen. Some almost shabby ones—due to the meagerness of the life of an officer's wife—and those that preserved in their stripes, corners, collars, and belts—the history of their eight years. All kinds of incidents—funny, annoying, and touching.

He stood and looked at them—with sorrow.

Picturing Alina weeping right here, in this room, her face quaking in her delicate hands, was unbearable! For some reason no one else's tears, no one's tears in his whole life, not even his mama's, or Vera's, had so gripped his throat in crooked spasms as had hers.

Now, if Olda had burst out sobbing it would have been totally different. Not that she would have.

Here was what it felt like: as if he and Olda had run together and clasped in an embrace and hadn't noticed that they'd stepped on a child's foot or that there was a rabbit jerking under their soles and screaming—but we didn't hear, we were breathless.

Somehow the thought of Olda did not now lift up his heart like the rising draft from a brazier.

No, there was no holding on to Olda.

Perhaps there had been a path for his path: with neither one nor the other. Go away and sort things out. Maybe there had, but he hadn't noticed in time: where had that turn come?

This woundedness of hers was what wounded him most of all.

These scissors of hers, snatched up, opened wide, like a throat in cry.

If they could reconcile, he could lift this weight from his soul. Forget all that had happened, as if it had never been. Reconcile—so that things would be easy again.

But the feeling of cast iron misery would not leave him.

The fracture of a life.

That he should not have fractured.

It would have been much easier, a good deal easier, if Alina had been here herself. If she had shouted at him, reproached him, shamed him. He would have explained himself in fifteen minutes, been healed, fastened on his sword and—dashed off to the front.

But precisely because she was gone, and she was so defenseless, only the open, mute yawn of the scissors, and you were such a hangman—he could remember of her only the good, only the very best, nothing bad. Precisely because she was gone, everything here tortured him so—on her behalf, without uttering a word.

Here was this fragile porcelain ink horn, now dry. Or this finely carved box. All these things reproached him because their mistress thoroughly loved them; they were small parts of her. And how many touchingly help-less traces of her enthusiasms taken up and abandoned: French textbooks and notebooks (abandoned); knitting (dropped); sewing (never finished);

amateur photographs (darkened, overexposed, bland, some glued into an album, more in a heap, unsorted); badminton (quit; she tried to talk Georgi into playing once and he hadn't liked it). Alina kept trying new things, testing herself, giving herself over to fantasies. As she put it, she wanted to soar, and precisely because she was always unsuccessful, and you were aware of this but she wasn't—that was what now gripped your throat obliquely.

Such acute longing is always the lot of those left behind, usually the woman's lot: here, just now, your sweetheart was here, and now he's gone—and bitterness blazes through your heart so.

Was he sorry for her? Unspeakably sorry for some reason? He couldn't understand it himself.

And you just couldn't distract your thoughts. The hours dragged on, and now you had to wait for Susanna. There was nothing to do, nothing to think, a cast iron mind.

He went to look for something to drink—a little silver glass engraved with a swallow, her birthday present to him. He went into the kitchen to look for something to eat—her funny colorful mitts she used for taking things off the fire. Her written "lunch menus" and "dinner menus"—she'd wanted to work out a system, and of course she'd given up. . . . Her case piled with boxes, cans, packing, the new crowding out the old, which wasn't thrown out either, just pushed back.

Longing—maybe not even for the person who'd left. This was too abrupt a longing, even a kind of . . . why? what for? . . . Was it some prevision of our universal separations?

When the soul is torn, nothing can satisfy or gladden. Emptiness is emptiness.

The doorbell rang. He shuddered: Was it she? No, she would have opened up herself.

He opened the door: the mailman. He handed him an envelope—and moved on.

Alina's hand!

And the stamp: the Voronezh-Moscow train, yesterday. Dropped in the train mailbox.

He opened it—what unrecognizably shaky handwriting, nearly every letter broken!—and this scared him even more! But then he realized she'd written it while the train was moving. Where was she going?

". . . You are twice, you are thrice unworthy of my love. You didn't see who you were living with. You had a veil over your eyes. I could have adorned any company! But my best possibilities remained undiscovered. My dreams and aspirations were trampled for good! And by none other than you!"

He broke off. Sat down at the dining table. Put down the letter. And stretched his arms over the light green embroidered tablecloth. And stared stiffly.

He might well have sat like that for a long time.

Probably gone to Borisoglebsk, to her mother's.

He remembered and picked it up again to read:

"... Of everyone who has wronged me in my life—you are the cruelest. So know that! Did I ever get any reward from you for the years I yielded to you in everything? For eight years you had me under lock and key. But my slavery is over now!"

He broke off again. And again stretched and stretched his arms the full length in front of him over the uncluttered tablecloth.

How everything reeled away from him. As if it were about some stranger.

He had never read a single letter of hers like this.

But he had never felt such emptiness inside either. Such infinite desolation!

"During this time I've had the bitter leisure to think through all the subtleties of you and me. Now I see there is spoilage in your soul. Delve into your conscience! See how dirty it is! I alone am your conscience and your salvation!"

Well, she had been writing him the same thing all winter, after all. It was strange that all day today here he hadn't recalled a single one of those reproaches. But here they were—again.

And—again?

And—forever now?

An unbreachable impasse.

If Olda were in Moscow now, would he rush to see her?

Oh, no.

Something with Olda wasn't right, either. . . .

Desolation. . . . Desolation.

Had he left more unread?

"... If you want me to give up on life, say so outright. I'll just disappear for everyone. Only you will know where they bury me. I beg of you, visit me at least once every ten years. . . ."

Well . . . As if this were no longer addressed to him.

He was always amazed at how it was people got drunk and why. Could they really not control themselves?

But now, drinking himself senseless would be pure health.

He sat.

And sat.

But why had he always been so certain that Alina loved him?

He smoked.

And paced.

Here he was sitting at his desk.

Among permanent objects that caught his eye, this one, so familiar: a slightly truncated glass pyramid, two Swiss meadow views glued on the back side, one above the other, and magnified through the pyramid's thickness.

The more often you saw it, the less you noticed. But this had been his mama's possession; it was left from his mama.

He had very little left from his mama.

There wasn't even a photograph of her out anywhere. Here it was, in a drawer.

His entire life was his Moscow childhood. But you could look and search all you liked and not find anyone here.

You just wouldn't.

He smoked.

And remembered.

He took out an envelope and letter paper.

"To Kalisa Petrovna Koronatova. Bolshoi Kadashevsky Lane.

"Gracious Madam Kalisa Petrovna!

"I was passing through Moscow on my way to the front. I don't know your current circumstances. But if they are favorable, might I visit you tonight?

"With my sincere respect,

"Georgi Vorotyntsev"

There was always an errand boy available at Chichkin's store next door.

* * *

DON'T EXPECT TO BEAT AND MILK THE SAME GOAT

* * *

[9 6]

Mikhail Vladimirovich Rodzyanko thought that no one in Russia had known as tragic a situation or had so tragically grasped the essence of events as he. History had put him up if not for quartering then for being ripped apart by enraged bulls. (Bull snouts appeared before him like the reliefs at the Round Market on the Moika.)

Seeing for himself not only the right to feel and judge for the entire country but also to decide and *be* for the whole country, Rodzyanko had the courage not to submit to or flatter the Tsar in any way but rather to speak the bitter truth in his reports, to point out which hated individuals should be removed and which moods of society he should heed. He himself, a firm monarchist, found it hard that he had to condemn the monarch's actions and struggle with his instructions—but for the good of the Homeland! Rodzyanko also had the courage not to submit to society or the Duma's left wing, however well disposed he was toward them; rather, he distinguished himself by being loyal to his oath, not deviating in the slightest from the monarchical principle, and refusing ever to enter into a conspiracy against the Tsar.

And for this, the Tsar could not abide his counsel and had stopped listening to it! And for this, the Kadet wing had stopped trusting him, and as far as a year back this sure-fire candidate for premier in a government of public trust, Rodzyanko, had been replaced in a determined Milyukov maneuver by the blandly insignificant Prince Lvov. (Replaced but not broken! Privately, he continued to consider himself the inevitable future Prime Minister! It was simply ridiculous to compare his formidable figure and that zemstvo sycophant-reconciler.) And for this (he'd been told), Goremykin had called him mad, and Krivoshein had added—and at a dangerous stage, so had the rightists—a double-dyed dimwit.

But from the height of his presidency, Rodzyanko saw Russia better than anyone. He saw how the Tsar, by not heeding his counsel, had ruined Russia and the entire cause. He also saw how the Kadets, hardened in battle, were prepared to destroy not only the Empress and Stürmer but the entire Russian state. Look now: what had the Tsar done with his interruption of Duma activities? He had cut asunder any possibility of settling the conflict peacefully. And what did the left wing want? Not to submit to the Tsar's decree and not disperse? But that would be an even worse mutiny! The President could not agree to that either.

And what was going on in the streets? In the streets of Petrograd, soldiers were killing officers!

The bulls had strained and ripped everything apart. They needed to be tied down by their stubborn necks!

What could have been done? What could have been done? Yesterday, just after sending the thunderous telegram, Rodzyanko was singed by Golitsyn's call that the Duma had been dissolved temporarily as of that morning. What could he have done in the middle of the night? Only pad from room to room.

The morning brought some success. Clever Brusilov immediately responded with a telegram confirming obliquely that he had received and lent his support to the petition. ("I shall do my duty before the Homeland and Tsar.") Ruzsky had probably done the very same, although he had not yet responded.

But Alekseev? Silence. That meant the Tsar had not sent the President a word in reply.

Meanwhile, his nighttime telegram had been prophetic! Uncontrollable anarchy was building that would be impossible to restrain! What he had perceptively predicted to the throne that night—look, had already burst out this morning. And where? In the Guards! And on the day the civil war began, the Tsar had pulled out the last bulwark of order—the State Duma!

The President alone saw in all its fullness just how insane a step this was. Once again, the President alone could attempt to correct things.

Here's what: he should send a new telegram! This time directly to the Tsar!

Yes, only a telegram like that could save and fix everything. If the Emperor would come to his senses.

Thus the President's solitary sitting in his study resolved itself with action once again: a telegram! Once again he wrote sweepingly on several blanks, two sentences on each, continuation to follow.

. . . Command me, Emperor, in the stead of Your supreme decree, to reconstitute the legislative chambers. . . . Command me, Emperor, to convoke a new government based on the principles set forth by me to You in yesterday's telegram. . . . Make these measures known without delay in a supreme manifesto. . . . Emperor, delay not! Should the movement be conveyed to the army, the German will triumph, and Russia's downfall will be inevitable, and with it the dynasty's. . . .

He had to cleverly combine the rebellion's repression and the creation of a responsible government at one and the same time.

And to finish. . . . Yes, he had to write it this frankly:

In the name of all Russia, I beg Your Majesty to implement what has been set forth here. The hour deciding *your* destiny and the Homeland's has come! Tomorrow may be too late!

Even Rodzyanko—what else could he do? How could he shout any louder?

No, he could shout louder. And end in a simply shattering way. But also without stepping down from the stronghold of monarchism:

I pray to God that in this hour responsibility not fall on the monarch.

Now a telegram like **that** was sure to go down in Russia's history!

Although it was an impudent thing to say. It might provoke the Emperor's ire and spoil everything.

Simply with burning tears, deeply regretting his pen's best sentence, Mikhail Vladimirovich very cautiously crossed it out.

But it remained in the draft.

He sent it off to the telegraph office at the Tauride Palace. They should tap it out straight from there in ten minutes.

Suddenly he realized he still could! He could still make one important effort available to him alone!

The president could not call the Tsar to the capital, but he could summon the Tsar's brother, the figure by the Tsar's side. On this insane day, that might work. Rodzyanko had great influence over Mikhail Aleksandrovich, who unquestionably recognized him as number two man in the state. They were connected as well as two former Horse Guards. And the grand duke's spouse, so influential over her husband, had always been in favor of the State Duma.

So Rodzyanko began calling—and he got through to Gatchina, where Grand Duke Mikhail was now at his wife's home during his leave, or rather, his transfer from one military position to another. Rodzyanko got through and began imploring and insisting to both of them because it was the grand duke's wife who would make the final decision: that he should go straightaway and secretly to the capital to meet with the Duma President. (He telephoned even more confidently because, in January, Mikhail himself had come to see the President "to discuss the country's situation and to confer," and it was clear that he had been sent by his advantage-seeking spouse, given the critical overall shakiness.) Today Mikhail didn't very much want to, and he wavered. But Rodzyanko managed to persuade Natalia Sergeevna. Fine, he would go.

Fine.

So! The President alone had done everything both possible and impossible. Now shouldn't he assemble the faction leaders—the council of elders? He gave the order.

They began to assemble, each one doubling in the mirrored wall upon entering his office—and Rodzyanko and his powerful shoulders were doubled for all of them.

The rank-and-file Duma mass was still walking around and buzzing through the palace, only from time to time seeing their leaders flitting by but receiving from them no instructions. Everyone already knew about the looting of the Arsenal, the seizure of Kresty, the murder of the officers—and only the Tauride Palace, although right next to the action, remained in a kingdom of slumber where events did not break through and only distant shots were heard.

Was what gathered in Rodzyanko's office the council of elders, really, or the Progressive Bloc bureau again? Save the addition of Chkheidze and Kerensky. Because immediately upon proclamation of the decree of dissolution, the leaders of the rightist factions had left and not reappeared.

Thus, was the Bloc bureau, which had already met to no avail, still supposed to come up with something? His entire soul resisted submitting to the unceremonious Tsarist decree. But did not submitting mean starting a revolution himself?

They sat as on ruins: all had been swept away, the entire long siege and then the attack organized by the Bloc. There was shooting in the streets, and killing, and carrying of red flags—and at such a moment there was neither a Duma nor a Bloc!

The second most important figure here, Milyukov, could not conceal his lack of confidence. In this circumstance, much too unexpected, he did not know what to anticipate. He was so afraid of making a mistake that he thought it better not to act at all for the time being.

Well, fine. They had been forced to agree not to function as the Duma. But at least they could agree that they would not fan out over Russia, couldn't they? That everyone would stay in Petrograd and remain available for meetings and coalitions?

Other than Kerensky twisting in his chair and Chkheidze beaming handsomely (he had lived to see the great day, and he was amazed the rest weren't rejoicing), all the elders were distraught. But they did have to do something with the Duma mass strolling about there and waiting. They could not take any decision definitively without assembling everyone. However, assembling everyone, having everyone enter the hall at the bell as usual, would mean open defiance of the sovereign's will — mutiny!

That was what Kerensky proposed: the bell and everyone to the hall!

But Rodzyanko knew state laws and you couldn't get him to make such a move.

But then there was no hope!

In the Ekaterininsky Hall, the Duma members were still walking and walking, agitated, especially with the fresh news of where else the military uprising had spread through the city.

But it had not come here! Here, around the Tauride Palace, everything was still oppressively calm, only the shots in the distance, and further still.

Shaken, Shingarev was holding his head in his hands and surprised at his own deep-chested voice:

"What is this going on? Such things . . . Such things in time of war could only be arranged by the Germans! Who incited these events? Who is guiding them? And why isn't the government doing something?"

For many months, cursing the government, they had only gloated over the fact that it could not cope with anything and had wished it would fail to cope even worse and bankrupt itself utterly. But today, when the mutiny, chaos, weapons looting, and freeing of criminals had begun, the Bloc's leaders, and every Duma member, now as ordinary citizens of the country, could expect from this government at least some minimal firmness, at least some attempt to establish order, couldn't they? But that day, in this terrible moment, this astonishing government had not shown the faintest signs of life!

They were like children who keep pushing at a cupboard, believing it unshakable — and suddenly it tips over with all the dishes.

But they had never tipped it over for real! Only in their dreams had they nurtured, and only in their shouts had they called for it to tip — but they had not done any tipping.

Suddenly men came running, terrified: a crowd 30,000-strong was moving on the Duma!

A crowd — and 30,000-strong? A monster like that was terrible to imagine. Why would they be coming to the Duma if not to storm it?

Right then new witnesses ran in and announced what they had just heard: the mutinous crowd was shouting many things, but among them it was shouting, *Let's put an end to the Duma!* There were franchised elements in the Duma, they said, so slaughter them here and now!

Franchised. . . . Shivers down their backs. Yes, other than the peasants, although they were rightists, and also the few workers, they, the rest here, although they were leftist, were nearly all franchised, after all, that is, well-off, that is, of course, with personal wealth.

It had become rather uncomfortable in the ominously quiet Duma.

Only Kerensky rushed and weaved about. When will they get here? When? With the popular rebellion breathing down its neck, the entire State Duma turned into a clumsy crowd, a flock of sheep nearly—and only did Kerensky find all his nerve endings attenuating and his abilities to discern multiplied a thousandfold: crave this crowd, don't fear it! It will bring the Tauride Palace's new glory!

He eagerly breathed in this air of insurrection! His best and highest hour had come!

His morning efforts had helped: their shouts there had made a shred of the crowd see reason and turned them toward the Duma. But no matter how he dashed between windows, he did not see their approach, and his messengers were late in reporting—and the deadly frightened Duma officers raced to the Ekaterininsky Hall. The crowd had arrived! It was already in the open area out front and on the front steps, and there was no force to restrain it. It would burst into the palace at any moment!

They reported to Rodzyanko, of course, but Rodzyanko was suddenly put out. He was used to coming in front of the Duma—and all Russia, even the whole world, at once—but he was not prepared to come out before this rowdy, restless crowd. What could he tell them in the Duma's defense and justification? That he had sent telegrams to the Tsar and commanders-in-chief? Only that. He was now taken aback.

But those few leftist leaders, so impudent, clamorous, and burdensome for the President, who had so impeded the entire Duma path for everyone—now they proved useful! Now they rushed to greet the crowd, running across the Round Hall: the featherlight runner Kerensky, and the bald drake Chkheidze, from whom one could not have expected such vim, and the seemingly sluggish and clumsy Skobelev. They raced one another, and chasing after them, not having the right to lag under any circumstance, to let drop the honor and branch of the Progressive Bloc, its bureau chairman, the quiet, taciturn, drab Shidlovsky. Even if he was franchised.

Kerensky outstripped them all and was the first to burst ahead, flying, while the other three kept neck and neck, the three pushing through all the doors simultaneously.

How many had come? Oh, if only it were more! Oh, if only they had seen all Shpalernaya filled farther than the eye could see! But only two or three hundred perhaps came, not that longed-for hydra of a crowd as was drawn in the revolutionary imagination—but it was still a crowd! Disorderly, without leaders or a unified will of any kind, just whoever came forward and shouted—but that's how crowds are! With and without rifles, soldiers from various regiments, it was evident even to the untrained eye, and armed civilians, whether workers or bourgeois, you couldn't tell, but they didn't know how to hold a rifle, let alone how to shoot, and watch out one didn't go off by itself—and not a single red flag, like at the very last demonstration—but what determined faces! What stark movements! Well, maybe not decisive or stark, but would they run off now at the first alarm? Maybe just the opposite—would they burst commandingly into the Duma and give orders?

Grasping all this in an instant, then noticing as well a high school pupil, two apparent chambermaids, and two or three little boys, Kerensky—before he could even think, both his feet barely on the front steps when the other three burst through the door—threw up his arm and exclaimed:

"Comrade revolutionary workers and soldiers! In the name of the State Duma . . ."

He had been an annoying obstacle in that Duma, an *enfant terrible*, an unanticipated exception, but now he felt the entire timid Duma join him from behind—and he, the leader of a handful of Trudoviks, now embodied the entire Duma!

". . . allow me to welcome your irrepressible revolutionary impulse against the old, rotten order. We are with you! We thank you for coming here specifically! There is no force that can resist the mighty laboring people when it rises in its fury! . . . The people's representatives assembled in this building have always zealously sympathized. . . ."

Oh, how easy it was to speak. They didn't interrupt at all, and everyone to the last row could hear the orator's genuinely revolutionary voice, and the sentences themselves came forth, they came forth, perhaps a repetition of familiar ones, perhaps a combination of what had been said, and perhaps unprecedentedly new ones that had never been spoken in a single revolution on Earth! Kerensky would cast his eye over the faces—center, left, and right—and then look over their heads, farther, toward those thousands still to come—and he fired the first revolutionary salvo at the entire agitated people (the speech should not be too long)—and suddenly had a brilliant intuition. He happened to recognize the Volynian caps—he saw a few there, in the first row—and suddenly he shouted directly to them, in the voice of a congratulating military leader:

"Comrade Volynians! The State Duma thanks you for your loyalty to ideals! It accepts your offer to serve freedom and defend it from the dark Tsarist hordes! You four here, comrades, I appoint the first honorary revolutionary guard—at the doors to the State Duma! A great honor has befallen you! Stand to your post!"

He had never prepared for military commands, didn't know how to give orders, and had never trained that kind of a voice, but he felt that his voice and military bearing would arise of their own accord—and in an hour or two of accelerated revolutionary time, Kerensky was reborn, was steadily being reborn!

The Volynians singled out, who actually had not known where to go from there, were now glad to have found themselves a cause, and they obeyed, straightened their caps, straightened their belted greatcoats—and became sentries, all four in a row, with no idea who would come to replace them.

From the crowd came shouts of "hurrah!"

Now Chkheidze stepped forward to speak. He was touched that he had lived to see the revolution he had predicted in every speech, whether on a budgetary or transportation issue. These sentences had crossed his tongue so many times that now they repeated themselves without any effort; he let them spill out in a cracked voice, and shouted "hurrah!"—and a few willing voices shouted back at him.

But Skobelev was very much on his guard. It only seemed, here and now, like a hurrah, that they had posted the first revolutionary guard! But what kind of protection was this throng against the Tsar's troops? What kind of victory for freedom was this when a hundred obedient divisions might descend upon Petrograd tomorrow? However, his loyalty to social democracy forced him to take a risk. He spoke up. And the words flowed freely, it turned out, without lubrication.

Someone who looked like a sophisticated worker responded from the first row:

"You, comrades, are our true leaders. The people don't need ones like Milyukov for anything."

[9 7]

The morning's soldiers rebellion disrupted the entire expected course of events. Now whether the Duma had or had not been dissolved ceased to be the most important question, as it had seemed yesterday. Now, in general, the sequence of correct measures was unclear, what the government was to do and even *where* it was to do it, for the ministers' very movement about the capital had ceased to be safe or even feasible.

That morning the War Minister had telephoned the Prime Minister and both of them, at the two ends of the line, spent a long time trying to determine whether they should take measures and, if so, what kind. Naturally, it was seemingly from the government that a decision was expected, but since the capital was under martial law, the civil authorities were not responsible for anything, but neither was the War Minister, for the fullness of responsibility had been handed over to General Khabalov.

So difficult was it to think anything through in a two-way telephone conversation that they decided they needed to meet and confer. Prince Golitsyn, however, did not want to move through the streets himself and therefore scheduled the gathering of ministers to be held once again at his apartment on Mokhovaya. A good two hours was spent then on calling around to all the ministers and similarly complex explanatory conversations. At last, at eleven, the ministers began to assemble.

First to arrive was General Belyaev. His puny little figure was draped in a much too heavy general's greatcoat, and covering his small head was a much too large military peaked cap. He looked like a little boy in his tunic with its aiguillettes, monograms, and medals. But everything was compensated for by the tragic gravity of his somber, sunken eyes looking through his large pince-nez. Did the minister see and understand everything and have no need of explanations?

And the arrival of the Minister of Trade, Industry and Education, to say nothing of the Synod Procurator, did not solve anything.

The ministers did a poor job of convening. Again and again they summoned colleagues by telephone and would not begin without them.

Smoke filled the sky, and a servant explained that this was the District Court, which was quite close, three or four blocks away, half a verst, on fire! Rifle shots could be heard distinctly. A servant explained that this was people shooting on Liteiny and the streets beyond it, where crowds of soldiers were running around.

So it had become exceptionally dangerous to be right where they were, on Mokhovaya! The ministers' gathering and the apartment of the Prime Minister himself were under threat of attack by these bands. Now Prince Golitsyn deeply regretted not planning to gather at the Mariinsky Palace, a quiet area, but everyone had already been informed. Now he began telephoning that muddle-headed Khabalov, demanding a guard for his home, but Khabalov replied that he had no reserves. What was a Military District commander worth if he couldn't even protect the Prime Minister's apartment?

The ministers made their way with difficulty through the agitated, overflowing streets, some on wheels, some on foot. Finally, after noon by then, six or seven ministers had assembled, but all of them the kind who could not answer for what was happening. And the undoubtedly guilty Protopopov still had not appeared.

They gathered but did not convene, and they were very nervous. They drank tea or coffee, they sat down, they stood up, they gathered in twos and threes, some smoked, they looked out the window—Mokhovaya was still peaceful—and listened to the news the servant brought in. They called their ministries to find out whether they were working there—and apparently they all were.

Pokrovsky, the foreign minister, with his jogging gait, wandered among the ministers and, aiming his lowered mustache at one and then another, asked what they thought of the cabinet's resignation. After all, yesterday in the talks with Maklakov they had promised when the Duma dissolved to dissolve themselves as well. This morning Paléologue, the French ambassador, had been at his home and insisted that the Allies were awaiting a responsible administration; and in the afternoon he was expecting him and Buchanan—and they would insist on the same thing. What could he say?

Belyaev did the least moving around and speaking. He sat in the corner, now quite gloomy.

At last Protopopov walked in with the weary, crumpled face of a played-out actor. The look on his face said that he had predicted their rebukes but would rather not hear them.

He had no choice, though. All the ministers assembled here now pounced angrily on Protopopov, saying he was to blame more than anyone! He had led the cabinet of ministers astray with his soothing assurances, and now it could not be fixed! For a long time they wouldn't even let him say anything in his own defense. They dumped all their ministerial impotence, all the frustration they had experienced, on him.

Then again, Protopopov lacked his usual bounce. His proud, albeit balding head had sunk between his shoulders, and he looked out with ailing, joyless eyes. He tried to defend himself, but as someone certainly guilty, he did not once say, "my dear friends." That just yesterday the head of the Police Department had assured him that just yesterday all the ringleaders of all the revolutionary parties had been arrested. Therefore the revolution had been beheaded and what was happening could not be considered a revolution. What **this** had come out of was beyond comprehension. There was no way this was supposed to happen! And the upheaval in the troops? He was not responsible for that. That was the War Minister.

But everyone again shouted at Protopopov, and he hunched over, and his actor's head sank even farther between his shoulders, and he fell silent.

Belyaev, too, had to defend himself. He looked like a terrified hare with nowhere to run. Who could have predicted spontaneous movement from the troops? That could not have been envisioned. Now help would have to come from outside Petrograd.

Meanwhile, no guard had come to the Prime Minister's building. Nearby, on Liteiny, there was more and more rampaging and shots could be heard even here. It had become dangerous to remain here, let alone open a session.

They were the imperial government. They were also a small handful of distraught men who did not hold the reins to anything.

The pressure was wrenching. What was going on? And why were they here, in a darkened private apartment? As if they were some kind of conspiracy.

It had been a hollow summons. An incoherent, unnecessary meeting.

Prince Golitsyn paced decorously from room to room, not allowing himself to stoop or limp. He was more determined than ever to move the session to the Mariinsky Palace.

Right then the summoned Khabalov arrived.

The dictator made a painful impression, all in shadows, the skin on his face in folds. His large general's jaw trembled during the discussion, and so did his large hands, and his voice was hesitant. He didn't try to explain why all this had begun, how it had come about, what had happened in which districts—or what could be expected as the day progressed. But they didn't question him very hard, either, and Prince Golitsyn only rebuked him.

Soon after, Khabalov left, too, promising to send a guard immediately.

But then the rumor came in that a crowd was moving down Panteleimonovskaya.

So they decided unanimously to disperse immediately, one by one, and after three o'clock to assemble in the Mariinsky Palace.

Obviously, it was safer for the ministers to move about singly.

Seeing how badly off Khabalov was, Prince Golitsyn asked dark-eyed, doleful, huddled little Belyaev, although he himself was made of papier-mâché, to go to the city governor's offices and see with his own eyes what was what.

[9 8]

On Sunday, everything died down to such a degree that on Monday morning the women students gathered at the Bestuzhev Courses. After all, everyone had to see everyone and exchange news and decide something!

The first two-hour lecture went almost calmly, but by the end of it the lecture hall doors were being flung open and the fiery news was being shouted out from the corridors. The young women started running out and slamming doors, and the lectures fell apart.

Veronya and Fanechka felt guilty for being late and not taking part today. They'd decided to abandon their classes, run off, and agitate! They each got a large loaf of bread (since Saturday the City Duma had set up the sale of bread to women students in the classroom building), took one to Fanya's old folks, dropped it off, and brought one to the aunts, left it there so they wouldn't have to stand in line—and raced through Vasilievsky.

However, although from that side of the Neva even they could hear definite gunshots, here, on Vasilievsky, today, nothing revolutionary was happening. The pedestrians were going about their business, crowds were not gathering, and no one was looting anything or even singing songs.

The disgrace! Vasilievsky Island, which was one of the first to start smashing bakeries and demonstrating, now seemed to have fallen asleep and was not seeing crowds. Where were all those thousands of striking workers? The same lines were standing at the same bakeries, but now with time-old Russian docility.

The pedestrians? You weren't going to stop them and agitate. The young women tried to start people talking by the bread lines—the same human material. Were the striking workers sitting at home? You couldn't go around dragging them out of their apartments.

Return to class? Should the students assemble their own separate demonstration and go out? They didn't figure it out right away, but by now all the aware people had run off, and if anyone had stayed to finish listening to the lectures—they would remain to the end.

Taunt the police? But there were no police standing anywhere at solitary posts; they were only in large details or else sitting in ambush around their precincts.

Of course, you could take the easy way: under the guise of peaceable young ladies, cross the bridge, head for the center, and there merge with the general seething. (Sasha was at his Cavalry Remount Administration, which was not far from the center of events and, of course, he was losing no time, lucky man!) But their duty was to act here, where they were, on Vasilievsky Island.

The only decision left was to call out the troops—the Finland Regiment posted here and there around the island in detachments.

Both Veronya and Fanechka ran from one line of soldiers to another, where there was a barrier or a cordon near a factory, and fearlessly, taking advantage of their sex, walked right up to the lines, ignored the senior officers, and directly addressed the soldiers or the nice young ensigns—and explained that they were serving oppression and called on them to cross over to the people's side—and they also shamed the ensigns individually. Not a single officer drove them away, and no one pushed them, and the ensigns actually blushed. But the soldiers' passivity disappointed them no end. They made no reply, as if they hadn't heard or seen, but some frowned, even swore, and not at all nicely.

A great deal of time was spent on this fruitless agitation, one line being posted far from the next, Vasilievsky Island being big, and all of it being on foot. The young women ran themselves ragged and met with other similar failures—for everyone it had been in vain.

And so the day passed—without result.

But from the center they heard gunshots more and more clearly! And there was a whiff of smoke! Smoke from a fire—that was great!

They ran by Fanya's folks' place to have a bite to eat and get the news over the telephone. Raisa Isakovna had not budged from the telephone. There was real **revolution** in the city! That word could now be spoken!

The young women decided that since green wood won't light, they'd had enough. They'd fulfilled their duty and could head for the city and join in.

On the Palace Bridge they were already known as agitators and might not be let through. They crossed by the Nikolaevsky.

[9 9]

Staff Captain Sergei Nekrasov of the Moscow Life Guards Regiment, holder of the St. George for the Battle of Tarnavka, was now serving as adjutant in a reserve battalion. Up until this morning he had believed that all these upheavals were demands for bread, and as soon as they baked enough things would calm down. Even at the telephone since morning, receiving alarming reports from the center, he still couldn't believe how serious the situation was. He understood the shooting on Sampsonievsky and Lesnoi as a scare tactic, an attempt to make people see reason.

But none of the senior officers in the battalion had remained. Captain Dubrova had reluctantly taken command of the battalion. At the officers' club were the two Nekrasov brothers and a few ensigns who had not been detailed anywhere due to their inexperience. Also drawn to the club were the soldiers, about thirty of them, who trickled in one by one to the barracks from patrols routed and scattered in various places, who came here out of loyalty. These were the best soldiers, the old-timers.

The doctor and orderly were bandaging the first wounded.

But when Sergei Nekrasov saw out the window of the officers' club, across the parade ground, four officers fire back at the crowd, and then run—and Shabunin collapse—he instantly realized that this was a major and genuine revolt.

With frontline speed, linked ideas ran through his head: they had to fire immediately, out the windows, and win back the regimental parade ground! Summon every able man here! But they couldn't fire from the club itself. His fellows in the regiment would never forgive him the reciprocal devastation. On the other hand, they could fire from their adjutant apartment, above the club, upstairs.

He wouldn't have had time to arrange this if the crowd hadn't hesitated and stood there after the murder of the first officer.

Nekrasov made his appeal—and about twenty officers and soldiers rushed after him—circled around to the other entryway and up the stairs to the second floor. There turned out to be even more of them than needed. There were only five windows looking out on the parade ground from the adjutant apartment, and no more than three could fire from each window. Given the excess of people, one-legged Captain Vsevolod Nekrasov stood guard at the entryway, on the Sampsonievsky side.

They smashed out the lower window panes with their bayonets and started firing on the crowd from a kneeling position.

From here they could see a dense gathering from the Lesnoi gates all the way to the arsenal, where the crowd had killed a guard and looted the weapons depot. At the sudden coordinated firing from Nekrasov's party, the crowd started falling back, some back to the gates onto Lesnoi Prospect and some to the side, behind the woodpile and arsenal.

Thus they stopped the intruders.

However, the shooters had also been discovered; the rebels opened fire, as they had quite a few rifles—and a few minutes later all the windows had been smashed out, and the defenders had been sprinkled with shards and plaster dust from the back wall, which was brick and battered by bullets.

One here was wounded; later, another as well.

A few minutes later they suddenly saw a crowd of their own unarmed soldiers run out of the barracks on the left, from the 3rd Company—and dash across the parade ground on the diagonal to join the outside crowd. The stormy, unreliable 3rd Company had exploded at the battle they were seeing.

Stop them! Or else it's the end of the Moscow Regiment!

Fire at their own soldiers . . .

After losing a few fallen, the others hesitated, turned around, and ran back to their barracks.

In the somber, frosty day they could see there, past the woodpiles, past the shelters, the crowd outside: black figures and a certain number of soldiers milling about (sometimes you could see their heads over the woodpiles, but no one fired at them), maybe conferring, preparing.

Then they came running on the attack.

But the coordinated fire of Nekrasov's party sent them surging back.

This was repeated a few times—and each time they were beaten back.

During the lulls, the regimental medics picked the wounded up off the parade ground and carried away Shabunin as well.

Both he and Verigo were mortally wounded. They lay dying in the infirmary.

And so the intruders seemed to have been stopped and were kept off the parade ground. The remaining loyal soldiers covered the Sampsonievsky iron gates.

But the service entrances were left uncovered by fire—and little by little the crowd outside sneaked into the closest barracks, and the soldiers from the 3rd Company sneaked out to join the workers.

A few times, at long intervals, the mutineers renewed their heavy fire at the windows. There was a hellish lot of them, and the Nekrasov party numbered all of fifteen. It was getting harder and harder to put up a defense.

Then again, things quieted down again.

A protracted defense was becoming hopeless. But as long as they had the forces and the ammunition, they had to hold on.

A rumor reached them that the crowd of rebels was leaving but had promised to return with weapons in order to dislodge them with grapeshot.

In fact, the crowd didn't leave but rather converged behind the shelters.

Then his brother Vsevolod came and said that Captain Yakovlev had returned to the battalion and ordered all fire halted.

They conveyed the scene as well. Upon Yakovlev's return, Captain Dubrova had handed over the battalion to him, but he himself was almost paralyzed and fell on a chair, having lost control over his arms and legs, and he was propped up and carried to the pediatric hospital next to the barracks. This was his contusion at Tarnavka.

Sergei Nekrasov could not accept the order to cease fire from Yakovlev, an administrative captain! He had been trained to fight even when all was lost—unto death. At the Battle of Tarnavka, their Moscow Regiment, having taken forty-two weapons from the Germans (they marched in files for four versts under artillery fire over open ground), entrenched itself with a trench ring and for two full days held its spoils against the advancing corps until relief arrived.

Staff Captain Nekrasov did not accept that a defense could be abandoned while there was still the strength to hold it. They had not ended the battle, so why would they admit defeat?

He himself would have liked to understand what was happening in the city. But there was nowhere to find that out. As they told him, the regimental telephone, which had rung constantly since early morning, had now been turned or cut off.

At that point Nekrasov realized there was still one telephone—at the former regimental commander's, General Mikhelson's, in the same building, off the other staircase. He left observers in the demolished, disfigured, trampled, and freezing apartment and sent the rest to the club to warm up, while he and his brother went to see the general.

The general had also had windows smashed out in two places, and now they were stuffed with rags, and he and his wife had dressed and prepared in the event of evacuation. Yes, his telephone was working, and he was constantly calling military men he knew in different parts of the city. Everywhere in Petrograd was even worse than here. Nowhere had a single seat of resistance formed that they might join. In the center no one was resisting the uprising at all.

No one? Not at all? This was incomprehensible!

The old general advised the two brother captains to cease fire here, too. They shouldn't exacerbate relations with the soldiers.

This was terrible! Tomorrow or the day after, troops would arrive from the front. They would easily put down this Petrograd revolt. But what would the battalion of the Moscow Regiment say? How would it wash away this stain?

The officers' club preserved by the brothers spread from room to room in dignity, monumentalness, and even luxury: the gunfire had been diverted to the second floor and to the side, and nothing had been damaged here. Everything was intact! The crystal chandeliers, the double-window-row hall of columns, the portraits of Emperors, the portraits of all the former commanders of the Moscow Regiment on the billiards room walls, the library, and the regimental museum, all the windows, drapes, and carpets, the dining room, the regimental silver, and the furniture.

Only the servants had fled at the gunfire and the officers had not been fed.

And a few dozen loyal, bashful soldiers were sitting, unusually, on officer territory.

Surrendering was out of the question in this brick fortress!

But they could not expect relief from anywhere.

Or to fend off the attack on the officers' club after dark.

Actually, for now there was no shooting and no one was attacking anymore.

The war was unreal, too.

Paunchy, corpulent Captain Yakovlev, his face red as a poppy, had gathered all the officers present in the library. They stood there.

Yakovlev announced:

"Gentlemen, resistance is futile. We cannot fire on our own soldiers. All the reserve Guards battalions in the city have rebelled. The city is in rebel hands. Only the Grenadier Life Guards have not been touched by mutiny. For now the way to the Petersburg side is open, and anyone who wishes to may go there. You are free to leave. Anyone who has family here in the annex, take them away quickly, while the way is free."

Some officers stood there in tears. After the rebellion would there be demotions? A court-martial? The shame, the shame, the shame. . . .

Only the word "revolution" had not yet occurred to anyone.

[1 0 0]

They had barely run across the Liteiny Bridge and joined the Moscow Regiment men and the Vyborg worker crowd—when many throats began to shout: "Let's go rescue Kresty! Kresty!"

Kresty? Kirpichnikov had heard of it before. The famous prison where they held politicals. Oh well, he'd taken a liking to liberating prisons, so why not go there?

Whether he did or didn't go or agree—nothing depended on him anymore. The crowd was already rolling along with God knows who at its head. They obeyed whoever they heard or wanted. But some of the crowd went another way. Not only was Kirpichnikov not the marshal, he was recognized by only a few Volynians, the ones crowding nearby, and some of the Lithuanian and Preobrazhensky men who had noted him back in the yard.

This second prison was taken easy as pie; they'd now learned how. No need to fight or break down doors. They shouted threats, promised to blow it up, and fired in the air, each man had all his pockets stuffed with cartridges, and besides rifles some also had Brownings, officer trinkets, which were child's play to fire.

Besides the prison guard at Kresty there was also a small detail of the Moscow men who made no attempt to fight but simply traded places: ours walked in and they walked out.

The warders held out the bunches of keys, just so no one touched them. Were they really guilty? Like our brother, we have no choice; we all serve. Well then, go around to all the floors and open all the doors!

You should have seen the prisoners' joy when the door was opened wide, out of the blue, and—Come out, they said, you're free! Completely! Right now! Some were dumbstruck, others gasped, still others dashed to grab their few belongings fast and run out before anyone changed his mind about asking them. The rest—shaven, convicts probably—danced a dance and let rip a string of obscenities the likes of which you'd never heard.

Some wearing prison robes and shoes, some wearing their own things, empty-handed or carrying bundles—they filed out, ran out into the freezing cold.

But time presses us, too: we had to go on freeing more and more, so they couldn't stuff them back in anymore. Herein lay the salvation of the first to rise up: free as many of the people as possible!

And then—hey, even more prisons! Look! The Women's is nearby! Look! The Military! People ran there, too.

No, Kirpichnikov thought, prisons aren't going to make you stronger. And there's no point running from factory to factory; they don't need us to be free. But we do need to tear away our brother soldier, the Moscow Battalion. After all, that's what they'd been intending. Why did they get sidetracked to this prison? They'd just added a detour. But power is soldiers, and that's where we need to hurry! Where did Kruglov get to with the truck and machine guns?

There are fewer and fewer of us. When did we lose Markov? Didn't notice. And Orlov. Vakhov was still on hand—the fellow wasn't too quick in service, but he was loyal.

On the streets there were many crowds, artisans, ordinary residents, and various soldiers helter skelter, not a single party in formation, and ours more like a gang. You weren't going to line up anyone; to a sergeant's trained heart, it was actually frustrating.

They asked questions about the Moscow men. No, not yet, they were holding out locked in.

Not everyone wanted to go. Where are we wandering off? We've been on guard duty for four days, and our feet won't drag us. Right then, too, a cart drove by with cases of bread, so lots of people ran after the cart.

Many others turned toward the Liteiny Bridge: Back to the barracks! Enough!

But you weren't going to save yourself by going back. A rumor had gone around that there, on Liteiny Prospect, our men were already being crushed. He had a sinking feeling. Would this end well? Have we started something that's beyond us? Oh, we're done for—and all for naught!

But there were still about fifty men left, to go after the Moscow men. So they moved down Sampsonievsky. A cluster, quite random, Kirpichnikov knew no one, only his Vakhov was by his side and also a few men from the training detachment, and they were Volynians, but not ones he knew.

It was actually painful. That morning Kirpichnikov had been their undisputed leader. He wouldn't have started—no one would have—and the first step had been overwhelming. And now whether Kirpichnikov was leading this gang or it was proceeding on its own now, there was no telling.

There were plenty of civilians, workers, on Sampsonievsky, and others with rifles already—they'd provided for themselves!—but no soldiers in sight. That meant the Moscow men were still behind locked doors. They'd called these workers to join them—and some had gone and some hadn't.

He'd run out of steam.

All the victories today had been won without a fight. The only serious defense past the Liteiny Bridge hadn't had time to open fire. And so they were proceeding now in the hope they wouldn't shoot—but right then he heard serious shooting. Four hundred paces or so before the regimental gates, where narrow Sampsonievsky widened, all the men stopped—both the soldiers and the civilians with their thready songs—and refused to go any farther.

A few even stepped away and started back.

The shooting was fierce and coming from different places, but Kirpichnikov determined that it was on the other side of the large brick building, and bullets weren't flying this way. That building behind the iron fence enclosed the regimental yard.

Kirpichnikov called to his fellow soldiers:

"Let's go! Let's go! Don't lose heart! Let's take them from the rear right now!"

Some fresh young boy shouted:

"Whoever holds freedom dear, forward!"

Twenty or so men went forward, but the rest didn't budge.

They went but pressed close to the walls and fences or fell behind the snow piles. These fresh soldiers had never been shot at.

"They're not shooting here!" Kirpichnikov told them. "Quick! To the gates!"

They didn't believe him. And the shooting was fierce, though over their heads.

They fled in various directions and hid. Sampsonievsky was deserted.

Kirpichnikov found himself in the snow by a fence, too. And no one to be seen nearby.

He started back to where he'd left them—but almost no one was there. Even Vakhov was gone.

The place was nothing like Kirpichnikov had ever known. It didn't even look like Petersburg. How far he had drifted.

He wasn't going to take the gates of the Moscow Battalion. He had no one.

They were shooting robustly. Who? At whom?

And where had everything scattered?

And what was happening there, in the Volynian barracks?

He wandered back along the fence. Alone.

[1 0 1]

The wheeled reserve battalion, whose barracks were at the very edge of Sampsonievsky Prospect, nearly on Lesnoi, looked nothing like Petrograd's other reserve battalions. This was no holding tank of unprepared, untrained, underage soldiers commandeered for the army and then left to languish in inactivity, but rather highly developed soldiers of fighting age and healthy combat officers. The battalion was apparently the only military unit in the capital with front-line spirit. It trained and sent motorized companies—with machine guns on motorcycle sidecars with a truck convoy—to the front. Companies like this were something new and intended for joint actions with the cavalry in the major spring offensive coming up. Exercises proceeded intensely and solidly, for ten to twelve hours a day, without a break for Sundays, so much was there to teach these eager, interested soldiers. Intently engaged in its work, the battalion barely noticed what was going on in the capital, or even the country.

Although in late February a decree from the District commander had been read out to the battalion officers about which district their battalion was supposed to ensure the protection of in the event of major disturbances in Petrograd, the officers, the majority of whom had already done a great deal of fighting and had been called back from the front, viewed this decree with both mistrust and disdain. They had no desire to perform police duties and shouldn't have to.

Nor did what was going on in the city in these early March days reflect on the battalion. It did not post sentries on city streets, everything on Lesnoi was calm, exercises were not interrupted for a day, and the fact that factory crowds were going from here to the city to raise a rumpus—that only made it quieter here.

However, on overcast Monday the 12th, frequent and scattered shooting had been heard from the city, four to five versts away, since early morning. Later it got closer and crossed to this side of the Neva, and even closer—obviously around the Moscow barracks already. But even this did not seem serious enough to drop exercises and prepare for battle when they didn't know who they would be fighting or why.

Suddenly they heard wild singing, and down Sampsonievsky, from the south, a large, disorderly, agitated crowd approached consisting of civilians and soldiers and sailors out of ranks, with red flags.

The duty officer, Lieutenant Nagursky, hoped the crowd would pass them by—but somehow it didn't. It flowed this way, toward the fence and the watch. Through their small window they could see many crude, impudent, heated faces. Nagursky had no choice but to go out to meet them. He took his sergeant-major along and went out. Behind him, out of curiosity and for support, stepped the student Yelchin, one of the volunteers.

There was no one in charge in the crowd, and no one wanted to talk separately, but several voices shouted—harshly, disrespectfully, demanding, not asking, that the soldiers from the wheeled units be immediately released, for the holiday of freedom.

Lieutenant Nagursky had fought throughout the war and had raised a company to the attack and led it to the death, and he was used to the three stars on his epaulets ensuring the obedience of the soldier mass. Right now he keenly felt a completely new correlation: his stars ensured no superiority whatsoever. He could not give this crowd any orders, not even order it to line up and look outwardly decent, or tell the soldiers to stand tall and hold their rifles uniformly. In half a minute he had fallen from what he was used to being and felt an idiotic lack of confidence, not finding even the right tone of voice for this crowd. For some reason he didn't order them to get out and not dare speak such effronteries, but in a tone of justification explained that he couldn't let the soldiers out of the barracks without permission from the battalion commander. (He immediately realized what a useless response this was. They would demand the battalion commander let them go! His resourcefulness had failed him right off.)

So he stood there, a step away from the front edge of the crowd—no, half-encircled by it already—and tried to find the more intelligible faces among the agitated ones and worthier but comprehensible words for them. Suddenly Yelchin shouted to him in alarm.

"Your honor! They've cut off your weapon!"

Nagursky looked down, and not believing his eyes felt—and there were only the ends of his straps hanging, but his dagger had been cut away and so had his holster and revolver! Nagursky nearly howled with insult and shame, as if he had been indecently undressed in front of the crowd, and frustrated that he hadn't noticed it himself. He spun his head around, searching the hands of those near him—but none of them had his weapons! They'd taken them away, stolen them, in a purely thievish manner!

Brought down even further, to the next depth, with even less dignity, he began begging, imploring—he didn't know who—to give back his weapons! His honor! Without them he . . . Who could he turn to and how? They were neither gentlemen nor brothers. . . . He started touching the greatcoated, dark-rabble chest of one and then another in front of him, trying to guess his offender or a sympathizer—and suddenly cried out from a powerful, painful blow to the temple, something sharp to the head! And he staggered.

It was one of the nearby workers, who had thrown a large bolt at him across the backs of others, knocked off his cap, and torn a gash in his temple, making him stagger. Immediately, fists came thundering down on him from all sides.

Yelchin the volunteer, without measuring or considering, rushed to save him without any weapon at all, with his hands, to drag the injured lieutenant out of the jumble as quickly as possible! But before he could do anything he was stabbed from behind and lost consciousness.

That same dagger they'd taken away from the lieutenant had been driven into his back. He collapsed face first, at the crowd's feet.

Now the sergeant-major, on the contrary, retreating, began shooting at anyone near Nagursky and Yelchin. And he saw he was hitting his mark.

Meanwhile, other soldiers came running at his shots, also shooting, in the air.

The crowd quickly retreated, leaving the wounded in the snow.

The duty company came out of the gates with their rifles atilt and drove the crowd on farther.

Nagursky and Yelchin were carried through the gates. Both were still alive.

[1 0 2]

General Khabalov could not grasp just two things. What should he do with the city of Petrograd? And what should he do with himself?

As for himself, berated by Golitsyn, perhaps something like this: prop his head on both hands over a colored map of the city and examine it continuously. This concentrated activity may not have led him out of his impasse, but it did help him slowly figure something out.

On this excellent map, which indicated all the city's tiny streets, and especially each police station, and the location of each reserve battalion, all sixteen districts of the military guard were colored with different colored pencils, and now it was distinctly clear that the military uprising had been able to take place in the eighth district specifically because it was supposed to be protected by the Volynian Battalion, which was the one that had mutinied.

Then, it could not have been envisioned that military units would have to remain so long in their details, far from their barracks—and complaints were now coming in from various locations that the troops had not been fed since yesterday.

The ammunition situation was very bad. The depots on the Vyborg side were already in the rebels' hands, and they couldn't get through to the others.

Khabalov began telephoning energetically. None of his Guards battalions turned out to have any ammunition in reserve. He telephoned Kronstadt to send ammunition, and preferably troops as well. But the Kronstadt commandant replied that he was worried about his own fortress and had nothing to send.

Then they telephoned to the peaceful Petersburg side, to the Pavlovsky and Vladimirsky military schools. These did have ammunition reserves, but how could they be sent to the active battalions? After all, the cartridges might fall into rebel hands en route! Indeed. They rejected this scheme.

The 1st Infantry should have had a lot—but there was no way to get to the Okhta.

What about shells? Two artillery batteries had moved up closer to HQ, but they only had eight. The shells, too, were on the Vyborg side and even farther away, at the Kushelevka station.

If you thought about it, what good were shells in urban upheavals? Where would you fire one in a city?

Why on earth had Kutepov's detachment not pushed the rebels toward the Neva as they'd been ordered? Khabalov found the failure of Kutepov's detachment particularly depressing.

One thing gave him hope, that apparently some kind of reserve was going to gather on Palace Square. They'd been promised. First, two Preobrazhensky companies. And one company of Guards riflemen. And also one Kexholm company. It turned out now, as he kept trying to get through, that apparently the Izmailovsky and Jägers might be able to send some, too. And also, in reserve, an Oranienbaum machine-gun half-company, although it was not prepared to shoot. And also two batteries, still and all, though without shells, but they would intimidate.

No, Khabalov was assembling quite decent forces. If only they hadn't refused to obey orders. There was no confidence they would obey.

But the unreliable Pavlovsky Battalion could be left alone. Let it sit in barracks.

However, there was also a report that the officers of the Izmailovsky Battalion were inclined to enter into an agreement with Rodzyanko. And why not? That might not be a bad idea and the best, bloodshed-free solution.

Right then General Belyaev, darkened, small, and angry, arrived at the city governor's offices. Khabalov and Tyazhelnikov, following procedure, gave him all the reports on what was going on and showed him on the map. Belyaev began giving instructions, but in general terms, without naming districts or streets, just "pacify, suppress, and establish order," so that there was no way to tell what exactly should be done. And what about the detachment on Palace Square?

Actually, the War Minister immediately announced that he was appointing General Zankevich to command all the troops in Petrograd, that is, the head of the General Staff, the most senior of the generals at the minister's disposal.

He announced this and even summoned Zankevich here, to HQ—and sent Khabalov's thoughts flying. In what sense had Zankevich been appointed commander of all troops? In the sense of command of the Guard, to replace Pavlenko, who had fallen ill? Or in the sense of overall command of District troops? And Khabalov, was he to remain in his post or had he been replaced? It had not been clearly stated, and Khabalov did not feel altogether comfortable asking. Zankevich and the General Staff, yes, they reported to the War Minister, but the District did not. Khabalov had been appointed by the Emperor himself and was responsible to GHQ.

He was so tired, so weighed down by all that was happening, that he would willingly have gone into reserve right now. But he had not been told to leave his post, and the War Minister could not dismiss him.

That the troops were being given to Zankevich—that was much easier.

Khabalov made bold to convey to Belyaev the sensible thought that had been conveyed to him by the Izmailovsky men. Shouldn't we enter into relations with the President of the State Duma?

Small, almost bald Belyaev gave him an acutely guarded look through his pince-nez but said nothing, and there was no way to understand him.

While the generals were busy among themselves, it turned out that Grand Duke Kirill Vladimirovich had arrived at the city governor's offices and Balk had received him. The grand duke took a seat in an armchair by the main table and reproached the city governor for systematically failing to report to him—and demanded a detailed report on the situation.

All the ten or fifteen grand dukes always hovered like supernumerary generals of some vague high position.

The city governor reported as he understood that matters were quite terrible and he thought that by night the entire capital would be in the rebels' hands.

Slender Kirill Vladimirovich, clean-shaven with just a fluffy mustache and a smooth neck and face, and small, demanding eyes, questioned him as someone with power.

What about the Cossacks?

No, we're not bringing them out. Unreliable.

The grand duke almost shut his eyes. He leaned his head back. And almost groaned:

"Yes. . . . All the grand dukes had asked *him* for a constitution, but he wouldn't hear of it."

He learned that Belyaev was here and went in to see him. And advised him on how to save the state: remove Protopopov immediately.

To Khabalov he expressed his displeasure. Why was he not reporting on the military situation?

Khabalov murmured to the grand duke as best he could about the actions taking place. (If only he himself could understand them!)

The grand duke asked what he should do with his Guards crew.

Khabalov summoned his courage. If His Imperial Majesty was certain the crew would act against the rebels, then let it join the reserves by the Winter Palace. But if they stated they would not fire *against their own*, then better they remain in barracks.

The grand duke worked his lips and frowned. No, vouch for the entire crew—that he couldn't do. But he would send a more reliable training detachment.

[1 0 3]

Although three leftist speakers had announced encouragement for the uprising from the front steps, in the name of the Duma, that was hardly the mood inside the palace. It was just that almost no one—neither the center nor the Kadets (the extreme rightists had already made themselves scarce)—approved of this uprising. So far they'd been spared; a crowd 30,000-strong had not come to rout them. But it could at any minute.

There was also a rumor that government troops were breaking through from Liteiny Prospect onto Kirochnaya. And they would not have a pat on the back either for the Duma, which had been required to disperse but hadn't and had also allowed irresponsible statements from the front steps.

A few deputies displayed great impatience. The independent and impetuous Cossack Karaulov, in the spirit of proud liberty, loudly demanded opening a formal session of the Duma, submitting to no dissolution whatsoever. The nervous progressive Bublikov, who before this had been little noticed but was now enflamed, with a seething gaze and a pointy black mustache, dashing from group to group, also suggested:

"You're afraid of responsibility, gentlemen? But by this boundless obedience you are irrevocably forfeiting your dignity! You must throw down a challenge to the imperial government!"

Kerensky, cloaking himself in extraordinary new rights, called on the duty officers to sound the electric bell calling the deputies to the hall of sessions. But the officers did not obey him.

Now Rodzyanko had appeared in the Ekaterininsky Hall, his large head towering over the deputies. In his stentorian voice he invited all the Duma members to the Semi-Circular Hall, for a private meeting.

This was a relatively small hall, behind the main session hall, in a semi-circular part of the palace that jutted into the park, where auxiliary meetings were held and where the entire Duma could not fit; there wasn't even room for the three hundred or so present, and many had to stand.

This good idea had been suggested to Rodzyanko in the last moment of his slow deliberations. Defying the Supreme will and illegally assembling the dissolved Duma for a session he did not dare do. He had sworn an oath and he was a loyal subject. But what prevented the deputies, since the rooms had not been locked, from assembling for a *private* meeting, a meeting of private individuals, demonstratively bypassing the main hall? (Not assembling at all was impossible; everyone demanded and expected this.)

Here they were pouring into the Semi-Circular. Here they were convening, like men who had suffered ruin, who had lost their own permanent places, pushed out, driven together. How expansive and firm they had felt for years, here, in the next room, in this very building, and now they themselves could not recognize either the building or themselves. They didn't even have the strength or time to rage at the government. Taken unawares, they were listening closely to some apparently new sound, like the rustling of a great landslide just beginning, to something not even the ear could take in, something too ominous for the ear, something explainable only in the chest.

The entire council of elders was now seated at the table, so as not to offend any faction—although was there a single one of them who knew what to do?

Actually, Kerensky apparently did. Had he, by some innate sense, suddenly begun to understand the meaning of events? He had begun acting imperiously. Here he'd just come and sat down at the presidium table, perfectly erect—somehow the narrow erectness of his head was especially remarkable—and suddenly an inner voice told him something no one else could hear, and at that summons, he stood up with complete certainty and quickly walked out with utter certainty, not explaining anything to anyone. Even that shadow flitting by said that after all their session was not as important as what he was going to do there now, exiting.

But Rodzyanko, who seemingly had already lifted Russia's full burden so many times in the Duma—here was when he lifted it for the first time, here was when he truly felt its weight. Previously, all the weight had been in how to balance between the Duma majority and the Supreme authority enough so as to satisfy the former and not anger the latter too much. Previously the entire weight had been to measure out his expressions, but today, in total obscurity and ignorance, in the unprecedented absence of both the Duma and the government, the President had had before the others to discern and do something, but he was not capable of that.

What could he tell his Duma members? That the government was not showing the slightest signs of action, as if it did not exist at all, although delaying the revolt's suppression was impermissible. That he personally had done everything humanly possible, had sent telegrams to the Emperor and the commanders-in-chief both, and still there had been no response from His Majesty. Now, given the obscurity of the correlation of forces, the Duma had no basis for expressing itself definitively.

The Duma members were not encouraged. They huddled. Indeed, the situation was like a rebus.

Rodzyanko's deputy, the leftist Kadet Nekrasov, suggested that all power should immediately be handed over to a strong general whom the Duma trusted, immediately go to the government and force it to appoint such a general.

However, not only did he not embolden his colleagues, he dragged them down still further. Was it because it was a leftist who had asked for a general, and so what deep trouble they were all in?

First no one undertook to speak, and then several asked for the floor at once. Also to ask for a military dictatorship. No! But to elect from among themselves an organ for direct consultations with the rebellious army and the rebellious people! (But what if before they could do that the street burst in here?) And of course, the importunate Chkheidze today, as always, maligned the Duma for its bourgeois cowardice, perhaps more condescendingly than usual, for he was already overcome with joy at events.

But Kerensky was still gone. He was rushing around somewhere, finding out something important, correcting or averting something. Here the vigilant Karaulov shot forward to speak. In November he had warned the Duma about the *fourth* path, revolution. With the perspicacity of the Terek Cossack patrols, he had always picked up on and never let go of any suspicious rustling in the distance. And he now began treating the deafened Duma members with the sharpness with which he had once regaled the government. How can this be? Where are all our daring words? For a full year we have been abusing the government as fools, scoundrels, even traitors, and now we're going to go to those same fools and ask for assistance? No! Enough blather! We have to do something ourselves! And if we can't, then we're worthy of being driven out of here!

But **what exactly** should be done, he didn't say.

Seemingly, Milyukov should have spoken before anyone else. But he kept putting it off and apparently was prepared to yield even to Duma unknowns whom no one had ever seen on the dais and for whom the time limit was never sufficient. He kept putting it off because he was waiting for some kind of clarification, for more determinacy to events. Milyukov was not inclined to fits of passion and enthusiasm; he was a man ad ratio, to make judgments he had to have clear premises, grouped and verified facts from which he could draw an indubitable resultant. (For this he had always, though not today, written down the opinions of all the speakers.) But as long as there were only vague street flickerings going on and the position of all types of power remained unclear, Milyukov, the weightiest, most respected and sensible man here, could not indicate to the Duma a positive decision. If one were to peer deep into the essence, this could also be desperately bad: an undesired revolution gotten out of hand. This was no place for showy speeches to the public and the firecracker bombs with which he had previously deafened state power. This meeting was like groping with blind hands, and it was useful at least to listen to others in order to sum up better. Now his inevitable turn to speak was coming up, and he had to maintain his authoritative look and opinion so that no one would suspect the slightest distress in him.

So here's the thing. Pavel Nikolaevich did not agree with anyone who had spoken before, and maybe not even with anyone who spoke after. Of course, it would be quite improper to ask the government for a military dictator. But it would also be inappropriate to form their own Duma committee for a dictatorship. The Duma could not take power into its own hands because, lest the gentlemen members forget, it was a legislative body and therefore could not take on executive functions. And here were the arguments from state law that could be used to validate this assertion of certainty. . . . But we could also not take power or even take any definite decisions because we didn't know the precise extent of the disturbances, or the correlation of forces among local troops, or the role of workers and public organizations in these upheavals. So the moment to create a new authority had not come, and the heated voices ringing out in the corridors to enter the White Hall and declare themselves a Constituent Assembly were nothing but a reckless incitement to chaos. The most sensible thing was to take no decisions whatsoever for now and wait it out. Wait it out.

At that moment Kerensky suddenly burst into the hall with a dramatic look continuing to grow in importance. Burst in and hastened to speak, and—something that could never happen in this Duma in normal times—they quickly ceded him the floor, as a matter of procedure, forcing out the overall leader, who, however, yielded calmly. Kerensky stepped up to speak, even trembling from an excess of knowledge, responsibility, and determination, as if in this trembling shuffling off to his listeners his burning thoughts:

"Gentlemen! I am constantly receiving more and more new information! We cannot delay for a minute! The troops are in upheaval! More and more new regiments are going out on the street! I am about to take a vehicle immediately and go from regiment to regiment! I will stop them by conviction alone! But I have to know what I am authorized to tell them. Can I say that the State Duma is unconditionally on their side? That it is standing at the head of the movement now under way?"

He was trembling with half-closed eyes, practically swaying from his own words; then he opened his eyelids wide and hurled sheaves of fire. How many years had he moved among them—a minor lawyer, a haughty, machine-gun speaker—and they hadn't known him, hadn't understood what had turned out to be his talent as a commander, his strength and even imperiousness.

Now this popped out, cut through—and astonished. No one objected to why *he* specifically should go to the regiments.

However, he was asking too much of this Duma! He wanted to draw the parliament out to head up the street and the storming crowd that was freeing criminals?

The meeting faltered. They could find no form for suddenly authorizing Kerensky to jump into a vehicle and race from regiment to regiment.

Milyukov, insulted by the neglect, once again stepped in and contemptuously declined Kerensky's suggestion: a trip like that would convince no one and calm nothing. The right thing was to wait it out, gather more new information, and only then take decisions.

The debates, nearly derailed, apparently could flow normally again and for a long time, and Milyukov apparently was supposed to conclude his speech, although Kerensky physically could no longer bear to keep standing and sitting—and not moving. It's unimaginable how he would have coped with himself if at that moment the head of Duma security hadn't run in with a shout, disheveled and with one torn epaulet. Instead of protecting them all, he himself was asking for protection, saying they had nearly killed him! He was shouting that the impossible was happening at the front doors. They wanted to break in, someone had been injured, and they were asking him whether he was for or against the people.

The honorable assembly was singed: They want to break in—break in here? Straight to them? There was nothing to protect them, not even deputy immunity? **They want to come in**—that was a terrible statement.

But—like someone pulled out of this swamp by a newfound practical application—Kerensky fluttered up and dashed off without even a backward glance at the president.

By now everyone believed that their Kerensky knew what to do, their Kerensky would fix it! This calmed them a little but didn't lift their great alarm. What were they to do? What should they decide? It seemed there was no time left. It seemed they were struck like this for the first time!

Under the knout of the advancing, storming crowd, the debates took on a different character. Milyukov's rational suggestion to wait no longer enjoyed any success. The impetuous Kadet Adzhemov spoke out stormily against his party leader, that they could not put this off, that the Duma was itself a force and should act worthily. Some centrist argued that first they needed to learn the crowd's intentions. Were they coming to continue the State Duma's sacred work or were they simply storming them in favor of the Germans? In the former case, they were the People; in the latter, rabble. Someone else had doubts. How could the Duma be adapted to wielding any kind of authority?

A gloomy, alarmed, and far from formal Rodzyanko asked them not at all loudly, between speakers, to speed up the discussion. (He himself could not take a decision, and this session was preventing him from thinking.)

Finally, they decided — if it can be called a decision — they decided without a vote but simply by converging in the middle, to form Duma members into a committee but not invest this committee with any authority in advance and wait and see how events unfolded. However, not being the full Duma, they could not vote and elect, so the council of elders should comprise this committee.

In any event, no one was to leave Petrograd! This was everyone's clear desire for everyone else, that they not leave those remaining in the minority to untangle all this.

At this the meeting broke up for the time being, and the members promised each other not to leave the Tauride Palace. (Someone did slip away, though.)

The council of elders exited single file to convene in Rodzyanko's office.

Meanwhile, outside, Kerensky (once again fearlessly not dressed for the cold) handled the situation beautifully. The Volynians posted by him were no longer guarding the palace, and they themselves were nowhere to be found, there was no sentry left, and some rough mugs were starting to slip into the palace. But right then, a fat, energetic face presenting himself to Kerensky as Preobrazhensky Sergeant Kruglov announced that he had come with a party from the 4th Company after taking the barracks of the Moscow Regiment and offered to take over all the Tauride Palace watches.

Up until now men had been arriving ragtag. This was the first organized party, and the sergeant was clearly one of those who would not spare his own father for the revolution. His eyes looked out quite decisively and harshly over his prominent cheekbones and determined jaw. Men like this should not be given over to spontaneity but put into service — Kerensky understood this instantly — and then and there ringingly put him in charge of all the Tauride Palace watches.

Kruglov immediately posted four men on the front steps and with the others went to occupy the Duma telegraph office.

At that moment Kerensky was pierced by a thought that he himself could not even understand. Had he guessed? Or had the rumor been transformed in him that somewhere certain ministers were being arrested? He was pierced by the thought that the moment had come to arrest powerful enemies who might interfere with the course of explosive events. That was what they did during the French Revolution! Should he look for someone? Suggest something? Send someone?

But before he could think this through and find or send anyone, four workers with rifles and four soldiers led toward him two unarmed and frightened young ensigns. It turned out that across from the Tauride Palace, by the Main Waterworks, it was their watch that the arriving mutinous crowd had demanded removed. But the ensigns had not complied and had resisted surrendering their weapons — and here they'd been brought in like criminals for execution.

With the same avidity and grasp with which Kerensky was entering into his revolutionary role, which had been prepared for him his whole life, written for him his whole life, he drew himself up even straighter and taller, extended his commanding arm down from the front steps, and even leaning back at the beauty of the moment, announced:

"Gentlemen ensigns! I understand you! However, in view of the events we are witnessing, I order you to remove the watch in accordance with the workers' demand!"

The particularity of the revolutionary moment is that one doesn't have to try to encompass every aspect of an issue but should seize upon the most striking! Not surrender to doubts that the city water supply is in need of protection even now, but burst ahead to meet the demands of the agitated workers. In the revolutionary moment, he wins and rises above who decides instantly and strikingly!

In two voices, close to tears, the youths complained that they would be executed under the law for removing the watch.

At this the commanding hand turned into a sparing hand, and the triumph of the decree turned into the triumph of forgiveness:

"I, State Duma Deputy Kerensky, personally take responsibility for this order. I guarantee your immunity"—there was a shudder near his Adam's apple—"with my own life!"

The ensigns lost their resolve—and conceded.

And Kerensky immediately forgot all about them.

[104]

The Preobrazhensky Regiment was known to all as the Russian army's *premier* regiment. This had been Peter's favorite regiment—and its march had been heard back under Petrine ears. This regiment had elevated Elizabeth to the throne. From reign to reign it had been premier, the hope of the dynasty, and it was no coincidence that the present Emperor, as heir, had commanded a battalion of none other than the Preobrazhensky Regiment. Some of the regiment's barracks and its officers' club were even next to the Winter Palace, on Millionnaya—the only one of all the regiments in such proximity. (And an internal corridor connected their barracks to the palace.)

Although the regiment itself was now far away on the Southwest front, where it was suffering cruel losses, the officers of the reserve battalion, who had gathered now in this most proximate officers' club, some having ended up here after being wounded, but many—from the Petersburg public who had avoided previous mobilizations and now using their pull—also felt like true Preobrazhensky men, happy to shoulder all this long glory.

But yesterday, it was their Preobrazhensky detachment that had arrested the mutinous Pavlovsky soldiers, and now the Preobrazhensky officers were ashamed.

These last few months the atmosphere in their club had been quite free, and officers had met there who detested the Empress and sympathized with the Duma and reforms. Like many in the Petersburg Guards, they had welcomed the news of Rasputin's murder with champagne. Today they had expressed without the least diffidence their sympathy for the popular movement. After all, the people were asking for bread. How could they oppose them? They had no wish to stain their own reputation and the Preobrazhensky's by being lumped with the suppressors. If the regiment was premier in Russia, then all the more reason it should be on a level with civic consciousness. The government was made up of ghosts.

On 12 March, all officers free from details had had breakfast in the club on Millionnaya, and now no one had left, sensing the unusual sweep of events. The battalion commander, Argutinsky-Dolgorukov, was not there—not that anyone took him seriously—and the battalion adjutant, Lieutenant Maksheev, was informed of all dispatches and shared them willingly. Today he himself had been the first to receive the news that two of their companies, one having a noncombat role, had mutinied in the barracks on Kirochnaya, and he himself had had to make efforts to summon Colonel Kutepov, assigning him to Khabalov's disposal, to put this down. Maksheev did all this, but against his own conscience and convictions. Colonel Kutepov's convictions had already been revealed here, in the club, and they were the views of a blind old-timer.

An unusual situation had come about. Somewhere in the center of the rebellion, one Preobrazhensky unit was seething. Another, with Kutepov, was on its way to put them down. Meanwhile, the majority of the battalion's officers were sitting here, having no other orders, and were in a way neutral, even those who, shaken, had come from the barracks of the mutinous companies, or else had not been there yet and now could not go there. They were sitting in the room next to the billiards room and to the muffled click of balls were discussing with vehemence what they should do. They could not sit idle. The thirst to be useful to society did not contradict their thirst to carry on the glory of their regiment.

They had to and did understand that today's storming and shooting in the streets, probably, was not a crude revolt, but an unconscious pull toward justice and light, and the rays of light were coming from the State Duma. How could they exploit this impulse and create a responsible administration made up of Duma members? They wondered why the military authorities didn't simply reach an agreement with Rodzyanko—and the whole horrible conflict would end immediately. They needed to help unlimited autocratic power make the shift to constitutional power. But how?

A picture drew itself: after all, this was the same as the Decembrists' objective! Again—the Decembrists. Their objective had not been met to this day.

Like their forefathers the Decembrists—who had led soldier parties onto the square and demanded freedom—was that what they should do now?

404 \ THE RED WHEEL

But how?

Right then, all of a sudden, Lieutenant Maksheev, the most vehement speaker among them, was called to the telephone and given an order from District HQ to bring out all available remaining Preobrazhensky forces onto Palace Square fully armed to form the command's reserve. Further instructions would be issued later.

But they didn't need further instructions! Oh, what luck! They were being led out on the square by order of the command. Here it was, the decision, and here it was, the opportunity! They were acting on orders, perfectly legitimately—but the officers knew they were going to win freedom! Perhaps today the great day would come for Russia, and perhaps the dream of generations would or would not come true—before their very eyes.

Two companies constituted the available forces. They passed out cartridges and filled their pouches.

They came out with a large complement of officers, more than there needed to be: many wanted to participate.

The thought came straightaway: We are too few! What is this—two companies? We should have assembled all the battalions of the 1st Guards Division—the Semyonovsky! The Izmailovsky! The Jägers! A detachment like that then might not even have to act. By its mere presence it might achieve the State Duma's demands.

But how were they to inform the others?

A private motorcar was just passing down Millionnaya. The young officers stopped it. It turned out to be a stockbroker. They immediately put him out and commandeered his vehicle. Three of them got in and dashed off, to those three battalions.

A fine start!

Since this morning the Petersburg gloom had lasted many hours, even with a bit of fog. And after noon it was still overcast, but the sun shone through more clearly.

The huge, familiar square between the decorous Winter Palace and the broad sweep of the General Staff was deserted and could have held the entire Petersburg Guards, now dispersed to the different fronts, or today's entire untrained, maladroit Petersburg garrison. Nearly the entire square was covered by intact snow, sliced in only a few directions by sleigh and automobile wheels, and cleared at the edge, along the sidewalks.

With their synchronized soldier boots, the Preobrazhensky column flattened the snow across the untrodden expanse, to the right of the Aleksandr Column, closer to the Winter Palace.

And halted facing the angel on the column, their backs to the Winter Palace.

Right then they noticed that following them, from the east, was what looked like thinned smoke from a distant fire. A far-off, unusual, continuous noise reached them, often interrupted by rifle fire.

Thrilling music! In the huge capital, somewhere, something was already being done—and the Preobrazhensky's preliminary inaction on this expansive deserted square, before the many-eyed but dead General Staff, had become a solemn act! Here they had listened, here they had looked, here they had prepared and resolved! Russia's great historic moment was palpable! A profoundly exceptional moment in the life of the regiment as well.

This mood held them for a long time. The command was given—At ease!—and the officers paced in front of and behind the formation and spoke among themselves. The solemn square itself called for maneuvers, marches, some insane deed. But they had to wait and somehow sort out what was going on.

The mood kept intensifying like the visible struggle between the sun and clouds. With Victory pulled by six horses, right above the arch on the other side, facing this way.

Nothing had been explained to the soldiers, nor was there any call to do so prematurely, so their enthusiasm wouldn't then wane. The very form of the summons to the soldiers had been difficult and awkward; it had gone beyond the bounds of the military command, and no one had experience of this sort.

The soldiers stamped their feet, smoked, and talked among themselves; they, too, understood somehow why they were standing here and also that noise and smoke from the left—but how?

There was also a danger of *standing there too long*. The Decembrists lost everything by standing there much too long.

Rosenschild reminded the officers that on *that* December day, on Palace Square, troops also gathered—but troops loyal to Nikolai.

So that their standing there, especially under Khabalov's order, was shot through with significant ambiguity.

Palace Square could also become Senate Square. They had only to gather the forces and draw together.

It was strange that Khabalov was not sending any more instructions of any kind either.

The two companies standing idle in the middle of the deserted, snowy square attracted attention, naturally, and behind their backs, on the sidewalk by the Winter Palace, the curious began gathering, including a few colonels and old generals. They aspired to giving advice. An inspector general from the reserve troops pointed out to the officers that their battalion could not represent the true Preobrazhensky Regiment. That would be an impertinence.

But another general expressed the opinion that they should go on the attack against the Tauride Palace because the hydra's head was there. But from the awkward silence he realized he had missed the mark, and he gradually retreated.

The officers' mood did not lift. Less and less did they themselves understand why they were standing there and for so long.

Although the sun did finally break through and triumphantly set the square's untouched snow to sparkling, and the Admiralty Spire so nearby did turn to gold, as did, farther off, St. Isaac's imposing cupola, none of this looked like spring, or breathed warmth; instead, the typical frost of a brief winter afternoon took hold.

It took hold of toes in boots. And hands, if they'd been holding a rifle the whole time, even if in a glove.

The soldiers stamped their feet, tapped one leg against the other, and shifted rifles from hand to hand.

Captain Skripitsyn proposed going to Khabalov's headquarters, to the city governor's offices, for intelligence, since there was just a half-square and Nevsky to cross to get to it.

In half an hour he was back. He told them that HQ was amazingly disorderly and distraught, starting with the fact that anyone who wanted to was free to enter and no one was checking. The police generals looked terrified, and Khabalov was a lump of dough. Skripitsyn himself had spoken with him and, without expressing the officers' intention, warned him that the soldiers' mood was such that they were unlikely to shoot, even very likely would not. Generally speaking, the only way to pacify the Petersburg people was through just concessions, not gunfire. Khabalov hemmed and hawed and could say nothing definitive or give any orders.

All this standing around was clouding the mood. Twice, though, spirits were boosted by the arrival of small detachments of Jägers, and later a company from the Petrograd Regiment. But they too had no clear instructions from Khabalov's headquarters, only to come here. They lined up on the Preobrazhensky's left flank.

The sun could no longer do anything but set.

The soldiers were starting to freeze. The officers as well.

They had no idea what this handful was supposed to do.

From the other side, from the mutinous rumble—soon it would be two hours since anything had come up, approached, or been clarified. The revolt was limited to a few neighborhoods and was felt outside that area only by the rumble of gunshots and the smoke of a fire.

In order to figure out whether the mutiny was winning or losing and what exactly was seething or going on there, the officers took turns running back to their club and calling acquaintances in that district to find out.

Then suddenly! From the other direction, from the Field of Mars, from the other end of Millionnaya, they heard the sounds of a military band! Yes, it seemed so. Yes, exactly. Now you could even make it out: it was the Pavlovsky march being played over and over.

It was the Pavlovsky men coming! This way!

They were marching to music, which meant not hostilely. The Preobrazhensky ranks themselves took heart and stood tall without any command. But now the commands were given. Everyone stand to! Attention!

The Preobrazhensky soldiers had not thought to bring their band to the square, there being so few of them, and so with even greater avid hope they gawked at the approaching music.

However, as the Pavlovsky men crossed the Winter Palace canal, they abruptly stopped playing their own march for the Preobrazhensky march! This was how they came out on the square, stretching out their long formation—the entire combat battalion, that is, a few thousand! A few thousand snub-nosed, round-faced men—and they stretched and strutted onto the square—and hurrahs from the two formations mixed with the welcoming march! They filed their full length past the Preobrazhensky men, ending up west of them, on their right flank, and turning their columns' head toward the General Staff.

As if to draw the beginning of the Decembrist carré.

[1 0 5]

The guilty Pavlovsky marching company on Konyushennaya Square and the remaining companies on the Field of Mars—they all knew, of course, that nineteen instigators had been taken to the fortress in the night. The feeling ran through all the companies that those instigators had been taken in their place—and the punishment lay on them all. Also, the battalion commander, although wounded by a bystander and not a Pavlovsky man, nonetheless lay dying in the hospital, and his death aggravated the field company's fate.

There was a turnabout in mood among these few thousand, explainable only if one knew the result, but by no means predictable in the moment. These few thousand Pavlovsky men, who were maintained no better or more attentively than any of the other reserves in Petrograd, and who yesterday toward nightfall had been complicit in the first unthinkable step of military revolt, today, early in the morning, when the military revolt spilled out onto the adjoining streets, shouting, shooting, and lighting fires, they had not rushed to greet it, had not attempted to disperse or flee, had not erupted in the stone barracks, but had sat calmly and gloomily, making no unnecessary movements, and unusually were not taken out on the Field of Mars for exercises—and only across its expanse could they see well through the windows the mushroom of smoke from the great fire spreading ominously and triumphantly beneath the clouds.

The Pavlovsky should continue, shouldn't they? Herein, obviously, lay the way to save all those accused and rescue the rest from guilt—just attach themselves to the rebellion and it would be as if there had never been any guilt? Shouldn't they help the revolt more fervently than anyone else?

No, their Sunday mutiny remained without consequences. It was not their mutiny that had carried out a revolution.

The reserve soldiers, a ragtag battalion, could not be assumed to have had a mature concept of the regiment's honor. It was probably just that their sense of shared guilt—combined with their permanent habit of subordination—had kept them in a state of depression for half the day. But the officers, even newly minted ensigns like Vadim Andrusov and his friend Kostya Grimm, who because of the turbulent times had spent all night in the barracks, no one having been released, already understood that a funereal mark lay across the audacious, ringing Pavlovsky name, that as of 11 March—the shooting at the crowd and the uprising—the Pavlovsky men were no longer what they had been for more than a century.

They fell asleep and awoke in a foul mood.

Perhaps it was having the officers spending the night in the barracks, not like with the Volynians, that determined the gloomy restraint of the Pavlovsky soldiers that morning.

But in what gloom had Captain Chistyakov, who replaced the murdered commander, spent that night? The entire regimental burden had weighed on him, and early that morning a revolt had begun across the Fontanka, a dozen blocks from here, that immediately affected three battalions, and later more. The captain learned very quickly that the District command was utterly lost, had grown dumb in the face of danger, and could give him no instructions. He had to find his own solution, and he felt no decision was worse than going mad from sitting in the barracks in anticipation of what might happen.

Captain Chistyakov was an unmitigated officer, wholly invested in his service, screwed and cemented into the regulations. Whether he was simply standing, sitting, or walking, in his movement or nonmovement, in what he did or didn't say, above all he was constantly serving. The soldiers sensed this very strongly, even the rawest recruits. They might not like him for his piercing look and mercilessness, but they could not help but yield, submit to this living coalescence of regulations and commands.

These last months the captain had been undergoing treatment. His left arm was still in a sling, but even this disablement, rather than impair, had expressed even more plainly his agility and fitness for service.

Losing all hope in Khabalov's headquarters (where they wanted nothing more from the Pavlovsky than that they sit tight in their barracks), Chistyakov kept telephoning officers he knew in other battalions, conferring about what to do. He chose tested men. *What* to do they all understood identically: put down the revolt. Only they didn't know how and were uncertain of their soldiers due to the large number of new recruits.

After the soldiers' dinner, gathering his officers for a council and listening to how they perceived the soldiers' mood (no one expressed himself too hopelessly), Captain Chistyakov ordered the entire battalion (except for the marching company) to line up in full battle gear on the Field of Mars facing the barracks.

Confident, ringing commands were sounded through the companies. The soldiers in the compromised battalion hurried up to fit out, some were given rifles and live ammunition, and they pushed and shoved on the stairs and went outside. Wondering, brightening, rejoicing.

They formed four rows in their usual places, company after company. Up in front was the music detachment. The sky was brightening, and there was the sun.

The battalion realized it was no longer blamed. It was forgiven and there would be no punishment.

They sorted themselves out and dressed their ranks according to the last commands: Order arms (for whoever had one)! And everyone "at ease." Captain Chistyakov, with his bandaged arm, wearing a greatcoat nipped in at the waist, paced triumphally in front of the formation, not letting the tiniest detail escape his long-firing eyes—there were still ignoramuses, you see.

Everyone was expecting a speech, a send-off, but he only shouted:

"Fine young men of the Pavlovsky! Your Tsar and Emperor is expecting you to do your duty!" And he commanded the entire field: "Right face!" And to the band: "March!"

With cheerful confidence, the column turned, horns thundered the Pavlovsky march—and rising with the march to the stature of its famous regiment, to the drawn-out, swelling music, which doubled a man, in the joy of these victorious sounds—they were off! They were off, and the officers were in place. They were off, down the Field of Mars to the corner of Millionnaya, and there—

"Left turn!"

and filling Millionnaya with their music, their tread, and their thousands—to Palace Square!

It didn't matter if a revolution was under way in the city. All roads are open to a regiment marching to music.

[106]

An hour before, all that was going on in the capital had little affected General Zankevich—regardless of how it might end. In the mighty wings of the General Staff, with its tall, formal windows on Palace Square, quiet everyday shuffling of papers went on related solely and exclusively to the Army, both at the front and in the rear: provisioning, organization, and appointments. Zankevich glanced out and saw that a red-trimmed Preobrazhensky battalion unit had arrived and stood there on the square, but that did not affect him. Although Zankevich was both daring and battle-tested, he was neither bored nor languishing in his inaudible work because it led him down a brilliant road. He was a fine military tactician, and quite early on, given his age, just three weeks ago, he had replaced Belyaev as Chief of General Staff.

This same Belyaev had suddenly summoned him now to the city governor's offices, and he could tell from the summons that something was amiss. In the five minutes it took him to cross Nevsky, he girded himself for an imminent thrashing. Belyaev—the *Dead Head*—dictated his new appointment from vacant eye sockets.

But where were the troops? And where was the enemy located?

The enemy wasn't located anywhere, no one knew where he was moving, and he had unknown numbers in the northeastern part of the city, but Zankevich could have only those now being assembled. As for any of the fifteen or so battalions that did not want to come, let them remain in the barracks; it would be calmer that way.

So whom do we have? The Preobrazhensky. A company each of Izmailovsky and Petrograd soldiers. A machine-gun half-company. Two batteries without shells. And also, it had been promised, they'd send something from the Guards crew? Rather meager.

Meanwhile, having accepted the appointment, he had to act energetically and not sour, like that Khabalov. Until he's appointed, an officer in the service can only look out the window at what's happening. Once appointed, though, he has to astonish everyone with his enterprise and drive.

Right then the Winter Palace reported over the telephone that the entire Pavlovsky Battalion was entering the square—with music, a banner, and officers!

Zankevich's heart pounded like Napoleon's. Who was he if not a Pavlovsky man? He was heart and soul an officer of the Pavlovsky Regiment who had once never even dreamed of rising higher. Not that long ago, at the front, he had even been the Pavlovsky Regiment's commander! And in the reserve battalion, all the former wounded knew him, of course!

His heart was pounding: a portentous coincidence! He had been appointed to command, and the Pavlovsky men had come of their own accord! Coincidences like this lead to great deeds! An hour ago unprepared for anything, ten minutes ago filled with doubt—and now he had already determined irrevocably to pour all his strength into this day!

He grabbed a droshky standing by the city governor's offices and raced—not straight to the square, no, he raced home, quite nearby, to put on his full-dress Pavlovsky uniform with the white piping, his winter regimentals. He lost ten minutes on this—but what an effect!

In the same droshky he flew on a calculated course through the arch of the General Staff, made a handsome, showy arc, and sped toward the Pavlovsky formation, toward their right flank.

Standing at full height in the droshky, saluting.

Hasty commands rang out, the battalion stood at attention, and when the general greeted them, the response came forth from three thousand harmonious throats.

Stopping in front of his own Pavlovsky men, General Zankevich gave a brief but ringing speech that the Preobrazhensky could hear as well. If the revolt won, only the Germans gained from that. He was calling on them, Guards heroes, to serve Russia and the Tsar and to prove their loyalty to Guards traditions!

"Are there many here who know me? We shed blood together at the front!"

"Yes sir!" the Pavlovsky men shouted. "Yes sir!" ecstatically. "Willing to do our best! We'll try!" came selflessly from the ranks.

Splendid! Just like Napoleon: move straight to the Liteiny area and rescue Kutepov! They just had to wait a little for reinforcements and the Guards crew.

Zankevich the victor moved on. He stepped down and began striding in front of the Preobrazhensky formation. He called over the gentlemen officers and asked, "Well, how is it?"

Suddenly he perceived not merely the joy torn from the soldiers' breasts but a calculated caution, was it?—or doubt? or even muffled distaste?—from the Preobrazhensky officers.

What and how was this? He felt out the officers with his eyes and questions.

And he got his answer. The gentlemen officers *had no hope* that their soldiers would act against the State Duma. Would that they not swell the numbers of the opposing side. It would just be unnatural to go against the State Duma. The correlation of sides was by no means that simple.

The young officers watched in an aloof, even indignant way. They bore no resemblance whatsoever to defenders of the government.

Quickly, Zankevich began to cool, falter. In the excitement, he had let his mood soar and simply hadn't had time to think as far as the fact that there was no enemy. Behind the running rebels stood the State Duma and public opinion, whom General Zankevich would never think or want to fight. This was not the way to promotion for a general.

A talented man had to be doubly cautious. Whether or not to manifest zeal—he still had to take a closer look. Advance, yes—but on whom?

[1 0 7]

Returned from his walk and alone in his rooms, Nikolai immediately reread Khabalov's telegram. Yes, the Volynians had mutinied—more than a company—and they had been able to pull in another company, only it was unclear whether from the Lithuanian battalion or the Preobrazhensky. Not that many, three reserve companies—but what an ineradicable disgrace for the Guards! However, there was this: Khabalov had asked to be sent reliable units from the front *immediately*. "Immediately" was the word that had slipped past the Emperor's eyes when he read the telegram the first time, on the stairs.

But three reserve companies—was the matter serious enough to pull troops from the front?

The Emperor hesitated. To the point, he did not know this General Khabalov at all, did not know his qualities. This general had not been at the front, having most recently served as governor of Ural Province, and there was the memory of him coming to welcome the Emperor at the head of the Ural Cossacks, whom Nikolai loved dearly for their pleasant manner of speech, and they had also brought the most delicious caviar and cured sturgeon as gifts. Thus, it was only in connection with those enormous sturgeon fillets that he could recall Khabalov at all. And then, almost by chance, on someone's recommendation, he had been appointed to the Petrograd Military District, which wasn't even independent and had only recently split off from the Northwest Army Group. What was he to make of this "immediately" now? Was the need that acute? Or had he lost his head?

All would have come clear to Nikolai if he'd had a fresh telegram from his faithful Alix. But there had been nothing, which was reassuring. Alix was always on guard and would not let anything dangerous slip. How many times had she always warned him of everything in time? Her letters were never full of feminine chatter but rather contained a great deal of practical information and energetic advice.

Actually, her last telegram yesterday was as follows: "very concerned regarding city."

However, if it had gotten worse, she would have sent another today.

Naturally, one would have liked a reassuring line from the trusty Protopopov. But there had been none. Actually, given Protopopov's resourcefulness and perspicacity, this could be the evidence that all was well.

So, should he undertake something or not? A tortuous question, as always, but despite his entire large suite, the Emperor did not have a single practical advisor, a single bright mind. Weighing most on his heart was the fact that these last few days Nikolai had not been able to be with Alix and had had to go through all this and decide everything himself.

There was only his chief of staff. But he was an office man. Albeit a good soul and pious—not someone the Emperor could be open to, in any case.

And here he was, hastening to the royal home, the conscientious and diligent Alekseev bearing fresh telegrams.

The first he offered was from Belyaev. Aha! It was an hour later than Khabalov's and very brief. The War Minister informed him that the disturbances that had begun that morning in a few troop units were being firmly and energetically suppressed by the companies and battalions that remained loyal to their duty. The insurrection was not yet suppressed, but he was firmly confident of the imminent onset of calm. Merciless measures were being taken. The authorities were maintaining total calm.

Here there was a contradiction with Khabalov: no troops for assistance were requested; they would deal with this themselves and quickly. What's more, Belyaev held a higher post and had a better overview, and his telegram had come an hour later. If to this one added that during these hours the Duma, the chief instigator, had already been cut off from its activities, then more than likely one could expect calm.

Only something nagged. Yes, this: "the companies and battalions that remained loyal." Oddly expressed, if the garrison was almost entirely in hand.

Due to his own nature and temperament, as well as his relations with Alekseev, the Emperor could not simply say to him, "Mikhail Vasilich, this is all very unclear and is making me very uneasy. What are we to do?"

He merely touched his collar and looked at the general with wide open eyes and an implicit question.

But Alekseev's eyes, due to his eyelids' very arrangement, were constantly squinting and half-closed, and you couldn't see through to his mental state.

And also—he had held onto the second telegram and, with an unvarying and sour and preoccupied expression, now handed it over.

What? Again from that ill-starred fatty Rodzyanko? This time, though, without a maneuver with the commanders, addressed to the Emperor directly. Judging from the time, it had arrived right between the other two, between Khabalov's and Belyaev's, also this afternoon.

But what was it? What kind of unimaginable thing had he brought? Again: the government was powerless. (But this was what they had been shouting constantly, for years.) That one could not rely on the troops. (As if he commanded them and well knew.) That civil war had begun and was heating up! That officers were being killed in the reserve battalions, which were evidently on their way to storm the Ministry of the Interior and the State Duma!

The Duma, too? It was a telling picture, though.

And further—further he did not report or ask but ordered—the insane Samovar ordered—his own Emperor to issue such and such orders immediately. Immediately restore the Duma's activities. Immediately form a new government as he had insisted in yesterday's telegram and without delay proclaim these decisions in a manifesto, otherwise the movement would infect the army and ruin for Russia and the dynasty would be inevitable.

He was going too far! When people demanded—and with such threats—the proclamation of a manifesto conceding power, it reminded Nikolai painfully of another situation and another Manifesto—which at the time was granted utterly in vain, out of fear.

Not only Rodzyanko's tone but his demand for an immediate manifesto turned the Emperor's heart against his telegram.

And what was this at the end? The fatty asked, "in the name of all Russia," of course—and the hour had come that would decide the fate of both the homeland and the Emperor himself. Tomorrow might be too late.

Had he lost his mind? How was it this had come from his clumsy head and no one else's? A bellow of despair and fear, as if he had pinched his paw. His cry was out of proportion.

His insistence and tone completely repelled the Sovereign. There was also the implication that he was promoting himself as the new government's head. And at the same time he had the audacity to threaten that the Emperor's personal fate was being decided!

This barred the path to any kind of response.

There was also a third telegram, from Evert. More than half of it was a repetition of Rodzyanko's of yesterday—the same circuitous maneuver. From Evert himself: he was a soldier and did not get mixed up in politics, but he could not help but see the extreme disarray in transport and the failure to deliver provisions. Military action had to be taken to secure rail traffic.

He could simply have reported this in the course of his service. Rodzyanko had nothing to do with this.

He looked at Alekseev, in whose sharp-browed, sharp-mustached, slightly frowning face he knew a certain expression neither plaintive nor pitiful, the expression of a man gone sour, completely off kilter and aggrieved.

"Do you have something to say to me, Mikhail Vasilich?"

Suddenly, for some reason, at that moment, it occurred to him as never before that Alekseev looked like Chekhov's "man in a case." Wearing his uniform and cap, behind his mustache and glasses, he was cautiously hiding, reluctant to poke his head out unless absolutely necessary—and even when asked did so with caution and only in conjectural sentences:

"Your Majesty . . . Might the circumstances of this moment . . . Might the sensible thing be to yield to the public's demands? So the public might find a solution to all the crisis situations? Everyone would calm down immediately. . . ."

And the work at headquarters would continue without interruption.

Alekseev the simpleton did not have the foggiest notion of the magnitude of the question he had touched upon! Or its duration. He had served for a year and a half as Chief of the General Staff, but the bones of his own skull had never felt the crown's pressure or the weight of the Cap of Monomakh. Centuries-long tradition did not weigh upon his shoulders with both hands, nor had he himself agonized for two decades over the question of Autocracy's meaning, limits, and duration, or about his responsibility to his ancestors, descendants, and nation. That this was a mystic sin to hand over to the mob the authority invested in him from God. Or about the people's unreadiness for any other form of government.

"The public's demands"! The mood of the clamorous, uprooted, irresponsible intellectuals who had gathered in their circles in the Tauride Palace or at the Moscow congress. They thought it was so simple for the Tsar to have the ministers report not to him but to the Duma, when this was a rupturing of the entire principle.

Disrupting any established order is always dangerous. A careless innovation could bring down an ancient edifice in a matter of weeks. But reorganizing state administration—and during a war like this? That would mean disrupting everything at once. The decisive year of the war was coming. How little sense it made to speak of reforms.

But how was he to express all this to Alekseev? And to what end? He should have understood from the Emperor's look, from his eyes.

Nikolai remained silent.

Understanding this silence, Alekseev said in his mumbling little voice:

"Forgive me, Your Majesty. If no responsible government is allowed, then it becomes even more essential to appoint a dictator for the rear."

Well yes, this was Alekseev's suggestion of last summer: a single supreme minister over questions of fuel, transport, food supplies, military factories, the entire economy—like a Supreme Commander at the front. But having rejected it once, now he was supposed to approve it under these unusual circumstances? He needed to think about it all the more.

He remained silent.

The Emperor would sooner have thought whether to send as many troops to assist as Khabalov had requested. But Alekseev was not evincing that kind of agitation and did not suggest it himself. Besides, knowing him, of course, he was opposed to such a measure—weakening the front and removing regiments.

It would be awkward to be the first to express this, as if he had taken excessive fright. Alekseev speaking of a responsible administration while the Emperor spoke of troops to suppress?

But his heart did sense that something should be undertaken.

With restraint before the eye slits of the chief of staff, the Emperor spoke:

"Mikhail Vasilich. . . . Perhaps, after all . . . someone should be sent in? To Petrograd. Some cavalry unit."

He was prepared to retreat. But Alekseev was not all that surprised. He furrowed his brow.

"Perhaps. For example, from outside Novgorod, from the Selishchi barracks, a cavalry brigade."

"Think about it, Mikhail Vasilich," Nikolai felt immediately relieved. "Give the order. Tonight we will confer once again since some news will have been added."

Relief. He could not have done nothing!

Alekseev left feeling unwell, his head retracted into his shoulders.

It was time for evening tea.

Right then they brought the post from the train. A letter from Alix— yesterday's, but a long one! (Not perfumed this time, the last thing on her mind.)

Nikolai kissed it and began to read.

[108]

Reinforcements for Kutepov's detachment kept arriving from some-where nonetheless. A party of scouts, fifty or so, and the single officer there reported that they were from Tsarskoye Selo, from His Majesty's 1st Riflery Regiment. Why scouts specifically rather than a combat company? There was no one he could ask. Before the officer could finish making his report, Kutepov's gaze had already determined that the party was of indif-ferent quality. As was immediately confirmed. The colonel greeted the men, and they responded quite listlessly—and it is the response to the greeting that tells the tale, that first expresses the soldiers' mood. Right after the response someone, hiding, threw out from the ranks: "We haven't had our dinner today." You may as well not take a party like that; all you could do was take them and lead them into the nearest courtyard and set them straight there.

Before he could deal with them, a squadron rode up that turned out to be a Guards cavalry regiment. Without waiting for an order from the colonel, its captain immediately reported that his horses were poorly shod, his men hadn't eaten, and they were tired from their long journey and needed a rest. All this may have been so, but the officer should not have re-ported this first thing or in front of the formation. With contempt and in a loud voice, Kutepov replied that he was amazed by what he'd said and was relieving him of his command. This was not a situation to be requesting a rest. To command the squadron he immediately appointed a lieutenant—and ordered him to move across the Simeonovsky Bridge toward the Ciniselli Circus, and then figure out the situation in the Field of Mars area and, if necessary, take decisive action.

Here, on Liteiny, it was too tight for cavalry, and the cavalry wasn't that good. But Khabalov's unrescinded order to move toward Palace Square still loomed, so here, then, would be an attempt at such a movement. In the last four hours, Khabalov had neither changed nor repeated a single order, nor confirmed receipt of a single report. Kutepov had to act as if he had no su-perior in the capital.

So the reinforcements had not reinforced them, there were no troops to move forward, and he could not bring himself to remove the backmost Pre-obrazhensky company from the encirclement lest he expose the rear. Their frontmost company and a half-company of Kexholmers were operating on the side-streets off to the right. With just a half-company of Kexholmers, Kutepov advanced to the Hall of the Army and Navy.

At that moment, though, the firing on them intensified. Not only from the Munitions Works but evidently also from the bell tower of St. Sergius All Artillery Cathedral (the smoke from the burning District Court, getting closer and thicker, impeded a proper view). The inexperienced soldiers, who had never been under fire, began hiding in the gates' setbacks and rushing toward the Hall of the Army itself. Forward movement ceased.

Fortunately, a Red Cross division was housed right there on Liteiny, in Count Musin-Pushkin's home. Kutepov asked them to immediately take in the wounded. To the wounded Kexholmers they added two wounded men from the square at the Cathedral of the Transfiguration.

A serviceable machine gun was found, and Kutepov placed it so as to cover the corner of Sergievskaya and the Munitions Works.

He sent an order to the Preobrazhensky company on the right to act more decisively.

A battle could well have been waged, and they could even have blocked the Liteiny Bridge and pushed the rebels into a trap formed by the Neva— had they had triple or quadruple the forces that were both equipped and fed.

Right then a new company came up: the 4th Riflery Regiment from Tsarskoye Selo. Arriving simultaneously was a dispatch about some new crowd moving past the Summer Garden toward the Panteleimonovsky Bridge. That was opportune! Five minutes ago there had been absolutely nothing with which to defend the left flank—and now Kutepov sent this new company there, to the left, to the corner of Panteleimonovskaya and Mokhovaya to meet the crowd with fire.

Scarcely had he sent them off when there was a report from up ahead that on Sergievskaya, around the corner, a number of vehicles were converging, evidently for an attack. The modern style of war! An important moment! Kutepov dashed ahead to prepare the Kexholmer half-company to disperse the vehicles. Scarcely had he positioned them and explained when several vehicles flew out from Sergievskaya at the turn onto Liteiny, one after another, plastered on the outside with workers carrying rifles and with red scraps. They were driving straight this way, firing haphazardly as they went, not taking time to select a target.

The readied half-company opened fire from walls and gateways, and all the vehicles were knocked out in a minute and stopped, though one kept racing down Liteiny, losing those who had fallen on the pavement, and then turned with a squeal, having taken fire, with broken windows and an evidently wounded driver, and fled back to Sergievskaya. The rest, abandoning their vehicles and their dead, ran off in the same direction.

Good job fighting them off, Kexholmers! Well done!

Now they had a new job: taking away the dead somewhere. They already knew of an empty carriage shed by one of the buildings and dragged them there. The dead smelled strongly of alcohol.

These vehicles ought to be started up and fitted out.

Liteiny Prospect was by now accustomed to the colonel's tall figure, which had not taken a single bullet.

Kutepov thought, Not bad! He had already made it through several critical moments, holding his ground, consolidating, and even advancing. In their desperate moments, reinforcements had arrived.

Suddenly on the left, from Panteleimonovskaya, a company commander from the latest Tsarskoye Selo riflemen appeared at a run—a pale staff captain with a single torn-off epaulet.

He stopped and reported, panting. He had led his company to the corner of Mokhovaya, but there his soldiers had mixed in with the crowd, which took away his sword and tried to beat him, but he had run away.

There was reinforcement for you. . . .

Yes, the rebels here had a great numerical advantage.

[1 0 9]

There are readers whom even an earthquake can't tear away from a book; they hold onto it even in that instant. Such dear eccentrics, known to all, were in attendance today as well at the Public Library, in their customary places. But otherwise the library's gloomy halls and vestibules were deserted, as if it were a holiday, and those who had come in the morning had left in a hurry, so only the clerks themselves enlivened the silence and emptiness of the halls: either looking out the window on Sadovaya and Nevsky or rushing to the telephones to learn more distant news, or to each other to share it.

Vera did not jump up or go around to look at first. She sat in her chair deep behind the shelves, where the window faced the Aleksandrinsky Theater and did not provide much sustenance. No matter what happened outside, the work wouldn't do itself, and there were orders and promises. But her excited, overjoyed co-workers ran over to her with the news—and pulled her away, too. The news was truly stunning, although no one knew what would come of it. Never before had there been uprisings of entire battalions! This could be the start of something totally unprecedented. And the Duma! Dissolved, it had refused to disperse! And not somewhere in Vyborg but in the Tauride Palace itself. This was like having the banner of revolution unfurled over the capital. Everyone abandoned their current job and even left work altogether. Vera, too, was very excited. Was it really we who have come to live in this time? . . . But actually, all this could be wiped out in an hour or two of penal troops passing through.

At an open window pane the shooting could be heard louder and louder, closer and closer. Rumors filtered in about fires and the killing of policemen and—officers!

Oh, she wished this dawn had come differently somehow. Why set buildings on fire and—kill? And the fact that they would begin with the killing of army officers fighting for Russia was unimaginable. What horror was this?

Vera was very happy she had sent her brother away yesterday. He would certainly have gotten into some trouble here and might have fallen among those unfortunates.

Although it still wasn't clear how he might have intervened. The insurrectionists were our own flesh and blood, and how else could it be if Shingarev was among the insurrectionists?

Right then she was called to the telephone.

No sooner had she picked up the receiver, and no matter how the telephone distorted the voice, something powerful and warm immediately rested on her heart.

"Yes, hello. . . ."

Her co-workers were standing beside her, waiting for a report of news. But from Vera's first voice they realized there wasn't any. And they stepped away.

It was Dmitriev calling! My God, how she rejoiced! The telephone, which pulled his voice through the wire, compressing it, stripping it of its color, conveyed some different voice conventionally taken for real. Nonetheless, the intonation remained, the slowing down, the stretching out, the pauses, the fast and loud—and Vera listened to them.

He was calling just to call. There was no reason. Having learned of events, he was calling because he was worried about her. After all, she didn't know what stray bullets were, and those senseless, invisible pellets, of which it only took one. In short . . .

"Vera Mikhailovna, I'm calling—to ask you . . . not to go outside today."

My God, why was he asking? What right did he have to ask? (She did not say that.)

"But how else am I to get home, Mikhail Dmitrich?"

Well, just home, that was very close, by crossing Nevsky. But today's general distraction could lure her on a long walk—so you see . . . don't.

Vera became flustered and couldn't find a way to joke or to answer seriously. She nearly fell silent.

And he maintained a natural silence waiting for her answer.

But her silence felt unnatural.

Then he also begged her forgiveness. But he wanted, simply for his *own* peace of mind, for Vera Mikhailovna to promise him she wouldn't go anywhere today.

Vera replied agreeably, according to the way she felt:

"All right."

And from the other end, a lowered voice:

"Thank you."

But the conversation had become so awkward that she now said brightly:

"And how about you? Where are you calling from?"

Right then the thought flashed that this was just what she shouldn't ask, that it was she who could ask him less than he her, that there was this entire shaded off, unmentionable area.

But no, all was well. He was calling from the Obukhov factory.

Weren't they striking?

Yes, of course, everyone was striking, they had scattered, no one was there. But two smelters had agreed to work with him a little. There was a small casting, a test. And—how strange it all looked in a deserted factory, a deserted foundry.

He described it. With a slowness, as he always did.

She listened and listened.

When she replaced the receiver and was on her way, they asked, What's new?

But Vera had nothing to tell them. They had spoken without exchanging any news.

But how new that had been! How grateful she was to him!

A guardian hand had reached all the way across the city and said, Stay home.

Even though he was not free to speak this way, my God, how good it was that he had. After all, he hadn't made it up, which meant that was what he thought.

And she agreed submissively, joyfully. She would stay home.

She would have gone straight home anyway—but this, after all, was completely different. It was as if she had received a prohibition. As if she had lost her freedom of movement.

How good.

In the last few hours of work, sunshine slipped slantwise through the passage between the theater and library. The day seemed warmer and springlike.

But when she went outside—oho, what a chill.

The entire Ekaterininsky Square was filled with people, and Nevsky—down the sidewalks and the pavement—was filled with a crowd directed and stopped by no one—no police, no troops, no crews in sight. There were lots of soldiers, and in large clusters, but even Vera's untrained eye could tell that these were unusual soldiers, free somehow, not in formation, and some had rifles, but more didn't. And a mass of schoolboys. And university students, some with rifles as well, and one wearing a cartridge belt across his chest.

Somewhere far away people were shooting, but here no one was, and it was quite peaceful and amicable. Vera was walking freely and just examining all the faces.

It was a singular, happy state, as if a cloud of happiness had descended and swathed, intoxicated them all. There were distraught faces and curious ones (mostly curious, so everyone was examining each other, as if seeing them for the first time), and there were ecstatically happy ones. But most of all, there was the simple exchange of a good, amiable mood, the interchange of voices everywhere, and animated talk—this was all strangers talking to each other; there aren't ever so many familiar faces.

Vera had encountered something like this in crowds of believers near churches after holiday mass, but it was unusual to see the same fraternal feeling in a dry Petersburg crowd that had never been held together by anything.

Everyone knew, as one, that life would be very good and bright very very soon!

[1 1 0]

As all this had begun that morning, Obodovsky in the Military Technical Committee continued, of course, to sit and work, but it had started to wear on and tear at his insides.

After the shooting yesterday on Nevsky and once the disturbances had seemingly been suppressed, he reproached himself for the division in him. How could he have hesitated in the preceding days, let his sympathies be divided, and think it was more important to end the war and only after that . . . But after that you wouldn't achieve anything! He didn't share this with anyone except Nusya, and no one could reproach him, but it was as if with his own doubting feelings he had brought down defeat.

But today, when news item after news item had flowed in about how the military insurrection was spreading through the capital, Obodovsky determined very quickly, based on his experience in '05, when others still didn't dare say it, that this was **revolution!** This was it!

Now—no one had reproached him nor he anyone else—Revolution had spilled over, and its victory had gripped his heart. It had continued on its way all the same, so why reproach or try to calculate what it would affect? Just so it didn't stop now! Just so it kept going! This was a moment people wait centuries for. This was a moment that could not be put off for the sake of anything! It would not come again for another two centuries.

And another thing: How was it that we, having waited tensely for it and believing for years, how could we not have prepared or guessed that it had come? All these days—we hadn't guessed, after all.

And something more: Why had it been so easy? The wall had held all that time—and suddenly freedom went over it so easily, almost effortlessly? Had that mightiness really been so weak? But wait, it would still show itself.

Dmitriev telephoned from the Obukhov factory. He managed to talk two workers into continuing the bronze castings today. Well done! Obodovsky himself continued to work as well.

But from time to time he would lean back in his chair and shut his eyes tight.

Or listen to the gunfire through the window pane.

Or news over the telephone.

Or look out the window at the red scraps flashing by on clothing.

It was already taking hold of him. He was still working—but it was taking hold. When Nusya called to say there was nothing happening on the Petersburg side, he recounted to her what he was feeling and warned her that he might not come for dinner, that he might not be there to spend the night, and she shouldn't worry.

Nusya understood. If this was revolution, what kind of sleep could there be!

A couple of times Pyotr Akimovich went outside and onto the avenue, which was aboil with this human concoction of every rank, status, and age, strangers' congratulations, just like at Easter, sometimes tears in eyes—his were flowing, too—this mounting, all-encompassing brotherhood. What marvelous feeling, what breadth of soul, what miracle was the revolution? Just yesterday had these same people felt nothing of the kind for each other? Where had this come from, sweetly, boundlessly overflowing?

He could mingle like this for hours and look at the liberated faces and listen to the liberated voices, but this would do nothing to advance things, and the active army was at war after all, and men were sitting in trenches . . . and Obodovsky went back to his seat and his papers and drawings.

How terrible that this was during a war! But what wouldn't you forgive the revolution for its blindingness! A revolution is like an epidemic; it doesn't choose its moment and doesn't ask us.

He went outside yet again and saw a large military procession with a band and red banners. Although the ranks weren't even, and there were no officers, and the regimentals were ragtag, but it was unimpeded! Such a stream of soldiers! It was more than his mind could grasp.

After that there were no more processions. Showy but pointless vehicles broke through. You could see they had no purpose and were merely wasting fuel. And they fired, fired rifles, all in the air, all pointlessly, and most often it was adolescents who had taken guns from somewhere and were dancing around the crowd with them.

Madmen! After all, tomorrow or the day after they would have to defend Petrograd against Tsarist troops, and in two weeks maybe against the Germans if the front was opened to them, but hundreds of cartridges were flying into the air in vain.

The officers, meanwhile, were being disarmed. Obodovsky bit his lips, as if he himself had been insulted personally. He imagined that for an officer such an insult would be insufferable. But some had handed over their swords and were smiling?

He sat down at the telephone to call and seek out assistants, colleagues, and confederates. Around the Arsenal, around the ammunitions depot of the Munitions Works, and wherever else they looted or might loot—what else could be saved? Was there any chance of posting sentries?

But he didn't find any civil officials on the job, and where was he to find and organize a proper military guard?

There cannot be a revolution without chaos and destruction; that is its distinguishing feature. But while saving the revolution itself, he should have given it a good slap on its holy wrists!

But they didn't have the forces! Obodovsky was nobody, especially not a military official or even a military man at all, and he was no one's superior. He could only rely on chancing to convince and convert someone. But almost no one was at their jobs! Everyone had given themselves the privilege of running off or going outside as onlookers.

For a few hours Obodovsky sat nervously over the telephone, accomplishing very little. But meanwhile, with every passing half-hour, he felt it acutely, that the revolution was degenerating, degenerating, and because of the war, all of Russia with it!

It was horrible, horrible that this was in time of war, and therefore from the very first minute they should set up barriers and even fences against their Cherished Hope and not let it wreak destruction but transform it into action!

Obodovsky was nobody under the setting Tsar or the rising revolution— not a minister, not an official, not a general, not a delegate—but he was a man of action, and without asking anyone he could and should find himself a place. It was injudicious for him to keep sitting here, at the Military Technical Committee, when the fiery war had spread to Petrograd itself.

Where might the center be? Where would other men of action be choosing to assemble, where they could save or organize something, redirect the elemental toward reason?

At the State Duma, obviously. Nowhere else came to mind. Even though he managed to get through to some second-tier members in the Tauride Palace, no one had given him an adequate reply. That was where he needed to go right now, from the working day to the working night.

But right then he made one more call to GAU—the Chief Artillery Administration—which he had called several times during the day, and it turned out that the last people had dispersed, both the gentlemen officers and the clerical staff, and here the porter was alone and powerless. Ruffians had burst in and were dragging away cases, they'd used axes to open a case of compasses, and there were rugs and mirrors here, too, but no police.

Oh, the scoundrels! The scoundrels! Obodovsky grabbed his overcoat and hat. Dragging off new compasses? He would show them now over those compasses, no matter how many of them there were, even if there were a thousand men!

And with cranelike strides, noticing nothing on the streets, he raced toward GAU.

[1 1 1]

*   *   *

Whoever set fire to the District Court and when—there were no witnesses.

At the very height of the fire, the crowd didn't want to let the fire crew through, so it left. People stood around, gawked, approved. Exulting at the fire was Khrustalev-Nosar, who had been freed from prison two hours before. Neighborhood schoolboys were dragging off files, for fun. Dragging off files with convicts' photographs. A young man from the judicial offices stood there and, emboldened, was loudly shaming the crowd, saying the notarial archive was burning, and what a disaster that was, and why it was needed. A sullen workman spat and gave him a good tongue-lashing:

". . . y'know what you can do with your archive. We'll divvy up the houses and lands without an archive."

At the same time, across from the court, they had stormed the office of *The Russian Banner* and were ripping that Black Hundreds newspaper and brochures into tiny shreds on the pavement.

After the court's windows burned out and the ceilings collapsed, they let the firemen through. Several units arrived simultaneously and moved in a few ladders. But it was too late.

Now drunks were trying to get in the firemen's way, but the public pulled them off and calmed them down.

*   *   *

Down Suvorovsky Prospect raced one of the first trucks, full of armed soldiers. From the Rozhdestvensky side-streets people came running to look. Standing in the first row in the back, a young sergeant with a red scrap on his raised bayonet shouted:

"Hurrah! Down with the tyrant! Down with every kind of gentle-manobility!"

"Well done, Volynians!" people shouted to them from the sidewalk. But the old women crossed themselves in fright.

*   *   *

On the corners of Basseinaya, Zhukovskaya, and Nadezhdinskaya, soldiers clustered with the domestic servants who had come out, telling stories and swearing.

Several civilians in bowlers and felt hats, their sabers belted over their overcoats, rode down Kirochnaya on horses taken from the gendarme division barracks.

*   *   *

Train passengers couldn't find porters or transportation at the station. Here and there were overturned droshky cabs. Some looked for sleighs for their baggage, some got a burlap sack, put their things on it, and dragged it over the snow.

Near the stations, all the stores were closed and no one was at the windows.

*   *   *

But Sadovaya looked as usual, its stores and shops open, and there were crowds of buyers at the Apraksin and Shchukin markets, the sellers were coaxing, peddlers with trays were trying to outshout one another, joking and laughing.

*   *   *

Once they began robbing the Arsenal, they stole 40,000 rifles and smashed open many boxes of guns that day.

While on Nevsky they looted a hunting store. Cleaning out all the weapons.

*   *   *

Down Suvorovsky—again a truck of soldiers. Its deep horn wailed non-stop—and the crowd converged. They were throwing rifles and sabers off the side of the truck as they went. Young men were picking them up and then figuring out how to strap them on. Meanwhile, adolescent boys were going wild with joy and snatching them all up before anyone else.

A half-company led by a sergeant was marching harmoniously and strictly. But—nothing red. In the crowd:

"What's this, against the people?"

"Course not."

"So why aren't they yelling?"

*   *   *

The curious had gathered near gates and entryways—residents, officials, young ladies, and even officers with ladies. Watching was both dangerous and interesting. Sometimes their clusters would move forward toward the crowd, for a better look. Then they'd run back, and so would the officers with their ladies on their arm.

Residents roamed the streets filled with curiosity and dread.

They learned from the people they came across what was happening there and whether they could pass.

*　　*　　*

The Lithuanian Fortress—the women's correctional prison department—someone had tried to attack it back on Sunday night. Clusters of people gathered in the darkness, ran across, and fired shots. All the buildings around took fright and put out their lights.

But only on Monday, in the afternoon, did an armored vehicle and a detachment of soldiers show up. They opened fire, glass flew, and doors were smashed in. The defending watch was nowhere to be found. The prison warden, who would not surrender the keys, was beaten up and carried away bloodied.

They started releasing the prisoners. And dragged off all kinds of things they found in the storerooms.

Somewhere below, rusty-colored smoke began rising, maybe from the cellar (and turned into a three-day fire).

*　　*　　*

Over the course of the day, seven prisons were stormed. In addition to the House of Preliminary Detention (freeing the financier Rubinstein, for whom a motorcar came immediately), Kresty (freeing Gvozdev and the entire Workers' Group), and the Lithuanian Fortress, four more.

On the streets, prisoners and convicts, wearing robes and prison garb, strolled gaily, embracing each other and the soldiers.

Every last one was freed, no questions asked. Coming out into freedom along with the politicals were all the criminals (of whom there were many more). In those very same hours robberies, arson, and killings began throughout the city.

*　　*　　*

Through a window pane of the locked Mikhailovsky School, Cadet Lykoshin, a general's son, shouted onto Nizhegorodskaya Street:

"Comrades! We're with you, too! But they won't let us out!"

Then Cadet Yuri Sobinov, an artist's son, gave him a good slap in the face.

*　　*　　*

Workers had disarmed the guard at the Finland Station and seized it. They tore down the signal posts and train traffic came to a halt. Sestroretsky gunsmiths also occupied the Beloostrov Station.

Putilov workers seized the weapons stores and used those weapons to drive away the last police details near the factory.

*　　*　　*

On the streets, they started disarming officers everywhere, peacefully: Give us your sword and revolver and on your way, your honor.

Officers continued to walk through the crowded streets, saluting each other—but none of them had swords. Either their sheaths were empty or they had nothing. (Hidden? Left at home?)

Two civilians, cultivated men in fine overcoats, were walking along in animated discussion—and each carried a bared officer sword. (Had they seized it themselves? Taken it from whoever had taken it away?)

*　　*　　*

Rifles were going off so often and so much everywhere—it was as if they had a will of their own.

Trucks were seen on the streets more and more often, but where were they coming from? In three years of war, never had they been seen so often. They moved through the crowd like large, bristly animals. The soldiers were wearing cartridge belts across their chest, hanging from their shoulders, in their sash, or wound round the rifle barrels. Their faces displayed joy, impatience, and a surge of hatred.

"Hurrah!" they shouted continuously to the crowd. And the crowd flowed toward them with red shreds and scraps:

"Hurrah!"

A mighty armored Akhtyrets, equipped with a cannon as well as machine guns, was clattering down Nevsky. On its steel body was a red flag.

*　　*　　*

A military vehicle tried to pass through the crowd on Znamenskaya Square; an officer was driving and he sounded the horn. But the crowd wouldn't part.

"Stop, motorcar! You may not pass! Get out!"

A university student walked up and put his hand on the wheel.

"We're confiscating your vehicle."

The officer, sharply:

"Who are 'we'?"

"The rebels. Please don't irritate the crowd or force us to commit violence."

The captain got out, distraught.

Young men and that university student crammed into the vehicle—and off they went, bashing on the siren continuously.

But they wouldn't let the captain step away. Another student:

"Now you have to give us your sword."

The captain turned deep crimson and exclaimed:

"No! That would strip me of my honor!"

"But we need weapons," the student argued.

The captain took the measure of him and those who had stepped close in a circle:

"Then kill me! But I won't give you my sword."

A hardy soldier squeezed through and with one hand warned off the young men.

"Brothers. If the officer gives you his sword, he is stripped of his officer rank. One sword isn't going to help you, but should a man perish?"

"Who are you to stand up for him?"

"I'm against the leaders, too! But I won't let an officer be insulted."

He freed him. They let him go.

(But far?)

*   *   *

On Suvorovsky, some soldiers went up to an officer and tore off his epaulets.

He moved off a few paces to the side—and shot himself.

*   *   *

In the Preobrazhensky yard, Ivan Redchenkov and his countryman Mitka Pyatilazov were lounging around and occasionally going out through the gates onto Suvorovsky Prospect—but it was a free-for-all there, people shooting wherever they felt like shooting.

No one had fed them all day, the cooks had fled, and the regiment had oozed away, without a command about who was to go where, but the new recruits were afraid to go. Half an hour and you didn't feel the chill, but after a day, it definitely got to you. They'd been told they couldn't go into the barracks, for supposedly if insurrectionists seized one of them, they would be finished off.

*   *   *

The Izmailovsky Battalion's duty officer was standing at the gates responding to mutinied soldiers who came up to him, saying they couldn't enter the battalion building. He was stabbed then and there by two bayonets and tossed to the ground. (Later they undressed him and tossed him naked into the pantry.)

[112]

On the Petersburg side, that entire day had passed like a carefree, peaceful holiday, a holiday for everyone on a weekday. From the telephones across the Neva they knew what was going on, but no one was allowed across the bridges. From the Liteiny side it had spread to the Vyborg, but nothing went this way. Across the Neva and the Great Nevka—that was where everything was being decided, where all the shooting was. Here, meanwhile, large city crowds were just out strolling and passing rumors around, but the police were nowhere to be seen, and the Grenadier Battalion was only at the bridges.

Aleksei Vasilievich Peshekhonov, one of the leaders of the populist socialist party (which was very small now and today consisted of nearly only its leaders), should definitely have been writing his article for Korolenko's magazine, but he couldn't sit still at home, and time and again he would abandon this article, put on his heavy coat with the fur collar, go out, and mingle with the public.

The mood was excited, and people willingly struck up conversations with strangers because they were overflowing with the tremendous general joy. Peshekhonov himself was speechless with this joy. Had he ever thought he'd live to see this happy day? In all his fifty years he had done nothing but go to the people, over and over—as a teacher, as a zemstvo statistician, and then as a member of the Peasant (but urban) Union, always with the slogan, "Bread, light, and freedom!" And now—had something begun at last? Had the people woken up?

But at the same time he was grieved that the public—such indeed was our public!—limited itself to general curiosity and joy. No one was making any attempts to break through the cordons on the bridges and join the rebels, or to start decisive actions here, on the Petersburg side.

Finally, on he didn't know what number walk, at sunset already, Peshekhonov saw on that skewed square where Arkhiereiskaya, Bolshaya Monetnaya, and Malaya Vulfova streets converge, a cluster of people, a hundred or so working lads and girls and small fry that apparently was intending to do something. Here's what: they were inching closer and closer, as if intending to break the line of Grenadiers blocking the way to their barracks and further toward the Grenadier Bridge leading to the Vyborg side.

A young worker pulled some red fabric out from under his shirt, attached it to a stick—and raised it! He called the others to follow him, shouting and waving his arms.

But the young people were still shifting from foot to foot, unable to decide.

Aleksei Vasilich did not hesitate for a minute. He felt the excitement of that sacred moment so familiar to all old freedom lovers, a moment that does not very often fall to our lot. Not bending under the weight of his heavy coat, stepping firmly in his galoshes (the left, which was falling down, he had fortunately held up with some paper in the toe of his boot), he strode, strode across the empty space—and confidently stood under the red banner beside the young worker.

Whether it was his appearance—elderly, respectable, but also rather common—that had its effect, or a tipping point had been reached, but half the cluster started off, and Peshekhonov was in the first row!

Some did stay where they were, though. And some dashed around the corner, for fear shooting was just about to break out.

But even if it did, it wouldn't be so bad to perish for the people's freedom!

Peshekhonov, his head held proudly back in his beaver cap, did not lag behind the flagbearer, and so they walked side by side, together.

They had only about a hundred yards to go, and no one was shooting—there weren't even any hostile movements in the line of Grenadiers—but the cluster melted away; he could feel it with his back and tell by peripheral vision. A few people were left around the banner. Damn our Russian slave mentality!

They had to go back and bolster these young men's courage and daring and shame them. Peshekhonov delivered a short speech to them, pointing out their civic duty.

The Grenadiers heard but didn't intervene. They stood at ease, conversing in their line, and smiling and nodding to each other at the demonstrators. A young officer was pacing past the line, issuing no commands.

Even a line like that these young people couldn't bring themselves to break! O tempora, o mores! Oh, how low had the generation's martial spirit fallen!

It was no longer the standard-bearer but Peshekhonov who led these young workers a second time, and a third, and a fourth—and each time they lagged behind, stepped back, turned around, and gave out. Everyone here already knew him and called him "father."

The soldiers took pity on Peshekhonov and when he was close whispered to him, "Let them come! . . . We won't get in their way. . . . Our rifles aren't even loaded!"

But in vain. . . . The red flag had already been hidden away.

Peshekhonov was so tired of all this, so deeply offended, that without waiting for anyone or looking around at anyone, he simply walked on alone, past the formation, partly even wishing a martyr's death in order to bitterly shame those who had chickened out.

What happened? The Grenadiers didn't budge, and Peshekhonov passed unimpeded through their line—and on and on, past the old yellow-stone barracks with the columns—and even all the way to the Grenadier Bridge—without anyone detaining or calling out to him.

Here he was already, standing right in front of the bridge, facing a new line of Grenadiers that might also have let him through.

But a bitterness came over him, and he saw in this whole instance a vivid symbol that expressed in just a few strokes all of Russian history.

And he turned back.

[1 1 3]

The name was cobbled together from everyone's suggestions: "The Provisional Committee of the State Duma for the maintenance of order in Petrograd and for relations with institutions and individuals." How much wisdom and caution had been invested here! Provisional! For the maintenance of order! The most law-abiding objective. And only for relations—certainly not for actions or administration. And institutions meant only legitimate ones; this meant not the revolutionary parties.

Seemingly, the faction elders could not have given themselves a more prudent and loyal name.

Nonetheless, Mikhail Vladimirovich's troubled heart sensed that this was not law-abiding, that the Duma did not have the right even to a committee like this—and this was a revolutionary act. The President wanted to hold his Duma deputies in his broad embrace, like foolish children, away from the abyss—but instead they dragged him there.

(The Duma's Social Democrats interrupted and rapped on the door: Could they invite the party comrades who had been freed from prison to Room 13, to the budget commission, to meet with them? In his thoughts he somehow did not pause to ask whom this was for and to what end. So Rodzyanko told them, All right, have your meeting.)

But it was reassuring that the prudent Milyukov, who had been so obstinate at the private meeting, now had agreed to this committee and did not see anything so terrible in it.

Later they agreed at the private meeting that Duma deputies would submit without qualification to this committee—and in this way at least the Duma would create a unified, firm will in this dangerous hour. This was important for the sake of order.

They announced this to the remaining Duma deputies, who had been roaming the halls at random. So now the Committee existed.

Rodzyanko left for his office and solitude in order to marshal his stormy thoughts and the harrowing news from the city, to think through and make sense of things. He attempted yet again to telephone Prince Golitsyn at home and at the Mariinsky Palace, but without success. He was nowhere to be found.

Rodzyanko felt like King Lear when everything around him was disappearing and perishing and the storm was raging. He felt like a mighty ship that was nonetheless weakened somewhat by these blows.

He paced around his office and mentally conversed with the weak and unwise Emperor. He repeated to him the words of his telegrams and even stronger admonitions, trying to convince him that he could not have acted otherwise—but also that the Emperor would have no choice but to concede. He wanted to imagine the Emperor's replies, but the replies just would not come distinctly to his ears; they were elusive, as always.

Why, oh why, had the Emperor not responded to his two desperate telegrams?

Suddenly, the telephone rang. And he heard, distinguishable even in the telephone, the soft, kind voice of Grand Duke Mikhail Aleksandrovich informing him that he was already in the city.

Oh, what a relief! But how had he gotten there? Easily?

Rather simply: by train from Gatchina, and from the Warsaw Station in his own motorcar, which picked him up, and he had passed through the streets fairly freely. Now he was in his private apartment awaiting Mikhail Vladimirovich's instructions.

He even spoke humbly, the dear grand duke! He had always listened well to the President—and this gave him hope now! The Emperor was inaccessibly distant and deaf, but his only brother was right here, in the mutinous city, and could be utilized as a great lever.

But *how*? The plan was as yet unclear even to the President himself. They especially could not clarify this over the telephone; the young ladies at the exchange would hear—and tell. They could not even meet at the Duma because many here were themselves drawn toward the abyss, and Rodzyanko's task was to save Russia! They had to meet, but not here; best of all at the Mariinsky Palace, where the government resided, because this plan could not be decided without the government, and there they could finally locate the ministers, if they hadn't dozed off entirely or died.

He and the grand duke agreed to meet there at around eight o'clock, which would be two hours after dark, and by that time the crowds had usually calmed down and dispersed, and it would be easier to get through.

Rodzyanko told no one about the meeting other than his deputy Nekrasov and the Duma secretary, Dmitryukov, whom he planned to take along.

Half an hour later, though, he was told that a rumor was going through the Duma halls that Grand Duke Mikhail Aleksandrovich would be coming to the Tauride Palace today at nine and would be proclaimed emperor. Pfah!

Another persistent rumor had been roaming the Duma for an hour already, that troops loyal to the government were converging near the Winter Palace.

Oh, the plot was thickening. Naturally, the government was not going to remain idle. And now, in a few hours, they would restore order in the capital—but the Duma? The Duma had inadmissibly crossed the line.

He repented. And doubted all he had done. The President was alarmed fourfold.

Now, outside, a great noise reached him, shouts penetrating even deep inside the thick-walled palace. Duma officers ran in to report that outside a desperate, armed horde had approached, and neither Kerensky nor Chkheidze had been able to calm them, and they were demanding the President of the State Duma! Otherwise they would sweep aside all the guards and break in.

Rodzyanko's giant chest began to flutter. This was danger, but it was also his duty: to save the Duma!

Not going out was impossible. The most trusted Duma deputies were prompting Rodzyanko that Kerensky was still going out to the crowd and he had to be pushed back and put in his place. The people should see the State Duma's true master!

Yes, go out. But what should he say when he did? He couldn't deliver mutinous speeches or flatter the crowd with mutinous promises—but he had to satisfy this crowd somehow. After all, these were obviously the representatives of the insurrectionist units.

Rodzyanko had a fortuitous thought and picked up the drafts of the telegrams he'd sent. His insult mounted. Why had the Emperor not responded to Rodzyanko's honest appeal? Should he complain at last to the people themselves, to his Russia? Tell them directly about his terrible situation? They would understand! An officer quickly handed him his overcoat and wrapped his scarf familiarly and carefully around his neck. And so the President set off, unbuttoned, hatless, the sphere of his nearly bald crown—in a long, troubled stride.

He went out on the front steps, under the outside columns, to this roar, directly facing what was truly a horde bristling with rifles, and so ineptly that the bayonets were poking in all directions. There were here, besides the soldiers, many civilians—university students, workmen, adolescents, and rabble, and even two in prisoner robes. At Rodzyanko's appearance they sent up another roar, and not very respectfully, perhaps even menacingly, but this he could cover with his mighty voice, just so they didn't gut him with a bayonet. Had this horde burst in, they would have stabbed and shot him and the other Duma deputies in five minutes, and they had no one and nothing to defend them. There were no government troops or gendarmes. The situation was exceptionally dangerous.

Rodzyanko correctly resorted to his trump: the State Duma had always stood and was continuing to stand on guard of the people's interests. Here were the telegrams he had sent to the Tsar (he had wanted to say, respectfully, "the Emperor," but to please the crowd he let his tongue slip away from him: "Tsar"). And he began reading. Out loud. And his voice carried. He began reading without making any adjustments or repeating the text to himself, and suddenly these sentences, written from the heart and entirely permissible in an appeal to the Emperor, here sounded like a terrible tocsin, a revolutionary rumble, as if the first mutineer had been not that tousled, half-mad sailor in the Guards crew but the State Duma President himself:

"The government is in total paralysis and incapable of restoring order. . . . Russia is threatened by humiliation and disgrace. . . . Delay is akin to death. . . . They are killing officers . . . There is no hope for the garrison's troops. . . . A civil war has flared up . . . Should the movement be conveyed to the army, the collapse of Russia and the dynasty are inevitable. . . ."

Horrified, several times he wanted to stop. But he'd been carried off like a sled racing downhill, and for some reason he couldn't avoid a single sentence, as if he had to be crushed then, as against an approaching pillar.

"In the name of all Russia. . . . The hour deciding our homeland's fate has come. . . . I pray to God that in this hour responsibility not fall on the monarch."

He himself shuddered at the power of what he'd read. (This last sentence—had he sent it or not?)

So all this that was so horrible, that he himself had seen for the first time, he read out loudly, threw out to those greatcoats, pea jackets, jackets, and smocks—to tear to shreds. . . .

Indeed, he had satisfied them. They began to roar, to roar without threat, amicably now—and their bayonets were lowered, and no one was aiming to gut him.

And so the President beat back this horde and saved the Duma, and he repaired to the palace now saved from devastation. (However, certain unknown and poorly dressed characters who had nothing to do with the Duma did cross his path here and there along the way. They were standing around in small clusters, whispering and scrutinizing.)

All of a sudden Rodzyanko felt that he had committed something like treason. That he should not have taken the telegrams with him onto the front steps. What an unfortunate idea! He should not have read them.

He returned to his office ashamed and depressed. In the large mirror—less and less light was coming through the windows as the day drew to a close—he examined the lump of his worried, clear-cut, and aged face. He began pacing—straight toward the huge mirror and then turning a sharp back to it. He paced to calm himself, but he recalled those characters in the palace passageways and was again alarmed and called in the senior duty officer (who resembled him, also large and broad-faced).

The latter reported that, yes, there were certain socialist figures and also some released from the prisons today by the crowd, the guard had let them through, and the officer didn't have the forces to drive them out; doing so might cause a scandal.

Yes. . . . Yes. . . . He would have to accept this. . . . Now was no time to start a row.

Rodzyanko stayed in his office to pace and think, awaiting bad news.

And so it happened. A duty officer came running with more bad news: they had brought in the arrested Shcheglovitov!

How? Who could do that? The President of the State Council? The other legislative chamber, like the Duma? A prisoner? Incredible! Rodzyanko jumped up in fury and ran to the rescue.

In the Cupola Hall, Shcheglovitov wore no winter coat or hat, just a simple house coat, his head nearly bald and red from the cold. You mean he hadn't undressed here but had been brought this way through the cold? An impudent, shortish university student with a revolver and saber at his side was leading the convoy, and two hefty soldiers in the back were holding their rifles atilt. They were not joking.

A crowd had gathered around the unprecedented spectacle. Both the public and quite a few soldiers from somewhere were already inside!

Tall Shcheglovitov, with a sparse fringe of gray hairs but a thick dark mustache, was wiped of his usual businesslike expression, without any prominent facial features, and was breathing heavily. And silent, having seen Rodzyanko, too.

"Ivan Grigorich! What's happened to you? What is this misunderstanding?" Rodzyanko rumbled in his bass voice and spread his arms, intending to casually take the prisoner away (he did not extend his hand, though).

But the student made a warning gesture: Don't come any closer. And the soldiers did not make way.

Right then, heard from off to the side was Kerensky's rising, roosterish voice, which swept along at the solemn significance:

"Ivan Grigorievich Shcheglovitov?"

Shcheglovitov looked at him tensely, perplexed, and as if he hadn't heard his cry. His large mustache barely moved.

"Yes."

The pause held long enough for Kerensky to engage a new, exultant voice:

"In the name of revolutionary law, you are under arrest!" he declared excessively sonorously and too readily, without surprise. "You will be held in the Tauride Palace!"

What, in fact, was this? Since when, and why, did he comport himself as the top man? Once again Rodzyanko spread his arms cordially while simultaneously giving Kerensky a little push.

"Ivan Grigorich, please come to my office."

But the student raised an impatient hand.

"No! No!" Kerensky exclaimed piercingly. "He is not your guest here and I refuse to release him!"

What business was this of his? He was talking as if he had done the arresting or was the general prosecutor!

Someone here had been general prosecutor, that is, minister of justice, for nine years, but it was Shcheglovitov. And now—according to statute, he was the peer to Rodzyanko! And treated as a criminal . . . ?

Anxious not to relinquish his victim, Kerensky proclaimed:

"You are the man who could deal the most dangerous blow to the revolution's back! And at such a moment, we cannot leave you at liberty!"

From his elephantine height, Rodzyanko looked at this puny man contradicting him here, in the Duma!

And all of a sudden he deflated like a sack. All of a sudden he realized that his former power here had ended. Even his Duma duty officers were nothing here.

A strapping Preobrazhensky sergeant with little eyes and a ruddy beard across his broad jaw stood himself at Shcheglovitov's side and gave him a shove to keep moving, understanding which way Kerensky had indicated with a light sweep of his arm.

Kerensky himself pushed ahead in front of them like a fiery bird.

The two revolutionary students and the soldiers holding rifles atilt stepped out.

People on all sides watched the procession fearfully. The Duma deputies all knew Shcheglovitov.

But they were accustomed to knowing or despising him as someone embronzed. And here he was walking under compulsion, not nodding to anyone.

[1 1 4]

Making their way one by one unrecognized through the agitated capital, the ministers once again assembled just after three in the afternoon, now in the Mariinsky Palace.

Here there was a company of soldiers concealed in a space near the porter's room, while in front of the palace were two field guns, and on Mariinskaya itself there were as yet no mutinous movements of any kind.

The small second-floor hall of the Council of Ministers had a splendid view of the square, one of the eternal views of Petersburg: past the expansive, spacious part that covered the Moika was Clodt's distant, elegant Nikolai the First, from the back, and farther off the magnificent enclosure formed by St. Isaac's Cathedral, where for a brief while the sun played on the cupolas. How many times had they seen this permanence—and grown used to it and not appreciated it as acutely as they did today, when it threatened to topple. The ministers had assembled in bad moods, too, at times, when things had seemed to be going badly, but now, oh, if only it were like before, when the obedient capital flowed peacefully down the sidewalks, in cabs, and on streetcars—and policemen stood unbendingly at the intersections.

It was the same dark red hall with the formal portraits and chandelier, the dark wine-colored velvet of the armchairs and the floor-length cloth on the big table (today this red color, although muted with a noble darkness, took on a hostile and vanquishing meaning). The same expanse for crossing the hall, approaching the windows, speaking privately in twos and threes. Here there was no sense that the ministers were hiding, as at Golitsyn's apartment, here they felt as if they were in their accustomed safety, and here they assembled more fully than there.

Their ranks, however, had thinned. Besides the ailing Grigorovich, for some reason the ever indispensable Rittikh was not there, and he had not warned them, had not telephoned that morning, and he was not at home. Nor was the orotund Synod Procurator there.

A serious and nervous tension. Somehow they had to decide immediately, and do something—immediately. But they had absolutely no idea what. The military suppression of the revolt was being managed without them, by Belyaev, who indeed had gone to the city governor's offices to give instructions. But the other ministers—what could they do during a revolt?

The telephone connection had been maintained with the Tauride Palace. Sitting there was a duty officer from the Council of Ministers chancellery, who kept them informed of events. So that the ministers always knew what was going on in the eye of the storm—though they could not imagine, let alone believe it.

An unauthorized, private meeting of Duma deputies. . . . A self-constituted Committee to establish order. . . .

But what about the government?

Why had they assembled here? Perhaps they should have stayed at their respective ministries.

Everyone was off balance, but more nervous than the others, cracking his knuckles, with the weary face of a losing gambler, burdensome and even odious to all his colleagues, was Protopopov. Everyone felt it was because of him that they were sinking to the bottom. After all, the brunt of the Duma's hatred struck at him, and it was he who was sinking them. It was he who had failed to bring about order in the capital. And now he had lost his artificial, triumphantly arrogant appearance, his look of special significance and knowledge, had ceased to seem and pretend but rather openly showed that he was finally breaking down.

And now he got a call from General Globachev, the Okhrana chief, from the Petersburg side: Nothing has happened yet, but what should I do about our colleagues? And our priceless, top secret archives?

What could Protopopov reply? No Minister of the Interior, none of his predecessors, had ever faced anything like this—not Pleve the rock, not the iron Stolypin. Destroy them? It might be too soon. Risk leaving them behind? It might be too late. Wait.

He was handed a note saying that the residence of the Miniser of Interior had been stormed and he could not return home; his wife had taken refuge with the building supervisor.

Everything was collapsing at once! Protopopov couldn't stifle a morbid moan and grabbed his balding temples with both hands. His gaze kept revolving.

They turned to him, and he eagerly complained out loud.

They murmured a few condolences—or else this was each one transmitting a shared fear for himself. After all, at any minute even their ministries could be like that.

They kept not starting the session, not starting, kept walking past one another, exchanging a few brief words.

The immediate opinions were that they should resolve to inform the Emperor that the capital was lost. (But was it really?) And that . . . they should be given the right to enter into negotiations with the Duma. The government did not feel it had that manifest right, to speak with its own parliament.

Finance Minister Bark said no telegrams would have time to turn around, and there was no point waiting for any replies. They had to decide everything now themselves.

But this council was powerless to decide!

Finally, the short, artificial, dark-eyed—no, sinisterly dark—Belyaev came in. They so wanted to believe in his strength, that he was a general, but he was so obviously a puppet. They so wanted to hear some perhaps victorious news from him, but he had none to tell. Instead, he took Golitsyn aside and started expounding to him in a half-whisper. That the only way to save the government and the entire situation was to get rid of Protopopov, to remove him.

Did Prince Golitsyn really think otherwise? But the government did not have the right to remove one of its own ministers. Only the Emperor personally could appoint and dismiss a minister. No minister could even resign without permission.

Protopopov could tell they were talking about him—besides, they couldn't help but look askance at him. His handsome, suffering, now entirely unconfident eyes drilled into them.

Oh well, they might as well start the general discussion. They sat at the table.

In a measured voice, and with all the restraint of his high-society ways, Prince Golitsyn began to say that for the only possible salvation of the government, one of its members had to make a patriotic sacrifice and voluntarily resign without waiting for the Emperor's permission.

He wouldn't say *who*, and he kept spinning in circumlocutions, but apart from possibly the half-deaf Minister of Education, from his first word it was to such an extent clear to everyone that they all looked frankly at Protopopov—with revulsion for him and with hope of saving themselves. His resignation might save them all.

Protopopov blazed up, although his flaccid skin was not inclined toward flushing, and began looking around wildly in this all-round siege, which he had not expected. Everyone looked at him with banishing gazes, as if they had conspired.

He couldn't stand them either! He despised them all! But all the protective figures had taken a step back into muteness and gloom—and here Protopopov sat, unprotected and powerless.

Suddenly he was so alone, so excruciatingly alone, and he felt so sorry for his handsome life and great career, which had not reached its zenith—it was as if he had played out a tragic role before a side-show public.

But he did not relieve the ministers by offering his own name.

Then the floor went to the black owl, Belyaev. Small, with protruding ears, he looked out gloomily from the depth of his eye sockets through the screen of his pince-nez, and spoke without vocal force. He apologized to Aleksandr Dmitrievich for his military frankness. But today he had seen several prominent individuals (he did not say where or whom, but this device always produced an impression of authenticity), and all of them had stated that the disorders were going on out of a common hatred for Protopopov. If he left, everything would quiet down. They could not tarry a minute. They could not taunt the crowd, which was electrified.

Protopopov burned—and gasped. He could not even reply properly. More than anything, he was insulted.

Then Prince Golitsyn politely and formally *requested* in the name of the entire Council of Ministers that Aleksandr Dmitrievich sacrifice himself and resign his post—which would have a calming effect on the infuriated crowd.

No one dared force him! He could resist! But the nervous burning that had held him these last few days suddenly drained completely. Protopopov sank and dropped his head—and it was like this that they finished him off.

He had to fall ill. It was his duty to fall ill immediately and thereby save Russia's government.

There were no one's eyes, no one's soul to support him! And who was here? There were no lofty souls here! Protopopov raised his head in despair and felt like bursting into either laughter or sobs.

"Well, gentlemen, allow me! Well, if you would like this so much, I can declare myself ill!"

They were not horrified at his sacrifice and did not shudder at their betrayal; everyone was obviously relieved. For them, all their problems had been solved.

And this hurt Protopopov even more and made his throat tighten bitterly.

"Oh, what bad and evil men you are!" he made his habitual joke.

Prince Golitsyn said:

"I am very grateful to you, Aleksandr Dmitrich, in the name of the Council of Ministers, for sacrificing yourself."

Protopopov could barely refrain from laughing-sobbing. He leapt up with his head thrown back, so they wouldn't see his eyes, and breathing heavily, spoke:

"I can even commit suicide for you! That is all I have left—to shoot myself!"

And he exited the hall.

Everyone breathed more freely, and no one rushed after him. They didn't believe him.

The government was saved. The meeting continued.

But although Protopopov had opened a way out for them, that way would just not open. What was to be done after all?

They didn't even have an obvious way to announce Protopopov's resignation.

They couldn't win the capital back without outside assistance.

But was that assistance in the offing?

They also had to appoint a deputy Minister of the Interior. It was paradoxical, after all, to be left at such a moment without a Minister of the Interior!

But what was even more paradoxical was that no one had prepared and no one could come up with any candidate, even the most provisional. Golitsyn proposed energetic General Manikovsky, the quartermaster—whom they brushed aside. The chief military prosecutor? The State Council secretary?

They started making telephone calls and offers—and no one would agree.

Meanwhile, their official called from the Tauride Palace with news that Kerensky and Rodzyanko were giving incendiary speeches.

Pokrovsky leaned back in his chair by way of contradiction.

"I cannot believe that Rodzyanko, the chamberlain, is at the head of a revolutionary gang. Something is amiss!"

But all they could do was sit in their chairs and have desultory, disorderly, pointless discussions. Under them the capital, firm ground, and the palace floor were being washed, swept away, and they could come up with nothing. Despair and impotence.

It was reported to Prince Golitsyn that a crowd was approaching his private home on Mokhovaya, apparently with the intention of storming it.

There you had it—and now he, too, had no other solution! In a minute neither might any of the others!

It was too bad they had not declared a state of siege. Last night would not have been too late!

Declare it now? A state of siege was convenient because it lifted any responsibility from the government and shifted it all over to the military. But how could they declare it to an already rebellious city? There was even an unexpected problem: Who would print such a decree and where? And would they be allowed to hang it throughout the city?

The dispatches from the Tauride Palace had stopped; evidently the official had been removed from the telephone.

However, Stishinsky, a prominent old member of the State Council, walked in, all in disarray, and announced: "State Council President Shcheglovitov has been arrested in his apartment and taken away to the State Duma!"

This struck them like a thunderbolt. The man in the highest state post—and he had been arrested? One legislative chamber had arrested another? What was going to happen? Did that mean the same could be done to *them*?

Hands were wrung. At this someone called someone outside and conveyed a confidential proposal from the rightists in the State Council that they give a command to the pilots stationed at Tsarskoye Selo to fly at the Tauride Palace and drop bombs on the revolutionary nest.

They dared to repeat this circumspectly at the conference table, but everyone staggered back. And big-eared little Belyaev said that as War Minister he would never allow such an order.

No, the farther this went, the more the ministers saw that the situation was unsalvageable here, from the inside.

They needed a dictator from the outside, with troops.

And to send the Emperor a telegram requesting troops.

But allow me, gentlemen, Pokrovsky reminded them, the Duma has demanded our resignation in exchange for its dissolution. It would be dishonest to violate the terms.

Yes, it was true. Yes, most sensible of all, and easiest of all, would be for them to resign and not worry about anything anymore.

But they couldn't all fall ill at once, like Protopopov. That meant they had to petition the Emperor for the government's collective resignation.

The distant, taciturn, unreachable Emperor.

Send him a telegram to that effect.

Pokrovsky and Bark composed it readily and swiftly.

The Council of Ministers dares present to Your Majesty . . . with a declaration of a state of siege in the capital, such as has already been imposed. . . . Petitions for the appointment of a military leader with a popular name. . . . Under the present conditions the Council of Ministers cannot cope with the situation that has transpired and proposes disbanding itself after appointing as prime minister an individual who enjoys society's confidence. . . .

Prince Golitsyn signed with conviction.

[1 1 5]

After he came back across the Liteiny Bridge, Kirpichnikov failed to assemble his men, all of whom had gone off somewhere. The host of people seethed, not like in the morning; now everyone was daring—but his men weren't there. In the morning, however many there had been, he had led them, the entire horde, but now there were thousands upon thousands, and not only did they not listen to him, they no longer took notice of this puny sergeant walking with them.

After all, when they'd smashed the Arsenal on Simbirskaya, they'd probably collected a few thousand Brownings alone, and they were all in the hands of little boys, who were all shooting. And you couldn't take that away; a little boy is worse than any good-for-nothing soldier. You can bark at him and he doesn't listen. But what's the point of shooting in the air when they needed to win freedom?

From time to time he would shout at them.

In the morning, Kirpichnikov and his friends were concerned about getting the first case of cartridges released from the warehouse, so as not to start out bare-handed. But now even all those civilians, whoever felt like it, were laden with a rifle and cartridges.

The fire on the corner was sending up flame, soot, and above that, smoke.

Some detachment had turned onto Liteiny Prospect, although it was not well formed, and not orderly by any stretch, but it was a detachment nonetheless, and Kirpichnikov's sergeant-major heart rejoiced: they still understood formation!

What was left? With his new small handful, Kirpichnikov joined their ranks at the back. Off they went. But up ahead there was shooting, and the formation scattered quickly. Across Fuhrstadtskaya, Kexholmers stood in a deployed front against the free troops.

All the free troops were frightened, and no one wanted to keep going.

Kirpichnikov had done more than anyone today, so he shouldn't have had to step forward. But he burned with resentment that all was going to be lost like this. Stop once and all was lost, you see.

He went back to try to assemble and convince in turn the soldiers and the civilians that they should all proceed as a solid crowd and not shoot but wave their hands and caps and try to persuade people—then there would be no need to fire at them.

Some he convinced, but more than that—the crowd was pressing hard, converging from every street, and so much of the crowd flowed down Kirochnaya that it moved on that line of soldiers like a swarm.

So they waved their sheepskin caps and their peaked caps and shouted to them and tried to persuade them—and moved up.

The ensigns ordered them to shoot—but the Kexholmers wouldn't.

As the crowd advanced, they killed those ensigns with their revolvers. And the Kexholmer ranks evaporated.

The crowd flowed on down Liteiny, unhampered.

Civilians passed along the information that a Semyonovsky regiment lay in ambush behind the church and apparently had eight machine guns.

They also passed on that here, in a tearoom, there was an ambush—and two more machine guns.

The men drifted in all directions, there was no controlling them: maybe to storm the ambushes, or to make off, or just to loiter around the streets.

But one thought gnawed at Kirpichnikov. Before it got dark, they should go to the Field of Mars and get the Pavlovsky men to join.

His shouting rounded up something of a small crowd, but you weren't going to line them up. They were moving, and that was good.

They crossed the Panteleimonovsky Bridge, but civilians talked them out of going farther, saying there was a major ambush on the Field of Mars and they would all be shot.

Once again, they scattered every which way.

But something had to be done.

It was dark already, and the rows of streetlamps were lit up faultlessly through all the streets of the capital, as if there were no turmoil whatsoever.

Only the ones planted with bullets didn't shine.

[1 1 6]

Colonel Kutepov set out alone with large, swift strides in that direction, toward Panteleimonovskaya, where the crowd had disheartened the Tsarskoye Selo riflemen, although he hadn't—hadn't been able to—come up with any idea of what he would do, one man against a mixed armed crowd. It was simply that he hadn't been able to recruit a soldier from a single line, but he couldn't just stand by and do nothing—so all that remained was to continue on his way.

Once again he was lucky (actually, he'd had luck all day today if one weighed the disposition of forces and means using military logic). At the corner of Panteleimonovskaya, two more companies of reinforcements approached him: the Semyonovsky battalion's Life Guard and two young ensigns, Soloviev and Essen the 4th.

Kutepov turned the Semyonovsky men around toward Panteleimonovskaya so that he himself could lead them there. They reported that an ensign on Liteiny, a Preobrazhensky ensign, had been shot on his way to report to him on the actions on the other side of the Cathedral of the Transfiguration.

However, even this was no faster than in war, quite the front-line pace, and Kutepov had time to consider and decide without hesitation, although the advantage of surprise tended toward the adversary. He ordered the Semyonovsky ensigns to move the company down Panteleimonovskaya, block it off, and in the event of a hostile crowd appearing, to open fire on it. Two blocks behind him, where there was a Kexholmer half-company, he himself heard a loud shout:

"Don't shoot! Don't shoot!"

and disregarding his rank and height, he ran there.

From far off he saw on Liteiny another tall officer, who was shouting this, and on his chest, on his greatcoat, there was a large red ribbon.

The Kexholmers truly were not shooting, as if transfixed. This was an officer, after all! And he kept getting closer.

Running up, Kutepov cried out abruptly to open fire.

Then the officer ran, to reach the Kexholmer zone faster—but he was shot and collapsed.

The companies assigned and distributed by Kutepov held on, they held a dozen blocks of stone buildings—but they could no longer advance. Reports were coming in from all sides that the next blocks were filled with half-armed crowds of workers and isolated soldiers run riot. Gunfire was intensifying on all sides.

Meanwhile, the day was drawing to a close. The sun, which had peeked in after midday, had again clouded over, and anyway by now it was due to go over the walls of Liteiny's stone canyon. The light was waning, and the day was moving toward twilight and its close.

What should Kutepov do now? Khabalov had not sent a single courier with an order or explanation to him all day, and those Kutepov had sent had not returned, and for some reason the city governor's offices had not answered his telephone calls at all. Kutepov went to Musin-Pushkin's home himself to telephone—and couldn't get through. The central telephone exchange informed him that for the last hour the city governor's offices hadn't answered anyone and hadn't once picked up the receiver.

Did that mean the city governor's offices had been stormed?

The telephone operators didn't know, although they were close by them. They themselves, on Morskaya Street, had been guarded by infantry and cavalry so far, and there had been no fighting whatsoever. What else did they know around them? They also knew that some units had formed up on Palace Square but then left, and some were standing there now. Who were these units supporting? The telephone operators themselves didn't know.

Kutepov had been sent—and forgotten. All his companies had been forgotten.

Now twilight was falling, but it was a twilight still lit by the District Court fire.

Before Kutepov could finish his telephone inquiries, he heard a large noise in the home itself. He dashed downstairs—and the frightened Semyonovsky men ran through the door and pressed close, then they carried in, one after the other, the mortally wounded ensigns Soloviev and Essen the 4th.

Then the Preobrazhensky men pressed in, all with rifles—and the building quickly filled with armed soldiers. Kutepov couldn't stop them, no matter how he shouted, and he himself was in a helpless position and couldn't squeeze out the door against the flow.

His entire defense on the avenue had collapsed.

By the time he came out on Liteiny, it was dark.

The entire avenue had been filled by a crowd flooding out of the cross-streets. The crowd was running and shouting—and shooting at the street-lamps or hurling things in order to smash them.

Among the shouts Kutepov heard his own name accompanied by foul language. But they didn't pick him out.

His detachment had ceased to exist.

He went into Musin-Pushkin's home and ordered them to lock the doors. And to feed equally everyone who was there with the sifted flour bread and sausage they had bought that morning in a shop on their way.

[1 1 7]

On a day like this, isolated in inaction and impotence, Krivoshein needed someone close to talk to. He had no one in his family, and he himself wasn't going anywhere in this storm—and no one better than Rittikh would come. His longtime assistant of many years in the Agriculture Ministry, so responsive and helpful, who remembered all the details of the entire long, patient, structural work, the entire tradition, how the ministry was structured, fashioned, and expanded into a "Ministry for Asiatic Russia" and how they had fought with Kokovtsov over finances, and how the year before last Krivoshein had been dismissed, so prematurely considering the work's aims, while Rittikh, who had spent time under two random ministers, had finally himself accepted the post. For Krivoshein, Rittikh was who he would have been today had his career not broken so unluckily; today it was he, Krivoshein, who should have had to drag himself into the session of the insignificant, now powerless government or gone to take shelter with someone reliable, and whose memory should have been crowded with numbers of freight cars—freight cars of flour that had arrived, that were en route, and that were being loaded at various distant stations—and the reassuring sum, if the numbers all worked out, would let themselves be divided into the number of mouths to feed—and the frustration and despair that this shooting, running around, and shouting would not let it be divided up.

Yes, this was exactly what had now occupied Rittikh's carefully combed and ministerially representative head, and Krivoshein put his arm protectively around his shoulders.

"As loyal Rittikh remained . . ."

The desperate exclamations of his forced eloquence before the Duma had yet to die in Rittikh's throat, how he, only just last week, had hopelessly called on *them*: Would anyone approach the rostrum, not a party orator but a man who loves Russia selflessly? (No one did.) In his last speech, he composed his last words—not prophetically? "Perhaps for the last time has the hand of fate raised the scales on which Russia's future is weighed."

Now he had been taken by a chill that this might be prophetic.

Now—and especially so—it seemed to Krivoshein that he had always predicted just this. **All of this** will come crashing down! He had always had a presentiment that a monarch who had isolated himself from his own country could not help but fall. He even precisely recalled one marvelous steamer ride—the kind of moment that makes up the charm of our existence. In May '14, right before the war, there was a dinner on the Islands for a narrow circle: Grand Duke Pavel Aleksandrovich and his enchanting morganatic spouse, who had just arrived from Paris, Count Witte and his wife, and Shcheglovitov—and after that dinner, on that white night, they set off by steamer with a gypsy chorus for a ride around the Gulf of Finland. And just as suddenly as now for Rittikh on the dais, a prophecy had entered Krivoshein's breast, or else it was a very beautiful moment in life and the princess was beautiful, and he was drawn to say something—which he did, on the deck: "You lived so peacefully in Paris. Why did you come to Petersburg? War is approaching, and it will not end well. There will be an explosion, a tragic one perhaps for the throne."

Actually, this was impressive as far as predictions go, but right now there were no grounds for thinking that that explosion, tragic for the throne, had already taken place. All this Petersburg upheaval might just as easily be pacified in a day or two.

But here they were sitting in his office, hour after hour, and occasionally they looked out the window at the noisy and unusual sight of armed groups running past (hadn't Krivoshein warned of the foolishness of a mass call-up of extra soldiers?), but they received more information over the telephone from various places. At least the telephones were working smoothly, so they were getting what was going on there and what measures were being taken—and all the news was that the revolt was winning. It was as if throughout the capital, from the very first hour, there had been no trace of state authority, as if state power had turned out to be a specter of the Petersburg twilight.

Even if this was supposed to have happened, though, why today specifically? What had led to this? After all, there had been no event. And it had happened a few hours before the Duma's dissolution, so the Duma had nothing to do with it.

A stable thirty years, half a life here, large paintings by Flemish and Lombardy masters hanging in heavy frames, and Russian landscapes, and an antique Russian chandelier (Krivoshein liked pre-Petrine homeware), soft, rounded furniture and docile carpets underfoot—an unshakeable six-story building with a marble staircase and an elevator, an unshakeable daily existence. Krivoshein loved the good things in life and knew how to arrange things for himself, and knew how to have his Petersburg apartment, and his dacha, and his trips abroad. There was a time for everything. Not all that nearby—two and a half stone blocks to the burned District Court, so it was unlikely the fire would reach there, although there was a fiery cast to the air and the strong smell of smoke—the building had been shaken along with everything else that had been shaken, and if It could collapse, then why not this building?

Here they were, two men of state, the elder of whom having been predicted for head of the Russian government more than once, here they were, on the fourth floor, two helpless civilian residents with a telephone—and they could have no influence on anything, but they themselves could be cast into that fire at any moment.

Rittikh was certain the ministers' arrests would begin.

Arrests? Surely not that! Krivoshein did not want to allow that.

But for now, in the interval between news and cups of tea, should they sit? Pace?

Rittikh grabbed his head, which was smoothly placed down to the last hair.

"I'm ashamed, Aleksandr Vasilich. I'm ashamed to be a member of this government."

He had not realized this just today. He had been burdened by his colleagues ever since his appointment in November. He had barely been able to sit through the cabinet's last meetings. All those days he had been superfluous there, too energetic, and now did not regret that he had not sought out their lifeless, spineless, hidden meeting.

Had that government really been so worthless? Three ministers there had continued on out of those who had worked under Krivoshein. Rittikh, too, was a working minister.

But here was what made it worthless: the ill-prepared nonentity for the Prime Minister's seat. The secretive nonentity in the War Minister's seat. And the hysterical nightmare that was Protopopov. Not even the foreign minister was any good. And this was all in combination, and during days such as these!

Protopopov seemed to have thrown dust in everyone's eyes and wormed his way into power like a pale undead. After all, even Krivoshein had once recommended him as a vice minister. . . .

Yes, an anemic government. Indecisive. Its hands tied.

"Yes"—Krivoshein took his gray head in his fingers—"this is what they have brought us to by opposing every step, every reform!"

"But Aleksandr Vasilich, you can't achieve reforms if you're foaming at the mouth, as they are."

They were speaking of different "they's."

Very attentive to society's judgment, Krivoshein, as much as he could, had tried to bring representatives of the zemstvos and city administrations into discussion of ministerial affairs (paying them out of the budget), thereby moving his ministry into society.

Whereas Rittikh had not admitted society's judgment over himself. It had been enough for him to make an effort over food supplies for a rumor to spread that he was a German, a Germanophile, and had artificially created the food difficulties.

If now things were to falter and society demanded calling him to account, Rittikh would not admit that society's judgment. He would not agree to face such a trial.

But that extreme did not seem likely. The upheavals in Petrograd were nothing; the entire army was outside. The urban upheavals did not mean the fall of state authority.

Rittikh thought otherwise. It was worse.

Their understandings had diverged further.

But they needed to await further news. The torturous hours dragged on and on. Meanwhile, between two pieces of news . . . Should they recall Kokovtsov again? Even the Russian-German treaty of 1904, so exceptionally disadvantageous for the Russian economy. An unprecedented instance when a great country had voluntarily donned its own economic lasso. The failures of the present war stemmed largely from there. And how Kokovtsov for many years had held back Russia's development by hoarding lifeless gold.

Naturally, they recalled Stolypin. The further the years moved away from him, the higher he rose. Such strength of spirit, such strength of spirit—yes, if only we could borrow some of it!

Actually, Krivoshein noted that his reasoning was now much more statesmanly and dispassionate than the alarmed Rittikh's. And although he didn't expect anything that bad, he did understand and suggested:

"How about it, Aleksandr Aleksandrych, really, spend the night here with me. They won't show up here, but who knows, they might come to your place, so be careful, please. . . ."

Rittikh readily agreed.

Twilight was falling, and the ominous flashes from the fire were reflected in the air more vividly. Smoke wafted over Sergievskaya.

It was like the end of the world.

He persuaded his guest that he should go lie down right away. He was going to need his strength and rest.

While he himself paced and paced around his study on a diagonal marked in the carpet. First he would stand transfixed in front of the fiery window. Then he would sink into a corner of the sofa.

But wasn't he himself more to blame than anyone? Why hadn't he taken the Prime Ministership when the Tsar had offered it to him? After all, he understood everything and knew how better than the others. Why hadn't he taken it? He would have delivered Russia. Ever vacillating as to whether or not to accept, he missed having a hand in the wheel's progress. He had cleared the way for himself—and hadn't accepted.

Regret pressed on him that he himself had not taken charge.

And relief that things had not gone wrong under him.

But now, as best as he could grasp, a unique moment had come. The Tsar would now be forced to appoint a strong Prime Minister, a genuine Prime Minister. And the Duma would also need the same—but it didn't have one.

That January Krivoshein had had secret meetings with Vasili Maklakov and someone else from the Bloc. And it was clear they would be agreeable to Krivoshein. Only recently, Ryabushinsky's newspaper had once again come out with this: "We would agree to Krivoshein!"

Yes, Rittikh was right. The public's appetites could be unbearable. The Kadets could never forgive Krivoshein for having demonstrated the foolishness of the Kadets' land program in practice, so easily and efficiently. Nonetheless! This eternal standoff between "us" and "them." One day this veil of misunderstanding would have to be torn. And both sides of the Russian energy united.

Apparently, the moment for this had come.

Now Krivoshein swore to himself that, if offered, he would no longer be afraid and would accept.

The burden, grief, and joy of responsibility!—as Stolypin used to say.

After his resignation, life seemed to have stopped. This inactive year and a half had meant ossification. But he still had strength! He did! And here he was—ready.

And as God sees, not for himself—although it was pleasant to have weight and influence.

Rather, for Russia.

To unite "us" and "them" at last.

Frightening smoke and gleams from the fire shot down Sergievskaya.

Propped on his desk was a portrait of the Emperor presented upon Krivoshein's dismissal, in a Karelian birch frame with silver Fabergé ornaments.

Ten years of unforgettable benevolence.

But they had not seen each other again since the day, in autumn '15, when Krivoshein offered his resignation—and the Emperor had been unable to conceal his delight.

But what was it like for him now?

Emperor, Emperor! Why have you cut yourself off so? Why have you buried yourself in your Mogilev silence?

[1 1 8]

As soon as Himmer arrived at work at his Turkestan Land Reclamation Administration—may it wither away—that morning, he immediately attached himself to the shared telephone, not letting anyone else speak. Who could have found out as much as he could! He made the round of a dozen numbers, and another round, and again, and his impatience passed simply into rage when the telephone operators responded listlessly, indifferently, "Busy," "Busy" . . . Wasn't their blood boiling as well?

He learned that the Duma had been dispersed—and had not dispersed nonetheless. Yes, this one thing did constitute quite a revolutionary step! What about the fact that the Liteiny area, the focus of barracks and military institutions, the bastion of the government, had been the first revolutionary district?

Might that decisive hour have arrived for which generations had worked? . . .

All the employees abandoned their work and surrounded Himmer in their superior's office (their superior was away) and avidly snatched at the head-spinning news he threw out to them in between conversations.

But everyone who could be telephoned had been, and spending any more time at his desk simply seemed like a mockery. And so, without beginning any work whatsoever, Himmer ran to watch the revolution.

There were no such scenes on the Petersburg side, though, just people in an excessive quantity loafing on the sidewalks and gawking. Himmer was overcome by a spiritual languor due to his pathetic status as a detached nonparticipant in the great events.

The most reliable thing would have been to force his way across the bridges. But gunfire could be heard too clearly, and in a moment like this, the enraged soldiers would not spare him even on the bridge. Crossing the Neva over the ice was even more dangerous; they would shoot at the snow from a distance, an open target.

Had Himmer really been destined to go shoot or simply fight? His purpose, his longing, was to give himself to the revolution as a literary force and a powerful theoretician. Men, after all, the ordinary limited, shaken inhabitants, after all, even if and when they did learn the events themselves and their entire course, they would still not be able to understand and interpret them.

But here was an idea! Best of all would be to head for Gorky's. All the news would converge at his place if it converged anywhere.

So it was. Gorky was at home, and a few people were sitting in the dining room, pacing through the rooms, discussing, conjecturing—and calling, calling, calling for news.

They learned about the Provisional Committee of the State Duma and about the seizure of the Vyborg side, but as it was these were all scraps, scraps, episodes, nothing whole, who saw what out the window, in the center.

So what, should they go there themselves? Shall we go, Aleksei Maksimovich? Why not? Let's go, he mumbled into his mustache.

But right then a rumor came in that they weren't letting anyone across the bridges on foot, only in military-issue vehicles.

They were left in woefully tedious anticipation.

From one of Gorky's windows there was a fine panorama, lit by the sun, a section of the Neva and the Peter and Paul Fortress as well. Beware the

Peter and Paul Fortress. Major forces had been assembled there. It was quite ominous. At any minute it might bring down the fire of its cannons on the revolutionary crowd!

Someone brought the rumor that a few vehicles near the Trinity Bridge had already been fired upon from the Fortress.

That's what it meant to ride in a vehicle.

Clouds of smoke wafted over the Neva from the great fire on the other side.

Meanwhile, Shlyapnikov arrived—on foot from the Vyborg side. He had been in various places on the Petersburg side and had visited colleagues, and there was free movement everywhere. He'd wanted to go to Vasilievsky, but on the Exchange Bridge the soldiers hadn't let him through, and for a long time he wrangled with them, but they were only letting through officials of various departments and ranks.

Why hadn't he gone straight from the Vyborg side over the Liteiny Bridge that way, toward the fire? Why that circle?

And Shlyapnikov knew nothing. Astonishing! Not that the revolt had moved to the Vyborg side, not that the Duma had been dissolved but had not dispersed, and not that a Provisional Committee had been created. There's ignorance! Well, you can have a laugh at those Bolsheviks, those dimwits.

So then, should they go to the Tauride Palace perhaps?

The light was already fading.

They went, Himmer and Shlyapnikov.

But Aleksei Maksimych didn't go anywhere; his friends and family members wouldn't let him: We won't let our literature die out there!

[1 1 9]

Over the Nikolaevsky Bridge, another life awaited Veronya and Fanya. Left behind was the dozing Tsarist city they detested—and here they had stepped foot into a city of revolution! What this revolution looked like and what this revolution constituted was still not clear. They had never seen one! Still hanging on building walls and fences were the same proclamations by Commander Khabalov with calls for order and with threats—but only his notices. Nowhere were his bristling hordes. There was no guard at the other end of the Nikolaevsky Bridge, or the embankment, or Annunciation Square—no police guards anywhere and only rare patrols, whereas the freely scurrying public, with their motley, concerned, joyous faces, included a greater number of soldiers without formation or command and many who had been recovering in hospitals and were now talking excitedly and waving their bandages.

But there was no rally per se, no red flag—so the young women chose to turn toward the center, closer to events. Before them, though, a little to the right, they saw thick clouds of smoke, and they were told that the Lithuanian

Fortress was burning and the prison was being liberated. Hurrah! That's where the girls ran—to liberate the women's prison!

Before they could get there, though, in front of the Potseluev Bridge on the Moika, they encountered a procession of already liberated women prisoners—a file of twenty or thirty, all wearing prisoner gowns and shoes—and they walked that way down the snowy street, and even though there was not a hard frost—my God!—they had to be clothed somewhere, fed and warmed! Veronya and Fanya rushed toward the file greatly agitated and confused. So how are you? What's happening? Women, comrades, how can we help you? But the prisoners either had not awoken from their release or had already answered enough on their way. They didn't even turn their heads but dragged along apathetically, single file, no one answering anything, and only one telling them crudely where they could go.

As if struck, Veronya and Fanya froze, shied away, and let the entire file pass. The fact that they were dressed too nicely had probably offended the prisoners.

Now they felt self-conscious about going to the prison. And they were dissuaded from going to the center by amiable passersby with revolutionary joy on their face: the regime rules there and you should go to the worker and army districts instead. So the young women headed over the Fontanka.

Their expectations were vindicated. Soon they began to hear gunfire: a few adolescents ran past them, firing shiny new black pistols in the air and immediately reloading them from their pockets as they went, something they'd picked up somewhere!

Soon they did see a rally. A student with an officer's saber strapped on climbed onto a firm mound of snow and spoke very well about freedom, although it was impossible to determine his party orientation—maybe ours, but maybe SR. Listening to him were a few dozen quite random people—wounded soldiers, lower middle-class people, one official. The young women could have stayed and spoken as well, and maybe debated with the student, but now that they had abandoned their own island and duty anyway, they wanted to see more, to take it in and move!

So on they went, on they went.

There was a little scene by a building: a pale man in civilian dress with white hands pressed to his chest was standing there and opposite him was a cluster of about a dozen people of various sorts. Someone shouted, "Let's take him, comrades!" But a lady asked, "But will you take him to the State Duma?" "We know where we'll take him!" they shouted at her. While they were talking, the pale man dashed through a gateway, into a courtyard. And the entire bunch went after him, shouting. A shot rang out and the lady on the sidewalk explained to the young women that this was a young policeman who had changed clothes and who lived on their courtyard.

The young women cringed: this was the first death they'd come close to seeing.

Right then there were shouts:

"Ah, the jig's up! Filthy coppers, black hundreds!"

They walked on. Across the Fontanka it was even livelier. There was another rally—from an unharnessed horse-cart, and with several speakers now. But the young women didn't stop. They knew perfectly well what was being said here, and they wanted to see and even act.

Here was joy! People were carrying bolts of red bunting out of a dry goods store, and clearly they hadn't bought it. Straight from the threshold they threw the bolts at the public so that they flew over their heads and came unwound, and then fell on someone's shoulders or on the pavement. Everyone ran for the bunting and tore at it as if it were more precious than bread. Some carried entire pieces farther on to pass out while the rest ripped it up right there, and someone even took pins from the dry goods store.

How was it the young women hadn't had that idea before? Now they made large rosettes for their chest and coat. Some made bows, some ribbons. But Fanechka also tore off a long wide ribbon and pinned it slantwise across her shoulder, the way Tsarist dignitaries wore their insignia. Funny!

Some took it for banners, some made red cockades for their caps, and some snatched a scrap and fastened it to a soldier's bayonet—and he liked that and carried it like that, and everyone shouted loudly.

From that spot, from the passing out of red fabric, when they themselves and all the people around them became colorful, and no one chased the red or came down on them with whips, it was as if everything around them had begun to sing and change with great joy.

The young women noted that they were no longer shuddering from nearby shots; each even gave them a merry jolt. Especially since no one had fallen wounded.

An officer was walking nervously and quickly across Trinity Square, not making eye contact. Two university students and two workers, all in red bows, barred his way.

"Mister officer! Surrender your weapon!" one student shouted imperiously.

The officer shuddered, looked from side to side, saw no one to help, looked ahead at them, hesitated for thirty seconds, struggling or trying to get his nerve—and pulled out his sword with an abrupt jerk—and held it out to the student by the grip. He took it and the others shouted:

"And his gun! His gun!"

They walked through the Izmailovsky companies. The young women didn't know what distinguished Izmailovsky soldiers from others, but some soldiers were roaming the streets freely in groups, almost all with rifles, in no kind of formation or parties but in clusters.

A cavalry soldier rode by with red in his horse's mane and bridle, accompanied by a noisy bunch of adolescents, some holding onto the stirrups, some skipping alongside.

Before their eyes, the crowd was becoming redder and redder from the pinned-on red and more and more numerous and animated.

Suddenly they heard a steady and alarming automobile horn, as if it had collided or run over something or wanted to convey danger. Everyone recoiled from the middle of the street—and it appeared, an open-top motorcar. The driver was wearing driving glasses and a leather jacket, stern, unapproachable, and sitting in the vehicle itself were a few soldiers, bayonets pointed up, and also taciturn. But the most frightening thing was on the front fenders on each side a soldier leaned forward with his feet on the steps and holding his rifle forward and steadily aiming at anyone who might interfere.

Sowing horror, the ominous vehicle raced through, no one knew where or why, but very fast.

This vehicle made something else leap up and change in their mood—even redder, more fervent, merrier.

Fanechka said:

"I want to shoot!"

Veronika was astonished.

"Shoot who?"

"Not at anyone. Just shoot! Shoot in the air. That means the people won't shoot, the people are magnanimous, not like the Tsar's satraps!"

Right then a loud din broke out along with ovations all along the street. Another vehicle was coming, this time a truck, not scarily, without its horn, slowly, not aiming at anyone, and hanging on the front of the cab was a large red banner, and in the back about twelve men were standing close together—soldiers with little red flags on their bayonets, and students and workers with rifles, too, and one sister of mercy—and all of them were waving their arms at once with their red and their caps, shouting and appealing to all sides, but since they were all doing it at once, you couldn't understand them, and the people were responding from the sidewalks and shouting to them all at once, too, so even less could be understood, not a word, but the rejoicing! The rejoicing!

Veronya and Fanechka, too, throwing up their arms, shouted to them, too, and waved, and flowed behind the many others down the street behind the truck's slow passage, collecting a crowd.

This way they poured onto the square in front of the Technological Institute—and here there was a crowd! Here there was an enormous rally, a mass of student caps, and workers in their usual dark garb, but how much red on everyone! There were also another dozen or so large homemade flags above the crowd, large pieces of red bunting only just torn off and attached to random sticks. My God, here was where the people's celebration was! The entire crowd was swaying like wet clay—and Zabalkansky Prospect sent another gushing stream to join it.

Veronya shook Fanechka by the arms so they would both believe that this was really happening.

"Fanya! Have we really lived to see this? Fanya! Is this all really true? And no blood is spilling! And it was achieved so easily? Could this really be turned back now?"

Their chests were bursting from the tremendous, indivisible rejoicing. They could never be any happier than this!

Down Zabalkansky, surrounded by a howling public, crawled one more vehicle — this time a large flatbed truck rattling its drive chain. On its platform stood about twenty-five people, but in a third way, like frozen statues, not greeting the crowd but displaying themselves, like statues. The entire front row, leaning over the drivers' backs, had rifles at the ready. Farther back, one man had a red flag, another a bayonet-less rifle raised high, which he was shaking, another with a rifle-less bayonet, another with a kerchief, a red scarf — and they rode slowly like that, stiff, greeted by the crowd on all sides.

The entire square melded into a long wail of triumph.

"I want to get on the truck!" Fanya shouted into her ear.

It was already dusk. While the young women had been making their way across the square, and the crush's streams had borne them onto Zagorodny Prospect, the streetlamps had already turned on. But nothing had changed in the young women's movement — they were being carried farther and farther somewhere, for some reason.

People had smashed a pharmacy window and door and were dragging out bottles. Probably in search of alcohol.

In a side-street a bunch of young men were beating an old man — a yardman, it was said.

Informed, he must have; so now he's getting it.

At the Tsarskoye Selo Train Station they encountered a slow-witted soldier who was walking alone and very reluctantly carrying a bayonet-less rifle.

"Soldier boy! Give me your rifle!" Suddenly Fanya had a good idea.

He looked at her a little wall-eyed.

"Do you know how to shoot?"

"I'll learn!" Fanechka exclaimed cheerfully.

"Well then, here!" He held it out to her without hesitation. She grabbed it and was about to go. "Wait up!" He unhitched his belt and removed his heavy pouch. "What are you going to shoot? Here!" He also held the belt out to her, leather, and so unexpectedly heavy she could barely lift it.

She stuck it in her pocket and it twisted her whole coat around.

The rifle, too, turned out to be so heavy, Fanechka didn't know how to carry it. She just started dragging it by the barrel, trailing the butt over the mounds of trampled sidewalk snow.

They understood less and less where they were going under the infrequent streetlamps; it was dark — but more and more interesting! Although they had done nothing today, they felt like genuine participants in a great Revolution! And the most important thing was still to come, still ahead!

They were aware that it was coming now, a new era was coming on. Now all men would be brothers, everyone equal, and everyone happy.

At this, a truck drove out from the Semyonovsky parade ground carrying several men. As it was pulling out it stopped—and a shout rang out:

"Comrade Maria!"

Veronika shuddered. It had been a long time since she'd been called that. She looked and under a streetlamp recognized Kesha Kokushkin, from the Obukhov factory. He had a wide, teeth-baring grin.

"Sit with us! Comrades, this is a party worker! Let's take her along!"

No one there argued since there was room—even if she hadn't been with the party. They reached out and boosted up both Veronika and Fanechka with her rifle.

Dakhin turned out to be standing there, too, and he had wild, mean eyes. And they were off!

From that moment, something spectacularly new and unusual began for the young women. Everything was shaking underfoot, and the engine was rumbling. As the truck went, they were tossed about, thrown forward, pitched back, flung to the side—and they could only hold onto the sides or one another—strangers, chance fellow travelers, but united in the enchanted shared movement and in their great shared cause. These touches and squeezes of the hand conveyed the full might of the risen masses. There were several workers here, several soldiers, and again two university students—but even with the students there was neither the desire nor the time to exchange words, seek out friends, or learn anything. If there was meaning in anything, then it wasn't in quiet words but in the loud shouts you could never burst out with while walking down the sidewalk, but from here, from the truck, they burst out on their own, ripping the entire excess of delight from deep down. The moment the road evened out, and the truck's movement steadied, and they weren't being tossed about, their hands let go and shot up, and they waved right and left. And so they congratulated everyone—everyone!—walking down the street, and they in turn were congratulated from below!

Where they were going, only the driver could know, but it didn't matter. The purpose wasn't even a question for them: the riding in itself was the *purpose*. Only swift wheeled travel, only that could compare with the pace of events and express the whole delight! The whole triumph! They didn't talk to each other in the back of the truck, but they amicably expressed as one their shared delight until they were hoarse, and if anyone did say anything to anyone, it was immediately lost.

They made a sharp turn—oh, that was onto Vladimirsky—and dashed onto Nevsky, nearly running over the scattering people—and on Nevsky they nearly collided with a truck like theirs coming from the Moscow Train Station. But they didn't collide because the other pulled back, and ours started to go even faster, and as a sign of delight that they hadn't collided and sending each other revolutionary greetings—both our students fired their guns in the air—and the other truck answered with shots.

Now they were driving down Liteiny, and the soldiers started shooting their rifles, too—in the air or at the top floors of tall buildings—and Fanechka grabbed them by the shoulders, holding on and shouting in their ear at the same time:

"I want to! To learn! To shoot!"

But her rifle was lying around underfoot.

One student held out his gun and showed her how. She squinted, pulled the trigger, and screamed! But she had to give the gun back.

Shots were the only way to show outwardly, to throw out to the street her vast delight; she didn't have enough throat left. Veronya struck up a song:

> Onward, without fear or doubt,
> To deeds of valor, friends!
> To the dawn of sacred expiation . . .

Nothing came of it, no one chimed in, or they didn't know the words. Simply—each shouted however he wanted.

There were lots of people on Liteiny, and the soldiers were running in packs, so they had to drive a little slower. Right then they drove past a large fire that was burning itself out, the red-hot caved-in and surviving walls glowed and puffed, so that the heat reached all the way to the middle of the street. Then they got a good look at each other for the first time, as if it were daytime, at their trip companions, their fellow travelers on this beyond-happy, insane ride, and everyone saw on each other the indescribable joy of liberation—and an even greater joy rocketed them up. After they had raced farther, as if into darkness, between the rows of streetlamps, they tried to shout something more to each other, and Dakhin pressed Veronika's hand and shouted, too.

They no longer noticed their route; the driver knew it. They turned somewhere, yes, along the embankment, and for some reason stopped—yes, at the Trinity Bridge. Three older men ran up to them and started trying to prove that they were important revolutionaries and they needed to be driven off to the Tauride Palace. What a mockery! How important could they be when all was won? And what could be more important than the general triumph and this ride of theirs? All of them, fourteen or fifteen gullets at once, from above they explained to the revolutionaries—and meanwhile the driver rattled off once again.

But while they were stopped, one soldier taught Fanechka how to shoot her rifle. And a Cossack climbed up and joined them. Then they raced across the deserted Trinity Bridge—toward an oncoming vehicle, and headlamps struck headlamps, and they might have collided, but luckily they missed—and both vehicles shouted and fired into the air—and they raced through the Petersburg side, no one having any idea where they were going now. At that point the scene became even more fantastic—first darkness, then onrushing streetlamps, then shoals of people rushing in and out, then turns of the vehicle—turns of the entire city, with its embankments, lights, and fires—not a drive but a dance of happiness whose tempo their guns and rifles counted off in the air, and the Cossack twirled furiously and spun his saber overhead, miraculously neither stabbing anyone nor chopping off anyone's head.

[1 2 0]

Scarcely had the most serious disturbances begun today on the Petrograd streets when certain beating hearts began aspiring to find that important place where the meaning of events should be focused and guided. And some hearts, perhaps wrongly, were pulled into the hollering, shooting, half-crazed crowd, although it was clear that the sole possible governing center for events was the Duma.

The Social Democrats, too—Frankorussky, a multifaceted man of initiative, and Shekhter-Grinevich, an Internationalist-Initiativist, a leftist Initiativist, even—independently of each other, in different parts of the city, realized this—and they were among the first to make their way to the Duma, at around two o'clock, and separately get inside, circumventing the guards under various pretexts—and once inside happily greeted each other and stated their purpose.

They were thrilled to recognize that their reasoning had been correct and that something had to be done—**here.** But for now they felt timid in these empty halls with the polished floors. They stood in the Ekaterininsky Hall behind the columns and quietly conversed. They could very easily have been thrown out.

Then they were joined by the Bundist Erlich, with the same course of conversation. They became more cheerful.

Then, the economist Groman, not a deputy but a prominent figure in Duma circles, recognized them, came up, and began talking. And they felt increasingly legitimate.

Afterward, separating from the general movement of deputies, Social Democratic deputies began approaching them and discussing the news and prospects. The arrivals were now quite in their element.

The larger discussion of principle expanded into how, in this perturbed, troubled condition into which the city had fallen, they could not expect initiatives from the franchised bourgeois Duma, nor could they entrust that initiative to it. Indeed, since something genuine had begun, they themselves had to act decisively, in the spirit of the glorious traditions of 1905. One of the boldest initiatives of that time, by Trotsky and Parvus, had been the Soviet of Workers' Deputies. Nothing better or more vivid and appropriate came to mind right now. It would be marvelous right now to revive the Soviet of Workers' Deputies.

Problem was, where were they to come up with the workers themselves if they were running through the streets? But it was all the more the duty of socialist intellectuals to represent workers' interests here. And how could deputies be elected from the factories as long as a general strike was going on and there was no one at the factories?

No, their conscious initiative group had gathered, and now they needed to declare themselves the Soviet of Workers' Deputies. At least provisionally.

They had to dare—herein lay the pathos of great moments!

And best to declare the Soviet not in some random location that no one would ever know but here, in the Duma, where everyone would come and take an interest!

Eureka!

The initiative group took heart and was already speaking louder, not standing around like guests. And right then they saw reinforcements thronging toward them: members of the Workers' Group released from prison: Gvozdev, Bogdanov, Broido, and the unattached internationalist Kats-Kapelinsky.

Gvozdev, it should be said, was in shock, and his ingenuous face said that he was not going to be able to seize the moment. But the rest had already swung around afresh.

It was so remarkable! The Workers' Group! Now with them they would have the irreproachable Soviet of Workers' Deputies! Add Chkheidze and Skobelev as honorary members, and that was it.

The idea swiftly took on substance.

They went to see Chkheidze to ask his blessing and to get themselves a room in the Tauride Palace.

The burdened Rodzyanko waved them off and allowed them to use the budget commission's room in the right wing.

Not that they couldn't have freely occupied it without asking. Such uncertainty or bewilderment had descended on the Tauride Palace, instantly somehow there was no master, the duty officers and clerks had absconded somewhere, and those who were still in place were not getting involved.

There was not just one room here but two connecting rooms: no. 13, for the commission chairman, and no. 12, for the commission itself, not bad, quite spacious. They seated themselves with pleasure around the large oak table.

They started discussing where to begin. Paper, ink, pencils, telephone—they had all that now. It had come with the room. But they had to figure out how to distinguish themselves from the franchised deputies. Clearly: with revolutionary red.

Here's what: obtain from the supply unit coarse red cotton cloth, rip it up—and tie bands and bows on themselves.

Very good! They went to get the cloth.

So, there was paper, and there was ink. Should they write an appeal to the people?

But first should they add others, from the most important factories? Or simply seek out appropriate worker deputies—somewhere on the streets? But to do this wouldn't they have to disperse and leave this space they had occupied—for total disorder, confusion, and shooting? Personal forays could be substituted for, first, by the telephone, and second, by this very Appeal—which could be sent with secondary individuals.

And so: "Citizens! (And the French Revolution rang out!)—The worker representatives in session at the State Duma . . ."

"And soldiers!"

Yes, why be shy of it? ". . . and soldiers . . ."

That's right. They had to hurry to pull in the soldier masses, who were continuing to behave in a revolutionary fashion on the streets—but that was until they started going hungry. Then they could be turned from the moving force of revolution into a grave danger to it. If they were to head off to get fed in the barracks, that would be the collapse of the revolutionary front, and wouldn't they be falling into a trap there? But the Soviet of Workers' Deputies didn't have the funds or organization either for feeding the mutinous soldiers. (They themselves would have liked to run out to the buffet, which was at the end of the corridor. . . .) Here's what they should do: compose a second appeal to the populace as well, for the populace to take care of feeding soldiers who were close to their homes. Excellent?

For the creation of such a proclamation and its mass printing and distribution throughout the city, the young Soviet created from its numbers a Food Supplies Commission under Frankorussky's chairmanship. If food supplies had provoked the popular outburst, they shouldn't be allowed to extinguish it. Frankorussky went to find another free room and occupied it without asking permission.

Right then, out of thin air, a comic figure burst in: a wobbly, gray-haired man in a civilian coat, his scarf hanging, and over it, askew, on his belt—an officer's sword.

Before they could laugh they recognized him—besides, he himself joyously told them his name out loud:

"I am Khrustalev-Nosar. Don't you recognize me?"

And he beat his chest.

And it was clear why he had come: to head up their Soviet. After all, he was—and had as yet not been replaced as—chairman of the disbanded Soviet of Workers' Deputies of 1905. His appearance meant that he was laying claim to the chair now.

But this was too much! He wasn't needed here at all. Why should he be, and where had he come from? Hadn't he been abroad? Yes, he'd spent ten years in Paris and had been back half a year and gone to prison in a criminal case—and that meant today he'd been freed and here he was.

Oh no, this was taking it too far! The new Soviet's members simply ignored him, simply refused to notice or invite Nosar to the table.

But someone else showed up, also astonishing them: Nakhamkes-Steklov! Astonishing because for the last war years he had moved completely away from revolutionary interests. He'd broken all ties with his comrades, served calmly in the Union of Towns, under his own name, his wife had kept a beauty salon on Bolshaya Konyushennaya, and he himself, as a franchised resident, had strutted about in the best suits—even now he was wearing one, and a fashionable overcoat. He had not been expected here now. He was burly, tall, large-headed, broad-shouldered, ruddy-bearded, and handsome, and he held himself proudly. He did not have to sneak into the Tauride Palace. Naturally, they let him in as a member of the Duma.

And now he had found them here. He did not burst in madly like Nosar but rather entered with a firm, proprietary step, thoroughly surveyed those present and in the corners in case someone was hiding there—and strode toward the oval oak table and sat down—and immediately his seat seemed to become the chairman's.

"So, comrades. What are we deciding to do?" He had a powerful, lush voice, too, to go with his burliness.

Meanwhile, Kapelinsky was thinking in keenly revolutionary fashion: they had to think above all about military actions! They had to assemble the Revolution's HQ right here, under the Soviet of Workers' Deputies. And for this they had to find at least two or three, if not military men, if not officers, then at least . . . And they sorted through the possible candidates convulsively.

Bam! Yes, Maslovsky, that is, Mstislavsky! An SR known even to the authorities, for the period of reaction he had found himself a place as a librarian at the General Staff Academy. True, not an officer, but by the nature of his work almost like an officer. Generally speaking, he might figure this out perfectly well and come himself; after all, the Academy was three blocks from the Duma. But he hadn't turned up.

At first his telephone didn't answer for a long time, but Kapelinsky kept dialing, kept pestering the young lady telephone operators. Finally, someone picked up the receiver. It was he! And Kapelinsky, nearly hopping in front of the wall telephone, into the receiver there, said:

"Sergei Dmitrich! We've lived to see it! Haven't we? Quickly, come join us quickly! The Tauride, Room 13! Or if you like, shall we send a motorcar for you? We have motorcars now!"

* * *

JUST LET ME GET MY PAW ON THE CART,
AND I'LL HOP ON MYSELF

* * *

[1 2 1]

All that had gone on yesterday and today had made Vadim Andrusov's own life seem a puzzling spectacle. Up until yesterday's shooting on Nevsky, there had been nothing but military service, which he had grown used to somehow in the past few months after all. Yesterday, this unfortunate shooting had shifted everything. The entire evening afterward in the battalion barracks, as well as in the city, he'd had to defend himself, saying that the Pavlovsky men hadn't been the first to start shooting on Sunday, that they'd been compelled to by a crafty bullet from behind—but only his friend Kostya Grimm believed him completely. This feeling of having been scorched by his inability to justify himself had already shifted all Andrusov's emotions.

He spent the night in his barracks, in the training detachment, on Tsaritsyn Street, behind the Field of Mars, and it was still unknown whether the neighboring 4th Marching Company, in the Konyushennaya barracks, was going to mutiny again, whether they would have to go out against them that night or Monday morning.

But the night and morning passed calmly, even though gunfire was heard in the morning coming from the Liteiny side. Then Andrusov was called in and ordered to go to the regimental guardhouse immediately and free a prisoner, Baron Clodt, and everyone else in there as well. The guardhouse was on the other side of the Field of Mars, across its entirety, close to the rebellious blocks, which was probably why they'd been freed. Andrusov knew Baron Clodt slightly, at third hand and by hearsay. His appearance was not at all baronial or even Guards-like. He was feeble, dark, and gnarled, was known even in the Pavlovsky regiment for his exceptional drunkenness, and was now in the guardhouse for brawling.

Although the noise and shooting had drawn close, the guardhouse watch was kept under lock and key. Andrusov ordered everything opened up and everyone released. They opened four cells and released everyone. The soldiers who had come with Andrusov and who had crowded around here a little earlier raised Baron Clodt on their shoulders, laughing, for they understood everything, and someone shouted that he was a victim of the Tsarist regime—and they carried him like that for twenty paces or so, and then set him down.

One episode after another seemed to loosen in their minds the various ties that bound them, prohibitions, and so did this freeing from the guardhouse, which astonished the guard detachment and Andrusov himself as well. All these shifts and disturbances were rather intoxicating, although he hadn't drunk anything. His feet carried him and his thoughts came more easily.

Afterward they spent a few hours in the barracks, almost ordinary hours, only without training exercises—and then the performance started up again when suddenly the Pavlovsky Battalion, without its 4th Company, was formally lined up with a band—and marched off to Palace Square to music.

The music was so unreal at a time when music seemed the last thing on the entire city's mind.

All was solemn on Palace Square, too—at first. General Zankevich sped out on a sleigh and delivered an ardent speech, and this too was like a continuation of the spectacle. The mood was such that now they would move somewhere.

Preobrazhensky and Izmailovsky men and one other company stood there.

Then a Guards Crew company in black uniforms came up.

A few Jägers rode up.

Two batteries drove up.

A large force assembled, but after Zankevich left, not a single officer galloped up again with any order. A host had assembled on the snowy square, on the rectangle around the Aleksandr Column—and here they'd stood in the cold for half-hour after half-hour. And the sun kept going down.

The Pavlovsky officers paced around, questioned their neighbors, and spoke to one another, trying to determine what was what. And the answer came quite incomprehensibly and discordantly: Would there be action and, if so, what kind? What kind was needed?

As for attacking—no one had attacked them either. Neither friend nor foe had poked his nose out from anywhere, no one had even been watching them from the thousands of windows of the General Staff except for maybe the idling servants from the Winter Palace.

All of a sudden, a Guards crew, having learned or decided something and not told anyone, with a sailor's contempt for dry land, made a sharp turn, tore their black column out of the square—and exited across Nevsky, westward, to their own side.

All the ranks faltered a little. It was cold and they weren't being fed, so why were they being kept here? The soldiers were muttering almost out loud.

But before things went as far as disaster, the battalion commander's order arrived. The Pavlovsky men turned around, bent their left shoulder forward, and now without music, passed through the Winter Palace's main latticed gates, which had been opened wide for them. Andrusov perceived this, too, as a continuation of the unusual spectacle.

Compared to the sweep of the palace, the gates seemed very narrow, and it was even hard to tell where they would put the three thousand Pavlovsky men. However, they did not hurry and went in; they all went in and there disappeared.

As a frustrated child of art, Andrusov rejoiced that now they would be led through marvelous halls always closed to the public, and he would see interiors not accessible even to professors at the Academy of Fine Arts.

No interiors like that were revealed to him, though. The courtyard was the same as any building's, not a palace's, and even more so—vaulted, thick-walled, broad corridors through which they were led on (but how nicely heated it was here!)—so even the ordinary soldiers moderated the shuffling of their boots out of respect for the significance of these stones. Even the simplest of simpletons understood that they had been admitted to the residence of the Tsar himself!

However, their enticing passage through the first floor was brief. They were directed down a staircase, which, although marble, was like an ordinary building's, and its width was not enough for them to observe formation, so everyone got jumbled up.

They descended to a huge cellar that was also warm but dimly lit, with small windows somewhere high up on the sides, but the vaults were wrapped in rather somber shadows and the dim electric lamps were few and far between. This cellar was nearly empty, with an occasional bench, and nothing more than that (and no wine barrels, either), only capitals of support columns.

The companies, and then the platoons, were given orders and commands that were reflected in a muffled echo, and many boots shuffled, voices droned, and rifles clattered. What now? They weren't going to stand here, even "at ease"—which meant sit where you're standing. Actually, even the stones here weren't very cold and you could sit on your greatcoat.

They sat down. It was an unusual kind of sitting. Three thousand soldiers in a huge, dimming cellar, no permission to smoke, and talking—no one felt like talking loudly and the only good thing was that it was warm, and they left it at that. They spoke in muffled voices.

No light whatsoever was coming through the outside window now, and the cellar lamps rarely did, so there were lots of black shadows on and behind the columns and along the walls.

Andrusov couldn't shake his half-intoxicated, displaced condition, and as a joke he thought about getting up the nerve to go roaming through the palace to look at the architecture and sculpture.

But the general constraint and gloom now began conveying itself to him from the low vaults, the thickness of the impenetrable walls, and the darkness of the recesses, but most of all from the oppressed soldiers themselves. At first when they'd come here, everyone thought it was a good thing. It was warm here and you could sit. But they sat for half an hour, and another half an hour, and nothing changed, and food wasn't brought, and it was hard to imagine anyone bringing it here, to these close cellar quarters. The aboveground windows turned pitch black, and outside it was growing dark, too. The fear of a trap was probably being born in the soldiers' hearts. You mean we're spending the night here? Why had they been driven into these casemates? And held without a reason or an order?

Wasn't it for their death? Wasn't it in revenge for yesterday's insurrection by the 4th Company? Maybe they were going to drown them here with water. Or crush them with stones. Or unleash the machine guns on them. Now even a child's mind could put two and two together. They got nothing for the revolt yesterday and were brought here today with music—and driven into the casemates like silly fools. Did that mean the entire battalion straight into the dungeon?

Somewhere the whispering started, the word was passed on, it got a little louder—and suddenly everyone was filled with certainty:

"Brothers! They've led us on!"

"Brothers—to our death!"

"They'll blast us!"

"Suffocate us!"

If any officer tried to shout them down (not Andrusov)—they wouldn't listen to him. The hubbub rose and a shout in thousands of throats—and the entire mass jumped up, slamming their rifle butts—and wandered back from memory the way they'd come—squeezing and pushing to be first to get out. Desperate voices wailed:

"They led us on!"

"To be killed!"

And so it began, a jumble of pushing and shoving. There was no question of fending it off—you just had to keep from being flattened yourself.

The Pavlovsky men crowded, and pushed, and squeezed in mass terror. Oh, God, just let us escape this one time! And return one more little time to our beloved barracks—and once we're there we'll know what to do!

[1 2 2]

At the moment of the crowd's attack, Colonel Balkashin, commander of the Wheeled Battalion, was not at the battalion and arrived only later, when the wounded had already been taken to the hospital, where they pulled the dagger out of Yelchin's back.

There were ten companies in the battalion: two already raised and ready to be sent to the front; four combat companies in the process of formation; and four reserve. They had settled here in the barracks (the entire installation, both barracks and fence, was made of wood and could be shot through), where there were six machine guns, with another eight in the battalion storehouse. What was inconvenient and vulnerable about the location was the fact that the battalion's weapons store and all its garages were more than a verst away, at the top of Serdobolskaya Street, near the Lanskaya station.

Balkashin began making the rounds of the companies training. They all knew about the attack and were seething, and there was no need to do a lot of convincing that the crowd could not have been playing better into the Germans' hands. In each company Balkashin asked that they maintain order, and everyone shouted in one voice: "We will! We will!"

Besides, they loved him personally, and he knew that.

Immediately he put two companies on duty and ordered them to go out and block Sampsonievsky Prospect, facing in opposite directions—but to try to refrain from opening fire and to settle matters peacefully.

He rotated the companies every two hours.

For a long time the crowd did not approach. Balkashin had time to get lots of bullets from Serdobolskaya Street and to arm everyone, especially the machine-gun detachment.

However, isolated shots rang out occasionally from the tall factory buildings not far away, and it was hard to respond since they didn't know where to fire.

For the first few hours there was also a telephone connection with District headquarters, but they couldn't give Balkashin any definitive orders there or advice. The right thing to do was something he would have to figure out himself, here, based on the situation.

Balkashin understood that his small unit, cast so deep and far into the workers district, and also being in wooden barracks, all its fighting spirit notwithstanding, could not undertake battle with the local tens of thousands, who were already significantly armed. He could only try to hold out until help arrived, and for that he had to do more threatening than shooting.

By day's end, no one at all had responded from District headquarters, for as long as there had been a connection with other telephones.

After that, any telephone connection with the city had broken off—cut? The Wheeled Battalion, which that morning had been in the capital of their homeland, suddenly found itself an encircled landing party in a hostile land.

Before dark, huge crowds advanced on the battalion from both ends of Sampsonievsky. They pressed on the companies on duty, shouted, and agitated but didn't shoot—and all the more so it meant the battalion couldn't fire into the crowd. All they could do was retreat.

Then, in order to prevent the crowd from breaking into the yard, Balkashin moved one more company onto the piece of the avenue that was left and started shooting salvos in the air.

The crowd came to a halt.

But it made no sense to keep the companies that way any longer and in the dark. Gradually, he led everyone into the yard, left a duty platoon behind the gates, and in the yard placed machine guns opposite the entrance.

Now the crowd converged freely, spilled over, and moved down Sampsonievsky, but was careful not to touch the Wheeled Battalion units. However, they scoffed, shouted, and agitated for them to kill their officers.

Before long the crowd should disperse—and in this way Balkashin hoped to last the night with his battalion.

He prepared two scouts from the training detachment—to let them out when it got quieter and darker—and have them go through the troubled city to District headquarters for further instructions.

Farther down the avenue, the crowd had lit bonfires and posted pickets, evidently.

But Balkashin had been hasty in reassuring himself. By back alleys, through snowy vacant lots, backyards and side-streets, clerks arrived from Serdobolskaya. The crowd had flooded in there (yes, he had been counting on them not finding it, and he didn't have a second force to protect it), swept the sentries aside, looted the garages—and driven off with all the trucks and motorcycles! (How cleverly they spirited them away! Not a single motorcycle passed down Sampsonievsky. They would have noticed there and figured it out.) But the crowd didn't get as far as the weapons store.

He had no choice but to send a company or so there, too.

He called in Lieutenant Verzhbitsky and two second lieutenants.

[1 2 3]

But in Moscow, nothing special had happened. The Moscow newspapers were as ordinary as you please. No special agent telegrams of any kind had been posted. However, the newspaper editorial offices, first one, then another, had received stunning private telephone reports from Petrograd—and immediately each such telephone call had multiplied through Moscow in twenty reports to friends, who made further calls, or they had calls from elsewhere, and meanwhile more and more reports kept coming in from Petrograd. And all this had twisted into an exciting, invigorating tangle. Even if you didn't believe half the telephone news, even half was more than enough!

At first, Susanna Iosifovna, who had been visiting ailing friends in the morning and at the stores afterward, during the middle of the day, for a long time knew none of this, and there were no signs of it of any kind anywhere in the city. Later she picked up the news from friends—and took a cab to get home faster, returning before four o'clock. David wasn't home, and she learned from the maid that he had stopped receiving visitors long before and hadn't gone to the bank. He had sat by the telephone a lot and now had gone to his lawyers' club without promising to return for sure for dinner. Her son had telephoned from the university, too, that there was news. News! He and the other students were discussing it and she shouldn't wait for him, either.

This joyous anticipation of great events—perhaps the fall of eternal chains?—scorched Susanna! She, too, would have clung to the telephone now if the maid hadn't told her that Colonel Vorotyntsev had telephoned in the morning—and would telephone after four.

What should she do? The obligation had been accepted, and who could have predicted that everything would swirl up like this? She had to receive the colonel, in fact best to do it now, when David wasn't there, because the visit would irritate David. So that staying on the telephone for a long time was inconvenient, that's the trouble.

The heart's laws do not heed public events. They are more insistent. He would be there any minute, and she had to focus her feelings and be absorbed into the discord between these spouses. A conversation like this was a complex tactical battle, and for being Alina's confidante, Susanna had to conduct it as well as possible.

She found Alina's excessive trust in her and this entire mission placed on her a burden—but Alina herself was like a blind woman, everything was inapt, and how could she not help her in this trying moment?

How could she help, though? All these familial intercessions were utterly pointless, after all. No one instance resembled another, and a bystander couldn't give infallible advice. Advice won't extricate you. This was always long and hard, and in shipwrecks of the heart only the drowning can save themselves. If wisdom was not what was needed, then at least clear vision was. Alina had always had a heightened focus on herself, and now she could only keep insisting that her husband adored her, keep referring to his former letters. What was amazing in them was that they seemed written not to a living woman, his woman, but to a woman in general. And not only that. On that visit in the autumn, Susanna caught his looks of alarm or awkwardness over his wife's remarks. But there was also a contradiction between his unpolished look, gripped by battles, his look of decisiveness and his quick eyes—and his relaxed behavior throughout this entire story. As if his new attachment did not give him more resolve.

Actually, Susanna knew from herself delicate sensors of emotions that forestalled someone speaking his mind directly. She was hoping to get a good look at her visitor.

He kept not calling, though, and not calling. Susanna Iosifovna was relieved to realize he wasn't going to.

When her wristwatch (these were now coming into fashion) said ten 'til five, Susanna sat down confidently at the telephone, swallowing up more and more news, even if it was contradictory, and then passing it on to her close friends.

For all the contradictions, an epic was in progress in Petrograd! And it could not subside so simply, could not ebb without leaving some trace or scar.

She didn't notice how long she'd sat there—maybe an hour, maybe two. Her son still wasn't there, but David had returned—wildly joyous and excited, as if he'd brought a hurricane! What was happening! What was happening! Dinner? Well, let's be quick about it.

Susanna pressed the buzzer for the cook.

"In Petrograd—it's a revolution! There's what!" David made a slashing gesture. "The State Duma has refused to disperse. It's brilliant! A revolution in Petrograd, Zusenka!" And he hugged her, kissed her.

He rushed to his study immediately, looking for something, and she was right behind him.

"Basically—when are we going to stop waiting like slaves? History isn't made apart from us, it's made by us alone! Can we fail to act when others are accomplishing this for us? Are we really not going to support them? Are we really not going to blow up our godforsaken Moscow?"

It had been decided among them that this evening the councilors—not all of them, of course, but the progressive wing—would assemble at the City Duma, along with other progressive figures in Moscow with famous names. And David was going! Naturally, the entire City Duma couldn't be swung around to supporting this. It was too much of a quagmire, and the re-actionary electoral law had taken its toll. Besides, those who did gather were masters at speaking fervently and then calling it a day, which added up to nothing. But somehow they had to constitute themselves as the embryo of a new authority, without asking permission. Of course it was frightening! In a Moscow that had not yet changed in the slightest, based solely on telephone reports from Petrograd, to take this step and declare themselves revolution-aries! But decades of development had led to this! A committee? Obviously. But right now they would start proposing, warily, a public committee, a pro-visional committee, self-demeaning names of some sort. Whereas what they should do was summon up their courage and cross the Rubicon. Korzner decided to give a speech and blaze forth with a proposal:

"The Committee of Public Salvation!"

His eyes glittered indomitably. He raised his fist.

Courage! Courage! This was what Susanna loved.

[1 2 4]

Over these past few days, measles had run through the 1st and 2nd Cadet Corps but not the Naval Corps of His Imperial Highness the Heir Apparent, and the young naval cadets had been allowed to go into the city on Satur-day and Sunday, as usual. On Sunday evening, when they came back from leave and had already gone to bed, the bugle sounded and called them to the hall to line up. They were told that the Emperor had ordered an end to the city upheavals, and watches had been immediately assigned to pro-tect their enormous building on Vasilievsky Island between the Neva and Bol-shoi Prospect from the crowd. The watches were given rifles and real bullets, which the majority had never held before. The watch, which was changed every four hours, required so many men that they posted boys as well.

That night, though, nothing happened at all. For a long time, Monday passed calmly. There were no crowds to be seen on nearby streets, and a de-tail of the Finland Regiment was blocking the Nikolaevsky Bridge. But after three o'clock in the afternoon, young cadet Goridze from his watchpost on the embankment side watched in horror as entire black and gray crowds of armed men started in their direction—first over the ice, and then over the bridge as well. And the Sea Cadet Corps was one of the first buildings along the embankment.

The watches of naval cadets went inside.

The crowds tried to break through the gates and the main doors. They shouted that they had been fired at by machine guns from this place. Outside, shots rang out. A few of the young cadets responded in kind. The crowd realized they couldn't take it here without a battle.

Then they declared they wanted to send in truce envoys.

The door was unlocked for the truce envoys, and in walked a handful of soldiers and sailors, who struck Vice Admiral Kartsev in the head with a rifle butt and grabbed him. And the crowd surged on and on through the open door.

The teachers and company commanders rushed to rescue the younger boys and threw the rifles into cold stoves and elsewhere besides—and put the boys in the different classrooms, as if lessons were under way.

The invaders ran from floor to floor looking for machine guns. Their jaws dropped at the hundred-year-old artillery models. In the picture gallery, they poked out the eyes of all the emperors and admirals with their bayonets. They smashed whatever came to hand.

And ransacked the kitchen.

And left.

There was nothing left to eat, the school had been looted, and the vice admiral had been led off into captivity. It was clear from everything that there would be no studying tomorrow, so the cadets were allowed to go home, without their broadswords, but in uniform.

Goridze and his friend K* made their way across teeming Annunciation Square; on their epaulets was the heir's monogram, and the ribbons on their caps were blowing around. "His Imperial Highness." One petty bourgeoise saw it and spat in the boy's face at close distance.

K* wiped it off.

That woman didn't know it, and K* only secretly dreamed, that he would one day be an admiral in this country.

[1 2 5]

Evidently every Revolution has the following puzzling characteristic: when it is coming it doesn't show us all its beautiful face in the very first minute. It can come wearing the mask of the ordinary, so that it is already coursing through our usual life before we find out that It has come.

That was how it had been all these last few days. Sure, the bread riots, sure, they'd looted the shops, sure, they'd torn the police to shreds. It may have been cheerful, but only as individual happy episodes. So it had been yesterday, after the shooting on Nevsky, although his chest had tightened angrily and he'd felt like punching not some individual official but the regime itself in the face, and Lenartovich had even promised out loud not to forgive them this—but **how** "not to forgive"? What should he do? By evening it had seemed that once again everything was going to fall back into its usual foul order, that it had been put down.

Last night, Sasha had gone to Likonya's for her nameday party as if there was nothing going on—and there, among perfect strangers, he had been doomed to being the outsider and because of that awkward, unsuccessful, and the last thing Likonya needed. He felt humiliated. He tried to remind Likonya what a tragic day it was, but nothing got through to her. He tried to ask her how it would be between them, and she suddenly responded candidly, "Sasha, I'm a bad person. You have to know I'm capable of betrayal."

This candor had been the evening's acquisition. This candor had shocked him because people just don't talk like that! But this admitted slide toward betrayal, instead of arousing revulsion in Sasha, aroused him even more to get the better of her! To possess her!

The more impossible the . . .

But in the morning he woke up with the aftertaste of humiliation—he wished he hadn't gone there yesterday!

He dragged himself, as usual, to his ossified Administration to serve out the tedious hours over his papers.

When the first news suddenly started pouring through the telephone, it took Sasha more than a minute, more than an hour to see that the Revolution was finally ripping the mask off its inspired face.

Nonetheless, he did realize it before others. At the midday break, without clearing the papers from his desk, he slipped out of his institution with no intention of returning that day. Maybe ever.

Where had the people found this unexpected strength? And why had the enemy suddenly proved so weak?

What was to be done now on the street? How was it to *make* a revolution? Something should be stormed—best of all, police stations, as the most loyal nests of the regime? Or get those who had not yet revolted to join in? Sasha guessed that the revolution was first of all a matter of pace, how many new supporters it managed to attract in an hour.

He was prepared—heart and impulse—afraid of nothing. But what about his greatcoat, epaulets, and sword? Had they once again torn him away from what was precious? In the eyes of everyone on the street he was now a watchdog of the regime. What should he do? Run home to Vasilievsky and change into civilian clothes? But he couldn't race on foot through all these upheavals, and it was dangerous, you'd get caught up in something en route anyway. Was his military uniform once again keeping him from real life? But no! He would drag his uniform into real life! Just like this, as he was, an ensign with a sword, throw himself into the revolution.

A few excited boys were running, each carrying a rifle and revolver. One had his rifle already dragging over the sidewalk, doing him no good, so the ensign relieved him of it. And for some reason they understood that he was *not opposed*, and also gave him the revolver, but no bullets.

Farther on he saw a dozen soldiers without their sergeant roaming aimlessly down the pavement, all of them holding their rifles differently, their greatcoats flapping (and their pockets loaded down with bullets and each also carrying a zinc cartridge box), both young boys and some a little older, and you could tell that they were at a loss as to where to go and why. Their eyes passed over the strange young officer as an irrelevance—but he had the inspiration to give them a shout! He shouted and for the first time didn't recognize his own manner or voice or how it had come about so easily and ringingly, as if he had grown up on commanding—and the whole business was close to his heart:

"Men! Where are you going? Let's go storm something!"

He shouted like someone with the right to ask questions and give orders—and all of a sudden they understood immediately and obeyed him and responded readily. For the first time in his entire military life, Lenartovich felt like a real officer and even maybe a born officer.

Afterward all that day, this personal feeling grew in him alongside the general exultant sensation of Revolution. He was astonished now that for four years he hadn't known or guessed this about himself. Before, he'd even wondered whether he wasn't a coward. He couldn't forget how he'd been scared to death and dug his face into the potato beds at Neidenburg. Everywhere, he had always avoided and shied away from danger however he could, and then he'd been clever enough to clear out of the front, but his inner sense had always told him that no, he wasn't a coward. Inside he knew it, it was just that he wasn't going to die for other people's interests but would save himself from someone else's war for his own. Only today, amid the whistling of senseless aimed and unaimed bullets, when the police had returned fire from the windows and doors, Sasha had not forgotten his joyous private thought that he, in fact, was not the least bit afraid! That he was actually merry in this danger and wouldn't even mind getting wounded or killed on this beautiful, merry day.

The soldiers soon began calling him "our ensign" and obeyed him with zeal and alacrity such as they had not obeyed cheerless, compulsory commands. "We have us an ensign!" they shouted to other soldiers or the public, and this called forth shouts of ecstasy, and their party swelled. If Sasha made mistakes in his orders, the older soldiers ignored those commands and figured out what should be done instead, while he felt himself more and more agile, quick-witted, and daring, and a hundred times bigger as he commanded.

At first, to be sure to pull them along, he told them to go somewhere close he knew—the police station on Ligovka near Chubarov Lane. This wasn't the most important place in Petrograd to attack, of course, but it was easier to gather up people's anger at this. Actually, there were no unimportant places; in each, the great work of Revolution was being done. They had to wage a battle for the stone building, scatter from shots fired from windows, hug the walls, run around the corner, and shoot so many bullets—they were overflowing with bullets—that the shots set the riddled building on fire. Then take the staircase by storm and fight on it. Then triumph over the filthy cops, their punishment, their pleas, and take them away, and he didn't think they'd set fire to the documents, no one had expressed that thought, but the papers burned and burned, through the doors and curtains, from room to room, and smoking out the victors. But even smoked out, Sasha stood on the street in brash good cheer, admiring the fire.

In this way he had begun today to take revenge for his Uncle Anton! And for the hanged members of People's Will! In this way in many places in Petrograd, at the same time, unbeknownst to but reinforcing one another, Justice was triumphing for several generations at once. The hour of universal vengeance.

What rapture he saw beside him on the soldiers' faces!

Some importunate intellectual in a fur coat and cap was trying to persuade Sasha to move on the Semyonovsky barracks, saying this tenacious, trained Tsarist regiment was refusing to join the revolution, so it had to be removed, even if by force.

It wasn't far from there, and Sasha felt perfectly capable of perorating even in front of a battalion, and he believed in the strength of his conviction. Nonetheless, he realized that his detachment, in the event of resistance, lacked sufficient numbers and cohesion.

Other passersby were giving different, contradictory advice as to where to go and what to do—but Sasha and the men of his beloved detachment, whom he knew by neither face nor name, but were simply those who kept by his side, stood there admiring it burning.

This was a symbol of the destruction of the old and of renewal, and pride filled their chests and heads to the point of drunken numbness, when the body doesn't feel scratches or bruises and is unafraid of wounds.

They were joined by a few workers wearing peaked caps and pea jackets, and carrying rifles shouldered on straps. They persuaded Sasha to go liberate the Transit Prison, which was also not that far from there, and they knew the way, although it was unusual. They climbed over railroad fences, crossed the tracks, and came out right at the prison—there were even two of them nearby, though the House of Detention had been liberated without them.

But they never had to strike. The prison guard immediately surrendered, opened the doors and gates wide, and went to unlock the cells. But the very process of liberation, of being the liberator and seeing the joy, dancing, and cursing of the freed prisoners, afforded them incomparable enthusiasm.

And brothers hand to you their sword.

Sasha had not expected such an honorable and joyous role for himself.

They were held up because some of the freed men were taking their revenge on the prison authorities, beating some and cleaning out the prison's equipment and provisions storeroom. Actually, the latter was not without benefit for Sasha's party, too. Everyone was good and hungry and ate eagerly.

Then they thronged through the side-streets to Staro-Nevsky—and arrived quite opportunely for the storming of the Aleksandr Nevsky police station; the seizure was not yet over here and the fire had only begun. The firemen nearby refused to join the revolution, for which they had their fire-tower set on fire; it burned quite strikingly, high and long, on into the evening, so that they couldn't wait for it to be over.

Seemingly, Sasha was on the periphery of events. He saw nothing central, but he turned out to be an important worker for the Revolution anyway. Most of all, he himself experienced such elation, such a singing feeling—this may have been the happiest day of his life!

With each hour and each new victory he was more and more convinced that the Revolution was certain to win out. Nowhere had they seen or heard of resistance from any troops.

Now, as the day was drew to a close and darkness fell, Sasha felt like getting to some more central revolution. He decided to make his way to the Duma to see someone there, to learn the news better than they had on the street from idlers and passersby. His party may have changed and moved around and spread out around the fire at the Aleksandr Nevsky station, but there were still about twenty men left who called him "our ensign"— and they went with him. After various adventures and stops with about ten of them, he reached the Duma—and left them to wait in the event of new actions, while he himself as an officer was able to penetrate inside.

[1 2 6]

Today's seemingly quiet and lonely day had been a shock for Vorotyntsev. He was so hopelessly upset and had arrived at such fretful incomprehension, such an alarming state of indecision, that he simply could not leave Moscow right now.

After that letter from Alina, there wasn't even any point in going to see Susanna anymore.

He thought, Here his mama and father had lived for so many years in discord—could he ever imagine his mama writing such a letter? Lashing out like that?

Never, probably.

His mama would understand this shock of his, probably. This sudden void.

Kalisa had cried inconsolably at his mama's funeral.

But further back, further back—the courtyard on Plyushchikha, and the blue-eyed girl five or so years younger who wore the little sheepskin coat and fluffy shawl got into the sleigh either with her brother or him when they took the ice-run. She was teased, but she never cried or took offense.

They were the children of the owner of the building where the Vorotyntsevs were lodging at the time and where Georgi would later visit occasionally in his youth. Kalisa grew up, her stoutness made her seem older than her years, and she was good-natured and amiable—she always shone with her smile and common Moscow speech, and his mama loved her. But when she was about nineteen she was married off to an elderly merchant in the Kadashi neighborhood. By then Georgi had finished school and was not serving in Moscow.

But there was a very awkward memory. A year before the Japanese war, Vorotyntsev, then already commanding a company, came home on leave, sometime in March, when there was a thaw. At that moment Kalisa was staying with her parents while her husband was on a distant journey. Somehow, in the evening, meeting Georgi in the courtyard, she invited him to eat a vyaziga pie she had just baked. He went to her place, for pie, as people say, but there was a full Lenten table, the fast was under way, and they sat for a long time, just the two of them, while her parents were out visiting. You'd think his officer world and her merchant world had nothing in common, that they'd have nothing to talk about, but she murmured on and on so easily, and he listened to her placid intoning. He gazed at her powder-white face and softly rounded shoulders—she was voluptuous, but not fat—and suddenly a shameless, insane, reckless flame overcame him: Here and now! It didn't matter she was married! He went on the attack and spooked her. He was already holding her by the shoulders and trying impatiently to persuade her, and she was fending him off and asking him to let her go—and right then, uninvited and unexpected, a visiting nun walked in. And everything collapsed.

Then came the Japanese war. He married, lived in Petersburg and Vyatka, and in '14, right before the war, met her in Moscow, in mourning. Her husband had gotten drunk and been poisoned by stove fumes, a wholly Russian death, and Kalisa remained in her husband's home in Kadashi, a childless widow, only a little past thirty and in full bloom. And again it was war.

But today, as he sat there, scorched, while his memory rummaged through his native Moscow, he suddenly remembered Kalisa. Talking to her would be easy; after all, he was completely tongue-tied all day.

The messenger brought her reply in her rounded handwriting saying she would be happy to see him, she was at home, and she would be expecting him at seven for dinner.

He was there at the appointed hour. It was a private home at the back of a courtyard, with a little garden. A servant opened up, but Kalisa Petrovna herself, wearing a blue velvet dress with a lace collar, met him on the landing of the staircase. He kissed her hand. She became flustered but talked nonstop and led him into the dining room.

Here there was a large antique sideboard with a mirror and carved pears and grapes on the side doors. A square oak table with eight heavy oak chairs around it. Over the table hung a bulky kerosene lamp made of figured pink glass, but an electric lamp had been woven into the chain, and it was burning. (In reserve on the walls were double candelabras filled with fresh candles; they did not trust electricity here.) There was also a gramophone by the wall with a huge horn, massive. Also to one side there was a special armchair with a half-reclined back, and on top toward the head it had a leather pillow also covered with a white antimacassar. Kalisa Petrovna noticed immediately:

"But you're so very tired, Georgi Mikhalych! Please take a seat in this chair until we go to the table. Rest."

Indeed, she had guessed: he really was terribly tired. A rest was exactly what he needed, first and foremost.

In the muffled silence even the slightest sounds could be heard, the creaking of his boots, the jingling of his spurs.

He sat down. Leaned back. Relaxed.

He felt shaken, as if he were ill. Whether something sluggish and vast filled him, or whether, on the contrary, he'd been thoroughly emptied so that nothing remained, but it was keeping him from living and doing anything. How well he had guessed: there was no need to talk here. Kalisa Petrovna asked him questions about the war—not questions so much as her own murmurings about what had happened to whom, in the war or right here, in Zamoskvorechie, nearby.

He made no attempt to conceal his despondency. He allowed it to express itself—in his aging face and shoulders.

While Kalisa, finishing up at the table and not asking him about anything, with just the repetitions of her voice entertained him in her way.

It was as if there were nothing unnatural in him coming to relax in a strange house. Reclining, he sat there silently.

He didn't smoke, imagining she didn't like the smell in the rooms. His insides even ceased demanding the hot smoke, previously such a balm for his nerves.

If he'd had to explain why he'd come, he couldn't have. Fortunately, though, he didn't have to. It was soothing to feel he had come to the right place. Not going somewhere was not an option, either.

And now, he didn't have to. Good.

But Kalisa Petrovna was already inviting him to the table. She saw his devastated condition but out of delicacy asked no questions and made no mention of it. She invited him to the table.

There was sturgeon in aspic. Golden cucumbers perfumed with currants. Marinated mushrooms of various kinds. A golden open-faced sterlet pie.

This wasn't right for supper. Wouldn't Georgi Mikhailovich prefer smelt soup? I have it, it's good.

This was when Vorotyntsev realized how hungry he was; he hadn't eaten anything all day, after all. Fish soup, too, and why not! Well, and a shot of starka, since you've come from the fighting. Another small shot. His hostess took a sip as well.

And he started eating everything in succession, gradually reviving. And Kalisa—in her easy but unhurried way—kept murmuring something about Moscow life without pressuring him to respond. She didn't know how to lighten his load.

Not a sound from the city street reached this old-fashioned dining room, this refreshment, the muffled silence here. It was as if this three-year war and the general decline had never happened and here was the inviolable daily life of Zamoskvorechie, which would live on a thousand years more.

Yes, rest. He looked into her luscious blue eyes with their inviting goodness. He was refreshed.

Here's what. For some reason he could tell this good-hearted stranger how hard things had become for him.

But he looked more and more at her full shoulders in the blue velvet, at her white neck with its necklace of faceted, transparent, honey stones—and suddenly he said, without tearing his eyes from her, across the corner of the table, as they were sitting:

"Kalisa Petrovna, do you know why I came?"

She looked at him ingenuously.

Agitated, and remembering his former agitation, he said:

"For your vyaziga pie."

"Oh!" And she threw up her hands. "I don't have one today. I had no idea."

And he watched her, plunging into her soft, defenseless eyes. She blushed and turned her face away.

"Oh, what a good memory you have. . . ."

He stood up and took a step—and his ten fingers grasped her arm above her elbows, both her plump shoulders. His fingers dug in—and there was no tearing them away.

And he said, looking down, in a muffled voice:

"Kalisa, darling. I'm going to stay with you today."

She lowered her head, revealing the back of her neck and the thick knot of her dark golden hair.

And she sighed.

"Oh, what a sin, Georgi Mikhalych. Both times during Lent, the third week. . . ."

[1 2 7]

This Shlyapnikov, although he occasionally wrote several paragraphs at a go, was, of course, no man of letters. His level was primitive; the trees of his party technique absolutely kept him from seeing the forest of revolutionary politics. Thus, no doubt, he had led his leaders in Switzerland to despair.

But one had to work with the human material one had. One way or another, right now Shlyapnikov was the sole member of the Bolsheviks'

Central Committee in Petrograd, and there was no choice but to seek an understanding with him, especially given the heated turn of affairs.

Several times already Himmer had sought an occasion to come to terms with him, but Shlyapnikov had avoided him simply because he knew his own incapacity for theoretical discussion. Now, though, it could not be put off, and he had to take advantage of this chance meeting. In order to achieve coordination of actions with the Bolsheviks, Himmer spent the entire time going from Gorky's apartment to the Tauride Palace conscientiously explaining to Shlyapnikov the situation that had come about.

Actually, the conditions for explaining weren't optimal. They nearly ran the whole way, trying to pass dangerous spots as quickly as possible. First, past the Peter and Paul Fortress.

Himmer explained to him that power had to be bourgeois at first because without preparation the proletariat was incapable of creating state power. For an isolated revolutionary democracy, especially in wartime conditions, the technology of state work was too much.

It had grown quite dark, and all kinds of excesses were possible. They were walking and running. The Trinity Bridge was free, they were letting everyone through, but it was rather deserted.

The danger lay specifically in the bourgeoisie refusing to take power. If it did, by its neutrality alone it would wreck the revolution. The bourgeoisie had to be *forced* to take power, exactly, even against its will. While recognizing, of course, that the creation of the Duma's Provisional Committee by no means implied solidarity between the Duma's bourgeois top leaders and the attacking people, but rather was an attempt to save the dynasty and the plutocratic dictatorship. They would have liked to conduct a line of struggle with revolution, but we had to inveigle them into power—and in that way force them to serve the mill of revolution.

Vehicles kept rushing by, fast, coming toward them—motorcars and trucks, with armed men shouting in them all. Several times Shlyapnikov rushed to stop them, and one time he did, he caught up and said something.

"What did you say to them?"

"That they should go occupy the Okhrana."

"Listen, that's all well and good, but we can't get held up like that. Instead, we should catch a vehicle and get it to take us quickly to the Tauride Palace."

They ran on, to the end of the bridge.

Invest the bourgeoisie with all the tasks of waging war—but then this would free up our position significantly. Even up to and including temporarily somehow, well, maybe, to tone down the antiwar slogans?

It was the most dangerous point in the situation. But Shlyapnikov said nothing. And that was good. Well, it's true, they were running.

They turned left down the embankment. Time and again they heard unintelligible rifle shots nearby. Who was shooting? What for? What at?

Where were the bullets flying? There was no making sense of it. It was striking the last place you expected.

They ran past the Summer Garden to the Fontanka and decided to turn
off the embankment in order to bypass the Liteiny Bridge and get there with
less fuss.

Shlyapnikov disagreed with one thing after the other, of course—probably
just in case, since he couldn't have his own understanding, but at least
Himmer got the impression that the Bolsheviks had not made the decision to unleash the whirlwind. In any case, they had no slogans or plan at
the ready.

Even better, the leading unattached socialists would be able to head
them off and steer the course of events.

They ran past the Munitions Works' brick wall, straight toward the District Court fire. Several cannons stood in its fiery light on Sergievskaya, but
their barrels were all pointing in different directions and were unmanned,
so they didn't make a very martial impression. There were also ammunition
cases, and a carriage leaning on them, two barrels, the broken off wall of
some kind of booth, a few boards, and scattered furniture and junk—all of it
resembling a barricade, except that the barricade had no defenders. And
the groups of soldiers standing here and there at the intersection had no
connection to it whatsoever.

The firefighters were battling the fire in vain. The curious had collected,
but no one was helping. Here and there walls had collapsed; vaulted windows had held on. A wide surrounding area of the street was full of puddles
of melted snow.

They crossed the intersection and hurried on down Sergievskaya. The
unintelligible shots continued here, too, but not a single bullet stung.

From then on, the closer they got to the palace, the greater the animation.
On the sidewalks and pavement a mixed crowd of civilians and isolated soldiers jostled, lots of young people, but they were able to get through. There
were no rallies among the crowd.

Right at the palace, in front of it and on the square, vehicles of all kinds
and types were parked, starting, snorting, stopping, and setting off; armed
men hopped into some and jumped out of others, and there were women
in nearly every one. Rifle bayonets flashed by, poked up, everywhere. They
were loading cases onto one vehicle, and from another, on the contrary, unloading food supplies. The most terrible chaos and clamor reigned, and
nearly everyone was giving orders that no one was obeying. It was impossible to engage a single vehicle in conversation.

All right, at least they'd arrived unharmed. Now to get inside? It wasn't
that easy. A sentry was posted and a civilian Cerberus was in charge of
letting people through.

As it turned out, a leftist journalist acquaintance recognized Himmer
and let them in.

[1 2 8]

The lighting both on Shpalernaya and in front of the façade of the spread-eagled Tauride Palace, with its widely flung single-story wings had always been considered sufficient. But not for events like today! The street-lamps on Shpalernaya seemed sparse, the street not bright, and the square in front of the palace even dim for such a multitude, although the lamps were burning on the colonnaded porch and all the windows were lit. Over the two-story middle of the palace corpus, like a glimmering head raised separately in the darkness, was the enigmatically dreary, matte cupola. The impression was one of obscurity, concealment, and mystery, that here something secret was going on. And one wanted to get in.

By contrast, what brought lighting to mind were the crimson glows, so unusual for the city, coming from different directions, although impeded by the tedium of the blocks of stone buildings. Nearby, past the Tauride Garden, the Provincial Gendarme Administration on Tverskaya was burning. Not far away, but in the opposite direction, the District Court was burning. And between them in a third direction and a little farther away, the Aleksandr Nevsky station.

But in the square in front of the Tauride Palace, the motliest public had collected and was crowding in more and more. Lots of soldiers, either in groups that knew each other or separately—an odd, unintegrated rabble of exactly those beings who are normally never without formation or command. And the very first sailors from the crews. And more and more young people—young men and women students, young men and women workers, and even schoolboys. (There were no street adolescents because there was no shooting near the palace.) Vehicles, both motorcars and trucks, kept driving up and crowding in idly.

Many people pushed ahead, trying to penetrate the main doors, but the outside sentry pushed them back and shouted at them. This crowd of pressing civilians included well-off men, sometimes in expensive fur coats, who gave oral arguments to those checking as to why they needed to go in, while some thrust their documents at them.

For a while they checked strictly, went to the commandant's room to make inquiries, and brought back permission to enter. Then the crowd pressed harder and pushed back the guards—and broke in if they could. Later the guards got the upper hand and occupied their former posts and once again instituted strict control over entering.

Inside it was warm and in the halls there was truly enough light for a national holiday. So vast were the palace's inner rooms that all these waves of those who burst in and those allowed in drifted off, broke up, were swallowed up, and although the palace did get busy, it certainly wasn't crowded. Within two hours, though, the palace lost all decorum and formality, as only Duma members could appreciate.

They were nearly the only ones without outerwear, having handed it to the doormen that morning, as usual. So they went around in their frock coats and gleaming shirtfronts, amid the gathered outsiders dressed in fur coats, top coats, greatcoats, pea coats, peaked caps, and tall fur hats. Besides, the Duma deputies were already missing many of their number, and those who remained were dwindling to an obscure dash of the no longer usual masters of this palace, whose beauty and expanse they had not appreciated before. And the leaders had not shown themselves in order to deal authoritatively with the situation. The Duma's clerks and duty officers were vanishing little by little. The palace no longer had a master.

But those who burst in usually didn't know what to do next. They wandered around in their boots (leaving snow and mud on the parquet, which made you slip) and examined the halls. Idle soldiers gathered as well in reticent clusters, discussing quietly. But then they summoned their courage, looking at the scurrying, hurrying, educated gentlemen and students, and began themselves to scurry and scour. At one end of one corridor they discovered the buffet—and started helping themselves without asking or paying. The new soldiers got wind of the buffet—and cleaned it out instantly; no one dared try to prevent them.

The Ekaterininsky Hall was the size of a city square, and certain groups didn't bother others at all. One man scurried along pompously on business, another agonized over the indeterminacy, yet another waited for something patiently, impatiently. And the young people gathered in their own clusters. Someone climbed onto a chair and started a small rally.

In the Cupola Hall a long table appeared at which several men sat while others began swarming them, leaning over them. They were writing out passes and allowing someone something and sending someone somewhere.

More and more frequently through the vestibule doors they brought detainees—wearing policemen's uniforms but more often civilian clothing, prisoners of all ages and types. They were escorted by workers, soldiers, sailors, and ordinary people—bayonets atilt, revolvers raised and sabers or daggers bared. The people in the entrance, halls, and corridors looked at these detainees with avid curiosity. What attracted and called forth their malicious joy was that the police hadn't been catching people; they themselves had been caught, or some other malefactors previously out of reach! They stared hard at them.

They already knew where to take ones like that: to the financial commission's room. There, several members were meeting under the chairmanship of the dashing and strident Karaulov: Adzhemov, Papadzhanov, and Mansyrev. In the presence of the convoy that brought them they hastily interviewed the men brought in—and were immediately compelled to issue and did issue an instantaneous and final order on the detainee's fate: let him go or take him into custody. Where to take the detainees afterward had also been chosen: the rooms on the second floor, near the gallery. (Kerensky did not take small-timers like that into the ministerial pavilion.)

The escorts always had weapons—they were the only people there with weapons—and they burned with the fire of feverish justice and were proud that they had had the good sense to capture them and bring them in. It was almost impossible to let them go with bayonets and revolvers like that around. Although the men had been seized merely because these armed men didn't like their look, or for a disagreeable word spoken, or for not letting them into their apartment to search—it made more sense for now to arrest them, counting on letting them go tomorrow, and thanking the convoys and praising them for working hard to consolidate the revolution.

Back in the early evening, the members of the legislative chamber had been stunned by Shcheglovitov's arbitrary arrest. But now, only a few hours later, the Duma deputies seemed to have reconciled themselves and adapted to this, and here had also taken on a raft of trials without possessing any legal authority whatsoever, flouting it in Kerensky's wake. He had drawn them all to being a law unto themselves.

Later in the evening, a large convoy entered the Cupola Hall to great commotion, bringing thirty men at once—men wearing the uniforms of gendarme officers, policemen, and civilian dress. The convoy was under the command of a gray-haired old man on crutches who had put on a lieutenant's uniform—probably his own old one that had been lying around for a long time. In the middle of the Cupola Hall he loudly announced that he was asking to report to the *leader of the revolution, Deputy Kerensky*.

And although Kerensky was not anywhere near—to this summons, out of thin air, he appeared!

Kerensky quickly revealed—indeed, it had always lived inside him!—the manner of holding himself strikingly and nobly before the revolutionary mass. Now he walked up—neither slowly (so he would not look arrogant) nor quickly (so as not to be ingratiating). He stopped in front of the old man with proud and erect bearing—but also with great attention, his head slightly tilted.

The invalid attempted to stand at attention as much as he could on crutches and salute. He reported distinctly, providing fierce food for the first revolutionary newspapers.

"I have the honor to report that I have captured, disarmed, and brought in thirty *enemies of the people*! I place their heads at your disposal, Mr. Deputy!"

Kerensky replied ringingly, with understanding and approval, as if he had been waiting for nothing but this report and this invalid.

"I thank you, lieutenant! And I am counting on you from this time forward."

He didn't ask who they were or why they'd been arrested or under what circumstances. And he didn't send them to the commission, which he knew all about, for questioning. But above all maintaining his bearing and the uniqueness of the moment, with a tone of revolutionary loathing, he quietly commanded, without knowing who would respond:

"Take them away."

And he exited with a self-importance that was neither too quick nor too slow.

The convoy shifted from foot to foot. The lieutenant thought about it. He thought they'd brought them this far, so what now?

And then someone from the crowd they'd attracted rushed through the convoy to strike the enemies of the people with his fists.

Others used their rifle butts. Drawing blood.

The convoy, too, joined in the beating.

The enemies didn't dare defend themselves. Some cried for mercy, some fell under the blows.

Then they were led away to the prisoner rooms, to the gallery.

[1 2 9]

That afternoon there was a lull in the Okhta area. On Okhta's Bolshoi Prospect, where people had been thick the last few days, there was now almost no one. You couldn't go directly onto the ice here. The bridge was blocked. There was shooting in the city, seething in the city, fires had been started there, but what was happening there, that no one knew.

But for those itching to get at the whole thing—a gang thronged in a large bend along the Polyustrovskaya Embankment and onto the Vyborg side. But the calmer folk stayed in Okhta, mostly in their homes, since there was a strike anyway.

But there weren't any policemen at their posts, or any patrols. They'd gathered at their stations and were sitting there, just peeking out the windows, coppers' ugly mugs.

The shooting continued in the city—but it was calm in Okhta.

And the day was over.

By evening the young Okhta men had flooded back, and those who had looted the Arsenal—they had rifles.

They gathered here and there: Why don't we pull out our own coppers? They've been finished off everywhere else, after all, and no help is going to reach them in time.

The 1st Infantry Regiment was stationed in Okhta—and wouldn't mutiny. They sent their lads to see them, and they replied, "Why the heck do we need that?" There's a good-for-nothing uniform for you.

People had also been sent to tell the soldiers: the whole Petersburg garrison has risen up, so what are you waiting for?

Finally, it seemed like they'd risen up, shown themselves, seemed like they'd knock down the fence—but no one was coming through the streets, no one was coming to help us.

Well, we won't wait! They thronged to the police station themselves, in a crowd, smashing streetlamps. (Listen to it ring, and see it go out—it does the heart good!)

At the corner of Georgievskaya and Bolshoi, people were surging toward the station—but they opened their windows wide and started taking shots.

Drop back!

But no one was wounded. (They may have fired upward.)

They flooded on, into the side-streets, and started waiting.

Waiting for the 1st Regiment to send a truck with soldiers.

It wasn't sending one.

While in the city, all the while, there was shooting and more shooting. The glow was vivid in the darkness. The glowing tears so at the soul: Hey, let's show 'em! How are we any worse! There, on the Petersburg side, the boys are going to gain their freedom—and we're going to stay like this?

What are we so timid for, boys? Let's gather up! All go at once!

Exactly, at once. What if we get going and they aren't coming around the corner?

Send word: at the whistle—all at once!

The whistle! I'll give you what for! This cuts cleaner than any shot! The whistle of Solovey Razboinik!

And men came running from all sides! They grabbed the policemen, who couldn't even get off a shot, and here we clung to the walls, we smashed their windows with rocks and ice and broke down the doors with whatever came to hand.

Everyone inside! And what won't a crowd do? Those policemen were quaking in their boots because they had nowhere to go? You're not going anywhere, yours are all far away!

The crowd didn't fire a shot.

They rounded them up, five to a copper, punched him in the face for starters—but only for starters. Then with arms pulled back and twisted—they dragged them outside, where there was room for easier beating. Some shouted and cursed; others moaned; still others begged.

No, you're not going to beg your way out of this now! Oh no, you've got it coming! You had your turn lording it over us, and now we're over you!

"Brothers! . . . For God's sake! . . . I have children. . . ."

Beat them, grind them to sausage, don't listen! Oh you, children! Keep beating with whatever's handy—sticks, rifle butts, bayonets, stones, boots to the ear, heads on the pavement, break their bones, stomp them, trample them, even dance on them!

From one more, his last:

"My brothers . . ."

And how did you grab us when we weren't your brothers? Hey, whoever's finished beating theirs, made 'em croak, come help us finish our dance!

And their papers—chuck 'em outside!

What for? Set fire to them and the walls, too!

Hey, here's when our life starts—only now!

We don't want to live with police anymore. We want to live in total freedom!

[1 3 0]

Count Musin-Pushkin's home on Liteiny had its solid oak doors locked, but inside it was jammed with Semyonovsky, Preobrazhensky, and Kexholm soldiers, whoever had managed to run in, and whatever wounded they had been able to pick up and carry inside.

Anyone who remained outside had to make themselves into rebels for the crowd, and fast.

If over the day two thousand had come under Kutepov's command, then there were about sixty wounded collected here.

The infirmary director and doctors asked the colonel at least to remove all the healthy soldiers from the building.

Yes, it had come to that.

But there was nowhere to assemble and line them up for the farewell—no such room or even hallway. The colonel assembled them on the stairs, himself standing on the middle landing, at the turn in the dark lacquered banister, and spoke first down, then up, unable to see them all at the same time.

He didn't have time to remember many of them by face, but did remember some. He'd had hundreds of Preobrazhensky men at the front with whom he'd passed through all the fields of death, but these chance half-soldiers, still not prepared for war, for some reason not a single recuperating acquaintance, and he himself here by chance, and their battle had been chaotic, jerky, barely resembling a battle at all—but all of a sudden Aleksandr Pavlovich was struck that all his previous battles might not hold a candle to today's, which he would remember for the rest of his days. Though he had lost it.

He addressed the shoulder-crammed staircase:

"Soldiers! In the name of the Sovereign Emperor . . . and in the name of Russia . . . I thank you for your honesty and steadfastness today. I would have awarded all of you a St. George . . . but I can't even nominate them . . . The enemy is doing his ruthless deed. He is striking us from behind in the middle of a Great War. I am compelled now to disband you all. Go through the streets and return to your barracks, and if you cannot resist, at least do not abet the enemy! . . . For now, hand in all your rifles and all your cartridges and stow them in the attic. Then divide yourselves up into small groups with your sergeant—and be on your way. And may God bless you!"

The staircase murmured warmly and unintelligibly, such as soldiers never respond. They weren't real soldiers, after all. But then they weren't in formation, either.

All the rest happened in Kutepov's absence, he having been called in to see Sergeant Essen the 4th.

All too young, he was dying. Clutching the colonel's arm, he asked him to tell his relatives and his regiment that at his first trial he conducted himself worthily and had not stained the immortal Semyonovsky Regiment.

Kutepov shook his hand in return. And wrote down the address. And stroked his pale, sweaty brow.

The other wounded men all fell silent and listened. They had all been here long since, stale, some three months gone from the front.

Then Kutepov went to find out where they'd put Sergeant Soloviev. He had already been given the last rites. No sign he was clinging to life, as there was in Essen, and he lay on his back stretched out, immobile. But his half-open eyes still expressed consciousness, and there was a smile on his lips — back before Kutepov and while he was there, a young, perfectly easygoing smile. Only stiffening.

Outside, meanwhile, the riled crowd, those who hadn't dispersed yet and remembered that their enemies had gone into this building, seethed. And shouted threats at the colonel and raised their fists and rifles.

If the building hadn't had the large banner of the Red Cross, they would have shot at the windows and doors long ago.

The couple who owned the building, afraid for their home but not saying so, made the colonel several suggestions, trying to convince the colonel to change into civilian clothing and leave that way.

If you looked closely, Kutepov had a unique and permanent expression on his face — as if he wanted to grin but had stopped the movement of his features and vivid lips between his stiff black mustache and beard. This freezing of features and his lush eyes seemed to express sorrow and reproach — or surprise? or doom?

He had been wounded five times, if you counted from the Japanese war. Kutepov took them both by the hand, as he had the dying Essen:

"Dear madam and sir, do not try to incline me toward an unworthy masquerade. I have never yet been ashamed of the Russian military uniform. As soon as the opportunity arises, I will quit your home."

He sent two of the remaining sergeants to scout out the whole situation outside and to see whether there was some unguarded exit.

Half an hour later one returned and reported that parties of armed workers were standing at all the possible exits and were especially waiting for the colonel in particular, and everyone already knew his name: Kutepov.

Oh well, he let this sergeant go and was left completely alone. In the little room assigned to him, he often put out the light and observed for long stretches what was happening on Liteiny, with its noisy through traffic, even automotive already.

Late that night, a Preobrazhensky lance corporal well known to the colonel penetrated the building and brought from his sergeant-major a bundle with a soldier's uniform. He assured him that they weren't guarding all that closely and he could get out in soldier's dress.

Aleksandr Pavlovich hesitated: This uniform was his, the Preobrazhensky. And then: No! It was a repulsive masquerade in any case.

He sent him away.

[1 3 1]

The movements of the Baltic fleet during the winter months were inhibited by the icy expanses, the dreadnaughts and the battleships moored for winter anchorage in the Helsingfors harbor, on a mooring anchor; only torpedo boats went far out to sea, protecting the approaches. However, due to the ice, the enemy could not descend upon them here either. And so, at anchorage in Helsingfors, there was only the watch service on the vessels, the usual steady routine, and also a few training hours per day—the most advantageous time for sailors. And for the officers, if they were ever to get to talk, to read and think—this was the time.

Captains First Rank Prince Mikhail Cherkassky, Ivan Rengarten, and Captain Second Rank Fyodor Dovkont on the *Krechet*, the Commander's headquarters vessel, had started holding regular discussions among themselves on political topics this winter. They were almost entirely of like mind, the Navy's "Young Turks." They loved their navy and themselves in this navy as men who could guide it to glory with authority—intelligent, responsive to events, with firm decisions and easy movements. But what they placed above all was whatever Russia needed. And if anyone knew and surely said to any of them at any minute that their death was needed for Russia's salvation, each was prepared to die that very minute.

Like a shining and beloved ache, this had grown in their soul from youth, along with us: Russia! The tractless land, the great and heartfelt people— washed with tears, and robbed, and in the dark, and in ignorance, and nearly always in the hands of unworthy rulers. The duty they had taken in with their mother's milk was to give the people everything we had deprived them of unjustly. The precious, bequeathed impulse: The Decembrists! Herzen! And the list of those who had suffered for the people, enlighteners, self-sacrificing insurrectionists. How much had been done for the people's freedom! Could it all really have been in vain? Each of the three men fervently loved the sacred liberation tradition of the past century and owed a debt to it and felt the strength inside to carry on!

Through their service, they had come together and risen around the Commander of the Baltic Fleet. Misha Cherkassky was now flag-captain for operations and Vanya Rengarten head of reconnaissance. And with the recent appointment of the young Vice-Admiral Nepenin as Commander, the significance of their posts and the promise of their possibilities had grown even more. Although *Adrian*—as they called the admiral among themselves—was not as thoroughly developed in the tradition of Liberation, what educated Russian had not had a shadow cast on him by its wings? Adrian was by nature impatiently direct, and honest, and he responded nobly to everything noble. So the three of them knew with a steady joy that even the admiral agreed with them. With increasing daring and success they openly expressed to him their opinions, trying to unite even more tightly.

In their secret three-way discussions, although minutes were taken, they had discussed this spring the general issues of a possible program for Great Russia. And of course, in detail the issue of the Straits, which were by no means an imperial aspiration but were a vital necessity—and a favorable situation was being created for the first time in two or three centuries for our taking the Straits. Most of all they discussed the present domestic political situation and how to lead Russia out of it.

All this endless Rasputin-Stürmer-Protopopov business, and possibly state treason, liaisons with the enemy—how could their homeland be pulled out of this filthy mess? Of the possible decisions, the most radical and sure path offered itself: eliminate the Colonel (Nikolai II) and thereby eliminate his entire clique. Sitting on their ships, they could not participate in this directly, but they could offer ideas, make contact, and use their position to influence. Such was the decision—not theirs alone, however all this did not lead to any action and somewhere got tangled up in an excess of sympathetic conspirators and a shortage of realistic ones.

But these last few days, and especially today, events in Petrograd had gushed out—and they couldn't stand idle anymore!

For communications, they summoned by disguised wire their trusted First Lieutenant Kostya Zhitkov. They themselves had met in the flag-captain's cabin since six o'clock in the evening. Misha Cherkassky set forth the plan of action as he had worked it out.

It is easy to read about historic events as if they'd been readied. But when they're happening, it's anything but easy to work out the simplest plan of action. Here, events had taken an ominous turn, and the moment was already slipping away. Clearly, the Duma, and all public figures, were sluggish and flabby and wouldn't be able to pounce on the situation that had arisen. It was essential to give them an impulse from without, to spur them to take up an active role. None of the three could leave his post on ship, but Kostya Zhitkov would go to see one or two public figures and convince them to arrange a private conference where he would report responsibly on the mood of authoritative circles in the navy. These figures could not help but select prominent individuals from among their number and send them to calm the Army group commanders and keep them from intervening. The objective was only that they not intervene, that the army remain neutral—but on the other hand, here the support of the Baltic fleet was assured. Wasn't this support for the mutinous capital? To encourage public figures to act quickly, asking no one's permission and electing a government responsible to the Legislative body. And simply bring all that had happened to the Colonel's attention: the government he had appointed no longer existed. Given this fact, the entire supreme camarilla should be disregarded and removed from power. The ages-old dream had come true! Russia was on a new path!

It was a marvelous plan—assuming they could count on Nepenin's firm support. However, knowing his impatient, freedom-loving attitude toward the camarilla, it was obvious they would have it. And in any case, Prince Cherkassky himself led naval headquarters.

The flag officers would then simply obey the Commander's orders. Try to neutralize the other officers who might cause harm to the spread of the idea, and if possible, attract them to our side. And the navy would be all ours!

So they sat in a locked cabin with two portholes, and although they couldn't see roaring Petrograd, they did feel the stirring touch of Russian history.

Although in a different manner, a different uniform, and a different century, they were intrepidly repeating the Decembrists' failed exploit.

[1 3 2]

It had taken off! Kayurov had been everywhere. He'd been to see the Wheeled Battalion, where the soldiers were lined up. He'd asked the soldiers, "Why are you standing there, comrades? Why aren't you joining in?" The soldiers gave him an off-smile, and the officers rudely suggested he move along. "Where am I supposed to move along to when the entire avenue is blocked off?"

He ran over to the Moscow barracks a few times. These had finally been taken, and our crowd filled the entire yard—and many weapons had been handed over to us, in fact, lots of soldiers surrendered them willingly, and they themselves climbed onto the bunks.

Now both Vaska Kayurov and Pashka Chugurin each had a rifle and an ammunition belt across his shoulder. When you walk around with a weapon, even if you don't know how to shoot, you have a completely different strength, and your feet carry you so much more lightly.

They went on to storm and set fire to two more police stations, picked off a few policemen, beat up the rest and arrested them—and put them in their own lockup.

The day rolled along like the great flood of an unexpected revolution. Then even the sun almost peeked in. The masses roamed and roved, congratulated each other, here and there thoughtlessly robbed shops. People's joy made them feel like having a bite to eat and especially obtaining spirits, but that took searching and devising since there had not been government wine shops for three years.

The mutinous mass's general exultation was dancing, and only infrequent shots from some stubborn defenders of the regime somewhere and the incomprehensible obstinacy of the Wheeled Battalion units were spoiling the mood.

Right then they brought Shlyapnikov's now ready leaflet: "Continue the general strike!" What a laugh!

Vasya Kayurov began to think, and it crossed his mind that now if the revolution won out, then lots of clever, deft people would turn up and they'd all start clutching at power. In the meantime, the Bolsheviks needed to get the jump on everyone before the other parties picked up the scent.

But what would it take to do that? Somehow he had to shout at the top of his lungs, like through a megaphone, shout to the whole working class and the entire soldiery. No, a leaflet wasn't what was needed, what was needed here was . . .

Kayurov felt as if he were about to burst, so he went to find comrades to confer with.

Vast was the Vyborg side, but for anyone who knew this place well, it was like one big neighborhood, and he knew everything and everyone. Everyone had gone their separate ways, but when Kayurov started cutting through the crowd, he found Khakharev. But none of them could find Shlyapnikov anywhere. Where had he gone?

They went back to Kayurov's apartment to confer.

"We have to, brothers," Kayurov was thinking. "In these instances the Tsar—he writes a Manifesto. That's what we should roll out—a Manifesto! From the Bolsheviks."

Explain that we're the ones who'll be leading them all forward now. Otherwise they'll snatch it away from us.

That may well be, but wishing is about zeal, whereas composing, writing takes a knack. Are we taught that?

Patterning was clever work, but Kayurov knew that writing was even cleverer.

"Oh, the way they knew how to when we were in Sormovo, I remember, in 1904: 'Let them shoot us, and let the newborn Tsarevich swim in our blood!' That's the ticket! We've gotta . . ."

"Pyotr Zalomov knew how!" his fellow Sormovo men recalled.

Khakharev sat down with a pencil to sketch it out while Kayurov paced around the room—and they proceeded to compose.

But an old idea kept coming back: how the workers' consciousness had been repressed, how they had oppressed us, robbed us. You know—the Tsar's gang, the revolutionary proletariat, the eight-hour workday, of course. Confiscation of monastic lands.

No, even fresher: the red banner of insurrection! Let's destroy the kingdom of lackeys!

No, they were missing something important.

MARCH 1917 / 491

"All right, let's go see Mitka Pavlov and consult with him, he's more literate. Maybe even Gavrilych is there."

Off they went. It was already growing dark.

Mitka Pavlov was another of them, from Sormovo, and even in 1902, when Pyotr Zalomov carried around "Down with autocracy," Mitka walked alongside holding the banner's edge, so it would be easier for people to read. Later, he wasn't taken on at the factory, and like Kayurov made ends meet in the co-operative, while at his apartment they concocted explosives for bombs. After the uprising he left straightaway for Petersburg, where he was accepted as one of their own, for ten years. He married and went to build aeroplanes. His apartment on Serdobolskaya stood amid vacant lots and sheds, so it was hard for police spies to tail him. Now this was the safe house and apartment of the Bureau of the Central Committee, and papers were secreted away in the chess table.

They arrived—and in his vestibule he had drying "Down with autocracy" and "Long live the revolution"—which the painter had written across bunting.

Also in the apartment sat meat-faced Molotov, from the Bureau of the Central Committee. He'd sat like that the whole day through and only learned what was happening where in the city from those who came. Kayurov told him a little, and he found it hard to believe.

Kayurov gave Mitka Pavlov his Manifesto to read.

Mitka added:

"Onward! There's no going back! A battle without mercy!"

But Molotov, the mama's boy:

"But what's this? What's this?"

He gathered up the paper, read it, and wiped his hands as if he'd been scorched:

"Isn't this jumping the gun, Comrade Kayurov?"

Kayurov took offense.

"No, it isn't! It isn't jumping the gun! But where's Gavrilych?"

Shlyapnikov had been here half the day but had left.

"It isn't jumping the gun! As it is we're going to miss the whole thing! The minutes are burning up!"

But Molotov took out a pencil, rubbed his hands—and started crossing things out.

[1 3 3]

It had crept up on him sort of imperceptibly and taken such an unexpected turn. As of that morning, the entire city of Petrograd, all its outlying areas, and the entire province had been in General Khabalov's hands. Then, over the course of the day, there had been no battles whatsoever apart from a few actions by Colonel Kutepov on Liteiny, about which he never could get a clear picture, and minor crossfire at the Moscow Battalion Life Guards. And all of a sudden, by day's end, Khabalov held neither the province, nor the outlying areas, nor the city and could attest to nothing more than a narrow strip between the Neva and the Moika—Admiralty Island, and also the Peter and Paul Fortress, which he had no idea what to do with, off to the side.

All day he'd been trying and trying to establish contact with the various military units in the various parts of the city. Nearly all the battalions had remained loyal, only they didn't dare send out their reserves or watches—and all this loyalty, and all these battalions, had imperceptibly slipped through his fingers, and here he had the strip between the Neva and Moika left. Only snatches of information had come in regarding everything outside this strip, so it was very hard to put together a picture.

Apart from all these units in the city, there were also the military schools: two infantry, the Pavlovsky and Vladimirsky, one cavalry, the Nikolaevsky, two artillery, the Mikhailovsky and Konstantinovsky, one engineering, and a drivers school and the different corps—Sea Cadet, Pages, and two other cadet corps—all of which came to more than two thousand bayonets, two hundred sabers, sixteen guns, and eight armored vehicles. Several times that day Khabalov had been reminded of the military schools, encouraged to incite them to action and assured that the young men were raring to put down the insurrection. But somehow that didn't feel right. No. After all, there were plenty of loyal battalions without that, and the plan for the city's defense did not have anything in it about bringing in the schools, there was no mention of it. And how afterward would society reproach him for involving young men in politics and internecine strife!

So all that day Khabalov had not called up a single military school. Let them study. Nor had he managed to summon a single ensign school from the outlying areas.

Reinforcements had been coming in of their own accord from time to time. At about five o'clock, as the sun was starting to set, a Guards reserve battery of eight guns in full order and with fifty-two live shells suddenly arrived from Pavlovsk, having been called up that morning. Its commander, Colonel Potekhin, although he used a crutch, was agile and evidently much obeyed.

Not bad. It was a good force. But where to use it in the city? Not to lob shells at buildings.

Other reserve units had gathered with Khabalov at the city governor's office in the second half of the day: one squadron, a gendarme division, and mounted and foot police. He had even larger forces descending upon Palace Square. He had the forces, yes, but the harder problem was where to move them. General Zankevich, who had flown there like an eagle, returned all wet and discouraged; they could not rely on the Preobrazhensky men. Just imagine!

Now there were differing points of view, and they were gradually worked through among the leading generals. (The overlap with Zankevich was still a great bother. Who was subordinate to whom? Who was leading the troops? He had no idea.) Tyazhelnikov suggested that they abandon the city center altogether, where there were no provisions for the troops, and fight through to the outskirts or even away from the city. And then from there attack in concentrated fashion. In any case, the more shaky troops taken out of the city, the less combustible material would remain in it itself.

That might well be so. But where were they to fight through to? To the Vyborg side and onward to Kushelevka for cartridges and shells? That was the very thick of the rebels. There would be a major bloodbath and their cartridges wouldn't last. To Tsarskoye Selo, to join up with the large garrison there? And there wait conveniently for help from the Field Army? Or entrench on the Pulkovo Heights? But that would mean abandoning the city altogether. And that was not envisaged by the defense plan, nor had Khabalov been so instructed. How would the Peter and Paul Fortress remain?

But maybe they could adopt the principle of solid all-round defense and defend Admiralty Island.

It was an extremely difficult decision to make, much too unusual and too crucial. Their heads were already clouded and heavy, and everyone's thoughts could barely take a step.

Meanwhile, the hours were passing, and the day was ending and turning gray, the day the Emperor had ordered them to put an end to the disturbances. But they hadn't.

The day was ending, and unreassuring information began coming in from Palace Square. The sailors of the Guards crew had stood there and left, removed by Grand Duke Kirill. The Preobrazhensky companies had left to have their dinner—and hadn't returned. The Pavlovsky Battalion taken to the cellars of the Winter Palace had panicked and broken out and gone to their barracks. And the machine-gun half-company had taken off somewhere. The Kexholmers, too. After that, whatever small remnants there were Zankevich had sensibly removed from the square entirely and led to the city governor's office.

But it should also be acknowledged that during these hours the rebels' command had not undertaken any actions against government forces either. According to reconnaissance reports, there were no large gatherings anywhere except at the Tauride Palace. By evening the crowds were gradually melting away from the streets.

So that with his remaining forces, Khabalov could have marched straight to the Tauride Palace.

But that had not been envisaged by the defense plan either. How's that? Strike a blow against the State Duma? The State Duma could not be viewed as an enemy or a rebel. Under no plan were any forces in Petrograd intended to be used against the State Duma.

But on the other hand, if there were some kind of oppositional center, then wasn't it precisely the Tauride Palace?

It was so odd. And unclear.

The generals discussed and discussed the plan for the city's defense. Actually, could they be certain that Admiralty Island was still in their hands? In the darkness, and given their poor reconnaissance, you couldn't keep track of that. They were known to have possession of only a few buildings: the city governor's office itself, the Admiralty, and the Winter Palace. Presumably (they had not been monitoring it), the General Staff building as well. Also, the telephone exchange at 24 Morskaya. Also the barracks of the Cavalry Regiment Life Guards. At one end of the zone was the Mariinsky Palace, but there were almost no forces for its defense. What was the right way to position their defense for the night? You couldn't guard all of it. And if they kept an entire company at the telephone exchange (for the convenience of residents, so that the telephone wouldn't get cut off), then it was impossible to have a solid defense for the core. Best of all would be to concentrate in some one building and defend that.

Which building to choose? General Zankevich suggested the Winter Palace, as a symbol of the monarchy. But General Khabalov, after some thought, preferred the Admiralty. It stood quite separately, surrounded by squares, which made its defense easier, and from it three directions leading to four train stations opened up—Nevsky, Gorokhovaya, and Voznesensky, which could be fired upon with the cannons they had. And it was close to the city governor's office, so we wouldn't be losing that.

It was already dark when they resolved to move everything to the Admiralty.

Shifting the troops wasn't hard because it was very close and there were no obstacles.

First the artillery dragged itself over, skirting the square.

The infantry went straight across.

Then the foot and mounted policemen.

The detachment crossed over drowsy and listless, having been idle all day.

It was harder for City Governor Balk. At first he assembled all his officials and announced that their activities had ended and they should disperse to their homes. (They asked whether they should come to work tomorrow. He said only if shooting in the streets did not prevent them from moving about safely.) He took with him only a few aides. The city governor's offices had already ceased to be the police center. Although the city telephones kept operating reliably as before, the connection to most police stations had already been cut.

It was impossible now to withdraw, and, in plain sight of outsiders, Balk began burning the secret correspondence from his drawers.

He ordered the building custodians to lock up the city governor's offices after everyone had left. And to report all incidents by telephone to the Admiralty.

There was no time for dinner. They just went.

Far off in the city they could hear rifle fire. And see a glow.

The motorcars with senior officials were supposed to make a detour past St. Isaac's Cathedral—but there, off more or less toward the Senate, a machine gun started firing. They had no idea where from or at whom.

And the day was coming to an end. Khabalov could not avoid wiring his dispatch to GHQ for the day.

. . . I have been unable to carry out His Imperial Majesty's command. . . . Most of the units have betrayed their duty, refusing to fight the rebels. Others have even turned their weapons against troops loyal to His Majesty. By evening, rebels hold the greater part of the capital. . . .

That was virtually so. Not just some mutinous units, but a collection of rebels, everywhere. The entire city was full of them.

. . . Small units remain loyal to their oath, and with them I will continue the fight. . . .

[1 3 4]

No one attempted to break into Turner's clinic—and Captain Nelidov and his ill-starred sergeants could move freely about the courtyard and vestibule, behind the locked gate.

But it had become clear that he had no chance of breaking through to their barracks with them as an intact detachment, through the seething streets, and with only one leg.

Even more closed was the chance of him venturing out alone.

The battalion telephone had stopped answering.

Nelidov started sending out unarmed scouts—in ones and twos. Their intelligence gave him a picture of the authorities' total collapse, the wild armed crowds all over the Vyborg side, and the impossibility of an officer showing his face.

About the battalion barracks themselves he learned toward nightfall that after some shooting they had surrendered and been opened to the crowd.

Meanwhile, a sergeant-major had brought the captain a list of all the sergeants and lance corporals present.

To what end?

Well, they all asked to be remembered and have it confirmed that not one of them had gone over to the rebels.

But they had easily given him up for slaughter. What prudent sergeants! No, it would have been better to leave them to fast.

There was no way a battle lay in store. Could they hold onto the clinic, and if so, to what end? How could he feed them here? He should let them all go back to barracks.

However, Nelidov did not want to give their weapons back to the barracks the insurrectionists had seized. He ordered the sergeants to disassemble all the rifles and hide them here, at the clinic. After which he released them all.

He himself remained sitting in the porter's room. He had no idea, had lost his way. What could he do? Had he been mobile and healthy—but he had a hard time getting around, after all—just barely, at a walk.

He had no family or home in Petrograd. He had only ended up here because of his injury anyway. He had bonded with his regiment and his place was at the front, apparently the only place still warm, where everyone was awaiting his return.

He did know people he could spend the night with, but they were on the other side of Nevsky. And he had no chance of reaching his battalion.

But it wasn't himself Nelidov was mulling over. He could lie down on the bare bench here, in the porter's room, and sleep, if the infirmary supervisors didn't ask him in, which seemed unlikely, as though they were shying away from the picket. No, Nelidov was trying to understand this insane mess. The capital had mutinied during time of war? Not just the capital, but the Cossacks were for the rebels? What impossible thing was happening and how would it end? Evidently there was no other solution than to call troops back from the front to put this down. But how much blood would be shed? What a stain on Russia. And what a loss for the front.

How many extremes and dangers had he been through during the war years—only to get bogged down here! It was frustrating and demeaning.

But after all, a few of them, combat officers, had petitioned to be issued armored vehicles and taught how to operate them, just in case. Even a wounded officer in an armored vehicle can be worth an entire company of rabble.

However, their petition had died, and the idea did not take hold with the authorities.

How clear this lapse was today!

Instead, he had had to train soldiers without rifles and affix the company's censor's stamp to three hundred soldier letters every day.

Despondent, Nelidov was sitting at the porter's when all of a sudden a worker came in wearing a black jacket and black cap. His clothing and certain rather sinister appearance that develops in factories, perhaps, said he was a typical worker, one of the very ones who had grabbed Nelidov by the arms today and wanted to kill him.

Nelidov thought, Well, here it is! He's going to turn me in now.

Tall, skinny, older perhaps, but strong—but on his shaven face, with its big mustache, there was a stern gravity. He did—and didn't—look like *them*.

The worker greeted the captain with a bow. He turned out to be an acquaintance or maybe a relative of the porter, whom he sat down and talked with while examining the captain. He said:

"No, your honor, you can't go outside. Why do you have that stick? Wounded at the front?"

Nelidov replied.

"You really can't go outside." The man shook his head. "Those bandits will shoot you on the spot. Why don't you go rest up at my place? We'll avoid the street."

His tobacco-infused voice and grave tone elicited trust. He had nothing better left. They went. The worker slowed down for the captain's wounded leg.

Through a back door, a dark courtyard, and another courtyard—they went around and ended up at the back of the worker's little house, an ordinary single-story worker's house, set well back in the third courtyard, meagerly illuminated.

The mistress was a broad and battered woman with a stern face.

She offered him something to eat, but Nelidov couldn't. He could barely stand.

They led him to a small, narrow bedroom with a single, narrow iron cot, a chest of drawers, a tiny kerosene lamp, and a single shuttered window.

The courtyard was like a trap, but his hosts elicited total trust, even though Nelidov barely managed to speak with them.

He noticed his hands were shaking, as if from a new contusion, but he was on fire, an inner fire. He seemed to be falling ill.

But he didn't tell his hosts. He undressed and lay down, lifting his atrophied leg with his hands as usual.

He thought he was too agitated to fall asleep. And he fell asleep immediately.

[1 3 5]

After his exploit against the grenadiers, Peshekhonov returned home, where several acquaintances, all from the Petersburg side, were waiting for him.

They had sat down to drink tea, of course—what kind of Russian conversation is it without tea?—and right then Peshekhonov's wife returned from making house calls. In their ordinary dining room with its pinkish tablecloth under a pinkish lampshade, they munched on petit fours, spooned strawberry and plum jam into saucers—and themselves seemed bewitched by the bright and unexpected luminescence of joy. They couldn't let themselves believe it—yet they also couldn't ignore the facts or deny the shift that had come about. Here they had only a holiday shift of mood—but there, across the Neva, were genuine battles, entire insurgent regiments—so why should there be any hesitation to use that word? Yes, this was **It**, long-awaited and long-dreamed for, even if it did get hurled back into the abyss, beheaded, hanged. It had come nevertheless, hadn't It?

But the enemy had all the footholds, and it was too soon to rejoice.

So they'd been sitting for maybe a couple of hours when, from the street, through the caulked windows, they heard powerful shouts.

Sitting any longer was out of the question! They abandoned their unfinished cups and hurriedly, dressing carelessly, and slipped their quaking feet into their galoshes, stepping on the edges, when they were already tramping down the staircase—and running, running down.

The shouts were coming from the square on Kamennoostrovsky, where Arkhiereiskaya crosses Bolshoi Prospect. They raced there.

The little square surrounded by a line of streetlamps was filled with joyous people who were shouting and waving—and in the middle, two open trucks loomed, each with a dozen or so men bristling with bayonets and red flags. There were women among them as well, and they too were brandishing revolvers.

Peshekhonov began pushing toward the closer truck, near a Belogrud building with little towers. The din was unimaginable. Everyone in the crowd was shouting at once, and also from the truck, and it was nearly impossible to understand. Gradually, Peshekhonov gathered that the revolutionaries had broken across the Trinity Bridge and wanted to "remove" the troops here and storm the police. Now they were asking where the police stations were and where the military units were quartered and which way they should go. But because they were all asking everyone and everyone was answering at once, they hadn't been able to clarify this for fifteen minutes already.

Peshekhonov felt so sorry for this naïve and good-natured, leaderless popular mass: the limit of imagination of their hatred was simply the police on their beat, who did nothing but preserve the usual order, which is always necessary in any civilized state. Whereas here, on the Petersburg side, since they had broken through here, sat a venomous spider web—the Okhrana— and that was what should be first in their sights—not so much to storm, but to seize! Very valuable secret documents, the key to disclosing informants and rendering the spider web harmless! Peshekhonov, grabbing on clumsily to the side of the truck, shouted to them so passionately that his cap nearly flew off about the Okhrana and how this was of the utmost importance and how they could get to the Mytninskaya Embankment! Some even leaned toward him and listened—but they could scarcely have heard or understood anything in that muddle.

He himself would have gone with them if he knew he was guiding them. He felt a brave heart grow in his no longer young chest and ignore the impossibilities of an intellectual's body.

No, he couldn't sit over tea any longer and discuss how something was happening somewhere! He had to participate himself! The Trinity Bridge was open, so there was no justification for inaction!

The trucks drove off. After jostling among the people some more, Peshekhonov saw his guest and asked him to tell his wife that he was heading for the Tauride Palace—and he started down Kamennoostrovsky.

The Tauride Palace was the movement's logically possible center. If the flame of revolution was blazing anywhere, it was there.

Right then he met up with someone else he knew who was heading in that direction. They went together.

Racing toward them down Kamennoostrovsky from time to time were revolutionary trucks, speeding by like wild, fantastic visions, lighting up under the streetlamps, darkening on the stretches. How beautiful and terrible was the Revolution's countenance! What an unexpected image!

One truck was tossing out papers of some kind. They picked one up and read it right there, under a streetlamp. It was the hectographed proclamation of the Provisional Executive Committee of the Soviet of Workers' Deputies. Oh ho! So things had gone that far! There was already a Soviet of Workers' Deputies! And we're missing out on everything here! The leaflet called on the population to feed and shelter the revolutionary soldiers, who had spent all day on the street trying to win their freedom.

But what about the Okhrana? Until the Okhrana was routed, no victory was secure. Tomorrow it would revive its activities! It might even be functioning this very minute!

Peshekhonov and his companion, now by the Trinity Bridge, with their weak cries but even more with their signals and broad arm waving, were able after all to attract and stop one vehicle. There was no one nearby shouting, so now they were able to explain about the Okhrana and how to get there—but the others were so agitated, it was as if they'd been wound up by internal springs, they found the delay impossible, and they were speeding somewhere toward a contemplated but invisible, nonexistent goal—and they dashed off, dashed off farther.

The Trinity Bridge was almost free of pedestrians, empty, while on the other side three fire glows were scarily crimson—two on the left and one far on the right.

On the other bank of the Neva they were expecting to encounter a revolutionary sea, all Petrograd on the streets—but nothing of the kind. It was just as scarily and sinisterly deserted on the French Embankment, all the palaces' windows dark, and only once did frantic vehicles race past in both directions.

They turned onto Liteiny, and this was where the principal fire was revealed to them, as they already knew. Since early morning the building of Judicial Determinations, the District Court, Bazhenov's beauty—the creation of a luckless architect who had seen everything of his either not built at all, or not completed, or perished—had been set on fire and was burning still. Its incandescent skeleton was still glowing, but everything inside had burned up. And there had been something to burn: what stores of notary acts alone, what archives of civil proceedings, what a library!

Peshekhonov contemplated these ruins. An investigator had called him here for questioning several times. And he'd faced trial here for his Peasant Union. Later he himself had appeared on other people's behalf. How much time had he spent in the dusty halls and dark corridors of this building, either in nervous agitation or in tedious anticipation. But here he saw these scorched ruins—and felt no gratification whatsoever.

On the contrary: alarm. A court should not burn. Without the courts a society cannot stand. And we're starting by setting fire to a court.

It was probably set on fire by the first criminals who gained their freedom. What would they do if not set fire to the court's poorly guarded building?

The whole day had passed like a light, bright holiday. Only in the night did these dynamic, frantic vehicles and these burning ruins appear like an ominous reminder that revolution is not a joke.

They lingered, stood there a while. It was already about nine when they walked up to the Tauride Palace.

Here, so many people were seething and scurrying in front of the square's iron grating—mostly soldiers, but also armed civilians. Vehicles started up for some unknown purpose were growling.

Getting inside was easy, even though there were guards posted.

Peshekhonov was even shy about looking with open eyes—and immediately seeing the seething headquarters of the revolution.

[1 3 6]

Early that morning the telephone rang in the Kerenskys' apartment—and was never quiet thereafter. No sooner had he replaced the receiver after a conversation than it rang again.

Last night they had met there—and gone their separate ways thinking it was all over and nothing was going to happen. But today the first call was from Somov, Sasha's school friend from Tashkent, later also an SR, and now also a lawyer. Somov demanded Aleksandr be woken up: there was an uprising among the soldiers of the Volynian Battalion. They'd killed officers and were marching through the streets! But while Olga Lvovna went to wake up Sasha, the telephone brought her back. It was Rodzyanko's secretary calling, saying he was asking Kerensky to come to the Duma urgently because a decree had been received for its dissolution.

With two hands on his cheeks, gently—she still considered her husband ill after last year's operation—Olga Lvovna woke up Sasha with the two deafening pieces of news from the two directions. He woke up instantly and caught fire in a moment. He could barely eat his breakfast and was glowing impatiently, already alight with thoughts, outstripped by his own impulse, and could no longer answer his wife's questions.

For the last few weeks clouds had hung over them—of losing deputy immunity, of being arrested, of being under investigation. They needed some kind of heroic and surprise solution! And now, had it come?

This was why they had moved to Tverskaya, next to the Tauride Garden, and the first floor, so that Sasha could get to the Duma without difficulty. His operation had been serious—tuberculosis of the kidneys—and might have ended much worse. He assured her that now he was entirely well, and it was true, he was once again lively as before, once again youthful and quick. Although two years older than Olga, he had always looked younger than she did, he was so impetuous.

For some reason her heart ached keenly when she saw him off across the threshold. She put her arms around his neck and asked him to be careful.

He laughed, freed himself, and left quickly.

While she was left with a bad presentiment. (We are given to shrink in presentiment but we are not given to guess it. Was something going to happen to her husband? Would they kill him? Would he not return? He truly would never return to this apartment again. But it would be of his own accord. Here was presentiment for you.)

And it was always thus. Sasha's revolutionary impulse was uncontrollable, and Olga could only try to keep up, while her departed father-in-law had held her to blame for everything, beginning with Aleksandr's exile under his father's roof in Tashkent. The Kerensky clan had had monks and priests, and the elder Kerensky had been devoted to the monarch and Church and could not understand where this contagion had suddenly come from in their clan. (Olga herself was a general's daughter.)

And the telephone! During breakfast alone the telephone had given a piercing jingle several times, and after, and constantly after that. Some reported, others inquired, all of Petrograd was being telephoned out, drained by telephones. The person who called most of all was Himmer. He knew Olga Lvovna well because he had spent the night with them occasionally while underground and was on very good terms with Sasha, and now, sitting in his remote office, he was hoping to learn the latest news from that apartment, as one of the city's central locuses of revolution.

But only Sasha could have the latest news, and he hadn't telephoned home all day. Nonetheless, other calls had brought news, stunning news, which Olga Lvovna conveyed to Himmer and everyone.

In the glow of this news, her bad presentiment gradually melted away.

Finally, she couldn't stay home hovering over the telephone any longer; the power of what was happening drew her outside. Leaving their two sons with the maid, Olga Lvovna headed for the Duma herself! There she would learn and see more, maybe even Sasha himself.

Many people were flashing by down Tauride Street, but the first she saw was a sprightly column of soldiers without an officer. The soldiers were waving jauntily and heading toward the turn onto Shpalernaya.

Having been a sister of mercy the last few years, Olga Lvovna had a simplicity with soldiers, so she ran up and asked one of them:

"Brother, what's happened? Where are you going?"

Although it was very noisy, the soldier heard her, bared his youthful teeth, and shouted:

"We're free now! We're going to the Duma!"

Oh, marvelous! Olga was going there, too! Alongside their formation, not lagging, prepared to walk hand in hand with this brother—in universal, Russia-wide love and exultation! Oh, marvelous!

Here they were already approaching the Duma. Up ahead both the street and the sidewalk were badly jammed up. The soldiers' formation came to a halt. So did Olga.

The immense crowd, as if in some church service, all facing the Tauride Palace façade, filled both Shpalernaya and the open area in front of the palace. People were curious, making noise—and waiting joyfully for something.

Up front, on fence ledges and trucks, on something else still, speakers would appear occasionally. They were hard or impossible to hear here, in back, but the waving of their arms could be seen and their exultation was conveyed to everyone.

It wasn't cold, and it was sunny, and she was wearing boots—so Olga Lvovna didn't notice standing there an hour, and two, and three, and probably more. It was impossible to leave this Easter-like service! Gradually there were modulations and movements in the crowd—and Olga Lvovna was also not standing in the last row anymore, rather she was being pulled steadily into the thick of it and eventually even onto the square.

As evening came on, trucks and loaded vans and wagons began pulling up, and the crowd somehow oozed away and let them in. They had brought and were unloading—either right here, onto the snow, in the square, or inside past the front steps—for some reason, battle gear, cartridges, barrels of butter, sacks of bread loaves, bundles of leather, cases of unknown content—all of which for some reason had to be unloaded at the Tauride Palace.

Meanwhile twilight had fallen and it was growing dark, but nothing had happened and the pressure of the mixed soldier-civilian crowd began to ease. Some left altogether; others burst inside in bunches. Olga Lvovna was already close to the front steps, and she too burst through in one of those bunches. A good thing because she was already freezing.

Inside the palace was just as much a jumble as outside: sparser, but the same kind of mixed, disorderly crowd that didn't know what to do, while by the walls of the round Cupola Hall everything that had been brought had been piled up or was still being piled up, and if people were telling the truth

and some of the boxes had gunpowder, all it would have taken was one cigarette flicked in that direction—and they were being flicked—for the palace
to blow up with all the triumphant masses even before they'd known their
freedom.

There was a guard around the explosive materials, but he was barely
holding his rifle and was nearly falling down. Olga Lvovna went up to him
and learned that he had been posted many hours before but had been forgotten and no one had come to replace him.

"Brother!" Olga Lvovna said. "Why don't I stand here for you and you go
get them to replace you."

The soldier was young but he knew his business and merely grinned.

"No, sister. I don't have the right to leave without an officer's permission."

Around her an unimaginable round dance was spilling and turning, and
there were hundreds of soldiers with rifles and nothing to do—but this little
soldier couldn't leave without an officer's permission!

Olga Lvovna earnestly undertook to help him—and went to look for an
officer herself. This took her a long time. Her eyes became alien to idleness
and did not examine just what was happening but sought out her purpose.
She had to elbow her way through and ask lots of questions, but ultimately
some officer agreed to go and found a soldier to replace him.

Then Olga was rewarded when from one vortex, going quickly through
the crowd, she picked out Aleksandr himself! She managed to cross his
path and stand in front of him, beaming.

To share with him the imminent great popular joy—and in the very Tauride thick! Just to watch him carry this day.

He was taut, pale, and young and in a great hurry, and he frowned hard
when he suddenly caught sight of her.

Did this proximity demean him in this historic moment? Suddenly, she
understood this and was embarrassed.

"Why?" he asked quietly.

"Just to rejoice!" she tried to vindicate herself. "Just because . . . I couldn't
stay home."

He shrugged.

"Well, as you like. Forgive me, I'm in a desperate hurry."

And he had already headed off.

"When are you coming home?"

"Oh no!" he smiled distantly. "We're all prisoners here now. No, that's
out of the question! Not today and not tomorrow. Don't wait."

"But what will you do?"

"Here—on the desks, on the couches." His smile was erased and he was
already walking away.

"Listen! There've been lots of calls!"

He brushed that off. That didn't matter now. Besides, telephone news
turned stale in half an hour.

She'd been hoping to meet rather differently, but still she was glad. On a day like this, she couldn't be mad at anyone or anything! What had her entire life been up until now—hers, both of theirs, their entire circle's? Their entire breath had been in the Liberation Movement.

And here it had soared up like a fountain!

Someone had already nicknamed the Ekaterininsky Hall the Temple of the People's Victory. In this formal, incomparable hall, where Potemkin had once thrown incredible balls in the empress's honor, between two paired rows of Corinthian columns, under seven dazzling chandeliers, each consisting of three shining circles—even today it was as if a ball had begun, but instead of Petersburg high society waltzing here, it was the round dance of democracy! A dance of guests unheard of here, who had not removed their outer clothing, or their greatcoats, or checked their rifles, a mixture of common soldiery and intelligentsia of all backgrounds, people who had suffered and survived long enough to see the greatest of celebrations, such as this hall had not known since the taking of Izmail. Above, on the balustraded gallery, strange visitors jostled, sending down smiles and waving.

So many familiar faces flashed by. The entire Petersburg intelligentsia! Olga Lvovna exchanged greetings with some at a distance, never getting close, as if she were moving in the intricate dance of the crush.

She was swept back toward the doors to the Cupola Hall—and there, by a column, she saw a large old man dressed in black and with a large, noble head who had just come in, saw him standing with his stick, erect, and looking at the hall in amazement. She saw—and immediately recognized him because she personally knew him well; his son's wife was Olga Lvovna's close friend: Herman Lopatin!

Herman Lopatin! Look who had been drawn here! He and no one else here! On such a day!

And didn't he deserve this holiday more than anyone? Hadn't he put more than anyone into the Movement? A personal friend of Marx and Engels! A member of the Soviet of the First International! Translator of *Das Kapital*. Author of a desperate and unsuccessful attempt to liberate the great Chernyshevsky from exile! And the legendary older brother of members of People's Will. Eighteen years of hard labor! And honorary judge in the dispute between Burtsev and Azef.

Who here now was worthier than he!

Pushing her way out of the spinning dance, Olga Lvovna headed joyously toward him; she could not have been rewarded with a better meeting now.

"Herman Aleksandrovich!"

He recognized her immediately and rejoiced as well. Actually, the simple momentary joy didn't last, couldn't last on his magnificently solemn, bearded face. Half a head taller than the crowd and gazing, enchanted, on this whirl, so that perspiration even appeared on his jutting forehead, capless—he wasn't even just standing but participating right now in a mystical rite.

"Now let-test me de-part . . . ," he said penetratingly, slowly, thickly, looking not even at Olga Lvovna but at the whirl of these heads, not all, not all
of which could understand the act's full significance.

It turned out, living outside of town and agitated by the morning news
from the city, after midday he had set out on foot because it was impossible
to find a cab, not that he wanted to, so he was obliged to come on foot and
not miss a single step or a single look. He had walked more than twenty
versts—at age seventy-two!

He stood erect. And kept looking through the small spectacles he was
wearing—at the hall, at the hall, and every so often at Olga Lvovna. He
spoke quietly, distinctly, not leaning toward her.

"This is the day for which I have sacrificed everything since my early
youth."

He stood there, occasionally shutting his eyes.

"Now I can die. Happier I will never be."

He shut his eyes again. And opened them.

"Though no. Now I would like to live a bit more. To see how quickly
everything arranges itself. Russia will come to life at last. A happy, free life."

Our Russia will blossom like a flower in a beautiful garden.

Afterward they found a place to sit; people let them have an armchair
and side chair. They sat side by side in silence.

Spilling over with happiness.

[1 3 7]

He reread and focused his mind on Alix's Sunday letter—and everything
around him immediately thawed out, warmed up, and became dearer! Instantly, he wasn't lonely!

A big letter—and he could picture each and every sweet detail of the previous day one after another. So tender she was toward the two letters she'd
received from him, and so lonely, with no one to talk to. Taking care of the
sick all the time, and with Anya ill and capricious; thank God, the two
younger girls were holding on and helping. Events in the city were not that
terrible, not at all like 1905. The whole problem was this lazy public, the
well-dressed men, girl students, and so forth who were inciting them to upheavals. And also, about the children (he was prepared to reread this endlessly): who had what temperature, and who hurt where. We just went to
the grave of our Friend—I brought you this bit of wood just over his grave,
where I knelt. The sun shone so brightly—I felt such peace and calm on
this dear place. Faith and trust. So happy you went to this dear Image. Your
loneliness must be awful; just that great stillness around is so depressing,
poor beloved one! Ever, your old Wify.

The splinter from the grave was now quite superfluous; Alix's worship of
Grigori was just a cult. But thank God her soul was at peace, and that peace

embraced Nikolai. Unsealing his wife's letter, he could always expect stern-
ness, and reproaches, and reproof—and his soul breathed easy when there
was none of that.

As a return gift he now wanted to thank her. And so immediately, in distinct, large letters on a telegram blank: Many thanks for your letter! Leaving
tomorrow at 2:30. (Now we will see each other soon, not long to wait! But in
order to assure her even more): Guard Cavalry from Novgorod ordered at
once for Petrograd. God grant the disorders among troops shall soon be
stopped. Always near you . . .

A telegram expresses so little, though! But if he sent a letter right away,
with the evening train, it would beat him there by nearly twenty-four hours.
My own treasure! Tender thanks for your dear letter. How happy I am at the
thought of meeting you in two days! After the news of yesterday from Petrograd, I saw many faces here with frightened expressions. Luckily, Alekseev is
calm. The disorders among the troops—I wonder what Pavel is doing; he
ought to keep them in hand. God bless you, my beloved Sunny. I cover
your sweet face with kisses, also the children. . . .

Barely had he sent it off when Alekseev was there again. But he looked
ill: one solid scowl, his eyes not visible at all, his shoulders tensed, red spots
on his cheeks.

"Ah, you have a full plate, Mikhal Vasilich! You came in vain, most
likely. You might have stayed on in the Crimea."

Although it was the right time, in reality, to make preparations for the
spring offensive.

But Alekseev had come, again holding blue telegrams, two of them.

And both from the War Minister. Quite fresh and sent twenty minutes
before.

It was odd. There was an interval of only seven minutes between their
sending. Some new event had taken place in those seven minutes?

This time Alekseev had hurried over with them immediately.

"Please, have a seat, I beg you."

In the first, Belyaev reported, contradicting his telegram of this afternoon,
that they had not yet been able to put down the military insurrection; on the
contrary, a number of units had joined the rebels. Fires had been started as
well, and there were no means for fighting them. And something he had not
asked for seven hours before: that the speedy arrival of truly reliable units was
essential—moreover, in sufficient numbers for simultaneous actions in various parts of the city.

So that's how it was. Nikolai cast a questioning glance at the collected
gloom that was the seated Alekseev.

In the second, seven minutes later, Belyaev reported that the government
had declared Petrograd under a state of siege and Khabalov had displayed
bewilderment.

But Khabalov had asked for troops seven hours earlier, when Belyaev was still being reassuring. Truly, what was going on in Petrograd and with men's minds?

There were no more telegrams in Alekseev's hands. Oh, how a telegram from Protopopov would clarify and help! But from Protopopov not a word.

His heart ached and ached. How hard it was not to understand anything, to be at this distance, while his family was right there, perhaps under threat. . . . There was no one to open up to in this aching alarm, and he could not confer with Alix!

However, the conversation with Alekseev now was perfectly simple and there was no reason to be self-conscious. Clearly, Mikhail Vasilievich, troops must be sent to Petrograd. Urgently. Lots of them. Immediately.

Pinched, gray, and motionless, Alekseev fully agreed.

How many regiments? Five, six?

Yes, and from different army groups so as not to weaken any of them.

Both cavalry and infantry?

Yes.

Go see to this, Mikhail Vasilievich.

Alekseev rose.

At least the main question had been decided swiftly and without hesitation. He felt better right away.

But there was still a question. Who was to be placed at the head of the troops sent in?

Who? As if there were no generals in the Russian imperial army! Generals of long, solid, brilliant service, for which appreciation had been expressed so many times in maneuvers and reviews, strewn with medals, and later for battles as well! But you couldn't name a decisive, experienced, and capable one just like that. He had to admit, there was, after all, no Suvorov among them. And would they really want a Suvorov for such an ignoble cause as routing a gang in the rear? He was even ashamed at the thought. No matter how serious it was in Petrograd, it wasn't that serious. They might just call up Gurko, whom he'd had in mind recently, but he would be sorry to tear him away from the Guards army, and there would be a delay until he could come.

"But here's what! Here's what!" it suddenly dawned on the Emperor. "Perhaps Nikolai Iudovich?"

Indeed, there was no one closer who could be appointed more quickly.

Alekseev frowned sourly—was it from malaise?

There's a thought! There's a marvelous thought! The Emperor was very pleased with his find. After all, Ivanov retained the rank of Army Group Commander, and he was not only an adjutant general but also a prominent and experienced military leader and endlessly devoted. He had three different classes of the St. George cross, and a gold sword with diamonds. And he was free from his position right now. And he was at hand (in a train car at the Mogilev train station), simply awaiting "orders" under GHQ, but he had not received orders of any kind yet, for a year. (People thought he was preparing there to lead the entire Field Army practically, but the Emperor simply felt sorry for him after his resignation from the Southwest Army Group. What was he to do with the old man? And so he lived here as a sign of honor.) Why, he is invited to my dinner; he will be here any minute! That is when I will tell him. (The satisfaction of being first to announce flattering news.) And afterward you will initiate him into the details.

There was one other memory linked with Nikolai Iudovich: it was his Awards Council that had awarded the Emperor his cross. And the Emperor had found that inexpressibly pleasant. He himself could never have brought himself to hint or ask—but how could he be the leader of the Russian army and not hold a St. George's cross? It wasn't that he had remembered that this very minute. No. But the grateful memory was always present in him.

"But in what capacity shall we appoint him?" Alekseev inquired providently. "What post?"

They thought. If he was to act in Petrograd, then there could not be two military authorities in Petrograd at the same time. And Khabalov had disgraced himself. That meant commander . . . no, even, maintaining his rank, Commander-in-Chief of the Petrograd Military District.

But the troops would be coming from various army groups, so they would have to be assembled somewhere outside Petrograd, Alekseev reasoned. What would he himself take along? At least some minor forces had to be sent with him from here.

That's right.

Alekseev, gripped with illness, reasoned:

"A battalion of St. George medalists?"

Again a marvelous idea! Men as brave as they come, not one with fewer than two crosses, and they were also at hand (symbolically guarding GHQ).

Stepping cautiously, Alekseev, being always free of duties to attend the highest dinner, went to give orders.

It was already time for dinner. Coming out to the men gathered, where they were starting to nibble and drink a glass standing, the Emperor saw Ivanov himself, simple and unpretentious, drowning in his shovel-shaped beard—but what a fine fellow: a string of crosses, a St. George sword, wearing his sashes and saber—very martial! And not old: sixty-five. Was that old for a general?

But it would be indecent here, in front of everyone, to announce his appointment to him. And it was impossible to interrupt the routine, stop the dinner, and take Ivanov to his quarters. Etiquette was etiquette, and the next hour and a half had to be devoted to dinner.

GHQ was considered to be permanently "on campaign" and therefore all breakable objects were excluded from the table; all the plates and drinking vessels were silver, gilded on the inside, and served by waiters in military uniform.

The Emperor could only give Ivanov his attention, seat him close, and begin asking questions about how Nikolai Iudovich had put down the insurrections in 1905.

Extremely flattered, the beaming general began recounting the tale, and he was an engaging storyteller! Everyone listened with consuming attention, guessing, as it were, the hint and the hope.

Nikolai Iudovich recounted broadly and amiably how he had put down the insurrections without a single shot, merely using his ability to deal with soldiers. The illustrious incidents at Harbin and Kronstadt. Nikolai Iudovich was a supporter of mild actions—not executions or field courts-martial (he did not approve a single execution)—and preferred to bring them to their knees, to reason, to apply the rod.

General Ivanov's entire bearded appearance as an ordinary man, an ordinary soldier, communicated a reliable reassurance. The entire suite cheered up, and the Emperor felt much more at ease.

The general beamed from the unusual universal attention—but he still didn't know what honorable appointment awaited him.

The Emperor even felt like sending Ivanov right away, today, before midnight, not waiting for tomorrow morning, but it would be cruel to demand the old man go so quickly. And there were also all kinds of preparations.

A tempting yearning drew the Emperor himself. How very long he still had until he went to Tsarskoye, not until tomorrow afternoon. How he had withered being without Alix and the children!

[1 3 8]

Especially in his first few minutes in the Tauride Palace, Himmer was exceptionally happy.

He had been in the State Duma previously only among the public, in the gallery. But now, everyone here was a visitor no more. Without removing his coat—not that the coatroom was open—in his fur coat, hat, and galoshes, Himmer walked through the Cupola Hall, through the Ekaterininsky—and examined with interest the unusual and wildly colorful public against the formal backdrop of the dozens of columns.

But within five minutes he had understood something quite remarkable. If you didn't count the soldiers and the other people roaming around pointlessly, there were quite a few intellectuals here, and they all recognized each other! Everyone already knew each other, if not personally, then by face, and each had already met everyone else sometime somewhere, if only at some meeting. Why should he be so surprised? Petersburg's socialist radical intelligentsia wasn't all that large, unfortunately, so here it was in its entirety, here it had converged.

Himmer met people he knew at every step, which meant he immediately entered into all the news and rumors. He was convinced yet again of what he had learned over the telephone: in all these days, other than the five-man Bolshevik PC and a few from the cooperative movement, the Workers' Group, no one in Petersburg had been arrested—which meant the authorities were bewildered! He found out right away that Tsarism's guiding lackey, the former minister of justice, under whom Beilis had been trampled, was sitting behind a locked door in the ministerial pavilion with fierce guards posted! This was remarkable and encouraging news! Then: that Protopopov, on the contrary, had managed to hide and not be taken. Then: various instances when police stations had been stormed and quite a few policemen killed. Then: that Rodzyanko had gone to the Mariinsky Palace for talks with the government and Duma deputies were very concerned about his safe return.

Yes, but the main thing! Sokolov came flying at Himmer like a black-bearded bomb to tell him the main thing: that a Soviet of Workers' Deputies had been formed! And Sokolov was a member of it! And Himmer would be a member, too, now!

He dragged him to the hallway in the right wing.

Himmer weighed this swiftly. Was that so? A Soviet of Workers' Deputies already? On the one hand, this was good, and why shouldn't he be part of it? But on the other, wasn't this like laying claim to power? But it was too soon, too soon; it would frighten the bourgeoisie.

In the room, at a big table, the radical party public was already seated, but there were still chairs free, for Himmer, too. Looming protectively over them all was the large, stately head of Nakhamkes. Was that so? Running through possible leaders for the burgeoning movement, Himmer had in fact forgotten about Nakhamkes. Through the war years he had behaved very circumspectly, kept hidden away, avoiding the party public, discussions and publications, and had lived quietly at his dacha on the Karelian isthmus. People had thought he'd turned completely bourgeois—but now?

Oh well, it was his right. He'd been a member of the 1905 Soviet. Judging from his figure, gestures, and character, he was going to lay claim to the leadership, naturally. All right, we'll share it. He wasn't going to master the theoretical path; here, no one could compare with Himmer.

But Himmer sat there a while as a member of the Soviet—and ate his heart out he was so bored. (Sokolov had fled even earlier.) What theory? They were all preoccupied with minute practice: how to choose deputies, when to open—and how to feed the roaming soldiers. If they weren't fed they'd sweep us all away, too. We had to find the food stores throughout the city, plunder them, and bring food to the Tauride Palace, and then we could consolidate the soldiers. Frankorussky and Groman kept running and in and out, sending trucks out.

Himmer had to agree they might be right. The immediate situation was such that they had to focus not on major policy, unfortunately, as his whole being and specialty drew him. If they began acting politically right away, that would only scare off bourgeois franchised circles and help the immoderate groups, the Bolsheviks and Interdistrict men. Yes! No! For now, the Soviet had to concentrate on the *machinery* of revolution, which could be mastered only by a revolutionary democracy. You could not get that from the bourgeoisie.

History's hour was just about to chime. Let all democracy busy itself with the machinery, but Himmer could not cripple himself. Right now he would have liked to do some political reconnaissance and orient himself in the mood of bourgeois circles. Right now the key was the bourgeoisie, not the Soviet. If even in the minds of the Duma left—as Himmer understood from his first minglings in the hall crowd—the question of seizing revolutionary power had not yet been aired, then how much more unprepared for something like this would the bourgeois circles be?

He left the Soviet and went out into the Ekaterininsky Hall—and suddenly saw Milyukov coming his way!

Not just coming—proceeding!

Not just proceeding: strutting! His step firm and his decisive gray head firmly planted. Oh, how right that was! You'd think, why shouldn't he sit in his comfortable office? Why mingle in this disarray? But he was right. In moments like this the leader has to show himself. Show that he exists, show that he is thinking for everyone. Look: he was walking—and thinking. In anticipation of some important hour? Some event? Amid the flickerings and troubling movement he was trying to follow a straight line, as if not noticing, seeking out, or seeing anyone. If people came up to him and started talking, he replied with such obvious reluctance that they left him alone. He had to think and walk alone.

What an intelligent, noble, and respectable appearance. This was who Himmer would have liked to speak with now! For all his bourgeois mistakes, this was the sole great man out of all the franchised. And they were equal theoretical minds! But Milyukov didn't know this, they were not at all acquainted, and he would not consider him noteworthy if he approached, would not have a conversation with him. Himmer's tentative, frail appearance besides was always a frustrating impediment.

So Himmer did not approach. With great regret. He went to do some reconnaissance—to the left wing of the palace, a direction in which the newly arrived public was not moving at all and where the Duma deputies and their procedures retained their authority. But one could walk there freely; there were no officers on duty.

Himmer freely entered the office of the Duma's vice president, Konovalov, who was very well known for his friendship with the leftists. Sitting in Konovalov's office was the indefatigable Efremov, the leader of the progressivists. So! Without verifying their acquaintance, he asked them directly and sternly who was going to create a revolutionary authority and how.

A very tidy, sleek, and fat factory owner wearing a gold pince-nez and blindingly clean-shaven, Konovalov could only blink and blink, not understanding, and mumble a few words, albeit politely. But Efremov, with his disheveled beard and pince-nez, looked sharply askance and merely snorted.

They had no idea what he was talking about. Oh, the mediocrity! He left them powerfully dismayed. Did that mean his dreams of forcing the bourgeoisie to seize power had been naïve?

But in the Ekaterininsky there was still the same jostling, mingling, and wandering (Milyukov was gone), and soldiers were spitting on the parquet floor. Brounshtein, a Menshevik he knew, ran up to say that soldiers throughout the city were still storming and looting, and this was undoubtedly a provocation by Black Hundred pogrom gangs, acting with the police. Plainclothes policemen were without a doubt marshalling the gangs! Brounshtein was trying to prove to each person he spoke with that anarchy had to be suppressed before a pogrom began against the Jews.

Doctor Vyacheslov also ran up. He too was a Menshevik, a leftist internationalist, a well-known doctor in leftist circles who never stopped talking politics even while doing his tapping, listening, and injecting of diphtheria serum. Now he was here, too, and running frantically on his short legs from one person to another, from acquaintance to acquaintance, grabbing each one excitedly by the lapels of his topcoat or frock coat.

"Listen! Fresh regiments are moving on Petrograd from without! We're going to be crushed! Is anyone organizing any resistance? What is defense headquarters doing? A session must be opened right away on the revolution's defense!"

As soon as he told one, he ran on to repeat this to the next.

Oh, hell! The hour for theory truly had not chimed, and what was needed was the machinery of revolution. Indeed, the situation of the entire revolution and all of them at the Tauride Palace was highly critical. While they were here, in the halls and corridors, trying to convince one another, the entire laboratory of revolution was floating in a void, universal anarchy, and the glow of fires. It wasn't just that there wasn't a battalion or company for its defense, there wasn't even a platoon of organized soldiers. The officers' disappearance was easily explained, inasmuch as they had been disarmed, harassed, and even killed all day long—but here it had become dangerous for the revolution. Right now in the Tauride Palace, quite a few officers flashed by, but all had either been brought in as prisoners or were fugitives who had fled here—and not a one of them led any kind of detachment. And the revolutionary democrats possessed no military knowledge

whatsoever. Even the uprising's success throughout the city was entirely unclear, contrived. Where was this victory and what did it consist of? While
the governmental spider web even here, in Petrograd, might be preparing a
fatal blow, perhaps from the Peter and Paul Fortress. After all, look how
many cannons had been aimed and how many soldiers were on the walls.
In a few hours, couldn't they just take the revolution with their bare hands?
Besides, the millions of armed forces in the field were still in the Emperor's
hands. While all we have here is some kind of defense headquarters.
Maslovsky the librarian and a few of the uninstructed. Had the train stations
been occupied against the possible arrival of Tsarist troops? No one in the
Tauride Palace knew the answers to this question, and who could have occupied the stations if there wasn't a single organized unit? Had the treasury
and telegraph been seized? No one had even given that a moment's
thought. What units of the garrison had not yet gone over at all to the side of
the revolution—and had someone been sent to agitate among them? No
one knew. A few expeditions had been fitted out here, in front of the Tauride
Palace, but based on their lax appearance, people said, it was hard to suppose they'd ever got anywhere.

Himmer, coming down from his theoretical height, himself began dashing from person to person, like Brounshtein and Vyacheslov. And suddenly
he saw something unusual. Standing in the Cupola Hall was a slim, smart,
armed young ensign with a graphically bold, clean-shaven face, an open
brow, shining eyes, and an unconcealed smile of joy. This could not be a
fugitive who had just avoided soldierly retribution. No, he was simply exulting in everything around him there, taking it all in and waiting confidently.

Right then, Himmer recognized him, only he couldn't recall his name.
Yes, this ensign had introduced himself to Himmer just a few days ago!
He'd been searching for paths to revolutionary work.

Himmer recognized him! He didn't remember his name, but he did remember his nickname. He walked up to the ensign and said quickly:

"Ah, Yasny! Is that you?"

The ensign beamed and straightened up even more, as if facing his formation leader. He began to speak, gasping from satisfaction, that he had
been acting all day, that this was so unusual, he was so glad to serve the revolution, he and his detachment.

Oh, he had a detachment? A revolutionary officer and an organized detachment as well! This was just what the Temple of the People's Victory
needed! Without explaining to him how complicated and dangerous it all
was—youthful enthusiasm had no need of that—Himmer immediately
grabbed him by the sleeve of his greatcoat and pulled him, pulled him to
defense headquarters in the left wing.

At the door they parted the waiting civilians and soldiers, the curious and
the messengers, and went inside. And Himmer kept pulling the ensign—
straight to Maslovsky.

Maslovsky was seated wearing a simple worn jacket, not even a tunic, his head tilted to the side, weary, sour, looking ten years older than his forty, his appearance demonstrating that this defense headquarters was repugnant to him, as was this defense, and he was going to sit a while longer and then leave, and he believed in nothing, and what was the point of this ensign?

And this was the defense headquarters chief! This was a tested SR!

However, next to him was the black uniform of a brisk naval lieutenant, who immediately welcomed the ensign.

But Himmer had had enough, he'd already done his work for the machinery. He said he knew this ensign from his revolutionary work and would vouch for him—and he left. Before the Soviet of Workers' Deputies opened session, he had to consider an overall political strategy, which he might have call to lay out.

The closeness in the right wing of the palace was thickening, workers and armed soldiers were crowded around, still not having removed their coats or caps. These weren't the assembled, already elected deputies, were they? Unfortunately, no. The punctilious Erlich was jostling around and asking whether they had *credentials* and who was a *deputy*? They didn't understand him. He still kept writing people down and pulling them into the Soviet room as deputy. At the same time he fastened a red ribbon to whomever he was bringing in if he didn't have one yet.

Himmer already had a credential from Erlich: "representative of the socialist literary group."

Sokolov was giving very loud instructions and running around a lot.

The Soviet had already commandeered two rooms. People took seats in spacious Room no. 12: the leading radical public at the big table, while for the soldiers and workers they put boards across the chairs along the walls and also brought in stools and chairs. Altogether they hadn't scraped up even fifty, which made it awkward to begin the Soviet.

The soldiers were sitting sedately and in silence mostly. They were shy in front of the educated men. Others who were more forward were telling their neighbors what had happened today and how.

But the faces were so stupid and undeveloped!

Himmer was horrified. Who had they summoned here? Were they really prepared for a serious meeting? Could theoretical problems really be laid out before them?

And what would they themselves go on about if they were allowed to speak? . . .

[1 3 9]

Although Rodzyanko had agreed under pressure to create and preside over this provisional Duma Committee, it gnawed at him that this was the wrong path, an illegal path, and circuitous, and not any kind of a solution to the question. So far he had not come up with any actions or sessions for this Committee. He brought along his legitimate Duma leadership—his one deputy, Nekrasov, Duma Secretary Dmitryukov, a leader of the faction, and the Octobrist Savich—to meet with the grand duke.

Rodzyanko had the following goals. To save the monarchy. Not to let the Duma itself mutiny. And, maybe, take government power himself, but only by direct, legitimate, formal means. He had been shaken by Shcheglovitov's arrest. He might be a political opponent, but he held exactly the same position in the upper chamber as Rodzyanko did in the lower, and his arrest was like the mirror image of Mikhail Vladimirovich's own arrest if matters continued in the same way. Shcheglovitov's arrest made it even more certainly clear to Rodzyanko that he had to seek a legitimate path. Otherwise all was lost. (And what should be done with Shcheglovitov now? Releasing him would only mean subjecting him to mob justice.)

Had the Emperor been at Tsarskoye Selo, Rodzyanko would have gone to see the Emperor. Now, he went to see the Emperor's brother, the only person here now who might help, bearing as he did the aura of the royal name.

Someone had already put a red flag on the President's motorcar—and in front of the excited soldierly mass it would be risky now to take the flag down. He would have to drive off like this with an unperturbed and even satisfied look. A soldier with a rifle, bayonet forward, lay on each fender. Although it was cold lying there and they could fall off, they had nearly fought for these places; everyone wanted it. Security for the motorcar was useful, too, but what a fearsome look it had!

The area up to the Trinity Bridge had been considered the revolution's *own* for the last few hours. Here the revolt had seethed, and a motorcar with a red flag passed freely.

To an onlooker, if anyone recognized the Duma president, he probably looked odd as the revolution's leader.

But he wasn't that, and he would have forbidden everyone from thinking so!

Near the Trinity Bridge, someone from a small group in their path waved his arm and detained the motorcar. They asked who he was. And let him through.

Farther along, the embankments were deserted, and no one stopped them, so they drove on quite freely. This desertedness in the early evening was unusual. A strange revolution. Ride through the city wherever you want. Rodzyanko ordered them to stop and remove the red flag. They hid it on the motorcar's floor.

They skipped past the Winter Palace, past the Admiralty, turned at Senate Square, which was just as deserted, passed by St. Isaac's, and came out on Mariinskaya Square. Here there was a somewhat larger crowd and traffic in both directions. By the palace entrance were two cannons and a sentry.

The new arrivals were let through without delay. The largest and heaviest of them all, Rodzyanko went up the stairs with a powerful and impatient tread, overtaking them all.

He noted with envy that procedure was being followed here. No suspicious outsiders, no one bursting in with a weapon, all attendants liveried and in their places. Only there was no overhead lighting, and all the passageways and halls were poorly lit.

From the rotunda, a forewarned attendant led the arrivals toward the State Council, pulled open the rosewood door incrusted with bronze and nacre for them—and right then Rodzyanko had the unpleasant realization that he was walking into the president's office, that is, Shcheglovitov's.

Another symbol. Shcheglovitov was locked up in the ministerial pavilion, the key in Kerensky's pocket, and Rodzyanko had now entered his office uninvited, as if acting as one with Kerensky.

But it was too late for second thoughts or a change of mind. Grand Duke Mikhail was already sitting here, not the least embarrassed at having been first to arrive, and was waiting. He rose to meet him readily, not royally. He was slim, with a long, narrow waist.

He had with him only his unfailing secretary, the Englishman Johnson. The Duma deputies exchanged greetings with the grand duke, and they took their seats at a separate hexagonal table with incrustations that was surrounded by six chairs.

Despite his jaunty, broad-spread blond mustache, the grand duke's unset face, as always, did not have its own tension or established thought but looked with open bafflement at his interlocutor.

His head had been shaven, like a soldier's, and had grown out only a little.

Rodzyanko knew his own steady influence on the grand duke and now, with the full weight of his authority, appearance, and voice, he began sternly trying to convince him. (However, as if only advising.)

Right then, having learned of his arrival, Prime Minister Prince Golitsyn and War Minister Belyaev came in. (Rodzyanko called the latter General Phull.) They were not really what Rodzyanko needed, and it was actually an odd situation: the heads of the other warring side, supposedly, here they were seating themselves peacefully at the same table. A sixth seat was found for Golitsyn, and short, jug-eared Belyaev sat to the side and behind, as if shrinking even more. Not the least constrained by these shadows' presence, Rodzyanko continued.

At that moment the duty of these responsible and highly placed men was to save the situation. Salvation was still possible now, this very minute—and it was in the hands of the grand duke alone!

All this was reflected on Mikhail's impressionable, responsive, and unfirm face. He seemed surprised—but exultant at the same time. A private citizen living in Gatchina, albeit an inspector general of the cavalry—but he had never expected he might save Russia. None other than he?

And although it was hard to see in those features Russia's imperious savior—yes, it was he! Or so Rodzyanko inspired him with mounting hope, quite indisputably. Exactly: due to the Emperor's absence and the difficulty of contacting him, the prerogatives automatically lay on His Imperial Highness. He must now, immediately, without seeking prior permission or waiting for confirmation, accept the dictatorship over Petrograd, compel the government to resign immediately and in full, and send the Emperor a telegram demanding that he grant a ministry responsible to the Duma. The Duma would form such a ministry instantly, in an hour.

Rodzyanko laid this all out relentlessly and insistently. He was not at all constrained by the presence of the head of the so-called government. This government they, the Duma, had already pursued out loud and openly, and this was yet one more time! Nothing worse could be imagined than this lackadaisical Mariinsky Palace. Then again, Rodzyanko had already tasted the Tauride Palace's swampiness and instability. Now he had to find a firm path between two dangerous swamps.

Both ministers were sufficiently bruised and so lost that they did not even attempt to object in their own defense. However, Rodzyanko heard a sharp objection behind him. It was Kryzhanovsky, now the State Council secretary and for years quite a prominent state official, who had just joined them. He now launched into rebukes against Rodzyanko for arresting Shcheglovitov.

Rodzyanko was struck, and quite offended, and he turned around and honestly started to explain that he hadn't arrested him, he hadn't been able to do anything because the crowd and for some reason Kerensky had the power. (He recalled Kerensky's "revolutionary law." From here, from the Mariinsky, it was especially clear: what kind of "revolutionary law" could there be in two hours? Up until that moment, this had been called terror.)

"If that is the case," the ever restrained Kryzhanovsky said even more indignantly, "if you are not the master even in your own Tauride Palace, then how can you take it upon yourself to be the master in Russia?"

Rodzyanko turned red and truly could come up with no objection (mentally having decided, his jaw clenched, that tonight he would rein in his Tauride).

Kryzhanovsky pressed just as aggressively, saying that the government had already sacrificed Protopopov. (What? The Duma deputies didn't know yet!) The government itself had sent a request to appoint a dictator for Petrograd but had sent it to the Emperor, who alone could decide this. (He was saying all this by implication for the grand duke.) But meanwhile the Duma was the guilty party and at the head of the revolutionary upheaval!

So inopportunely had he arrived and so energetically had he overturned—knocked out—the entire impression from Rodzyanko's plan. One couldn't come up immediately with any way to object.

Protopopov didn't matter now! Rodzyanko shrugged that off. It was too late, it should have been done a month before. The street was raging, and you couldn't feed it Protopopov anymore.

Meanwhile, an intimidated Prince Golitsyn plucked up his nerve and tried to justify himself to Rodzyanko, saying that he was not grasping at power one bit, that he had not sought his position and had accepted it reluctantly—and just today, an hour ago, they had sent the Emperor a collective request to resign. There had been no answer as yet, and they were sitting here, in the palace, risking arrest.

"So leave. What's the matter?" Rodzyanko made a broad gesture.

Oh, no, Golitsyn objected. The emperor's servant cannot leave his post on his own initiative. That would be desertion. That would be a disgrace!

Indeed, here there were boundaries that are forgotten when you know how vulnerable the ground has become and how the street is raging.

If the grand duke succeeded at restoring monocracy and order, the government would only be glad of it.

But Rodzyanko didn't need order with *this* government. The entire meeting was not going as he had hoped. And the Duma deputies he'd brought—though he may as well not have—were silent. Silent, too, was the most leftist Kadet, Nekrasov, in his wolfish reticence, as he often was.

The grand duke listened dazedly to the dissension, as if he were the last person it concerned and the main admonition had not been directed toward him. His gaze was bright and almost childlike.

Rodzyanko, though, did not tire, and once again he tried to prove that he was not a revolutionary but with his plan he was saving the monarchy. There was no other solution.

Golitsyn started trying to help with his own persuading. Yes, let the grand duke take on the dictatorship, albeit exceeding his powers—and then let him immediately dismiss the government, which was agreeable.

But the longer they went, the more the grand duke listened to them with sorrow rather than decisiveness. At last he spoke with sorrow and gentleness. He had always acted as necessary for the good of the homeland. He was prepared. And he had always sympathized with the Duma. However . . . What they were asking of him—that would be like . . .

He didn't say *what* it would be like. He didn't want to offend anyone.

And so he pulled back, smiling sadly, and felt obvious relief.

However, Rodzyanko knew what a stone this failure would be, what a stone again on his shoulders! With his indecisiveness, this ungainly grand duke had ruined everything! The final hours had been let slip—and everyone would regret this later! It would be too late for all Russia!

He argued with new force. Now His Highness had more time to assemble his garrison's unshaken units!

He argued some more—in vain.

He argued some more—to no avail.

Fine, then, so be it. Let His Imperial Highness not declare himself dicta-tor directly. But could he *talk it over* with his most august brother? Right now, on a direct line? And convey all this?

The grand duke might not have felt very much like talking, but now, out of politeness, out of respect, he agreed.

There was a shift so that they began right then, together, compiling a long text of what the grand duke should communicate to GHQ in his name. They were aided by Golitsyn, Belyaev, and Kryzhanovsky. The brother speak-ing with the Emperor was something everyone approved.

What should they call **all this**? *A movement.* It had taken on *massive pro-portions.* And the grand duke's own opinion that the entire Council of Min-isters should be dismissed—and Prince Golitsyn confirmed the same thing. (Meanwhile, there was no need to mention Rodzyanko, so as not to anger the Emperor yet again.) The grand duke thought the sole inevitability was that the Emperor would settle his choice on an individual *invested with the trust of* . . .

Society? No. The grand duke would not go that far. No . . . Invested with the trust of His Imperial Majesty but simultaneously enjoying respect among broad strata as well. . . . Lay the duties of Prime Minister on this in-dividual. A Council responsible to . . . ?

Rodzyanko had no doubt: the Duma! Otherwise no step forward would be taken. Otherwise, what was the point of this whole discussion? Given the current situation in the streets. . . .

The Duma deputies supported him. The others remained silent.

This weight was laid on Mikhail's shoulders.

From his apologetic look it was impossible to guess how he would con-vey this.

Well, fine, at least he agreed to say something.

The situation, then, was extremely grave, and would it not please His Im-perial Majesty to authorize his own brother to announce such-and-such a decision in the capital without further delay? . . .

The grand duke made no attempt to delay. He rose, thanked them, smiled fondly at everyone, and shook everyone's hand. He was now heading off to the General Staff, for a direct line with GHQ. Prudent Belyaev warned, however, that this might prove dangerous. The rebels were already near Palace Square and had already been making forays. But they could go to his official residence, the home of the War Minister, on the Moika, where he had the same kind of reserve equipment hooked up, and the grand duke would feel freer there. Excellent. He went with Belyaev.

The others dispersed as well.

Rodzyanko was sorely vexed by this weakness in the grand duke, by his inability to take statesmanly steps. Nonetheless, he had one last hope that something would come of this conversation. And that Mikhail would name *his*—Rodzyanko's—candidacy to the Emperor. (Had they been alone, he would have tried to persuade the grand duke to do this more directly.) Rodzyanko asked Belyaev to be sure to telephone the Duma afterward and inform them of the result.

In the rotunda, the Duma deputies stood a little longer with the ministers who had gathered for another evening session. All the ministers were in a hopeless, doomed state, and everyone was expecting the crowd to burst in at any moment. Not all of them had come in motorcars even to the Mariinsky Palace; some had come on foot, too, so as not to attract attention.

There was a rumor going around among them that Guchkov had arrived at the Mariinsky. And he could come, as a member of the State Council. But something grated: it was like a triumphant raid by a bitter enemy. People were saying he had that look.

Rodzyanko left feeling an active superiority over the insignificant, powerless government, which had fouled everything—and had now resigned. Oh, *his* government would not be like that! It would imperiously turn Russia around.

They were returning now without guards on the fenders, their menacing escorts having gone off somewhere. Their motorcar now was stopped several times by rebels or simply ruffians. But when they learned it was the President of the State Duma, they greeted him loudly and let him through.

One time they themselves stopped and the driver again attached the red flag in front.

It would be awkward to return without it.

[1 4 0]

After all the scrapes on Nevsky and memorable Znamenskaya Square, Kirpichnikov was once again alone. Again, not a single familiar face; they had all split up, moved around, taken off somewhere.

For the most part, the crowd had thinned out, the vehicles and trucks just the opposite, and they were carrying soldiers. People were shouting at these vehicles, gawking and waving.

Timofei stared at all this—and couldn't believe it. Had he alone really made all this happen? Had this whole devil's dance through the whole city really started just with him?

And now he was alone again.

These civilians could gaze and wave to their hearts' content; each had a home, and come nightfall, they'd all disperse. But where was a soldier to go?

A soldier goes to his barracks, that's clear. But where was Timofei Kirpichnikov, the first mutinous sergeant, the instigator of all the turmoil, to go? What if they were just waiting to grab him at his barracks? At night, in his sleep—would they grab him?

Better not to go there.

But he had nowhere else to go.

Timofei had ruffled all Petersburg—and he had not a single friend or intercessor in all Petersburg. This was going to end in a court-martial, and you had no one to hide out with.

Either way, as he pondered this his feet themselves bore him toward his barracks. Down Nadezhdinskaya.

Right then he saw some Volynians, three of them, standing around. Join them. They were smoking, cheerful. It was a pleasure for a soldier to have a smoke outside, since up until now it had been forbidden. No, they were strangers, he didn't know them at all. They were talking—about the havoc, about the looting.

You couldn't ask anyone questions, anyone's advice.

He stood around with them a while and continued on.

At the corner of Basseinaya he thought, there's nothing to be done for it, and turned toward his barracks.

Approaching laterally, sort of.

Fontannaya. A lonely spot now, no one about. Where were all those throngs? On the main streets.

Well, no one there.

How many times today had Kirpichnikov walked fearlessly into the soldiers' lines, into the shooting, how many times that morning had he overcome all the weight of fear—and now, all of a sudden, his heart began to sink.

This was no joke. The number one insurrectionist, and here he was on his way to the barracks alone, without support or protection, without checking: they'd grab him and that would be it.

He walked down Vilensky Lane—and again no one. No sentries at the gates.

What a bind! This morning here he'd led his entire training detachment in formation "to die for freedom"! He'd turned them in the lane's cramped space—and now he'd come back alone, in fear of arrest.

No, under his own steam he couldn't deliver his head into a trap.

What a bind! He wandered back down Fontannaya, now down Basseinaya to the other side, then down Grechesky—and again, there was no one there.

Nothing to do but spend the night in the snow then!

But the frost was quite nippy. You could freeze easily.

Only at the corner of Grechesky and Vilensky he met men from his training detachment.

"Well, how is it back at our barracks, boys?"

Only now did he notice his voice was completely gone, he'd lost it in the constant shouting.

"Nothing much."

"In order?"

"Sure. What of it?"

"Well, is everyone home? All's quiet?"

He didn't even try to explain what he'd been trying to sort out.

"Come on, then!"

The yard. Where Lashkevich had lain. They'd taken him away.

The staircase he'd thought to defend with machine guns only to hold out somehow in the barracks, he'd had no hopes beyond that, beyond that had seemed unshakable.

But they'd given it the barest shove, with the one training detachment—and off it went. Off it rumbled.

In detachment quarters they saw him and started shouting. Here was Kanonnikov. And Brodnikov. Hey, they said, sergeant-major! We thought you'd been killed.

They brought him hot tea.

Timofei sat on his cot—and sipped with such pleasure, sipped the sweet tea with such pleasure.

He regrouped himself. Wait, no duty officers? No. No, brothers, this is no good. They'll grab us like this. Well then, let's send patrols through the nearby streets. Only half get undressed for the night, and half sleep in your greatcoats and boots, with your rifles.

They grumbled, the men grumbled. Patrols? What ever for? What's the point—not getting undressed for the night?

[1 4 1]

Some of the Moscow Regiment officers, freed from their own subunits, left before night fell across the Great Nevka for the grenadier barracks.

The others walked around the officers' club, restless.

There had been no more attacks—and no more shooting.

Their own soldiers, and strangers, and civilians were already strolling freely around the parade ground.

Captain Yakovlev once again assembled the remaining officers in the library; except for the Nekrasov brothers, this meant nothing but ensigns. He announced that from now on they had to fight with words, not gunfire. For this, for the night, everyone now should disperse among the companies, whichever ones they came across, replacing those absent—and there persuade the soldiers to maintain order and even remain to spend the night.

Even the Nekrasovs were surprised, but the ensigns' eyes popped out. They'd just been shooting at those soldiers—and they were supposed to go singly to see them in their companies?

Yakovlev might be right, though: if they weren't running away from their battalion, there was no other choice. A strange feature of a war against your own. . . .

To the 4th Company went its commander, Staff Captain von Fergen, who had spent the whole day with the guard in the clinic by the Sampsonievsky Bridge. He was new to the company, just a month back from the front, but the company already knew and liked him.

The Nekrasov brothers would have gone to the 3rd Company, where there were mostly soldiers from the front, but how could they go there if they'd been shooting at them specifically that afternoon? They went to the 2nd Company, where there were also regular noncommissioned officers who had been wounded, whom the Nekrasovs knew well. With the captains was little Pavel Greve, an ensign, still a boy, recently from the cadet corps.

They went, only they left their revolvers at the club.

They stepped through the company door—and there was no howl, no attack, but the man on duty loudly gave an order and made his usual report, and Staff Captain Nekrasov ordered him at ease, although he apparently had not been standing at attention.

It was as if there had been no shooting in the yard. Here were soldiers wearing the Russian military uniform, even from the beloved Moscow Regiment, with their Russian language, many bearded reservists, unarmed recruits straight from their families—and they were waiting for an explanation and reassurance from their father officers. They gathered around closely in several rows. Trustingly even.

Vsevolod was leaning on his stick, and young Greve was languishing, so it was up to Sergei to speak. Now he realized that Yakovlev had been right: there had been no shooting today at all. It was a delusion. But their halftrained reserve battalion was standing there in an odd, quasi-wartime atmosphere.

Sergei Nekrasov, from his height able to see everyone well, raised his voice and suggested cleanly and ringingly that they calm down and go to bed. Tomorrow was another day. (He himself wanted this peaceful night for contemplation and for regaining his senses.)

That was enough for many of the men, too. They seemed to feel they had forgiven themselves for their agitation today, some not leaving the barracks and some running around the parade ground, and now they could disrobe for the night.

But it did not end that simply. Many soldiers did disperse to their bunks, but the sergeants, on the contrary, stepped in closer, to have it out. With them, too, were some of the soldiers.

They, the sergeants, they said, had had things worse than anyone, caught between two fires. On the one hand, there was their oath—did they think they didn't understand? But on the other hand, how could they fire on the crowd? There were women there, and little boys, and they were all Russians. Wishing the gentlemen officers no ill, they would always protect them from the crowd. But the *civilians*, they came up, pressured us, and demanded we disarm our officers, otherwise they'd bring the cannons and smash all the barracks with them.

Nekrasov met the eyes of Taramolov, with whom he had fought shoulder to shoulder at Tarnavka. They both had a George Cross from there.

"Well, Taramolov, you of all people, do you really believe it? What cannons? Who's going to be smashing anything?"

Taramolov didn't believe in the cannons and he smiled, but like everyone, he had a strong, unnameable reason, a reason that had put an end to the regiment's life as the officers had known it.

"Your honor, you can't pick off everyone and you can't shoot everyone away. Of course, you can't give *them* the weapons, and we wouldn't stand for that. And they do want to take away our weapons, maybe even slaughter you. But there's no shame at all in giving weapons to *us*, the men you lay with under German barbed wire. You should give them to us, and we'll protect you as one of us. We'll tell those civilians that we've disarmed you—and they can be on their way. Do you have any other ideas, your honor?"

Convinced by his speech, the handful of sergeants, supported by the soldiers, began to buzz confidently and good-naturedly. This good nature was a miracle after the day's shooting, which had divided them into enemies.

This good nature struck Sergei Nekrasov, too. What he never would have done under any threat, what he could not have imagined in his officer's career, in a few unprecedented hours it had been overthrown and turned out to be a movement of trust and friendship.

He exchanged looks with his brother Vsevolod. He, too, was convinced. He, in any case, wouldn't have to give his sword back and only had his stick with him.

Staff Captain Nekrasov straightened up. Squinted. Frowned.

He unfastened his sword. And held it out to Taramolov.

Little Greve unfastened his, too—and handed it over carefully.

And the men buzzed and buzzed with approval.

Once again Nekrasov felt he was with his own soldiers—together, as he had been throughout his service.

The soldiers dispersed to go to bed. The officers, too, now should have stayed to spend the night here.

But there was absolutely no room: the bunks were double-decker and all filled; after all, the companies had fifteen hundred each.

In the company office? Too crowded. There was room for one, on the clerk's bed.

But they had calmed the company down and could leave.

Although, why relinquish their weapons then?

And you couldn't ask for them back now.

With a sense of having been robbed and an acute sense of their mistake, they went outside.

Then again, this was not their company. Vsevolod had run a school for soldiers' children, and Sergei, as battalion adjutant, had been in charge only of staff clerks. So that they were free.

But where to now? They stood on the parade ground.

In their own adjutant apartment the windows had been smashed out, and cold and havoc roamed at will.

Crossing the dark parade ground were individual figures, strangers, who according to procedure and the time should not have been there.

One of the gates had been knocked down, after all. And the sentries were nowhere to be seen.

The Nekrasovs recalled how in the new officer annex there was the empty apartment of Staff Captain Stepanov, commander of the 3rd Company, who had gone to the Caucasus for treatment.

They went there.

They picked up the key from the officers' club porter and told him to tell the other officers.

[1 4 2]

Had the Emperor listened to General Alekseev's advice last summer, the entire rear would have been led long ago by a single minister-dictator and nothing like the present shortages and street disturbances would have occurred. Instead, all spheres of life in the rear and spheres of leadership were in a variety of uncoordinated hands.

And since this was so, then it would probably be better that those hands be hands trusted by the public rather than hands chosen in the secrecy of Tsarskoye Selo—to avoid any additional hostile tension with the public. Why not allow the sensible ministry everyone was asking for, made up of public figures? What talents had the Emperor espied in his randomly chosen ministers, that he should prefer them? (Allow it voluntarily, not the way the conspirators who had come to Sevastopol that winter had suggested.)

Now Rodzyanko was trumpeting, the calculating Brusilov was chiming in, and even the cautious, two-faced Ruzsky had joined this request with a delay of twenty-four hours. But was this the time, in this kind of turmoil, to take such a serious decision?

Now, due to this slip, he had to spend the whole day going from his official residence to the Emperor's home carrying ultra-important telegrams from the distraught generals. Now Ivanov had been put at the head of all the troops under way. As if Alekseev did not know him, having served sufficiently under him in the Kiev District and in the Southwest Army Group. Panicked and no kind of commander or strategist, he had been leaning toward surrendering Kiev, an utterly unmodern general, worthless even, who had only his

appearance, handsomely stroking his beard in silence and speaking pater-
nally with the soldiers. He was utterly unfit for his present role.

However, Alekseev also knew that it was in the choice of individuals, in
his personal appointments, that the Emperor could be especially insistent.
In these, Alekseev had been forced to concede. If he liked it so much . . .
Why should a chief of staff also correct an emperor's selection?

Indeed, you couldn't think of anyone that quickly; it was an unexpected—
and far-reaching—appointment.

Ivanov's shortcomings could be compensated for by requesting from the
army groups that they appointed true combat generals to lead the regiments
and brigades being sent.

He was reluctant to remove significant forces from the front right before
the offensive. After all, you couldn't send them back that quickly afterward.
Alekseev liked having all his regiments in their places.

Actually, he also understood, of course, that today the situation at the
front allowed him to remove as many troops as he liked.

He still felt shivery, and his chest and head were killing him. Struggling,
Alekseev sat at the table and searched for troops, taking some from the reserves, which was better, and some, reluctantly, even from the line of battle.

He took approximately two infantry and two cavalry regiments from three
army groups. From the Northwest it turned out to be convenient and quick to
send the solid brigade of 1812: the Life Borodinsky and Tarutinsky regiments
standing in reserve. In two nights and a day, at the dawn of 14 March, they
could be in Petrograd. Arriving almost immediately after them, also from the
Northwest, would be the Tatar Uhlan and Ural Cossack regiments. Twenty-
four hours later the Sevsky and Orlovsky infantry regiments, one hussar, and
one Don Cossack regiment would arrive from the West Army Group. Finally,
if it could not be avoided, he could remove from the Southwest, from Gurko's
army, his Guards regiments, even the Preobrazhensky itself.

It was simpler to present the choice of regiments to the Army Group
commanders themselves, but due to his meticulous manner of doing his
subordinates' jobs and knowing everything himself down to the dot, Alekseev did all the choosing and assigning himself. He could not live calmly for
an hour without knowing precisely which regiment was going to decrease.

After eight o'clock in the evening, Alekseev talked this over by telephone
with the chiefs of staff of the North and West army groups. Although sympathizing little with the entire undertaking, he did, however, issue an unam-
biguous order: send the troops with all possible haste, the moment was ominous, this was a matter of our continued future. And send *solid* generals.

Having made his decision, now he could not waver. Naturally, GHQ was
utterly ill-equipped for such a task—countering domestic disturbances.
This was not the best outcome of the civil crisis, but it was also perfectly possible. It promised certain success. There were no troops in Petrograd comparable in quality to those being sent. What was an uprising of a few un-

trained and almost unarmed reserve battalions in an isolated corner of the country when the entire Field Army remained loyal? And while all Russia remained calm? Not only that, but on the days of Petrograd's disorganization, GHQ, thanks to the Emperor's presence there, could take over not only military control of the army groups but also the country's entire administration.

After this, already after ten, Alekseev sent a telegram to the War Minister in Petrograd about Adjutant General Ivanov's appointment and the troops being sent with him to Petrograd and requesting that he create a headquarters for Ivanov.

This telegram had barely been sent by direct line to the War Minister's residence on the Moika when word came from there that Grand Duke Mikhail Aleksandrovich was asking General Alekseev to pick up the direct line.

The Tsar's brother! A surprise.

[1 4 3]

General Nikolai Iudovich Ivanov had risen from the very lowest strata. His background was not transparently known, so that some high-born ill-wishers asserted that he came from fugitive convicts, or that his father was a convict; others that he came from christened cantonists, which was why his patronymic remained Iudovich and his surname was the invented Ivanov. Once he had achieved high posts and the magazines printed his photographs where he was strewn with medals, they added a caption: "nobleman from Kaluga Province." But his appearance expressed an appealing common touch—his short-haired cabbage head, his shovel-shaped, black, gray-streaked beard, and his ingenuous forward gaze. Even in the routine of his day: he awoke very early and took a walk through the headquarters of the corps, port, district, or army group he commanded as if it were a peasant's yard, spying out flaws and giving proper dressing-downs. And the same common touch in his way of speaking and even more in his way of being wisely silent, stroking his beard. His paternal attitude toward the soldier was well known. Nor had he ever expressed any unpleasant notions to the Emperor; he was artless and sincere. How many medals Nikolai Iudovich had—from the Turkish war, from the Chinese suppression, and from the Japanese war, and especially from this one; only he and Nikolai Nikolaevich had the St. George's 2nd class. So firmly did Ivanov sit at the command of the Southwest Army Group that he had been staggered by his sudden removal from it a year before. (There was no other explanation for this than intrigue and vengeance on the part of the ungrateful Alekseev, whom he, Ivanov, had helped make his way.) It had been hard for him to say goodbye to his troops.

Remove him from this height they did, though—but where could they move him? He could not go lower, and equivalent posts were occupied, and the only higher posts were Alekseev and the Emperor himself. There was simply no replacement post to be found. But right then the Emperor's benevolence saved the day. General Ivanov was ensconced at GHQ in his own separate, comfortable, well-equipped train car (and he was not married), so that in the morning he could now dress down the various military officers he encountered at the Mogilev station, and the sum total of his duties for the past year had been to appear at a few imperial dinners.

Today, too, he had been invited. Bathing painstakingly and getting ready, belting up his quite healthy, albeit capacious body, he put on his tunic with all his crosses and medals, fastened on his gold sword with diamonds, and took the motorcar sent for him. He was received with more honor than ever and seated at the Emperor's left hand. By the Emperor's kindness he was invited to tell stories of the past, how he had successfully put down the upheavals in 1905.

At this the general inwardly began to grasp something untoward; during the stretch of his long life's school, he had always lived on the alert. But now there had also been bad news from Petrograd, to which the general had ascribed no significance, but at dinner it was not made clear. Putting all this together as he went, however, Iudovich in his stories began presenting himself a little more lightly, as a little more fatherly, not meant for an ominous moment—and hoped that all would end with this dinner and these stories.

After dinner, however, the Emperor called him in, lit his jointed cigarette holder—the meerschaum part for his papirosa, the gold fastener ball, and the amber part in his lips—and shaking it over the ashtray, which was in the shape of an antique Russian pitcher, formally announced to the general that he had been appointed Commander-in-Chief of the Petrograd Military District, replacing Khabalov, and must depart for there immediately, about which he would receive instructions from Alekseev.

How very flattering. And so unexpected. How peacefully Nikolai Iudovich had been living up until today, it turned out! It took the general's breath away hard. Facing the Emperor, he had to preserve an expression of directness and honest readiness to serve and suffer, but inwardly, everything sank. It was hard not to see that they wanted to get off the hook at his expense, that they were sending him not just into danger, but on an extremely awkward, difficult, and potentially disgraceful mission.

The more thought he gave this, the more ominously he understood all the dangers of his appointment: if Ivanov the artillery general successfully put down the upheavals, he would always be known as a punisher, and terrorists would kill him, and in any case society would brand him such that life would be a misery. All the more reproachful would his position be because the Emperor was unlikely to stand firm and could concede responsible government at any moment—and from a new ministry life would be all the more a misery for Ivanov. If the upheavals were so great that they could no longer be put down, then the general's position was even more dangerous. He would not be forgiven such a step against the Liberation Movement, and they might even hang him.

Whichever side one argued from, his journey was dangerous and unnecessary. However, being in the Emperor's service and being his agent, he did not dare betray his despondency or hesitation. What he decided privately was in any case to delay his journey as much as possible. Life experience told him that whenever you were being squeezed, the surest course was to draw things out.

Nor did he like getting his assignment from his former subordinate.

Alekseev gave him the St. George battalion to take along. Marvelous men, but what kind of army were they? They were used to being window dressing, and they were so few. True, Alekseev promised to add another machine-gun detachment en route. They studied the list of units being attached from the North and West army groups and when they might arrive—on 14 and 15 March. Was there any certainty in these units? Alekseev assured him that they were the most reliable. So, eight regiments all in all? Not enough! Ivanov insisted on sending another three regiments from the Southwest.

But the more units there were, the harder it would be to assemble them, and the later he himself would have to go. (Fortunately, no one as yet had indicated precisely when he was supposed to set off.) Moreover, the correct place for the units to disembark was not Petrograd, rather they needed to be positioned throughout the farther outskirts.

So would things be clearer in the morning? Tomorrow morning, General Ivanov would come again?

Alekseev was suffering from chills. He did not object.

Nikolai Iudovich left all these unpleasantnesses for now and went home to the station, to his cozy train car. It was high time he went to bed.

Events in Petrograd were proceeding apace, and by tomorrow this entire trip might not even be necessary.

[1 4 4]

Before Sasha had a chance to look around in the strange situation of the palace's entrance hall, where bundles of hand grenades lay alongside barrels of herring and crates of eggs, but more than anything rejoicing in how unusual it all was—this was a true sign of revolution!—a small, lean, browless, pinched man headed toward him. Himmer! There was luck for you! Their acquaintance had come in handy!

He recognized him.

"Ah . . . Yasny!" he greeted him animatedly. And he led and led him down a corridor, a rather crowded corridor—where?—to defense headquarters!

Defense headquarters? Sasha could not have landed more centrally! What else could a heart desire in revolution? He entered the room with shining eyes and shivers down his spine even—because the impossible had come to pass!

It was a spacious room under a shimmering chandelier, the office of someone important, an oak desk, and velvet on the other tables and chairs. There were only a few people in the room altogether—one sailor, a lieutenant, one infantry ensign, four soldiers with rifles who had not removed their greatcoats or fur hats, in that warmth, and one civilian in a worn jacket with a sour, heavy face. (The notion occurred to Sasha that this was a revolutionary who had just emerged from underground.) And it was he who proved to be senior here. Himmer pointed out Sasha to him and, after a few answers from Sasha, left.

Maslovsky looked at him exactingly and asked him which unit he was from and whether he had soldiers obedient to him. He was disappointed that he came from an institution but rejoiced that he did have soldiers, about fifteen of them, and they were all here. (Sasha responded confidently, but remembering the chance nature of his gang, he could not have guaranteed that half an hour later they would still be in front of the palace.)

Also among the headquarters accoutrements was a map of Petersburg jaggedly torn from a reference book and spread out on the desk in a well-lit spot. They were sitting around it any which way, and Maslovsky asked the ensign, and then the soldiers, and then even Sasha, what they knew about the disposition of military forces in the city.

Sasha, who had spent some time in an army milieu and so had seen officers working from maps and a military disposition being plotted—suddenly felt pity and pride for this *headquarters*. Pity that the revolution had to begin with something so insignificant—a torn-out civilian map and no colored pencils, plotting tables, or rulers—a headquarters on the level of soldiers and ensigns, and not a single person present with anything useful to say about a single hostile unit, and as to their own, everyone knew they had scattered and no longer existed—and at the head of them all was not a colonel or even an officer but a civilian. But pride that they would set to it with this— and just watch them win! A Revolution breaks all the rules, she's a hooligan, she's permitted the impermissible, even ignorance—and nonetheless she will win. Such is the inertia of history!

Right then someone entered and called out the soldiers to a meeting of the Soviet of Deputies. It turned out they had come not to a defense headquarters, but had been put here temporarily for a conversation, and now they were off to the Soviet.

Sasha had just been amazed that the headquarters had been made up of soldiers, and now there were no soldiers left.

Four of them remained, and of the weapons, three revolvers and two swords. Lieutenant Filippovsky didn't have even a dagger on him; on the other hand, he was a longtime SR and even from their combat organization, and Sasha was very drawn to him. But the ensign was some very silly man and not even from Petrograd. He'd just arrived today by train; he'd been traveling from Vologda and landed in this whole mess. He knew no one and nothing here but was prepared to do his part.

Because there were so few of them left now, Maslovsky and Filippovsky did not seclude themselves but did their discussing of what the situation was right there, out loud. The situation turned out to be the following. Vasili-evsky Island, which was occupied by a Finland battalion, had not been touched at all by the movement, and no measures whatsoever had been taken to demoralize it. The Petersburg side was only starting to come under control. On the Vyborg side, a wheeled battalion was resisting. Throughout the entire rest of the city the situation was quite obscure. All the Cossacks, the 9th Horse Regiment, a Guards crew, and the Semyonovsky men were in their barracks, neutral as yet, but they could come out at any moment on either side, and if they made a stand, it would be against us because the only units for us were those who had refused to submit and had scattered, which meant they no longer existed. There was no such thing as *our* troops. The Peter and Paul Fortress had been occupied by government troops, and its cannons had been aimed but had not yet fired. Nothing was known about a single military school, all of which might act against, which was more likely. That afternoon some troops had formed up near the Winter Palace, which meant they were Khabalov's, so everyone in that formation was no longer ours because ours had no formations. Khabalov's forces were an unknown quantity in general. They had assembled somewhere in the city's center and their intentions were unknown. That afternoon they had tried to move down Liteiny, but their progress had been halted by the crowds, and they wouldn't fire on the crowds so they were bottled up. But right now, with the darkness, the crowds were already dispersing and the streets were clearing out—and we had no defense left whatsoever, and our opponent was obviously going to shift to a decisive offensive. We can't defend ourselves with our soldiers. We simply can't form them up, and obviously we can't lead them away from the Tauride Palace because they won't go. Not only that, we have neither cavalry nor functioning artillery. There are cannons for decoration and four machine guns, but they can't fire them without glycerin, and there is no communication with anyone other than by city telephone. Although the telephone exchange on Morskaya is in Khabalovite hands and under their headquarters, amazingly it is answering all calls from the Tauride Palace! Probably so that they can eavesdrop on us. They could turn off the entire network and we would be left blind and cut off, but they would still have the military-police line on separate poles. Finally, who had all the southern train stations and what was going on there was also unknown. At any moment Tsarist troops could disembark there, and we were not only powerless to pre-vent that but would not even know about it.

The situation was utterly catastrophic; according to the rules of conven-tional war it was time simply to run away before they themselves were seized and hanged. But Revolution, she's a hooligan! Sasha experienced a wild joy even that everything was so bad. It was as inviting as music, and there was a certain special merriment, not from what was good but from what was bad: make merry at a catastrophe—and crush it! He had fought for half a day today, and he had won, and he knew the air of the streets now, and this same air was with them now, although it wasn't noted on the military maps.

"Permission to pace?" he asked his seniors and began nervously pacing, although he didn't smoke, and in this movement, across the carpet, which had already been tracked over by soldiers' melting boots, he foresaw finding something. That would be funny, if he could come up with their salvation now!

Right then another agile civilian ran in bringing one more infantry ensign and at the same time reporting that an armored car had entered the open area out front and was at their disposal.

There! An armored car! Things were improving.

But the new ensign couldn't help them; he didn't know where which units were. And the Vologdan didn't know a single Petrograd street. To hell with help and ensigns like that.

Filippovsky was smoking over the map, but Maslovsky wasn't smoking, nor was Lenartovich, but he, too, began pacing nervously.

"You," he told Filippovsky, "we will assign you the Tauride Palace defense. Somehow those anti-airplane guns have to be put in order and positioned. Otherwise, they'll swoop down on us!"

Filippovsky kept puffing smoke over the civilian map.

"You'll have to assemble volunteers from the soldiers in front of the palace and take two detachments to the Nikolaevsky and Tsarskoye Selo train stations, if not to occupy them, then for reconnaissance. Two of you will go," Maslovsky said.

Why, this was a wonderful assignment, to occupy all of one of the capital's large train stations! Sasha confirmed that he was prepared to go, but . . . but . . . He was still searching and was getting closer; some even greater objective was spinning in his head.

But in that time Maslovsky had stood up straight. Pricked up his ears. Stopped by the marble fireplace. As if he were listening closely. He held onto the mantelpiece with one hand and with the other began supporting his arguments.

"All the strength, of course, is on Khabalov's side. On ours we have only the revolutionary atmosphere. But that is exactly where he's losing! Because he's a slug and doesn't know the experience of revolutions. He's concentrating his troops in the very center of the city. That's a mistake! The capital is ablaze with this revolutionary atmosphere, and it's here that his troops will fall apart! The experience of revolutions shows that government troops win when they break out of the capital's contagious zone and then encircle it or, at least, attack from without."

How successfully he expressed this. That was such a beautiful, intelligent moment—on the one hand, everything was being lost from the delay, but on the other, they felt like speaking! From this tension an idea came to Sasha, although apparently there was no connection here. He stopped short, in the middle of the office, turned to Maslovsky, and said ringingly and proudly, distinctly aware of his own tone:

"Tell me, and where is the so-called government? Why don't we feel it anywhere?"

"In the Mariinsky Palace," Maslovsky replied.

He replied but nothing was born in him! Filippovsky raised his eyes to the smoke; he hadn't grasped Sasha's point.

"Then give me an armored car and a truck, too!" Sasha exclaimed with joyous insight so that no one could say it before he did. "I'll take my detachment and collect some volunteers, too, and **I'll go arrest the government**! Or drive them the hell out!"

Everyone looked at him with amazement. But also with mounting respect.

"There's probably a strong defense around the Mariinsky, though."

"If there's a strong defense, I'll shoot, give them a scare, and leave. But I've been on the streets all day today and I've already taken several buildings! I've been convinced it's very easy! The defenders of the old order will surrender in a minute!"

There's also no doubt that an attack is the best form of defense! If everything is so bad and unprotected for us, then let's attack!

Well, how about it? How about it? They exchanged glances and thought it over. Well, how about it! If you're suggesting it yourself. If you're prepared. . . .

Sasha was prepared for anything right now! Over the course of the day he had known the sweetness of action. And he wasn't afraid—not one bit. Anyone who acts boldly really isn't in the greatest danger.

True, he'd never had anything to do with an armored car in his life. But he'd had nothing to do with almost anything in the army. All this was to be mastered.

The main thing was daring and instantaneity and to go now, right now, and seize them before they expected anything. Arrest the government—and who among them would be left? Khabalov alone?

They liked this idea more and more. But Maslovsky seemed to be wavering as to whether the ensign was up to the task of arresting the government.

Suddenly the door opened, and without any introduction an officer walked in, gleaming, with excellent bearing, his spurs jingling, his boots striking, and reported:

"Cavalry Captain Sosnovsky from the Hussar regiment! I put myself at the disposal of the revolution!"

And—before whom? before his juniors, before a civilian—he lingered a little more in an excellently proffered salute, stunning them.

Everyone leapt up. Everyone immediately sensed a natural-born soldier! This was the beginning. The Tsarist officer class had begun to come over!

They introduced themselves, everyone shaking hands. And so attractive! A fluffy blond mustache, lively, clever eyes, the luxurious cascades of his voice, and his cheerful manner of speaking simply enchanted and encouraged them all.

Not losing any time, Maslovsky suggested that he head up the expedition to the Mariinsky Palace.

Sasha was not offended in the least. This subordination was by rights, and it would be even somewhat easier for him with the weapons and the orders. What he was perfectly free from was any kind of vanity, whether it's me or not, whoever's senior. He was experiencing a joy he had never known— the joy of serving, of surrendering wholly, nothing for himself.

For himself—even death. There is no death more beautiful than death for a revolution.

They quickly made the assignments. Sosnovsky and Lenartovich would take the armored car and the truck and collect soldiers—and go storm the Mariinsky Palace. While the two ensigns, if they added some volunteers to their detachments, would go to the Nikolaevsky and Tsarskoye Selo train stations, also in vehicles; there were some vehicles near the palace.

Also, have someone gather intelligence near the telephone exchange and Khabalov's headquarters?

With common purpose, Sosnovsky and Lenartovich strode down the hallway. Sasha took pleasure in the evenness of their movements, took pleasure in everyone liking him, that he was working for the cause, he was a genuine soldier and for that reason was party to events. Sosnovsky let drop an indiscreet joke concerning a girl student who flashed past them and even reached out toward her to detain her. (There's a hussar for you, just the time for that.)

The square outwise was growing thicker with vehicles and soldiers, and several bonfires had been started. They found the assigned armored car. The armored car's driver immediately agreed to go, but the truck's driver demanded a written order from Deputy Kerensky. They found someone else who agreed without anything in writing.

Sasha started shouting, "My detachment!" and went to where he'd left them, but there were other men there, not his. Then he started going from fire to fire and shouting simply for volunteers for an operation, naturally without naming what kind. They didn't come immediately but asked whether they'd be going on foot or in a vehicle. Learning it would be in a vehicle, some quit their fires and followed him. One shouted: "Only I'm on the fender!" And a second: "I'm on a fender, too!" That meant having the honor of lying on the uncomfortable fender with his bayonet thrust forward.

Before getting in, Sosnovsky once more said something inappropriate and vile on the topic of women and taking such liberties that Sasha was shaken.

But at this unworthy impetus his thoughts about Yelenka suddenly pushed forward. Sitting down beside the driver, to the already started, roaring engine, with a dozen soldiers behind him in the back and before tearing off, he thought of her with a new feeling: not in the demeaning remonstrances in which their last meetings had been spent, but with a powerful sense of his right to her: he had chosen her, and she would be his! According to his will, not hers!

No, there was something remarkable about war! Revolutionary war, of course.

[1 4 5]

On his way to the Tauride Palace, Himmer attached himself and chattered away. Shlyapnikov disliked terribly these abstruse, bookish theoreticians who couldn't hold a file or a chisel and would never pick up a revolver but would spin all kinds of yarns about the proletariat and how to make a revolution. You crossed the boundary at the Arctic Circle, dragged yourself around every night to one overnight halt after another, beset by homelessness and insomnia—while they in their clean clothing and clean apartments, with their passports, walked into a clean office—and were now the first to rush into the breach and seize places.

In the few hours from just before noon until twilight there had been a great Breakthrough, which even Shlyapnikov could still not comprehend, could not push himself that far, and now, en route to the Tauride Palace, looking around, he was still trying to grasp it. So, was it a clean break? Had everything that had been blocking us all these years—had it been breached?

But then, you see, the position of the parties and the position of individuals were about to change.

The rivalry among the parties was nothing new, a constant, but it was always in favor of the leftists, internationalists, and militants, so that they had to vie seriously only with the Interdistrict group, who time and again would grab the best and sharpest slogans, and in part with the Initiativists—while all the other Mensheviks, opportunists, defensists, and Gvozdevists were always on the outs, to say nothing of the Trudoviks and the populist socialists. (There were no SRs at all.) So, if the Breakthrough had occurred, then now, wait, and in a matter of hours or minutes an entirely new disposition of forces would be decided, who would seize what places. The old and genuine merits would count for nothing, and you had to grab on now.

Shlyapnikov as never before was responsible for not losing his head. He was responsible to those of his own who would be returning from Siberia, from abroad. Especially Lenin. Lenin would not forgive a failure of any kind.

It was good he had hurried to the Tauride Palace in the early evening hours, when the entire petty bourgeois and literary-socialist public was swaggering and blustering. There was no one from the worker districts, while these whom no one had seen for a long time were flying around like moths to a flame and rushing from room to room. Strutting with great self-importance were those *released from the prisons*, although some, like Rafes, had been in all of three weeks, and some two nights, like Kapelinsky. Chattering among the others like a birthday boy was Khrustalev-Nosar, with a sword at his side, who was thrusting himself at everyone with his explanations that as recently as this morning he'd been under threat of three years of hard labor and that since 1905 he had been the Soviet's unrelieved chairman. Also strutting around pompously was the very large Nakhamkes, who had sat through two war years in a comfortable, narrow-minded existence. Everyone was rushing around with red rosettes and bows, and they wanted to quickly open a session of the Soviet of Workers' Deputies at seven o'clock in the evening, and all the intellectuals were demanding their own credentials to the Soviet. Of course, genuine elections could not be held at the factories in today's turmoil, but not to wait for at least someone from the workers was simply indecent. Shlyapnikov was barely able to shame them into moving the opening to nine o'clock. (He had calculated mentally that as of now, given its present composition, the Bolsheviks would not have any positions, and even he himself would not get onto the Executive Committee.)

As soon as he'd persuaded them, he rushed to the free telephones to seek out and convene his own people. But they were all on the streets, in the events—and the Menshevik pests had pulled together to seize the historic roles.

Meanwhile, chairs and stools were being brought into the large room, and the curious were surging in from outside, so they had to post a guard at the doors. Some got issued credentials and some didn't. They assembled nearly fifty altogether. The Bolsheviks didn't make it, just one or two. It was amazing there weren't even any disruptive Interdistrict men, or their crazed Krotovsky. On the other hand, there was the equally crazed Dmitrievsky-Aleksandrovich, an SR.

Sokolov, Erlich, and Pankov all tried to be the one to open the meeting simultaneously. With the open tails of his frock coat flapping, Sokolov, of course, felt he was the chief organizer. But the others kept trying to outdo each other. Several were speechifying at once, and each started speaking sooner—and whose question had been first and whose third was not decided for a long time.

Then Chkheidze arrived looking cheerful and relaxed and with no pretensions to being the leader—a small, stooped man with a large bald spot and a beard twisted out of shape. But the Mensheviks fussed as if around an incomparable leader and sat him in the chairman's seat. Next to him sat another Duma leader, the young, chubby-cheeked Skobelev, his hair neatly styled, his strength not yet spent on anything, a rich sonny-boy, he had dillydallied, then done the Duma, and had chosen not to know the underground—much like nearly all those who had converged here.

Right before the opening, the boyish Kerensky, wearing a close-fitting suit, burst in and also sat next to them. But he immediately grew bored because this was not the audience for him. He shrugged his narrow shoulders, with darting eyes, threw out something about the triumph of the revolution—and left, busily and quickly.

Nakhamkes sat in his prominent seat and ran his fingers through his handsome reddish beard.

Fairly soon after, Chkheidze left, too. Order began to break down. Sokolov gasped and Skobelev got distraught, lacking any understanding or plan. Someone expressed the idea that to continue the glorious traditions of '05 it would be good to restore Khrustalev-Nosar as chairman.

Nosar immediately moved to speak, now without his sword. But his slipshod and confused speech garnered him no supporters.

At that, Shlyapnikov could not restrain himself, and so that the voice of the Bolsheviks would be heard, he spoke out sharply against, saying they could not choose just the one chairman; they had to choose the entire Executive Committee all at once. In any event, Nosar, that renegade of socialism and anti-Semite, could not be not only chairman of the Soviet but even among its honorary founders.

He immediately shook Nosar with "anti-Semite," and they would neither listen nor discuss it. An anti-Semite—that killed it.

But they did not try to select an Executive Committee, either. Frankorussky from the Food Supplies Commission seized the floor. He reassured them that based on the first inspection, the bread situation was far from catastrophic, all they had to . . .

But they didn't finish discussing the food question, either. Himmer in his delicate voice and Brounshtein demanded a discussion of the city's defense first and foremost.

And then, they shouted, wasn't there the broader question of repulsing Tsarist reaction?

But Shlyapnikov did not join this free-for-all. In his Bolshevik way, he was contemplating the main thing: how not to miss out on seizing more seats on the Executive Committee. For now both numbers and oratory had squeezed out the Bolsheviks, and the petty bourgeois pack was threatening to seize the workers' springboard.

But for now they were appointing a literary commission to write an appeal to the populace.

At this, some soldier scrambled up to tell how everything had happened today in his battalion, what he had seen himself, and how it had been in the barracks and on the street.

Then another followed, and they were barely stopped.

Meanwhile, Nakhamkes kept taking the assembly more and more into his own hands. He was a large figure with a powerful voice, and his look was very confident, as if he had carried the underground on his own shoulders. Some people do know how!

At last, it was already late, they got around to the elections for the Executive Committee. The game was immediately lost, of course, because Chkheidze was chosen chairman unanimously, and Kerensky and Skobelev deputy chairmen, and then it was impossible to put up a fight. The leadership had already gone to the opportunists! Immediately directed into the secretariat were Sokolov and Shekhter, and after him the rather idiotic Pankov, who was also an Initiativist, however—and Gvozdev, whom everyone here today had treated with great honor. When they started electing regular members of the EC, the most votes were garnered by Nakhamkes, Himmer, and Kapelinsky—an extra chance for nonparty members because party people only vote for their own. Still, the Initiativists supported the Bolsheviks, so Shlyapnikov and Zalutsky also got on the EC.

But the balance on the EC did not promise success. Shlyapnikov sat there while his seat burned under him. What could he devise? He envisioned Lenin destroying him for having been here at this moment and letting the leadership slip. Lenin's teaching had always been to seize the leading spots.

But what could Shlyapnikov have done? How could he have forced all of them here to obey him? He shrank against these loudmouths.

Ah! Here's what he came up with, whether it was good or bad: on the Executive Committee, besides the elected members, let there also be seats to be appointed by the parties, three apiece.

It passed. (He had calculated correctly that everyone would grasp at the extra seats.)

That meant the Bolsheviks would have another three, for five total.

But there would also be three Mensheviks. And three SRs.

The only advantage was that factions like the Interdistrict group would not have more than one.

[146]

After the shooting near the Moscow barracks, Vakhov went on to lose his last Volynians and his sergeant-major, Timosha Kirpichnikov, and was quite the orphan and completely lost his way; he didn't even know where to find the bridge they'd only just run across.

He proceeded like a blind man, down the agitated street, and everyone was going somewhere, either full of joy or just as lost as he was. He proceeded with his mouth hanging open. He had no idea what to do now, no idea where to go—but he noticed a Preobrazhensky sergeant with a broad jaw and little eyes who had also been leading since early morning—and Vakhov joined his detachment.

This detachment marched to this very noisy, cupolaed building, and there the Preobrazhensky men took up the watch.

But they didn't take Vakhov. What was he doing with strangers anyway? He began to languish in a bad way.

Should've gone back to his own men—but where were you going to look for them in this city? What if they weren't even in the city anymore but in the barracks? What if there was no one in the barracks and there was an ambush for rebels? So where should he go? It was seriously frightening. As long as they'd been racing through the city, shouting, shooting, and taking buildings on the fly, there was the strength of thousands and solidarity in it all, and it was fun, not frightening, like a wonderful outing, roaming however we wanted. But where was that crowd now? The civilians had had their fun and dispersed to their homes. But it's a soldier's head for this.

If he hadn't ever drifted away from his own men it wouldn't be so frightening. They couldn't make *everyone* answer, but he was all alone.

But here it was good: an enormous hall, like a field under a roof, and all the people! Vakhov sat on the floor by a wall and lay his rifle down so as to tuck it under the edge of his behind, so it wouldn't slip away—a soldier without his rifle is like a sheep—while he himself leaned back and started to doze off. His belly was grumbling. A whole day without food. Well, on the other hand he was warm and in safety. He could spend the night here, and things would be clearer in the morning.

No such luck! Nearby someone called out:

"Hey, Volynian!"

Vakhov opened his eyes and rejoiced:

"Well?"

He thought his men had found him and now they'd join up.

No, a soldier from another regiment was standing there with a civilian:

"Get up! You're going to be the deputy from the Volynian Regiment. None of yours are here. Go to the deputies' soviet!"

Where? Were you getting yourself into something even deeper? He regretted his place by the wall, so cozy, you weren't going to grab one like it later; you'd be in the middle of the floor, where everybody walked. Vakhov considered hiding, refusing, but they were ordering him, leaning over him. Where could you hide from them?

They went. Crossing a corridor.

There they pinned a big piece of red fabric to his greatcoat. Vakhov didn't want to let them.

"What do I need this for?"

You're driving that cloth right into me, like a splinter. A soldier's supposed to get something red put on his greatcoat? Fools like it red; soldiers like it plain.

But Vakhov could see that everyone here had it pinned on. Oh, all right.

He sat down on a bench by a wall, his rifle straight up between his knees. On his left, he looked—seemed like a workman. On his right, he looked—some kind of merchant. No one you could talk to.

And there, in the middle, around the table, all the educated ones were bunched up, not a single soldier among them, and not a workman to be seen—they were all from the same place, you know, and everyone was cut from the same cloth. They weren't making any explanations, it was as if they'd been discussing it for three days now and picked up on each other instantly. From where he was, on the outside, it was all pretty difficult, lots of words he didn't understand.

What had they called Vakhov in from the nice big space for? He wished he could spend the night there.

Everyone was trying to speak at once, to talk over each other, no one got a chance to talk things through, and they were leaping up from their chairs and pushing each other away at the table. Bedlam. Vakhov had never seen the like.

And everyone was so overjoyed, they were near to bursting. They were appointing each other for this and that, they were raising their hands and putting them down. What's it to you? You never raised your rifle under an oath, you'll all run off to your homes, like you were never here. But the soldier lays down his life for this.

Then they started talking sense: if troops do arrive, how can we fight them off? They weren't so joyful anymore, and Vakhov's heart started to ache badly. Surely they'd come, come to punish us! That was what these men were expecting. After all, there's no getting around punishment. Don't revolt in time of war! Truly, it was no joke: there was a war going on and we were laying our officers out dead? Had we lost our minds or something?

Then they started talking better: about how the soldiers needed feeding, apart from their units. Here, too, in this big building—feed them, too.

That'd be good. If they'd feed us here, we wouldn't have to slip back into the barracks just yet.

Right then, a young soldier burst forward from the doorway and squeezed between the chairs to the middle of the room, burst in as if he was being chased and they'd nearly caught him. He was holding his rifle in both hands and shaking it overhead—toward those in front, the main ones.

"Brothers and comrades! I bring you fraternal greetings from all the lower ranks in full of the Semyonovsky Regiment's Life Guard! Every last one of us has resolved to join the people against the accursed autocracy! And we vow to serve until our last drop of blood! We welcome the soviet of deputies and support it with our loyal bayonets!"

Vakhov thought this soldier was not very sensible, and he was still just a runt. Vakhov couldn't tell whether he'd really run all the way from the Semyonovsky barracks. That was pretty far. Or just the last block? Then why? And then: there hadn't been any Semyonovsky soldiers anywhere all day, they'd been sitting in their barracks, and this was the first to appear—and he was speaking for them all? The shooting was over and the bragging had begun. You couldn't tell by looking that he was speaking for everyone, and it would be odd to send such a young ne'er-do-well to speak for a whole battalion.

He had a very free tongue about him, as did the others, that was how they were talking here. Everyone all around cheered up and started clapping.

And so? If the retribution started against the soldiers, these ringleaders wouldn't be getting a pat on the back, either. If he stuck to them, maybe they'd devise some kind of relief.

A sapper started in after the Semyonovsky man and started telling how it had been, how today they'd decided to go against their battalion commander—and slain him. And they'd finished off Lieutenant Ustrugov. And besides that . . .

They applauded him.

The sapper's words weighed on Vakhov's heart. Now that was the truth.

Then someone from the Lithuanian battalion spoke.

And when they started calling out:

"What about you, Volynian? . . . Why don't you say something, Volynian? You were the first to start!"

Vakhov was cornered like a wolf. They turned toward him from all sides and goaded him on.

Pinned, he got up, only leaning on his rifle. And looked into these strangers' faces. How could he talk to them?

He would first have to explain that for a man, their whole Petersburg was worse than a primeval forest, these were the deepest, darkest woods, and for a peasant heart, there was nothing nice here, nothing but sadness. How in this forest all you had to hang on to was your division, your platoon. You knew your lance corporal, your sergeant, your cot, your mess. Following the military rules, like the blind following strings, was the only way to get through it. They wouldn't have broken those strings for anything in the world if they hadn't been sent into this savageness yesterday (yesterday, but it seemed ages ago), to fire on the people. In fact, their plan had been just not going on the detail and defending their staircase. There'd been no pact to kill Captain Lashkevich, so who killed him and how? By killing him they'd cut themselves off and there was suddenly no room for them in the whole world. Now, as night was falling, his mind couldn't take it in. Had all this really happened? It was as if Vakhov had gone on a rampage all alone with an ax—and it was too late now to throw it away, and it couldn't be forgotten, and his hands were spattered in that blood and that flesh—and it was frightening to go back to where they'd laid Lashkevich out.

But all this, he realized, he couldn't tell them. They hadn't felt the ax on its spree and they only applauded the murdered officers. He drew them along, drew them along:

"So you see, brothers, comrades . . . We Volynians were the first, of course . . . our training detachment. . . . We were the first, of course, and then everyone followed us. . . ." He felt more courageous here, among them: "And if we have to, we'll do it again. . . ."

And they finished up for him, shouting:

"Against autocracy!"

And so Vakhov made something up, not that much worse than the others, although not recognizing his own voice. Everyone there, even all the educated men, clapped for him and rejoiced.

As if they'd absolved him of any sin, this ax, this unspeakable ax.

And Vakhov felt a little easier. He was already leaning toward maybe going to his barracks.

Maybe he'd dodge it somehow, as though we're not us and I'm not me. Maybe somehow it would die down, and in his chest, too.

They couldn't drive a host that size to prison, could they?

[1 4 7]

Milyukov went out to walk around the Ekaterininsky Hall in hopes that additional observation and certain people's reports would provide the initial facts he was lacking for an accurate, synthetic judgment. In these hours of this universal shift and inquiry, there was demanded of him, at least preliminarily, a line that was socially resultant, but that line just wouldn't define itself. For the thought process itself, of course, there was little here of use. It was practically impossible to walk through Ekaterininsky Hall in a straight line, as they usually did here; time and again he had to either swerve or stop and let someone pass. A public had gathered that was unthinkable for the Tauride Palace and insulting: utterly undisciplined soldiers, without leadership, some smoking (and throwing their butts on the floor), some sitting on silk-upholstered chairs, some tramping around in dirty boots; here and there puddles were melting on the magnificent parquet, soldiers were dragging rifles behind them; then they would get tired of them and stack them in threes and fours cross-wise next to the columns, transforming the magnificent hall into the semblance of a bivouac. (Quite a fine bivouac, too, if they'd been prepared to repulse—but you see, they weren't.) In a few hours the quasi-legitimate public, which had been subdued for years, had come out of the woodwork and all been drawn to the Tauride Palace—and now here they were coming to life. But the Duma deputies, on the contrary, had become timid and disappeared—imperceptibly, because leaving the triumph of the revolution looked indecent. Very lively young women circled around, too, from quasi-revolutionary circles, of course. Now small rallies with speakers standing on chairs arose at various ends of the hall. But that was nothing! In the Cupola Hall they were carrying sacks of flour and storing them against the wall, as if it were a warehouse. Once again, this would not be bad for the Tauride Palace's possible (impossible) defense, but the look of it! My God!

Now, in the budget commission's room, this quasi-legitimate public had made something of itself; the mistake had been to let them in, but they hadn't had the strength to prevent them—and how could they be driven out now? While the main life, the higher content of these halls, which for twelve years had constituted the loftiest manifestation of Russian history, was melting away, retreating. In part, Milyukov wanted with his firm step to remind people of that life and defend it. While these members of the budget commission were pivoting at dizzying speed, the Duma deputies approached Milyukov with such distress or even foolishness that there truly was nothing to say in reply. There was just one marvelous plan—from the Duma journalists, who had come with the following proposal. Newspapers were not coming out in the city and the population knew nothing. It was essential to inform them immediately—and they were getting ready to publish such a newspaper today, early tonight. So could it be considered the organ of the State Duma's Provisional Committee?

An excellent idea, and Milyukov said yes. But immediately the question arose as to what printing press, in the descending chaos, would set it? Would they be able to convince or compel anyone?

Milyukov gave his consent—on behalf of the Provisional Committee. Was the Provisional Committee becoming a real force? Just a few hours ago, Pavel Nikolaevich had resisted creating that Committee. But the intervening hours had brought something new. Between midday and evening, the picture of events had changed quickly. Having crossed the mountain pass, there was now a general movement downhill, and it threatened to accelerate out of control. And while doing what we could to put the brakes on this acceleration, we still had to move forward, too. And not delay too much in doing so. If we didn't move to action, the masses were going to stop listening to us.

Not that long ago, this had been said just for effect. Pavel Nikolaevich had returned from his Crimean dacha after Christmas, and at a Moscow gathering he had been asked impatiently, "Why is it the Duma won't seize power?" At the time he had insulated himself by saying: "Bring us two regiments of soldiers, and we will."

But now, apparently, there were the regiments, so . . . ? The Duma, though, . . .

Was Milyukov not the Duma's principal figure? Who was the Duma, then, if not Milyukov? And what would the Duma be without Milyukov? But it was he today who had seen further than them all. He was glad the Duma was not in session yet; that would only narrow any productive new pathways. He especially objected to the suggestion that the Duma be declared permanently in session and made the state authority. That would be a clumsy extreme.

Now they needed something more flexible. The Duma's Provisional Committee? Milyukov himself had slowed it down by tagging it with a long name "for relations with institutions and individuals"—in the event punishment came, so as not to fall under the criminal heading. But now a few hours had passed and it had become clear that the Committee was not only permissible but even quite apt; it should even be made more dynamic. It could also serve as a regulative for all difficult circumstances.

It could be the seed of a new authority.

Could it be that the historic moment—to seize power—had come? How could this be known? Where could it be read for certain?

The whole art of politics, in essence, comes down to just this, you see: when to seize power, *how* to seize power, and how to retain power.

Yes, they had been waging a constitutional struggle, but that time had passed. Yes, now the Duma could hinder a real movement toward a ministry. So did seizing power mean stepping over both the fallen government and the Duma?

At this he experienced an awkward moment of a personal nature. In essence, only Milyukov was worthy of becoming the true head of the new Russia. After all, he was not simply the head of the leading party and the head of the Bloc but really only he could truly grasp, weigh, and direct.

However, history's diffident gesture is such that the worthiest candidate not only cannot name himself, declare himself, and imperiously move forward (the Americans do this remarkably honestly: openly nominate yourself!) but is compelled to stay in the background until it becomes natural to be nominated. Nonentities are always nominated to top positions, suiting all aspirants by their vapidity and absence of will.

Thus was Rodzyanko once elected Duma president. Everyone agreed that he was dull-witted and would be manageable. But he had betrayed their hopes when he had revealed an overly assertive disposition. From the Progressive Bloc's very creation, Milyukov had labored to instill and had instilled in everyone the notion that anyone but Rodzyanko should head up the desired future and dreamed-of public government, but instead . . . (everyone suggested) now Prince Georgi Lvov was a marvelous candidate (based on the same principle of vapidity) with a Russia-wide reputation.

Replace the Horse Guard with a Tolstoyan. (Who was not averse to conspiracies.)

Rodzyanko was unbearable. And not radical. Removing him from that post had been inevitable, and Pavel Nikolaevich did not regret that operation.

As for Lvov—we would see. Today he had been summoned urgently from Moscow.

Today the situation had been shifting by the hour, and you had to keep a keen eye on it. Now, while Rodzyanko was rushing to the Mariinsky Palace and Milyukov was pacing here, down the length of the Ekaterininsky Hall—quite a lot had changed. Although the word "revolution" was fluttering on people's lips, this was not yet a revolution. Not that we needed one by any means. But it looked as though we should not delay: we needed to prevent it.

The moderate public had always been opposed to a revolutionary coup anyway. But if everything was on such a swift downward plunge, then he had to be there in time to head up the movement and take it in hand. Real politics always demands zigzags and even drastic changes. But Rodzyanko—this was exactly what he opposed. His hulk occupied the president's seat, blocked the sole door of freedom, the sole way out—and he was resisting.

Here he had returned successfully from his journey, no one had detained him anywhere (though he had trumpeted that he was going into danger), and he had again placed his vast behind in that vast chair. He had made the trip for no reason at all and returned with nothing at all. Grand Duke Mikhail had not agreed to be dictator.

Did that mean seizing power themselves?

No! The Samovar could not bring himself to do that! He wouldn't himself, and he wouldn't let anyone else.

He was blocking the way no longer as Duma president and not yet as Committee chair but by virtue of his prominence and because even Army Group Commanders were in some kind of contact with him, if not in collusion. There was no getting around Rodzyanko.

Milyukov was sitting sideways to his large desk and was counting only on his own diplomatic designs. The objective and argumentation proved very difficult. He had to push Rodzyanko, as the main actor, to a seizure of power by the Committee—and simultaneously remove Rodzyanko from the main seat. It seemed undoable!

There was something big-doggish about Rodzyanko's head and face. His head's broad, heavy skull (his cheekbones and temples were as wide as his jaw). A fleshy face. Under the weight of fleshy eyelids—narrowed eyes. Any hair would have spoiled the picture, any hair would have been superfluous here—but he had none. He had been shaved on the closest setting—there was only a scattering around his crown.

Not a meeting of the Committee but just those who had assembled—the lone wolf Nekrasov, the dawdler Konovalov, the foppish loudmouth Shulgin, and the decisive and gloomy fool Vladimir Lvov. Milyukov had no worthy allies. He had to spin this all out himself.

"But Mikhail Vladimirovich, you are the one saying there is no more government, it's fallen apart. Think what a unique moment it is for the seizure of power! In literally two or three hours it might be otherwise, there might be a completely different balance."

Written on the face of that lout Konovalov was consent to everything. (What talentless hands we have making history! After all, this man had headed up the most progressive "Konovalovan" meetings!) Vladimir Lvov watched tensely and somberly, as if the entire weight of the decision rested on him. While Nekrasov was, as always, looking away, hiding his lips under his cunning mustache.

"It cannot be, Mikhail Vladimirovich, such a vast country—and to be without an authority? If the authority has already fallen anyway, in this ominous moment, who should lift it up if not us?"

Rodzyanko rested his large head on both hands, himself horrified at what was happening. But:

"I am not an insurrectionist, gentlemen! The uprising occurred because we were not heeded. But I have not made and do not want to make any revolution whatsoever! I cannot go against the Supreme Imperial Authority!"

"I!"—as if he alone existed and not the Duma or the Committee.

Shulgin (with his curled mustache and bowtie), mellifluously:

"Mikhail Vladimirovich! If we do not pick up the fallen authority, others will. Who is calling on you to go against the Supreme authority! We aren't touching the monarchy. You would be taking executive authority, and as a loyal subject. Everything will work out. The Emperor will name a new government, and we will hand over power to whoever they say."

Well, that's going a step too far, Milyukov thought.

"What if it doesn't work out?" the stunned Rodzyanko asked, and he seemed to be making an effort not to let his jaw drop.

"What if it doesn't work out? To hell with it!" Shulgin swore spiritedly; he liked acute situations. "But what kind of imperial government is it if it fled without resistance? They hadn't even been told to go yet—and they already have!"

"Take power ourselves," a discouraged Rodzyanko blazed and whispered, "that is a revolutionary act! I cannot."

"I" again! He had personally wedged shut the sole door to power—and couldn't bring himself to open it.

Milyukov had no means for undertaking an independent step; he could only through Rodzyanko. All that remained was to grind his bones over and over with arguments.

The entire Committee together had to push him from behind!

Irritation was already boiling in them all against this unyielding hulk. While he tried weakly to justify himself.

"But maybe the Emperor has given his consent to Mikhail Aleksandrovich for a responsible government. What if the head has already been appointed?"

Belyaev had not telephoned, however. They telephoned him at the War Minister's residence—but no one answered. Then a sergeant picked up: the War Minister had set out in some unknown direction.

[1 4 8]

What and where the government was and what and where the ministers were—of this the Empress had been unable to judge all day. There seemed to be no government of any sort left in Petrograd. If Protopopov had been killed, God forbid, then there was still the honest Belyaev. What about him? Not a single official communiqué or appeal had reached her palace all day, but random news kept trickling in from random people, and the news was terrible: the police had vanished, there were fires and looting in the city, and nearly the entire city was in rebel hands, and those loyal were resisting only somewhere in the center.

Only the telephones, to her surprise, had been functioning without interruption, and the local dacha trains were also running according to schedule, without interruption.

At Tsarskoye Selo, thank God, the usual stillness had been preserved.

Her ill children lay in their dark rooms.

The Empress moved among them, wringing her hands.

She had sent three desperate telegrams to GHQ that day. What else could she do?

But GHQ had been silent.

The Emperor was not alone there, however. Frederiks or his energetic son-in-law Voeikov, the palace commandant, who was kept for Frederiks's sake, he should have been in touch—long ago and first.

Just yesterday, at this same time, Aleksandra Fyodorovna had been reading her husband's naïve plans about moving the children to Livadia—and weighing the practical considerations about the difficulty of the move, even after the children recuperated.

Oh, on what strong wings would she take the children and their beds, too, right now—to Livadia!

Unfortunately, as always, bad presentiments had greater power over her than good ones, and now they were telling her they would never more see their sunny, fairytale Livadia! . . .

How many years had Aleksandra taken pride that she was a man among women wearing the trousers of state—and how powerfully and splendidly she would have coped had she had direct power and health! But now, in these hours, when she felt like a woman without any powers or advantages at all, how she needed a strong, confident, senior man by her side who could tell her what to do. But she had no one. . . .

She did! Pavel! Right here, in Tsarskoye Selo, in his palace, lived Grand Duke Pavel Aleksandrovich, the Emperor's uncle and inspector general of the entire Guard. Oh, how she would have liked Pavel's advice, protection, and help right now. After the murder of the man of God, though, she herself had forbidden Pavel, as the father of Dmitri, the murderer, access to her.

Oh, if only he asked permission now! If only he made the first move, she would summon him immediately!

But he didn't.

And why hadn't the dear, loyal, and brave Adjutant Sablin dashed here from the city to explain, encourage, and rescue her? When would he?

The main military official at hand, General Groten, newly appointed as if for spite, was still little acquainted with palace service.

Evening was coming on. Dear Lili, who had so brightened and eased this day for the Empress, had to return home to her seven-year-old child.

"What are you going to do, Lili?" the Empress asked sadly. "Wouldn't it be better for you to return to your Titi this evening?"

Elegant, slender Lili said anxiously:

"Allow me to remain with you, Your Majesty."

The Empress embraced and kissed her.

"But this I cannot ask of you."

"But I cannot leave you, either, Your Majesty."

The Empress was still obliged to sit with her capricious and implacable patient Anya for two hours a day. Now Lili could replace her and be with the children some of the time.

It was already dark outside. There was a telephone call from Petrograd saying it was alight with fires, there were revolutionary crowds everywhere, and there was no authority at all. This could spread to Tsarskoye at any time.

And GHQ was silent.

Whose assistance was there left to resort to? In this enraged and agitated Petrograd, who now could be the undisputed authority? Evidently only that repulsive, overly familiar, hostile, and foolish fatty Rodzyanko. How angry she had been with him before! But now the Empress could ask for protection only from this uncouth boor.

In Pavlovsk, two versts away, there was a Guards Cavalry-Artillery brigade, and it was commanded by the Emperor's aide-de-camp Linevich. The Empress telephoned him and asked him to go see Rodzyanko in the Duma and ask him for guarantees of the royal family's safety.

She did not have three fourths of her former pride left. The danger was streaming toward the palace walls.

She was tired of walking, and this panic was doing nothing to help. She and Lili lay down in the pink boudoir, where icons and paintings of the Annunciation hung. They talked over what might be and how events might go.

After eight o'clock, her lady's maid brought in a telegram from the Emperor. Oh, at last!

But what a calm tone! As if this volcano had never been. Nicky thanked her for the letter she had sent. (But not a word about her three telegrams today!) He reported that he was leaving for Tsarskoye tomorrow after two o'clock in the afternoon. That the cavalry guard from Novgorod had received orders to proceed to Petrograd immediately. And assurance that the disorders among the troops would soon be ended.

Oh, my God! Oh, what relief! How much alarm lifted from her soul! This was her first peaceful hour that entire day.

They remembered they hadn't eaten and decided to have tea.

And in fact, what was there to fear? Tsarskoye Selo was quiet. The Combined Guards regiment was serving irreproachably around the Aleksandr Palace. And stationed very nearby was a Guards crew, and they were not only our troops, they were true friends! And in general, there were Guards riflemen posted at Tsarskoye—a wall! Reserve battalions of select regiments, one of which bore the title of the imperial family.

And now the cavalry would arrive soon as well.

Should they cancel Linevich's trip to see Rodzyanko if he hadn't already left?

However, the day did not end as calmly.

At ten o'clock in the evening, General Groten was summoned to the telephone by Belyaev—who had shown up at last! Throughout this horrible day, he had not once made his presence known—so why now?

Belyaev was speaking not even for himself but conveying the advice of Rodzyanko: The Empress must immediately take the children away from Tsarskoye Selo. Tomorrow might be too late. The Petrograd crowds would reach there and attack.

Benckendorff arrived with his unfailing monocle, his narrow sideburns and mustache, even-tempered as always, and conveyed this all to the Empress. (But he was nervous.)

Once again everything had swirled up in an insane alarm! Rodzyanko was in no way a friend, but even before Linevich he had given advice, and there was a certainty to his advice. For some reason it seemed that this was all exactly what would happen!

But where could the Empress move with children running fevers of 39, and wracked by coughing and sore throats and ears?

There was only one thing to do: send a telegram to Mogilev (the telephone there was not working, of course), while the Emperor was there, and ask for his instructions.

Instructions about what? It was impossible to move in any case.

The Empress wrung her hands.

[1 4 9]

Mikhail Aleksandrovich wished he would never in his entire life have anything to do with affairs of state! So much of a sufficiency for a man— military service, sports, family! There was one unfortunate stretch, after his brother Georgi's death, when he had been considered heir to the throne. And then they had inured him to being heir by making him serve on the State Council, and for statesmanship practice he had even sat through sessions in the Council of Ministers. And although he never spoke up there, never did anything himself—underneath his uniform it weighed on him.

Once, though, in July 1904, one happy night at the Krasnoye Selo camp, they had brought him a telegram. He read it in his tent under a lamp—and in stormy joy shouted to his adjutant:

"Mordvinov! Get up! Champagne! The Empress has given birth to a boy! I'm not the heir anymore!"

Thus, at age twenty-six, he was released—and he remained simply a blue cuirassier, stationed at Gatchina, going on maneuvers, devoting himself to horseback riding, tennis, and skating, and attending the theaters, and he had the freedom to have a good time, and joke, and love. Most of all he loved sports in all its forms—for it strengthened his body (in his youth, Mikhail had been weak), and also provided excitement and risk. His dream was to fly an airplane, and he had already studied the mechanism but still hadn't gotten to know it to a tee. His cavalry agility was his pride. Never again did his brother involve him in affairs of state.

However, Mikhail had fallen seriously in love, and with a woman twice divorced who had two children from her previous husband, Wulfert. A grand duke marrying a woman like that was absolutely out of the question, a double transgression: she was not of his social status—a lawyer's daughter—and she was a divorcée. Falling irrevocably in love, though, Mikhail also made an irrevocable decision.

Since then, great tension had arisen with his brother the Emperor, and the constant ease between them was no more. Although Nikolai was ten years older and had statesmanly experience, and Mikhail sincerely respected him for his mind and tact, previously there had been a fraternal simplicity and ease, and after his unauthorized marriage that disappeared. Usually so gentle, Nikolai became consumed with anger and Mama raged—although Mikhail had the more right to be angry for having been put under the Senate's trusteeship as incompetent. Mikhail had then only just received command of a Horse Guards regiment! He had had to leave both his regiment and army service altogether, and, at the insult, Russia itself, and had spent two years in England, which might have been much longer had war not broken out. Natasha didn't want to return in any case—out of pride—and he would join the English army. Natasha had a keen mind and firm character, and Mikhail lived with her in harmony and total contentment, but what she did not understand was how he could not be a part of his homeland's army when it was fighting. That would be like ripping out his soul! Misha sent Nikolai a telegram requesting permission to return, was added to His Majesty's suite, and was given the rank of major general and the command of a native brigade made up solely of Caucasus volunteers (as there was no draft for people of the Caucasus), foolhardy daredevils. But Mikhail even himself in attacks did not avoid bullets and was agile on a horse and good to his subordinates, and his Native Division loved him.

Natasha was subsequently granted the title Countess Brasova. Nonetheless, the former simplicity between the brothers was never restored. Mikhail had felt this especially of late, when half the grand dukes, as if they'd lost their minds, kept trying to accuse the Emperor and went as far as Rasputin's murder, and they were all expecting Mikhail's support, which he did not lend. Right then, too, various public figures were seeking to influence the Emperor through his relatives—including, especially, Rodzyanko, whom Mikhail considered an outstanding man of state. To all of them, the Emperor's only brother seemed a very influential and important figure who had access to affairs of state—but Mikhail did not have access or the slightest desire; he was content with the life of a private individual and would never have wanted to discuss affairs of state even as an outsider. But here they had foisted it on him. (Natasha, too, took an interest in the State Duma and sympathized with the public moods.) In talking with these figures and Rodzyanko, Mikhail was easily convinced that they were right and that, of course, Nikolai could have dealt with a great many things much better. But if, out of sympathy for these good men, he tried to broach a conversation with his brother, and he even invited him to express himself, then Nikolai's first objections, weighed down with so many state circumstances, immediately deprived Misha of language and arguments. Not that he had ever had that kind of personality—to insist on his convictions.

Right now he was living peacefully and quietly in Gatchina with Natasha, her children, and their young son, one day at home, and every other day going to Galernaya to the office of the inspector general of the cavalry, his recent appointment—and now the city's upheavals had begun. How unfortunate it was that his brother had left for GHQ immediately before them. Had he been here, no one would have bothered Mikhail.

Today, when Mikhail was not planning to go to the city, Rodzyanko almost insisted that he come. Weren't their fears exaggerated? Yesterday, Sunday, in the afternoon, Mikhail had gone into the city, and he and his sister Ksenia had been at the Peter and Paul Cathedral for a requiem at his father's grave—and the streets had been perfectly quiet.

But Natasha convinced him that he had to go; evidently, it was an ominous moment. "You have to be on the scene!"

But at the Mariinsky Palace, while hearing out all the arguments from Rodzyanko, Golitsyn, and Kryzhanovsky and seeing their extreme agitation and discouragement, Mikhail, nonetheless, from the very first minute clearly sensed that they had made a mistake in turning to him. These were all respected men of state, which made it all the sadder to listen to them. How could he possibly take this on himself? When had his brother ever entrusted him with anything of the kind? He would be rightly amazed. Why should Mikhail go poking his nose into other people's business? This conversation was anything but easy in a room, but to hold it over telegraph equipment, when words unsuccessfully expressed and not corrected by intonation were leaking away, leaking unstoppably over the wire—and friendly brotherly advice was turning into some kind of ultimatum?

True, they wrote out what to telegraph, but didn't this look like an unauthorized seizure of power in the capital? My God, what did they want from him? He couldn't bring himself to object directly—he felt awkward for them—but how could they have gone this far? However, he did not have the firmness to refuse them outright. Something had to be done. He was trapped all right.

Oh, how he missed having Natasha by his side now, for advice. He was used to making sense of things with her.

But even in front of the iron cupola of the Rodzyanko head, Mikhail already knew that of course he wouldn't ask for a ministry responsible to the Duma. He knew how intolerant Nikolai was of that. And who here was truly right—Mikhail had never been able to understand that fully.

He certainly would not dare propose himself as the capital's dictator.

The War Minister's residence was on the Moika near Kirpichny Lane. Belyaev, in his more than fifty years never married, lived alone—an odd man of paper and pen.

There was a telegraph operator on duty by the equipment. They set up transmission and Belyaev himself went to the telephone to carry out one more of Rodzyanko's instructions: call Tsarskoye Selo and communicate that the Empress and children must leave as quickly as possible and get as far away as possible, this very night. That is how sweepingly events were unfolding!

Actually, Mikhail would have to speak not with his brother, of course, but with General Alekseev. And not speak but communicate through the telegraph operator the ideas that had been prepared for him.

He had to suggest a candidate for future Prime Minister. But they hadn't told him who. More than once, though, Mikhail had heard it, so he repeated this name: Prince Lvov.

This was the biggest thing Mikhail had determined to say: Would His Imperial Majesty not instruct his brother to immediately announce in the capital whatever decisions the Emperor would have?

Also, after Alekseev had received the telegram, something occurred to Mikhail and he gave some brotherly advice: the Emperor's scheduled return to Tsarskoye Selo should be postponed a few days.

A tape slowly advancing and printing letter by letter wasn't a conversation. It left no room for saying how alarming it was here, how inappropriate it was for Nikolai to show up here right now because it was simply impossible to be confident for his head. For anyone's head.

There, Alekseev carried off the tape to report. While here Mikhail, not stepping away from the equipment, sat in a relaxed pose. There—he had interfered once again. The last time, with Natasha's encouragement, he had interfered in November, in a letter: they had tried to persuade him very insistently on all sides. This change in the mood of the best-intentioned people had struck him. Dissatisfaction and condemnation had been expressed by men who had been such loyal subjects to date, so balanced, whose loyalty was above suspicion, that he was afraid for the throne and the state order. Who was left to support it? He was afraid for the Tsar's family and the entire dynasty. That was when Mikhail wrote his brother a letter. That the universal hatred for people seemingly close to the throne (he had in mind Rasputin and Protopopov but did not name them) had already united the most leftist and the most rightist. One had the impression that we were standing on a volcano and the least mistake could call up a catastrophe. But perhaps, if these people were removed and replaced with pure men, society would appreciate this concession and the path would be cleared for a military victory. Mikhail was afraid that these moods of society—which meant the entire country—were not felt as strongly in the Emperor's inner circle and he might be underestimating their danger. And whoever made the reports in his service was afraid to say the harsh truth. But Mikhail had determined to say it out of love.

As he did today.

Then Nikolai replied that *they* would always hate everyone, no matter who you appointed. Just two months ago they themselves had extolled Protopopov, as had our European allies. In fact they were trying to get it to be any way but how it was done in Russia. And remember that the *public* was not the Russian land.

The tape advanced. So it was that Nikolai once again rejected everything. He himself would give the orders about the government and everything when he arrived at Tsarskoye, and he was setting out tomorrow afternoon. Tomorrow Adjutant General Ivanov would leave for Petrograd as Commander-in-Chief of the Petrograd District, and tomorrow they would send four reliable infantry and four reliable cavalry regiments from the front.

This reply breathed firmness.

But look! The tape was still going. Now Alekseev himself, on his own behalf, was asking the grand duke, when they met in person, to once again repeat to His Majesty his request to replace the ministers and the means for selecting them. His Imperial Highness's intercessions were a priceless aid to the Emperor in decisive moments on which the course of the war and the life of the state depended.

Oho! What strong words! And somehow on the quiet from the Emperor. Alekseev, too, thought the same way everyone here had been trying to convince Mikhail.

Was it only the Emperor? . . .

No, something here was beyond comprehension. This was not for Mikhail to resolve. He would return to Gatchina and Natasha immediately and would again be an ordinary person.

Belyaev was quite heartened by the news that eight loyal regiments were on their way to Petrograd. And that he did not have to replace Khabalov or deal with him anymore. His pince-nez, which had been completely extinguished, was flashing once again. He had been right to reject that insane plan—to have the Tsarskoye Selo aviation detachment bomb the Tauride Palace. How could he accept that kind of responsibility? Now regiments would arrive and everything would be fine.

It was getting on toward midnight and time for the grand duke to go to the train station. But right then, unexpectedly, on the Moika, nearby, fierce shooting began.

Strange shooting. It didn't sound like a firefight. It was totally chaotic to the trained ear—but it would not die down. From time to time glass would jingle when someone happened to hit a window.

But breaking through the shooting was the easiest of all the past day's tasks. Belyaev begged him to wait a moment and not risk it, but the grand duke declined, saying it was silly to sit there. Especially since if they broke into the courtyard they might take away the motorcar and then you couldn't leave at all.

They pulled out of the courtyard flat out—and raced down a deserted Moika toward the Red Bridge.

Belyaev, who stayed behind, decided first to telephone the Mariinsky Palace and share the news with the ministers and say they had been ordered to remain in their posts. The secretary got through, summoned one minister and then another—and Krieger-Voinovsky supposedly came to the phone, but Belyaev could tell immediately that it was not his voice. And while they were holding the receiver, he heard a strange aside about looking through certain papers.

What a nightmare! The rebels were in charge at the Mariinsky already? The government had already been routed?

Then they might show up here, at the War Minister's residence, at any moment, of course! (He should still telephone Rodzyanko, but there was no time!)

The sole salvation for Belyaev was to move to Khabalov's headquarters before the route was cut off.

But shooting had started up again and very nearby! Were they already breaking down the gates?

It was too late to get going and take the motorcar. Motorcars were vulnerable, too. Motorcars got stopped!

General Belyaev threw on his peak cap and greatcoat and dashed out the service entrance. If there was no saving the War Minister's residence, then he would save himself.

[1 5 0]

They had appointed General Ivanov and taken the decision to send troops. Now all would be well and the Petrograd question solved, at least for today. Today—the evening might last longer—to rest, play dominoes with Grabbe and Nilov, read a nice history book in bed, and yes, sleep. That quiet late evening, all the organism's saving forces went on the alert so that nothing broke in and violated it!

But the sullen Alekseev dragged in once more bringing Ruzsky's telegram. After all, Ruzsky was being disingenuous. After waiting a full day, looking around at how unfavorably events were developing in Petrograd (he had received a copy of Belyaev's panicked telegram), he had aligned himself with Rodzyanko and also passed along Rodzyanko's unbalanced telegram—and also invoking the victory and food and transport difficulties, he dared report as a most loyal subject about the urgent necessity to calm the population, but measures of repression were more likely to exacerbate the situation than pacify it.

He did not write directly that he supported a responsible administration, but the upshot was that he did.

Even Alekseev himself, in his gold spectacles, with his sullen and dissatisfied look, as if the Emperor had caused him personal insult, was also leaning in the same direction.

The Emperor suspected that his entire suite, too, was thinking this way.

But he couldn't explain or reply to them all.

What a day, though! An hour passed, and Alekseev showed up again at the Tsar's residence, even more stooped, sour, and concerned. It turned out he had just had a direct conversation with Grand Duke Mikhail in Petrograd, who would remain by the line. He had asked him to report to the Emperor that the upheavals had taken on major proportions and the only way to calm them down—in his profound belief—was to dismiss the entire Council of Ministers. He believed the only solution was to choose someone respected by broad strata—but responsible solely to His Imperial Majesty. He even advised someone: Prince Lvov.

Ah, Misha, Misha, they twisted you around, too, and you're thinking with Rodzyanko's head. "Profound belief!"

It was as if they had all conspired, they had all formed a single ring of siege around the Emperor. Yes, and something else: Misha advised the Emperor against traveling to Tsarskoye during these days!

Nikolai was very much saddened by this interference of his brother's. It was the closeness of the advisor that stung his soul. Concealing this family issue from Alekseev, though, Nikolai replied immediately and hastened to reply—with dissatisfaction, to be communicated to his brother. That he was grateful to His Imperial Highness for the advice. But in view of the extraordinary circumstances he would not only not postpone his departure for Tsarskoye Selo but would leave the very next day. Once he had arrived, he would decide everything there regarding the government's composition.

Well, and please inform him about the troops being sent and about Ivanov. This was not a secret from the grand duke.

Alekseev left, but Nikolai, freed from the necessity of maintaining his imperturbability, began pacing around his office, his boots creaking, smoothing his mustache. This news from Misha had stung him. Why? Why had he interfered where it was none of his business? Why had he let himself be turned around? What power of speech these loudmouths had. They could overshadow anyone at all. It had gone this far: Misha, whose whole life had been taken up by his love and cavalry, unpretentious Misha, was giving him state advice, and what advice! To surrender his positions! Did he really have any state sense? He himself had been forgiven and returned to the army and to Russia less than three years ago.

After all, it was he who had once been heir to the throne. How would he have led?

Nikolai knew his own shortcomings before himself and God. He considered himself not only an unsuccessful Tsar but an unworthy Tsar as well. He had not a grain of vanity. He had never chased after popularity. However, more and more as the years passed, and because of the war, he had given himself over wholly to this calling, this burden—and now he knew its weight and pressure.

And now his brother Georgi appeared before him from his distant blue Abastumani, where he had died, a place never visited. He had died an untimely and senseless death, from a neglected cold.

But no more senseless than his hearty giant of a Father. Suddenly, somehow, their branch kept getting snatched away and borne out of life.

Georgi appeared not as the cheerful young companion of his Far Eastern journey, but with his penultimate, sad, and tubercular eyes—and so suddenly Nikolai ached for the brother he might have had. Who would he have been now, and what kind of possible fellow fighter? What kind of possible buttress in the dynastic discord?

Midnight was approaching and the day drawing to a close. It was amazing that in this entire most alarming day there had not been a single word from Alix.

This could only mean that the upheavals were not that dangerous and she did not want to alarm her husband for nothing. But then why had she not reassured him?

In twenty-two years, Nikolai had grown accustomed to, used to, attached to his daily conversations with her about his affairs or to her daily, multipage letters filled with state concerns and explanations about people, candidates, and situations. He had grown used to this as a matter of course and huddled over to slowly read and reread and contemplate these letters and draw conclusions. He was used to thinking and deciding only with Alix. His whole life, he had never had a friend and advisor more honest, more devoted, more intelligent, energetic, and perceptive than his wife.

The day was drawing to a close, but his worries were not; they were only spiraling up. Once again, stepping heavily in his boots, like a soldier even rather than an officer, poor Alekseev, even more concerned, stooped and burning with a fever, now brought Golitsyn's telegram, which had been written in utter distress.

First, the Council of Ministers had had the gall to present His Majesty with the urgent necessity of declaring the capital in a state of siege—actually, immediately qualifying this by saying that this had already been done on the War Minister's authority.

However, the Emperor had known about this for several hours already! He now glanced at the time notation and was stunned. The Golitsyn telegram brought to him had been en route for five hours! What had happened to the telegraph office? Whose sinister hands could have detained in this way the telegram from the Prime Minister to his Emperor?

There was no time now to find out, though. Read on.

The Council of Ministers was soliciting as his most loyal subjects for placement at the head of the remaining loyal troops a military leader from the Field Army with a name popular with the population.

Fortunately, this was exactly what had been done. They had figured well with Ivanov.

And finally: The Council of Ministers was proposing its own dissolution and appointing as Prime Minister an individual enjoying the general trust—and then there would be a responsible administration!

Only very rarely did Nikolai lose his temper, but apparently he was starting to now. This was beyond belief! Emperor's ministers, Emperor's servants, appointed by the Sovereign Supreme Authority, they had not only lost their head and any will but had taken it upon themselves to petition for the destruction of their own existence, something heretofore sought only by their enemies! In a moment of danger they wanted to desert, the whole lot of them.

The voice of the energetic, always cheerful, and confident Protopopov did not rise above them. Nothing separate had come from him all day.

Incompetent, weak old Prince Golitsyn! Was right now really the time for rearrangements? How many times and from how many mouths had the Emperor heard this—but never once from the Council of Ministers itself—that demand—tediously monotonous and headspinningly mad in its meaning—for a responsible administration!

He was not going to find sympathy here in Alekseev. Quite the contrary. Having grown used to the simplicity of their relations, Alekseev now, not waiting to be asked, in his muffled, grumbly voice, joined in to persuade him. What if the government itself requests this? To decide once and for all this accursed question of the rear—and prosecute the war to victory.

With old man Alekseev, except for that unfortunate instance with the Guchkov letter, Nikolai had always spoken respectfully, and how could he not like him for his tireless, diligent, and intent vigilance at headquarters! But now he didn't even feel like talking to him.

He coolly declined, saying he would respond to the telegram himself. And the sick old man left, gloomy and stooped.

Nikolai smoked—and paced. He felt as if he were under solid, all-round siege. On all sides, everyone was trying to get the same thing without understanding **what** they were asking. This would be anything but a small, passing concession. This was practically the abolishment of the Emperor. A republic.

Hovering over Nikolai right now in particular was the memory of October 1905. Then, too, it had seemed equally inevitable to concede; everyone around him was in favor of concession and no one supported him! And Nikolai had yielded. And how much grief he'd had from that! How he later regretted it! But what has slipped away you cannot later take back.

So today he would not allow himself to be frightened, would not allow himself to repeat that compliance: once again everyone had been misled by their emotions.

What a horrid condition: being so far from events and receiving information at such a delay and so fragmentary and ominous.

But most intolerable of all was being without Alix. Receiving all these terrible telegrams—without her. He felt like an orphan. My God, how could he live until tomorrow so he could go to her?

Suddenly a thought flashed. What if he didn't wait until tomorrow? What if he picked up and went earlier, sooner? What was keeping him here at GHQ? Alekseev's morning report and breakfast etiquette?

Who did he have around him? (Here they were still sitting over one last evening tea.) His suite. Seemingly essential, performing their duties, and dear—but utterly ineffective men, neither advisors nor aides. Minister of the Court Frederiks was already quite debilitated, at times feeble-minded, retained out of pity and tradition. Little Admiral Nilov was a good heart and zealous but hardly ever sober. Sleepy Naryshkin and obliging Mordvinov. Voeikov alone was energetic, and his mind operated practically, but most practically for his own benefit. Having cast a careful eye on him, Alix had warned Nikolai more than once that despite Voeikov's outward confidence, conceit, and ambition, on the inside he was a coward and always capable of betrayal.

With no one to fortify him, the Emperor wrote in his own hand the telegram in reply to Golitsyn: the new military leader and troops would arrive in Petrograd shortly. However, given the present circumstances, I consider any changes in personnel for the civilian administration (so as not to say "government" openly for the telegraph operators) inadmissible.

He himself carried the telegram to headquarters in order by his appearance to bring home once again to Alekseev that there would be no concessions concerning a "responsible administration."

It turned out that Alekseev was feeling badly enough that he had taken to his bed. The Emperor did not order him awakened. But he did order that he be told that *his decision was firm.*

However, before Nikolai could return to his quarters, preparing already to sleep, once again, with his heavy, no longer even military tread, Alekseev trudged over to see him. And began trying to dissuade him from sending the telegram.

Some part of all their brains had been stricken! They didn't realize what they were asking.

It had been hard for Alekseev to get out of bed and come.

And even harder for the Emperor to stand his ground.

But he summoned up all his will and withstood the entreaties.

He barely recognized his own firmness! Alix would have been proud of him!

However, all this recent firmness, which he had concentrated and held onto inside, all the exceptional strength of this day, could fall apart at any moment. He longed to come in contact with his wife's saving strength and glean new firmness as soon as possible.

Indeed, what if he didn't put it off until the middle of the day and left for Tsarskoye earlier? In the morning, for instance? . . .

He was already going to bed in the small bedroom he shared with the heir—filled with indecision, scarcely believing the day might end so simply—when his valet announced the arrival of Voeikov, who entered with a large, decisive step. (From the looks of him, there had never been a more confident and decisive man than he.)

Here's what had happened. An inquiry had just come in from Tsarskoye Selo over the telephone, though the connection was bad, from High Chamberlain Count Benckendorff: *Did His Majesty not wish for Her Majesty and the children to come meet him?*

A puzzle! . . .

Nikolai was stunned. Given the children's serious measles and the cold—they should come meet him? How was he to understand this? Just now, in her latest letter, she had begged off a trip to Livadia—in the spring, when the children were better—and now she was prepared to travel in the cold with them sick?

But he could not speak directly; the direct line to Tsarskoye had always operated intermittently and unintelligibly.

Oh, my God! How understandable it all was: the Empress was in a desperate position, and she feared for the children, feared this insurrection more than measles? So what was the situation there?

The practical Voeikov tried to make sense of it quickly. This was precisely what should be done. The family should leave Tsarskoye immediately, if only in motorcars, or aeroplanes! And then the train to the Crimea. Exactly so, Your Majesty.

But the Emperor could not picture such a thing: the children, the heir—they were pinned to their beds, so how could one risk taking them anywhere in this cold? This wasn't an insurrection; that was an exaggeration.

The Empress herself had not sent a single ominous telegram all day. Nor had Protopopov.

But my God! How lonely, confusing, and hard it was for her. How could he deliberate any longer whether to hasten his own departure?

Respond, if he could, or by telegram: by no means should you go! The Emperor was leaving immediately for Tsarskoye himself.

He had decided—and how his heart was relieved instantly! All the weight of this day, of these days—as if it had already slipped off and been survived! Together soon! United soon! All the torment! How was she doing there alone, poor thing. How?

He sent Voeikov to order the Tsar's trains brought up immediately! We are not going to bed at GHQ but leaving right away!

Might the rebels in truth be threatening Tsarskoye? But there was a good force of his own troops there! And a St. George battalion on its way. The regiments from the front would start arriving!

In his swift and accustomed way he was already gathering his small travel things.

But Voeikov returned to report a frustrating delay. The trains were technically not prepared to move, they could only be ready by night's end. But he could board the train cars at about one in the morning.

In an hour? Well, so be it. We're getting ready.

But again Alekseev! He had heard of the Tsar's instruction—and had once again risen from his bed and staggering, his spectacles pushed back, had come to try to convince the Emperor once again, this time not to go for anything!

So had Misha requested: just don't go to Tsarskoye.

So now Alekseev, too, was making the request: it was a dangerous moment, there was indeterminacy in Petrograd, and the Emperor's proper place was at GHQ. All Russia was at peace except for Petrograd, there were no disturbances anywhere else, and the entire Field Army was fine and under the strict command of the sovereign leader. How could the Emperor abandon all this and himself go into danger?

But it had already been joyously decided! The Emperor simply did not understand the unceremonious interference by the chief of staff in his personal affairs. What call holds more power over a man than the call of family?

And GHQ? GHQ remained in Alekseev's hands. The Emperor was leaving calmly.

[1 5 1]

As he walked out of the cabinet's fateful session, where he resigned his post, Protopopov wandered up and down the halls and staircases of the Mariinsky Palace, seeing neither the rugs nor the steps. He was in a despair and disconsolate loneliness such as he had never before known. Where should he go? His home had been pillaged—and it was no longer his home—he himself had resigned his shining post—so who was he now? It's easy to say "go shoot yourself"—but how could he squeeze the trigger? Not that he had a gun. How could he part with everything that was life, its colors and movement?

Fortunately, he wended his way to the office of Kryzhanovsky, who was in and who had the patience and time for a conversation, to listen to his passionate confession and complaints against the ministers, the Duma, and everyone—to support and placate him. He also discussed with Aleksandr Dmitrievich whether or not to end it all and assured him he shouldn't.

Kryzhanovsky himself was very much a man of state and had great experience. It was he who had once confidently acted as opponent to Witte, saying that the zemstvo was perfectly compatible with autocracy and should be allowed to develop. He was the author of the 1906 Constitution and, in its revision, the Law of 16 June 1907. Kryzhanovsky had nearly become Minister of the Interior. And so he had never once had occasion to occupy a genuinely major post—which today looked much safer. (However, he was worried about his imprudent diaries, which held the trace of many men and events of state; could he wait until tonight to burn them? Or was it already time?)

The more Protopopov unburdened himself, tiring himself out, lost in his fate, the more relieved he felt. Meanwhile, Kryzhanovsky contemplated Protopopov's position and indicated that the Mariinsky Palace might come under attack and would be in all the more danger if Protopopov remained here, as that would draw the crowd to the palace. Even more, this was extremely dangerous for Protopopov himself. But he, the deliverer, had a good idea of where Protopopov could hide: the building of State Control, very nearby, at 72 Moika. He telephoned and received permission to spend the night in that office. Oh, what a gift of fate and at such a moment! He didn't have to pick his way on foot through the chafing, swarming city but could slip out the Mariinsky Palace by the service entrance and dart two hundred paces back of it.

And look: they let him in. And look, the massive door was locked behind you—a well-meaning porter, an empty vestibule, an empty staircase—oh, you had to experience all these dangers, escape the hammer of fate, in order to experience an office building, in its evening desertion, as a corner of a saving paradise! In all Petrograd, one hardly could come up with a safer spot. Tonight they could storm all the palaces, all the ministries, and all the ministers' private residences—oh, but not one of those who had expelled him would dare sleep peacefully today! Meanwhile, Aleksandr Dmitrich would be utterly undaunted. For one night, but blissfully, like an angel. It would never occur to anyone to sack State Control! They took him to the office of the assistant to the chief controller.

Oh, what an immediate release of nerves! That agonizing inner trembling, which had not let up all day since the city governor's morning call, immediately calmed down. This drastic contrast, this ten-minute salvation, sent warm waves of grateful peace through your soul and somehow lifted you up, somehow lifted you up, and you were floating, and your feet couldn't feel the carpets. He had been so overwrought, so tormented—but the responsibility had come tumbling down, the danger had fallen away—and by contrast now he had no wish to think of anything bad, only to rest, dream, possibly—and let all his cares and disappointments be put off until the morning!

In the morning, everything might change, mightn't it? By morning, the saving troops might have arrived, mightn't they?

A whole twelve hours of safety stretched out before him! Reliable stone walls shielded him from the mutinous sea.

He paced around the office for a long time with satisfaction.

But there was a telephone on the desk.

The temptation of the telephone.

They couldn't find him. But he could find—he . . .

Whom could he find? In all Petrograd, there was no one he wished to telephone. His wife had been taken away to the custodian's. Badmaev? Yes, there was Badmaev, healer of body and soul. (That was where he'd like to be borne off to through the air—to Poklonnaya Hill to see Badmaev. But no, they'd find him there.) In the entire capital, in the entire corpus that comprised the world of the Russian state, no thread of sincerity tugged him to a single person enough that he would call him on the telephone. Protopopov had been repudiated by one and all.

But could he call Tsarskoye Selo?

Dear images crowded in. Even when he was on leave due to illness, he continued to visit the Tsarskoye Selo palace with informal reports to the Empress, and how much had he and she said about everything. Everything! Tsarskoye Selo was a heavenly, attractive island, a respite for the soul! My God, had he not tried to oblige the Empress? His reports to her were no less frequent than for the Emperor, and each time he left the Emperor he went to see her and repeated everything, in even more detail. How invariably kind the Empress had been with him always, and how she had trusted him—especially after the arrest of the Workers' Group, when he had averted a revolution. No, especially since he had conducted an energetic investigation into Rasputin's murder, the most ambitious action in his entire ministry, and had extracted a clue from Golovina, who had loved both the murderer and the murdered man. He himself at the time had not realized how cleverly and successfully he had acted.

And now, the Empress was doubtless awaiting news from him. Too much had happened, though. Oh, the proud, royal martyr with the irreconcilable soul! What would it be for her to learn of all this? Perhaps it was even better for her not to know right away.

After all, he was no longer a minister.

No, he could not call anyone from here; he would be immediately giving himself away and revealing his whereabouts. He resisted the telephone's temptation.

But now that the hydra-headed danger had retreated, the bile rose up more bitterly. He'd been cast off. Pushed out. Betrayed. And by whom? Not his Duma enemies but his own ministers. His colleagues. He should also, apparently, have been maneuvering among the ministers. Both Stürmer and Trepov had called him insane in front of the Tsar. (The Emperor himself had revealed this to him.) Stürmer had done many unpleasant things to him. And Trepov had asked the Emperor outright to dismiss Protopopov and had said to Protopopov's face: "Go! You're in my way!" Pathetic, dull-witted men—it was natural that Aleksan Dmitrich harbored no good will toward them, either. Having survived three Prime Ministers in five months, it was natural that he had circumvented them any way he could, not conveyed information on internal affairs, and tried to be the one to report this at Tsarskoye Selo, showing himself to be the best informed of all the ministers. He had recommended replacing Shuvaev with Belyaev, with whom he hoped to get on—and here today Belyaev, the hollow-eyed traitor, had been the first to push Aleksandr Dmitrich to resign! Protopopov had suggested a marvelous solution at Tsarskoye: Stürmer could "fall ill" in order to alleviate the Duma conflict—and here, today, they had forced him to "fall ill" himself.

But who doesn't come in for hatred aplenty? Why had they hated Rasputin so fiercely and crushingly? For his debauchery? Did many refrain from debauchery when that liberty was given them? And were those who had exposed him that much more pious? Hadn't the nobility caroused from time immemorial? How was a simple man to keep from losing his mind when high-born ladies bowed to him to the floor? There hadn't been that much of all that, either; they'd exaggerated. On the contrary, one should be amazed at how Rasputin retained his natural intelligence and gave so much sober advice, of which the Duma had never become capable. When Protopopov tried to persuade him to protect the royal name, he had listened. In November he had not accepted a bribe of 200,000 from Trepov to remove Protopopov and had said, "I don't need your money." That he asked countless times for privileges for anyone? But the moneymakers had tried to ensnare him. He himself had had no need of this, and they had profited more than he himself had.

The Mariinsky Palace came into view over the nearby roofs, well visible from the unlit office. The entire upper floor was flooded with electricity— to their own misfortune, as it drew the crowd to storm it.

Aleksandr Dmitrich was calming down.

You didn't want Protopopov? You didn't like Protopopov? Well, as you please.

What are they meeting about there? What are they deciding? What can they decide? They'd thought to save their own hides at the price of Protopopov?

Had his entire ministry really been nothing but a brief illusion? No, his soul protested against accepting this cruel fall! No, everything had not yet been smashed to smithereens! This was only a momentary trial! Tomorrow or the day after, the Emperor's victorious troops would enter the city—and the rabble would scatter in wanton horror, and the Duma leaders would fall to their knees, and the cowardly gang of ministers would beg forgiveness for this night. If only the Empress and Emperor would forgive him! Forgive him for this unwilling concession to nonentities, this forced and bitter resignation, out of tactical considerations, and in no way a betrayal of the Emperor's will!

The Emperor always forgave everyone so willingly. He found an excuse for everyone. Might he really not forgive his favorite? What marvelous, candid conversations they'd had (their views coincided on all issues)! How necessary it was always to know this tone (and Protopopov did)—never to be excessively insistent, never to communicate anything unpleasant with which the Minister of the Interior was constantly burdened (how the Emperor was cursed in Guards circles and what they wrote in their letters; the Emperor would not tolerate inspection of the mails).

Meanwhile, the Mariinsky Palace had gone out, gone out entirely, not a single window shone, which made it even darker in the office. Now in the sky on the right, from Nevsky, a distinct glow appeared.

Something was burning somewhere! Maybe even his home on the Fontanka. . . .

Oh well, it was fine here. True, the sofa's bolster wasn't that comfortable under his head, but was soft and spacious; meanwhile, the wall clock ticked quietly and reassuringly. Instead of undressing, he would have to cover himself in his own fur coat. Oh, that was all nonsense, all that could be borne.

The main thing was for the fateful dates predicted by Perrin to pass favorably. And now he would survive.

Once again he would return to the heights of the Ministry of the Interior. (Maybe even to Prime Minister?)

Once again they would gather in their Tsarskoye Selo intimacy—and talk everything over just as sweetly as before. Oh, this favor would return to him!

[1 5 2]

Neither Uncle Anton nor any of the old sacrificial revolutionaries had ever had, or could ever have dreamed of, such a fate: to race through the nighttime streets of overwrought and already authority-less Petersburg in some fairytale machine, through the streets as fast as a bird, with gunners on the fenders on either side aiming their rifles forward, another ten soldiers behind them—to race to capture the stronghold of government, seven hundred yards from Senate Square! Sasha was already so filled with happiness, his life had already soared to such a height, that it seemed to have been crowned, nothing better could ever happen, and now he could even part with it without regret.

Now *his* war had come! Previously he had safeguarded his head—for his hour only.

Up ahead rode the experienced Sosnovsky in the armored car, and he was selecting the route. They raced past the Summer Garden—and Sasha's heart pounded again from this symbolism. Here Anton Lenartovich had shot at Dubasov, here he had been caught, and here the Russian revolution's first shots—Karakozov's—had rung out and here was where Aleksandr Lenartovich had raced from for the final decisive storming of Tsarism!

He even felt a tearful pain in his eyes. How immortal it was! He could perish right now—but this deed would be inscribed and remembered: how Aleksandr Lenartovich had captured the stronghold of the last Tsarist government!

So Sosnovsky led them down the Moika's curving embankment, and they skipped across both Nevsky and Gorokhovaya without delay—and suddenly, noticing something up ahead, the armored car stopped short, but Sasha's driver couldn't brake right away—and he nearly ran into it and smashed into its rear end.

Sosnovsky stuck his arm out, indicating with circular movements to go back. The Moika embankment, narrowed by piles of snow, didn't have room for two vehicles to pass, and Sasha's driver, swearing vociferously, shifted into reverse—all the way to and onto Gorokhovaya itself. Right behind them with its menacing rear end came the armored car.

Sasha thought about climbing out and learning from Sosnovsky what exactly had happened, but the soldiers on the fenders were in the way, and the armored car, without slowing or explaining, turned around and tore down Gorokhovaya and then made a left down Morskaya.

In the middle of the Morskaya block, Sasha's vehicle caught up to the armored car, which was now moving cautiously, its headlamps turned off. Sasha's turned theirs off, too. Actually, on Morskaya there were quite a few streetlamps, and they both remained fairly visible to the palace, just as the palace was visible to them, the many windows of its two floors all shining, the rare window not lit. Were all the ministers sitting there now? Could they capture all the ministers at once?

Far past the palace, in the direction of the Mariinsky Theater, a fire's powerful glow flamed in the sky.

And directly in front of the palace were two cannons. There you had it! True, the barrels were aimed at St. Isaac's for now.

But an armored car was nothing against them.

Right then he heard a machine-gun round. At first, Sasha thought the armored car had started shooting, but no, when the round was repeated it became clear that it was aimed this way, and the bullets were cracking somewhere close by. (Sasha wasn't the least bit afraid! He suddenly discovered in himself that military sang-froid he had admired at times in true officers: during a battle, only thoughts of the battle!)

Sasha awaited Sosnovsky's decision. It was quite unexpected: the armored car turned on its headlamps and opened machine-gun fire—and so, with that light and that shooting made a sharp turn around the edge of the square to the right, back, past the Astoria, toward Gogol Street.

And vanished.

Sasha prevented the driver from moving. He didn't understand anything. He didn't understand at whom Sosnovsky had been shooting. And he didn't understand where Sosnovsky had gone—away from the palace altogether. They hadn't thought to agree on anything in advance. Sasha was now waiting for the end of the maneuver; he assumed that Sosnovsky would drive around the Nikolai I monument, get out of the cannons' line of fire, and emerge from the other side opposite the palace and take it in its pincers.

But Sosnovsky didn't come. He didn't come. He didn't show up.

It was utterly incomprehensible.

As it was also incomprehensible who had opened fire on them to start. They weren't shooting anymore. Sasha poked his head out, turned around, and asked his men in the back whether anyone was injured. No, no one.

The palace was shining; it hadn't turned off its lights at the shooting. Right in front of the main entrance, yes, the two cannons were quite visible—but without attendants. That was what Sasha realized. Without any attendants at all! So they couldn't fire or turn. Two sentries were standing at the main entrance and there was someone else next to them there. And that was all!

Whereas the square, as far as Sasha could see, from the palace to the monument, and farther into the open area past the monument, and on the other side of Morskaya, the square was neither empty nor full. It didn't have its usual pedestrian traffic, and no wonder near midnight, but a few clusters of people, not under the streetlamps but a little away from them, had collected here and there, at the mouths of the streets, by the walls, near the gates and front doors, and it was as if they were observing, paying attention, waiting for something, despite the cold. And taken together, this was a lot.

Were they preparing for an attack? On the palace? What were they waiting for?

Sasha decided on a sure plan: he had to drive his truck straight at the palace! Straight at the main entrance! That would take no more than a minute. Under direct fire? If he started suddenly, they wouldn't open fire right away and wouldn't have time to run out to the cannons. As he went he could also open unaimed rifle fire. And then all those clusters from the street mouths would swoop down in support. There was nothing more dangerous than the way he was stopped there now. Of course, without the armored car there were fewer chances of success, but . . . Not all of them might make it there, to the entrance, across the three hundred fifty or so yards, and even he might not make it—but this was the only right thing. Approaching with supposedly peaceful intentions was more dangerous because they wouldn't let them come close and would riddle them with holes.

All of a sudden, before Sasha could poke his head back and explain the mission to his soldiers, all the lights in the palace went out simultaneously. At once! All at once the palace was transformed from animated and bright into dark and hiding!

Why? Before its own attack, its own leap? But the palace couldn't leap, and it would be rather senseless for the garrison to attack. For defense then? In order to see and shoot better? So they should rush at it all the faster! But might it perhaps be out of fright, that someone's nerves had failed? Or were they trying to run out all the back doors in the darkness? Oh, they didn't have the forces to block all the exits!

The night was starry, chill.

Sasha poked his head back, but what was there to explain? He didn't have to inspire them; they were all volunteers. He simply shouted:

"Fire at the windows as we go, wherever you can!" And to the driver, touching his hand on the wheel: "Let's go! No headlamps."

The vehicle had not been turned off, and it started right away, crossing the square in a straight line. The light had diminished greatly, but with the square's streetlamps the driver could still make out and drive around a snow ridge he would have gotten stuck in.

Over their heads, their own rifles fired deafeningly and their shots blazed.

They were going fast, straight for the main entrance. Now was the decisive moment: would those people have time to jump out toward the cannons?

With his peripheral vision Sasha was able to notice that a few clusters were also running toward the palace, taking a short cut and joining them. So! A torch appeared overhead in one of the clusters. (He had time to think, How beautiful!)

Sasha felt like tearing his whole body off his seat and hurtling forward, outstripping the vehicle so as not to be riddled with holes!

But the vehicle was making good speed, and on the backdrop of the glow, the dark palace came up on them swiftly! Were they shooting at them or not? That you couldn't tell because of your own men, but only steps remained to the cannon muzzles—and there was no devastating fire blazing from them!

As they were passing them, going straight for the steps and arches of the main entrance, Sasha gave the command:

"Turn on the headlamps!"

In the depths of the arches, they shone on the guard tearing about, a few men, none of whom even tried to shoot back. They all held their hands and rifles in the air.

Hoping that his mounted men were keeping them in their sights but wouldn't fire on their own men, Sasha pushed a rifleman off the fender, hopped down, and with gun in hand ran up the steps.

Now there was nothing but the light being shone by the headlamps of their stopped vehicle. The guard continued to hold their weapons and arms ready for surrender; no officers among them.

"Open the doors!" Sasha shouted to them at the top of his lungs, as if afraid they would not obey.

And one sergeant did reach out—and opened—and held open for them the wide, tall, and heavy front door. Beyond that was darkness, a trap; the vehicles' headlamps only provided light for the first few steps.

Sasha's soldiers hopped out of the back of the truck. Now without his order they disarmed these few. But they were wary of going farther, inside.

Without hesitation, Sasha decided to go first and devised his order and how to leave his guard here outside. However, those clusters of civilians started running up, all of them men and young, whether or not workers, there was no time to look. Sasha took the first one who had a torch and led him inside.

The others came thronging behind him, soldiers and nonsoldiers intermixed.

In the entrance hall, with its red marble columns, he stopped. Resin torch in hand! On the left a formal marble staircase ascended and split. All the main offices and the government were probably there, upstairs. But there was a passage along the first floor, past the staircase.

Any large, unfamiliar building, if you just go and burst in there, disrupts you, pulls you in—your eyes dart over the staircases, passageways, and corridors, and you imagine the principal rooms in each direction. Where should they rush first? Where should they search? Whom should they seize? Where were the ministers? They probably hadn't left yet and were hiding somewhere! How could they ever seize them? Or was it more important to take the papers on their desks? Yes, seize the papers—that was more important! But where were their desks?

"Where's the doorman?" Sasha heard his own loud and angry voice.

Immediately a fat and frightened elderly doorman in livery stepped out in front of him into the light of the torch, while behind in the large mirror was his back.

"Where's the palace commandant?" Sasha shouted. "Where's the administrator? Who turned off the lights? I'll shoot you! Turn them on immediately!"

And without listening to justifications or explanations:

"Well, then, you two, with the bayonets, accompany him and arrest the commandant until the lights come on. Say that otherwise I'll shoot him!"

The two led the doorman into the darkness.

No, Sasha himself remained in the darkness, too, in the light of the truck, while the main light from the torch had chosen its way up, over the red carpet, without him—and with it an animated cluster of stray volunteers.

"Let's go!" Sasha commanded, and he too started upstairs, following the torch—and some followed him and some didn't. Right then he realized that his own soldiers, whom he'd come with, he didn't know by battalion, or last name, or face, that he had assembled them on the dark open space in front of the Tauride Palace—and had lost them just now in the same darkness. Now he could think equally of each man here that this one was from his detachment, or from the palace guard, or from somewhere else.

But next to him was a short, attractive, swarthy university student with puffy lips—and Sasha realized that right now this was the man he needed most.

"Let's go take a look and seize the main papers!" Sasha ordered him, and he expressed utter delight. "Stop, torch!" He called to the man in the lead.

But a second torch appeared at the bottom of the stairs and was also swaying this way.

Sasha realized he hadn't given the driver any orders, and he could easily drive off and leave them here.

But that no longer mattered. Without any urging whatsoever, some obscure volunteers came running, rushed up the stairs, and started howling joyously. If they would obey, he could now cordon off the palace and capture all the ministers. But they wouldn't and their attention was not on Sasha and his orders but had already outstripped him and run off somewhere. Where? Who were they? He couldn't tell, and farther on the staircase split.

Right then, a bright light went back on throughout the building all at once, lighting the white staircases and, up above, a pink hall.

Sasha saw that his volunteers from the square were already returning with antique chairs and tablecloths under their arms. Someone got up on the sill of a tall window and tore down the expensive drapery.

The material ripped, and a heavy curtain rod broke away and hung down, nearly killing the looter.

Voices were droning through the palace.

But Sasha had no one to combat this as well. He looked around and there was no one but this student.

Two soldiers of some kind were coming his way.

"Are you mine?" Sasha asked. "Then stand right here as guards. If the enemy shows up, shoot and then warn me. We'll keep going."

Farther on he saw a round hall with two tiers of white and gold columns. They rushed that way.

[1 5 3]

*   *   *

All day long, the 1st Reserve Regiment had held out on the Malaya Okhta. A crowd had broken into the barracks to take the rifles from their pyramids, but the soldiers themselves, without any officers, had escorted them out of the building and not surrendered their weapons.

*   *   *

Semyon, the nineteen-year-old student who had arrested Shcheglovitov, was telling the story: they'd come, but he wasn't home. They started questioning the doorman's wife. Where is he? She gave him away: "Oh, he's with his son-in-law, Kharitonenko." "And where is Kharitonenko?" She told them. They rushed there. They were so infuriated, they wouldn't let him put on his coat or cap and led him away. "But where are you taking me?" "To the State Duma." He agreed. They put him in a droshky.

Toward the end of the day and that evening, small armed clusters, at the head of which was always a university student, raced around searching the apartments of all the members of the Council of Ministers except for the liberals Pokrovsky and Krieger-Voinovsky. But no one was home. They didn't even find Prince Golitsyn. They took his briefcase from his desk and brought it to the State Duma.

*   *   *

The Semyonovsky regiment sat locked in their barracks past Zagorodny Prospect all day, until a mutinous crowd approached that evening. Then they flooded to join the crowd. Curses, shouts, and songs. They took the band along and went to the police station. They smashed it and killed a police officer. They set it on fire.

From the crowd—they packed the police officer's corpse in bundles of papers and threw it on the fire.

*   *   *

Toward day's end, throughout the city, all offices, stores, restaurants, shops, markets—any and all businesses—were closed. As were the movie houses or theaters. Everyone either holed up at home or thronged to the streets, with the crowds. There were cheerful, wild shouts and firing into the air everywhere.

The civilians and young people had so many weapons that the soldiers on Znamenskaya Square started taking weapons away.

And vice versa, with extra weapons being handed out to the crowd from several trucks.

Everyone was frightened by the motorcars where somber soldiers lay on the fenders, their rifles aimed forward. Occasionally, from trucks as well, they would aim in different directions and at the sidewalks. It was frightening.

Shocking and horrifying everyone who had not submitted to the revolution!

*　　*　　*

Toward nightfall they became much more violent toward officers and ripped the epaulets off some. On Nevsky a legless officer with a crutch refused to remove his epaulets—and was stabbed to death with a bayonet.

*　　*　　*

Most of all they were looking to beat up and kill policemen on the beat. During the chaotic and inept shooting, when stray bullets were ricocheting off walls, they decided unanimously that policemen were shooting from the rooftops. But they couldn't find them anywhere, which made them even more furious at the police.

*　　*　　*

People kept rushing around—university students with rifles, sailors with rifles, women with rifles. On the streets there was constant shooting—no one knew by whom or at what. When there was shooting, pedestrians would press up against the buildings.

In the evening the crowds thinned out. Many sat home and even put out the light or closed the shutters and lit their smallest bulbs or icon-lamps.

Through the streets, which were now freed of crowds, motorcars tore ever faster and more madly, motorcars, constant honking, shots, shouts. It was like an entire army on the move.

*　　*　　*

What came to pass was what each inhabitant of the capital, each of its two and a half million, was left to fend for himself: there was no one to guide and protect him. Released criminals and the urban rabble were doing as they pleased.

The criminals remembered the chambers of the justices of the peace where they were condemned and were storming them. At the 2nd Rozhdestvenskaya they set fire to all the case files of the justice of the peace, sheaves of papers, warming themselves simultaneously.

With particular animosity and sparing nothing, they stormed the apartments of police officers, which were known to all their neighbors. From one such apartment on the fourth floor they threw property and furniture out on the pavement and even tossed out a spinet. And then burned it all on a bonfire.

*   *   *

Some man (later it was learned he was enemy agent Karl Gibson, who had been released from prison) called on the crowd to storm the Okhrana—but led them away to storm Petrograd Military District counterintelligence on Znamenskaya Street. They led the counterintelligence clerks away to the Tauride Palace and jailed them as "Okhrana agents."

*   *   *

Petrograd spent all evening and night catching and killing its own police. During the nighttime, they would kill them on the streets without even taking them far, or drown them in ice-holes in the Obvodny Canal. Motorcar expeditions were fitted out to hunt down policemen.

The thought of the masses freed from the police matured swiftly. Why not storm private homes? In apartments, even if you didn't find an officer, oh yes, there was so much in goods you could snatch. They started going from apartment to apartment. "No officers here? Let us check." They ordered all gates and entryways kept open—for raids and searches.

On Znamenskaya Street, a doorman didn't unlock the gates immediately for a passing gang—and they killed him for it.

*   *   *

In one day, besides the District Court, they burned down the provincial Gendarme Administration, the Main Prison Administration, Lithuanian Fortress prison, the Okhrana, the Aleksandr Nevsky police station, and many, nearly all the stations. They also set fire to the police archive near the Lions Bridge.

There was a large fire on Staro-Nevsky. When it grew dark, while it was on fire, people were apparently jumping out of windows from a high floor. A large crowd stood there gawking. It turned out, it was dressed dummies they were throwing out: the police museum was burning.

People said that an officer at the Aleksandr Nevsky station had been skewered on bayonets and tossed on the fire alive.

*   *   *

But the Finland Battalion held out all day and night. That evening, they posted pickets between the Mining Institute and the Baltic Works, where there were a few paths across the Neva—and after the crowd stormed the Sea Cadet Corps, they stopped traffic and let no one through coming or going. Across the Neva there were patches of light from fires and muffled shooting. The roar of an exultant crowd and the roar of engines drew closer—but the Finland men would not let them across the Nikolaevsky Bridge.

* * *

Late that night, the revolutionary crowd surged as far as the Izmailovsky barracks. This wave flowed from the east—but in those same last minutes about two Izmailovsky companies left the barracks to reinforce the government troops and turned north, across the Fontanka, toward the center. And managed to get away. The two forces were separated by the massive, wide, and, at night, dark Trinity Izmailovsky Cathedral.

Surviving witnesses later asserted that in the surrounding darkness the cross on the cupola shone inexplicably. And anyone who noticed it removed his cap and crossed himself.

* * *

It had always been that the yardmen would stand by the gates until late, sit in their sheepskin coats, and a tardy passerby's muffled steps down the deserted street were safe.

Today, the yardmen had been swept away, all the windows were dark, and being about was frightening.

Here two men had been sitting in a gateway and for a good hour had been shooting diagonally across the street at the attic of a three-story building. They said there was a police machine gun there. (Although it never once responded.) They managed to hit someone's window. Crashing glass.

* * *

That night, after the looting of the Mariinsky Palace, many with similar desires were also drawn to the officers' nearby hotel, the Astoria. The windows were lit, six stories, and nothing but officers. Here was their prey!

However, officers would battle back. The storming never did come together.

* * *

News of the Petrograd soldiers' mutiny reached Oranienbaum by evening. Located there were two reserve machine-gun regiments, the sole machine-gun training for the entire Russian army. Mobilized there, too, were Petersburg workers with a revolutionary spirit. Now the soldiers were agitated. They gathered near their barracks and snapped up the machine guns, rifles, cartridge belts, and cartridges. In the hubbub and din, they decided spontaneously to come to the aid of the Petrograd regiments! Their officers tried to stop them—in vain, and they had their weapons taken away.

The machine gunners seized the railway station and ordered trains made ready for them—but couldn't bring themselves to go, fearing an intentional wreck. After midnight they started out in a large column down the highway to Petrograd. En route, they were joined by smaller military units, and they also broke open storehouses and took arms and provisions. They marched through Old and New Peterhof and Strelna. The column stretched out for many versts, led by its sergeants.

* * *

THE DOUGH-TROUGH IS LONG PATIENT, BUT IF IT OVERFLOWS, YOU CAN'T PUT IT BACK

* * *

[1 5 4]

The colossal Admiralty, which covered four city blocks and had four facades, seven main entrances, and seven gates, could hold ten and twenty such detachments, and several regiments, but silently dark in what was still the calmest part of the city, it had not been threatened by anyone and for its defense had no need even of the detachment that had come. This vagueness of mission, this decision's unclear advantage over some other not yet found, had not only vexed General Khabalov's headquarters but had unwittingly been communicated to the rank and file. After an entire day of inaction and the lost reserve of Palace Square, it was simply felt by every soul that something was being done wrong.

Even though ruffians were shooting throughout the city, but without a single organized military unit, without a single formation or line. The streets had freed up some with the evening, and Khabalov's detachment had all directions open to it, in fact. It could have taken the offensive against the Tauride Palace or without obstacle left the capital altogether. It could have gone and taken any building it chose and freed any persons that had been captured. No, Khabalov had already firmly set aside that thought, or couldn't understand it. Without difficulty or necessity he drove himself into the solemn and grandiose sarcophagus that was the Admiralty.

Here he was met with hostility by the aide to the chief of Naval General Staff, who had already been in contact with Navy Minister Grigorovich (who lived in the building but supposedly was ill right now): naval headquarters could not be turned into a military camp; that would entail putting a halt to current business.

General Khabalov looked down and went limp; now he had no idea whatsoever where to go.

However, General Zankevich intervened and patched things up diplomatically. The detachment was given the main entrance hall and the endless corridors of the first and second floors along Aleksandrovsky and Palace squares. The infantry and foot police were led into the corridors and the cavalry, mounted city police, and artillery into the large courtyards.

Khabalov's headquarters themselves and the city governor's group set up in the entrance hall, where there was plenty of furniture, chairs, and a telephone.

The Izmailovsky Battalion's training detachment continued to hold the telephone exchange, and the telephones operated without interruption. Only no one knew that headquarters had left the city governor's offices—and for a long time no calls came in at the new location.

From the first news they learned that the Okhrana had been looted and burned.

After that, the Council of Ministers ordered a strong guard be sent to the Mariinsky Palace.

But who could they send? They couldn't spread themselves too thin. Zankevich replied that there were too few troops and they couldn't stretch all the way to Mariinskaya Square. Wouldn't the esteemed ministers themselves like to come to the Admiralty?

Meanwhile, reinforcements were coming in—another couple of Izmailovsky companies, which was good. And here were squadrons from the Guards cavalry outside Novgorod, who had been summoned on Saturday. Where should they go now? There was nowhere to put them, and above all, there was nowhere to water the horses and nothing to feed them. They were sent to the Horse Guards' manège.

Right then a police cavalry sergeant reported that the horses were trembling from hunger and had to be fed.

But the fodder reserves had been left at the city governor's offices! Wouldn't you know it.

They sent some gendarme volunteers there for the forage—quietly, through Aleksandrovsky Square. The city governor's offices were calm and no one was there. They brought oats and wheat from there and for themselves also took sausage from a small shop on Gorokhovaya that hadn't been closed up.

They replaced the outside guard—it was, after all, ten degrees below zero and the soldiers were lightly dressed—with observation from second-floor windows. They lay boards and firewood at the iron gates and placed a gun behind each of the gates.

Soldiers were now sleeping in the corridors and on the steps with their rifles, nestling here and there. The officers were on chairs.

In the courtyard, the horses and the men attending them huddled in the freezing cold. So did the sentries.

A separate room with a door and a little food in the sideboard was finally found for Khabalov's headquarters.

Khabalov had apparently exhausted all his capacity to command. Did he at least have some plan or opinion? Yes. As he understood it, he had to hold out for another twenty-four hours, when major assistance would arrive from the front. But right now in the city there might be 40,000 rebels—maybe 60,000?—and he couldn't cope with a force like that.

Intermittent gunfire could be heard coming from all over the city, sometimes machine-gun fire. But not close.

So they froze in place in the vast and deserted Admiralty, in the city's deserted center. They had to hold out for a night here and then a day.

Also, around midnight, a local policeman telephoned from the city governor's offices that there, too, all was in order.

They hadn't had to leave.

Why were they here? In the emptiness of the naval corridors? It was like some dream.

At about eleven o'clock, Grand Duke Kirill suddenly flashed through the Admiralty. He gave no instructions and did not rebuke them for anything, but he surveyed the premises—and looked and looked. He said he was searching for two of his crew's companies, which apparently had gone missing since he had sent them to Palace Square that afternoon.

It was entirely possible that they had gone over to the rebels. . . .

The grand duke rode away and War Minister Belyaev, puffing, showed up on foot and without his coat in that cold. Frail and small, he walked across the tiled floor of the entrance hall with his hurried, clicking gait. He heard their report. He said nothing about military actions and had no words of praise or rebuke. He explained that his apartment in the War Minister's residence was now quite unsafe and he had withdrawn from there under fire. But the Mariinsky Palace had been seized by rebels, who were commandeering government documents there.

He secluded himself to make a telephone call.

After that he ordered that as long as military actions were not under way, they must address the populace immediately. Taking advantage of the fact that the Admiralty housed a functioning printing press and there were printers on duty, they must immediately print and post all over the city a new notice from the district commander. First, by supreme decree, a state of siege had been declared for the City of Petrograd, as of this 12 March. Second, henceforth, residents were forbidden to go outside after nine o'clock at night. Third, due to illness, the Minister of the Interior, Actual State Councilor Protopopov, would have his position filled by the appropriate deputy minister. (Belyaev had forgotten whom they had decided to appoint.)

Among the sullen generals, the Admiralty's defenders, the only opinion they could have about Protopopov was that the scoundrel had conveniently fallen ill and slipped away at the last possible moment.

Evidently, Belyaev had some instruction concerning the "supreme decree." Well, a state of siege could be declared, but it did not add any clear idea of what was going on. Fine, Belyaev wrote the draft right then and the printing press was ready, and Khabalov ordered a thousand copies printed. But with regard to not going out after nine o'clock, that drew such shameful disbelief that even Khabalov refused. Located where, seeing what with one's eyes, and having what in one's head could one write something like this? They could not let themselves in for such ridicule.

Fairly quickly the printed notices were brought. And then it dawned on them that they didn't know what to do with the notices. First, a city where they could post them did not exist. The city governor objected that the notice-posters would have to be protected by military details. Not only that, there was the simple fact that they needed glue and brushes! There was none of that here. And where were they to be had in the middle of the night?

You couldn't paste them up without glue, that was true.

Oh well, Khabalov instructed, let policemen attach a few notices right here, to the fence surrounding Aleksandrovsky Square. The rest could simply be scattered on Palace Square and at the head of Nevsky. They could also be attached to the Winter Palace's iron fence.

And that is what they did.

[1 5 5]

Sitting in the Preobrazhensky officers' club, in the room behind the billiards room (antique portraits and engravings, mahogany armchairs, banquettes upholstered in gray damask), even after supper, were about twenty disheartened and pained officers who were attempting to make sense of the unfortunate muddle of the day just ended. There were those for whom it was dangerous to return to the mutinous barracks on Kirochnaya. From the billiards room came the invariable clicking of balls—those persistent cues insensible and ignorant of all of life's upheavals outside.

How momentously and promisingly this day had begun! And what an ignominious fiasco it had ended in—there was no coming to terms with this! How could this have happened? Where was the mistake made? They tried to sort it out.

Should they not have gone then to explain everything to the soldiers? Rosenschild-Paulin now asked. Maybe that's where our mistake lay? Were we late in making the announcement?

But two captains sitting side by side on the sofa confidently objected that that would have caused a schism and tumult; a premature announcement could have spoiled everything.

What was there to announce anyway? That was the main problem: what was there to announce? The very objective was as vague and incomprehensible to the officers as it had been during the day and was now.

Then there was that exultant joy when the Pavlovsky Battalion had marched to music and their forces seemingly had increased tenfold—and all of a sudden the Pavlovsky had turned out to be *against* the people? How were they to accommodate and understand this?

Indeed, a Guards crew had also come, looming darkly, as if they, too, were opposed to the State Duma? What about the Jägers? . . . And the Kexholmers?

Ensign Holthoer, exercising junior officers' acknowledged right to open a discussion, now stated sharply that they should not have waited for any reinforcements but should have gone straightaway and arrested the entire Khabalovite leadership. If Captain Skripitsyn had been able to go there without being detained, then obviously attacking them would have constituted no difficulty even for a handful of men, let alone two companies. And the Preobrazhensky men would have thereby rendered an inestimable service to the Liberation movement. Right now, at this moment, there would be no one to fight with in Petrograd!

Act directly against government forces? No, they hadn't thought that way. It was an interesting idea, perhaps, but no one remembered Holthoer expressing it on the square.

No, it should have been done much more subtly—but how? Over the day they had lost both the freshness of their mood and the grandeur of their objective. Having accomplished nothing, only getting chilled and losing heart, everyone began dispersing, and the Preobrazhensky men, too, wanted to have their dinner and supper, so they returned to barracks—and now where could they go in the cold and at night? And to what end? You don't rouse soldiers easily, and the officers saw no sense in it.

But how had this Meaning dissipated in just a few hours? How had it fragmented and collapsed? What a pity! What a humiliating state of failure even!

The officers had their supper, but they all stayed at the Club and did not disperse. It was clear that on this day they should stay close to their barracks.

But go to the barracks themselves? Talk with the soldiers now? No, that, too, seemed clumsy, a missed opportunity.

The persuasive arguments were as follows. The soldiers were themselves of the people and by their nature could not be against the people. At the moment when the conflict bared itself in a gaping chasm, their conduct would be unambiguously determined. But our soldiers today were poorly trained in the military respect, and in the intellectual respect were even weaker, and they might not withstand such an immense upfront load on their psyches. There was no need to shed light on their objective prematurely but only at the very moment of action.

Tomorrow would not be too late to apply the battalion's forces. The conflict would continue, although the government's forces would be reinforced from without. Would such a dramatic, such a Decembrist, such an unrepeatable opportune moment ever come around again?

All of a sudden, into the room—wearing his Guards naval uniform, with the aiguillettes of an adjutant general and the gold Tsarist monogram on his epaulets, with three crosses, on neck and chest, pale—walked Grand Duke Kirill Vladimirovich.

How timely! The officers all rose and drew toward him. Here was the person they could learn something from and confer with! A rear admiral, commander of the Guards Crew, a prominent figure in the dynasty, the eldest son of the second branch, in the event of shocks, a possible candidate for the throne! And he knew a lot. What did he think?

But Kirill was in no hurry either to encourage or discourage the Preobrazhensky men. He stood tall, with a significant, arrogant look (but if you watched closely and understood—not so confident), and listened to their ideas, as he would subordinates'. His entire face was clean shaven except for a short bushy mustache.

Captain Priklonsky, exchanging looks with the others, summoned up the nerve to speak.

"Your Imperial Highness! We would consider it dishonest to speak with you without stating that we are on the State Duma's side."

Kirill did not shudder. He raised his eyebrows, but not in anger. He was searching for words. And suddenly he extended his hand to the captain.

"Gentlemen. I thank you for your candor. In my heart, I understand your sincere feelings." His eyes were cold, but his words were intended to express powerful emotions. "We pleaded and we implored, but it led to nothing."

Everyone stood there frozen in horror. Go on! Go on! The grand duke was just about to declare himself their leader—and lead them!

But he stood there just as cool and erect, even despite his very extreme final words:

"What they have led Russia to!"

He saluted, turned sharply—and started for the door. A few officers hurried to escort him to the coatroom.

He did not directly promise alliance and assistance; he did not say anything definite—but how he encouraged the Preobrazhensky men! If a grand duke could reason this way, what had things come to, indeed?

Why shouldn't the Preobrazhensky men open up even more, then? Directly! Why hadn't the State Duma itself ever learned of their high revolutionary mood today?

Right then, Second Lieutenant Nelidov interjected impetuously:

"Gentlemen! Look! It's not too late to fix this! All the Duma deputies are in place right now. The telephones are operating. My Uncle Shidlovsky is chairman of the Progressive Bloc's bureau. If you will only authorize me, gentlemen, I will telephone him immediately and officially, in the name of the battalion, I will declare Preobrazhensky support for the State Duma!" He was worked up. All the possibilities of the missed morning seemed to rise up anew. "If only my uncle is there now, he'll recognize my voice and believe me."

They exclaimed noisily, like at the table after a successful toast. Everyone liked this very much!

This was unanimous approval. They thronged to the telephone.

Fairly quickly the operator connected them. It was amazing that the telephone was functioning despite all the street events.

At the other end someone picked up the receiver, handed it over to someone else, and the third was Shidlovsky himself.

"Uncle Seryozha! Uncle!" Nelidov shouted joyously and even too much so into the receiver. "Do you recognize my voice? Listen!" And formally: "I am calling from the Preobrazhensky Officers' Club! I have been deputized to declare that the officers and soldiers of the Preobrazhensky Regiment have resolved to put themselves at the disposal of the State Duma!"

That was how it came out—a regiment, not a battalion. And his tongue itself turned that way and added the soldiers; without that it would not have sounded right.

Anyway, they had already convinced each other that the question of the soldiers had been decided.

[1 5 6]

What was there to be done?

What was to be done?

What to do!

Rodzyanko was stuck as between cliffs after Belyaev informed him that Mikhail had received a categorical refusal from the Emperor.

And those around him were pressuring, advising, and pushing him to take real power in the capital.

Milyukov had seated himself up close for this; he could be as tenacious as a tick until he proved his point. Rodzyanko was always a little afraid of overly long conversations with him, afraid of making excessive concessions.

But even simple-hearted Shidlovsky was similarly inclined. So was wishy-washy Konovalov. As was the rash and rather pointed Shulgin. To say nothing of Karaulov, the mad Cossack, when he had a moment to drop by. Even Nekrasov, who had looped the loop today with the President, was now tersely leaning the same way. (He liked to be silent for a long time and speak up at a later stage—and always be proven right.) After Mikhail's talks with the Tsar fell through (which was even better; events would take their own course, and what could be expected from the Tsar anyway?), all we could do was continue the State Duma's commission and take responsibility for protecting order.

This was nearly the entire Committee. But what Chkheidze and Kerensky thought was by no means known. For some reason they hadn't stopped by; they were meeting with other people in another wing of the palace.

And all the arguments seemed correct. The government was paralyzed, if it hadn't fled altogether. No instructions had been forthcoming from the Emperor either. Imperial power in the country did and somehow didn't exist. To what end had it been eclipsed? Imperial power was not being exercised over the capital in anything except for the sole, languid General Khabalov, who had not shown himself anywhere in anything either.

Meanwhile, anarchy was spilling through the city. What during the day had seemed the power of a people brought to the point of despair was now transforming them into a dangerous rabble. The police had been routed everywhere and no force protecting order remained. Reports came in of officers being stopped on the streets, insulted—and even killed. Two and a half million residents could not live without some authority over them; they had to obey someone. For the salvation of the inhabitants, and especially the officers, it would now be good to take on the protection of law and order. Who was going to safeguard the banks, the treasury, the wine and vodka warehouses? The guards had fled everywhere.

All this was so. But let's think. We shouldn't make a decision so immediately and quickly.

But we can't wait! The rabble is going to descend on the Duma itself and smash it! To save the Duma and to save the Fatherland there is no other solution than to quell the anarchy.

Lastly, while we're thinking and meeting, someone else is going to seize power. Over there, they are already concocting a Soviet of Workers' Deputies. And won't they snatch up power? There was good reason Chkheidze had not showed up here; he was their chairman.

All this was so. Rodzyanko looked over the faces again. (He tried to turn away from Milyukov.) All this was so. However, none of his advisors and none of the members of the Committee were taking upon themselves as much as Rodzyanko, nor were responsible in the same way he was. It was *he* who was their President, and the decision—and the responsibility—was his alone.

But this was audacity beyond his comprehension and rights.

But he had received no answer from GHQ.

But Mikhail had not given any definite answer.

But anarchy was raging through Petrograd.

And now, what Mikhail was unwilling to do, they suggested he do himself?

Every last man around was arguing for seizing power.

The President was squeezed as between cliffs.

Milyukov, that resolute cat in spectacles with the stiff, protruding mustache, did not say a government had to be created, one government instead of another, instead of an imperial government, a government responsible to the Duma. Rodzyanko would have agreed more readily to a Council of Ministers. But no, they were pushing him to seize unilaterally power greater than the government's, to declare the Committee's unprecedented power— essentially Supreme power?

That is, power virtually equal to the Emperor's!

That is, overthrow the state? Break his oath and vow? Act as the principal rebel against God's anointed?

But Rodzyanko was not a rebel!

But the Fatherland was dying, and Rodzyanko was responsible for it!

Might these persistent voices and besetting faces be making it hard for him to decide? He needed to concentrate, to think better than he had ever thought in his life. His own office, open to all Duma deputies, had ceased to be such a place.

"Here's what, gentlemen. If this is so, then leave me alone. For fifteen minutes, half an hour. I must consult my conscience."

They agreed, some reluctantly, especially Milyukov, who didn't want to break this off. They exited single file and went into Konovalov's office next door.

Unfortunately, he hadn't really walled himself off. There, behind that single door, he could still see and sense them: gathering, waiting, compelling. For them, the decision had essentially been taken.

And without their proffered advice, it turned out he had nothing to rest on.

Pray? He left that for later.

What had been bothering him all this time? What was so offensive? Here's what: **who** would be the authority? By what tacit plot and patient intrigues of Milyukov's had they pushed the Duma President out as a candidate for Prime Minister? Why Lvov? What reason was there for Lvov? What kind of state experience did he have? He wasn't even in Petrograd, while here every moment . . .

But Rodzyanko himself could not be the one to say this. Had this not occurred to anyone else? Everyone respected him so much, but no one had proposed him.

What was there to be done? What should he do?

He pictured the Emperor's all too familiar face—both gentle, and sometimes shining, but also hard to penetrate. Their last hard, difficult conversations had been at January and February audiences. Rodzyanko had never been able to check his booming anger, and the Emperor always had. But the last time his brow had darkened so much, Rodzyanko had thought a zigzag of lightning would flash across it any second.

What would he say when he found out that Rodzyanko had declared himself the authority?

Why had he not responded with a single word to yesterday's telegram, or today's? It was as if Rodzyanko were complaining to him about his health and not reporting that Russia was about to perish.

Weary by now of holding his head in his hands, he now stretched his hands overhead, interlocked.

Oh, how impossible it was to decide! How there was nothing, there was absolutely nothing to rest upon! Fifteen minutes passed. The large wall clock said midnight.

Suddenly (he had barely dropped his hands from his head), the door to Konovalov's office cracked open—and Shidlovsky's overgrown face poked in. He began talking not tediously, as he usually dragged on, but unusually for him, extremely agitatedly.

"Mikhail Vladimirovich! Forgive me for disturbing you in this moment. But there is extremely important news."

"Yes?" Rodzyanko asked not irritatedly but with hope. Some extraordinary news was exactly what he was lacking for his decision. Might this be it? Some small makeweight was missing on the scales, to one side or the other.

Shidlovsky came all the way in.

"They've just called from the Preobrazhensky Regiment. At the behest of the regiment's officers—my nephew Nelidov, he serves there. He asked me to tell you and everyone here that the officers and soldiers of the Preobrazhensky Regiment are putting themselves at the disposal of the State Duma!"

Rodzyanko was so surprised, he heard him out, sitting at his desk, but immediately stood up, the old Horse Guard. This sounded like the call of ten fanfares. Peter's beloved child, the Preobrazhensky Regiment, the first regiment of the Russian army, had offered him its support! Had bowed to the banner of the State Duma!

(It sounded just like fanfares; his mind didn't grasp that he should make the correction: the entire Preobrazhensky Regiment was at the front, while here was the rear reserve battalion.)

Rodzyanko sensed powerful waves of enthusiasm in his mighty chest. He himself stood as if on parade with the Preobrazhensky, he heard their march! And in a voice for the parade ground, not for Shidlovsky alone in his office, declared:

"Thank you for this news, Sergei Iliodorovich! I am taking power!"

He corrected himself:

"The State Duma is taking power!"

[1 5 7]

As he entered the Tauride Palace, Peshekhonov began encountering people he knew at every step, as if all the people he knew had intentionally agreed that evening to arrange a get-together for everyone under the vaults of the State Duma.

Not forgetting his burning concern, he asked each one whether seizure of the Okhrana had been envisaged and a vehicle had been sent. Most didn't know, but some said it had been. There was no one in charge to turn to. There were a great many people, but not one good head or any good sense.

In the Ekaterininsky Hall, soldiers had made themselves comfortable in various places, like in third class at a train station, lying on the floor, their rifles stacked cross-wise.

There were hundreds of individual soldiers, but no officers in sight, and only lowly-looking ones at that. It was both strange and alarming. Strange because there were many progressive, right-thinking officers in the capital, so how on such a day and given such events had they all hidden away somewhere? What fate awaited the mutinous soldier masses without their officers? How would they do battle?

In any case, there were thirty times more people here now than during the midday break on the busiest Duma day. And if you pushed through the denseness of the corridors and opened all the doors, then there were also people sitting, or meeting, or discussing in each room, ten or twenty men in each.

In the corridor, though, he didn't have to ask where the Soviet's door was; one of his party comrades, a populist socialist, appeared and grabbed him by the elbow.

"Aleksei Vasilich, quickly! We have no representative in the Soviet. They're creating everything without us!"

Peshekhonov let himself be driven on and brought in—and he joined the Soviet's session.

Near-sighted, he didn't get a good look at which one of his acquaintances shouted out his candidacy for the literary commission, to write the proclamation—and in this way, apparently, he wasn't occupying seats on the Soviet for his party, was he? But he didn't have it in him to object during the balloting—and here he was elected.

Immediately, hastening to business, the entire literary commission exited the general session, and so Peshekhonov also left without having had a chance to feast his eyes on the Soviet and affect its course.

Also on the commission, besides Peshekhonov, were Sokolov, Nakhamkes, Himmer, and Shekhter. Sokolov, who already knew everything here, boldly led them to occupy a room. The entire right wing had become ours, and it was all crammed full. So Sokolov led them to the left half, the Duma half, and there they commandeered Konovalov's office.

They seated themselves around his desk with the telephone, but fidgety, nimble Himmer asked to leave for five minutes, promising to gather news from defense headquarters, which was nearby. Indeed, it wasn't a bad idea, before composing the proclamation to the population, to at least find out what was happening in the fighting.

Himmer returned with a sheaf of news, although he admitted he had collected it not from members of headquarters but at the doors. The news was more ominous than joyous. On one hand, Kronstadt had gone over to the side of the people! (But no one had ever doubted Kronstadt, knowing its traditions.) On the other, the Tsarist ministers had gathered at the Admiralty, where they were guarded by artillery and many troops. So the hostile center was evident—it had preserved itself and was preparing a strike. There was also news about the Peter and Paul Fortress, but no one knew exactly: either it was going to surrender to the Tauride Palace or it had sent an ultimatum for the Tauride Palace to surrender or else it would open fire.

The latter was much more likely. In general, anyone who had felt personally for years the inexorable pressure of the Tsarist regime, who knew its claws, was more likely to believe that reaction was gathering the forces of rebuff—and that the blow would be crushing.

But here was the most terrible part: government troops were already arriving in Petrograd! At the Nikolaevsky Train Station either the 177th or the 171st Infantry Regiment had disembarked and was battling a revolutionary detachment on Znamenskaya Square.

Shekhter clutched at his head at each piece of news and could only repeat: "We're going to perish! Perish! . . ."

It would have been better if Himmer had not gone for this news; he had only spoiled the whole mood. What "revolutionary detachment" could hold out on Znamenskaya Square! They might be deputies from the regiments, they might be stray soldiers—but they could not be a battle-ready revolutionary detachment.

Under these impressions, the literary commission was overcome by inertia; they spoke up reluctantly and lapsed into silence. They were thinking, only not about the proclamation. Even Himmer was a little sluggish in his fidgeting, and Sokolov had lost his inexorable animation. Even Nakhamkes, for all his prominent courageous figure, had gone limp.

They might not all avoid imminent retribution.

"But comrades," fifty-year-old Peshekhonov, the oldest there, kept his spirits up and shamed them, "if we go on like this, we aren't going to get anything written before morning. Let's think!"

They could never have concurred if they'd started with a political assessment of the moment—what exactly had happened and what might be expected tomorrow. Even among the Mensheviks there were four lines of thought, and here was Peshekhonov as well. Even *why* it had happened—that was hard for them to agree on. Some proposed alluding to military failures, and others wouldn't agree because the army and defense should not be put in doubt. Then about the food shortage in the capital? Here, too, opposing voices were found. Nakhamkes believed that this would demean the significance of the revolutionary moment.

Then why? Indeed, why had it all begun? They themselves were at pains to explain it to themselves. **Why?** Why on those days specifically, when no one was expecting it? And why on one day all of a sudden, so swiftly?

But if the literary commission itself didn't understand this, then what would the popular masses understand? . . .

Right then a new obstacle arose. The next door opened and Duma deputies, members of the Provisional Committee, began exiting through it: Konovalov, to whom the office belonged, Milyukov, Nekrasov, and others.

Their news was that Rodzyanko had secluded himself, having asked for time to think.

They had to free up Konovalov's desk for him. They looked askance at their guests, though they did not dare drive them away, as the representatives of revolutionary democracy.

The literary commission moved aside and to the Duma deputies' loud conversation attempted to continue their discussion, while Himmer jotted something down in his lap.

". . . The struggle has not yet been taken to the point of victory. The old regime must be overthrown once and for all—and herein alone does Russia's salvation lie. . . ."

"Overthrown once and for all"—but they didn't know whether they would edit this proclamation more, or whether the 177th Regiment would press on from Znamenskaya Square and the Tauride Palace would scatter in all directions, because those warming themselves by the fires in the square or sprawled out in the Ekaterininsky Hall were not defenders. This was simply astonishing! There should be at least one company in the revolution's defense—but there wasn't a one.

". . . For a successful conclusion to the struggle in the interests of democracy . . . the Soviet of Workers' Deputies has been formed in the capital, made up of elected representatives from factories and plants. . . ."

At that point the telephone rang, and they demanded Shidlovsky and no one else, but he had gone out. Someone was calling for him. But the equipment was such that you had to hold your finger or a pencil under the lever or else the conversation would disappear. They taught Shidlovsky to hold the pencil.

He became very animated. It was clear that they were calling from the Preobrazhensky Regiment.

So it was! Shidlovsky finished up, beaming. He announced to everyone in the room that the Preobrazhensky Regiment in full was supporting the State Duma!

Phew! That made things much better.

He conferred with Milyukov and went to knock on Rodzyanko's door.

The literary commission, after an animated discussion of the Preobrazhensky Regiment, once again buried itself in its proclamation, encouraged. They had to formulate the main mission of the Soviet of Workers' Deputies and its main objective.

Soon Shidlovsky returned and announced emotionally that Rodzyanko had agreed to take power!

The Duma deputies present began to clap.

And so—a revolutionary authority had been created! The literary commission could not restrain itself and began to clap, too.

(Might the 177th Regiment already be pressing in?)

No, they could not stay here. The Duma deputies were talking too loudly. Although it was interesting to look and listen, our Soviet was still under way and that, too, was interesting. But they couldn't go back without a proclamation.

They ventured out to find another room. Meanwhile, in the Ekaterininsky, more and more people were going to sleep, and more and more cargo was being hauled into the Cupola Hall: machine-gun belts, guncotton, and sacks of something.

They found a small room, more like a storeroom, with old publications, and there, sticking at every word, barely got to the end of the proclamation.

Peshekhonov headed for the Soviet's session but didn't get that far. He was snatched away and dragged to the finance commission meeting, for which he'd also been coopted.

There they were discussing where the Soviet of Workers' Deputies was going to get the money for its work. Peshekhonov immediately grasped that this wasn't the problem they needed to be thinking about. Rather, they should be thinking how to safeguard the treasury and banks so they weren't looted.

[1 5 8]

The night had already claimed its rights in full: the warriors of Khabalov's motley detail were asleep on the floors and staircases. But the leadership—no, they still knew no rest.

The insatiably lively General Zankevich, making the rounds of the posts, got the impression that the soldiers' mood was unreliable, and not only were they not prepared for an offensive, they weren't even prepared to defend this strange Admiralty.

Once again he returned heatedly to his idea and reported to Belyaev that it made more sense and was more dignified to move to the Winter Palace—and defend it as the emblem of Tsarist rule.

Belyaev, Khabalov, and Tyazhelnikov all found it very hard to think anymore about new decisions. Hadn't they just gotten settled here—and now they were supposed to go somewhere else?

But Zankevich argued the following. Today the men went hungry, and tomorrow morning there'd be nothing to feed them. Whereas the Winter Palace had lots of supplies in its cellars, and they could cook hot food, and they could withstand any siege there. Whereas here, they'd been met hostilely, Grigorovich had not come out or sent a greeting or assistance. He had always acted in the Duma's favor.

Indeed, there was nobility and honor in this—to die defending the royal palace!

They agreed. Khabalov gave instructions to move.

It was after midnight when they woke the men and got them up, stamping around, and assembled in the vast and booming corridors. In the middle of the night, in the middle of heavy sleeping, the men were neither surprised nor upset and obeyed mechanically. They were so tired they wanted to sleep, but most of all, the awakened men wanted to eat.

The impression spread more broadly through the detachment that their leaders had no power and didn't know what they were doing.

The naval leadership very graciously escorted them out, glad at being rid of them.

They moved in darkness and silence, without loud commands from the officers. The artillery rumbled softly. The horses snorted.

They marched, their wheels rolling over Khabalov's notices, which they themselves had tossed there.

It was a magnificent, frosty night, and the stars flickered in utter vividness—over the same square where so very recently, one August day, a kneeling crowd had sung a hymn before the Tsar. But only this transport made it back.

In the darkness they didn't think to check whether anyone had turned off for their barracks or homes. Prominent police officers from the city governor's suite disappeared without saying goodbye. Indeed, men had been disappearing all night.

The Peter and Paul Fortress spire stood out against the dark sky, illuminated by the collective starry reflections.

A glance at the sky revealed the elegant figures along the perimeter of the Winter Palace roof.

Past the square, past the Aleksandr Column, were the dark, embracing wings of the General Staff.

And not a single passerby.

From the city they heard an isolated shot, and here and there the glows were dying down.

The infantry began filing through the Aleksandr II entrance. The artillery and cavalry, through the gates.

[1 5 9]

Chunky Rodzyanko came into Konovalov's office triumphantly, like the birthday boy—steady, prepared to receive congratulations, only red from his cheeks to his bare temples from the tension he'd endured.

He walked in and applause broke out. But not very much and not quite confident clapping. The procedure didn't come across in the simple room;

there were too few people and everything was swaying so much in the darkness, they weren't ready to exult.

But Rodzyanko took a few steps and stood in front of his Committee as he would have in front of the Duma hall and rumbled in his bass voice:

"I agree, gentlemen! If this is your wish, I agree. But on condition, naturally, of total subordination to me by all the Committee members! And all the Duma deputies in general."

Milyukov looked at this hulk hopelessly. Several others frowned as well. Here is what Rodzyanko had never understood—collegiality and the republican spirit. Here am I—and everyone else be damned.

"And especially"—Rodzyanko right then noticed Kerensky—"especially I'm expecting subordination from you, Aleksandr Fyodorych." And he looked at him expressively and eloquently.

This was Rodzyanko reminding Kerensky of their recent clash over Shcheglovitov. (He'd probably been preparing his release, right? But not out loud yet.)

Kerensky, who in his flights through the palace had slipped in here and now was awaiting the decision with interest—though he did not answer at all impudently but expressively nodded his mobile head and let his eyebrows play. The significance of the decision taken had dawned on him as well and held him here.

Even Milyukov was satisfied, despite the authoritarian form of the announcement. He had achieved what he'd wanted, an important step had been taken which he could not have taken himself, but only through Rodzyanko. Now this had to be established publicly and the paths of retreat cut off, so that this wouldn't be an abstract promise easily retracted.

The shy dozen of the Committee moved into the President's office and seated themselves there. Rodzyanko behind his massive presidential desk, but Milyukov, at the head of the cross-axis, essentially led the session.

It was a transitional moment. The Committee was no longer "for relations with institutions and individuals" but something new. Shouldn't they somehow inform the populace? Publicly express their intentions?

Milyukov already had a text at the ready, and here it was, for Milyukov this would never be cause for delay.

As was clear to everyone, given the difficult conditions of internal havoc called forth by the bankruptcy of the old government, the State Duma's Provisional Committee had been compelled—simply compelled—to take in its own hands—not power, no, that would sound presumptuous—but to take in its own hands the restoration of state and public order. And at the same time express confidence that the populace and the army would assist them in this difficult task.

(What task exactly? This was the most important part. Milyukov's thoughts ran ahead, and he was already readying the next little bridge, for the next step.)

The difficult task of creating a new government that would correspond to the desires of the populace (that is, not the Sovereign) and enjoy its confidence.

(The Provisional Committee was Provisional because it was only a small bridge toward the creation of a *government*, which would be different from this Committee in that it would have real power, and it was toward this power that Milyukov was moving. In order for a government to arise, the Committee would have to fade away—this so far Milyukov alone had seen.)

The Committee listened and had nothing to object. It was all quite sensible and moderate even. A government of confidence? That was all the Duma had always talked about. But this? "Bankruptcy"? Perhaps put this more gently, "the measures of the old government"? Fine, measures. Milyukov was a master at conceding wording while retaining essence. (Someone proffered, even if you called it a "marasmus," you wouldn't be wrong.)

Since it was all agreed—why, then, Milyukov excused himself and went out to the hall for a minute. (He had beaten out Kerensky!) There, journalists were waiting for him—and they snatched up the communiqué for the newspaper being published. Those wandering out of the Soviet of Deputies also heard and, in general, everyone was encouraged.

But Rodzyanko, still filled to the brim with the Preobrazhensky call, meanwhile asked Shidlovsky to go after the session to their officers' club and thank them in his name.

It was after midnight, but the Committee members not only did not disperse, they entered into a discussion of exactly what they should do. News continued coming in from everywhere that the populace was on the loose and marauding, beating up or killing officers, vandalizing property, and searching private apartments. There was no military force whatsoever to stop them or protect anyone. Did that mean they should issue yet another proclamation?

This time Milyukov did not have a draft. They started writing. Kerensky had vanished into thin air, and wild Karaulov was gone, therefore no harsh words were uttered but only the suggestions of moderate and sensible people. Nekrasov sat there wolfishly, impenetrably, not adding a single sentence of his own.

To the residents of Petrograd. To the soldiers. In the name of our common interests, spare our institutions and facilities such as the telegraph, water pumps, and electric power stations. (One could imagine if everything were plunged into darkness right now and the toilets stopped flushing!) And the streetcars! (They'd already caught it.) And what about the plants and factories? The Committee was assigning their protection to the citizens themselves.

What about the officers? They couldn't say directly. It would be on record that the officers were being harassed. Besides, it would look as if the Committee were defending the reactionary order. But this could be put in a more roundabout way, a very general way, that no attempts of any kind on the life and health of private persons were permissible. What about private property? Here's what to write: bloodshed and looting are a stain on the conscience of the people who commit these kinds of acts.

Shulgin shook his head and said venomously:

"We don't have many rights for starters if all we can do is appeal to the populace's conscience."

"But what more, sir!" The progressivist Rzhevsky heaved a sigh of relief. "What's more to you than conscience?"

They did manage to finish and sent the second proclamation to the journalists. . . .

But pride was rising in Rodzyanko's chest. No, he was not one of the timid set! Yes, he had taken this step, he had taken it for Russia's salvation. And now he had to bring order to the capital, and that meant above all assembling the disintegrated troops.

To do that, though, the Provisional Committee needed its own military commander.

He expressed this thought. They discussed it.

All the commanders were at the front. In Petrograd there were only useless chancellery generals like this Belyaev. And even those, unless you looked at Khabalov's staff, where were they to be found?

They started thinking, eight heads together. And one head had a bright idea: Engelhardt!

Engelhardt was wholly theirs, a member of the State Duma. In the past, he had been an Uhlan Guard, an equestrian fancier—and he had graduated from the Academy of the General Staff, although this had in no way guided his subsequent life. And he wasn't old.

How magnificent! What was his rank? Either lieutenant colonel or colonel. Excellent! Where was he now? Somewhere here. He'd been in a private meeting and had stayed on afterward.

Locate him!

And they did.

He arrived wearing a frock coat with a white shirtfront and bowtie; nothing about him conjured up anything military. But he was their own man, a Duma man, an Octobrist!

He had never risen to the society of the Duma leaders, but here he was, and all the leaders greeted him graciously. In an instant they had coopted him for the Provisional Committee (the thirteenth, as it turned out, whereas Rodzyanko had been driving them on to make it twelve!). And he was appointed. What would he be called? Inasmuch as Khabalov was still commander of troops, let him be "commandant of Petrograd"!

Now he would have to head up all the military units that had come over to the side of the people. Assemble and organize them anew. And if it came to that, then yes, lead military actions against the forces of reaction.

But gentlemen, right away? . . .

Yes, right away, with both hands, as a deputy, not even putting on a uniform. (Did he have a uniform at home? Yes.)

The long-whiskered Terek Cossack Karaulov burst in belatedly with cartridge pouches hanging from his Circassian coat. In what way was he not the commander? Here I am!

But the Terek Cossack lacked the educational qualification.

"And how can I do without a headquarters?" Engelhardt asked.

But wait, gentlemen, we already have a headquarters right here, right in Nekrasov's office.

Nekrasov's office? Rodzyanko was incredulous. A headquarters right here, behind this wall? And no one reported it?

He stared at his young and much too clever assistant.

But Nekrasov did not blush, and his blue eyes gazed just as impenetrably. His voice could be so sincere and ingenuous. "What's wrong? The comrades from the Soviet of Deputies requested space. . . ."

Rodzyanko stood up indignantly. No! He could not lead without knowing anything in his own house! He did not go around through the corridor but instead imperiously pushed the small, concealed, wallpapered door and stepped directly into Nekrasov's office.

Followed by Nekrasov, Engelhardt, and a few others. (Milyukov, strictly a civilian, did not go.)

There, too, they were not expecting this; they didn't think this door opened. And all of a sudden — Rodzyanko himself!

Some morose, frowning civilian in a crumpled jacket and with a crumpled face sat there. Some naval lieutenant with a slantwise shock. One ensign. A few people waiting. And a pile of rifles in the corner, on the floor. This was headquarters' full extent.

Rodzyanko surveyed all this disarray with louring displeasure. Might this be exactly what was needed, though?

He nodded to them.

"Gentlemen officers," he said through his teeth, not finding an appropriate form of address.

Before his majestic figure everyone had long since jumped up and stood up straight.

"The Provisional Committee of the State Duma has taken upon itself the restoration of order in the city. For this purpose, Colonel Engelhardt of the General Staff has been appointed the commandant of Petrograd, so I now ask you to accord this man your hearts and your obedience."

No one objected to this. But Rodzyanko's last words were also heard by a few others who had entered from the room opposite (why, they had seized all the rooms here!). At their head, a bald, short, hopping civilian with an unbuttoned frock coat and a tar-black rectangular beard burst out with this:

"We don't need you fat, enfranchised bellies! This is the defense head-quarters of the Soviet of Workers' Deputies, and it obeys no one!"

How was that? Rodzyanko was dumbstruck, as if from a blow to the fore-head. After all, in taking power he had just warned that it was on condition of universal and total subordination to him!

And all of a sudden insults like this? Impossible language like this?

And right next to his office?

But just then, from his office, he could hear the persistent ringing and ringing of the telephone. Rodzyanko had ordered his secretaries to connect only the most important calls for him. That meant it was important.

Without regret he left this absurd scene, this joke of a headquarters, and was followed by the other Duma deputies.

His big paw picked up the receiver and he answered commandingly—and strained to hear, but responded only monosyllabically.

Everyone there fell silent, focusing their attention, trying to catch what the conversation was about. Who was speaking—that they didn't under-stand right away, but evidently someone connected with the government and the Emperor.

All of a sudden Rodzyanko turned gray and his voice fell. He made sure he had heard correctly:

"Eight regiments?"

And instantly everyone knew where the regiments were coming from and going.

Eight combat regiments? Petrograd had about ten battalions that were like flocks of sheep!

The President was instantly covered with perspiration, even on his neck and chest. He had been too hasty! Now, if anyone was an insurrectionist, then he was insurrectionist number one.

What would it have cost Belyaev to call an hour earlier? He also could have . . . he also could have . . . What would it have cost to wait a little longer? Why had Milyukov gone running to the correspondents? And why had they distributed the proclamation?

Remorse rose up in the President. He wished he could liquidate this Committee immediately, before it was too late!

But he looked at his colleagues and didn't dare utter a word.

Silence struck everyone clear through. Rodzyanko uneasily surveyed these helpless men, of whom not a single one was a true soldier, to say noth-ing of a Horse Guard, and not a single one could stand shoulder to shoul-der with him—not the ruin Rzhevsky, not the simpleton Shidlovsky, not the other mice, not the fidgeter Shulgin—and Milyukov would be first in line to betray him.

For years the Duma had been attacking, exposing, and ridiculing—and the government had cowered, while the Supreme Authority had given no sign as to whether it was listening or not. A particular climate had been created in the Duma: speak forwardly about the *upper* strata and behave as freely as if there were no upper strata. They'd gotten used to pretending there weren't.

But here they were. Eight combat regiments.

The imperial hand had moved in—to slap them down here and now, along with their successes, their Committee, and their proclamations. . . .

[1 6 0]

Who better than Sergei Maslovsky had envisioned how to bring about a revolution? In 1905, he had written (anonymously) an instruction leaflet on the tactics of street fighting using barricades. Not that he himself had ever verified it in practice.

What had begun today had begun quite wrongly. If this were a serious revolutionary movement, then it was already wrong that it had begun not in the workers' neighborhoods, not around the factories, not even on every man's thoroughfare, Nevsky, but in the midst of the military blocks of the Liteiny section, the most reliable citadel of government. (For this reason the tumult in the professors' room at the Academy had been considerable.)

Yes, eleven years ago, coming up on his thirtieth, and after many personal failures, Maslovsky had joined the SR party and, one might say, been a participant in that revolution. But it had all been cruelly routed, and he himself had nearly been sent to the Peter and Paul Fortress. In the years following, he had found employment in a quiet position as librarian at the General Staff Academy (by knowing the right people; his father had been a professor there)—and here he was suffocating, like a hostage of the revolution in the camp of unbridled reaction and retrograde loyalty to the throne, and among the majority was supposed to move inexpressively and close-mouthed, to say what he did not think in a wooden voice, and to only a few could he caustically reveal his free thoughts. Petersburg revolutionary democracy knew of his revolutionary past and revolutionary essence, of course, but he encountered them rarely and did not act because his entire life had been lost in hopeless daily life. Since the war began, his librarianship had become a good shelter from the front, and Maslovsky had quite hidden away. And so he had to sit out this war in peace—but now something had begun.

Today lessons at the Academy had ended early, and the professors and military auditors, before dispersing to their homes, and having heard that officers were being disarmed on the streets, handed in their swords for safekeeping at the Academy's museum. Inwardly, Maslovsky laughed biliously at their helplessness. Here were your heroes, here were your knights of the throne! They could and were attempting to do nothing. He himself as well, then, left work, but he didn't have a sword; he wasn't an officer. And he lived in the building next door.

He and his wife decided that they should not go anywhere on a day like today because they might land in this mess, so they just looked out the windows at Suvorovsky Prospect. The avenue did not quiet down, and more and more new revolutionary-popular scenes kept unfolding. Swarms of adolescents circled, aimless shooting began, shouts of "hurrah," and caps in the air, as if the victory had already been won.

So Maslovsky, alarmingly agitated, sat home until dark fell, observing and calculating that tomorrow the situation would become clearer. But they made a mistake: his wife went out into the city to have a look and learn better—and right then the telephone rang. Maslovsky couldn't resist the temptation to pick up the receiver. What if it was something sensational that he could learn so easily? And he was caught. It was Kapelinsky calling from the Tauride Palace, and he was seething with joy, and summoning him, yes, him, the first of them all, to come immediately to the Tauride Palace to the organization's aid.

Oh, what a vexation! But since your whereabouts were known, you couldn't say you weren't at home. There was no going back. Nor could he stain his revolutionary reputation. His former glory had put him on the spot.

There was nowhere to hide. Maslovsky threw off his military uniform, put on a not-new jacket, a not-new overcoat, and his boots and galoshes— and started out, hunched over, for the Tauride Palace. It was close.

And there the party comrades, considering Maslovsky an educated military specialist, sat him down to direct the uprising's headquarters! A nice business, enough to shake you to the core: from being a peaceful citizen to suddenly running the headquarters of the city's entire uprising! You couldn't try to show them just how inappropriate this was for you. Everyone was telling each other: "We've lived to see it!" "We've lived to see it!" "At long last it's come!"

True, he had at his disposal a genuine naval lieutenant, Filippovsky, who was quite serious and energetic, and a few green ensigns. But was all this really a headquarters? No organization whatsoever, not even the least subordinated military unit, just some bustling motorists and soldiers without a command in the square in front of the palace. Based on the snatches of information brought in, the unjustifiably easy success of the revolutionary day had become by nightfall a total crisis, havoc.

Maslovsky got going and speaking to his comrades—automatically, making no attempt to master events. He was torn by the alarm of uncertainty. He tried on the death penalty or hard labor for size and was in despair that he had landed in this mess so foolheartedly. Maybe that night, by morning, there would be an opportune moment to slip away unnoticed.

But here, too, his soul was torn by well-meaning visitors to the headquarters room; after all, it was wide open to all who wished to enter, as was any room of the palace during these hours. Since the hour when the Tauride Palace's doors had been locked for the crowd and people had been let in only by selection, the palace had filled with "Petersburg society," the circles around revolutionary democracy, and simply sympathizers. And they (interspersed with journalists) went invariably to uprising headquarters and gave all kinds of advice: "But why don't you seize the aerostatic park? You would have aeroplanes!" "But why don't you order them to dig up the streets so the armored cars can't drive through? After all, Khabalov has a hundred armored cars, that's absolutely certain!" "But why haven't you blown up a few of the military-police telegraph poles to disrupt their communications?" "But why aren't you storming the Peter and Paul Fortress?"

And each one of them, of course, remembered and would testify at the trial, saying that it was Maslovsky who had led the uprising's headquarters! . . .

But right now there wasn't even any way to defend the Tauride Palace. True, someone did bring in weapons from somewhere — rifles, revolvers, bullets — and a few university students had gotten busy in the entrance hall loading cartridge belts. But they didn't have the machine guns themselves. There were two anti-aeroplane guns on the roof, and two in reserve — but they couldn't all fire. They sent one student to the pharmacy at least for vaseline for them — and he returned empty-handed. It was late already and everything was locked up. A *revolutionary* had shied from breaking down a door! . . .

Near midnight, rumors were brought from the corridors that Khabalov was just about to begin a general offensive. Which was natural. After all, he hadn't shown himself in any way all day; obviously there had been some calculation to that.

The entire revolution was hanging in the air, not a single point of it actually resting on solid ground.

They should expect the coming of retribution. But right now there was no escaping without incurring contempt from revolutionary circles.

Suddenly, at about one in the morning, the tightly wallpapered door in the office opened — and Rodzyanko himself appeared, steaming red, followed by a small suite of Duma deputies. Rodzyanko's look was incensed, even. He gazed with astonishment that someone was meeting here, though he had not given that order. And it seemed as though he might obliterate them right now with his bulk. However, he only announced, short of breath, that he was appointing Colonel Engelhardt commandant and everyone must obey him.

Commandant of *what*? The building? The city? Maslovsky didn't catch that, but he was already experiencing relief. However, before either he or his staff could stir, Sokolov burst through the open door of the connecting room on the other side and in his ringing lawyerly voice began insulting Rodzyanko. In the last few hours in the Soviet of Workers' Deputies, Sokolov had begun to feel that he, more than Rodzyanko, was master of this building.

Rodzyanko, steaming, with perspiration on his bald head, listened bewildered. And did not explode further. The big man even stepped back from the short bald man's sudden attack.

Sokolov kept fulminating and gesturing with his quick small hands.

"Headquarters have already been formed! Headquarters are functioning! What does Engelhardt have to do with this? To smash Khabalov and Protopopov we don't need your appointees, we need true revolutionaries! And we have them! There is nothing for your people to do here."

Probably no one had ever dared speak to Rodzyanko this way. Taken aback, he felt a dark cloud come over him and started grumbling without ceremony:

"Oh no, gentlemen. Now that I've agreed to take power, you will now be so kind as to obey me."

Oh, is that it? He's decided to take power? Maslovsky immediately realized that this was giving them all a fine chance. The Duma President! Legitimacy!

But the irrepressible Sokolov would not take the bit. He was drunk on his attained level of shouting. He shouted and sputtered that the Soviet of Revolutionary workers and mutinous soldiers alone would direct the defense, and the Duma Committee could send observers, but not leaders. Once again, he spoke insultingly of Rodzyanko so that the ensigns here couldn't stand it any longer and started pushing Sokolov out and objecting. Maslovsky, too, took to objecting.

He knew better than anyone that no headquarters of any kind had been formed here or was functioning—and it was marvelous that at this most terrible moment the Duma Committee and Engelhardt were going to accept all responsibility.

But Engelhardt, a Duma deputy little known to anyone, also turned out to be present—also in a civilian coat, feeling constrained and flushing awkwardly. After his rights had been confirmed and Rodzyanko and the Duma deputies had left, he had remained.

They had argued with and restrained Sokolov. What was here the Soviet of Workers' Deputies had already named the Military Commission. So, let it be just that, but a common organ of both the Soviet and the Duma Committee. Led by Engelhardt. They agreed.

Especially in the face of the inexorable news of the eight regiments sent.

They took their seats and decided they needed to publish a decree telling all military units and all solitary lower ranks to return immediately to their barracks; all officers were to join their units and take measures to instill order; and the leaders of individual units to appear tomorrow at the State

Duma to receive instructions. So, would we take the army into our own hands? How else could we fight? A revolutionary army could not be created instantly.

Puffing at his dark mustache, his shock of hair falling slantwise, Filippovsky sat down to write the decree. And then send it off to one of the seized printing presses.

But it was now hard to believe that after the murders the officers would return to their units and put them in order.

At this, Engelhardt had the thought to turn for help to the Preobrazhensky battalion, whose fortunate intervention had at midnight influenced Rodzyanko and where the officers, evidently, remained in place even now. So Engelhardt would go there! First to thank them, and then to rely on them. They alone could attack Khabalov.

A sensible idea! They agreed.

But Engelhardt thereby had disappeared and Maslovsky again remained to roast at the head of the cursed headquarters.

The ensigns were thinning out. He didn't know who he had left, but he couldn't go. All the visitors and public figures had dispersed from the Tauride Palace. And Duma deputies were no longer arriving.

To send parties of volunteers somewhere else—it was hard now even to find commanders and rouse soldiers. There had been no word of the many parties already sent out; they had trickled away and vanished.

On the other hand, that fine fellow Lenartovich had called to say he had seized the Mariinsky Palace! But not a single minister, and now he was busy there inspecting and seizing documents.

Nonetheless, this did not change the thick secrecy around Khabalov's intentions. Based on random dispatches, Maslovsky had begun to think that the entire Tauride section of the city was quietly being surrounded by a ring of machine guns.

There was a call from the Vyborg side saying the Wheeled Battalion was returning fire and refusing to surrender to the people.

They were requesting reinforcements for the Nikolaevsky Station. But no matter how many they sent, no one arrived. Where had they gone?

The Tauride Palace had spread out through its rooms and halls to sleep. But the Military Commission—Maslovsky and Filippovsky, the two of them—they couldn't leave or close their eyes.

The area outside in front of the palace was now deserted, not seething with volunteers.

And news came in that a crowd was gathering to storm the official wine storehouse on Tauride Street, nearby. That meant they needed to assemble and send a guard, or else the drunkards would make quick work of us, too.

But the Khabalov offensive had still not broken out, although it was already the dead of night, the streets were empty, and no one was blocking its way.

[161]

Enough stupidity in every wise man. Now, locked up hour after hour in the ministers' pavilion so familiar to him, where he had come so many times for Duma sessions, Shcheglovitov now understood very well what he should have done this morning: hide away, leave the city altogether—and even, maybe, without telling his beloved wife. Although concealment was unbearable!

But look . . .

After all, he had already received so much over the years—packages with little coffins, letters with little gallows, from Russia and the United States— that he could have predicted it: the first blow would have to fall on him. The hand of vengeance had to show itself the swiftest in revolution.

But this phenomenon—"revolution"—we don't know it in everyday life. It has no part in our accumulated life experience—and you make a mistake at the very first step. Especially if you've spent your entire life between taut legal strings. It had been hard to realize it this morning, from the first mutinies in the reserve battalions, that henceforth the concept of *law* would cease to exist, and even he, head of the Empire's upper legislative chamber, was no longer protected by any regulations whatsoever. Shcheglovitov was one of Russia's strongest jurists; his entire life juridicism had upheld him— and juridicism had failed him. Shcheglovitov was persistent, stern, and resourceful—as long as he stood on the path of the law. But once off it in the slightest—and he lost his way. He was sitting at his son-in-law's and there was an ordinary knock at the apartment—and behind the door were two Jewish students armed with sabers and revolvers together with two soldiers. The little student immediately shouted, "Shcheglovitov? You're under arrest!" The born jurist could not help but object. "By whom? By what order?" "By the will of the revolutionary people!" the student exclaimed insolently, and he put his hand on his saber.

Even an ordinary member of a legislative chamber, much less its head, could not be arrested by anyone's will until his immunity had been lifted. That much was clear. But here there was the advantage of four armed young men over a fifty-five-year-old civilian, so all he could do was obey, right? But they were hurrying him so frenziedly for some reason, dragging him by the elbows and pushing him from behind, that they didn't let him put on his coat or cap.

"In five minutes we'll be at the Tauride Palace and it's warm there!"

The Tauride Palace? Well, that wasn't so bad. That's a second legislative chamber, and there everything would be cleared up immediately.

But Rodzyanko? He had retreated like a coward and refused to free him. While that little nonentity of a lawyer Kerensky, who had never been any kind of jurist but had garnered for himself cheap fame with his demagogic speeches at political trials, had screamed piercingly and told the inflamed convoy to lead the prisoner on.

But with what conscience had Rodzyanko withdrawn?

But then, he too hadn't reacted in time, had he? Those brief moments when the fate of your life and body are decided—why can thought suddenly abandon us this way? You turn out to be a body sack, shut in by a simple door lock, and the key is in your enemy's pocket.

He recalled one strange night of his thirty years ago, in the spring of 1887. As the youngest in the Petersburg District Court, he'd been appointed to be present at the execution of the Ulyanov group in Schlüsselburg. He went there the night before and spent the night in the fortress and—as if he were the one they were supposed to execute—he did not get a wink of sleep all night. He was waiting and thirsting for a telegram granting a supreme pardon. In the morning, too, he delayed and delayed the execution by his authority, still awaiting a telegram. It didn't come.

Yes. Something similar.

Shcheglovitov was the same age as Aleksandr II's reforms, he loved their idea, had attended the Academy of Jurisprudence in their liberal air, and for many long years had not distinguished himself from that general stream of liberals. He became a professor of jurisprudence and published articles in defense of the law against outside pressure. (Although even then he saw the radical collapse of Aleksandr's judicial reform—the vindication of the Zasuliches and tens of others like them—and then he had censured lawyers who made a mockery of public trials, the same behavior Dostoevsky had ridiculed.) He had greeted ecstatically the Manifesto of 30 October as the opening of an era of legal norms—and in those same months he had been carried up to the heights of the judicial system, and from the very birth of this new state order he had become, and for nine years remained, minister of justice. A change in our official position should not change our convictions, but it cannot help but influence our views. What had been hidden from outside criticism becomes visible. Although even a year later, after the Second Duma, Shcheglovitov had argued against Stolypin's 16th of June amendments to the election law, now even more he believed it necessary to provide an ironclad defense of the constitutional order created and government policy—during the years when terror raged, when liberals not only applauded the murderers but even theoretically justified terror by saying that society was not satisfied with the state's governance. And so Shcheglovitov lost any liberal reputation he had, and he no longer even tried to maintain it. However, his emergency laws had always been *laws*: precise procedure was indicated, as were precise terms and responsible individuals. No one could be arrested **just like that,** the way they had him today. Several times during the revolutionary years he had been named a target for terrorists, and in 1908 he had sat at home in a two-month siege and one time avoided being killed only because he had by chance been detained in his entryway and had not come out to his carriage before three men attacked it.

Over the years, Shcheglovitov had seen the judicial ranks filled to bursting with lax loudmouths who made the court a poor defender not only of the state order but of citizens' very lives. However, he had not allowed himself impunity to forcibly shape the court and violate the law of judges' irremovability. He had merely resorted to ruses like enticing the unfit to retire with a pension, which was easier if the judge had manifested sins of personal conduct and might fall under disciplinary investigation. This was slow work, instilling in the courts the value of government stability. For a good thirty-five years, frenzied waves had eroded and destroyed that stability. The rest of society, and the gentry, and the highest state strata seemed to see all this—and not see it. No one wanted to believe that the foundations might collapse. The entire ruling elite rocked back and forth, languidly and serenely, and tried in their faintheartedness and spinelessness somehow to ignore the threats. In his bureaucratic colleagues Shcheglovitov saw only a climb out of one skin and into another, from position to position, while maintaining perfect indifference to the essence of the matter. So, having given many years to strengthening the Russian state order, Shcheglovitov was used to there being no one in Russia with whom he could ally, no one with whom he could act jointly; you just did everything yourself. How could he not be infected by this universal calm? Shcheglovitov also gave it its due. Wasn't it in this mood that he had failed to stop Kiev's judicial authorities in the case against Beilis, which should never have been opened? And when it began to take on world scope and it seemed too late to retreat, and given the disposition of passions Shcheglovitov himself was not unbiased either, he financed a visit by experts for the prosecution—although the trial proceeded within the strict framework of the law. A transcript was made of the entire trial, it was opened to reporters, as many witnesses and lawyers were allowed as the case required, and by the logic of the law the defendant was fairly acquitted.

But society pinned this trial to Shcheglovitov for all time. During those same years he lost the throne's support. The Empress would not forgive him for being irreconcilable toward Rasputin. Not only did he not flatter him but he did not give him any advantage, he did not even receive him out of turn, and he tore up the petitions that came through him. (Nonetheless, the slander was asserted in society that Shcheglovitov was Rasputin's stooge.)

Back in the summer of 1914, it was Shcheglovitov who had prevented the Emperor from changing the constitution in favor of autocracy and shifting the chambers back from being legislative to consultative: "I would consider myself a traitor to my Emperor if I said, 'Your Majesty, carry out this measure!'"

And in 1915, before the Duma swarms, an acquiescent Emperor forced his resignation. In his many interactions with the Tsar during the nine years of his ministry, Shcheglovitov was fated to drink his fill of the bitter taste of a man of state whose knowledge, intellectual powers, labor, will, and service turn to dust for a hesitant breeze. At times, he would heatedly try to convince the Emperor of some decision or would guide it along for months—and suddenly the Emperor would cancel everything under the influence of a random opinion he'd heard. The Emperor had always shunned strong personalities.

The rare conservatives in Russia had the courage to openly declare their beliefs. You could not assemble a congress of rightists from the entire country otherwise than by taking half off the street—poor, crude, unenlightened forces. Such a congress was assembled in December 1915, but no dignitaries or prominent officials attended; they were too embarrassed. The rightists preferred meeting in small, hidden circles and exchanging whispers. Having lost his balance due to his resignation, Shcheglovitov agreed to head up this congress.

This entire lonely, locked-in evening, and now night, Ivan Grigorievich had been roaming the rooms of the ministers' pavilion. The rather long but not overly large meeting hall, the cloth-covered table surrounded by armchairs and several small sofas. Two offices. A servants' room. A lavatory. How many times he had been here, but could he ever have supposed he would end up here in these circumstances?

He couldn't have supposed. But he should have foreseen.

For a year and a half Shcheglovitov had been observing this collapse—from the sidelines, powerlessly. As of the New Year, the Emperor had returned him to activity, made him President of the State Council—and Shcheglovitov had taken it on decisively, albeit with a sense of unease.

Here, in the deserted rooms of the spectral recent government, it was Ivan Grigorievich's plight to walk around—without food, drink, or company—locked up helplessly, after midnight now—and ruminate to his heart's content.

Shcheglovitov had in general held himself independent of the Court and kept his distance from the grand dukes. He had forbidden his beloved daughter Anna from becoming a lady in waiting, as she had been offered, believing that this was practically like being a maid. And when he was asked how he would regard the receipt of the title of count (Witte was delighted when he'd accepted his), Ivan Grigorievich replied that a foreign title would be ridiculous given his ancient Russian surname. (The Shcheglovitovs—the ancient line of Shaklovitovs—by Peter the Great's decree had had to change the letters slightly in order to distance themselves from the executed Shaklovitov, a favorite of Sofia.)

His daughter Anechka was his heart and soul. He had been widowed twice; his second wife had died giving birth to Anya. Ivan Grigorievich had been closely involved in her education. On Easter, at their estate, he made her exchange a triple kiss with each peasant family. When she got older, he took her to Italian opera and even chose her gowns.

But his third wife—beautiful and intelligent, a pianist, from society, and with an imperious personality—ruled him, directed him; he admitted this and could not change it. She and Anechka had disagreed and quarreled. And his heart had broken.

What would happen to Anechka when she learned of her father's arrest?

The last person with whom Ivan Grigorievich had spoken was Kerensky, holding a heavy key, comically and arrogantly offering to telephone Tsarskoye Selo for Shcheglovitov about the futility of resistance and advising them to surrender to the people's mercy.

This upstart was already ordering the Throne to surrender?

Shcheglovitov didn't even spare a full gaze at him.

Having observed erosion and destruction for two decades in the presence of universal apathy, he could expect everything bad. On the way here in the cab, Shcheglovitov had seen the agitated streets and the swarming palace there—and the scope of what was going on came clear to him.

That this was the collapse which should have been expected in a constantly rocked and undermined country.

He did not try to tell himself he would be freed tomorrow morning.

[162]

A year and a half of close contact with the Emperor had left Alekseev without any respectfully distanced attitude toward the monarch, any cloud of mystery or mystic threshold of superiority. For him, the Emperor was the most ordinary of men who loved Russia and the army but who was no strategist, rather actually a highly accommodating colleague receptive to Alekseev's decisions. Privately, Alekseev knew perfectly well that he was far from being one of the brilliant lot of military leaders and had been undeservedly promoted by the Emperor, but this did not prevent him from understanding that the Emperor was even less capable and weaker. By association, Alekseev began to sense this superiority in other spheres as well, such as here—how to deal with public disturbances.

Therefore, in conveying by telegraph the Tsar's response to his brother, Alekseev added his own message to the grand duke's request: when the Emperor returns to Tsarskoye Selo and they see each other, do not cool off. Petition once again for replacing the present Council of Ministers; but most important was *how* to choose them. (He could not bring himself to say that they should be responsible to the Duma, but that is exactly what he had in mind.)

Actually, it was now evident to Alekseev that each hour was precious and there should be no delay with concessions at this precious moment, while the Emperor would still be on his way to Tsarskoye Selo.

Here, in confirmation, a pleading telegram even arrived from the hapless Prince Golitsyn to dismiss them all and hand over power to a responsible administration. From various sides, everyone was asking decisively and unanimously for the same thing, something so simple. Why shouldn't he concede? This man had an amazing ability to dig in his heels!

Quartermaster General Lukomsky, too, tried to spur Alekseev not to surrender and to persuade him. As men nonetheless belonging to the educated strata, they understood each other; society's moan and anticipation, accessible to them, but to which the monarch was simply not attuned.

But Alekseev's arguments were in vain, and not dragging out the evening, he went to bed.

Right then, all of a sudden, the Emperor himself came to the quartermaster general's area, brought a telegram form for Golitsyn, and in particular communicated to Alekseev through Lukomsky that his decision was final and reporting anything more to him on this question was useless.

It was this communication that made Lukomsky begin trying to convince Alekseev to get up again and go cajole him. Did this stipulation of the Emperor's not hold the germ of a concession?

In his poor condition Alekseev once again wandered over to try to convince the Tsar that time that has slipped away can be irretrievable and the life of the state might depend on such moments. It had been right to send troops, but it was also right to concede on the government. It would be much better to get by without any bloodshed or violence and instead turn all the country's forces toward matters of war.

All once again in vain. Although the argument to avoid bloodshed had always struck a chord in the Emperor, now he wouldn't hear of a ministry, he had hardened so. His voice became muffled, without timbre or color, his cheeks sunken. He had returned from Tsarskoye Selo just as dispirited.

Fine, ultimately it was not Alekseev who had the foremost duty to decide matters of state for their entire dynasty.

He went to bed.

Meanwhile, though, the Emperor had taken the sudden, and in present conditions shocking decision to leave for Tsarskoye immediately. This very night!

After all, even his brother had sensibly asked him not to go! Why go, given this dangerous situation? Alekseev had been hoping yet tomorrow to dissuade the Emperor—and he was going today? No normal mind could take this in! How, at such a troubled moment, could the head of state and Supreme Commander abandon the center of command and the central hub for all military telegraphs, abandon the loyal 7 million-man front from the Baltic to the Black Sea, and this superior, firm position from which the armies' actions were directed? Go without any proper guard on unprotected rails to somewhere so proximate to the raging, mutinous capital?

Alekseev was also worried that when the Emperor was reunited with his spouse he could never again be convinced of the slightest concession; only here could you even try.

The chief of staff once again dragged his leaden boots along. And again in vain.

Alekseev could not recall this kind of firmness in the Emperor, this kind of blindness and deafness, in the last eighteen months.

All right, he's taken the bit—let him go.

Only he couldn't understand how they would be in contact in the morning, when the train was in motion.

He also sent instructions to the two army groups to guard the railroads connected to his route from disturbances.

Here the Northern Army Group reported that regiments had been assigned to Petrograd and would be there in twenty-four hours.

Well, everything seemed to be provided for and set. Now, at one in the morning, could Alekseev finally get all the way to bed?

The lieutenant colonel on duty reported to him on the conversation with the General Staff in Petrograd, that there was shooting throughout the city, telegrams could not be delivered, and all the telegrams since two in the afternoon lay at the telegraph office, where they were worried that the telephone might be cut off at any moment.

But right then they brought an even stranger telegram, not from a person but from the Petrograd telephone officials themselves saying that they were surrounded on all sides by rebels, who were firing machine guns. They had been unable to send the supreme dispatch over to the Prime Minister, or any other, and there was a danger they wouldn't have time to destroy all the old ones, so they wouldn't fall into the rebels' hands. They asked that he not send any more dispatches to Petrograd!

But the Tsar had already left for the train station and his train.

Well, he had dug in his heels, so let him go.

What could they do? Alekseev ordered no more telegrams sent to Petrograd, just to maintain the lines' technical repair.

They also delivered Khabalov's belated telegram, five hours en route instead of one, saying that most units had betrayed their duty, that by evening the rebels had taken control of most of the capital, and only a few fragments of various regiments that had converged near the Winter Palace remained loyal to their oath.

Alekseev sent this telegram as well after the Tsar, to the train. Let him read it.

[1 6 3]

The Winter Palace was uninhabited—and yet inhabited (some halls were now an infirmary and there were all the servants). After the chilly and dark Admiralty, these warm, brightly lit entrance halls with their mirrors and flowers and carpeted marble staircases, the first rooms with handsome upholstered furniture and expensive drapes—just the entry to the unending rows of rich suites alone was truly a place for a Tsar. It was a shame to destroy this beauty and adornment with a defense force.

But both the senior officers, who knew about the wealth of the palace's storerooms, and the rank and file, who were capable of guessing that this kind of luxury didn't exist without an abundance of supplies—they all had a presentiment that right now at least they would eat their fill for the day.

Naturally, the sofas here weren't for ordinary people, but the warm, polished parquet floors themselves were already luring them to sit and lie down. The men spread out. After putting the horses and weapons in the courtyards, the cavalrymen and artillerymen filed through the inner doors. The officers themselves, or else after conferring with the old good-natured palace footmen, looked for and pointed out to their own where to lie down.

They posted details by the many doors and went up to the second floor with machine guns, passed through fantastic deserted halls—one with a vacant throne, halls decorated with coats of arms, a white marble colonnade with St. George the Bringer of Victory, a malachite hall, broad corridors hung with the portraits of hundreds of generals from the Napoleonic war—and took up positions along the endless long walls at the windows onto the square and the embankment.

The night should pass somehow and safely, without gunfire, and in the morning they could ask the superintendent to unseal the windows, which were tightly shut for the winter, so as not to smash out windows more than necessary.

It was an odd shift. The permanent resident of this palace, whose grandeur this luxury was supposed to protect and elevate, had long since disdained this place, abandoned it in vain, didn't live here, but when the decisive moment came, this was exactly where the last loyal men had come.

Everyone who crossed the threshold of this palace, even if through back or side doors, had experienced the special nature of the place.

General Khabalov had his headquarters set up on the first floor in large rooms with carpets, paintings, and upholstered sofas and chairs. They hadn't even gotten settled, hadn't had time to think through a new plan of action and defense, when the palace superintendent, Lieutenant General Komarov, roused from his sleep, belatedly came to them and decisively protested their unauthorized military invasion by right of force and stated categorically that he could not allow them to stay here without the permission of the court minister, Count Frederiks, who, as they knew, was in Mogilev.

If any of the commanding generals here were impressed by this, it wasn't Khabalov (or Tyazhelnikov). All the past day Khabalov, rather than command, had been frozen in anticipation of what would happen of its own accord. But what could happen was only worse leading to worst. He understood this and now was surprised at nothing. He had humbly accepted that they were unwanted guests in the Admiralty and unwanted guests here in the Winter Palace. For many hours he had felt the detachment as a weight on himself and he had not been happy at any reinforcements, which only increased that weight. Actually, the weight hadn't increased; despite all the reinforcement the same number remained, fifteen hundred men, maybe two thousand, while the rest melted away imperceptibly. And still the same small supply of cartridges. And no forage whatsoever. And no food whatsoever. And with these half dozen companies he was prepared to wander off to some next place.

Belyaev, too, somehow did not feel like a minister, especially against the royal palace procedures. Truth is, he was lost. He himself had barely escaped the shooting and he, too, had nowhere to go back to. They'd probably already descended on the War Minister's residence to arrest him. (But if you think about it, what bad thing had he had time to do in his brief ministerial administration? Why did the State Duma have such an unjustly bad attitude toward him?)

But energetic Zankevich, who had come up with this whole symbolic move and who understood that they had no other choice, began arguing insistently with the palace superintendent. We need to get permission? We will, but for now we're staying here.

And there was a connection—by the special (as yet undamaged) line to Tsarskoye Selo. It wasn't Mogilev, but all permissions could be obtained from Tsarskoye Selo.

They began telephoning there.

General Groten, the palace commandant's Tsarskoye Selo assistant, came to the telephone, and then the high chamberlain, Count Benckendorff. No, there was no connection with Mogilev right now, and they were powerless to learn Count Frederiks's opinion. His Majesty could not be disturbed by a report before morning. Even less could they themselves decide this matter.

General Zankevich's first thought was that they didn't have to, and they would stay right here. Just one thing: give us permission to feed our detachment out of the palace stores.

To his surprise, even this small thing Benckendorff did not have the right to decide, either. He assured him that there was very little food in the palace at all, and they had to feed the 350 people in the infirmary, and the infirmary's medical personnel, and it was in days such as this that their reserve had to last. There were also the palace servants. He called General Komarov to the telephone—and he said the same thing. But still, couldn't they try to allocate something at least? . . .

On their own initiative, the footmen had already brought the staff itself hot tea and bread.

They changed places at the telephone. Even though it was the middle of the night, General Groten spoke confidently and overbearingly.

"What's happening there in Petrograd?"

City Governor Balk replied:

"It's all happened. Now, General Khabalov and his troops can't find anywhere to put themselves."

"I wonder," Groten persisted, "whether order has come to the city yet."

They began explaining to him in detail. His tone changed.

"Then I am asking you in the morning to inform me in a timely fashion whether the rebellious forces are heading for Tsarskoye Selo."

And something else. He asked them to enumerate what forces General Khabalov now had. Which cavalry? Magnificent, so send mounted gendarmes immediately to Tsarskoye Selo to perform reconnaissance service.

These new negotiations began as well. General Kazakov, commander of the gendarme division, argued that their barracks had been among the first occupied by rebels, in the morning, and the men and horses had not been fed for what would soon be twenty-four hours. The horses had not had frost nails driven into their horseshoes, and if they went twenty-five versts, they wouldn't be able to perform reconnaissance service.

But General Khabalov didn't care. Whichever way it was, he wasn't insisting on anything.

But the War Minister, supposedly the senior general there, took no part in all these disputes. He asked where there was another telephone and went there and in seclusion called Rodzyanko at the State Duma, warning him that troops had been sent to Petrograd from the front. In his last call from the Admiralty he had been in no hurry to report this news to the mutineers, so they wouldn't increase their resistance. But that had been a mistake. The State Duma could not be viewed as the government's enemy. Belyaev was now speaking with Rodzyanko quite graciously, even giving him a helpful precaution. He willingly reported that he was calling from the Winter Palace, where Khabalov's last troops now were. He had not been able to communicate the news about the troops earlier because of the firing on the War Minister's residence and having had to retreat from there. This news he was conveying now with embarrassment for the army, as if he himself were not the War Minister. Yes, and so: four infantry regiments and four cavalry, under the overall command of Lieutenant General Ivanov.

Meanwhile, the disheartened commander of the Guards cavalry regiment, whose squadrons were quartered in the Horse Guards manège, reported to Khabalov. Several delegates from the squadrons had come to him saying they didn't want to stay there without food or forage and were now leaving for their barracks outside Novgorod, and the officers could do what they liked.

These officers had also now gravitated as a cluster here, increasing Khabalov's staff just as his detachment kept decreasing.

But Khabalov didn't care. Come what may, no general's will could fix anything.

The entire detachment, from senior to junior, was listless and drowsy and waiting for a decision—and also waiting for food. No one said anything about it, but a dragging uncertainty was descending upon them.

And all of a sudden! Throughout the palace, throughout its rooms, corridors, and courtyards, the news flashed that the Tsar's brother had arrived, Grand Duke Mikhail Aleksandrovich! No one had announced this, but the news passed swiftly to everyone.

And animated everyone! And revitalized them! Their agonizing, aimless day-long tromping and shifting had tormented the men worse than their hunger. There was no soldier so foolish as to not understand that the cause was being lost by the hour, that the city had been taken over by the rebels— and the position of these men who were still loyal for some reason was becoming increasingly hopeless and pointless.

But now, the Tsar's brother himself had raced to them, to the Tsar's palace, in this difficult moment for the last loyal troops, in the middle of the night! To head up their battle to the death! And if necessary, to die with them for this sacred royal place.

Everyone took heart! They felt a new influx of patience, meaning, and courage coming from somewhere! They turned out to be exactly in the main place for which their entire oath and entire service had been taken!

The Tsar's brother was almost the same thing as the Tsar himself!

They waited for him to put them in formation, step forward, and speak to them! And also to feed them.

[1 6 4]

From the War Minister's residence, after the unsuccessful telegraph conversation with GHQ, Grand Duke Mikhail Aleksandrovich, accompanied by his secretary, Johnson, rode to the Warsaw Station, still counting on catching the last night train to Gatchina.

But between the Trinity Izmailovsky Cathedral and the station everything was rocking in a mutinous muddle. There were roaming crowds, noisy trucks driving around, people shooting, someone being dragged off for reprisal and beaten—the revolt had reached the Izmailovsky blocks, which up until nightfall had been quiet, when they had been able to drive by there calmly—but now that was out of the question. They wouldn't let him get as far as the station.

After a few attempts to wait them out and drive around, then attempts to break through directly onto the Gatchina highway—although fifty versts over a snowy nighttime road in the freezing cold was also a risk—the grand duke had to admit with vexation that he was stuck in Petrograd and would have to spend the night somewhere. Mikhail Aleksandrovich cursed the indefatigable Rodzyanko. (Then again, Natasha had said, Go!) He cursed his entire useless trip; obviously, he had only offended his brother, and now they were quarreling.

How he wished he could join Natasha now! But there was no avoiding spending the night somewhere in Petrograd. Johnson's place? That district was positively seething. To his administration on Galernaya? There, too, he had no idea what was going on in the dark narrow streets. In fact, it was dangerous now to drive down any street in Petrograd, even at night, even at high speed. They could be stopped. He didn't mind dying with dignity at the front, but he did mind falling into the rebels' filthy hands. And it wasn't every even close acquaintance you could disturb after one in the morning for a night's lodging. But here's what! The Palace Square area remained calmer. The thought flashed to go simply to the Winter Palace, although he had never had the habit of staying there.

Imagine his surprise when he found not a palace dark and dozing, with only servants, but a palace alit and filled with troops! A surprising night indeed.

With a light, easy step, Mikhail Aleksandrovich ascended to the third floor, to one of the offices—and was immediately run down by Komarov, the palace superintendent, who complained of the troops' forcible takeover and said they should be put out immediately, otherwise a battle would break out in the morning and the immortal treasures of the Winter Palace would suffer. The superintendent despaired of communicating with Mogilev, Tsarskoye Selo had not undertaken to give him precise instructions, and he certainly did not have sufficient power of his own. He was immeasurably glad at the grand duke's arrival (to whom, in any case, any decision had now been shifted). But it would be best to put them out.

As when faced with any important decision, Mikhail Aleksandrovich felt burdened. But what had been proposed seemed quite fair. Mikhail Aleksandrovich could not take responsibility for the destruction of the Winter Palace, that pearl of the Romanov dynasty, especially now as he anticipated reproaches from his brother, angered by his interference today in affairs of state. Indeed, what kind of misbegotten idea had this been to bring troops into the Winter Palace? As if the entire capital had converged on this one building and there was nowhere else to do battle. The uprising episode would be over in a few days, but what if the eternal Winter Palace were destroyed? No!

And what kind of conversations would there be afterward about the people being fired upon from the Romanovs' family home? The Winter Palace against the people? How clearly he saw the decision on clever Natasha's face. Natasha had always instilled in him that it was beautiful and noble to sympathize with a social movement. She had even received many of them in her own salon. Right now she would have categorically stated that there could be no discussion!

He saw Natasha's decision—and immediately felt better. My God, how he needed her at every moment! How he loved her, how he had loved her from the first moment she had appeared, the wife of his regimental officer, and immediately they had been drawn to each other, and she had become his lover long before she was his wife. What heat. What talent. What a mind!

He ordered Belyaev and Khabalov summoned to him.

They came. Small, beetle-browed, big-eared Belyaev, hunched and in a black mood since they'd seen each other two hours before. And the inexpressive Khabalov, heavy as lead, a slow-moving ruin.

Due to his great natural gentleness, Mikhail Aleksandrovich did not start scolding them for their failure. But he did indicate that they had made a mistake that had to be corrected immediately: take the troops away from the palace.

Two hours ago the grand duke might simply have been Belyaev's guest and drunk tea in his office, but General Belyaev did not derive from this any right to discuss or dispute the opinion of the Emperor's brother. It was not he but Zankevich who had thought of this Winter Palace; Belyaev had not considered this building more suitable than any other and he had no grounds to object.

And Khabalov, apparently, did not have the strength to stir his tongue at all or express any opinion whatsoever.

They left to give orders. The grand duke started preparing to get some sleep; the footman had already made a bed up for him in one of the rooms.

So—leaving. But where was there to go?

Someone suggested moving to the Peter and Paul Fortress.

True, the Peter and Paul Fortress had been theirs all day. There was a garrison there of several Kexholm companies, and they had not waged any battle whatsoever.

They called there. (The telephones were working without interruption; the Izmailovsky men were still holding the telephone exchange.) Baron Staël, assistant to the fortress commandant, came to the telephone. They asked him whether there was a chance of getting through to them without a battle, and what was happening in the fortress? Stal replied that the fortress was free, but on Trinity Square they could see armed mutinous crowds, and they had armored vehicles and barricades, apparently, on the Trinity Bridge.

Not gladdening.

The embankment as far as the Trinity Bridge and the Trinity Bridge itself, even the square beyond it—in half an hour their own intelligence would scope it out. But since an officer from the fortress had spoken, what was there to verify?

Getting through? They had sixty shells for the cannons and fifteen hundred men. But if they had not been able to come up with the spirit to attack during the day past, when they were not yet racked by hunger and lack of sleep, then now there wasn't the faintest hope of a surge in anyone.

A first-class fortress stood right there, across the Neva, a stone's throw away—but there was no enthusiasm for dragging themselves to it.

All the generals were tired, and everyone sank into despondency.

Where to? Back to the Admiralty. . . .

They roused the men. Told them to line up. As they were, unfed.

They roused and lined up the men, without waiting for the Emperor's radiant brother to emerge.

And commanded that they go out in the freezing cold and back the way they'd come.

The stars were shining and the frost was taking hold. The city had subsided and there was no shooting of any kind. The city had finally fallen asleep.

The soldiers grumbled: Where are they taking us now? Why did we let them? What kind of brainless commanders do we have?

The cavalry stepped quietly. The cannon wheels crunched over the snow.

In the cold and uncomfortable Admiralty, they sat down any which way. Their heads slumped into sleep.

Soon it would be morning.

*

* *

Neither crust nor roof for a serf.
A muzzle is all he's worth.

[1 6 5]

That evening, Himmer had set himself the goal of getting everywhere and seeing and knowing everything. At least one person in this grandiose muddle ought to know everything—so let that person be Himmer!

At first it seemed only proper for him to end up on the literary commission, and he agreed to it willingly. But never had he thought that he would be stuck there for over two hours. Whether it was a game of vanity, or that everyone was stupid by the dead of night after that day, or the ominousness of the military situation, but they wasted strength, time, and arguments on that half-page document as if they were composing a draft for Russia's new constitution. Himmer himself would have written this proclamation in fifteen minutes, and it would have been brilliant. As it was he kept trying to write in his own hand, sentence after sentence, and quickly, but they kept demanding that he account for what he had written and criticized it to pieces—and he kept having to start over from the beginning. When the slow-moving, respectable Peshekhonov and the obstinate, bullying Nakhamkes really dug their heels in against each other, Himmer put down the piece of paper and said, "Just a minute"—and he would run off.

He had to find out (a) what was going on at defense headquarters, (b) what was going on in the Duma Committee, and (c) what was going on at the center of the Tsarist troops.

This last he had no way to learn from anyone—but no one in the Tauride Palace knew this either. There was a constant crowd standing in front of the Military Commission. They weren't allowed inside, and benches had been placed like barricades—but even so, once Himmer pushed his way into the main room, he found it full of idle outsiders. Maslovsky kept turning the map of Petrograd profoundly and listening to all the out-of-turn statements and pressing questions. The rumor of Kronstadt going over was uncon-

firmed; the rumor of the Peter and Paul Fortress's capitulation was unconfirmed; but also unconfirmed was that the 170-something-th Regiment
was battling its way here from the Nikolaevsky Station. Whether it had not
arrived and disembarked at all or whether it had been been talked out of
fighting on Znamenskaya Square—this no one had been able to clarify.

On the other hand, the news of the Duma Committee itself had flooded
into the literary commission's meeting, and Himmer sincerely applauded it.
This was precisely the idea he had been pushing the last few days: force the
bourgeoisie to seize power! And here it had! Without that, it would be a
military insurrection, an urban mutiny; it would have no authority in society and would be easily put down. But now the franchised public had lent
legitimacy to the accomplished coup and taken on all responsibility for it!
That was what was needed! Now the status of Tsarist authority was greatly
weakened and the status of the revolution greatly strengthened!

However, another danger had arisen: the danger of the creation of a
bourgeois dictatorship. But that is exactly what democracy and the Soviet of
Workers' Deputies could prevent, advantageously located as it was behind
the Duma Committee's back and even on its own premises.

In the face of Tsarism, they had to force the bourgeoisie to seize power.
And behind the bourgeoisie's back make sure this power did not become real.

Himmer finally tore himself away from the unfortunate literary commission and left Shekhter to retype the proclamation—and he, Sokolov, and
Nakhamkes raced to the session of the Soviet, which was still ongoing, although it was now past two in the morning. The Soviet's work was in full
swing! But there were already signs of disintegration. There were no longer
people sitting on all the chairs or all the benches; some were standing talking and showing their impatience. Outsiders had seeped into the room, and
they weren't keeping to the walls but moving on the assembly and mixing
with the deputies. Everyone by now was having a hard time understanding
one another and keeping to their feet.

For the last hour, it turned out, a debate had been under way as to
whether Soviet members should or shouldn't join the State Duma's Provisional Committee. There was Kerensky's viewpoint and Chkheidze's
viewpoint (although Kerensky was no longer showing up at the Soviet
and Chkheidze was present only from time to time). According to Kerensky, they should definitely join (he was already in full swing there). Chkheidze thought that the organ of the Progressive Bloc should not be adorned
with their presence and sanctified with the authority of social democracy;
he himself had joined this Committee only until nightfall, until the appeal
to the Soviet.

Finally, after their exhausting debates, they were inclining to say that
they should join. Join and make sure that not a single important action was
undertaken without the Soviet of Workers' Deputies, that they did not push
through remnants of Tsarism behind the backs of the mutinous people.

Now the Soviet could disperse or consider itself dispersed, but it fell to the Executive Committee to rage. First, Himmer stated (vying with Sokolov) that they were just about to bring the proclamation and it had to be discussed. Second, the question had arisen of where to print it. Third, an even more general question, that the Soviet of Deputies could not exist and act without having its own newspaper. Petersburg had been without the printed word for three days and needed to get its first information from the hands of democracy.

But then an even broader question arose: What about other newspapers? Debates had heated up already on this issue, and some sat back down. Sokolov defended the principle of a free press and said that the faster normal conditions of life were restored, the firmer the revolution would stand. But Nakhamkes spoke cumbersomely about how premature and dangerous it would be to give freedom to all the press; this could lead to Black Hundred and counterrevolutionary propaganda in print.

The Executive Committee passed his proposal to allow the issuing of newspapers only depending on their orientation.

This vote transported Himmer! What was ravishing here was the fact that none of those who voted had had a single moment's doubt as to whether the Soviet of Workers' Deputies should decide on the freedom of newspapers. It never occurred to anyone, no one uttered a peep about how this question should be conceded to the authority of the Duma Committee!

This was an act in defense of the revolution, and it could not be left to a government from the Duma wing! There wasn't even any need to bring it to its attention.

Who were the press workers going to obey if not the Soviet? They had to appoint a commissar for the printing presses—and take them into their own hands. Immediately nominated and recognized as commissar for the printing presses was paunchy Bonch-Bruevich, who was wearing a cartridge belt, both to give himself a military look and to tuck up his belly. He declared that the printing press for the *Kopeika* newspaper had already been seized and he was going there right now—and would print the proclamation. (They listened to the proclamation one time through yawning and passed it without debate or vote.)

Peshekhonov butted in with a philistine objection that it was impermissible to seize private printing presses—and he was laughed at and dismissed by everyone.

Himmer started assembling others of like mind about how to seize control of the editorial office of the Soviet's newspaper in preparation and create their own majority there.

It was already after three in the morning, but the session of the Executive Committee or even the full Soviet had not ended, and things were unraveling into a multivoiced, chaotic discussion among random people that seemingly could not end now in any sane way unless a shell exploded in the cupola of the Tauride Palace. They were so carried away, it was as if the entire fate of the revolution was already assured and all that remained was to decide the republic's future direction.

Once again Himmer ran off to the Military Commission for news and again made his way through the sentries and the bench barricades—but he found the same Maslovsky and Lieutenant Filippovsky; the well-known engineer Obodovsky showed up, too, nervous from the confusion, and found the same scene of total ignorance of the situation, lack of planning, lack of an apparatus, and lack of a defense, not a single military unit at their disposal, and only rumors that regiments were on the move to Petrograd from Oranienbaum and Tsarskoye Selo. No one knew what kind or for what purpose, but more than likely for suppression. The rumor started up again about the Peter and Paul Fortress, that they were calling from there and feeling out how they might surrender to the State Duma.

Here is where the State Duma's status helped, and Rodzyanko helped! Excellent!

Actually, Himmer no longer feared the Peter and Paul Fortress or those regiments. Although that night the Tauride Palace had apparently been holding on by a thread, directly in front there were a few fires, a few puffing military vehicles, and a couple of untended cannons. Nothing to stand up to a single organized company. But the night was passing and Khabalov had not sent such a company.

Someone brought a pot of cutlets, without forks, and some white bread to the Military Commission. Himmer found himself a seat as well.

[166]

Near Rodzyanko's office there was a semicircular room with upholstered furniture known as Volkonsky's office, after the former vice president; lately it had not been an office and had been used for private conversations and small meetings.

It was very convenient for conversations but for spending the night not at all. It didn't have a single large sofa. Squirming on a small one was Konovalov; Milyukov removed his boots and lay down on the sole table there, on his own fur coat (all the Duma deputies had retrieved their outerwear from the coatroom; with such a throng, it was dangerous to leave anything there)—and they were already asleep. That Konovalov was sleeping was nothing to be surprised at. A healthy, solid, not old man, he moreover had always had a trace of somnolence about him, even when he was working in earnest. But it was amazing that Milyukov had fallen asleep so swiftly and soundly. You would think the Progressive Bloc's leader wouldn't be able to sleep on a night like this, that his thoughts, plans, or regrets should be tearing him apart, or that he should have been handing out instructions to his supporters—but here he was, showing just how much his nerves were not yet frayed, sleeping in an uncomfortable position, not even turning over, and snoring evenly and confidently.

The room's overhead light was on.

How many years had the leading Duma deputies worked together, shared sessions, conversations, lunches, and dinners, but they had never seen each other in their simple everyday guise, with loosened ties, or having removed their boots, in just socks, or finding out who snored and who didn't.

Shulgin and Shingarev, having discussed the fact that it was too far for them to go for just half a night, far over to the Petersburg side, to Monet-naya, and also under fire, nonetheless had missed their chance to grab a sofa or curved-backed loveseat, as Kerensky had in one of the rooms. Shingarev lay down on the floor somewhere, on a bed of unneeded papers; manners had simplified in the one day. But Shulgin couldn't find a place for himself and had to spend the night sitting up, in an upholstered chair at a small oval table.

In the next chair sat the most agreeable neighbor, Vasili Alekseevich Maklakov. He did not have that far to go to get home, but he, too, for some reason had stayed at the Tauride Palace.

There was something about this moment—a paradox, a conundrum, an alarming anticipation—that robbed them of any desire to go home to their own bed, but kept them here to observe, think, and get a better sense of it all. The day's excitement was still rocking inside them so that without great effort they sat there, even though it was two hours after midnight.

What was also good was that seemingly no one could break in here, into this room. The Duma had experienced the surge of these masses, or mugs, or rabble for just a few hours, and now in their own Duma halls they had already come to view with joy a familiar Duma face as a fellow countryman on foreign soil.

Who could fail to understand that the most extraordinary day in their life had just passed! It still had to be made sense of and packaged. Actually, Shulgin, not without malevolent pleasure toward himself as well, warned:

"Mark my words, Vasili Alekseich, this is our first night of discomfort, but far from our last."

Maklakov with his appealing smile:

"What aim could be nobler than observing people's ways?"

This was not just a joke; Shulgin felt this as well. Yes! Never mind this sitting position, what he really wanted was to observe. And think lofty thoughts. Somehow watch everything going on from a very very high summit. After all, this was that joyous push, that jump, which for some reason, despite all considerations of safety, our heart has always thirsted for.

He reminded him:

"Yes, that was your thesis, after all: if our authority can't become thought, let thought become our authority!"

Indeed, Maklakov had many theses. He had this one, too, published in *The Russian Gazette*: When that longed-for moment comes when we settle up with *Him*! For the past few months, Maklakov had not tried very hard to conceal that he'd had prior knowledge of the plan to kill Rasputin and had himself even given Yusupov the lead bludgeon from his advocatory collection. Somehow this had not been viewed as breaking the law.

Maklakov, with his deep and attentive gaze, greeted that sentence with seeming surprise. That was his?

He replied quietly and clearly—they were alone talking in the room— which made his soft "r" even more distinct each time:

"Yes, but I find the sword repugnant. I don't want the sword. After all, we have always wanted to avoid revolution. This is why we tried to bring down the government, in order to avoid revolution. And now . . ."

But Shulgin was transported by a romantic readiness:

"First of all, this isn't a revolution yet. We'll see about that. But if it has happened—so be it! An unintended path, an unexpected turn—but therein lies history! We love to read about the great events of centuries past. Why don't we love to live through them ourselves? Consider it from the opposite direction. After the retreat of 1915, we all said that a government could not be forgiven *this*! Which was why we all joined the Bloc. A government that managed to retreat to Kovno and Baranovichi and allowed panic to ensue even in Riga and Kiev—what right did it have to remain in power? Here it's been removed in a single blow. And we're even required to rejoice. Even if the new government isn't led by *those invested with the people's trust*—it will no longer be in its former disgrace, no! We never had the strength to break this strap that was choking us—and suddenly, in one day, they've all run away?"

"How can I put it . . ." Maklakov said slowly. No argument had ever been able to draw him to a single side; he had always maintained a cool balance and paid attention to opposing arguments. "We also have to understand what direction we're going in and whether we're continuing Russia's cause. After all, wasn't the Bloc's slogan 'Everything for the war'? That hasn't been rescinded, has it? And today, all that happened—was that for the war? Or for the Germans? If our factories and plants start being smashed now, that's the end of our defense and the war."

The day's stormy events seemed to have left Maklakov on the sidelines. He didn't speak at the private meeting or join the Duma Committee. The gradual handover of power taking place still hadn't drawn him into its vortex, although he was the undisputed principal candidate for minister of justice. For now, though, he could ponder aloofly and freely:

"The Russian people are magnificent material. In capable hands. But left to their own devices, they can be savages. How can we learn to correct our shortcomings without destroying the edifice of state itself?"

"I beg your pardon!" Shulgin exclaimed. "Who on earth is laying a finger on the entire edifice of state? It is unshakable for all time! This is just a Petrograd episode, and in two days' time things will return to normal. There are troops on their way from the front, aren't there?"

"But the Duma is at the head of the rebellion," Maklakov pointed out.

"Well, not at the head! We're at the head of popular trust. Although"—he laughed and corrected himself—"they've stolen all the silver spoons in the buffet. Yes, the Russian people have to be in good hands. But the monarchy constitutes those hands."

"The monarchy runs the country best, yes. But a parliamentary system corresponds better to society's mood. Autocracy is equipped for storms. But in peaceful times it degenerates. Obviously and inevitably."

"Yes, there's no time to lose," Shulgin agreed in his own way. "The central will must be strengthened, otherwise it might fly off in all directions. Someone has to think and act lightning fast. Force them to obey. But where is that someone?" He sighed.

They didn't know anyone like that. Milyukov? It was even ridiculous to say, looking at him sleeping, without his spectacles.

Maklakov looked at the carpet under his feet, searching in the patterns:

"In troubled times, people have come forward out of vanity, envy, and spite. Out of the inability to be fair. Truly great men, that is, those who see Russia farther than others, they take little part in events such as these. Any party struggle cures men of being fair."

What was this anyway, nearly three in the morning and nowhere to sleep— not that they felt like sleeping. Their insomnia left them feeling useless.

Maklakov added, half-audibly:

"We all felt we were approaching some sort of Rubicon. And now we have. And if Russia starts to totter, no power can stop it. . . ."

How much worse armchairs were than side chairs, they had never understood. You can move three or four chairs together and then you have a bed. But you can never make a bed out of the best armchairs; the arms get in the way.

But don't we sometimes wait to change trains and sleep sitting up? They had to learn to sleep in an armchair as well. The next day was hardly likely to be calmer than this.

Maklakov weighed this rather gloomily:

"What is most dangerous is that from the very first steps we have not been leading events. And where are they heading? If the soldiers don't return to barracks, what can we do with them?"

And fitting his head to the back of his armchair:

"We brought Acheron into the battle, and by doing so, we ourselves will be changed."

[1 6 7]

They wouldn't let the old general sleep, though! At about two in the morning, the adjutant woke Nikolai Iudovich in his train car to say that the Emperor was suddenly leaving Mogilev and was already on his train and had summoned him.

What else had happened? Was something amiss? He dressed and belted up with shaking hands.

Superiors always did this. They summoned you because it was more convenient for them. Ivanov, too, would awaken his subordinates at five in the morning like this. The Emperor was on his train but the train wasn't moving, so he'd summoned him.

The imperial train was dark inside, without a single light, its wide windows tightly curtained. There was no one close on the platform. Only the convoy sentries, carrying daggers and wearing shaggy black fur hats.

No, the Emperor had urgent business for the summoned adjutant general. A new telegram had just arrived from Khabalov saying that the majority of Petrograd units had refused to fight the rebels and some were even fraternizing with them, turning their weapons against troops loyal to His Majesty. Now the capital was nearly entirely in rebel hands and they had converged to defend the Winter Palace as a last bastion.

(Oh ho! Oh ho! Things had gone that far! . . . Why should Ivanov go now, and where? . . . What District was he supposed to command?)

Every time you force yourself to get up, your nature resists what they want to foist on you. Gradually, though, your spirits overcome your nighttime indolence, and you begin to figure out what you need to do.

You needed, through some circumlocution, to obtain the Emperor's consent for not overly decisive actions. Iudovich saw he could present the matter this way: the military units would be arriving from different places. In troop trains they were vulnerable and unprepared for battle. Deploying and coordinating them correctly would take time; they should be held at the farthest ring, not brought into the capital right away. This mode of action had the advantage that excessive bloodshed could be avoided and internecine strife would not begin prematurely.

The Emperor had always been in favor of peaceableness, something he and Ivanov agreed on. And here he'd been cheerful since evening because he was already on the train and on his way to Tsarskoye. Without arguing, somewhat distractedly, he responded: "Yes, of course."

This was all Iudovich needed! This "yes, of course" he could now deploy for versts and days of peaceable actions. He had the right to interpret this "yes, of course" as the main course of action. Not only that, besides Petrograd, his expedition had another goal: to protect Tsarskoye Selo, the Empress, and their most august children from the threat of rebellious troops.

The Emperor's train was not pulling out soon, the Emperor spoke readily, and the general sat with him for a long time. They talked about how all
this would gradually get settled. (It was not easy for Iudovich to imagine
how, if the capital was in the rebels' hands, but they didn't say exactly *how*.)
Nikolai Iudovich set out the various difficulties entailed by the troops' possible unreliability, by strikes, and by food supplies in the capital. Obviously
he needed the ministers to carry out his requests without delay.

The Emperor livened up and even seized on this. Both he and General
Alekseev had wanted to have a dictator, a single firm authority in the rear.
So here's what:

"Tell General Alekseev in the morning to telegraph the Prime Minister
to say that all your demands must be carried out by the Council of Ministers
immediately and without question."

The Emperor had overdone it; Iudovich had not thought that far, nor did
he want to. It had taken the old man's breath away: he was becoming not
only commander-in-chief of the Petrograd District but Supreme Dictator of
all Russia? No, Nikolai Iudovich had not asked for such an honor in troubled circumstances. He was even more frightened.

"But how will General Alekseev believe me?"

"He will!"

"Your Imperial Majesty, you know I have served as an officer honestly
and without self-interest for forty-seven and a half years . . ."

But it was done. The appointment was irrevocable.

In parting, the Emperor suggested that tomorrow morning he and the
general see each other again in Tsarskoye Selo (where the general would arrive today?).

Iudovich did not object that he might not make it that soon . . .

[1 6 8]

But even at four o'clock in the morning, it was amazing, the Executive
Committee had not become master in the Soviet's rooms. Even though the
general session had ended long since, everyone was standing around, droning, refusing to disperse—a cluster of soldiers, and workers who weren't
workers but district representatives, or simply those who planned to spend
the night here—making it impossible for the Executive Committee to meet
and speak frankly. Heavy with insomnia and exhaustion, already gnawed by
unsated appetite, their heads somber, they wandered around, not all of
them, but the Executive Committee's remains. Where else could they set
up to meet?

They dragged along in an awkward file. Chkheidze was shuffling. This
day had been too much for him; never a Caucasus eagle, he was, besides,
already past fifty. This day had fortified him as the triumphant patriarch,

here his flock had gathered in multitudes, but what exactly they had been doing, deciding, and resolving—he, happy and worn out, could only nod or shake his head, I agree or I don't know. Basically, he agreed with everything done in the Soviet and did not agree with anything that was done in the Duma Committee. It was a feast for him to preside in the Soviet, and here he was being led by the arm for the same thing.

In the Cupola Hall, a machine was pounding away, loading cartridge belts. The cartridges lay in heaps.

The rooms of the Duma wing were locked one after the other and the keys inserted from the inside.

The Ekaterininsky Hall looked like one big bedroom. On the silk-upholstered benches and on the floor lay hundreds of soldiers, their heads resting on their rifles, pouches, fur hats, and arms. There was snow melt under their boots. Or this could have been a large field where warriors, caught at night in a crossing march, had collapsed without even posting sentries.

But sound the alarm and these warriors would not be able to assume any kind of formation.

The worn-out Executive Committee members dragged themselves up the stairs to set up in the session hall galleries. But there, it turned out, in the adjoining rooms, they were holding arrested policemen and gendarmes, and the watch would not allow even the members of the Executive Committee to pass.

So should they just go to the big meeting hall?

Yes. There were no obstacles here.

In the White Hall, which had heard so many shattering speeches, where public Russia's agitation had rolled out, which had thundered with so much applause and driven correspondents' pencils along at such a rate, there was now almost no light, it having been sensibly turned off by duty officers, only the feeble, solitary lights over the doors. The hall had sent its seething on to the capital and was itself resting. Individual figures were resting here and there, their silhouettes visible against the amphitheater's chairs. Someone lay in the sloping aisles. And someone else lay at the bottom of the boxes. You couldn't drive them away, either.

But one box, the correspondents', remained free. The Executive Committee entered it, arranged the chairs more comfortably, and began their session.

Besides the firecracker Himmer, portly Nakhamkes, and sturdy Shlyapnikov, there apparently wasn't a member left who could have withstood this new session. Chkheidze stumbled in, sat down—and nodded off.

Nonetheless, the session reconvened.

But now looming over them on the wall, mockingly, behind the President's rostrum, in an expensive, massive frame with a wreath, was a Repin portrait of the Tsar twice life-size! Right now, in this sleepy nighttime moment, when the entire revolutionary people were prostrate with weariness, its last wakeful Executive Committee was seemingly observed by the equally wakeful, irritating Tsar with the slantwise ribbon across his uniform shoulder. Granted, in a respectfully idiotic pose, toes turned out, a service cap in his lowered hand, as if he had come to report and not inspect.

Nonetheless, it was terribly irritating. The very same Tsarist portrait about which Chkheidze had once exclaimed to the Duma deputies, "There he is, looking at you with his insane eyes!" No, the Tsar's eyes were not insane, they were not menacing, and not even majestic, but—agaze. Nevertheless, it had to be removed immediately. It was intolerable!

Shlyapnikov insisted on not delaying and immediately bringing onto the Executive Committee representatives from the parties by name. Of the Bolsheviks now he immediately dictated: Molotov, Shutko . . .

The others objected. Give us a chance to think! In any case, the Mensheviks, SRs, the Bund—they have yet to name theirs. . . .

No, they couldn't finish the discussion. They didn't have the strength and abandoned it until tomorrow.

But this was urgent. They had to appoint district commissars so that in the morning . . . They started naming candidates for commissar. Shlyapnikov himself volunteered for the Vyborg side, they had thought to appoint Peshekhonov to the Petersburg side since he lived there, although he had gone off somewhere. But they didn't have the memory, imagination, strength, or tongues for all the districts. They stumbled. So what, should they accept the Tsarist division of police stations? Well, there was no sense changing them in haste.

Shlyapnikov drove on for the immediate arming of Petrograd's workers.

They argued whether to have a workers' militia at each factory or district-based musters of armed workers.

However, Shlyapnikov got his way: they agreed to arm one-tenth of the workers. They assigned this to him.

While they were discussing and debating—from all ends of the hall, figures began converging on their box—clumsy, sleepy soldier mugs. What's this chit-chat about?

You couldn't talk in front of them. All right, we're finishing up anyway.

And so, in this famed hall, the chandeliers' light passed into deep gloom, the debates to the journalists' box, the public galleries to prisoners' cells, the self-confident daytime Duma deputies to nighttime soldier specters.

Some left. But Himmer threw his heavy quilted coat on the floor of the State Council box—and lay down there.

Meanwhile, the President of the very same State Council was sitting, a prisoner, across the corridor—in the ministerial pavilion.

At five in the morning the Duma hall fell dark and quiet.

But its glass ceiling would start to whiten very soon.

The ceiling that had caved in exactly ten years before.

[1 6 9]

SCREEN

Blunt-nosed, six-storied, with a rounded roof, the Astoria,
some of its windows lit,
how visible it is going past the monument to Nikolai I
down Voznesensky Prospect, resting right on the Admiralty's
  tower.
Night. Streetlamps here and there.
Almost no one on the square in the half-dark. Only clusters
  conferring.

Closer.
  Clusters of soldiers talking among themselves
  with a backward glance,
  a quick glance back at the Astoria.
  Clearly the rabble is not all from the same unit. Some have
    rifles, some sticks.
  And five or so sailors.
  They were staring at the hotel.
  In some rows the windows are lit, in some dark.
  The lower shop windows are all dark.
  Another backward glance.
  = A deserted, half-dark square.
  Only nervous clusters of soldiers
  facing both Astoria facades.
  You're just what we need!
  And the signal! Hands wave!
an abrupt two-fingered whistle!
  And they rush it from both sides of the corner!
  From wherever,
  all with rifles, sticks, and crowbars!
  And the broad windows more than twice a man's height, the top
    a semicircle — not quite windows and not quite doors —
  but entire windows and behind them it's hard to see without any
    light. What's there?
  Well, show us how you break? And with the rifle butt!
Smash!
  Some parts broke, some didn't, a dark ragged hole,
  but all the glass didn't succumb right away. That's not how glass
    gets broken, more like plywood.
  The same at another spot!

Smash! Crash!

    The same at a third! Several hands at it.

    Ripping out holes, not a passage or an opening. Watch out or
        you'll cut yourself.

    They piled on at that window and hit it with whatever came to
        hand.

    But if you turn a bayonet-less rifle around and grab the barrel,
        and then the butt reaches high,

    and does its damage there. What a hole!

    Someone shot a bullet in the air!

A shot.

    But the hole was too small.

The shot

    was more for fun.

    But there it was dark.

    Someone crawled through and they dragged something out of
        the darkness,

    dragged—something heavy—outside.

    A hefty tub with an exotic little tree.

    They broke its trunk on the jagged edges of the glass—

    and threw the tub on the pavement, more for a joke.

    Big deal! Nothing to rummage in here.

    The smarter ones went left, ran left,

    past one more broken window,

    past another,

    on and on!

    The soldiery rushes to get ahead. Maybe there is enough for all
        here, and maybe there isn't, and whoever is in front has a
        better chance!

    The door! Here it is. You can't mix that up. This is where the
        bigshots go! Locked.

    They piled on, no getting in.

    Smash it! With your butts! Your sticks! Hey, sailors!

Bash! Crack!

    The breaks are too small, no crawling through.

    Bring your butts here, tear it apart! Go! Go!

Crack! Crash!

    The eye could now see their prosperity, there was light, but the
        hand couldn't reach—another door, locked!

= But inside a general was running around waving his arms!

    Around the black brim of the general's cap, in gold letters:
        "Astoria"!

    Right away, he said, I'll open it right away, just don't smash it, for
        God's sake!

"But why are you locked up?"
"Why are you all locked up in there, you scum?"
He opened one half of the door. They nearly got crushed in the
    passage, shoving each other, trying to be first.
"Who is it's staying here?"
"Who is it's staying here? Offhitsers?"
It's light here!
The general spread his arms in front of the staircase, gasping for
    breath.
*"Gentlemen officers are staying here. All kinds of gen-
    tlemen. Come to your senses, gentlemen soldiers!
    They're asleep, you see. Come in the morning."*
"Ha ha ha ha! . . . Ha ha ha ha! In the morning?"
*"We'll tug at their beds! We'll drag their little bodies
    all gentle!"*
"Got young ladies with 'em, I bet?"
And they ran forward, but coming at them is another whole
    gang! Other soldiers! Sailors, too! And with weapons! And
    coming straight at us!
About to run straight into each other! So the whole gang stopped.
And that oncoming gang, it stopped.
One of ours waved a rifle—and one waved there, matching.
They figured it out!
"It's a mirror the whole wall long, don't be afraid!"
Hearty laughter.
"Look, how they live!"
= But it was the sailors, the quickest of the lot, who had the idea
    first and were already up the stairs like a shot!
Up! Up there, where someone was getting away in what looked
    to be an officer's uniform.
"Get 'em! Get the gold epaulets!"
The soldiers went up in a pack. There! Six floors. Plenty of room
    for having a good old time!
= But the sharpest of them, here, downstairs, set to that servant:
*"And the wine, where d'you keep it? The wine! Show
    us the wine!"*

* * *

BAD LIFE, GET OUT!
GOOD LIFE, COME ON IN!

* * *

[1 7 0]

"Your Imperial Highness! Your Imperial Highness, wake up!"

The voice was so kind, so homey—rather than rouse him he practically entered into his dream. But the warm huskiness repeated and repeated—and finally made him wake up. This old, gray-haired, Winter Palace footman, with luxurious, flowing side-whiskers, who had long since grown accustomed to the idea of no one from the Tsar's family spending the night here, instead of the joy of not disturbing the high-born guest's sleep, had decided to enter the room and lean over the bed.

"Your Imperial Highness! The palace has become dangerous. After the troops left, some gangs tried to break through different doors a few times. Only the locks are holding them back. What forces do we have to fight them off?"

The cold and nasty waking got through to Mikhail. Now this he had not expected! That gangs would invade the palace. What gangs could there be in the capital?

"Gangs from where?"

"God knows where." The footman was distressed. "A few have gathered up and gone wild. Soldiers, too. And all kinds of rabble. I suppose they know how many treasures we have here. What cellars."

Now fully awake, stretched out on his back, Mikhail lay in satin, in an alcove. Between the parted curtains he could vaguely see the footman's large head—there, behind him, some small light on the table, a candle, he hadn't dared light a lamp.

But why should Mikhail, barely out of sleep, be supposed to understand what he was to do with the doors or how to protect himself? This kind of guard should have been provided for by someone, and what about General Komarov?

"Oh, my God, Your Imperial Highness!"—the footman—whom Mikhail remembered from childhood, he had been at the Gatchina palace at one time, and at the Anichkov, only he forgot his name—clucked in the same warm, muffled, and homey voice of a nanny. "Please do not think I am burdening you with this concern. I took it upon myself to interrupt your sleep only in alarm over your safety. You see, we have no armed guard and we're all old men. Tonight they broke into the Mariinsky Palace. Who is to prevent them from breaking in here? They might have done so already except they think, well, there are troops here now."

Mikhail turned quickly.

"The Mariinsky? When?"

"Oh, it was after midnight. They called us."

"So . . ." And he himself had just been meeting there! "And the Council of Ministers?"

"I can't know, Your Imperial Highness. Probably they were saved by having dispersed."

And still Mikhail did not fully understand! The old man added:

"You cannot stay in the palace now, Your Imperial Highness. They'll break in and find you. It is more dangerous for you here than anywhere else. You need to . . . before dawn . . . move . . . go . . . They'll recognize you by daylight."

Only now did the full bitterness of it fill his roused chest and awakened head: flee? He was supposed to flee his family roof at night, right now, in secret and in haste?

Mikhail's bed had been made up for him on the third floor, next to his father's inviolable bedroom where he had lived when he was the heir—but he had not spent a day here since that crushing day when Mikhail's grandfather—already missing a leg and spilling blood on the marble of the stairs and the parquet floors—was barely carried to the first couch, for the last minutes of his life.

After that, his father had had to hide in Gatchina from new attempts on his life. He had fled.

In the twenty-three years of his reign, his brother had barely lived in this palace; he had fled to Tsarskoye, fled to Peterhof.

And here Mikhail, who had come for just the night, was being suggested the same thing: flee.

How easy to arise in the night at the battle alarm—and immediately gallop off into the darkness, in strict regimental formation. But what torture and pain it was when you were woken up to a trembling candle to be driven out of your family home!

Mikhail lay on his back as if pinned, unable to rise, not even his head, but he understood more and more clearly.

Now it was so clear to him. Yes, he had been naïve to come to the Winter Palace to sleep. He had placed himself in danger of brigandage.

Sleep in palaces as if time had not passed?

Had he been sitting with Natasha now at Gatchina, he would know no distress. Oh, Rodzyanko, big-headed Rodzyanko! He'd lured him into an ambush! Not only had he summoned him into this chaos, he'd also abandoned him without protection. After all, his vehicle was allowed anywhere and could have taken him to the train station. And now, here? . . .

Danger from a drunken, dissolute gang was humiliating, one could not fight them as equals and surrounded by combat friends. No matter what he did, no matter what action he took, there would still be disgrace, insult, and loss. Mikhail wasn't afraid of a galloping German grenadier, but a resentful Russian foot soldier seemed terrible. He felt that.

But what could he do? He drew himself up. Drive through the city now? That was hardly safer than remaining in the palace. A motorcar would have no protection at all against that kind of gang.

Where to then? Headquarters, on Galernaya? Also too well-known a place. To the home of his adjutant, Count Vorontsov? Not close.

So there was nothing he could do? There was no solution at all?

Gentle-faced, in his nightshirt, the grand duke looked at the old footman with distraught astonishment.

Oh, he had already thought it all through, the old man. His Imperial Highness could neither drive nor walk through the city; it was dangerous in either case. But perhaps he could think of some quite reliable family very close to the palace? Best of all would be on Millionnaya, because the exit there was good.

If he hadn't said "on Millionnaya," Mikhail might not have grasped the idea and his thoughts would have long wandered. But no sooner had he let his mind go from house to house down Millionnaya than he remembered: his own Horse Guard, Colonel Prince Putyatin, the palace's equerry! No. 12.

The old man rejoiced and went to telephone and wake up Johnson the secretary, while he asked the grand duke to dress, and if possible, by candle-light. Right now they should not turn on the overhead light in the outer rooms and attract attention; let the palace appear to sleep.

The candle remained in its saucer on the wall, and in the unaccustomed lighting of the large palace room, Mikhail dressed, trembling slightly.

By candlelight, everything looked different: the sculpting of the ceiling, the curtains, the antique furniture—as it had in the early part of the last century, under his great-grandfather. It breathed that age and the age before that even. Mikhail did not even suspect how deeply he felt this connection to the dynastic nest; although now, today, he had immediately refused to allow troops to set up here—because this was not a place for battle. This palace was a treasure of memories.

Actually, if the troops had remained, then might he not have had to flee?

Poor men, where did they wander off to? Perhaps he should have kept them?

The footman returned, encouraged. He had awakened Princess Puty-atina by telephone. The prince himself was not there, he was at the front, but the princess was proud to welcome His Imperial Highness and would stay awake in anticipation of his arrival.

The secretary had already risen and would join them in a moment. Awaken anyone else?

"Your Imperial Highness"—the footman's voice trembled—"if you will entrust me with your exit, then there is no need to initiate anyone else. One Hermitage guard and the Hermitage theater's doorkeeper will also know. You will exit onto Millionnaya just a few buildings from no. 12. You could give instructions to walk through the second floor; I could open all the empty halls on the formal side for you, but that would take longer. You could also go through the infirmary."

"Fine, my dear man, lead me through the infirmary. And from there as you know."

The footman dropped in gratitude to the grand duke's hand. He was nearly sobbing, which only doubled the bitterness in Mikhail's heart. Yet again it was conveyed to him that he was not simply changing his place of lodging and taking cover for a few hours but doing something important and irrevocable that his mind could not grasp.

The old man brought along another candle fitted into a lamp. But the one here he extinguished as he exited.

He went in front and held the lamp up so that the sphere of the shuddering light would spread more widely.

Mikhail walked a couple of steps to the side and back of him.

And behind him was Johnson.

They took the Admiralty side of the third floor and reached a corner stairway, where dim lamps were lit. They descended to the second. And walked through the entire enfilade given over for an infirmary, with windows on the square.

This infirmary had been opened by Aleksandra Fyodorovna in the very first days of the war and had been here ever since. Many hundreds of wounded men had passed through it.

The footman lowered his lantern and carried it near his knee. Nightlights burned here and there on the walls and by the duty nurses' small tables. The patients were asleep and no one was tossing and turning; there were no freshly gravely wounded men because there had not been major battles for a long time and the long-term patients had nearly finished their treatment. One or two who got up here and there did see the young general's passage; they may have been surprised, but they didn't recognize him. The nurses did, apparently.

Passing through the infirmary halls helped ease his heart's agonizing pang of farewell. Here we all are, together, Russians forged by a single war and the single chain of bandaged wounds. We are all on the same side. And those gangs—we are not those gangs.

The halls had such high ceilings that the nightlights didn't help you see the ceilings from below. There had not been balls here for many years, but Mikhail had seen them as a young man and remembered. In those days, the walls had been decorated with branches of tropical trees and flowers from the Tsar's hothouses. Along the flights of stairs and the mirrored walls rows of palms would be set out and all this flooded with the shimmer of chandeliers and candelabras—and the colorful uniforms, embroidered with gold and silver, were brilliant, as were the women's priceless diadems and necklaces. Everything always opened with a polonaise. And only here, the only place except for Poland, did they dance a quick mazurka.

All that had vanished long ago—all the spinning, all the people, and all the lights had gone out—and now even the night lamps remained behind them. From the last infirmary room the old man unlocked the door and they crossed the covered bridge to the Hermitage. And once again he raised his lantern, lighting the way.

Lighting the Petersburg views—the gallery hung with views of old Petersburg in gold frames. Old Petersburg.

The windows of the hanging garden flashed by, the defenseless winter jasmine and lilac drifted with snow.

And another bridge-passage, another threshold of parting, and they crossed into the New Hermitage.

Again a fateful presentiment entwined with and squeezed his heart. Why couldn't he return in a week in the full light of day and pass through confidently, his spurs jangling?

But the sense was of farewell. Even in the total silence, his spurs jangled just a little.

Now they were walking through the picture galleries. As they went, and to the lantern's light, he could not see a single one properly, let alone remember; Mikhail mixed up these halls and all he could see on the walls were huge still-lifes, animals, stalls with game, fish, fruits, vegetables—an outsized, monumental, screaming abundance that does not at all gladden a pinched soul.

In the middle of the halls were porphyry vases and porphyry floor lamps.

With his two free hands Mikhail covered his face and made a washing gesture.

Each new room, each row of paintings crammed with dead game, dead fish, and insensible fruits blocked out the dear domestic part of the palace he'd left, where his unforgettable father had lived and where his mother now no longer returned.

And he wondered why had they collected all this. Why hadn't they lived more simply?

In a hall at the curve of the building were coins and medals, coins and medals . . .

They started through a gallery that could not be confused with anything else: the loggias of Raphael.

The raised lantern floated up ahead—the old man's arm had not grown numb—as if purposely showing the biblical scenes on the walls.

Mikhail turned to check on Johnson—and saw his own menacing shadow floating through the loggias, like the vision of yet another ancestor to yet another descendant.

But he had to keep going, relentlessly. Carrying this shadow, for the edification of he knew not whom.

They made one more turn, into the foyer of the Hermitage theater, across the long, glassed-in passage over the snowy Winter Channel, French windows to the floor.

Outside, a distant fire was reflected across the sky.

The loyal old man halted and turned.

"Your Imperial Highness! If we now leave by the service stairs, we will be in the courtyard, but that only has access to the embankment and you would have to double back, and it's far. But take this corridor and go through the Preobrazhensky barracks and you will come directly out on Millionnaya, and there you have another four buildings or so and to cross only Moshkov Lane. What would you have?"

What doubt? Wasn't what he meant by this to ask whether the grand duke was afraid of the Preobrazhensky Guards?

"Will you have me escort you through the barracks?"

"No need," Mikhail answered quietly.

The Preobrazhensky are our men.

He suddenly put one arm around the old man, who began to sob and caught his hand to kiss it.

This sobbing of the footman tore through the last film of consciousness. What had happened?

Had he sensibly taken cover? Or had he fled? Or left the roof of seven generations of Romanovs—as the last of them?

The great-grandson of the Emperor who lived here, the grandson of the Emperor who was killed here—was he fleeing for all of them, taking them with him?

He didn't notice at which threshold this happened. Which crossing.

Taking a military stride, he started down the final corridor.

MAPS

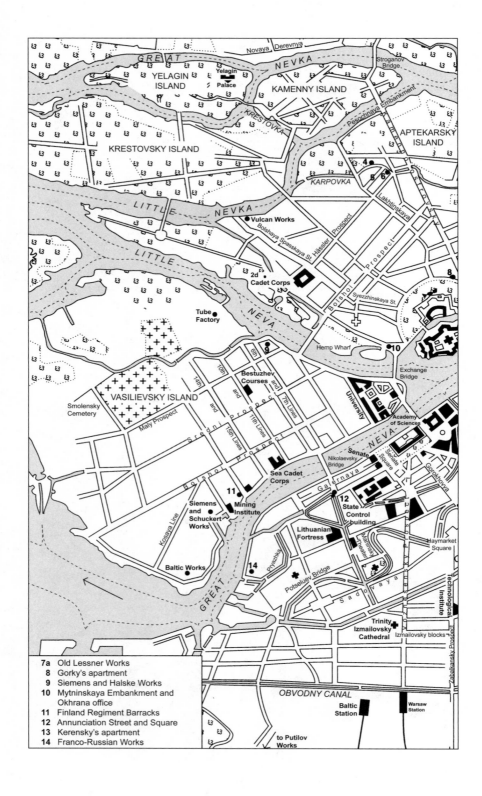

GRE AT — Novaya Derevnya — NEVKA — Stroganov Bridge

YELAGIN ISLAND — Yelagin Palace

KAMENNY ISLAND

KRESTOVKA

Pesochnaya Embankment

APTEKARSKY ISLAND

KRESTOVSKY ISLAND

KARPOVKA

4
5 6

Lakhtinskaya

LITTLE — NEVKA

Vulcan Works

Bolshaya Spasskaya St.

Bolshoi Prospect

Hässler St.

LITTLE — NEVKA

2d Cadet Corps

Syezzhinskaya St.

8

Tube Factory

NEVA

Hemp Wharf

10

9

6th

10th

14th

Bestuzhev Courses

and

7th Lines

Exchange Bridge

VASILIEVSKY ISLAND

Srednii Prospect

and

11th Lines

9th Prospect

15th Lines

University

NEVA

Smolensky Cemetery

Maly Prospect

Academy of Sciences

Senate

Senate Square

Sea Cadet Corps

Bolshoi Prospect

Nikolaevsky Bridge

Galernaya

Gorokhovaya

11

Mining Institute

12
State Control building

Kosaya Line

Siemens and Schuckert Works

Lithuanian Fortress

Mariinsky Theater

Haymarket Square

Baltic Works

14

Pryazhka

Potseluev Bridge

Sadovaya

Technological Institute

GRE AT

Trinity Izmailovsky Cathedral

Izmailovsky blocks

Zabalkansky Prospect

OBVODNY CANAL

Baltic Station

Warsaw Station

to Putilov Works

7a Old Lessner Works
8   Gorky's apartment
9   Siemens and Halske Works
10 Mytninskaya Embankment and
    Okhrana office
11 Finland Regiment Barracks
12 Annunciation Street and Square
13 Kerensky's apartment
14 Franco-Russian Works

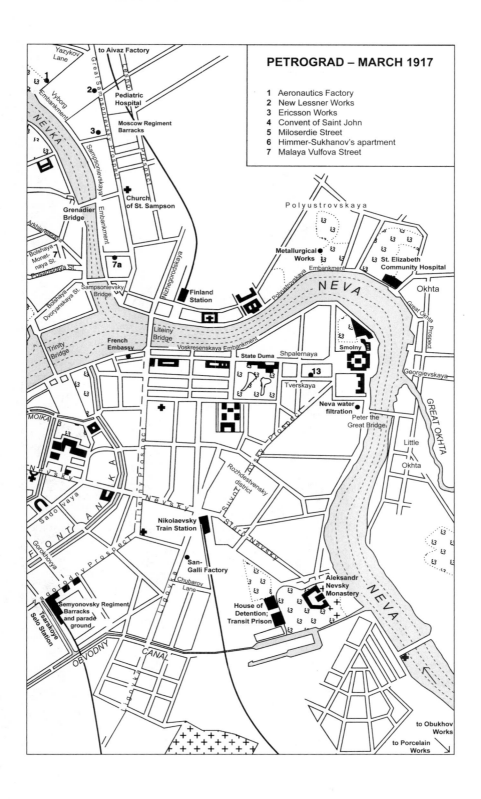

PETROGRAD – MARCH 1917

1 Aeronautics Factory
2 New Lessner Works
3 Ericsson Works
4 Convent of Saint John
5 Miloserdie Street
6 Himmer-Sukhanov's apartment
7 Malaya Vulfova Street

Yazykov Lane

to Aivaz Factory

Vyborg Embankment

Great Sampsonievsky

Pediatric Hospital

Moscow Regiment Barracks

NEVKA

Sampsonievskaya

Embankment

Church of St. Sampson

Grenadier Bridge

Arkhiereiskaya

Bolshaya Monet-naya St.

Posadskaya St.

7a

Bolshaya Dvoryanskaya St.

Sampsonievsky Bridge

Nizhegorodskaya

Finland Station

Polyustrovskaya

Metallurgical Works

St. Elizabeth Community Hospital

Okhta

Embankment

Polyustrovskaya

NEVA

Liteiny Bridge

Trinity Bridge

French Embassy

Voskresenskaya Embankment

State Duma

Shpalernaya

Smolny

Great Okhta Prospect

Georgievskaya

GREAT OKHTA

13

Tverskaya

Neva water filtration

Peter the Great Bridge

Little

Okhta

MOIKA

Nevsky

Sadovaya

FONTANKA

Liteiny Prospect

Nevsky

Rozhdestvensky district

Staro Nevsky

Prospekt

Nikolaevsky Train Station

Gorokhovaya

Zagorodny Prospect

San-Galli Factory

Chubarov Lane

Semyonovsky Regiment Barracks and parade ground

Tsarskoye Selo Station

OBVODNY CANAL

House of Detention; Transit Prison

Aleksandr Nevsky Monastery

NEVA

to Obukhov Works

to Porcelain Works

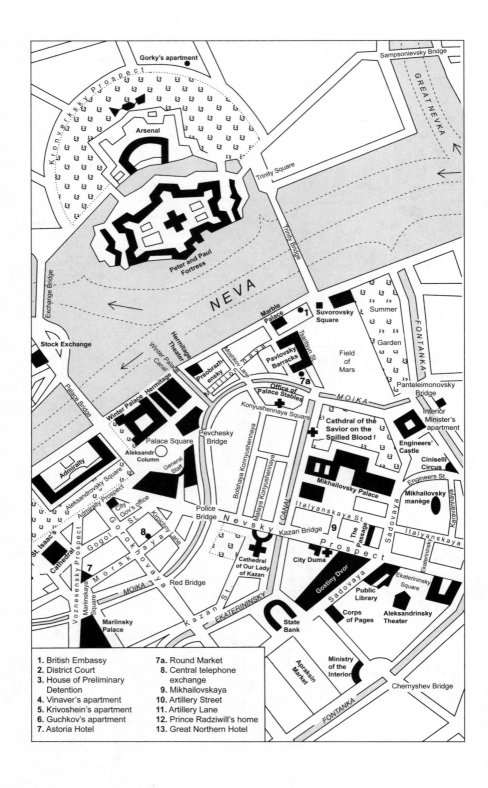

Gorky's apartment

Kronyerksky Prospect

Arsenal

Peter and Paul Fortress

Trinity Square

Trinity Bridge

GREAT NEVKA

Sampsonievsky Bridge

NEVA

Exchange Bridge

Stock Exchange

Winter Palace Canal

Palace Bridge

Hermitage Theater

Moshkov Lane

Preobrazhensky

Marble Palace

1 Suvorovsky Square

Tsaritsyn St.

Pavlovsky Barracks

7a

Field of Mars

Office of Palace Stables

Summer Garden

FONTANKA

MOIKA

Panteleimonovsky Bridge

Hermitage

Winter Palace

Palace Square

Aleksandr Column

General Staff

Admiralty

Pevchesky Bridge

Konyushennaya Square

Bolshaya Konyushennaya

Malaya Konyushennaya

Cathdral of the Savior on the Spilled Blood

Interior Minister's apartment

Engineers' Castle

Ciniselli Circus

Mikhailovsky Palace

Engineers St.

Mikhailovsky manège

Karavannaya

Aleksandrovsky Square

Admiralty Prospect

City Gov's office

Gorokhovaya St.

Kirpichny lane

8

Nevsky

Police Bridge

CANAL

Italyanskaya St.

Kazan Bridge

9

Italyanskaya

The Passage

Sadovaya

St. Isaac's

Cathedral

Voznesensky Prospect

Gogol St.

Morskaya

7

Prospect

Cathedral of Our Lady of Kazan

City Duma

Gostiny Dvor

Sadovaya

Ekaterininskaya

Ekaterininsky Square

Mariinskaya Square

MOIKA

Red Bridge

Kazan St.

EKATERININSKY

State Bank

Public Library

Corps of Pages

Aleksandrinsky Theater

Mariinsky Palace

Apraksin Market

Ministry of the Interior

FONTANKA

Chernyshev Bridge

1. British Embassy
2. District Court
3. House of Preliminary Detention
4. Vinaver's apartment
5. Krivoshein's apartment
6. Guchkov's apartment
7. Astoria Hotel

7a. Round Market
8. Central telephone exchange
9. Mikhailovskaya
10. Artillery Street
11. Artillery Lane
12. Prince Radziwill's home
13. Great Northern Hotel

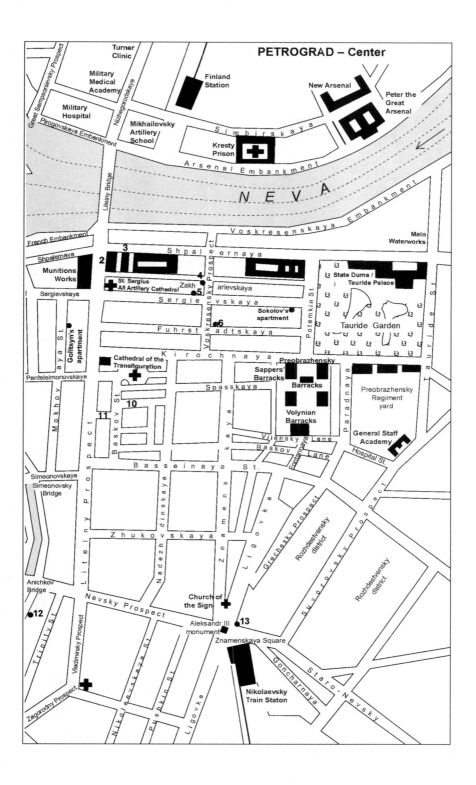

PETROGRAD – Center

Turner Clinic
Military Medical Academy
Military Hospital
Mikhailovsky Artillery School
Finland Station
New Arsenal
Peter the Great Arsenal
Kresty Prison

Great Sampsonievsky Prospect
Nizhegorodskaya
Pirogovskaya Embankment
Liteiny Bridge

S i m b i r s k a y a
A r s e n a l E m b a n k m e n t

N E V A

V o s k r e s e n s k a y a Embankment
Main Waterworks

French Embankment
Shpalernaya
Munitions Works
Sergievskaya

3
2
S h p a l e r n a y a
St. Sergius All Artillery Cathedral
Zakh
4
5
arievskaya

State Duma / Tauride Palace

Voskresensky Prospect
S e r g i e v s k a y a
Sokolov's apartment
F u h r s t a d t s k a y a
6

Potemkin St.
Tauride Garden

Tauride St.

Golitsyn's apartment
Mokhovaya St.

K i r o c h n a y a
Cathedral of the Transfiguration
10
11
Baskov St.

S p a s s k a y a

Preobrazhensky
Sappers' Barracks
Barracks
Volynian Barracks
V i l e n s k y L a n e
B a s k o v L a n e

Paradnaya
Preobrazhensky Regiment yard
General Staff Academy
Hospital St.

Panteleimonovskaya

Znamenskaya
Fontannaya Lane

Simeonovskaya
Simeonovsky Bridge

Liteiny Prospect
B a s s e i n a y a St.

Nadezhdinskaya

Z h u k o v s k a y a
Znamenskaya

Ligovka

Grechesky Prospect
Rozhdestvensky district
Suvorovsky Prospect
Rozhdestvensky district

Anichkov Bridge
12
N e v s k y P r o s p e c t
Vladimirsky Prospect

Church of the Sign
Aleksandr III monument
13
Znamenskaya Square

Trinity St.
Nikolaevskaya St.
Pushkin St.
Ligovka
Zagorodny Prospect

Nikolaevsky Train Staton
Goncharnaya
Staro-Nevsky

Index of Names

Abramovich, Aleksandr Emelyanovich (Shaya Zelikovich) (1888–1972): Bolshevik since 1908, emigrated to Switzerland, then returned to Russia in Lenin's carriage. Collaborator of the Comintern.

"Acetylene Gas." *See* Gutovsky.

Adzhemov, Moisei Sergeevich (1878–1953, USA): Deputy in Second, Third, and Fourth Dumas. Prominent member of the Kadet Party.

Aleksandr II (1818–1881): The "Tsar Liberator," presided over the emancipation of the serfs, the introduction of the zemstvos, modernization of the judicial system, easing of the burden of military service. Assassinated 13 March 1881 by members of the Narodnaya Volya (People's Will) organization.

Aleksandr III (1845–1894): Became emperor following the assassination of his father, Aleksandr II. Discontinued and in part reversed his father's program of reform. Father of the Franco-Russian Alliance.

Aleksandr (Aleksan) **Aleksandrovich** (Aleksanych, Sanych). *See* Rittikh.

Aleksandr Dmitrievich (Dmitrich). *See* Protopopov.

Aleksandr Fyodorivch (Fyodorych). *See* Kerensky.

Aleksandr Gavrilovich (Gavrilych). *See* Shlyapnikov.

Aleksandr Ivanovich (Ivanych). *See* Guchkov, Aleksandr; Spiridovich.

Aleksandr Mikhailovich ("Sandro"), Grand Duke (1866–1933, France): Grandson of Nikolai I, friend of Nikolai II in his youth. Married Nikolai's sister Ksenia.

Aleksandr Pavlovich. *See* Kutepov.

Aleksandr (Aleksan) **Vasilievich** (Vasilich). *See* Krivoshein, Aleksandr.

Aleksandra Fyodorovna ("Alix"), Empress (1872–1918): Born Princess Alix of Hesse and by Rhine. Married the future Nikolai II in 1894. Nickname "Sunny" in letters with her husband. Murdered together with her husband and children by the Bolsheviks.

Alekseev, Mikhail Vasilievich (1857–1918): Infantry general, chief of staff, first on the Southwestern, then on the Northwestern Front. From 5 September 1915, chief of General Staff. On sick leave 21 November 1916 to 7 March 1917. Advised the Tsar to abdicate in March 1917. Supreme Commander until 3 June 1917. After the October Revolution organized the first White Army on the Don.

Aleksei ("Baby," "Sunshine") (1904–1918): Son and youngest child of Nikolai II and Aleksandra Fyodorovna, hemophiliac. Murdered together with his parents and sisters by the Bolsheviks.

Aleksei Maksimovich (Maksimych). *See* Gorky.

Aleksei Vasilievich (Vasilich). *See* Peshekhonov.

Anastasia (1901–1918): Youngest daughter of Nikolai II and Aleksandra Fyodorovna, murdered with her whole family by the Bolsheviks.

Belogrud, Andrei Ivanovich (1875–1933): Russian architect.

Belyaev, Mikhail Alekseevich (1863–1918): General. Vice Minister of War June 1915–August 1916. Minister of War January–March 1917. Arrested by the Provisional Government, liberated, arrested again and shot by the Bolsheviks.

Benckendorff, Pavel Konstantinovich, Count (1853–1921, Estonia): Cavalry general, general aide-de-camp, high chamberlain of the Court.

Bernatsky, Mikhail Vladimirovich (1876–1943, France): Economist, Kadet, held different posts in the Provisional Government, then in White governments during the Civil War.

Bezobrazov, Vladimir Mikhailovich (1857–1932, France): Cavalry general. Commander of the Guards Army.

Blok, Aleksandr Aleksandrovich (1880–1921): The best-known Russian poet of his time; Socialist Revolutionary supporter, secretary of the Extraordinary Commission of Inquiry of the Provisional Government.

Blondes, David Abramovich: Jewish physician's assistant residing in Vilna, accused of "ritual murder" in 1900, first found guilty, then acquitted on appeal in 1902 in what became known as the Blondes Case.

Bobrinsky, Vladimir Alekseevich (1868–1927, France): Deputy in Second, Third, and Fourth Dumas. Moderate rightist, then leader of the nationalist group, in whose name he signed the program of the Progressive Bloc.

Bogdanov, Boris Osipovich (1884–1960): Menshevik, secretary of the Workers' Group, defensist; after the October Revolution spent forty years in and out of prisons, labor camps, internal exile.

Bonch-Bruevich, Vladimir Dmitrievich (1873–1955): Publisher and publicist. Close to Lenin. Wrote for *Iskra*, specialized in history and sociology of religion. Many official functions after October.

Boris Vladimirovich, Grand Duke (1877–1943, France): Major general, ataman of the Cossacks, cousin of Nikolai II.

Botkin, Evgeni Sergeevich (1855–1918): Physician to the imperial family. Murdered with them by the Bolsheviks.

Brasova, Natalia Sergeevna (Natasha; Natalia Sergeevna; née Sheremetievskaya, divorced Mamontov, divorced Wulfert) (1880–1952, France): Morganatic spouse of the Grand Duke Mikhail Aleksandrovich (1912).

Brilliant, Hirsch (pseud. Sokolnikov, Grigori Yakovlevich) (1888–1939): Bolshevik since 1905, emigrated in 1909, returned to Russia in Lenin's carriage. Condemned in one of the Moscow show trials, died in prison.

Broido, Grigori Isakovich (1885–1956): Menshevik, member of the Workers' Group, became Bolshevik in 1918. Had an undistinguished career.

Bronsky, Moisei (Mieczyslaw), alias Warszawski (1882–1938): Polish Social Democrat. Later Bolshevik, close collaborator of Lenin before the Bolshevik Revolution, modest career afterward. Executed.

Brounshtein (Braunstein, Brownstein-Valerianov), **Mikhail Adamovich** (1886–1938): Revolutionary who would be sentenced in 1931 for an alleged Menshevik conspiracy and later executed.

Elizaveta Fyodorovna ("Ella") (1864–1918): Sister of Empress Aleksandra Fyodorovna. Born Princess of Hesse and by Rhine. Married to Grand Duke Sergei Aleksandrovich; after his assassination took the veil. Murdered by the Bolsheviks.

Enescu (Enesco), **George** (1881–1955): Romanian composer and violinist.

Engelhardt, Boris Aleksandrovich (1877–1962): Deputy of the Fourth Duma, military officer who sided with the Revolution but fled Soviet Russia in 1918. Emigrated to Latvia; following its Soviet annexation in 1940, lived in exile in the USSR.

Erlich, Henryk Moiseevich (1882–1942): One of the leaders of the General Jewish Labor Bund. In 1917 a member of the Executive Committee of the Soviet of Workers' Deputies. Lived in Poland, fled to Soviet territory in 1939, where he was sentenced to death for espionage.

Ernst, Grand Duke of Hesse and by Rhine (1868–1937): Brother of Empress Aleksandra Fyodorovna.

von Essen, Sergei Antonovich (?–1917): Semyonovsky Regiment ensign, killed attempting to quell the February Revolution.

Evert, Aleksei Yermolaevich (1857–1918 or 1926?): Infantry general, commanded 46th Army, then Western Front (from 31 August 1915). Recalled by the Provisional Government; murdered.

von Fergen, Aleksandr Nikolaevich (?–1917): Decorated for bravery in Great War, served as staff captain in the Moscow Regiment when killed by soldiers during February Revolution.

Filippovsky, Vasili Nikolaevich (1882–1940): Navy lieutenant, Socialist Revolutionary. Died in a labor camp.

Flakserman, Galina Konstantinovna (Lia Abramovna) (1888–1958): Wife of Himmer-Sukhanov, Bolshevik. Her apartment was a key meeting place for Bolsheviks planning the October 1917 coup d'état.

Frederiks, Vladimir Borisovich, Count (1838–1927, Finland): Vice Minister of the Court 1893–1897, Minister from 1897.

Friend (the, our). *See* Rasputin.

Fyodorov, Sergei Petrovich (1869–1936): Doctor, surgeon, professor of the Military Medical Academy, who attended to Nikolai II and his son Tsarevich Aleksei. Continued to practice in the USSR.

Gavrilych. *See* Shlyapnikov.

George V (1865–1936): King of England (since 1910), cousin of Nikolai II.

Georgi Aleksandrovich (1871–1899): Younger brother of Nikolai II; died of tuberculosis.

Georgi Mikhailovich, Grand Duke (1863–1919): Older brother of Grand Duke Aleksandr Mikhailovich ("Sandro"), murdered by the Bolsheviks.

Gessen (Hessen), **Iosif Vladimirovich** (1865–1943, USA): Lawyer, member of the Second Duma, advocate for Jewish rights. In the 1920s and 1930s, in France, published 22-volume *Archive of the Russian Revolution*.

Gippius (Hippius), **Zinaida Nikolaevna** (1869–1945, France): Famous Russian symbolist poet.

Globachev, Konstantin Ivanovich (1870–1941, USA): General in the Corps of Gendarmes and the last chief of the Petrograd Okhrana.

Mikhail Aleksandrovich, Grand Duke ("Misha") (1878–1918): Younger brother of Nikolai II, refused the crown in March 1917 after Nikolai's abdication. Murdered by the Bolsheviks.

Mikhail Vasilievich. *See* Alekseev.

Mikhail Vladimirovich. *See* Rodzyanko.

Mikhailichenko, Aleksei Yakovlevich (1867–1924, Belgium): Career military officer, served in the Moscow Regiment from 1890, promoted to colonel in 1913. After the Revolution joined the White forces opposed to Bolshevism; evacuated in 1920 from Batum.

Mikhelson, Aleksandr Aleksandrovich (1864–?): General, commander of Moscow Regiment 1913–1915; following leg injury, worked in the General Staff.

Milyukov, Pavel Nikolaevich (1859–1943, France): Politician and historian, professor at the University of Moscow, dismissed in 1895; emigrated (1895–1905); main founder of the Kadet Party (1905) and its recognized leader; editor-in-chief of the *Rech*; leader of the Progressive Bloc and its spokesman in the Duma; Minister of Foreign Affairs in the first Provisional Government; emigrated in 1920.

Misha. *See* Mikhail Aleksandrovich.

Mniszech, Marina (Maryna Mniszchówna) (1588–1614): Daughter of Polish noble who in 1605 married the False Dmitri, pretender to the throne in the Time of Troubles, and after his death was a warlord; seen in Russian historiography as the embodiment of ambition.

Molotov (real name Skryabin), **Vyacheslav Mikhailovich** (1890–1986): Bolshevik since 1906; for a long time Stalin's right-hand man; untouched in all the purges. Foreign minister before and during World War II.

Montenegrin sisters, Stana (Anastasia) (1868–1935, France) and Militsa (1866–1951, Egypt): Daughters of the Montenegrin king, each married to a Romanov: Stana to Grand Duke Nikolai Nikolaevich and Militsa to his younger brother Pyotr. Attracted to mystics, the Montenegrin sisters introduced Rasputin to the royal couple.

Mordvinov, Anatoli Aleksandrovich (1870–1940, Germany): Colonel, member of the Emperor's suite, chamberlain; emigrated after Revolution; wrote memoirs.

Motya: diminutive for Matvei Ryss.

Münzenberg, Wilhelm (Willi) (1889–1940): German-Swiss Social Democrat, secretary of the Socialist Youth International (1915–1919), then Communist Youth International (1919–1920). Reichstag deputy 1924–1933. Emigrated to France in 1933; hanged in 1940.

Nabokov, Vladimir Dmitrievich (1869–1922, Germany): Lawyer. Active participant in Zemstvo congress 1904–1905; one of the founders of the Kadet Party. Signer of the Vyborg Appeal. Secretary general of the Provisional Government. Emigrated, assassinated by a Russian right-wing extremist. Father of the writer Vladimir Nabokov.

Nadya. *See* Krupskaya.

Naine, Charles (1874–1926): Lawyer. Leading Swiss Social Democrat, internationalist (at Kienthal), then moved to the right.

Nakhamkes (Steklov), **Yuri Mikhailovich** (1873–1941): Early Social Democrat; from 1903 close to the Bolsheviks, contributor to the *Social-Democrat* and *Pravda*;

after February, a "Revolutionary defensist," then returned to Bolshevism; after October, active in journalism and historical works; died in the purges.

Naryshkin, Kirill Anatolievich (1867–1924): Childhood friend of Nikolai II, member of the Emperor's suite. Arrested by the Bolsheviks, died in prison.

Nekrasov, Nikolai Vissarionovich (1879–1940): Kadet deputy in Third and Fourth Dumas. One of the organizers of the Zemgor. Held ministerial posts in the Provisional Government, left Kadet party and allied with socialists. Arrested in 1930, worked as a hydraulic engineer building canals and dams; freed; arrested and executed in the purges.

Nekrasov, Sergei Sergeevich (ca. 1890–after 1978, USA): Graduated Odessa Cadet Corps in 1912, joined Moscow Regiment; brother of Vsevelod Nekrasov; after the Revolution fought in a White Guards regiment, promoted to colonel.

Nekrasov, Vsevolod (?–?): Captain in Moscow Regiment; brother of Sergei Nekrasov; stayed in Petrograd after Revolution; further fate unknown.

Nelidov, Boris Leontievich (?–1929, France): Moscow Regiment officer, made colonel; disabled veteran; evacuated after Revolution; lived until 1926 in Bulgaria, then France. (Not to be confused with second lieutenant Nelidov of the Preobrazhensky Regiment, nephew of Sergei Shidlovsky.)

Nepenin, Adrian Ivanovich (1871–1917): Admiral, decorated for bravery in Russo-Japanese War. Led Russia's Baltic Fleet during the Great War.

Nikolai I Pavlovich (1796–1855): Youngest son of Paul I; the premature death of Aleksandr I and renunciation by his older brother Konstantin put him on the throne in December 1825; repressed the revolt of the Decembrists on the day of his crowning. His reign was conservative and firmly authoritarian.

Nikolai II Aleksandrovich (1868–1918): Last emperor of Russia. Murdered with his wife and children by the Bolsheviks.

Nikolai Iudovich. *See* Ivanov.

Nikolai Mikhailovich, Grand Duke (1859–1919): Older brother of Grand Duke Aleksandr Mikhailovich; a historian of note. Shot by the Bolsheviks without trial.

Nikolai Nikolaevich (Junior) ("Nikolasha"), Grand Duke (1856–1929, France): Supreme Commander 1914–1915. Viceroy of the Caucasus (September 1915–March 1917). Was again named Supreme Commander by Nikolai II at the moment of abdication, but not confirmed by the Provisional Government. Emigrated in 1919.

Nilov, Konstantin Dmitrievich (1856–1919): Admiral, adjutant general in the Emperor's suite. Executed by the Bolsheviks.

Nobs, Ernst (1896–1957): Swiss Social Democrat. President of the Swiss Confederation in 1949.

Novitsky, Pyotr Vasilievich (1867–after 1917): Landowner, veteran of the Russo-Japanese War, conservative lawmaker in the Third and Fourth Dumas; in 1917 supported monarchy; his fate thereafter is unknown.

Okolovich, Konstantin Markovich (1872–1933, Latvia): Priest, served in Vilna; right-wing member of Fourth Duma from Minsk province; emigrated.

Olga Lvovna. *See* Baranovskaya.

Olga Nikolaevna (1895–1918): Oldest daughter of Nikolai II and Aleksandra Fyodorovna, murdered with her whole family by the Bolsheviks.

Olga Pavlovna (Protopopova, née Nosovich): Wife of Protopopov.

Paléologue, Maurice (1859–1944): French ambassador to Russia 1914–1917.

Pankov, Grigori Gavrilovich (1885–1963): Worker, took part in 1905 revolutionary activity; in 1917 a member of the Petrograd Soviet, supported October Revolution; chairman of the Bryansk Executive Committee 1920–1922. Held labor posts in 1920s and 1930s.

Parvus, Aleksandr Lvovich (nom de guerre of Israel Lazarevich Helfand) (1867–1924, Germany): Played prominent part in 1905 Revolution. Invented theory of "permanent revolution." Successful businessman; funded revolutionaries (especially Bolsheviks).

Paul I (Pavel I Petrovich) (1754–1801): Son of Peter III and Catherine the Great, emperor from 1796. Tried to undo his mother's policies elevating the position of the nobility. Murdered by a palace conspiracy in March 1801. The Pavlovsky regiment and military school were named after him.

Pavel Aleksandrovich, Grand Duke (1860–1919): Son of Aleksandr II, uncle of Nikolai II. Cavalry general. Shot by the Bolsheviks without trial at the Peter and Paul Fortress.

Pavel Nikolaevich. See Milyukov.

Pavlenko (Pavlenkov), Vladimir Ivanovich (1865–1920, Greece): Career military officer, was put in charge of the Petrograd garrison in Chebykin's absence. Fought on the side of the Whites in the Civil War, died in a military hospital.

Pavlov, Dmitri (Mitya, Mitka) Aleksandrovich (1879–1920): Worker from Sormovo, member of Social Democrat party from 1899; a leader of the 1905 Moscow armed uprising. After Revolution fought on the side of the Red Army, died of typhus. Gorky memorialized him in a short sketch, Mitya Pavlov.

Perrin, Charles Louis (Perin, Carl Louis): Palm reader, astrologist, occultist, author of Perin's Science of Palmistry (1902).

Peshekhonov, Aleksei Vasilievich (1867–1933): Social populist, banished in 1922, buried in Leningrad.

Petrunkevich, Ivan Ilyich (1843–1928, Czechoslovakia): Lawyer. One of the organizers of Zemstvo congresses. Prominent member of the Kadet party. In 1904–1905, president of the "Union for Liberation"; deputy in the First Duma, signer of the Vyborg Appeal, editor-in-chief of the Rech. Emigrated in 1920.

Philippe, Nizier-Anthelme (1849–1905): A French "healer" patronized by the imperial couple in 1901–1902.

von Phull (General Phull), Karl Ludwig August Friedrich (1757–1826): Prussian general; in the Russian service after 1806, devised plan for fighting the Patriotic War in 1812.

Platten, Fritz (1883–1942): Locksmith, then designer, secretary of the Swiss Social Democrat Party; at the Zimmerwald and Kienthal conferences; organizer of and companion in Lenin's return to Russia. Founded the Swiss Communist Party in 1918; from 1923 lived in the USSR, where he died in exile.

von Pleve, Viacheslav Konstantinovich (1846–1904): Headed the Police Department in the 1880s, put down the terrorism of the People's Will organization; in 1902 was named Minister of the Interior and pursued a hard line against revolutionaries; murdered by a Socialist Revolutionary.

Pokrovsky, Nikolai Nikolaevich (1865–1930, Lithuania): Last Foreign Minister of the Russian Empire. Banker. Emigrated, taught finance at Kaunas University.

Polivanov, Aleksei Andreevich (1855–1920): Infantry general, close to Guchkov, retired by General Sukhomlinov; Minister of War 1915–1916, overcame the munition crisis, offered his services to the Red Army, died of typhus.

Posnikov, Aleksandr Sergeevich (1846–1922): Professor of economics and law; member of the Fourth Duma; proponent of communal land ownership and farming; opposed to Stolypin and his vision of private land ownership and individual farmsteads.

Potemkin, Grigory Aleksandrovich, Prince (1739–1791): Field marshal and Russian politician, favorite of Catherine II, who named him the Prince Tauride for his conquest of Crimea and Tauride Province and offered him a palace by the same name. Unoccupied after his death, the palace was refurbished in 1906 to house the imperial Duma and its services.

Pozharsky, Dmitri, Prince (1578–ca. 1642): Leader of the popular militia that dislodged foreign invaders and marauding armies during the Time of Troubles and cleared the way for establishing the Romanov dynasty.

Protopopov, Aleksandr Dmitrievich (1866–1918): Deputy in the Third and Fourth Dumas, Octobrist, vice president of the Duma in 1914; accused of spying for Germany (in Sweden during the summer of 1916 at the time of an English trip of a Duma delegation). Last imperial Minister of the Interior; incarcerated by the Provisional Government, shot without trial by the Bolsheviks.

Pumpyansky, Leonid Moiseevich (1889–1942): Social Democrat, Menshevik, arrested in February 1917 together with the Workers' Group; after the February Revolution served under the Provisional Government. Left Soviet Russia in 1922 and came to Estonia in 1925, where he was an economist and manager in the machine-building and oil shale industries. With the 1941 invasion he evacuated to the USSR. He is believed to have died of natural causes.

Purishkevich, Vladimir Mitrofanovich (1870–1920): Monarchist, right-wing leader, deputy in the Second to Fourth Dumas, where he was known for oratory flare and outrageous behavior. Co-murderer of Rasputin. Joined White Volunteer army, died of typhus.

Pustovoitenko, Mikhail Savvich (1865–?): General, close aide of Alekseev, served in GHQ (General Headquarters); emigrated after the Revolution; further fate unknown.

Putyatin, Mikhail Sergeevich (1861–1938, Paris): General of the Emperor's suite, administrator of the Imperial residence at Tsarskoye Selo.

Putyatin, Pavel Pavlovich (1871–1943): Colonel, equerry of the Imperial Court. His apartment on Millionnaya 12 would become the site of the dissolution of the Romanov dynasty. Died in emigration.

Samovar: derogatory nickname for Rodzyanko.

Samsonov, Aleksandr Vasilievich (1859–1914): Cavalry general, Cossack origins. Commanded the 1st Army in East Prussia in August 1914, which suffered a crushing defeat by the Germans at Tannenberg; committed suicide after the battle.

Sasha: short name for Aleksandr. *See* Ziloti, Aleksandr.

Sashenka: short name, term of endearment for Aleksandra. *See* Kollontai, Aleksandra.

Sashka, Sanka: short and colloquial names for Aleksandr. *See* Shlyapnikov.

Savich, Nikanor Vasilievich (1869–1942, France): Deputy in Third and Fourth Dumas; actively helped White armies during the Civil War; evacuated in 1920.

Sazonov, Sergei Dmitrievich (1860–1927, France): Vice Minister (1909), then Minister of Foreign Affairs September 1910–July 1916.

Shakhovskoy, Vsevolod Nikolaevich (1874–1954, France): Minister of Commerce and Industry 1915–1917; emigrated after the Revolution.

Shaklovitov, Fyodor (d. 1689): Ancestor of Shcheglovitov. Executed for conspiracy against Peter the Great after trying several times to have the regent Sofia crowned.

Shcheglovitov, Ivan Grigorievich (1861–1918): Jurist; Minister of Justice 1906–1915; President of the State Council. Shot by the Bolsheviks with Khvostov and Nikolai Maklakov as part of the Red Terror.

Shidlovsky, Sergei Iliodorovich (1861–1922, Estonia): Left-wing Octobrist. Vice president of Third Duma; chairman of the Progressive Bloc's bureau.

Shingarev, Andrei Ivanovich (1869–1918): Physician and head of a zemstvo hospital. Deputy to Second, Third, and Fourth Dumas. Member of Kadet Party leadership. Minister of Agriculture in the first Provisional Government, then Minister of Finance in the second. Imprisoned by the Bolsheviks, murdered together with Kokoshkin at the Mariinskaya Hospital.

Shirinsky-Shikhmatov, Aleksei Aleksandrovich (1862–1930, France): Senator, member of the Government Council, arrested in 1917, released, emigrated, active in monarchist movement.

Shklovsky, Grigori Lvovich (1875–1937): Social Democrat since 1898, emigrated to Switzerland in 1909; diplomat after the Revolution. Executed in the purges.

Shlyapnikov, Aleksandr Gavrilovich (Gavrilych) (1885–1937): Born into a family of Old Believers. Bolshevik from 1905. Worked in factories abroad, 1908–1914. Collaborated closely with Lenin during the war, returned clandestinely to Russia via Scandinavia on various occasions, oversaw the work of the Bolshevik Russian Bureau. Trade union leader; first Commissar of Labor after the Bolshevik Revolution. One of the leaders of the Workers' Opposition movement in the Party, 1920–1922. Expelled from the Central Committee in 1922. Held minor posts subsequently. Excluded from the Party in 1933, arrested 1935, executed.

Shulgin, Vasili Vitalievich (1878–1976): Duma deputy, leader of the right. Member of the Progressive Bloc. With Guchkov, received Nikolai II's abdication. Emigrated, made a clandestine trip to the USSR. Captured in Yugoslavia in 1944, spent twelve years in a prison camp, welcomed by Khrushchev, lived out his days in the USSR.

Shurkanov, Vasili Yegorovich (1876–1917 or later): Worker. Deputy in Third Duma, police informer from 1913. Arrested after February, further fate unknown,

Shutko, Kirill Ivanovich (1884–1941?): Bolshevik from 1902, active in October Revolution; held posts overseeing cinema, culture. Friend of the painter Kazimir Malevich. Arrested in 1938, executed.

Shuvaev, Dmitri Savelievich (1854–1937): Infantry general; Intendant General of the Armies. Minister of War March 1916–January 1917. Served, taught courses in Red Army after the Revolution. Retired after 1927; arrested in 1937 and executed.

Shvedchikov, Konstantin Matveevich (1884–1952): Bolshevik since 1904; after the Revolution, industrial career, in cinematography.

Skobelev, Matvei Ivanovich (1885–1939): Social Democrat from 1903; Menshevik, deputy in the Fourth Duma. Patriot during the war. Minister in Second Provisional Government July 1917. Joined Bolshevik Party in 1922. Worked in foreign trade organization. Expelled from the Party in 1937; died in the purges.

Skripitsyn, Boris Vladimirovich (?–1923): Preobrazhensky Regiment officer; shot by the Bolsheviks.

Sofia Alekseyevna (1657–1704): Daughter of Aleksei Mikhailovich's first marriage, regent of Moscow 1682–1689, deposed by her brother-in-law Peter the Great; first favorable, then very hostile to the Old Believers.

Sokolov, Nikolai Dmitrievich (1870–1928): Lawyer, Bolshevik sympathizer. Drafted Order No. 1, which in effect destroyed discipline in the Russian army in March 1917. After the Revolution worked as a lawyer in various Soviet agencies.

Soloviev, Nikolai Konstantinovich (?–1917): Semyonovsky Regiment ensign, killed attempting to quell the February Revolution.

Somov, Viktor Viktorovich (1881–1938): Member of Social Revolutionary party; helped shelter his friend Kerensky's family before their escape from Soviet Russia. Worked as a dentist in the USSR. Was arrested and executed during the purges for alleged secret ties to Kerensky.

Sosnovsky, Captain (pseud. of Iosif Rogalsky): Convict who in February 1917 fled prison, committed murder, dressed up in military uniform, led street action against the government, joined the Transport Ministry under the Provisional Government.

Spiridovich, Aleksandr Ivanovich (1873–1952, USA): Major general, responsible for Nikolai II's security until the assassination of Stolypin. Commander of the Kronstadt garrison, then civilian governor of Yalta during the Great War. After February, arrested on order of Kerensky, then released; emigrated to France. Left behind important historical texts.

Stankevich, Vladimir Bogdanovich (Vlada Stankevicius, Vladas Stanka) (1884–1968, USA): Lawyer, philosopher, military engineer, publisher of a textbook on fortifications; one of the leaders of Russian military efforts during 1917; arrested by Bolsheviks, emigrated; settled in Berlin, then Kaunas; after World War II worked in Berlin helping displaced persons; then left for USA in 1949.

Steklov. *See* Nakhamkes.

Stempkovsky, Victor Ivanovich (1859–1920 or later): Octobrist deputy in Third and Fourth Dumas. Worked on land reform in 1917 under the Provisional Government and attempted to do so in the early Soviet years. Arrested in 1920, sentenced to death; subsequent fate unknown.

Trotsky (pseud. of Bronstein), **Lev Davidovich** (1879–1940, Mexico): Revolutionary Social Democrat from 1897. Chairman of the Petersburg Soviet during the 1905 Revolution. Returned to Russia after February and engineered the Bolshevik seizure of power in October 1917. Founded Red Army and led it through the Civil War. Lost struggle for power and expelled from USSR in 1929; murdered by a Soviet agent.

Trubetskoy, Sergei Nikolaevich, Prince (1862–1905): Philosopher, zemstvo activist. In June 1905, at the head of a delegation, he gave a speech on a program of moderate reforms in front of Nikolai II. Died of heart attack in the office of the Minister of the Interior. Father of the well-known linguist Nikolai Trubetskoy.

Tsereteli, Irakli Georgievich (1882–1959, USA): Social Democrat; deputy to second Duma; exiled in 1913, returned after February Revolution; important Menshevik leader. Emigrated after the sovietization of Georgia.

Turner, Genrikh (Henry) **Ivanovich** (1858–1941): Doctor, father of orthopedic surgery in Russia; founder of Petrograd's Turner Clinic. After the Revolution, remaining in Soviet Russia, he founded a practice in 1926 for disabled children. Was the son of an Englishman, John Turner, who emigrated to Russia.

Tyazhelnikov, Mikhail Ivanovich (1866–1933, France): Led the HQ of the Petrograd Military District. After the Revolution, fought for the Whites, then emigrated.

Ulyanov, Aleksandr Ilyich (1866–1887): Older brother of Lenin, member of the People's Will organization, hanged 8 May 1887 for preparing an attempt on the life of Aleksandr III.

Vanya: diminutive for Ivan.

Vasili Alekseevich (Alekseich). *See* Maklakov, Vasili.

Vasili Vitalievich (Vitalich). *See* Shulgin.

Vasiliev, Aleksei Tikhonovich (1869–1930, France): Police official, Actual State Councilor; headed Police Department, led the investigation into the Rasputin murder; jailed in 1917.

Velyaminov (Voronotsov-Velyaminov), Vasili Konstantinovich (?–1919): Volynian Regiment lieutenant; after the Revolution joined the White cause in the Civil War; killed in Chernigov province.

Vera. *See* Guchkova; Komissarzhevskaya; Vera Vorotyntseva (under Principal Non-Historical Characters).

Viktoria Fyodorovna (née Victoria-Melita de Saxe-Coburg-Gotha) (1876–1936, Germany): Wife at first of Ernst, older brother of Aleksandra Fyodorovna; then divorced; then married Grand Duke Kirill Vladimirovich against the wishes of Nikolai II.

Vinaver (Winawer), Maxim Moiseevich (1863–1926): Lawyer born in Warsaw, founder of the Kadet Party, deputy in the First Duma, signer of the Vyborg Appeal; in 1919, member of a White government in Crimea; emigrated to France that same year.

Voeikov, Vladimir Nikolaevich (1868–1947, Sweden): Palace Commandant, General of the Emperor's suite, son-in-law of Count Frederiks, chairman of the first Russian Olympic committee. Had the reputation of a capable but self-serving organizer. After the Revolution lived in Finland.

Voronkov, Mitrofan Semyonovich (1868–after 1918): Kadet lawmaker from the Don, fought Bolsheviks during the Civil War.

Vyacheslov (Vecheslov, pseud. Yuriev), **Mikhail Georgievich** (1869–1934 or later): Doctor, Menshevik, one of the early revolutionaries. After the Revolution served in Afghanistan.

Vyrubova (Taneeva), **Anya** (1884–1964, Finland): Lady-in-waiting to the Empress. For some years her closest friend and intermediary between the imperial couple and Rasputin. Victim of a railroad accident in 1915, arrested in 1917, liberated, rearrested, emigrated.

Witte, Sergei Yulievich (1849–1915): Minister of Finance 1892–1903. Urged civil reforms and modernization. President of the Council of Ministers October 1905–April 1906, when he resigned (replaced by Goremykin). Author of an important memoir.

Yakovlev, Pyotr Mikhailovich (1878–1931): Captain. Entered service in the Moscow Regiment in 1896. After the Revolution, retired, then joined the Red Army, taught military courses, held low-level jobs; arrested, charged with helping old regimental church to hide its silverware from government expropriation; executed.

Yusupov, Feliks Feliksovich (1887–1967, France): Governor general of Moscow, son-in-law of Aleksandr Mikhailovich, co-murderer of Rasputin.

Zalomov, Pyotr Andreevich (1877–1955): Worker active in the revolutionary movement during 1901–1905; the prototype for Pavel Vlasov in Gorky's novel *The Mother*.

Zalutsky, Pyotr Antonovich (1887–1937): Originally a Socialist Revolutionary, a Bolshevik from 1907. Trotskyist in the 1920s, deported 1934, presumably executed.

Zankevich, Mikhail Ippolitovich (1872–1945, France): General, fought in the Great War; in 1917 was chief of the General Staff in Petrograd. Fought against the Bolsheviks in the Civil War.

Zasulich, Vera Ivanovna (1849–1919): Populist terrorist, tried in 1873 for an attempt on the life of the governor of St. Petersburg, acquitted, fled abroad, became one of the Menshevik leaders, opponent of the Bolshevik regime.

Zenzinov, Vladimir Mikhailovich (1880–1953, USA): Hailed from a family of wealthy merchants. Member of Social Revolutionary party, active in 1905 Revolution. Elected to Constituent Assembly, opposed Bolshevism, emigrated. Worked as a correspondent.

Ziloti (Siloti), **Aleksandr Ilyich** (1863–1945, USA): Russian pianist and conductor, founder of a series of musical events including the "Ziloti concerts" (since 1903); lived in the United States after 1922. Cousin of Sergei Rachmaninov.

Ziloti, Maria Ilyinichna (Masha) (1871–1938): Sister of Sergei and Aleksandr Ziloti, wife of Aleksandr Guchkov.

Ziloti, Sergei Ilyich (Seryozha) (1862–1914): Composer, army officer, brother of Aleksandr Ziloti. Died during the Great War.

Ziloti, Varvara Ilyinichna (Varya) (1868–1939): Sister of Sergei and Aleksandr Ziloti, wife of Konstantin Guchkov.

Zinoviev, Grigori Evseevich (pseud. Radomyslsky, Ovsei-Gershon Aronovich, born Apfelbaum, Hirsch) (1883–1936): Bolshevik from 1903. Chairman of the Petrograd Soviet after the October Revolution, Politburo member, leader of the Comintern. Helped depose Trotsky, then was deposed by Stalin, expelled from the Party, tried and executed in 1936.

Zubatov, Sergei Vasilievich (1863–1917): Minister of Police, encouraged workers to collaborate with his administration.

Principal Non-Historical Characters

Adalia and Agnessa: Aunts of Aleksandr (Sasha) and Veronika Lenartovich, who brought them up after the death of their parents. Deeply populist, to the left of the Kadets, Aunt Adalia did not belong to any political party; Aunt Agnessa, however, was an anarchist, at times a maximalist, had been in prison and in Siberia, and was entirely devoted to the Revolution. The two sisters symbolize the Russian intelligentsia united by its hatred for the aristocracy, its scorn for police, and its desire for freedom of the people.

Alina Vorotyntseva, née Siyalskaya: Wife of Colonel Vorotyntsev. Trained as a pianist, she devoted herself entirely to her husband's career during the eight years of her marriage preceding the war of 1914. When he was sent to the front, Alina, who had no children, was left alone in Moscow and became extremely active, organizing concerts for the troops. During the war, she felt she had come alive again as a person, until she learned that her husband was having an affair with a famous woman from Petrograd.

Andozerskaya, Olda Orestovna: She was said to be the most intelligent woman in Petersburg. Professor of world history, she nonetheless supported the monarchy, a rare case in learned circles. In November 1916 she met Colonel Vorotyntsev, who was passing through Petrograd. They began a passionate affair, which continued through correspondence during the winter of 1916–1917.

Anton Lenartovich: Uncle of Sasha and Veronika Lenartovich, brother of aunts Adalia and Agnessa. Born in 1881, the year Aleksandr II was murdered by a member of the People's Will organization, Uncle Anton participated actively in the events of 1905. After the failure of this first revolution, he turned to terrorist action. Arrested and tried, he was given the death penalty and hanged.

Dmitriev, Mikhail Dmitrievich: Engineer at the Obukhov Works in Petersburg. Designer of a cannon for the trenches that was not built because of strikes.

Kovynev, Fyodor Dmitrievich: Originally from the Don, he lived in Petersburg. His prototype is Fyodor Kryukov, believed to be the real author of the novel *And Quiet Flows the Don*, whereas Soviet officialdom ascribed the novel to Mikhail Sholokhov.

Likonya (Yelenka, Yolochka): School friend of Veronika Lenartovich, although their friendship was broken. A devotee of the arts, she is the opposite of the ideal of revolutionary militancy. Nonetheless, Sasha Lenartovich was charmed by her.

Obodovsky, Pyotor Akimych: Mining engineer, charged by the All-Russian Union of Engineers to form a committee of military technical assistance in the central War Industry Committees. A revolutionary, prosecuted twice, he was imprisoned, exiled, and even managed an escape abroad, always faithfully supported by his spouse, Nusya (Nina). Although he did not give up on his ideas, Obodovsky did not believe the revolution should take place before the end of the war.

Sasha (Aleksandr) Lenartovich: Student, enrolled in the army at the beginning of the hostilities. Raised by his aunts in the revolutionary tradition of the intelligentsia and in respect for Uncle Anton's memory, he militated against the aristocracy and was opposed to war. In August 1914 he met Colonel Vorotyntsev at the front, where he did not display courage or military valor.

Susanna Iosifovna Korzner: Wife of a well-known lawyer in Moscow, David Korzner. Jewish, she militated for the improvement of the life of Jews in Russia. Specializing in "lectures and proclamations," Susanna forged a friendship with Alina, who offered to become her page-turner for musical concerts for the troops.

Vera (Vorotyntseva, Vera Mikhailovna): Sister of Colonel Vorotyntsev. Lived in Petersburg with their old nurse. Worked at the Public Library. Fourteen years younger than her brother, she spent her childhood without him and was very influenced by the traditional peasant world of her nurse. In love with the engineer Dmitriev, she led a solitary life, while he was embroiled in a complicated love affair.

Veronika Lenartovich (Veronya): Sister of Sasha Lenartovich. Although brought up in the family revolutionary tradition, she escaped its influence and showed no interest in politics. Eventually, however, she became a fierce militant, to the great satisfaction of her aunts and her brother, which led her to drift away from her school friend Likonya.

Vorotyntsev, Georgi Mikhailovich: Graduated at the top of his class from the military academy. Colonel. After his studies in Petersburg, he and his wife Alina lived in garrisons in the Vyatka region until he was sent to Moscow. After a brief rise that took him to GHQ (General Headquarters), he was sent on a mission in East Prussia. He escaped the encirclement of the Samsonov army at Tannenberg in August 1914. Eventually he was "exiled" to a regiment because of his positions on war strategy. In early November 1916, on a mission in Petrograd, he met Professor Andozerskaya and they began a passionate affair.

Yasny: nickname of Sasha Lenartovich.

Zinaida (Altanskaya): Former student of Fyodor Kovynev, when he was teaching in Tambov. She shared with him a passionate and complex love affair.

ABOUT THE AUTHOR

Aleksandr Solzhenitsyn (1918–2008) is widely acknowledged as one of the most important figures—and perhaps *the* most important writer—of the last century. A Soviet political prisoner from 1945 to 1953, he set himself firmly against the anti-human Soviet system, and all anti-human ideologies, from that time forward. His novel *One Day in the Life of Ivan Denisovich* (1962) made him famous, and *The Gulag Archipelago*, published to worldwide acclaim in 1973, further unmasked communism and played a critical role in its eventual defeat. Solzhenitsyn won the Nobel Prize in 1970 and was exiled to the West in 1974. He ultimately published dozens of plays, poems, novels, and works of history, nonfiction, and memoir, including *Cancer Ward*, *In the First Circle*, and *The Oak and the Calf* (a memoir that is continued in *Between Two Millstones*). Few authors have so decisively shaped minds, hearts, and world events as did Solzhenitsyn.